CANDIDE

and Other Writings

CANDIDE
and Other Writings

VOLTAIRE

Edited, with an Introduction, by
HASKELL M. BLOCK
State University of New York at Binghamton

THE MODERN LIBRARY · New York

THE MODERN LIBRARY

is published by

RANDOM HOUSE, INC.

Manufactured in the United States of America

CONTENTS

PHILOSOPHICAL WRITINGS

DIALOGUES AND SHORTER PIECES

INTRODUCTION

By Haskell M. Block

Great writers like Voltaire never grow old. Their works are forever energetic and vital, capable of engaging successive generations of readers and of adding to each new generation something it would not otherwise have. Few writers have been so varied and capacious, so mindful of human dignity and depravity, of the eternal conflict between the forces of light and darkness for the possession of men's bodies and minds. To our own age he speaks with impassioned clarity in words that sting and burn if we will let them. Voltaire knew the ways of the police state. He had bitter experience of hired thugs, paid informers, police spies, and their ruthless and fanatical masters; he was all too keenly aware, even in the civilized eighteenth century, of the torture chamber and the stake, of brain-washing and forced confessions or recantations. His incessant struggle on behalf of liberty and humanity takes on added meaning in our own day of concentration camps, slave labor, and thought control. It was not only to combat savagery and stupidity that Voltaire labored, but to lead men toward the pursuit of happiness on earth At two centuries' distance his voice is not merely a cry of defiance and protest, but a call to action. Freedom for Voltaire is not a state but a process, not a resting place but a way of thinking and living. It is precisely in the dynamics of his mind and art that his permanence lies: Voltaire is always our contemporary, and never less so than he is today.

It was not always thus, and to understand the heritage of Voltaire, to realize more fully what he is to us, we must also know something of what he was to his own day, who he was, and what he made himself become. He was born François-Marie Arouet in Paris in 1694. His parents were well-to-do members of the upper middle classes. His father was an eminent notary who numbered many of the nobility among his clients and who moved in an atmosphere of intelligence and refinement. Young Arouet attended a fashionable Jesuit academy where he received a thorough grounding in the Latin and Greek classics. His more worldly education may have been first acquired in the salons of his mother and her friends. While still a boy he began writing verses and gained recognition among his schoolmates for his wit and spirited satire. When he left school at the age of 16, his practical-minded father overrode his literary ambitions and directed him to the study of law. Soon afterward, we find young Arouet in Holland caught up in a madcap love affair with a Mademoiselle Du Noyer, who for a time seems to have responded to his passion. Encouraged, the young lover planned an elopement but was forestalled by the French Ambassador and quickly shipped back to Paris, to face an indignant father who threatened to have him transported to America. In Paris the youth was more spirited and adventurous than ever. He completed a play, *Œdipus*, performed in 1718 with great success, and in the dedication the author first signed his name "Voltaire." In his early career it was primarily as a playwright that Voltaire made his reputation among his contemporaries, even though today his plays are largely of historical interest only.

At this time too the young writer was to suffer his first experience of the arbitrary whim of an autocratic government. For eleven months, from 1717 to 1718, he languished in the Bastille in consequence of satiric poetry directed against the Regent, the Duke of Orleans. On his release he plunged into literary activity and soon cut a brilliant figure in polite society. His career was interrupted in 1725 by an open quarrel with an arrogant aristocrat, who subsequently had Voltaire beaten. To forestall a duel, the authorities imprisoned Voltaire, and released him only when he offered to leave at once for England.

Voltaire's English exile lasted from 1726 to 1729. He made the most of his opportunity, learning English well, and meeting the leading literary figures of the day—Swift, Pope, Congreve, Bolingbroke, and many others. He acquired an insight unusual for a foreigner into English traditions and institutions, and was astonished by the contrast they provided with the French. Implicitly, Voltaire's *Philosophical Letters* are a powerful indictment of the *ancien régime*; for in praising English law, English tolerance, English philosophy, science and art, he exposed the weaknesses of his own society in the light of a superior standard of value. No wonder that soon after its publication in 1734 the book was condemned by the French parliament and burned by the hangman in the public square. Yet the *Philosophical Letters* is not only a work of combat; Voltaire was genuine in his praise of Bacon, Newton and Locke, and the impact of British empiricism is writ large in his philosophical and scientific speculations of the ensuing years. Like most of the thinkers of his day, Voltaire was filled with admiration for Newton as that philosopher who reduced Nature to law by discovering the universally operative causes of natural phenomena. The method of experimental science, well established by the middle years of the eighteenth century, played an ever-increasing role in Voltaire's reexamination of the principles of social morality and his rejection of the most cherished prejudices of his time. It may well be that in his *Philosophical Letters* Voltaire exaggerated the superiority of the English to his countrymen, but his attitudes and underlying standards of judgment were in many instances to remain with him for the rest of his life: from the *Philosophical Letters* to the *Philosophical Dictionary* is but a short step.

In 1733 Voltaire met and fell in love with Madame du Châtelet, a spirited and intelligent woman twelve years his junior. They worked together at scientific and philosophical investigations, and it was to her chateau at Cirey, in Lorraine, that Voltaire fled in 1734 after the condemnation of the *Philosophical Letters*. It was here that he did much of the wide reading that was to serve him so well in later years. Drama, satiric poetry, popular science, metaphysics, history, all belong to the decade of the 1730's, spent largely at Cirey, and culminating in 1739 with the seizure of the first chapters of Voltaire's history, *The Age of Louis XIV*, upon their publication in Paris.

Voltaire's historical writings owe much to the reading shared with Madame du Châtelet. He encouraged her to accept a more adequate conception of history than was provided by the universal historians or the chroniclers of the past, concerned either with demonstrating the wisdom of God in history or with recording the spectacular events of previous reigns. If Voltaire may be considered the father of modern history, and the claim is not too large to make, it is because he was the first to conceive of history as the total interpretation of the customs and manners of past civilizations. His history was evaluative as well as descriptive; in his judgment of ancient times his highest praise was for China and India, and in the west, for Greece and Rome. In modern times he held that the apogee of civilization was reached in the age of Louis XIV. It is important to recognize that in taste and temperament, the balanced rationality and polish of French society in the later seventeenth century represented an ideal for Voltaire, a glorious epoch whose perfection was embodied in poetry in the plays of Racine, in literary criticism in the rules of Boileau, in manners in the court at Versailles, and in government in the benevolent autocracy of Louis XIV. Voltaire's history is in large part propaganda for a way of life, an attempt to educate his reader to the ways of the most refined and cultivated of modern civilizations, seen not in its political and military triumphs, but in the achievement of its arts and institutions. Voltaire's concern with institutional and historical forces is altogether unusual in the history of his day, but it is also noteworthy that he wrote history with a passion for accuracy, refusing to omit any labor that might help him to obtain and verify his facts. Particularly after 1745, when Voltaire became Royal Historiographer, he had access to innumerable private documents and state papers that made possible a degree of authenticity virtually unknown in histories of the past. Yet he selected with discrimination and arranged his material so as to compel the reader's attention by the liveliness of his narrative and the precision of his language. Voltaire is one of the masters of historical style, an artist and a social philosopher in the same instant that he is recorder and interpreter of facts and their consequences.

By 1745 Voltaire was a famous man in the eyes of his con-

temporaries. The following year he was elected to the French
Academy, and he did not scruple to insure his success by dedicating a play to the Pope. Duplicity with Voltaire was an important
element of literary strategy. If at times he seems to contradict
himself, to lie, conceal, or play a double game, it is because Voltaire the public man was often a very different writer from Voltaire the intimate correspondent. His newly won favor at court,
under the sponsorship of Madame de Pompadour, was important;
almost at once he received royal titles and commissions, and
honors on all hands. In retrospect, we can see that the years of
fame lay ahead of him. If Voltaire had died in his early fifties, it
is not likely that we should consider him today as more than a
minor literary figure of the early eighteenth century. Voltaire
would no doubt be astounded to learn that it is primarily by
his fiction that he survives in literature. The publication of his
short stories and *nouvelles*, beginning with *Zadig* in 1747, belongs to the latter part of his career.

Zadig and *Candide* are by common consent the best of Voltaire's tales, yet it is sometimes forgotten that he wrote over
twenty-five fictional compositions; many of these are waiting to
be rediscovered. Voltaire's *contes* belong to a narrative form
characteristic of the eighteenth century, the philosophical tale,
best represented in English literature by Samuel Johnson's moral
fable, *Rasselas*, or William Beckford's extravaganza, *Vathek*, first
written in French and remarkably close in style to the manner of
Voltaire. From Montesquieu and from imitators of the recently
translated *Arabian Nights*, from Swift and other writers of *voyages imaginaires*, Voltaire learned the art of exposing and satiriz-
ing contemporary abuses through allegory, parody, or burlesque.
A recurrent figure in the *contes philosophiques* is the wise, ob-
jective, and impartial commentator, usually an oriental sage,
whose experiences and reflections serve to unmask the follies
and vices of the times. Voltaire's tales are intensely topical, far
more than most present-day readers can realize, for the mask and
the disguise are implicit within the very structure of the story.
Yet what in other writers was merely low gossip or pornography
or flat travel narrative became in the hands of Voltaire an in-
cisive weapon for the analysis of philosophical argument. *Zadig*

(from the Arabic *Saadiq*, meaning "the truthful one") is essentially an examination of the impact of destiny on human affairs, of the conflict and confluence of fate and chance, the ordained and the fortuitous, the constrained and the free. The hero is a philosopher in quest of happiness, yet he is made to endure cruel persecutions at the hands of vicious men. Each chapter of Voltaire's tale provides yet one more example of human pettiness and meanness or stupidity. The climax of the narrative comes in the hermit's demonstration of human insufficiency: the inevitability of evil and suffering in a world of crime and misfortune. Yet Zadig does not end by submitting to the bleak fatalism the hermit would impose in accordance with the immutable decrees of Providence. Zadig's final and unanswered "But" carries with it a protest in the name of suffering humanity against the injustice of man's lot, and the eventual good fortune of Voltaire's hero is to some degree an optimistic qualification of the hermit's harsh assertion of the littleness of man amid the immensity of the universe.

Candide, Voltaire's masterpiece, appeared in 1759, twelve years after *Zadig*. It is unquestionably darker in implication, more ferocious in its satire and irony than the earlier work. Voltaire maintains the same variety of incident and rapidity of pace, but the setting is the Western world which we know, given extension by Voltaire's bold manipulation of the picaresque pattern. Candide himself is no rogue but a naive and good-hearted fellow, uneducated in the ways of the world. Those he meets are virtually without exception knaves or dupes: his education is our education; his achieved wisdom becomes that of the reader, to serve as a practical means of enduring a life that is at best painful and difficult. The shallow optimism Voltaire attributes to Leibnitz is an easy target and in the grotesque caricature of Doctor Pangloss, an amusing one as well; but it is with the man-made causes of human evil—that is, that part of evil which man can ameliorate —that Voltaire is primarily concerned. Lisbon may be reduced to dust by earthquake, but this is an event wholly beyond man's control and to be borne as best we can. Most human ills are derived from institutions and from the ways of man himself: hereditary privilege, war, the aristocracy, the church, the Jesuits, slavery, savage self-interest, all provide the most desperate evidence in support of Martin's view that God has abandoned this globe— or globule—to some evil creature. Candide ends without embracing this black pessimism, but he agrees completely with Martin's insistence on work without theorizing as the only way to make life endurable. To cultivate our garden, we must direct our attention to that which it is in our power to improve. Voltaire's conclusion should not be taken as a defense of quiescence or of indifference to the plight of humanity. All the world, he asserts, is our garden; let us work to make it better than it is.

In our preoccupation with the ideological implications of Voltaire's satire, we sometimes take too little account of his wonderful craftsmanship. Voltaire was a master of pace and dialogue; few writers have known how to tell a story with such verve and polish. The economy of means in *Candide* is breath-taking. There is not a line or word which does not do its work. The animation and gusto of Voltaire's humor depends on the most consummate literary skill: on understatement and magnification; on irony and parody; on the abrupt and dramatic subversion of probability and of our sense of normal expectation. No sooner does Candide become the hero of the Bulgarians than he is thrown into irons and flogged. The surprising and the fortuitous move side by side in a world which may be something like the world we know, but in which the irrational and the catastrophic are the rule. Each episode in *Candide* has its own completeness and relentless inner logic. The sheer abundance and variety of incident serve to propel the action and to keep the reader constantly on the edge of expectation and surprise. Yet in all this speed and restlessness there is an underlying unity controlling Voltaire's selection of detail: not a single chapter or episode fails to unmask the illusion of shallow optimism and to reveal the inevitability and permanence of vice and suffering in human experience, from Patagonia to Turkey and in all the nations of Europe. The hard and uncompromising view of reality *Candide* presents is mitigated only by the deft humor of Voltaire's wit and the brilliance of his style. If *Candide* has become an endless source of delight to generations of readers, it is so not only because of the urgency of its wisdom but because of the power of Voltaire's art.

Candide is its author's masterpiece, but the same qualities that establish its pre-eminence in eighteenth-century fiction are also present in Voltaire's other tales and in his dialogues and short satiric sketches. Many of these may have been the product of more ambitious pursuits. *Micromegas* is clearly the offspring of Voltaire's scientific investigations at Cirey from 1734 to 1739, and it is very likely that the first draft of this work dates from this last year. Although the tale was not published until 1752, it may well be the first of Voltaire's *contes* in order of composition. It is significant that here, as in *Candide*, Voltaire's demonstration of human ignorance and the inadequacy of science to explain the nature and end of cosmic events moves side by side with a spirited assault on false pride and inhumanity. Nowhere is Voltaire's abhorrence of war as a plague and curse of mankind so clearly expressed as in his description of the horrible quarrel over a lump of clay, in which not a single one of the "miserable little creatures" whose throats are cut knows what it is all about. In a society that claimed to worship God and to live in accordance with the dictates of Christianity, Voltaire could not understand how men could behave like brute beasts: it is precisely at such points of contradiction in practice and belief that his humor is most trenchant. In his dialogues too we can see the same simplicity and directness mingled with thinly veiled irony and exuberant satire. Voltaire's ingenious account of the sickness and death of the Jesuit Berthier, editor of a journal that ceaselessly attacked the *philosophes* of the enlightenment, is at the same time a reduction of the Jesuit opposition through ridicule and humor. By making men laugh at the fanatical and intolerant, he could also expose the real dangers that lay in the persecution of those who would free men's minds from superstition and error. In *André Destouches in Siam*, war, hypocrisy, savagery in the name of religion, political and legal corruption, all the inconsistencies and depravities of contemporary France are mercilessly exposed through the simple device of reversing the usual presentation of European manners as seen by the naive oriental or the Indian savage. Voltaire's dialogues were often mere bagatelles, light and flippant in manner, generously enlivened by epigrammatic wit. Yet in their vivid sense of reality and their intellectual vigor, these short pieces are little masterpieces. They may vary in tone from the facetious to the philosophical and meditative, yet they all move with the same ease and fluidity and apparent artlessness that conceal the most precise and deliberate craftsmanship. Voltaire's art of dialogue is above all an art of movement within design, a triumph of dynamic discipline.

As he approached the age of sixty, a fundamental change began to take place within Voltaire; more and more he felt impelled to enter into the battle between enlightenment and oppression that he saw waged daily around him. It was in 1752, during the unfortunate period of attachment to his friend and fellow-philosopher, Frederick the Great, that Voltaire conceived the plan of his *Philosophical Dictionary*. This project was to occupy him intermittently for the ensuing twenty years. Firmly established in an environment where he could work unhampered by persecution from church or state, first in 1755 at "Les Delices" near Geneva, and then, more securely, after 1759, at Ferney, in French territory but just outside the Swiss frontier, Voltaire set out more boldly than ever to crusade on behalf of humanity and justice. Such events of the 1760's as the torture of Calas, the condemnation of Sirven, and the execution of La Barre aroused in him an almost pathological indignation. In the last decades of his life Voltaire's irritability literally goaded him into action against the intolerance and persecuting spirit of his countrymen. He responded with a fanaticism of his own that drove him to inundate France and the rest of Europe with tracts, sermons, pamphlets, satires, diatribes and denunciations of every description. Much of this writing is propaganda of a local and immediate character, far more journalistic than literary. Yet even in calmer years, the journalist and the man of letters were never far apart in Voltaire's activity. His scientific and philosophical writings are essentially essays in popularization; and if he discovered few facts, he knew how to assimilate the discoveries of others and to make them accessible to the ordinary reader. He designed the

Philosophical Dictionary as a little book, to be carried in the pocket as a work of ready reference, in sharp contrast with the massive effort of Diderot's *Encyclopedia,* an enterprise which Voltaire admired and supported, but which he felt was paid for at too great a price in the absorption of Diderot's energies. Yet he did not spare himself when he came to the same task of enlightening his countrymen, of proclaiming the necessity of freedom of thought and of expression at a time when intolerance and censorship seemed to be gaining renewed strength. It is to Voltaire's credit that no external pressure or private interest obliged him to take up the defense of Jean Calas. That so barbarous a deed as the torture of Calas on the wheel by the religious fanatics of Toulouse could occur in a supposedly civilized nation outraged and infuriated Voltaire and incited him to action. His *Treatise on Tolerance,* written in the heat of his attempts to rehabilitate Calas, served to alert all Europe to the dangers of bigotry and fanaticism. So long as these dangers persist, Voltaire's eloquent essay will command our attention. His "Prayer to God" transmutes his angry prose into impassioned poetry, for it offers not simply a denunciation of intolerance and religious hatred, but a positive assertion of human brotherhood and the essential dignity of all men.

If the parliamentary decree of 1765 clearing the name of Calas enheartened Voltaire, the execution of the Chevalier La Barre at Abbeville the following year all but drove him mad. There is no doubt that he suffered physically as well as mentally in the face of this new outburst of intolerance. La Barre had been accused of mutilating a crucifix and of singing disrespectful songs during a religious procession. He was condemned to be burned alive after first having his tongue torn out and his right hand cut off. His sentence was subsequently modified, so that he was beheaded before his body was thrown into the flames. A copy of Voltaire's *Philosophical Dictionary* was burned with him. It is clear that Voltaire felt personally implicated in this new atrocity. He could not understand how Frenchmen of means and education could amuse themselves in conversation or at the opera, or how they could sleep at night while a religious fanaticism rivaled only by the Inquisition transformed his countrymen "from monkeys into tigers." He wrote seriously to D'Alembert and Diderot of leaving France once and for all: "In truth, now is the time to break your ties and to go off to another place with the horror that has penetrated us. . . . It is no longer time for joking; witticisms do not go well with massacres." Almost at once Voltaire set to work on his commentary on the treatise of Cesare Beccaria, *Of Crimes and Punishments*. Voltaire knew that criminal procedure with its tortures, secret witnesses, and disproportionately cruel sentences itself constituted one of the strongest obstacles to the reformation of men's minds. In his *Commentary* he insists repeatedly on the importance of public hearings for the accused, on their right to be considered innocent until proved guilty, and on the right of the accused to confront those witnesses that testify against them. His endeavors on behalf of a more equitable and humane criminal law, often forgotten amid his other achievements, are an important facet of his almost desperate struggle to "crush the infamous." Increasingly from 1765 to the end of his life in 1778, we find his adjurations to his fellow philosophers ending insistently: "*écrasez l'infâme.*" The forces of infamy were not, as some have supposed, all religion, but rather that religion which encouraged fanaticism and superstition, intolerance and hatred. Voltaire may not have shared the belief in a personal God and in retributive justice of the more orthodox, but there is no doubt that he believed in the existence of God, without presuming to fix the relationship of God to man. Late in life Voltaire asserted that he had lived as a good Christian. He may not have been a saint, but there can be no doubt that in his fearless dedication to the rights of others and in his constant struggle to liberate men from the bondage of closed systems of whatever sort, he stands forth as one of the great champions of humanity.

The massiveness of Voltaire's achievement almost stuns the imagination. Few writers of any time or place can rival his variety and scope, the multiplicity of his forms and themes, the energy of his mind and art. For us today, far more vividly than any other writer of the eighteenth century, he mirrors the central crises and cleavages of his age. He emerges unmistakably as its foremost representative, as the symbol of an era in European thought. In his insistence on reason and common sense in human affairs, in his hatred of cruelty and his essential love of mankind, Voltaire is in the forefront of a spiritual revolution that is yet far from won. Men still cry out for enlightenment, and the "infamous" are always with us. The Nazis melted down Voltaire's statue in Paris during the occupation. Others, more subtle in their efforts to enslave men's minds, are forever challenging the premises of individual liberty and human dignity which are our heritage as free men. Voltaire knew that the struggle against barbarism and inhumanity is the enduring price of civilization. His legacy is ours, to keep and to share. The best of Voltaire's writing has entered into the best of Western literature, a perpetual source of the keenest pleasure and delight, and of something more.

EDITORIAL NOTE

Voltaire is a difficult writer to present within the pages of a single volume, least of all in the totality of his vast and varied output. I have attempted to provide an indication of Voltaire's range and complexity by selecting those works which have most clearly become a vital part of our intellectual and artistic heritage. This is necessarily a restrictive point of view, but it is one that Voltaire would have understood and appreciated. Again and again he urged his own editors not to print every line he wrote: "a man should not go to posterity with such heavy baggage." I have taken him at his word.

The text of this edition has been prepared in the hope of making some improvement over previous English versions. All of the selections are complete. There are no excerpts of letters or parts of chapters as are so frequently found in editions of the French writer. It is surprising and somewhat disquieting to learn how inaccurate the texts of virtually all English editions of Voltaire have been. In the eighteenth century, translations of his writings appeared almost immediately after French publication. Voltaire's English translators could not know that he would subsequently revise his work, omitting some sentences, rewriting others, and sometimes deleting entire episodes or chapters. The eighteenth-century translations were often out of date even before they had been completed, yet year after year down to our own day, they have been reprinted, uncorrected. Thus Voltaire's delightful tale, *Zadig*, has never before appeared in English in an accurate translation, and I have no doubt that many of the selections included in twentieth-century reprints of the *Philosophical*

Dictionary are either not by Voltaire or do not belong to that work. In every instance I have collated the texts of this edition with those of the best French critical editions whenever they were available.

It is hoped that the translations in this collection will help to make a beginning toward an accurate edition of Voltaire in English. In every section of the volume I have provided new translations wherever they were necessary. I should add that the translations from Voltaire's *Notebooks* are the first from that work to appear in an English edition. The *Notebooks* were first published in 1952; [1] they provide a rare and curious illustration of Voltaire in the workshop. Where older translations have been used, they have been thoroughly revised. In particular, for all of the fiction except *Candide,* I have modernized the version of Robert Bruce Boswell.[2] The translation of *Candide* is by Richard Aldington. Other recent translations have been included where suitable. I am especially grateful to Martyn P. Pollack for the selections from his excellent version of *The Age of Louis XIV,*[3] and to Floyd Gray for his assistance in the translating of Voltaire's correspondence.[4]

I am deeply indebted to the admirable critical editions of André Morize (*Candide*); Gustave Lanson (*Philosophical Letters*); Georges Ascoli (*Zadig*); Raymond Naves (*Philosophical Dictionary, Dialogues, Letters*); and Theodore Besterman (*Letters, Notebooks*). The editions and critical interpretations of George R. Havens, Norman L. Torrey, and Ira O. Wade have been extremely helpful throughout. I am grateful to my colleague, Joseph E. Tucker, for his encouragement and aid, and to all others who helped me in the preparation of this edition.

[1] By the Institut et Musée Voltaire; ed. Theodore Besterman, by whose permission these selections are included.
[2] *Zadig, and Other Tales.* By permission of G. Bell & Sons, London.
[3] Everyman's Library. E. P. Dutton & Co., New York, and J. M. Dent & Sons, London.
[4] Versions of some letters are based on those in S. G. Tallentyre's *Voltaire In His Letters,* John Murray, London.

FOR FURTHER READING

The best individual studies in English are: John Morley, *Voltaire* (London, 1913); Henry N. Brailsford, *Voltaire* (London, 1935); Norman L. Torrey, *The Spirit of Voltaire* (New York, 1938). Valuable French studies include Gustave Lanson, *Voltaire* (Paris, 1910); Raymond Naves, *Voltaire* (Paris, 1942). Interesting illustrative material is provided by René Pomeau, *Voltaire par lui-même* (Paris, 1955).

General studies of the eighteenth century available in English and especially helpful in understanding Voltaire are: Ernst Cassirer, *The Philosophy of the Enlightenment* (1932; trans. 1951); Paul Hazard, *European Thought in the Eighteenth Century. From Montesquieu to Lessing* (1946; trans. 1954); George R. Havens, *The Age of Ideas* (New York, 1955).

FICTION

ZADIG,

OR DESTINY

An Oriental Tale[1]

DEDICATORY EPISTLE TO THE SULTANA SHERAH, BY SADI

*The 18th day of the month Shewal,
in the year 837 of the Hegira*

Delight of the eyes, torment of the heart, and light of the soul, I kiss not the dust of your feet, because you scarcely ever walk, or only on Persian carpets or on roses. I present you with the translation of a book written by an ancient sage, to whom, being in the happy condition of having nothing to do, there occurred the happy thought of amusing himself by writing the story of Zadig, a work that says more than it seems to say. I beseech you to read it and judge it; for although you are in the springtime of life, and courted by pleasures of every kind; although you are beautiful, and your talents add to your beauty; and although you are praised from morning to night, and so have every right to be devoid of common sense, yet you have a very sound intelligence and a highly refined taste, and I have heard you argue better than any old dervish with a long beard and pointed cap. You are cautious yet not suspicious; you are gentle without being weak; you are beneficent with due discrimination; you love your friends, and make no enemies. Your wit never borrows its charm from slander; you neither say nor do evil, in spite of abundant facilities if you were so inclined. Lastly, your soul has always appeared to me as pure as your beauty. You have even a small stock of philosophy, which has led me to believe that you would take more interest than any one else in this work of a wise man.

It was originally written in ancient Chaldean, which neither you nor I understand. It was translated into Arabic for the entertainment of the famous Sultan Oulougbeg, about the time when the Arabs and Persians were beginning to compose *The Thousand and One Nights, The Thousand and One Days*, etc. Ouloug preferred to read *Zadig*; but the ladies of his harem liked the others better.

"How can you prefer," said the wise Ouloug, "senseless stories that mean nothing?"

"That is just why we are so fond of them," answered the ladies.

I feel confident that you will not resemble them, but that you will be a true Ouloug; and I venture to hope that when you are weary of general conversation, which is of much the same character as *The Arabian Nights* except that it is less amusing, I may have the honor of talking to you for a few minutes in a reasonable way. If you had been Thalestris[2] in the time of Alexander, son of Philip, or if you had been the Queen of Sheba in the days of Solomon, those kings would have travelled to you.

I pray the Heavenly Powers that your pleasures may be unalloyed, your beauty unfading, and your happiness everlasting.

I

THE ONE-EYED MAN

In the time of King Moabdar there lived at Babylon a young man named Zadig, who was born with a good disposition, which education had strengthened. Though young and rich he knew how to restrain his passions; he was free from all affectation, made no pretense of infallibility himself, and knew how to respect human weakness. People were astonished to see that, with all his wit, he never turned his raillery on the vague, disconnected, and confused talk, the rash slander, the ignorant judgments, the coarse jests, and all that vain babble of words which went by the name of conversation at Babylon. He had learned in the first book of Zoroaster that self-conceit is a balloon puffed up with wind, out of which issue storms and tempests when it is pricked. Above all, Zadig never prided himself on despising women, nor boasted of his conquests over them. Generous as he was, he had no fear of bestowing kindness on the ungrateful, following the noble maxim of Zoroaster: *When you eat, give something to the dogs, even though they should bite you.* He was as wise as man can be, for he sought to live with the wise. Instructed in the sciences of the ancient Chaldeans, he was not ignorant of such physical principles of Nature as were then known, and knew as much of Metaphysics as has been known in any age, that is to say, very little. He was firmly persuaded that the year consists of three hundred and sixty-five days and a quarter, in spite of the new philosophy of his time, and that the sun is the center of the world; and when the leading magi told him with contemptuous arrogance that he entertained dangerous opinions, and that it was a proof of hostility to the government to believe that the sun turned on its axis and that the year had twelve months, he held his peace without anger or disdain.

Zadig, with great riches, and consequently well provided with friends, having health and good looks, a just and well-disciplined mind, and a heart noble and sincere, thought that he might be happy. He was to be married to Semira, a lady whose beauty, birth, and fortune made her the first match in Babylon. He felt for her a strong and virtuous attachment, and Semira in her turn loved him passionately. They were close to the happy moment which was to unite them, when, walking together towards one of the gates of Babylon, under the palm trees which adorned the banks of the Euphrates, they saw a group of men armed with swords and bows advancing in their direction. They were the satellites of young Orcan, the nephew of a minister of state, whom his uncle's courtiers had encouraged in the belief that he might do anything he liked. He had none of the graces or virtues of Zadig; but, thinking that he was worth a great deal more, he was desperate at not being preferred to him. This jealousy, which proceeded only from his vanity, made him think that he was madly in love with Semira, and he determined to carry her off. The ravishers seized her, and in their violence wounded her, shedding the blood of one so beautiful that the tigers of Mount Imaus would have melted at the sight of her. She pierced the sky with her lamentations. She cried aloud:

"My dear husband! They are tearing me from the one I adore."

Taking no heed of her own danger, it was of her beloved Zadig alone that she thought, who, meanwhile, was defending her with all the force that love and valor could bestow. With the help of only two slaves he put the ravishers to flight, and carried Semira to her home unconscious and covered with blood. On opening her eyes she saw her deliverer, and said:

"O Zadig, I loved you before as my husband, I love you now as one to whom I owe life and honor."

Never was there a heart more deeply moved than that of Semira; never did more lovely lips express sentiments more touching, in words of fire inspired by gratitude for the greatest of benefits and the most tender feeling of the most honorable love. Her wound was slight, and was soon cured; but Zadig was hurt more severely. An arrow had struck him near the eye and made a deep wound. Semira's only prayer to Heaven now was that her lover might be healed. Her eyes were bathed in tears night and day; she longed for the moment when those of Zadig might once more be able to enjoy her glances; but an abscess which attacked the wounded eye made her fear the worst. A messenger was sent to Memphis for Hermes, the famous physician, who came with a large number of attendants. He visited the sick man, and declared that he would lose the eye; he even foretold the day and the hour when this dreadful event would happen.

"If it had been the right eye," said he, "I might have cured it, but wounds of the left eye are incurable."

All Babylon, while bewailing Zadig's fate, admired the profound scientific knowledge of Hermes. Two days afterwards the abscess broke of itself, and Zadig was completely cured. Hermes wrote a book, in which he proved to him that he ought not to have been cured. Zadig did not read it; but as soon as he could go out, he prepared to visit her in whom rested his hope of happiness in life, and for whose sake alone he desired to have eyes. Now Semira had gone into the country three days before. On his way he learned that this fair lady, after loudly declaring that she had an insurmountable aversion to one-eyed men, had just married Orcan the night before. As this news he lost consciousness, and his grief brought him to the brink of the grave; he was ill for a long time, but at last reason prevailed over his affliction, and the very atrocity of his suffering served to console him.

"Since I have experienced," said he, "such cruel caprice from a girl brought up at Court, I must marry one of the townspeople."

He chose Azora, who came of the best family and was the best behaved girl in the city. He married her, and lived with her for a month in all the bliss of a most tender union. The only fault he noticed in her was a little frivolity, and a strong tendency to find that the handsomest young men had always the most intelligence and virtue.

II

THE NOSE

One day Azora returned from a walk in a state of vehement indignation, and uttering loud exclamations.

"What is the matter with you, my dear wife?" said Zadig; "who can have put you so much out of temper?"

"Alas!" she replied, "you would be as indignant as I, if you had seen the sight which I have just witnessed. I went to console the young widow Cosrou, who just two days ago raised a tomb to her young husband beside the stream which forms the boundary of this meadow. She vowed to Heaven, in her grief, that she would dwell beside that tomb as long as the stream flowed by it."

"Well!" said Zadig, "a truly estimable woman, who really loved her husband!"

"Ah!" returned Azora, "if you only knew what she was doing when I paid her my visit!"

"What then, fair Azora?"

"She was diverting the course of the brook."

Azora gave vent to her feelings in such lengthy invectives, and burst into such violent reproaches against the young widow, that this ostentatious display of virtue was not altogether pleasing to Zadig.

He had a friend named Cador, who was one of those young men in whom his wife found more merit and integrity than in others; Zadig took him into his confidence, and secured his fidelity, as far as possible, by means of a considerable present.

Azora, having passed a couple of days with one of her friends in the country, on the third day returned home. The servants, with tears in their eyes, told her that her husband had died quite suddenly the night before, that they had not dared to convey to her such sad news, and that they had just buried Zadig in the tomb of his ancestors at the end of the garden. She wept, and tore her hair, and vowed that she would die. In the evening Cador asked if she would allow him to speak to her, and they wept together. Next day they wept less, and dined together. Cador informed her that his friend had left him the greater part of his property, and gave her to understand that he would deem it the greatest happiness to share his fortune with her. The lady shed tears, was offended, allowed herself to be soothed; the supper lasted longer than the dinner, and they conversed together more confidentially. Azora spoke in praise of the deceased, but admitted that he had faults from which Cador was free.

In the middle of supper, Cador complained of a violent pain in the spleen. The lady, anxious and attentive, had all the essences on her toilet table brought, to try if there might not be some one among them good for pain of the spleen. She was very sorry that the famous Hermes was no longer in Babylon. She even condescended to touch the side where Cador felt such sharp pains.

"Are you subject to this cruel malady?" she asked in a tone of compassion.

"It sometimes brings me to the brink of the grave," answered Cador; "and there is only one remedy which can relieve me: it is to apply to my side the nose of a man who has been only a day or two dead."

"What a strange remedy!" said Azora.

"Not more strange," was his reply, "than the scentbags of Mr. Arnoult as an antidote to apoplexy."

That reason, joined to the extreme merit of the young man, at last decided the lady.

"After all," said she, "when my husband shall pass from the world of yesterday into the world of tomorrow over the Chinavar bridge, the angel Azrael will not grant him passage any the less because his nose will be a little shorter in the second life than in the first."

She then took a razor, and went to her husband's tomb; after she had watered it with her tears, she approached to cut off Zadig's nose, whom she found stretched out at full length in the tomb. Zadig jumped up, and, holding his nose with one hand, stopped the razor with the other.

"Madam," said he, "do not cry out so loudly another time against young Cosrou; your intention of cutting off my nose is as bad as that of turning aside a stream."

III

THE DOG AND THE HORSE

Zadig found by experience that the first month of marriage is, as it is written in the book of Zend, the moon of honey, and that the second is the moon of wormwood. He was some time afterwards obliged to give up Azora, who became too difficult to live with, and he sought for happiness in the study of nature.

"There is no happiness," he said, "equal to that of a philosopher, who reads in this great book which God has set before our eyes. The truths which he discovers are his own: he nourishes and cultivates his soul, he lives in peace, he fears no man, and no tender spouse comes to cut off his nose."

Full of these ideas, he retired to a country house on the banks of the Euphrates. There he did not spend his time in calculating how many inches of water flowed in a second under the arches of a bridge, or whether a cubic line of rain fell in the month of the mouse more than in the month of the sheep. He did not contrive how to make silk out of cobwebs, nor porcelain out of broken bottles; but he studied most of all the properties of animals and plants; and soon acquired a sagacity that showed him a thousand differences where other men see nothing but uniformity.

One day, when he was walking near a little wood, he saw one of the queen's eunuchs running to meet him, followed by several officers, who appeared to be in the greatest uneasiness, running hither and yon like men bewildered, searching for some most precious object which they had lost.

"Young man," said the chief eunuch to Zadig, "have you seen the queen's dog?"

Zadig modestly replied: "It is a bitch, not a dog."

"You are right," said the eunuch.

"It is a very small spaniel," added Zadig; "it is not long since she has had a litter of puppies; she is lame in the left frontfoot, and her ears are very long."

"You have seen her, then?" said the chief eunuch, quite out of breath.

"No," answered Zadig, "I have never seen her, and never knew that the queen had a bitch."

Just at this very time, by a usual quirk of fortune, the finest horse in the king's stables had broken away from the hands of a groom in the plains of Babylon. The grand huntsman and all the other officers ran after him with as much anxiety as the chief of the eunuchs had displayed in his search after the queen's bitch. The grand huntsman accosted Zadig, and asked him if he had not seen the king's horse pass that way.

"It is the horse," said Zadig, "which gallops best; he is five feet high, and has small hoofs; his tail is three and a half feet long; the bosses on his bit are of twenty-three carat gold; his shoes are silver of eleven pennyweights."

"Which road did he take? Where is he?" asked the grand huntsman.

"I have not seen him," answered Zadig, "and I have never even heard anyone speak of him."

The grand huntsman and the chief eunuch had no doubt that Zadig had stolen the king's horse and the queen's bitch; they had him brought before the Assembly of the Grand Desterham, which condemned him to the knout, and to pass the rest of his life in Siberia. Scarcely had the sentence been pronounced, when the horse and the bitch were found. The judges were now under the disagreeable necessity of amending their judgment; but they condemned Zadig to pay four hundred ounces of gold for having said that he had not seen what he had seen. He was forced to pay this fine first, and afterwards he was allowed to plead his cause before the Council of the Grand Desterham; he expressed himself in the following terms:

"Stars of justice, fathomless gulfs of knowledge, mirrors of truth, ye who have the gravity of lead, the strength of iron, the brilliance of the diamond, and a close affinity with gold. Inasmuch as it is permitted me to speak before this august assembly, I swear to you by Ormuzd that I have never seen the queen's respected bitch, nor the sacred horse of the king of kings. Hear all that happened: I was walking towards the little wood where later on I met the venerable eunuch and the most illustrious grand huntsman. I saw on the sand the footprints of an animal, and easily decided that they were those of a little dog. Long and faintly marked furrows, imprinted where the sand was slightly raised between the footprints, told me that it was a bitch whose dugs were hanging down, and that consequently she must have given birth only a few days before. Other marks of a different character, showing that the surface of the sand had been constantly grazed on either side of the front paws, informed me that she had very long ears; and, as I observed that the sand was always less deeply indented by one paw than by the other three, I gathered that the bitch belonging to our august queen was a little lame, if I may venture to say so.

"With respect to the horse of the king of kings, you must know that as I was walking along the roads in that same wood, I perceived the marks of horseshoes, all at equal distances. 'There,' I said to myself, 'went a horse with a faultless gallop.' The dust upon the trees, where the width of the road was not more than seven feet, was here and there rubbed off on both sides, three and a half feet away from the middle of the road. 'This horse,' said I, 'has a tail three and a half feet long, which, by its movements to right and left, has swept away the dust.' I saw, where the trees formed a canopy five feet above the ground, leaves lately fallen from the boughs; and I concluded that the horse had touched them, and was therefore five feet high. As to his bit, it must be of twenty-three carat gold, for he had rubbed its bosses against a touchstone. Lastly, I inferred from the marks that his shoes left upon stones of another kind, that he was shod with silver of eleven pennyweights in quality."

All the judges marvelled at Zadig's deep and subtle discernment, and a report of it reached the king and queen. Nothing but Zadig was talked of in the antechambers, the presence chamber, and the cabinet; and, though several of the magi were of opinion that he ought to be burned as a wizard, the king ordered that he should be released from the fine of four hundred ounces of gold to which he had been condemned. The registrar, the bailiffs, and the attorneys came to his house with great solemnity to restore him his four hundred ounces; they kept back only three hundred and ninety-eight of them for legal expenses, and their servants claimed their tips.

Zadig saw how very dangerous it sometimes is to be too wise, and resolved on the next occasion of the kind to say nothing about what he had seen.

Such an opportunity soon occurred. A state prisoner made his escape, and passed under the windows of Zadig's house. On being questioned, Zadig said nothing; but it was proved that he had looked out of the window. For this crime he was condemned to pay five hundred ounces of gold, and he thanked his judges for their leniency, according to the custom of Babylon.

"Good Heavens!" said Zadig to himself, "what a pity it is when one takes a walk in a wood through which the queen's bitch and the king's horse have passed! How dangerous it is to stand at a window! and how difficult it is to be happy in this life!"

IV

THE ENVIOUS MAN

Zadig sought consolation in philosophy and friendship for the evils which fortune had brought him. In one of the suburbs of Babylon he had a house tastefully furnished, where he had gathered all the arts and pleasures that were worthy of an honest man.

In the morning his library was open to all men of learning; in the evening his table was surrounded by good company. But he soon discovered how dangerous learned men are. A hot dispute arose over a law of Zoroaster, which prohibited the eating of a griffin.

"How can a griffin be forbidden," said some, "if no such creature exists?"

"It must exist," said the others, "since Zoroaster forbids it to be eaten."

Zadig tried to bring them to an agreement by saying:

"If there are griffins, let us refrain from eating them; and if there are none, there will be all the less danger of our doing so. Thus, in either case, Zoroaster will be obeyed."

A learned scholar who had composed thirteen volumes on the properties of the griffin, and who was moreover a great theurgist, lost no time in bringing an accusation against Zadig before an archimagian named Yebor,[3] the most stupid of the Chaldeans, and consequently the most fanatical. This man would have had Zadig impaled for the greater glory of the Sun, and would have recited the breviary of Zoroaster in a more complacent tone of voice for having done it; but his friend Cador (one friend is worth more than a hundred priests), sought out old Yebor, and addressed him thus:

"Long live the Sun and the griffins! Take good care that you do no harm to Zadig; he is a saint; he keeps griffins in his backyard, and abstains from eating them; and his accuser is a heretic, who dares to maintain that rabbits have cloven feet and are not unclean."

"In that case," said Yebor, shaking his bald head, "Zadig must be impaled for having thought wrongly about griffins, and the other for having spoken wrongly about rabbits."

Cador settled the matter by means of a maid of honor who had borne him a child, and who was held in high esteem in the college of the magi. No one was impaled, though a good many of the doctors commented on the fact, and prophesied the downfall of Babylon in consequence.

Zadig exclaimed: "On what does happiness depend! Everybody in this world persecutes me, even beings that do not exist." He cursed all men of learning, and determined to live henceforth only in the best society.

He invited to his house the most honest men and the most charming women in Babylon; he gave elegant suppers, often preceded by concerts, and enlivened by interesting conversation, from which he knew how to banish that straining after a display of wit, which is the surest way to have none and to mar the most brilliant company. Neither the choice of his friends, nor that of his dishes, was prompted by vanity; for in everything he preferred being to seeming, and thereby he attracted to himself the real respect to which he made no claim.

Opposite Zadig's house lived Arimaze, a person whose depraved soul was painted on his coarse countenance. He was consumed with malice, and puffed up with pride, and, to crown all, he set up for being a wit and was only a bore. Having never been able to succeed in the world, he took his revenge by railing at it. In spite of his riches, he had some trouble in getting flatterers to flock to his house. The noise of the carriages entering Zadig's gates in the evening annoyed him, the sound of his praises irritated him yet more. He sometimes went to Zadig's parties, and sat down at his table without being invited, where he spoiled all the enjoyment of the company, just as harpies are said to infect whatever food they touch. One day a lady whom he wanted to entertain, instead of accepting his invitation, went to sup with Zadig. Another day, when he was talking with him in the palace, they came across a minister who asked Zadig to supper without asking Arimaze. The most inveterate hatreds are often founded on causes quite as trivial. This person, who went by the name of "the Envious man" in Babylon, wished to ruin Zadig because he was called "the Happy man." Opportunities for doing harm are found a hundred times a day, and an opportunity for doing good occurs once a year, as Zoroaster has observed.

The Envious man went to Zadig's house, and found him walking in his garden with two friends and a lady, to whom he was addressing frequent compliments, without any intention other than that of saying them. The conversation turned upon a war, which the king had just brought to a prosperous conclusion, against the prince of Hyrcania, his vassal. Zadig, who had displayed his valor during the short campaign, had much to say in praise of the king, and still more in praise of the lady. He took out his note-book, and wrote down four lines, which he made on the spur of the moment, and which he gave to his fair companion to read. His friends begged him for a sight of them; but his modesty, or rather a natural self-respect, made him refuse. He knew that impromptu verses are never of any value except in the eyes of her in whose honor they have been composed, so he tore in two the page on which he had just written them, and threw the pieces into a thicket of roses, where his friends looked for them in vain. A shower came on, and they went indoors. The Envious man, who remained in the garden, searched so diligently that he found a piece of the page which had been torn in such a way that the halves of each line that were left made sense, and even made a rhymed verse, in shorter metre than the original; but by an accident still more strange, these short lines were found to contain the most dreadful libel against the king. They read thus:

> "By the greatest crimes
> Set on the throne,
> In peaceful times
> One foe alone."

The Envious man was happy for the first time in his life, for he had in his hands the means of destroying a virtuous and amiable man. Full of such cruel joy, he had this lampoon written in Zadig's own hand brought to the king's notice, who ordered him to be sent to prison, together with his two friends and the lady. His trial was soon over, nor did his judges deign to hear what he had to say for himself. When he was brought up to receive sentence, the Envious man crossed his path, and told him in a loud voice that his verses were good for nothing. Zadig did not pride himself on being a good poet, but he was in despair at being condemned as guilty of high treason, and at seeing a beautiful lady and his two friends in prison for a crime that he had never committed. He was not allowed to speak, because his notebook spoke for him. Such was the law of Babylon. He was then forced to go to his execution through a crowd of inquisitive spectators, not one of whom dared to pity him, but who rushed forward in order

to scrutinise his countenance, and to see whether he was likely
to die with a good grace. His relatives alone were distressed; for
they were not to be his heirs. Three quarters of his estate were
confiscated for the king's benefit, and the Envious man profited
by the other quarter.

Just as he was preparing for death, the king's parrot escaped
from its perch, and alighted in Zadig's garden, on a thicket of
roses. A peach had been carried there by the wind from a tree
close by, and it had fallen on a piece of writing paper, to which it
had stuck. The bird took up both the peach and the paper, and
laid them on the monarch's knees. The king, whose curiosity was
excited, read some words which made no sense, and which appeared to be the ends of four lines of verse. He loved poetry, and
princes who love poetry are never at a loss. His parrot's adventure set him thinking. The queen, who remembered what had
been written on the fragment of the page from Zadig's note-
book, had it brought to her.

The two pieces were put side by side, and were found to fit
together exactly. The verses then read as Zadig had made them:

> "By the greatest crimes I saw the earth alarm'd,
> Set on the throne the king all evil curbs;
> In peaceful times now only Love is arm'd,
> One foe alone the timid heart disturbs."

The king immediately commanded that Zadig should be
brought before him, and that his two friends and the fair lady
should be let out of prison. Zadig prostrated himself with his face
to the ground at their majesties' feet, asked their pardon most
humbly for having made such poor rhymes, and spoke with so
much grace, wit, and good sense, that the king and queen desired
to see him again. He came again accordingly, and pleased even
more. All the property of the Envious man who had accused
him unjustly was given to Zadig, but he gave it all back, and the
Envious man was touched, but only with the joy of not losing his
wealth. The king's esteem for Zadig increased every day. He made
him share all his pleasures, and consulted him in all matters of
business. The queen regarded him from that time with a kindness
that could become dangerous to herself. to her royal consort, to

Zadig, and to the whole State. Zadig began to think that it is not so difficult after all to be happy.

V

THE GENEROUS MEN

The time was now arrived for celebrating a great festival, which recurred every five years. It was the custom at Babylon to announce in a public and solemn manner, at the end of such a period, the name of that citizen who had done the most generous act. The grandees and the magi were the judges. The chief satrap, who had the city under his charge, made known the most noble deeds that had been performed under his government. The choice was made by vote, and the king pronounced judgment. People came to this festival from the farthest corners of the earth. The successful candidate received from the monarch's hands a cup of gold decorated with precious stones, and the king addressed him in these terms:

"*Receive this reward of generosity, and may the Gods grant me many subjects who resemble you!*"

The memorable day had arrived, and the king appeared upon his throne, surrounded by grandees, magi, and deputies sent by all nations to these games, where glory was to be gained, not by the swiftness of horses nor by physical strength, but by virtue The chief satrap proclaimed with a loud voice the actions that might entitle their authors to this inestimable prize. He said nothing about the magnanimity with which Zadig had restored all his fortune to the Envious man; that was not considered an action worthy of disputing the prize.

First, he presented a judge who, having made a citizen lose an important law-suit, by a mistake for which he was in no way responsible, had given him all his own property, which was equal in value to what the other had lost.

He next brought forward a young man, who, being madly in love with a girl to whom he was engaged to be married, had resigned her to a friend who was nearly dying for love of her, and had paid her dowry as well.

Then he introduced a soldier, who in the Hyrcanian war had given a still nobler example of generosity. Some of the enemy's troops were laying hands on his mistress, and he was defending her from them, when he was told that another group of Hyrcanians, a few paces off, was carrying off his mother. With tears he left his mistress, and ran to rescue his mother; and when he returned to his beloved, he found her dying. He wanted to kill himself; his mother pointed out that she had no one but him to help her, and he was courageous enough to endure to live on.

The arbitrators were inclined to give the prize to this soldier; but the king interposed, and said:

"This man's conduct and that of the others is praiseworthy, but it does not astonish me. Yesterday Zadig did something that made me marvel. Some days before, my minister and favorite Coreb had incurred my displeasure and been disgraced. I uttered violent complaints against him, and all my courtiers assured me that I was too easy with him; each vied with his neighbor in saying as much evil as he could of Coreb. I asked Zadig what he thought of him, and he dared to say a word in his favor. I am free to confess that I have heard of instances in our history of men atoning for a mistake by the sacrifice of their goods, giving up a mistress, or preferring a mother to a sweetheart, but I have never read of a courtier speaking a good word for a minister in disgrace, with whom his sovereign was angered. I award twenty thousand pieces of gold to each of those whose generous acts have been recounted; but I give the cup to Zadig."

"Sire," said he, "it is Your Majesty alone who deserves the cup, for having committed an act of unprecedented magnanimity, in that, being a king, you were not angry with your slave when he went counter to your passion."

The king and Zadig were both admired by all. The judge who had given away his fortune, the lover who married his mistress to his friend, and the soldier who had preferred his mother's safety to that of his sweetheart, received the king's presents, and saw their names written in the Book of the Generous. Zadig had the cup. The king gained the reputation of a good prince, which he did not keep long. The day was celebrated with feasts that lasted longer than the law directed. Its memory is still preserved in Asia. Zadig said:

"At last, then, I am happy." But he was deceived.

VI

THE MINISTER

The king had lost his prime minister, and chose Zadig to fill his place. All the beautiful ladies in Babylon applauded the choice; for since the foundation of the empire there had never been such a young minister. All the courtiers were offended; and the Envious man spat blood on hearing the news, while his nose swelled to an enormous size. Zadig, having thanked the king and queen, proceeded to thank the parrot also.

"Beautiful bird," he said, "it is you who have saved my life, and made me prime minister: the bitch and the horse belonging to Their Majesties did me much harm, but you have done me good. On what do human destinies depend! But," added he, "a happiness so strangely acquired will, perhaps, soon disappear."

"Ay," replied the parrot.

Zadig was startled at the response; but, being a good naturalist, and not believing that parrots were prophets, he soon reassured himself and began to carry out his duties as best as he could.

He made every one feel the sacred power of the laws, but made no one feel the weight of his dignity. He did not curb the free expression of opinion in the divan, and each vizier was welcome to hold his own without displeasing him. When he acted as judge in any matter, it was not he who judged, it was the law; but when the law was too harsh, he tempered its severity; and when there were no laws to meet the case, his sense of equity supplied him with decisions that might have been taken for those of Zoroaster.

It is from Zadig that the nations of the world have received the great principle: "It is better to risk saving a guilty man than to condemn an innocent." He held that laws were made as much for the sake of helping as of intimidating the people. His chief skill lay in revealing the truth which all men try to obscure. From the very beginning of his administration he put this great talent to good use. A famous merchant of Babylon had died in India, and made his two sons heirs to equal portions of his estate, after having married off their sister; and he left a present of thirty thousand gold pieces to that one of his two sons who should be judged to have loved him the most. The elder built him a tomb; the younger increased his sister's dowry with a part of his own inheritance. Everybody said: "It is the elder son who has the greater love for his father, the younger loves his sister better; the thirty thousand pieces belong to the elder."

Zadig sent for the two brothers, one after the other. He said to the elder:

"Your father is not dead; he has been cured of his last illness, and is returning to Babylon."

"God be praised!" answered the young man, "but his tomb has cost me a large sum of money."

Zadig then said the same thing to the younger brother.

"God be praised!" answered he; "I will restore to my father all that I have, but I hope that he will leave my sister what I have given her."

"You shall restore nothing," said Zadig, "and you shall have the thirty thousand pieces; it is you who love your father best."

A very rich young lady had made a promise of marriage to two magi, and, after having received a course of instruction for some months from each of them, found herself pregnant. Both still wanted to marry her. "I will take for my husband," she said, "the one who has put me in a position to present the empire with a citizen."

"It is I who have done that good work," said one of them.

"It is I who have had that privilege," said the other.

"Very well," answered she, "I will recognize that one as the father of the child who can give him the best education."

She gave birth to a son. Each of the two magi wished to bring it up, and the case was brought before Zadig, who summoned the magi to his presence.

"What will you teach your pupil?" he asked of the first.

"I will instruct him," said the doctor, "in the eight parts of

speech, in dialectic, astrology, demonology, the difference between substance and accident, abstract and concrete, monads and
pre-established harmony."

"For my part," said the other, "I will try to make him just
and worthy of having friends."

Zadig exclaimed: "*Whether you are his father or not, you shall
marry his mother.*" [4]

VII

THE DISPUTES AND THE AUDIENCES

Thus it was that Zadig daily showed the subtlety of his intellect
and the goodness of his heart. He was admired, yet he was
also loved. He passed for the most fortunate of men; all the
empire resounded with his name; all the women made eyes at
him; all the citizens extolled his justice; the men of science regarded him as their oracle, and even the priests confessed that he
knew more than the old archimagian Yebor. Far from wishing to
prosecute him for his opinions on the subject of griffins, they believed only what seemed credible to him.

Now there was a great controversy in Babylon, which had
lasted fifteen hundred years, and had divided the empire into
two bigoted sects; one maintained that the temple of Mithras
should never be entered except with the left foot foremost;
the other held this practice in abomination, and always entered with the right foot first. Everyone waited impatiently for
the day on which the solemn feast of the holy fire was to be
held, to know which side would be favored by Zadig. All had
their eyes fixed on his two feet, and the whole city was in agitation and suspense. Zadig leaped into the temple with both his
feet together, and afterwards proved in an eloquent discourse
that the God of Heaven and Earth, who is no respecter of persons, cares no more for the left leg than for the right. The
Envious man and his wife contended that there were not enough
figures of speech in his discourse, that he had not made the
mountains and hills dance enough.

"He is dry and without imagination," they said; "one does

not see the ocean fly before him, nor the stars fall, nor the sun melt like wax; he lacks the fine oriental style."

Zadig was content with having the style of a reasonable man. He was a favorite with all classes, not because he followed the right path, nor because he was reasonable, nor even because he was amiable, but because he was grand vizier.

He also happily put an end to the hot dispute between the white and the black magi. The white asserted that it was impious, when praying to God, to turn towards the east in winter; the black were confident that God abhorred the prayers of those who turned towards the west in summer. Zadig directed that men should turn in whatever way they pleased.

He likewise found out the secret of taking care of all his business, both public and private, in the morning, and he employed the rest of the day in improving Babylon. He had tragedies presented which moved the audience to tears, and comedies that made them laugh; a custom which had long passed out of fashion, and which he had the good taste to revive. He did not pretend to know more about their art than the actors themselves; he rewarded them with gifts and distinctions, and was not secretly jealous of their talents. In the evenings he amused the king much, and the queen still more.

"A great minister!" said the king.

"A charming minister!" said the queen.

Both of them agreed that it would have been a great pity if Zadig had been hanged.

Never was statesman in office obliged to give so many audiences to the ladies. The greater number came to speak to him about no business in particular for the sake of having particular business with him. The wife of the Envious man presented herself among the first; she swore by Mithras and the Zendavesta, and the holy fire, that she detested the conduct of her husband; then she told him in confidence that this husband of hers was jealous and treated her brutally, and gave him to understand that the Gods punished him by refusing him the precious effects of that holy fire whereby alone man is made like the immortals. She ended by dropping her garter. Zadig picked it up with his customary politeness, but did not offer to fasten it again round the lady's knee, and this little fault, if it can be considered such, was the cause of the most dreadful misfortunes. Zadig thought no more about the incident, and the Envious man's wife thought about it a great deal.

Other ladies continued to present themselves every day. The secret annals of Babylon assert that he yielded to temptation on one occasion, but that he was astonished to find that he enjoyed his mistress without pleasure, and that his mind was distracted even in the midst of the tenderest embraces. The fair one to whom he gave, almost unconsciously, these tokens of his favor was a lady in waiting to Queen Astarte. This tender daughter of Babylon consoled herself for his coldness by saying to herself:

"That man must have a prodigious amount of business in his head, since his thoughts are absorbed with it even when he is making love."

Zadig happened at a moment when many people say nothing and others only utter terms of endearment, to suddenly exclaim: "The queen!" The fair Babylonian fancied that he had at last recovered his wits at a happy moment, and that he was calling her: "My queen!" But Zadig, still absent-minded, proceeded to utter the name of Astarte. The lady, who in this agreeable situation interpreted everything in a flattering sense, imagined that he meant to say: "You are more beautiful than Queen Astarte." She left the seraglio of Zadig with magnificent presents, and went to relate her adventure to the Envious woman, who was her intimate friend. The latter was cruelly piqued at the preference shown to the other.

"He did not even condescend," said she, "to replace this garter which I have here, and which I will never use again."

"Oh!" said her more fortunate friend, "you wear the same garters as the queen! Do you get them from the same maker?"

The Envious woman fell into a deep meditation, and made no reply, but went and consulted her husband, the Envious man.

Meanwhile Zadig became aware of his constant absence of mind whenever he gave an audience or administered justice; he did not know to what to attribute it; it was his only subject of annoyance.

He had a dream. He seemed to be lying at first on a heap of dry herbs, among which were some prickly ones which made him uncomfortable, and afterwards he reposed luxuriously upon a bed of roses, out of which glided a snake that wounded him in the heart with its pointed and poisoned tongue.

"Alas!" said he, "I lay a long time on those dry and prickly herbs; I am now on the bed of roses; but who will be the serpent?"

VIII

JEALOUSY

Zadig's misfortune arose out of his very happiness, and especially out of his merit. He had daily interviews with the king and with Astarte, his august consort. The charm of his conversation was doubled by that desire to please which is to the mind what ornaments are to personal beauty; his youth and graceful manners insensibly made an impression upon Astarte, of which she was not at first aware. Her passion grew in the bosom of innocence. Astarte gave herself up without scruple and without fear to the pleasure of seeing and hearing a man who was so dear to her husband and to the State; she never ceased singing his praises to the king; she was perpetually speaking about him to her women, who even went beyond her in their commendations; everything served to fix more deeply in her heart the arrow of which she was unconscious. She bestowed presents upon Zadig, into which more love-making entered than she supposed; she meant to speak to him as a queen satisfied with his services, but the expressions she used were sometimes those of a woman of tender sensibility.

Astarte was much more beautiful than that Semira who so hated one-eyed men, or that other woman who had wanted to cut off her husband's nose. Astarte's familiar manner, her soft speeches at which she began to blush, her eyes which, despite her efforts to turn them away, were ever fixed upon his own, kindled in Zadig's heart a fire which filled him with astonishment. He fought; he called to his aid the philosophy which had never before failed him; he drew from it nothing but a clearer perception, and received no relief. Duty, gratitude, and outraged majesty presented themselves to his view as so many avenging deities; he struggled, and he triumphed; but this victory, which had to be repeated every moment, cost him groans and tears. He no longer dared to address the queen with that sweet freedom which had had such charms for both of them; a cloud overshadowed his eyes; his conversation was constrained and abrupt; his eyes were downcast, and when, in spite of himself, they turned towards Astarte, they encountered those of the queen moistened with tears from which there shot forth arrows of flame. They seemed to say to each other:

"We adore one another, yet we are afraid to love; we both burn with a fire which we condemn."

When Zadig left her side it was with bewilderment and despair, his heart oppressed with a burden which he was no longer able to support: in the violence of these disturbances he let his friend Cador discover his secret, like a man who, after having endured the most excruciating pains, at last makes his malady known by a cry which a keener spasm than any before wrings from him, and by the cold sweat which pours over his forehead.

Cador addressed him as follows:

"I have already guessed the feelings that you would hide from yourself; the passions have symptoms which cannot be misinterpreted. Judge, my dear Zadig, since I have been able to read your heart, whether the king is not likely to discover there a sentiment that will offend him. He has no other fault but that of being the most jealous of men. You resist your passion with greater strength than the queen, because you are a philosopher, and because you are Zadig. Astarte is a woman; she lets her looks speak for her with all the more imprudence because she does not yet believe herself blameworthy. Assured of her innocence, she unfortunately neglects appearances which it is necessary to observe. I shall tremble for her so long as she has nothing with which to reproach herself. If you came to a common understanding, you would be able to throw dust into everyone's eyes; a growing passion, forcibly checked, breaks out into the open; but love when gratified can easily conceal itself."

Zadig shuddered at the suggestion of betraying the king, his benefactor; and he was never more faithful to his prince than when guilty of an involuntary crime against him. Meanwhile the queen pronounced the name of Zadig so often, she blushed so deeply as she uttered it, she was sometimes so animated, and at other times so confused when she addressed him in the king's presence, and she was seized with so profound a fit of day-dreaming whenever he went away, that the king began to be alarmed. He believed all that he saw, and imagined all that he did not see. He particularly remarked that his wife's slippers were blue, and that Zadig's slippers were blue; that his wife's ribbons were yellow, and that Zadig's cap was yellow. Terrible indications these to a prince of such delicate sensibility! Suspicion soon became certainty in his envenomed mind.

All the slaves of kings and queens are so many spies over their hearts. It was soon discovered that Astarte was tender and that Moabdar was jealous. The Envious man got his wife to send the king her garter, which was like the queen's; and, to make the matter worse, this garter was blue. The monarch thought of nothing now but how to take his revenge. One night he determined to poison the queen, and to have Zadig strangled at day-break. The order was given to a merciless eunuch, the usual executioner of his vengeance. Now there happened to be at the time in the king's chamber a little dwarf, who was dumb but not deaf. He was allowed to wander about when and where he pleased, and, like a domestic animal, was oftentimes a witness of what happened in the strictest privacy. This little mute was much attached to the queen and Zadig, and he heard with no less surprise than horror the order given for their death. But what could he do to prevent this frightful order, which was to be carried out within a few hours? He did not know how to write, but he had learned how to paint, and was particularly skilful in making likenesses. He spent part of the night in portraying what he wished the queen to understand. His sketch represented in one corner of the picture the king in a furious rage, giving orders to his eunuch; a blue bowstring and a cup on a table, with garters and yellow ribbons; the queen in the middle of the picture, expiring in the arms of her women, and Zadig lying strangled at her feet. A rising sun was represented on the horizon to indicate that this horrible execution was to take place at the earliest glimpse of dawn. As soon as this task was finished he ran to one of Astarte's women, awoke her, and made her understand that she must take the picture that very instant to the queen.

In the middle of the night someone knocked at Zadig's door; he was roused from sleep, and a note from the queen was given him; he doubted whether or not it were a dream, and opened the letter with a trembling hand. What was his surprise, and who could express the consternation and despair with which he was overwhelmed, when he read these words: "Fly, this very moment, or you will be seized and put to death! Fly, Zadig; I command you in the name of our love and of my yellow ribbons. I have done nothing wrong, but I foresee that I am going to die like a criminal."

Zadig, who had scarcely strength enough to speak, sent for Cador, and then, without a word, gave him the letter. Cador forced him to obey its injunction, and to set out immediately for Memphis.

"If you dare to go in search of the queen," said he, "you will only hasten her death; if you speak to the king, that step again will lead to her destruction. Her fate shall be my care; follow your own. I will spread the report that you have taken the road to India. I will soon come and find you, and I will tell you all that shall have passed at Babylon."

Cador, without a moment's delay, had two of the swiftest dromedaries brought to a secret gate of the palace, and made Zadig mount one of them; he had to be carried, for he was almost ready to expire. Only one servant accompanied him; and soon Cador, plunged in astonishment and grief, lost sight of his friend.

The illustrious fugitive, when he arrived at the edge of a hill which commanded a view of Babylon, turned his gaze towards the queen's palace, and fainted. He recovered his senses only to shed tears and to wish that he was dead. At last, after having occupied his thoughts awhile with the deplorable fate of the most amiable of women and the best of queens, he returned for a moment to himself, and exclaimed:

"What, then, is human life? O virtue! of what use have you been to me? Two women have basely deceived me, and the third, who is innocent and is more beautiful than the others, is about to die! All the good that I have done has always brought upon me a curse, and I have been raised to the height of grandeur only to fall down the most horrible precipice of misfortune. If I had been wicked, like so many others, I should be happy like them."

Overwhelmed with these gloomy reflections, his eyes shrouded with a veil of sorrow, the paleness of death on his countenance, and his soul sunk in the depths of a dark despair, he continued his journey towards Egypt.

IX

THE BEATEN WOMAN

Zadig directed his course by the stars. The constellation of Orion, and the bright star of Sirius guided him towards Canopus. He marvelled at those vast globes of light, which appear only like feeble sparks to our eyes, while the earth, which is in reality nothing more than an imperceptible point in nature, appears to our covetous eyes something grand and noble. He then pictured to himself men as they really are, insects devouring one another on a little atom of mud. This true image seemed to annihilate his misfortunes, by making him realize the insignificance of his own existence and that of Babylon. His soul rushed into the infinite and, detached from his senses, contemplated the unchangeable order of the universe. But when, afterwards returning to himself and once more looking into his own heart, he thought how Astarte was perhaps already dead for his sake, the universe vanished from his eyes, and he saw nothing in all nature save Astarte dying and Zadig miserable. As he gave himself up to this alternate flow of sublime philosophy and overwhelming grief, he approached the borders of Egypt; and his faithful servant was already in the first village, looking for a lodging. Zadig was, meanwhile, walking towards the gardens which skirted the village, and saw, not far from the high road, a woman in great distress, who was calling out to heaven and earth

for help, and a man who was following her in a furious rage. He
had already reached her before Zadig could do so, and the woman
was clasping his knees, while the man overwhelmed her with
blows and reproaches. He judged from the Egyptian's violence,
and from the repeated prayers for forgiveness which the lady
uttered, that he was jealous and she unfaithful; but after he had
closely observed the woman, who was of enchanting beauty, and
who, moreover, bore a little resemblance to the unhappy Astarte, he felt moved with compassion towards her and with
horror towards the Egyptian.

"Help me!" she cried to Zadig in a voice choked with sobs;
"deliver me out of the hands of this most barbarous man, and
save my life!"

Hearing these cries, Zadig ran and threw himself between
her and the barbarian; and having some knowledge of the Egyptian tongue, he addressed him in that language, and said:

"If you have any humanity, I entreat you to respect beauty
and weakness. How can you mistreat so cruelly such a masterpiece of nature as lies there at your feet, with no protection but
her tears?"

"Ah, ha!" answered the man, more enraged than ever; "then
you are another of her lovers! and on you too I must take revenge."

Saying these words, he left the lady, whom he had been holding by the hair with one hand, and, seizing his lance, made an
attempt to run the stranger through with it. But he, being cool
and composed, easily avoided the thrust of one who was beside
himself with rage, and caught hold of the lance near the iron
point with which it was armed. The one tried to draw it back,
while the other tried to wrench it out of his hand, so that it was
broken between the two. The Egyptian drew his sword, Zadig
did the same, and they forthwith attacked each other; the former
dealing a hundred blows in quick succession, the latter skilfully
warding them off. The lady, seated on a piece of turf, read-
justed her coiffure, and looked calmly on. The Egyptian was
stronger than his antagonist, Zadig was the more dexterous. The
latter fought like a man whose arm was guided by his head, the

former like a madman who in blind frenzy delivered random strokes. Zadig, attacking him in his turn, disarmed his adversary; and while the Egyptian, rendered still more furious, tried to throw himself upon him, the other seized him with a tight grip, and threw him on the ground; then, holding his sword to his breast, he offered to give him his life. The Egyptian, out of his mind, drew his dagger and wounded Zadig, at the very instant that the conqueror was granting him pardon. Aroused, Zadig plunged his sword into the other's heart. The Egyptian uttered a horrible cry, and died struggling violently. Then Zadig advanced towards the lady, and said in a respectful tone:

"He forced me to kill him; I have avenged you, and delivered you out of the hands of the most violent man I ever saw. What will you have me do for you now, madam?"

"Die, wretch," she replied; "die! You have killed my lover; would that I were able to tear out your heart."

"Truly, madam, you had a strange sort of lover there," returned Zadig; "he was beating you with all his might, and he wanted to have my life because you implored me to help you."

"I wish he were beating me still," answered the lady, with loud lamentations; "I well deserved it, and gave him good cause for jealousy. Would to heaven that he were beating me and that you were in his place!"

Zadig, more surprised and indignant than he had ever been before in his life, said to her:

"Madam, beautiful as you are, you deserve to have me beat you in my turn for your unreasonable behavior, but I shall not take the trouble."

So saying, he remounted his camel, and advanced towards the village. He had hardly gone a few steps when he turned back at the clatter of four messengers riding post haste from Babylon. One of them, seeing the woman, exclaimed:

"That is the very person! She resembles the description that was given us."

They did not bother themselves with the dead body, but at once caught hold of the lady, who kept calling out to Zadig:

"Help me once more, generous stranger! I beg your pardon for having reproached you: help me, and I will be yours till death."

Zadig no longer felt any desire to fight on her behalf.

"Apply to someone else," he answered, "you will not catch me again."

Moreover he was wounded and bleeding; he needed help; and the sight of the four Babylonians, probably sent by King Moabdar, filled him with uneasiness. So he hastened towards the village, unable to imagine why four messengers from Babylon should come to take this Egyptian woman, but still more astonished at the conduct of the lady.

X

SLAVERY

As he entered the Egyptian village, he found himself surrounded by the people. Everyone was crying out:

"This is the fellow who carried off the lovely Missouf, and who has just murdered Cletofis!"

"Gentlemen," said he, "may Heaven preserve me from ever carrying off your lovely Missouf! she is too capricious for me; and as for Cletofis, I have not murdered him, I only defended myself against him. He wanted to kill me because I had asked him most humbly to pardon the lovely Missouf, whom he was beating unmercifully. I am a stranger come to seek a refuge in Egypt; and it is not likely that, in coming to ask for your protection, I should begin by carrying off a woman and murdering a man."

The Egyptians were at that time just and humane. The people conducted Zadig to the town hall. First they had his wound dressed, and then they questioned him and his servant separately, in order to learn the truth. They came to the conclusion that Zadig was not a murderer; but he was found guilty of homicide, and the law condemned him to be a slave. His two camels were sold for the benefit of the village; all the gold that he carried was distributed among the inhabitants; his person was exposed for sale in the market-place, as well as that of his travelling companion. An Arab merchant, named Setoc, made the highest bid for him; but the valet, as more fit for hard work, was sold at a much

higher price than the master. There was no comparison, it was
thought, between the two men; so Zadig became a slave subordinate to his own servant. They were fastened together with a
chain, which was passed round their ankles, and in that condition
they followed the Arab merchant to his house. Zadig, on the way,
consoled his servant, and exhorted him to be patient; and, according to his custom, he made some general reflections on human
life.

"I see," he said, "that my unhappy fate has spread its shadow
over yours. Hitherto at every turn I have met with strange re-
verses. I have been condemned to pay a fine for having seen
traces of a passing bitch; I thought I was going to be impaled
on account of a griffin; I had been sent to execution because I
made some complimentary verses on the king; I was on the
point of being strangled because the queen had yellow ribbons;
and here am I a slave along with you, because a brute chose to
beat his mistress. Come, let us not lose courage; all this perhaps
will come to an end. Arab merchants must have slaves; and why
should not I be one as well as another, since I am a man like
any other? This merchant will not be merciless; he must treat his
slaves well, if he wishes to make good use of them."

Thus he spoke, but in the depths of his heart he was thinking
only of the fate of the queen of Babylon.

Setoc the merchant left, two days later, for Arabia Deserta,
with his slaves and his camels. His tribe dwelt near the desert of
Horeb. The way was long and painful. Setoc, on the journey, took
greater care of the servant than of the master, because the former
could load the camels much better; and any little distinctions
made between them were in his favor.

A camel died two days before they expected to reach Horeb,
and its load was distributed among the men, so that each back
had its burden; Zadig had his share. Setoc laughed to see how all
his slaves were bent almost double as they walked. Zadig took the
liberty of explaining to him the reason, and gave him some instruction in the laws of equilibrium. The astonished merchant
began to regard him with other eyes. Zadig, seeing that he had
excited his master's curiosity, increased it by teaching him many
things that had a direct bearing on his business, such as the spe-

cific gravity of metals and commodities in equal bulk, the properties of several useful animals, and the way in which those might be rendered useful which were not naturally so, until Setoc thought him a sage. He now gave Zadig the preference over his comrade, whom he had before esteemed so highly. He treated him well, and had no reason to repent of it.

Having reached his tribe, the first thing Setoc did was to demand repayment of five hundred ounces of silver from a Jew to whom he had lent them in the presence of two witnesses; but these two witnesses were dead, and the Jew, assured that there was no proof of the debt, appropriated the merchant's money, and thanked God for having given him the opportunity of cheating an Arab. Setoc confided his trouble to Zadig, who was now his adviser in everything.

"At what place," asked Zadig, "did you lend these five hundred ounces to the infidel?"

"On a large stone near Mount Horeb," answered the merchant.

"What kind of a man is your debtor?" said Zadig.

"A rogue," replied Setoc.

"But I mean, is he hasty or deliberate, cautious or imprudent?"

"Of all bad payers," said Setoc, "he is the hastiest man I ever knew."

"Well," pursued Zadig, "allow me to plead your cause before the judge."

Thereupon he summoned the Jew to trial, and thus addressed the judge:

"Pillow of the throne of equity, I come here to claim from this man, in my master's name, repayment of five hundred ounces of silver which he will not restore."

"Have you witnesses?" asked the judge.

"No, they are dead; but there still remains a large stone upon which the money was counted out; and, if it please your lordship to order someone to go and fetch the stone, I hope that it will bear witness to the truth. We will remain here, the Jew and I, until the stone arrives; I will send for it at my master Setoc's expense."

"Very good," answered the judge; and he then proceeded to other business.

At the end of the sitting he said to Zadig:

"Well, your stone has not arrived yet, has it?"

The Jew laughed, and answered:

"Your lordship would have to remain here till tomorrow before the stone could be brought; it is more than six miles away, and it would take fifteen men to move it."

"Now then," exclaimed Zadig, "did I not say that the stone would bear witness? Since this man knows where it is, he acknowledges that upon it the money was counted." The Jew, disconcerted, was soon obliged to confess the whole truth. The judge ordered him to be bound to the stone, without eating or drinking, until the five hundred ounces should be restored, and they were soon paid.

Zadig the slave and the stone were held in high esteem throughout Arabia.

XI

THE FUNERAL PYRE

Setoc was so enchanted with his slave that he made him his intimate friend. He could no more get along without him than could the king of Babylon; and Zadig was glad that Setoc had no wife. He found in his master an excellent disposition, with much integrity and good sense; but he was sorry to see that he worshipped the host of heaven, that is to say, the sun, moon, and stars, according to the ancient custom of Arabia. He spoke to him sometimes on the subject with judicious caution. At last he told him that they were material bodies like other things, which were no more worthy of his adoration than a tree or a rock.

"But," said Setoc, "they are immortal beings, from whom we derive all the benefits we enjoy; they animate nature, and regulate the seasons; besides, they are so far from us that one cannot help worshipping them."

"You receive more advantages," answered Zadig, "from the waters of the Red Sea, which bear your merchandise to India. Why may it not be as ancient as the stars? And if you adore what is far away from you, you ought to adore the land of the Gangarides, which lies at the very end of the world."

"No," said Setoc; "the stars are so bright that I cannot refrain from worshipping them."

When evening came, Zadig lit a large number of candles in the tent where he was to dine with Setoc; and, as soon as his patron appeared, he threw himself on his knees before those wax lights, saying:

"Eternal and brilliant lights, be ever propitious to me!"

Having offered this prayer, he sat down to table without paying any attention to Setoc.

"What is that you are doing?" asked Setoc in astonishment.

"I am doing what you do," answered Zadig; "I adore these candles, and neglect their master and mine."

Setoc understood the profound meaning of this parable. The wisdom of his slave entered into his soul; he no longer lavished his incense upon created things, and worshipped the eternal Being who had made them.

There prevailed at that time in Arabia a dreadful custom, which came originally from Scythia, and which, having established itself in India through the influence of the Brahmins, threatened to invade all the East. When a married man died, and his beloved wife wished to be sanctified, she would burn herself in public on her husband's corpse. A solemn festival was held on such occasions, called *the Funeral Pyre of Widowhood*, and that tribe in which there had been the greatest number of women consumed in this way was held in the highest honor. An Arab of Setoc's tribe having died, his widow, named Almona, who was very devout, made known the day and hour when she would cast herself into the fire to the sound of drums and trumpets. Zadig showed Setoc how contrary this horrible custom was to the interests of the human race, for young widows were every day allowed to burn themselves who might have presented children to the State, or at least have brought up those they already had; and he made him agree that so barbarous an institution ought, if possible, to be abolished.

Setoc replied: "It is more than a thousand years since the women acquired the right to burn themselves. Which of us will dare to change a law which time has consecrated? Is there anything more venerable than an ancient abuse?"

"Reason is more ancient," rejoined Zadig. "Speak to the chiefs of the tribes, and I will go and find the young widow."

He was introduced to her; and after having insinuated himself into her good graces by commending her beauty, and after having said what a pity it was to commit such charms to the flames, he praised her again on the score of her constancy and courage.

"You must have loved your husband wonderfully?" said he.

"I? Oh no, not at all," answered the Arab lady. "I could not bear him. He was brutal and jealous; but I am firmly resolved to throw myself on his funeral pyre."

"Apparently," said Zadig, "there must be some very delicious pleasure in being burned alive."

"Ah! it makes nature shudder to think of it," said the lady; "but I must put up with it. I am a pious person, and I should lose my reputation and be mocked by everybody if I did not burn myself."

Zadig, having brought her to admit that she was burning herself for the sake of other people and out of vanity, spoke to her for a long time in a manner designed to make her a little in love with life, and even managed to inspire her with some kindly feeling towards himself.

"What would you do now," said he, "if you were not moved by vanity to burn yourself?"

"Alas!" said the lady, "I think that I should ask you to marry me."

Zadig was too much occupied with thoughts of Astarte to take any notice of this declaration; but he instantly went to the chiefs of the different tribes, told them what had passed, and advised them to make a law by which no widow should be allowed to burn herself until after she had had a private interview with a young man for the space of a whole hour. Since that time no lady has burned herself in Arabia. To Zadig alone was the credit due for having abolished in one day so cruel a custom, that had lasted so many centuries. Thus he became the benefactor of Arabia.

XII

THE SUPPER

Setoc, who could not part from the man in whom wisdom dwelt, brought him to the great fair of Bassora, where the greatest merchants of the habitable globe would go. It was no little consolation to Zadig to see so many men of different countries assembled in the same place. It seemed to him that the universe was one large family which gathered together at Bassora. The second day after their arrival Zadig found himself at table with an Egyptian, an Indian from the banks of the Ganges, an inhabitant of China, a Greek, a Celt, and several other foreigners, who, in their frequent voyages to the Persian Gulf, had learned enough Arabic to make themselves understood. The Egyptian appeared exceedingly angry. "What an abominable country Bassora is!" said he; "I cannot get a loan here of a thousand ounces of gold on the best security in the world."

"How is that?" said Setoc; "on what security was that sum refused you?"

"On the body of my aunt," answered the Egyptian; "she was the best woman in Egypt. She always accompanied me on my journeys, and died on the way here. I have turned her into one of the finest mummies to be had; and in my own country I could get whatever I wanted by giving her in pledge. It is very strange that no one here will lend me even a thousand ounces of gold on such solid security."

In spite of his indignation, he was just on the point of devouring an excellent boiled chicken, when the Indian, taking him by the hand, exclaimed in a pained voice, "Ah! what are you about to do?"

"To eat this chicken," said the man with the mummy.

"Beware of what you are doing," said the man from the Ganges; "it may be that the soul of the departed has passed into the body of that chicken, and you would not wish to run the risk of eating your aunt. To cook fowls is plainly an outrage upor nature."

"What do you mean with your nonsense about nature and

fowls?" returned the wrathful Egyptian. "We worship an ox, and yet eat beef for all that."

"You worship an ox! Is it possible?" said the man from the Ganges.

"There is nothing more certain," replied the other; "we have done so for a hundred and thirty-five thousand years, and no one among us has anything to say against it."

"Ah! A hundred and thirty-five thousand years!" said the Indian. "There must be a little exaggeration there; India has only been inhabited eighty thousand years, and we are undoubtedly more ancient than you are; and Brahma had forbidden us to eat oxen before you ever thought of putting them on your altars and on your spits."

"An odd kind of animal, this Brahma of yours, to be compared with Apis!" said the Egyptian. "What fine things now has your Brahma ever done?"

"It was he," the Brahman answered, "who taught men to read and write, and to whom all the world owes the game of chess."

"You are wrong," said a Chaldean who was sitting near him; "it is to the fish Oannes that we owe such great benefits; and it is just to render homage to him alone. Anybody will tell you that he was a divine Being, that he had a golden tail and a handsome human head, and that he used to leave the water to come and preach on land for three hours every day. He had several children who were all kings, as everyone knows. I have his portrait at home, to which I pay all due reverence. We may eat as much beef as we please; but it is certainly a very great sin to cook fish. Moreover, you are, both of you, of too common and too recent an origin to argue with me about anything. The Egyptian nation counts only one hundred and thirty-five thousand years, and the Indians can boast of no more than eighty thousand, while we have almanacs that go back four thousand centuries. Believe me, renounce your follies, and I will give each of you a beautiful portrait of Oannes."

The Chinaman here put in his word, and said:

"I have great respect for the Egyptians, the Chaldeans, the Greeks, the Celts, Brahma, the ox Apis, and the fine fish Oannes, but it may be that Li or Tien,[5] by whichever name one may choose to call him, is well worth any number of oxen and fishes. I will say nothing about my country; it as as large as the land of Egypt, Chaldea, and India all put together. I will enter into no dispute concerning antiquity, because it is enough to be happy, and it means very little to be ancient; but if there were any need to speak about almanacs, I could tell you that all Asia consults ours, and that we had very good ones before anything at all was known of arithmetic in Chaldea."

"You are a set of ignoramuses, all of you!" cried the Greek; "is it possible that you do not know that Chaos is the father of all things, and that form and matter have brought the world into the state in which it is?"

This Greek spoke for a long time; but he was at last interrupted by the Celt, who, having drunk deeply while the others were disputing, now thought himself wiser than any of them, and affirmed with an oath that there was nothing worth the trouble of talking about except Teutath and the mistletoe that grows on an oak; that, as for himself, he always had some mistletoe in his pocket; that the Scythians, his forefathers, were the only honest people that had ever been in the world; that they had indeed sometimes eaten men, but that no one ought to be prevented by that from having a profound respect for his nation; and finally, that if anyone spoke evil of Teutath, he would teach him how to behave.

Thereupon the quarrel grew warm, and Setoc saw that in another moment there would be bloodshed at the table, when Zadig, who had kept silence during the whole dispute, at last rose. He addressed himself first to the Celt as the most violent of them all; he told him that he was in the right, and asked him for a piece of mistletoe; he commended the Greek for his eloquence, and soothed the general irritation. He said very little to the man from China because he had been the most reasonable of them all. Then he said to the whole party:

"My friends, you were going to quarrel for nothing, for you are all of the same opinion."

When they heard him say that, they all loudly protested.

"Is it not true," he said to the Celt, "that you do not worship this mistletoe, but him who made the mistletoe and the oak?"

"Assuredly," answered the Celt.

"And you, my Egyptian friend, revere, as it would seem, in a certain ox him who has given you oxen, is it not so?"

"Yes," said the Egyptian.

"The fish Oannes," continued Zadig, "must give place to him who made the sea and the fishes."

"Granted," said the Chaldean.

"The Indian," added Zadig, "and the Chinaman recognize, like you, a First Principle; I did not understand very well the admirable remarks made by the Greek, but I am sure that he also admits the existence of a supreme Being, upon whom form and matter depend."

The Greek who was so much admired said that Zadig had seized his meaning very well.

"You are all then of the same opinion," replied Zadig, "and there is nothing left to quarrel over;" at which all the company embraced him.

Setoc, after having sold his merchandise at a high price, brought his friend Zadig back with him to his tribe. On their arrival Zadig learned that he had been tried in his absence, and that he was going to be burned in a slow fire.

XIII

THE ASSIGNATIONS

During his journey to Bassora, the priests of the stars had determined to punish Zadig. The precious stones and ornaments of the young widows whom they sent to the funeral pyre were theirs by right; it was in truth the least they could do to burn Zadig for the ill turn he had done them. Accordingly they accused him of holding erroneous views about the host of heaven; they gave testimony against him and swore that they had heard him say that the stars did not set in the sea. This frightful blasphemy made the judges shudder; they were ready to rend their garments when they heard those impious words, and they would have done so, without a doubt, if Zadig had had the means to pay them compensation; but in their extreme pain, they contented themselves with condemning him to be burned in a slow fire

Setoc, in despair, exerted his influence in vain to save his friend; he was soon obliged to hold his peace. The young widow Almona, who had acquired a strong appetite for life, thanks to Zadig, resolved to rescue him from the stake, the misuse of which he had taught her to recognize. She turned her scheme over and over in her head, without speaking of it to anyone. Zadig was to be executed the next day; she had only that night to save him. This is how she set about the business like a charitable and discreet woman. She anointed herself with perfumes; she enhanced her charms by the richest and most seductive attire, and went to ask the chief priest of the stars for a private audience. When she was ushered into the presence of that venerable old man, she addressed him in these terms:

"Eldest son of the Great Bear, brother of the Bull, and cousin of the Great Dog" (such were this pontiff's titles), "I come to confide to you my scruples. I greatly fear that I have committed an enormous sin in not burning myself on my dear husband's funeral pyre. In truth, what had I worth preserving? A body liable to decay, and which is already quite withered." Saying these words, she drew up her long silk sleeves, and displayed her bare arms, of admirable form and dazzling whiteness. "You see," said she, "how little it is worth."

The pontiff thought in his heart that it was worth a great deal. His eyes said so, and his mouth confirmed it; he swore that he had never in his life seen such beautiful arms.

"Alas!" said the widow, "my arms may be a little less deformed than the rest; but you will admit that my neck was unworthy of any consideration," and she let him see the most charming bosom that nature had ever formed. A rosebud on an apple of ivory would have appeared beside it nothing better than bed-straw upon box-wood, and lambs just out of a bath would have seemed brown and pale. This neck; her large black eyes, in which a tender fire glowed softly with languishing lustre; her cheeks, enlivened with the loveliest crimson mixed with the whiteness of the purest milk; her nose, which was not at all like the tower of Mount Lebanon; her lips, which were like two settings of coral enclosing the most beautiful pearls in the Arabian sea; all these charms made the old man believe that he was twenty years old.

With stammering tongue he made a tender declaration; and Almona, seeing how he was smitten, asked pardon for Zadig.

"Alas!" said he, "my lovely lady, though I might grant you his pardon, my indulgence would be of no use, as the order would have to be signed by three others of my colleagues."

"Sign it all the same," said Almona.

"Gladly," said the priest, "on condition that your favors shall be the price of my compliance."

"You do me too much honor," said Almona; "only be pleased to come to my chamber after sunset, when the bright star *Sheat* shall rise above the horizon; you will find me on a rose-colored sofa, and you shall deal with your servant as you may be able."

Then she went away, carrying with her the signature, and left the old man full of amorous passion and of distrust of his powers. He employed the rest of the day in bathing; he drank a liquor compounded of the cinnamon of Ceylon and the precious spices of Tidor and Ternat, and waited with impatience for the star *Sheat* to appear.

Meanwhile the fair Almona went in search of the second pontiff, who assured her that the sun, the moon, and all the lights of heaven were nothing but faint marsh fires in comparison with her charms. She asked of him the same favor, and he offered to grant it on the same terms. She allowed her scruples to be overcome, and made an appointment with the second pontiff for the rising of the star *Algenib*. Thence she proceeded to the houses of the third and fourth priests, getting from each his signature, and making one star after another the signal for a secret assignation. Then she sent letters to the judges, requesting them to come and see her on a matter of importance. When they appeared, she showed them the four names, and told them at what price the priests had sold Zadig's pardon. Each of the latter arrived at his appointed hour, and was greatly astonished to find his colleagues there, and still more at seeing the judges, before whom they were exposed to open shame. Zadig was saved. Setoc was so delighted with Almona's cleverness, that he made her his wife. Zadig left after throwing himself at the feet of his beautiful liberator. Setoc and he parted company in tears, swearing an eternal friendship, and promising that whoever should first gain a great fortune would share it with the other.

Zadig traveled in the direction of Syria, thinking all the while of the unfortunate Astarte, and continually reflecting on the fate that persisted in toying with him and persecuting him. Imagine! he said to himself: 400 ounces of gold for having seen a dog go by; condemned to execution for four bad lines of poetry in praise of the king; about to be strangled because the queen had slippers the color of my cap; reduced to slavery for having helped a woman who was being beaten; and on the point of being burned for having saved the life of all the young Arab widows!

XIV

THE BRIGAND

On arriving at the frontier which separates Arabia Petræa from Syria, as he was passing near a rather strong castle, a party of armed Arabs sallied forth. He saw himself surrounded. Someone cried out to him: "All that you have belongs to us, and you belong to our master."

Zadig, by way of answer, drew his sword; his servant, who had plenty of courage, did the same. They routed and slew the Arabs who first laid hands on them; their assailants now numbered twice as many as before, but they were not daunted, and resolved to die fighting. Two men defended themselves against a multitude. Such a conflict could not last long. The master of the castle, whose name was Arbogad, having seen from a window the prodigies of valor performed by Zadig, conceived such an admiration for him that he hastily descended, and came in person to disperse his men and deliver the two travelers.

"All that passes over my lands is my property," said he, "as well as whatever I find on the lands of other people; but you seem to me such a brave man, that I exempt you from the general rule."

He made Zadig enter his castle, and ordered his people to treat him well. In the evening Arbogad desired Zadig to dine with him.

Now the lord of the castle was one of those Arabs who are known as *robbers*; but he sometimes did a good action among a multitude of bad ones. He robbed with fierce rapacity, and gave away freely; he was intrepid in battle, though gentle enough in society; intemperate at table, merry in his cups, and above all, full of frankness. Zadig pleased him greatly, and his animated conversation prolonged the repast. At length Arbogad said to him:

"I advise you to join under me; you cannot do better; this trade is not a bad one, and you may one day become what I now am."

"May I ask you," said Zadig, "how long you have practised this noble profession?"

"From my tenderest youth," replied the lord of the castle. "I was the servant of a pretty sharp Arab; I felt my position intolerable; it drove me to despair to see that in all the earth, which belongs equally to all mankind, fortune had reserved no portion for me. I confided my trouble to an old Arab, who said to me: 'My son, do not despair; there was once a grain of sand which complained of being a mere unheeded atom in the desert; but at the end of a few years it became a diamond, and it is now the most beautiful ornament in the King of India's crown.' This story made a great impression on me. I was the grain of sand, and I determined to become a diamond. I began by stealing two horses; I then formed a gang, and put myself in a position to rob small caravans. Thus by degrees I abolished the disproportion which existed at first between myself and other men; I had my share in the good things of this world, and was even recompensed with usury. I was held in high esteem, became a brigand chief, and obtained this castle by violence. The satrap of Syria wished to dispossess me, but I was already too rich to have anything to fear; I gave some money to the satrap, and by this means retained the castle and increased my domains. He even named me treasurer of the tribute which Arabia Petræa paid to the king of kings. I fulfilled my duty well, so far as receiving went, and utterly ignored that of payment. The Grand Desterham of Babylon sent here in the name of King Moabdar a petty satrap, intending to have me strangled. This man arrived with his orders; I was informed of all, and caused to be strangled in his presence the four persons he had brought with him to apply the bowstring to my neck; after which I asked him what his commission to strangle me might be worth to him. He answered me that his fees might amount to three hundred pieces of gold. I made it clear to him that there was more to be gained with me. I gave him a subordinate post among my brigands; today he is one of my smartest and wealthiest officers. Take my word for it, you will succeed as well as he. Never has there been a better season for theft, since Moabdar is slain and all is in confusion at Babylon."

"Moabdar slain!" said Zadig; "and what has become of Queen Astarte?"

"I know nothing about her," replied Arbogad; "all I know is that Moabdar went mad and was killed, that Babylon is one vast slaughter-house, that all the empire is laid waste, that there are some fine blows to be struck yet, and that I myself have done wonders in that way."

"But the queen?" said Zadig; "pray tell me, know you nothing of the fate of the queen?"

"I heard something about a prince of Hyrcania," replied he; "she is probably among his concubines, if she has not been killed in the insurrection; but I am more curious about plunder than about news. I have taken a good many women in my raids, but I keep none of them; I sell them at a high price if they are handsome, without inquiring who or what they are, for my customers pay nothing for rank; a queen who was ugly would find no purchaser. Maybe I have sold Queen Astarte, maybe she is dead; it matters very little to me, and I do not think you should care any more about her than I do."

As he spoke thus he went on drinking lustily, and mixed up all his ideas so confusedly, that Zadig could get no clarification from him.

He remained speechless, overwhelmed, unable to stir. Arbogad continued to drink, told stories, constantly repeated that he was the happiest of all men, and exhorted Zadig to make himself as happy as he was. At last, becoming more and more drowsy with the fumes of wine, he gradually fell into a tranquil slumber. Zadig passed the night in the most violent agitation.

"What!" said he, "the king gone mad! the king killed! I cannot help pitying him! The empire is dismembered, and this brigand is happy! O fortune! O destiny! A robber is happy, and the most lovable being that nature ever created has perhaps perished in a frightful manner, or is living in a condition worse than death. O Astarte! what has become of you?"

At break of day he questioned all whom he met in the castle; but everybody was busy, and no one answered him: new conquests had been made during the night, and they were dividing the spoils. All that he could obtain in this noisy confusion was permission to depart, of which he availed himself without delay, plunged deeper than ever in painful thoughts.

Zadig walked on restless and agitated, his mind completely taken up by the unfortunate Astarte, the king of Babylon, his faithful Cador, the happy brigand Arbogad, and that capricious woman whom the Babylonians had carried off on the borders of Egypt, in short, by all the disappointments and misfortunes that he had experienced.

XV
THE FISHERMAN

At a distance of several leagues from Arbogad's castle, he found himself on the bank of a little river, still deploring his destiny, and regarding himself as the model of misery. He saw a fisherman lying on the bank, hardly holding in his feeble hand the net which he seemed ready to drop, and lifting his eyes towards heaven.

"I am certainly the most wretched of all men," said the fisherman. "I was, as everybody said, the most famous seller of cream cheeses in Babylon, and I have been ruined. I had the prettiest wife that a man of my condition could possess, and she has betrayed me. A squalid house was all that was left me, and I have seen it plundered and destroyed. Having taken refuge in a hut, I have no resource but fishing, and I cannot catch a single fish. O my net! I will cast you no more into the water, it is myself that I must cast therein."

Saying these words, he rose and advanced with the appearance of a man about to throw himself headlong and put an end to his life.

"What is this?" said Zadig to himself; "there are men then as miserable as I!"

His eagerness to save the fisherman's life was as prompt as this reflection. He ran towards him, stopped, and questioned him with an air of concern and encouragement. It is said that we are less miserable when we are not alone in our misery. But according to Zoroaster this is due, not to malice, but to necessity; we then feel ourselves drawn towards a victim of misfortune as a fellow-sufferer. The joy of a happy man would be an insult; but two wretched men are like two weak trees, which, leaning together, mutually strengthen each other against the storm.

"Why do you give way to your misfortunes?" said Zadig to the fisherman.

"Because," answered he, "I see no way out of them. I was held in the highest regard in the village of Derlback, near Babylon, and I made, with my wife's help, the best cream cheeses in the empire. Queen Astarte and the famous minister Zadig were passionately fond of them. I had supplied their houses with six hundred cheeses, and went one day into town to be paid, when, on my arrival at Babylon, I learned that the queen and Zadig had disappeared. I hastened to the house of the lord Zadig, whom I had never seen; there I found the police officers of the Grand Desterham, who, furnished with a royal warrant, were sacking his house in a perfectly straightforward and orderly manner. I flew to the queen's kitchens; some of the lords of the table told me that she was dead; others said that she was in prison; while others again declared that she had taken flight; but all assured me that I should not be paid for my cheeses. I went with my wife to the house of the lord Orcan, who was one of my customers, and we asked him to protect us in our distress. He granted his protection to my wife, and refused it to me. She was whiter than those cream cheeses with which my troubles began, and the gleam of Tyrian purple was not more brilliant than the carnation which animated that whiteness. It was this which made the lord Orcan keep her and drive me away from his house. I wrote to my dear wife the letter of a desperate man. She said to the messenger who brought it:

" 'Oh! ah! yes! I know something of the man who writes me this letter. I have heard people speak of him; they say he makes excellent cream cheeses; let him send me some, and see that he is paid for them.'

"In my unhappy state I determined to have recourse to justice. I had six ounces of gold left; I had to give two ounces to the lawyer whom I consulted; two to the attorney who undertook my case, and two to the secretary of the first judge. When all this was done, my suit had not yet commenced, and I had already spent more money than my cheeses and my wife were worth. I returned to my village, with the intention of selling my house in order to recover my wife.

"My house was well worth sixty ounces of gold, but people saw that I was poor and forced to sell. The first man to whom I applied offered me thirty ounces for it, the second twenty, and the third ten. I was ready at last to take anything, so blinded was I, when a prince of Hyrcania came to Babylon, and ravaged all the country on his way. My house was first sacked and then burned.

"Having thus lost my money, my wife, and my house, I retired to this part of the country where you see me. I tried to support myself by fishing, but the fishes mock me as much as men do; I catch nothing, I am dying of hunger, and had it not been for you, my illustrious consoler, I should have died in the river."

The fisherman did not tell this story all at once; for every moment Zadig in his agitation would break in with: "What! do you know nothing of what has happened to the queen?" "No, my lord," the fisherman would make reply; "but I know that the queen and Zadig have not paid me for my cream cheeses, that my wife has been taken from me, and that I am in despair."

"I feel confident," said Zadig, "that you will not lose all your money. I have heard people speak of this Zadig; he is an honest man; and if he returns to Babylon, as he hopes to do, he will give you more than he owes you. But as for your wife, who is not so honest, I recommend that you not try to recover her. Take my advice, go to Babylon; I shall be there before you, because I am on horseback, and you are on foot. Apply to the noble Cador;

tell him you have met his friend, and wait for me at his house. Go; perhaps you will not always be unhappy."

"O mighty Ormuzd," continued he, "you make use of me to console this man; of whom will you make use to console me?"

So saying, he gave the fisherman half of all the money he had brought from Arabia, and the fisherman, astonished and delighted, kissed the feet of Cador's friend, and said: "You are an angel sent to save me."

Meanwhile Zadig continued to ask for news, shedding tears as he did so.

"What! my lord," cried the fisherman, "can you then be unhappy, you who do good?"

"A hundred times more unhappy than you," answered Zadig.

"But how can it be," said the good man, "that he who gives is more to be pitied than him who receives?"

"Because," replied Zadig, "your greatest misfortune was need, and because my misery has its seat in the heart."

"Has Orcan taken away your wife?" said the fisherman.

This question recalled all his adventures to Zadig's mind; he repeated the catalogue of his misfortunes, beginning with the queen's bitch, up to the time of his arrival at the castle of the brigand Arbogad.

"Ah!" said he to the fisherman, "Orcan deserves to be punished. But it is generally such people as he who are the favorites of fortune. Be that as it may, go to the house of the lord Cador, and wait for me."

They parted; the fisherman walked on thanking his stars, and Zadig moved on still accusing his own.

XVI

THE BASILISK

Having arrived at a beautiful meadow, he saw there several women searching for something very carefully. He took the liberty of approaching one of them, and asked her if he might have the honor of helping them in their search.

"Take care not to do that," answered the Syrian; "what we are looking for can only be touched by women."

"'That is very strange," said Zadig; "may I venture to ask you to tell me what it is that only women are allowed to touch?"

"A basilisk," said she.

"A basilisk, madam! and for what reason, if you please, are you looking for a basilisk?"

"It is for our lord and master, Ogul, whose castle you see on the bank of that river, at the end of the meadow. We are his most humble slaves; the lord Ogul is ill, his physician has ordered him to eat a basilisk cooked in rose-water, and, as it is a very rare animal, and never allows itself to be taken except by women, the lord Ogul has promised to choose for his well-beloved wife, whichever of us shall bring him a basilisk. Let me continue the search, if you please; for you see what it would cost me, if I were anticipated by my companions."

Zadig left this Syrian girl and the others to look for their basilisk, and continued to walk through the meadow. When he reached the brink of a little stream, he found there another lady lying on the turf, and not in search of anything. Her figure appeared majestic, but her face was covered with a veil. She was leaning over the stream; deep sighs escaped from her mouth. She held in her hand a little stick, with which she was tracing characters on the fine sand which lay between the grass and the stream. Zadig had the curiosity to look and see what this woman was writing; he drew near, and saw the letter Z, then an A; he was astonished; then appeared a D; he started. Never was there surprise to equal his, when he saw the two last letters of his name. He remained some time without moving; then, breaking the silence, he exclaimed in a trembling voice:

"O noble lady! pardon a stranger who is in distress if he ventures to ask you by what astonishing chance I find here the name of Zadig traced by your adorable hand."

At that voice, at those words, the lady raised her veil with a trembling hand, turned her eyes on Zadig, uttered a cry of tenderness, surprise, and joy, and, overcome by all the varied emotions which simultaneously assailed her soul, she fell fainting into his arms. It was Astarte herself, it was the queen of Babylon, it was she whom Zadig adored, and whom he reproached himself for adoring; it was she for whom he had wept so much, and whose fate he had so feared. For a moment he was deprived of the use of his senses; then, fixing his gaze on Astarte's eyes, which opened once more with a languor mixed with confusion and tenderness, he cried:

"O immortal powers, who preside over the destinies of feeble mortals! Do you give me back Astarte? At what a time, in what a place, and in what a condition do I see her again?"

He threw himself on his knees before Astarte, and placed his forehead in the dust of her feet. The queen of Babylon lifted him up, and made him sit beside her on the bank of the stream, while she repeatedly dried her eyes from which tears would soon begin again to flow. Twenty times at least did she take up the thread of the discourse which her sighs interrupted; she questioned him about the strange chance that brought them once more together, and she anticipated his answers by other questions. She began to relate her own misfortunes, and then wished to know those of Zadig. At last, both of them having somewhat appeased the tumult of their souls, Zadig told her in a few words how it came to pass that he found himself in that meadow.

"But, O unhappy and honored queen! how *is* it that I find you in this remote spot, clad as a slave, and accompanied by other women slaves who are searching for a basilisk to be cooked in rose-water by a physician's order?"

"While they are looking for their basilisk," said the fair Astarte, "I will inform you of all that I have suffered, and for how much I have ceased to blame heaven now that I see you again. You know that the king, my husband, took it ill that you were the most amiable of all men; and it was for this reason that he resolved one night to have you strangled and me poisoned. You know how heaven permitted my little mute to warn me of the order of his sublime majesty. Hardly had the faithful Cador forced you to obey me and to go away, when he ventured to enter my chamber in the middle of the night by a secret passage. He carried me off, and brought me to the temple of Ormuzd, where his brother, the mage, shut me up in a gigantic statue, the base of which touches the foundations of the temple, while its head reaches to the roof. I was as if buried there, but waited on by the mage, and in want of none of the necessaries of

life. Meanwhile at daybreak His Majesty's apothecary entered my
chamber with a draught compounded of henbane, opium, black
hellebore, and aconite; and another official went to your apartment with a bowstring of blue silk. Both places were found
empty. Cador, the better to deceive him, went to the king, and
pretended to accuse us both. He said that you had taken the
road to India, and that I had gone towards Memphis; so officers
were sent after each of us.

The messengers who went in search of me did not know me
by sight, for I had hardly ever shown my face to any man but
yourself, and then in my husband's presence and by his command. They hastened off in pursuit of me, guided by the
description that had been given them of my person. A woman
of much the same height as myself, and who had, it may be,
superior charms, presented herself to their eyes on the borders of
Egypt. She was evidently a fugitive and in distress; they had no
doubt that this woman was the queen of Babylon, and they
brought her to Moabdar. Their mistake at first threw the king
into a violent rage; but soon, taking a nearer look at the woman,
he perceived that she was very beautiful, which gave him some
consolation. She was called Missouf. I have been told since that
the name signifies in the Egyptian tongue *the capricious beauty*.
Such in truth she was, but she had as much artfulness as caprice.
She pleased Moabdar, and brought him into subjection to such a
degree that she made him declare her his wife. Thereupon her
character developed itself in all its extravagance; she fearlessly
gave herself up to every foolish whim of her imagination. She
wished to compel the chief of the magi, who was old and gouty,
to dance before her; and when he refused she persecuted him
bitterly. She ordered her master of the horse to make her a jam
tart. In vain did the master of the horse protest that he was not
a pastry cook, he must make the tart; and he was driven from
office because it was too burned. She gave the post of master of
the horse to her dwarf, and the place of chancellor to a page. It
was thus that she governed Babylon. All regretted that they had
lost me. The king, who had been a tolerably reasonable man until
the moment when he had determined to poison me and to have
you strangled, seemed now to have drowned his virtues in the

exorbitant love that he had for the capricious beauty. He came to the temple on the great day of the sacred fire, and I saw him implore the gods on behalf of Missouf, at the feet of the image in which I was enclosed. I lifted up my voice, and cried aloud to him:

" 'The gods reject the prayers of a king who has become a tyrant, who has wanted to put to death a reasonable wife to marry a woman of the most extravagant whims.'

"Moabdar was so confounded at these words, that his mind became disordered. The oracle that I had delivered, and Missouf's domineering temper, sufficed to deprive him of his senses. In a few days he went mad.

"His madness, which seemed a punishment from heaven, was the signal for revolt. There was a general insurrection, and everyone ran to take up arms. Babylon, so long plunged in effeminate idleness, became the scene of a frightful civil war. I was drawn out of the cavity of my statue, and placed at the head of one party. Cador hastened to Memphis, to bring you back to Babylon. The prince of Hyrcania, hearing of this dreadful news, came back with his army to form a third party in Chaldea. He attacked the king, who fled before him with his wayward Egyptian. Moabdar died pierced with wounds, and Missouf fell into the hands of the conqueror. It was my misfortune to be myself taken prisoner by a party of Hyrcanians, and I was brought before the prince at precisely the same time as they were bringing in Missouf. You will be pleased, no doubt, to hear that the prince thought me more beautiful than the Egyptian; but you will be sorry to learn that he destined me for his harem. He told me very decidedly that as soon as he should have finished a military expedition which he was about to undertake, he would come and keep me company. Imagine my sorrow. The tie that bound me to Moabdar was broken, and I might have been Zadig's, if this barbarian had not cast his chains around me. I answered him with all the pride that my rank and my feelings gave me. I had always heard it said that heaven has endowed persons of my condition with a greatness of character, which, with a word or a look, can reduce the presumptuous to a humble sense of that deep respect which they have dared to disregard. I spoke like a queen, but found myself treated like a servant. The Hyrcanian, without deigning to address to me even a single word, told his black eunuch that I was a saucy wench, but that he thought me pretty; so he ordered him to take care of me, and subject me to the diet of his favorites, that I might recover my complexion, and be rendered more worthy of his favors by the time that he might find it convenient to honor me with them. I told him that I would sooner kill myself; he answered, laughing, that there was no fear of that, and that he was used to such displays; whereupon he left me like a man who has just put a parrot into his cage. What a state of affairs for the first queen in all the world,—I will say more, for a heart which was devoted to Zadig!"

At these words he threw himself at her knees, and bathed them with tears. Astarte raised him tenderly, and continued thus:

"I saw myself in the power of a barbarian and a rival of the mad woman who was my fellow-prisoner. She told me what had happened to her in Egypt. I conjectured from the description she gave of your person, from the time of the occurrence, from the dromedary on which you were mounted, and from all the circumstances of the case, that it was Zadig who had fought on her behalf. I had no doubt that you were at Memphis, and resolved to go there.

" 'Beautiful Missouf,' said I, 'you are much more pleasing than I am, and will entertain the prince of Hyrcania far better than I can. Help me to escape; you will then reign alone and make me happy while ridding yourself of a rival.'

"Missouf arranged with me the means of my flight, and I departed secretly with an Egyptian woman slave.

"I had nearly reached Arabia, when a notorious robber, named Arbogad, carried me off, and sold me to some merchants, who brought me to this castle where the lord Ogul resides. He bought me without knowing who I was. He is a voluptuary whose only object in life is pleasure, and who is convinced that God has sent him into the world to sit at the table. He is excessively fat, and is constantly on the point of suffocation. His physician, in whom he believes little enough when his digestion is all right, exerts a despotic sway over him whenever he has eaten too much. He has persuaded him that he can cure him with a basilisk cooked in rose-water. The lord Ogul has promised his hand to whichever of his female slaves shall bring him a basilisk. You see how I leave them to vie with one another in their eagerness to win this honor, for, since heaven has permitted me to see you again, I have less desire than ever to find this basilisk."

Then Astarte and Zadig gave expression to all that tender feelings long repressed—all that their love and misfortunes could inspire in the noblest and most passionate hearts; and the genii who preside over love carried their vows to the sphere of Venus.

The women returned to Ogul's castle without having found anything. Zadig, having obtained an introduction, addressed him in these words:

"May immortal health descend from heaven to guard and keep you all your days! I am a physician, and am come to you in haste on hearing the report of your sickness, and I have brought you a basilisk cooked in rose-water. I have no matrimonial intentions towards you; I only ask for the release of a young slave from Babylon, who has been several days in your possession, and I consent to remain in bondage in her place, if I have not the happiness of curing the magnificent lord Ogul."

The proposal was accepted. Astarte set out for Babylon with Zadig's servant, having promised to send him a messenger immediately to inform him of all that might have happened. Their parting was as tender as their recognition. The moment of separation and the moment of meeting again are the two most important epochs of life, as is written in the great book of Zend. Zadig loved the queen as much as he swore he did, and the queen loved Zadig more than she professed to do.

Meanwhile Zadig spoke thus to Ogul:

"My lord, my basilisk is not to be eaten, all its virtue must enter into you through the pores. I have put it into a little leather case, well blown out, and covered with a fine skin; you must strike this case of leather as hard as you can, and I must send it back many times; a few days of this treatment will show you what my art can do."

The first day Ogul was quite out of breath, and thought that he should die of fatigue. The second day he was less exhausted, and slept better. In a week's time he had gained all the strength, health, lightness, and good spirits of his most robust years.

"You have played ball, and you have been temperate," said Zadig; "believe me, there is no such creature in nature as a basilisk but with temperance and exercise one is always well, and the art of combining intemperance and health is as chimerical as the philosopher's stone, judicial astrology, and the theology of the magi."

Ogul's chief physician, perceiving how dangerous this man was to medicine, conspired with his private apothecary to send Zadig to look for basilisks in the other world. Thus, after having already been punished so often for having done good, he was again about to perish for having healed a gluttonous nobleman. He was invited to a grand dinner, and was to have been poisoned during the second course; but while they were at the first he received a message from the fair Astarte, at which he left the table, and took his departure. "When a man is loved by a beautiful woman," says the great Zoroaster, "he always gets out of trouble in this world."

XVII

THE TOURNAMENTS

The queen had been received at Babylon with the enthusiasm which is always shown for a beautiful princess who has been unfortunate. Babylon at that time seemed more peaceful. The prince of Hyrcania had been killed in a battle; and the victorious Babylonians declared that Astarte should marry the man whom they might choose as sovereign. They did not desire that the first position in the world, namely, that of husband of Astarte and king of Babylon, should depend upon intrigues and cabals. They took an oath to acknowledge as their king the man whom they should find bravest and wisest. A great field, surrounded by amphitheatres splendidly decorated, was formed several leagues away from the city. The combatants were to go there fully armed. Each of them had separate quarters behind the amphitheatres, where he was to be neither seen nor visited by anyone. It was necessary to enter the lists four times, and those who should be successful enough to defeat four cavaliers were thereupon to fight against each other, and the one who should finally remain master of the field should be proclaimed victor of the tournament. He was to return four days afterwards with the same arms, and try to solve the riddles which the magi would propound. If he could not solve the riddles, he was not to be king, and it would be necessary to begin the jousts over again, until a knight should be found victorious in both sorts of contest; for they wished to have a king braver and wiser than any other man. The queen, during all this time, was to be strictly guarded; she was only allowed to be present at the games covered with a veil, and she was not permitted to speak to any of the competitors, in order to avoid either favoritism or injustice.

This was what Astarte let her lover know, hoping that for her sake he would display greater valor and wisdom than anyone else. He took his departure, entreating Venus to fortify his courage and enlighten his mind. He arrived on the banks of the Euphrates the evening before the great day, and caused his coat of arms to be inscribed among those of the combatants, concealing his face and his name, as the law required. Then he went to rest in the lodging that was assigned him by lot. His friend Cador, who had returned to Babylon, after having vainly searched for him in Egypt, sent to his quarters a complete suit of armor which was the queen's present. He also sent him, on her behalf, the finest steed in Persia. Zadig recognized the hand of Astarte in these gifts; his courage and his love gained thereby new energy and new hopes.

On the next day, the queen having taken her place under a jewelled canopy, and the amphitheatres being filled with ladies and persons of every rank in Babylon, the combatants appeared in the arena. Each of them came and laid his device at the feet of the grand mage. The devices were drawn by lot, and Zadig's happened to be the last. The first who advanced was a very rich lord named Itobad, exceedingly vain, but with little courage, skill, or judgment. His servants had persuaded him that such a man as he ought to be king; and he had answered them: "Such a man as I ought to reign." So they had armed him from head to foot. He had golden armor enamelled with green, a green plume, and a lance decked with green ribbons. It was evident at once, from the manner in which Itobad managed his horse, that it was not for *such a man as he* that heaven reserved the sceptre of Babylon. The first knight who tilted against him unhorsed him; the second upset him so that he lay on his horse's rump with both his legs in the air and arms extended. Itobad recovered his seat, but with such a bad grace that all the spectators began to laugh. The third did not condescend to use his lance, but after making a pass at him, took him by the right leg, turned him half round, and let him drop on the sand. The squires of the tourney ran up to him laughing, and replaced him on his saddle. The fourth combatant seized him by the left leg, and made him fall on the other side. He was accompanied with loud jeers to his quarters, where he was to pass the night according to the law of the games; and he said as he limped along with difficulty: "What an experience for such a man as I!"

The other knights acquitted themselves better. There were some who defeated two antagonists one after the other, a few went as far as three, but the prince Otame was the only one who conquered four. At last Zadig tilted in his turn; he unseated four cavaliers in succession in the most graceful manner possible. It then remained to be seen whether Otame or Zadig would be the victor. The arms of the former were blue and gold, with a plume of the same color, while those of Zadig were white. The sympathies of all were divided between the knight in blue and the knight in white. The queen, whose heart was throbbing violently, prayed to heaven that the white might be the winning color.

The two champions made passes and wheeled round with such agility, they delivered such dexterous thrusts, and sat so firmly on their saddles, that all the spectators, except the queen, wished that there might be two kings in Babylon. At last, their chargers exhausted, and their lances broken, Zadig had recourse to this stratagem: he steps behind the blue prince, leaps upon the croup of his horse, seizes him by the waist, hurls him down, takes his place in the saddle, and prances round Otame, as he lies stretched upon the ground. All the amphitheatre shouts: "Victory to the white cavalier!" Otame rises, indignant, and draws his sword. Zadig springs off the horse's back, sabre in hand. There they are, both of them on foot in the arena, beginning a new conflict, in which strength and agility by turns prevail. The plumes of their helmets, the rivets of their arm-pieces, the links of their armor, fly far afield under a thousand rapid blows. With point and edge they thrust and cut, to right and left, now on the head, and now on the chest; they retreat, they advance, they measure swords, they come to close quarters, they wrestle, they twine like serpents, they attack each other like lions; sparks fly out every moment from their clashing swords. At last Zadig, recovering his coolness for an instant, stops, makes a feint, and then rushes upon Otame, brings him to the ground, and disarms him, and Otame exclaims: "O white cavalier! it is you who should reign over Babylon."

The queen's joy was at its height. The cavalier in blue and the cavalier in white were conducted each to his own lodging, as well as all the others, in due accordance with the law. Mutes came to attend them and to bring them food. It may be easily guessed that the queen's little mute was the one who waited on Zadig. Then they were left to sleep alone until the morning of the next day, when the conqueror was to bring his coat of arms to the grand mage to be compared with the roll, and to make himself known.

In spite of his love Zadig slept soundly enough, so tired was he. Itobad, who lay near him, did not sleep a wink. He rose in the night, entered Zadig's quarters, took away his white weapons and his coat of arms and left his own green armor in their place. As soon as it was daylight, he went up boldly to the grand mage, and announced that such a man as he was victor. This was unexpected, but his success was proclaimed while Zadig was still asleep. Astarte, surprised, and with despair at her heart, returned to Babylon. The whole amphitheatre was already almost empty when Zadig awoke; he looked for his arms, and found only the green armor. He was obliged to put it on, having nothing else near him. Astonished and indignant, he armed himself in a rage, and stepped forth in that guise.

All the people who were left in the amphitheatre and arena greeted him with jeers. They pressed round him, and insulted

him to his face. Never did a man endure such humiliating mortification. He lost patience, and with his drawn sword dispersed
the mob which dared to insult him; but he knew not what
course to adopt. He could not see the queen, nor could he lay
claim to the white armor which she had sent him, without compromising her; so that, while she was plunged in grief, he was
tortured with rage and anxiety. He walked along the banks of the
Euphrates, convinced that his star had marked him out for utter
misery, reviewing in his mind all his misfortunes, from the adventure with the woman who hated one-eyed men up to this present
loss of his armor.

"See what comes," said he, "of awaking too late; if I had slept
less, I should now be king of Babylon and husband of Astarte.
Knowledge, conduct, and courage have never served to bring me
anything but trouble."

At last, murmurs against Providence escaped him, and he was
tempted to believe that the world was governed by a cruel destiny, which oppressed the good, and brought prosperity to cavaliers in green. One of his worst grievances was to be obliged to
wear that green armor which drew such ridicule upon him; and
he sold it to a passing merchant at a low price, taking in exchange from the merchant a gown and a nightcap. In this garb
he paced beside the Euphrates, filled with despair, and secretly
accusing Providence for always persecuting him.

XVIII

THE HERMIT

While walking along, Zadig met a hermit, whose white and venerable beard descended to his waist. He held in his hand a book
which he was reading attentively. Zadig stopped, and bowed
deeply to him. The hermit returned his greeting with an air so
noble and mild, that Zadig had the curiosity to enter into conversation with him. He asked him what book he was reading.

"It is the book of destinies," said the hermit; "do you want to
read some of it?"

He placed the book in Zadig's hands, but he, learned as he was in several languages, could not decipher a single character in the book. This increased his curiosity yet more.

"You seem to me much vexed," said the good father.

"Alas! and with only too much reason!" answered Zadig.

"If you will allow me to accompany you," rejoined the old man, "perhaps I may be of service to you; I have sometimes brought consolation to the souls of the unhappy."

The hermit's aspect, his beard, and his book, filled Zadig with respect. He found in conversing with him the light of a superior mind. The hermit spoke of destiny, of justice, of morality, of the greatest good, of human frailty, of virtue, and of vice, with an eloquence so lively and touching, that Zadig felt himself drawn towards him by an irresistible charm. He earnestly urged him not to leave him, until they should return to Babylon.

"I myself ask the same favor of you," said the old man; "swear to me by Ormuzd that you will not part from me for some days to come, whatever I may do."

Zadig swore not to do so, and they set out together.

The two travellers arrived that evening at a magnificent castle, where the hermit asked for hospitality for himself and for the young man who accompanied him. The porter, who might have been taken for a distinguished nobleman, introduced them with a sort of disdainful politeness. They were presented to one of the principal domestics, who showed them the master's splendid apartments. They were admitted to the lower end of his table, without being honored even with a look from the lord of the castle; but they were served like the others, with elegance and profusion. A golden bowl studded with emeralds and rubies was afterwards brought them wherein to wash their hands. For the night they were led to fine sleeping apartments, and in the morning a servant brought each of them a piece of gold, after which they were courteously dismissed.

"The master of the house," said Zadig, when they were again on their way, "seems to me to be a generous man, but a little too proud; he practices a noble hospitality."

As he said these words, he noticed that a very wide sort of pocket which the hermit was wearing appeared stretched and stuffed out, and he caught sight of the golden bowl adorned with precious stones, which the hermit had stolen. He did not at first venture to say anything about it, but he experienced a strange surprise.

Towards noon, the hermit presented himself at the door of a very small house, inhabited by a very rich miser, of whom he begged hospitality for a few hours. An old servant, meanly clad, received them roughly, and showed the hermit and Zadig to the stable, where some rotten olives, mouldy bread, and stale beer were given them. The hermit ate and drank with as contented an air as on the evening before; then, turning to the old servant who was watching them both to see that they stole nothing, and who kept urging them to go, he gave him the two pieces of gold which he had received that morning, and thanked him for all his attentions.

"Pray," added he, "let me speak a word to your master."

The astonished servant introduced the two strangers.

"Magnificent lord," said the hermit, "I cannot refrain from offering you my most humble thanks for the noble manner in which you have treated us; deign to accept this golden bowl as a slight token of my gratitude."

The miser almost fell backward from his seat, but the hermit, not giving him time to recover from his sudden surprise, departed with his young companion as quickly as possible.

"Father," said Zadig, "what is all this that I see? You do not seem to me to resemble other men in anything that you do; you steal a bowl adorned with precious stones from a nobleman who entertained you magnificently, and you give it to a miser who treats you with indignity."

"My son," replied the old man, "that pompous person, who receives strangers only out of vanity, and to have them admire his riches, will become wiser; the miser will be taught to practise hospitality. Be astonished at nothing, and follow me."

Zadig was still uncertain whether he had to do with a man more foolish or more wise than all other men; but the hermit spoke with a tone of such superiority, that Zadig, bound besides by his oath, could not help following him.

In the evening they arrived at a house built in a pleasing but simple style, where nothing suggested either prodigality or avarice. The master was a philosopher who, retired from the world, pursued in peace the study of wisdom and virtue, and who, nevertheless, felt life no tedious burden. It had pleased him to build this retreat, in which he welcomed strangers with a generosity free from ostentation. He went himself to meet the travellers, and first left them to rest in a comfortable apartment. Some time afterwards he came in person to invite them to a good and well-cooked meal, during which he spoke with much good sense about the latest revolutions in Babylon. He seemed sincerely attached to the queen, and expressed a wish that Zadig had appeared in the lists as a competitor for the crown.

"But men," he added, "do not deserve to have a king like Zadig."

The latter blushed, and felt his grief redouble. In the course of conversation it was generally agreed that events in this world do not always happen as the wisest men would wish. The hermit maintained throughout that we are ignorant of the ways of Providence, and that men are wrong in judging of the whole by the very small part which they are able to perceive.

They spoke of the passions. "Ah! how dangerous they are!" said Zadig.

"They are the winds that swell the sails of the vessel," replied the hermit; "they sometimes sink the vessel, but it could not make way without them. Bile makes men angry and ill, but without bile they could not live. Everything here below is dangerous, and yet everything is necessary."

They spoke of pleasure, and the hermit proved that it is a gift of Divinity.

"For," said he, "man can give himself neither sensations nor ideas, he receives them all; pain and pleasure come to him from without like his very existence."

Zadig marvelled how a man who had acted so extravagantly could reason so well. At length, after a conversation as instructive as it was agreeable, their host led the two travellers back to their apartment, blessing Heaven for having sent him two men so virtuous and so wise. He offered them money in a frank and easy manner that could give no offense. The hermit refused it, and told him that he must now take leave of him, as he planned to leave for Babylon before morning. Their parting was affectionate, Zadig especially felt full of esteem and love for so likable a man.

When the hermit and he were alone in their rooms, they passed a long time in praising their host. The old man at daybreak awoke his comrade.

"We must start," said he; "but while all the household is asleep, I wish to leave this man a token of my regard and affection."

Saying these words, he seized a candle, and set fire to the house. Zadig uttered a cry of horror, and would fain have prevented him from committing so dreadful a deed, but the hermit dragged him away by superior force, and the house was soon in flames. The hermit, who was now at a safe distance with his companion, calmly watched it burning.

"Thank God!" said he; "there goes the house of my dear host, destroyed from basement to roof! Happy man!"

At these words Zadig was tempted at once to burst out laughing, to overwhelm the reverend father with reproaches, to beat him, and to run away from him; but he did none of these things; still overawed by the hermit's dominating influence, he followed him in spite of himself to their last quarters for the night.

It was at the house of a charitable and virtuous widow, who had a nephew fourteen years of age, full of pleasing qualities, and her only hope. She did the honors of her house as well as she could, and in the morning she bade her nephew conduct the travellers as far as a bridge which, having broken down a short time before, was now dangerous to cross. The lad hastened to walk before them. When they were on the bridge, the hermit said to the youth:

"Come, I must prove my gratitude to your aunt."

Then he seized him by the hair, and threw him into the river. The boy sank, rose for a moment above the water, and was then swallowed up by the torrent.

"O monster! Most wicked of all men!" exclaimed Zadig.

"You promised to be more patient," said the hermit, interrupting him. "Know that under the ruins of that house to which Providence set fire, the master has found an immense treasure;

and that this youth, whose neck Providence has twisted, would have murdered his aunt within a year and you within two."

"Savage, who told you so?" cried Zadig; "and though you may have read this event in your book of destinies, are you allowed to drown a child who has done you no harm?"

While the Babylonian was speaking, he perceived that the old man had no longer a beard, and that his countenance assumed the features of youth. The dress of a hermit disappeared; four beautiful wings covered a form majestic and glittering with light.

"O messenger from heaven! Divine angel!" cried Zadig, falling on his knees; "art thou then descended from the empyrean to teach a feeble mortal to submit to the eternal decrees?"

"Men," said the angel Jesrad, "judge of everything without knowing anything; of all men you were the one who most deserved to be enlightened."

Zadig asked if he might have permission to speak.

"I distrust myself," said he, "but may I venture to ask you to resolve my doubt? Would it not have been better to have corrected this youth, and to have made him virtuous, than to drown him?"

Jesrad answered: "If he had been virtuous, and had continued to live, it would have been his destiny to be murdered himself, together with the wife he was to marry, and the son whom she was to bear."

"What!" said Zadig, "is it necessary then that there be crimes and misfortunes and that misfortunes fall upon the good!"

"The wicked," answered Jesrad, "are always unhappy; they serve to try a small number of righteous men scattered over the earth, and there is no evil from which some good does not spring."

"But," said Zadig, "what if there were only good, and no evil at all?"

"Then," answered Jesrad, "this earth would be another earth, the chain of events would be a different order of wisdom; and this different order, which would be perfect, can only exist in the eternal dwelling place of the supreme Being, which evil cannot approach. He has created millions of worlds, not one of which can resemble another. This immense variety is an attribute of his immense power. There are not two leaves of a tree upon this earth, nor two globes in the infinite fields of heaven, which are alike; and everything that you see on this little atom where you have been born must be in its place, and exist in its own fixed time, according to the immutable decrees of Him who embraces all. Men think that this child who has just perished fell into the water by accident, that it was by a similar accident that that house was burned; but there is no such thing as accident; all that takes place is either a trial, or a punishment, or a reward, or a foretelling. Remember that fisherman who thought himself the most miserable of men. Ormuzd sent you to change his destiny. Feeble mortal, cease to dispute against that which you must adore."

"But," said Zadig——

As he said, "But . . . ," the angel was already winging his way towards the tenth sphere. Zadig on his knees adored Providence and submitted. The angel cried to him from on high:

"Make your way towards Babylon."

XIX

THE RIDDLES

Zadig, in a state of bewilderment, and like a man at whose side lightning has struck, walked on confusedly. He entered Babylon on the day when those who had contended in the lists were already assembled in the grand vestibule of the palace to explain the riddles, and to answer the questions of the grand mage. All the knights were there, except him of the green armor. As soon as Zadig appeared in the city, the people gathered round him; they could not satisfy their eyes with the sight of him, their mouths with blessing him, or their hearts with wishing him to be king. The Envious man saw him pass, shuddered, and turned away, while the people escorted him to the place of assembly. The queen, to whom his arrival was announced, became a prey to the agitation of fear and hope; she was devoured with uneasiness, and could not comprehend why Zadig was unarmed, and how it came to be that Itobad wore the white armor. A confused murmur arose at the sight of Zadig. All were surprised and delighted to see him again; but only the knights who had taken part in the tournament were permitted to appear in the assembly.

"I have fought like the others," said he; "but another here wears my armor, and, while I must wait to have the honor of proving it, I ask permission to present myself in order to explain the riddles."

The question was put to the vote; his reputation for integrity was still so deeply impressed on the minds of all, that there was no hesitation about admitting him.

The grand mage first proposed this question:

"What, of all things in the world, is alike the longest and the shortest, the quickest and the slowest, the most divisible and the most extended, the most neglected and the most regretted, without which nothing can be done, which devours everything that is little, and enlivens all that is great?"

Itobad was to speak first; he answered that such a man as he understood nothing about riddles, that it was enough for him to have conquered by the might of his arm. Some said that the answer to the riddle was fortune; according to others it was the earth, and according to others again light. Zadig said that it was time:

"Nothing is longer," added he, "since it is the measure of eternity; nothing is shorter, since we lack it for all of our projects. There is nothing slower to one who waits, nothing quicker to one who enjoys. It extends to infinity in greatness, it is infinitely divisible in minuteness. All men neglect it, all regret its loss. Nothing is done without it. It buries in oblivion all that is unworthy of posterity; and it confers immortality upon all things that are great."

The assembled agreed that Zadig's answer was the right one.

The next question was:

"What is it which we receive without acknowledgment, which we enjoy without knowing how, which we bestow on others when we know nothing about it, and which we lose without noticing the loss?"

Everybody had his own explanation. Zadig alone guessed that

it was life, and explained all the other riddles with the same
ease. Itobad said on each occasion that nothing was simpler, and
that he would have come to the same conclusion with equal
facility, if he had cared to give himself the trouble. Questions
were afterwards propounded on justice, the chief good, and the
art of government. Zadig's replies were pronounced the sound-
est.

"What a pity," it was said, "that one whose judgment is so
good should be so bad a knight!"

"Illustrious lords," said Zadig, "I have had the honor of conquering in the lists. It is to me that the white armor belongs.
The lord Itobad seized it while I slept; he thought, apparently,
that it would become him better than the green. I am ready to
prove upon his person at once before you all, in this robe and
armed only with my sword, against all this fine white armor
which he has stolen from me, that it was I who had the honor
of vanquishing brave Otame."

Itobad accepted the challenge with the greatest confidence.
He felt no doubt that, armed as he was with helmet, breastplate,
and arm guards, he would soon see the last of a champion clad
in a nightcap and a dressing gown. Zadig drew his sword, an·
saluted the queen, who gazed on him with feelings of joy an
fear. Itobad unsheathed his weapon without saluting anyone. H
advanced upon Zadig like a man who had nothing to fear, anc
made ready to split his head in two. Zadig adroitly parried the
stroke, opposing the strongest part of his sword to the weakest
part of that of his adversary, in such a way that Itobad's blade
was broken. Then Zadig, seizing his enemy round the waist,
hurled him to the ground, and, holding the point of his sword
where the breastplate ended, said:

"Let yourself be disarmed or I will kill you."

Itobad, who was always surprised at any disgrace which befell
such a man as he, let Zadig do what he pleased. He peacefully
relieved him of his splendid helmet, his superb breastplate, his
fine arm guards, and his glittering thigh-pieces, put them on
himself again, and ran in this array to throw himself at Astarte's
knees.

Cador had no difficulty in proving that the armor belonged to

Zadig. He was acknowledged king by unanimous consent, and most of all by Astarte, who tasted, after so many adversities, the delight of seeing her lover regarded by all the world as worthy of being her husband. Itobad went away to hear himself called his lordship in his own house. Zadig was made king, and he was happy. What the angel Jesrad had said to him was present in his mind, and he even remembered the grain of sand which became a diamond. The queen and he adored Providence. Zadig left the beautiful and capricious Missouf to travel the world at will. He sent in search of the brigand Arbogad, gave him an honorable post in his army, and promised to promote him to the highest rank, if he behaved like a true warrior, and to have him hanged, if he followed the trade of a robber.

Setoc was summoned from the heart of Arabia, together with the fair Almona, and set at the head of the commerce of Babylon. Cador was loved and honored as his services deserved: he was the king's friend, and the king was then the only monarch upon earth who had one. The little mute was not forgotten. A fine house was given to the fisherman, while Orcan was condemned to pay him a large sum, and to give him back his wife; but the fisherman, now grown wise, took the money only.

The fair Semira was inconsolable for having believed that Zadig would be one-eyed; and Azora never ceased lamenting that she had wished to cut off his nose. He soothed their sorrow with presents. The Envious man died of rage and shame. The empire enjoyed peace, glory, and abundance; that age was the best which the earth had known. It was ruled by justice and by love. All men blessed Zadig, and Zadig blessed Heaven.

THE WAY THE WORLD GOES

VISION OF BABOUC

Written by Himself[6]

Among the genii who preside over the empires of the world, Ithuriel holds one of the first places, and has the province of Upper Asia. He came down one morning, entered the dwelling of Babouc, a Scythian who lived on the banks of the Oxus, and addressed him thus:

"Babouc, the follies and disorders of the Persians have drawn down upon them our wrath. An assembly of the genii of Upper Asia was held yesterday to consider whether Persepolis should be punished or utterly destroyed. Go there, and make full investigation; on your return inform me faithfully of all, and I will decide according to your report either to chastise the city or to wipe it out."

"But, my lord," said Babouc humbly, "I have never been in Persia, and know no one there."

"So much the better," said the angel, "you will be the more impartial. Heaven has given you discernment, and I add the gift of winning confidence. Go, look, listen, observe, and fear nothing; you will be well received everywhere."

Babouc mounted his camel, and set out with his servants. After some days, on approaching the plains of Sennah, he fell in with the Persian army, which was going to fight with the army of India. He first accosted a soldier whom he found at a distance from the camp, and asked him what was the cause of the war.

"By all the gods," said the soldier, "I know nothing about it;

it is no business of mine; my trade is to kill and be killed to get a living. It makes no difference to me whom I serve. I have a great mind to pass over tomorrow into the Indian camp, for I hear that they are giving their men half a copper drachma a day more than we get in this cursed service of Persia. If you want to know why we are fighting, speak to my captain."

Babouc gave the soldier a small present, and entered the camp. He soon made the captain's acquaintance, and asked him the cause of the war.

"How should I know?" said he; "such grand matters are no concern of mine. I live two hundred leagues away from Persepolis; I hear it said that war has been declared; I immediately forsake my family, and go, according to our custom, to make my fortune or to die, since I have nothing else to do."

"But surely," said Babouc, "your comrades are a little better informed than yourself?"

"No," replied the officer, "hardly anybody except our chief satraps has any very clear idea why we are cutting each other's throats."

Babouc, astonished at this, introduced himself to the generals, and they were soon on intimate terms. At last one of them said to him:

"The cause of this war, which has laid Asia waste for the last twenty years, originally sprang out of a quarrel between a eunuch belonging to one of the wives of the great King of Persia, and a custom-house clerk in the service of the great King of India. The matter in dispute was a duty amounting to very nearly the thirtieth part of a florin. The Indian and Persian prime ministers worthily supported their masters' rights. The quarrel grew hot. They sent into the field on both sides an army of a million troops. This army has to be reinforced every year with more than 400,000 men. Massacres, conflagrations, ruin, and devastation multiply; the world suffers, and their fury still continues. Our own as well as the Indian prime minister often protest that they are acting solely for the happiness of the human race; and at each protestation some towns are always destroyed and some provinces ravaged."

The next day, on a report being spread that peace was about

to be concluded, the Persian and Indian generals hastened to give battle; and a bloody one it was. Babouc saw all its mistakes and all its abominations; he witnessed stratagems carried on by the chief satraps, who did all they could to cause their commander to be defeated; he saw officers slain by their own troops; he saw soldiers despatching their dying comrades in order to strip them of a few blood-stained rags, torn and covered with mud. He entered the hospitals to which they were carrying the wounded, most of whom died through the inhuman negligence of those very men whom the King of Persia paid handsomely to relieve them.

"Are these men," cried Babouc, "or wild beasts? Ah! I see plainly that Persepolis will be destroyed."

Occupied with this thought, he passed into the camp of the Indians, and found there as favorable a reception as in that of the Persians, just as he had been led to expect; but he beheld there all the same abuses that had already filled him with horror.

"Ah!" said he to himself, "if the angel Ithuriel resolves to exterminate the Persians, then the angel of India must destroy the Indians as well."

Being afterwards more particularly informed of all that went on in both camps, he was made acquainted with acts of generosity, magnanimity, and humanity that moved him with astonishment and delight.

"Unintelligible mortals!" he exclaimed, "how is it that you can combine so much meanness with so much greatness, such virtues with such crimes?"

Meanwhile peace was declared. The commanders of both armies, neither of whom had gained the victory, but who had caused the blood of so many of their fellow-men to flow, only to promote their own interests, began to solicit rewards at their respective courts. The peace was extolled in public proclamations, which announced nothing less than the return of virtue and happiness to earth.

"God be praised!" said Babouc, "Persepolis will be the abode of purified innocence. It will not be destroyed, as those wretched genii wished: let us hasten without delay to this capital of Asia."

On his arrival he entered that immense city by the old approach, which was altogether barbarous, and offended the eye with its rustic want of taste. All that part of the city bore witness to the time at which it had been built; for, in spite of men's obstinate stupidity in praising the ancient at the expense of the modern, it must be confessed that in every art first attempts are always rude.

Babouc mingled in a crowd of people composed of all the dirtiest and ugliest of both sexes, who with a dull and sullen air were pouring into a vast and dreary building. From the constant hum of voices and the movements that he remarked, from the money that some were giving to others for the privilege of sitting down, he thought that he was in a market where straw-bottomed chairs were sold; but soon, when he observed several women drop to their knees, pretending to look fixedly before them, but giving sidelong glances at the men, he became aware that he was in a temple. Grating voices, harsh, disagreeable, and out of tune, made the roof echo with ill-articulated sounds, which produced much the same effect as the braying of wild asses on the plains of the Pictavians,[7] when they answer the summons of the cow-herd's horn. He shut his ears; but he was about to shut his eyes and nose, when he saw workmen entering this temple with crowbars and spades, who removed a large stone, and threw up the earth to right and left, from which there issued a most offensive smell. Then people came and laid a dead body in the opening, and the stone was put back above it.

"What!" cried Babouc, "these folk bury their dead in the same places where they worship the Deity, and their temples are paved with corpses! I am no longer surprised at those pestilential diseases which often consume Persepolis. The air, tainted with the corruption of the dead and by so many of the living gathered and crammed together in the same place, is enough to poison the whole earth. Oh, what an abominable city is this Persepolis! It would seem that the angels intend to destroy it in order to raise up a fairer one on its site, and to fill it with cleaner inhabitants, and such as can sing better. Providence may be right after all; let us leave it to do as it will."

Meanwhile the sun had almost reached the middle of its course. Babouc was to dine at the other end of the town with a lady for whom he had letters from her husband, an officer in the army. He first took several turns around Persepolis, where he saw other temples better built and more tastefully adorned, filled with a refined congregation, and resounding with harmonious music. He observed public fountains, which, badly placed though they were, struck the eye by their beauty; open spaces, where the best kings who had governed Persia seemed to breathe in bronze, and others where he heard the people exclaiming: "When shall we see our beloved master here?" He admired the magnificent bridges that spanned the river, the splendid and serviceable quays, the palaces built on either side, and especially an immense mansion where thousands of old soldiers, wounded in the hour of victory, daily returned thanks to the God of armies.[8] At last he entered the lady's house, where he had been invited to dine with a select company. The rooms were elegant and handsomely furnished, the dinner delicious, the lady young, beautiful, clever, and charming, the company worthy of their hostess; and Babouc kept saying to himself every moment: "The angel Ithuriel must not care about the world if he thinks of destroying a city so delightful."

As time went on he perceived that the lady, who had begun by making tender inquiries after her husband, was, towards the end of the dinner, speaking more tenderly still to a young magician. He saw a magistrate who, in his wife's presence, was bestowing the liveliest caresses upon a widow; and that indulgent widow kept one hand round the magistrate's neck, while she stretched out the other to a handsome young citizen whose modesty seemed equal to his good looks. The magistrate's wife was the first to leave the table, in order to entertain in an adjoining chamber her spiritual director, who had been expected to dine with them but arrived too late; and the director, a man of ready eloquence, addressed her in that chamber with such vigor and unction, that the lady, when she came back, had her eyes moist and her cheeks flushed, an unsteady step, and a stammering utterance.

Then Babouc began to fear that the genie Ithuriel was in the right. The gift that he possessed of winning confidence let him into the secrets of his fair hostess that very day; she confided to him her partiality for the young magician, and assured him that in all the houses at Persepolis he would find the same sort of behavior as he had witnessed in hers. Babouc came to the conclusion that such a society could not long hold together; that jealousy, discord, and revenge were bound to make havoc in every household; that tears and blood must be shed daily; that the husbands would assuredly kill or be killed by the lovers of their wives; and, finally, that Ithuriel would do well to destroy immediately a city given up to continual disorders.

He was brooding over these dark thoughts, when there appeared at the door a man of grave countenance, clad in a black cloak, who humbly entreated a word with the young magistrate. The latter, without getting up or even looking at him, gave him some papers with a haughty and absent air, and then dismissed him. Babouc asked who the man was. The mistress of the house said to him in a low tone:

"That is one of the best lawyers we have in this city; he has been studying the laws for fifty years. The gentleman yonder, who is but twenty-five years of age, and who was made a satrap of the law two days ago, has employed him to draw up an abstract of a case on which he has to pronounce judgment tomorrow, and which he has not yet examined."

"This young fool acts wisely," said Babouc, "in asking an old man's advice, but why is not that old man himself the judge?"

"You must be joking," was the reply; "those who have grown old in toilsome and inferior employments never attain positions of great dignity. This young man enjoys a high office because his father is rich, and because the right of administering justice is bought and sold here like a farm."

"O unhappy city, to have such customs!" cried Babouc; "that

is the height of confusion. Doubtless those who have purchased the right of dispensing justice sell their judgments; I see nothing here but unfathomable depths of iniquity."

As he thus expressed his sorrow and surprise, a young warrior, who had that very day returned from the campaign, said to him:

"Why should you object to judicial appointments being made matters of purchase? I have myself paid a good price for the right of facing death at the head of two thousand men under my command; it has cost me forty thousand gold darics this year to lie on the bare ground in a red coat for thirty nights in a row, and to be twice wounded severely by an arrow, of which I still feel the smart. If I ruin myself to serve the Persian emperor whom I have never seen, this gentleman who represents the majesty of the law may well pay something to have the pleasure of giving audience to suitors."

Babouc in his indignation could not refrain from condemning in his heart a country where the highest offices of peace and war were put up to auction; he hastily concluded that there must be among such people a total ignorance of legal and military affairs, and that even if Ithuriel should spare them, they would be destroyed by their own detestable institutions.

His bad opinion was further confirmed by the arrival of a fat man, who, after giving a familiar nod to all the company, approached the young officer, and said to him:

"I can only lend you fifty thousand gold darics; for to tell you the truth, the imperial taxes have not brought me in more than three hundred thousand this year."

Babouc inquired who this man might be who complained of earning so little, and was informed that there were in Persepolis forty plebeian kings, who held the Persian empire on lease, and paid the monarch something out of what they made.

After dinner he went into one of the grandest temples in the city, and seated himself in the midst of a crowd of men and women who had come there to pass away the time. A magician appeared in a structure raised above their heads, and spoke for a long time about virtue and vice. This magician divided into several parts what had no need of division; he proved methodically what was perfectly clear, and taught what everybody knew already. He coolly worked himself into a passion, and went away perspiring and out of breath. Then all the congregation awoke, and thought that they had been listening to an edifying discourse. Babouc said:

"There is a man who has done his best to weary two or three hundred of his fellow-citizens; but his intention was good, and there is no reason in that for destroying Persepolis."

On leaving this assembly, he was taken to witness a public entertainment, which was given every day of the year. It was held in a sort of hall, at the further end of which appeared a palace. The most beautiful women of Persepolis and the most illustrious satraps, seated in orderly ranks, formed a spectacle so brilliant that Babouc imagined at first that there was nothing more to be seen. Two or three persons, who seemed to be kings and queens, soon appeared at the entrance of the palace; their language was very different from that of the people; it was measured, harmonious, and sublime. No one slept, but all listened in profound silence, which was only interrupted by expressions of feeling and admiration on the part of the audience. The duty of kings, the love of virtue, and the dangers of the passions were set forth in terms so lively and touching that Babouc shed tears. He had no doubt that those heroes and heroines, those kings and queens whom he had just heard, were the preachers of the empire. He even proposed to himself to persuade Ithuriel to come and hear them, quite convinced that such a spectacle would reconcile him forever to the city.

As soon as the entertainment was over, he wanted to see the principal queen, who had delivered such pure and noble sentiments of morality in that beautiful palace. He procured an introduction to her majesty, and was led up a narrow staircase to the second story, and ushered into a badly furnished apartment, where he found a badly dressed woman, who said to him with a noble and pathetic air:

"This calling of mine does not afford me enough to live upon;

one of the princes whom you saw has made me pregnant, and I shall soon be brought to bed; I am in want of money, and you cannot lie in without that."

Babouc gave her a hundred gold darics, saying to himself: "If there were nothing worse than this in the city, I think Ithuriel would be wrong in being so angry."

After that he went, under the escort of an intelligent man with whom he had become acquainted, to pass the evening in the shops of those who sold objects of useless ostentation. He bought whatever he liked, and everything was sold him in the most polite manner at far more than it was worth. His friend, on their return to his house, explained to him how he had been cheated, and Babouc made a note of the tradesman's name, in order to have him specially marked out by Ithuriel on the day when the city should be visited with punishment. As he was writing, a knock was heard at the door; it was the shopkeeper himself who had come to restore his purse, which Babouc had left by mistake on his counter.

"How is it," cried Babouc, "that you can be so honest and generous, after having had the nerve to sell me a lot of trinkets for four times as much as they are worth?"

"There is no merchant of any note in this city," answered the shopkeeper, "who would not have brought you back your purse; but whoever told you that you paid four times its proper value for what you bought from me, has grossly deceived you; my profit was ten times as much; and so true is this, that if you wish to sell the articles again in a month's time, you will not get even that tenth part. But nothing is fairer; it is men's passing fancy which settles the price of such baubles; it is that fancy which affords a livelihood to the hundred workmen whom I employ; it is that which provides me with a fine house, a comfortable carriage, and horses; it is that which stimulates industry, and promotes taste, traffic, and plenty. I sell the same trifles to neighboring nations at a much higher price than to you, and in that way I am useful to my country."

Babouc, after a moment's reflection, scratched the man's name out of his notebook.

Babouc, much puzzled as to what opinion he ought to have of Persepolis, determined to visit the magi and men of letters; for, inasmuch as the former devote themselves to religion and the latter to wisdom, he had great hopes that they would obtain pardon for the rest of the people. So early next morning he went to a college of the magi. The head of the monastery acknowledged that he had an income of a hundred thousand crowns for having taken a vow of poverty, and that he exercised a very extensive power by virtue of his profession of humility; after which he left Babouc in the hands of a brother of low degree, who did the honors of the place.

While this brother was showing him all the magnificence of that home of penitence, a rumor spread that he had come to reform all those religious houses. He immediately began to receive petitions from each of them, all of which were substantially to this effect: "Preserve us, and destroy all the others."

To judge by the arguments that were used in self-defense, these societies were all absolutely necessary; if their mutual accusations were to be believed, they all alike deserved extinction. He marvelled how there was not one of them but wished to govern the whole world in order to enlighten it. Then a little fellow, who was a demi-mage, came forward and said to him:

"I see clearly that the work is going to be accomplished; for Zerdust has returned to earth; little girls prophesy, while having themselves pinched in front and whipped behind. Could you not protect us from the grand lama?"

"What nonsense!" said Babouc. "From the grand lama? From the pontiff king who resides in Thibet?"

"Yes," said the little demi-mage, "from him, and none else."

"Then you wage war on him, and have armies?" asked Babouc.

"No," said the other, "but he says that man is free and we do not believe a word of it. We have written three or four thousand books against him, that he does not read. He has hardly ever heard us spoken of, he has only had us condemned, as a master might order the trees in his garden to be cleared of caterpillars."

Babouc shuddered at the folly of those men who made a pro-

fession of wisdom; the intrigues of those who had renounced
the world; the ambition, greed, and pride of those who taught
humility and unselfishness; and he came to the conclusion that
Ithuriel had very good reasons for destroying the whole breed.

On his return to his lodging, he sent for some new books in
order to soothe his indignation; and he invited some literary
men to dinner for the sake of cheerful society. Twice as many
came as he had asked, like wasps attracted by honey. These
parasites were as eager to speak as they were to eat; two classes
of persons were the objects of their praise, the dead and themselves,—never their contemporaries, the master of the house excepted. If one of them happened to make a clever remark,
the countenances of all the others fell, and they gnawed their
lips in pain that it was not they who had said it. They did not
disguise their real feelings so much as the magi, because their
ambition was not pitched so high. There was not one of them
but was soliciting some petty post or other, and at the same time
wishing to be thought a great man. They said to each other's
face the most insulting things, which they took for flashes of wit.
Having some knowledge of Babouc's mission, one of them
begged him in a whisper to annihilate an author who had not
praised him enough five years ago; another asked for the ruin
of a citizen who had never laughed at his comedies; and a third
desired the abolition of the Academy, because he himself had
never succeeded in gaining admission. When the meal was finished, each went out by himself, for in all the company there
were not two men who could endure or even speak a civil
word to each other, outside the houses of those rich patrons who
invited them to their table. Babouc deemed that it would be no
great loss if all that breed of vermin were to perish in the
general destruction.

As soon as he was rid of them, he began to read some of the
new books, and recognized in them the same temper as his
guests had shown. He saw with special indignation those ga-

zettes of slander, those records of bad taste, which are dictated by envy, baseness, and hunger; those cowardly satires in which the vulture is treated with respect while the dove is torn to pieces; and those novels, devoid of imagination, in which are displayed so many portraits of women with whom the author is totally unacquainted.

He threw all those detestable writings into the fire, and went out to take an evening walk. He was introduced to an old scholar who had not made one of his late company of parasites; for he always avoided the crowd. Knowing men well, he made good use of his knowledge, and was careful to whom he gave his confidence. Babouc spoke to him with indignation of what he had read and what he had seen.

"You have been reading poor contemptible stuff," said the learned sage; "but at all times, in all countries, and in every walk of life, the bad swarm and the good are rare. You have entertained the mere scum of pedantry, for in all professions alike those who least deserve to appear always obtrude themselves with most impudence. The men of real wisdom live a quiet and retired life; there are still among us some men and books worthy of your attention."

While he was speaking thus another man of letters joined them; and their conversation was so agreeable and instructive, so superior to prejudice and conformable to virtue, that Babouc confessed he had never heard anything like it before.

"Here are men," he said to himself, "whom the angel Ithuriel will not dare to touch, or he will be ruthless indeed."

Reconciled as he now was to the men of letters, Babouc was still enraged with the rest of the nation.

"You are a stranger," said the judicious person who was talking to him; "abuses present themselves to your eyes in a mass, and the good which is concealed, and which sometimes results from these very abuses, escapes your observation."

Then he learned that among learned men there were some who were free from envy, and that even among the magi virtuous men were to be found. He understood at last that these great societies, which seemed by their mutual collisions to be bringing about their common ruin, were basically beneficial institutions; that each community of magi was a check upon its rivals; that if they differed in some matters of opinion, they all taught the same principles of morality, instructed the people, and lived in obedience to the laws; like tutors who watch over the son of the house, while the master watches over them. Becoming acquainted with several of these magi, he saw souls of heavenly disposition. He found that even among the fools who aspired to make war on the grand lama there had been some very great men. He began to suspect that the character of the people of Persepolis might be like their buildings, some of which had seemed to him deplorably bad, while others had filled him with admiration.

Said Babouc to his literary friend:

"I see clearly enough that these magi, whom I thought so dangerous, are in reality very useful, especially when a wise government prevents them from making themselves too indispensable. But you will at least acknowledge that your young magistrates, who buy a seat on the bench as soon as they have learned to mount a horse, must display in your courts of law the most ridiculous impertinence and the most perverse injustice; it would undoubtedly be better to give these appointments gratuitously to those old lawyers who have passed all their lives in weighing conflicting arguments."

The man of letters made reply:

"You saw our army before your arrival at Persepolis; you know that our young officers fight very well, although they have purchased their commissions; perhaps you will find that our young magistrates do not pronounce wrong judgments, in spite of having paid for the positions they occupy."

He took Babouc the next day to the High Court, where an important decision was to be delivered. The case was one that excited universal interest. All the old advocates who spoke about it were uncertain in their opinions; they quoted a hundred laws, not one of which had any essential bearing on the question; they looked at the matter from a hundred points of view, none of which presented it in its true light. The judges were quicker in giving their decision than the advocates in raising doubts; their judgment was almost unamimous; and they judged well, because they followed the light of reason, whereas the others went astray in their opinions, because they had only consulted their books.

Babouc came to the conclusion that there is often some good in abuses. He saw on that very day how the riches of the financiers which had given him so much offense, might produce an excellent effect, for the emperor, being in want of money, obtained in an hour by their means a sum that he would not have been able to procure in six months through the ordinary channels; he saw that those big clouds, swollen with the dews of earth, restored to it in rain all that they received from it. Moreover, the children of those self-made men, often better educated than those of the most ancient families, were sometimes of much greater value to their country; for there is nothing to hinder a man from making a good judge, a brave soldier, or a clever statesman, in his having had a father who could figure well.

By degrees Babouc forgave the greed of the financiers who are not in reality more greedy than other men, and who are necessary. He excused the folly of those who impoverished themselves in order to be a judge or a soldier, a folly which creates great magistrates and heroes. He pardoned the envy displayed by the men of letters, among whom were to be found men who enlightened the world; he became reconciled with the ambitious and intriguing magi, among whom great virtues outweighed petty vices. But there remained behind abundant matter of offense, above all, the love affairs of the ladies; and the ruin which he felt sure must follow filled him with anxiety and fear.

As he wished to gain insight into human life under all conditions, he procured an introduction to a minister of state, but on his way he was trembling all the time lest some wife should be assassinated by her husband before his eyes. On arriving at the statesman's house, he had to wait two hours in the antechamber before he was announced, and two hours more after that had.

been done. He fully made up his mind during that interval to report to the angel Ithuriel both the minister and his insolent servants. The antechamber was filled with ladies of every degree, with magi of all shades of opinion, with judges, tradesmen, officers, and pedants; all found fault with the minister. The misers and usurers said: "That fellow plunders the provinces, there's no doubt about it." The capricious reproached him with being eccentric. The libertines said: "He thinks of nothing but his pleasures." The factious flattered themselves that they should soon see him ruined by a cabal. The women hoped that they might soon have a younger minister.

Babouc heard their remarks, and could not help saying:

"What a fortunate man this is! He has all his enemies in his antechamber; he crushes under his heel those who envy him; he sees those who detest him grovelling at his feet."

At last he was admitted, and saw a little old man stooping under the weight of years and business, but still brisk and full of energy.

He was pleased with Babouc, who thought him a worthy man, and their conversation became interesting. The minister confessed that he was very unhappy; that he passed for rich, but was really poor; that he was believed to be all powerful, yet was constantly thwarted; that almost all his favors had been conferred on the ungrateful; and that in the continual labors of forty years he had scarcely had a moment's peace. Babouc was touched with compassion, and thought that if this man had committed faults and the angel Ithuriel wished to punish him, he had no need to destroy him; it would be enough to leave him where he was.

While the minister and he were talking together, the beautiful lady with whom Babouc had dined hastily entered; and in her eyes and on her forehead were seen symptoms of grief and anger. She burst out into reproaches against the statesman; she shed tears; she complained bitterly that her husband had been refused a post to which his birth allowed him to aspire, and to which his services and his wounds entitled him. She expressed herself so forcibly, she complained with so much grace, she overcame objections with such skill, and reinforced her arguments with such eloquence, that before she left the room she had made her husband's fortune.

Babouc held out his hand, and said:

"Is it possible, madam, that you can have gone to all this trouble for a man whom you do not love, and from whom you have everything to fear?"

"A man whom I do not love!" she cried. "My husband, let me tell you, is the best friend I have in the world; there is nothing that I would not sacrifice for him, except my lover, and he would do anything for me, except give up his mistress. I should like you to know her; she is a charming woman, full of wit, and of an excellent disposition; we dine together this evening with my husband and my little mage; come and share our enjoyment."

The lady took Babouc home with her. The husband, who had arrived at last, overwhelmed with grief, saw his wife again with transports of delight and gratitude; he embraced by turns his wife, his mistress, the little magian, and Babouc. Unity, cheerfulness, wit, and elegance were the soul of the dinner.

"Learn," said the fair dame at whose house he was dining, "that those who are sometimes called women of no virtue have almost always merits as genuine as those of the most honorable man; and to convince yourself of it come with me tomorrow and dine with the beautiful Theona.[9] There are some old vestals who pick her to pieces, but she does more good than all of them together. She would not commit even a trifling act of injustice to promote her own interests, however important; the advice she gives her lover is always noble; his glory is her sole concern; he would blush to face her if he had neglected any occasion of doing good; for a man can have no greater encouragement to virtuous actions than to have for a witness and judge of his conduct a mistress whose good opinion he is anxious to deserve."

Babouc did not fail to keep the appointment. He saw a house where all the pleasures reigned, with Theona at their head, who knew how to speak in the language of each. Her natural good sense put others at their ease; she made herself agreeable without an effort, for she was as kind as she was generous, and, what enhanced the value of all her good qualities, she was beautiful.

Babouc, Scythian though he was, and though a genie had sent him on his mission, perceived that, if he stayed any longer at Persepolis, he should forget Ithuriel for Theona. He felt fond of a city whose inhabitants were polite, good-humored, and kind, however frivolous they might be, greedy of scandal, and full of vanity. He feared that the doom of Persepolis was sealed; he dreaded, too, the report he would have to give.

This was the method he adopted for making that report. He gave instructions to the best metal-worker in the city to cast a small image composed of all kinds of metals, earth, and stones, the most precious and the most worthless. He brought it to Ithuriel, and said:

"Will you break this pretty little image, because it is not all gold and diamonds?"

Ithuriel understood his meaning before the words were out of his mouth, and determined that he would not think of punishing Persepolis, and would not interfere with *the way the world goes;* "for," said he, "if all is not well, still, it is passable." So Persepolis was allowed to remain unharmed, and Babouc was very far from complaining like Jonah, who was angry because Nineveh was not destroyed. But when a man has been three days in a whale's belly, he is not so good-tempered as after a visit to the opera or to the play, or after dining in good company.

MICROMEGAS[10]

A PHILOSOPHICAL TALE

I

JOURNEY OF AN INHABITANT OF THE WORLD OF THE STAR SIRIUS TO THE PLANET SATURN

In one of those planets which revolve round the star named Sirius there lived a young man of great intelligence, whose acquaintance I had the honor of making on the occasion of his last journey to our little ant-hill. He was called Micromegas, a name which is exceedingly appropriate to all great people. He had a stature of eight leagues, and by eight leagues I mean twenty-four thousand geometrical paces of five feet each.

Here some mathematicians, a class of persons who are always useful to the public, will immediately take up the pen, and find out by calculation that since Mr. Micromegas, inhabitant of the country of Sirius, is twenty-four thousand paces in height from head to foot, which make one hundred and twenty thousand statute feet, whereas we denizens of the earth have an average stature of hardly more than five feet, and, since our globe is nine thousand leagues in circumference, they will find, I say, that the world which produced him must have a circumference precisely twenty-one millions six hundred thousand times greater than our little earth. Nothing in nature is simpler or more a matter of course. The states of certain rulers in Germany or Italy, around which you can walk in half an hour, as compared with the empire of Turkey, of Russia, or of China, can give but a very faint idea of the prodigious differences which nature has set between every sort of being throughout the universe.

His Excellency's height being what I have said, all our sculptors and painters will readily agree that his waist may be about fifty thousand feet round, which would constitute a very fine proportion.

As for his mind, it is worthy to rank with the most cultivated among us; he knows many things, some of which are of his own invention. He had not yet reached his two hundred and fiftieth year, and was studying, as was customary at his age, at the Jesuit school in his planet, when he solved, by the strength of his own intellect, more than fifty propositions of Euclid; that is eighteen more than Blaise Pascal, who, after having, according to his sister's account, solved thirty-two for his own amusement, afterwards became a rather mediocre geometrician, and a very poor metaphysician. When he was about four hundred and fifty years of age, and already passing out of childhood, he dissected a great many little insects less than a hundred feet in diameter, such as are invisible under ordinary microscopes; he composed a very curious book about them, but one which brought him into some trouble. The mufti of that country, much given to hair-splitting and very ignorant, found in his work statements which he deemed suspicious, offensive, rash, heretical or savoring of heresy, and he prosecuted him for it avidly. The question in dispute was whether the substantial form of the fleas of Sirius was of the same nature as that of the snails. Micromegas defended himself with spirit, and had all the women on his side; the trial lasted two hundred and twenty years. At last the mufti had the book condemned by judges who had never read it, and the author was forbidden to appear at court for eight hundred years.

He was only moderately afflicted at being banished from a court which was full of nothing but trickery and meanness. He composed a very funny song ridiculing the mufti, which in its turn failed to give the latter much annoyance; and he himself set forth on his travels from planet to planet, with a view to improving *the mind and heart*, as the saying is. Those who travel only in post-chaises or family coaches, will doubtless be astonished at the sort of conveyance adopted up there; for we, on our little mound of mud, can imagine nothing that surpasses our own experience. Our traveller had such a marvelous knowledge of the laws of gravitation, and all the forces of attraction and repulsion, and made such good use of his knowledge, that, sometimes by means of a sunbeam, and sometimes by the help of a comet, he and his companions went from one world to another as a bird hops from bough to bough. He crossed the Milky Way in a very short time; and I am obliged to confess that he never saw, beyond the stars with which it is thickly sown, that beautiful celestial empyrean which the illustrious parson, Derham,[11] boasts of having discovered at the end of his telescope. Not that I would for a moment suggest that Mr. Derham mistook what he saw; Heaven forbid! But Micromegas was on the spot, he is an accurate observer, and I have no wish to contradict anybody. Micromegas, after many turns and twists, arrived at the planet Saturn. Accustomed though he was to the sight of novelties, when he saw the insignificant size of the globe and its inhabitants, he could not at first refrain from that smile of superiority which sometimes escapes even the wisest; for in truth Saturn is scarcely nine hundred times greater than the earth, and the citizens of that country are mere dwarfs, only a thousand fathoms high, or thereabout. He laughed a little at first at these people, in much the same way as an Italian musician, when he comes to France, will laugh at Lulli's performances. But, as the Sirian was a sensible fellow, he was very soon convinced that a thinking being need not be altogether ridiculous because he is no more than six thousand feet high. He was soon on familiar terms with the Saturnians after their astonishment had somewhat subsided. He formed an intimate friendship with the secretary of the Academy of Saturn,[12] a man of great intelligence, who had not indeed invented anything himself, but who gave an excellent account of the inventions of others, and who could turn a little verse neatly enough or perform an elaborate calculation. I will here recount, for the gratification of my readers, a singular conversation that Micromegas one day held with Mr. Secretary.

II

CONVERSATION BETWEEN AN INHABITANT OF SIRIUS AND A NATIVE OF SATURN

After His Excellency had laid himself down, and the secretary had approached his face, Micromegas said:

"I must confess that nature is full of variety."

"Yes," said the Saturnian; "nature is like a flower-bed, the blossoms of which——"

"Oh," said the other, "have done with your flower-bed!"

"She is," resumed the secretary, "like an assembly of blondes and brunettes, whose attire——"

"Eh! What have I to do with your brunettes?" said the other.

"She is like a gallery of pictures, then, the outlines of which——"

"No, no," said the traveller; "once more, nature is like nature. Why do you search for comparisons?"

"To please you," answered the secretary.

"I do not want to be pleased," rejoined the traveller; "I want to be instructed; begin by telling me how many senses the men in your world possess?"

"We have seventy-two," said the academician; "and we are always complaining that they are so few. Our imagination goes beyond our needs; we find that with our seventy-two senses, our ring, and our five moons, we are too limited, and, in spite of all our curiosity and the tolerably large number of passions which spring out of our seventy-two senses, we have plenty of time to become bored."

"I can well believe it," said Micromegas; "for in our globe, although we have nearly a thousand senses, there lingers even in us a certain vague desire, an unaccountable restlessness, which warns us unceasingly that we are of little account in the universe, and that there are beings much more perfect than ourselves. I have travelled a little; I have seen mortals far below us, and others as greatly superior; but I have seen none who have not more desires than real wants, and more wants than they can satisfy. I shall some day, perhaps, reach the country where there is lack of nothing, but hitherto no one has been able to give me any positive information about it." The Saturnian and the Sirian thereupon exhausted themselves in conjectures on the subject; but after a great deal of discussion, as ingenious as it was vague, they were obliged to return to facts.

"How long do you people live?" asked the Sirian.

"Ah! a very short time," replied the little man of Saturn.

"That is just the way with us," said the Sirian; "we are always complaining of the shortness of life. This must be a universal law of nature."

"Alas!" said the Saturnian, "none of us live for more than five hundred annual revolutions of the sun;" (that amounts to about fifteen thousand years, according to our manner of counting). "You see how it is our fate to die almost as soon as we are born; our existence is a point, our duration an instant, our globe an atom. Scarcely have we begun to acquire a little information when death arrives before we can put it to use. For my part, I do not venture to lay any schemes; I feel like a drop of water in a boundless ocean. I am ashamed, especially before you, of the absurd figure I make in this universe."

Micromegas answered: "If you were not a philosopher, I should fear to distress you by telling you that our lives are seven hundred times as long as yours; but you know too well that when the time comes to give back one's body to the elements, and to reanimate nature under another form, which process is called death,—when that moment of metamorphosis comes, it is precisely the same thing whether we have lived an eternity or only a day. I have been in countries where life is a thousand times longer than with us, and yet have heard complaints at its brevity even there. But people of good sense are to be found everywhere, who know how to make the most of what they have, and to thank the author of nature. He has spread over this universe abundant varieties with a kind of admirable uniformity. For example, all thinking beings are different, yet they all resemble each other essentially in the common endowment of thought and desires. Matter is infinitely extended, but it has different properties in different worlds. How many of these various properties do you count in the matter with which you are acquainted?"

"If you speak," replied the Saturnian, "of those properties without which we believe that this globe could not subsist as it is, we count three hundred of them, such as extension, impenetrability, mobility, gravitation, divisibility, and so on."

"Apparently," rejoined the traveller, "this small number is sufficient for the purpose which the Creator had in view in constructing this little habitation. I admire his wisdom throughout; I see differences everywhere, but everywhere also a due proportion. Your globe is small, you who inhabit it are small likewise; you have few senses, the matter of which your world consists has few properties; all this is the work of Providence. Of what color is your sun when carefully examined?"

"A very yellowish white," said the Saturnian; "and when we split up one of its rays, we find that it consists of seven colors."

"Our sun has a reddish light," said the Sirian, "and we have thirty-nine primitive colors. There is not a single sun, among all those that I have approached, which resembles any other, just as among yourselves there is not a single face which is not different from all the rest."

After several other questions of this kind, he inquired how many essentially different substances were enumerated in Saturn. He was told that not more than thirty were distinguished, as God, space, matter, beings occupying space which feel and think, thinking beings which do not occupy space, those which possess penetrability, others which do not do so, and so on. The Sirian, in whose world they count three hundred of them, and who had discovered three thousand more in the course of his travels, astonished the philosopher of Saturn immensely. At length, after having communicated to each other a little of what they knew, and a great deal of that about which they knew nothing, and after having exercised their reasoning powers during a complete revolution of the sun, they resolved to go on a little philosophical journey together.

III

JOURNEY OF THE TWO INHABITANTS OF SIRIUS AND SATURN

Our two philosophers were ready to embark upon the atmosphere of Saturn, with a fine collection of mathematical instruments, when the Saturnian's mistress, who got wind of what he was going to do, came in tears to remonstrate with him. She was a pretty little brunette, whose stature did not exceed six hundred and sixty fathoms, but who made up for her smallness of size in many pleasant ways.

"Oh, cruel one!" she exclaimed, "after having resisted you for fifteen hundred years, and when I was at last beginning to surrender, and have passed scarcely a hundred years in your arms, you leave me and start on a long journey with a giant of another world! Go, you have no taste for anything but novelty, you have never felt what it is to love; if you were a true Saturnian, you would be constant. Where are you going so fast? What do you want? Our five moons are less fickle than you, our ring is less changeable. So much for what is past! I will never love anyone again."

The philosopher embraced her, and, in spite of all his philosophy, joined his tears with hers. As to the lady, after having fainted away, she proceeded to console herself with a dandy who lived in the neighborhood.

Meanwhile our two inquirers set forth on their travels; they first of all jumped upon Saturn's ring, which they found pretty flat, as an illustrious inhabitant of our little globe has very cleverly conjectured; [13] thence they made their way from moon to moon. A comet passed quite near the last one, so they sprang upon it, together with their servants and their instruments. When they had gone about a hundred and fifty million leagues, they came across the satellites of Jupiter. They landed on Jupiter itself, and remained there for a year, during which they learned some very remarkable secrets which would be at the present moment in the press, were it not for the inquisitors who have discovered therein some statements too hard for them to swallow. But I have read the manuscript which contains them in the library of the illustrious archbishop of ——, who, with a generosity and kindness which cannot be sufficiently praised, has permitted me to see his books.

But let us return to our travellers. Quitting Jupiter, they traversed a space of about a hundred million leagues, and, coasting along the planet Mars, which, as is well known, is five times smaller than our own little globe, they saw two moons, which attend upon that planet, and which have escaped the observations of our astronomers. I am well aware that Father Castel will write, and pleasantly enough too, against the existence of these two moons,[14] but I rely upon those who reason from analogy. Those excellent philosophers know how difficult it would be for Mars, which is such a long way off from the sun, to get on with less than two moons. Be that as it may, our friends found the planet so small, that they were afraid of finding no room there to put up for the night, so they proceeded on their way, like two travellers who disdain a humble village inn, and push on to the nearest town. But the Sirian and his companion soon had cause to repent having done so, for they went on for a long time without finding anything at all. At last they perceived a faint glimmer; it came from our earth, and stirred pity in the minds of those who had just left Jupiter. However, for fear of repenting a second time, they decided to disembark. They passed over the tail of the comet, and meeting with an aurora borealis close at hand, they got inside, and arrived on the earth by the northern shore of the Baltic Sea, July the 5th, 1737, new style.

IV

WHAT HAPPENED TO THEM ON EARTH

After having rested for some time, they ate for their breakfast a couple of mountains, which their servants prepared for them as nicely as possible. Then wishing to inspect the country where they were, they first went from north to south. Each of the Sirian's ordinary steps was about thirty thousand statute feet; the Saturnian dwarf followed panting far behind, for he had to take about a dozen steps when the other made a single stride. Picture to yourself (if I may be allowed to make such a comparison) a tiny little toy spaniel following a captain of the King of Prussia's guards.

As the strangers proceeded rather quickly, they made the circuit of the globe in thirty-six hours; the sun, indeed, or rather the earth, makes the same journey in a day; but it must be borne in mind that it is a much easier way of moving to turn on one's axis, than to walk on one's feet. Behold our travellers, then, returned to the same spot from which they had started, after having set eyes upon that sea, to them almost imperceptible, which is called *the Mediterranean*, and that other little pond which, under the name of the *great Ocean*, surrounds this mole-hill. Therein the dwarf had never sunk much above the knee, while the other had scarcely wetted his ankle. They did all they could, searching here and there, both when going and returning, to ascertain whether the earth were inhabited or not. They stooped, they lay down, they groped about in all directions; but their eyes and their hands being out of all proportion to the tiny beings who crawl up and down here, they had not the slightest sensation which could lead them to suspect that we and our fellow-creatures, the other inhabitants of this globe, have the honor to exist.

The dwarf, who sometimes judged a little too hastily, at once decided that there was not a single creature on the earth. His first reason was that he had not seen one. But Micromegas politely gave him to understand that that was not a good argument:

"For," said he, "you, with your little eyes, cannot see certain stars of the fiftieth magnitude which I distinctly discern; do you conclude from that circumstance that those stars do not exist?"

"But," said the dwarf, "I have felt about very carefully."

"But," rejoined the other, "your powers of perception may be at fault."

"But," continued the dwarf, "this globe is so ill-constructed, it is so irregular, and, as it seems to me, of so ridiculous a shape! All here appears to be in a state of chaos; look at these little brooks not one of which goes in a straight line; look at these ponds, which are neither round nor square, nor oval, nor of any regular form; and all these little sharp-pointed grains with which

this globe bristles, and which have rubbed the skin off my feet!"
(He alluded to the mountains.) "Observe too the shape of the
globe as a whole, how flat it is at the poles, how it turns around
the sun in a clumsy slanting manner, so that the polar regions
are necessarily wastelands. In truth, what chiefly makes me think
that there is nobody here, is that I cannot suppose any people of
sense would wish to live here."

"Well," said Micromegas, "perhaps the people who inhabit it
are not people of sense. But in point of fact there are some signs
of its not having been made for nothing. Everything here seems
to you irregular, you say; that is because everything is measured
by the line of Saturn and Jupiter. Ay, perhaps it is for that very
reason that there is so much apparent confusion here. Have I
not told you that in the course of my travels I have always noticed the presence of variety?" The Saturnian had answers to
meet all these arguments, and the dispute might never have
ended, if Micromegas, in the heat of discussion, had not luckily
broken the thread which bound together his collar of diamonds,
so that they fell to the ground; pretty little stones they were, of
rather unequal size, the largest of which weighed four hundred
pounds, and the smallest not more than fifty. The dwarf, who
picked up some of them, perceived, on bringing them near his
eyes, that these diamonds, from the fashion in which they were
cut, made excellent microscopes. Accordingly, he took up a little
magnifier of one hundred and sixty feet in diameter, which he
applied to his eye; and Micromegas selected one of two thousand
five hundred feet across. They were of high power, but at first
nothing was revealed by their help, so the focus had to be ad-
justed. At last the inhabitant of Saturn saw something almost
imperceptible, which moved half under water in the Baltic Sea;
it was a whale. He caught it very cleverly with his little finger,
and placing it on his thumb nail, showed it to the Sirian, who
burst out laughing a second time at the extreme minuteness of
the inhabitants of our globe. The Saturnian, now convinced that
our world was inhabited, jumped to the conclusion that whales
were the only creatures to be found there; and, as speculation
was his strong point, he wanted to determine the source of the
movement of so insignificant an atom and whether it had ideas

and free will. Micromegas was greatly confused over it; he examined the animal very patiently, and the result of his investigation was that he had no grounds for supposing that it had a soul lodged in its body. The two travellers then were inclined to think that there was no being possessed of intelligence in this habitation of ours, when with the aid of the microscope they detected something as big as a whale, floating on the Baltic Sea. We know that at that very time a flock of philosophers were returning from the polar circle, where they had gone to make observations which no one had attempted before.[15] The newspapers say that their vessel ran aground in the gulf of Bothnia, and that they had great difficulty in saving their lives; but we never know in this world the real truth about anything. I am going to relate honestly what took place, without adding anything of my own invention, a task which demands no small effort on the part of a historian.

V

EXPERIENCES AND CONJECTURES OF THE TWO TRAVELLERS

Micromegas stretched out his hand very gently towards the place where the object appeared; thrusting forward two fingers, he quickly drew them back for fear of being mistaken; then, opening and closing them, very skilfully seized the ship which carried those gentlemen, and placed it likewise on his nail without squeezing it too much, for fear of crushing it.

"Here is an animal quite different from the first," said the Saturnian dwarf. The Sirian placed the supposed animal in the hollow of his hand. The passengers and crew, who thought that they had been whirled away by a tempest, and supposed that they had struck upon some kind of rock, began to bestir themselves; the sailors seized casks of wine, threw them overboard on Micromegas's hand, and afterwards jumped down themselves, while the mathematicians seized their quadrants, their sectors, and a few Lapland girls, and descended on the Sirian's fingers They made such a commotion, that at last he felt something tickling him; it was a pole with an iron point being driven a foot deep into his forefinger. He judged from this prick that it had proceeded somehow from the little animal that he was holding; but at first he suspected nothing more. The microscope, which scarcely enabled them to discern a whale and a ship, had no effect upon a being so insignificant as man. I have no wish to shock the vanity of anyone, but here I am obliged to beg those who are sensitive about their own importance to consider what I have to say on this subject. Taking the average stature of mankind at five feet, we make no greater figure on the earth than an insect not quite the six hundred thousandth part of an inch in height would do upon a bowl ten feet round. Imagine a being who could hold the earth in his hand, and who had organs of sense proportionate to our own,—and it may well be conceived that there are a great number of such beings,—consider then, I pray you, what they would think of those battles which give the conqueror possession of some village, to be lost again soon afterwards.

I have no doubt that if some captain of tall grenadiers ever reads this work, he will raise the caps of his company at least a couple of feet; but I warn him that it will be all in vain, that he and his troupe will never be anything but infinitely little men.

What marvelous skill then must our philosopher from Sirius have possessed, in order to perceive those atoms of which I have been speaking! When Leuwenhoek and Hartsoeker first saw, or thought they saw, the minute speck out of which we are formed, they did not make nearly so surprising a discovery. What pleasure then did Micromegas feel in watching the movements of those little machines, in examining all their gestures, in following all their operations! How he shouted for joy, as he placed one of his microscopes in his companion's hand!

"I see them," they exclaimed both at once; "do you not observe how they are carrying burdens, how they stoop down and rise up?"

As they spoke, their hands trembled with the pleasure of seeing objects so unusual, and with the fear of losing them. The Saturnian, passing from the one extreme of scepticism to an equal degree of credulity, fancied that he saw them engaged in the work of propagation.

"Ah!" said he, "I *have surprised nature in the very act.*"

But he was deceived by appearances, an accident which happens only too often, whether we make use of microscopes or not.

VI

WHAT HAPPENED TO THEM WITH MEN

Micromegas, a much better observer than his dwarf, perceived clearly that the atoms were speaking to each other, and he called his companion's attention to this fact; but he, ashamed as he was of having made a mistake on the subject of generation, did not at all care to believe that such creatures as they could communicate ideas. He had the gift of tongues as well as the Sirian; he did not hear the atoms speak, so he concluded that they did not do so; besides, how could those imperceptible beings have vocal organs, and what could they have to say? To be able to speak, one must think, or at least make some approach to thought; but if those creatures could think, then they must have something equivalent to a soul; now to attribute the equivalent of a soul to this species appeared to him absurd.

"But," said the Sirian, "you fancied just now that they were making love; do you imagine that they can make love without being able to think or utter a word, or even to make themselves understood? Moreover, do you suppose that it is more difficult to produce an argument than a child? Both appear to me equally mysterious operations."

"I no longer venture either to believe or to deny," said the dwarf; "I no longer have any opinion about the matter. We must try to examine these insects, we will form our conclusions afterwards."

"That is very well said," replied Micromegas; and he straightway drew out a pair of scissors with which he cut his nails, and immediately made out of a piece of his thumb-nail a sort of large speaking-trumpet, like a huge funnel, the narrow end of which he put into his ear. As the wide part of the funnel included the ship and all her crew, the faintest voice was conveyed along the circular fibres of the nail in such a manner, that, thanks to his perseverance, the philosopher high above them clearly heard the buzzing of our insects down below. In a few hours he managed to distinguish the words, and at last to understand the French language. The dwarf did the same, but with more difficulty. The astonishment of the travellers increased every instant. They heard mere mites speaking tolerably good sense; such a freak of nature seemed to them inexplicable. You may imagine how impatiently the Sirian and his dwarf longed to hold conversation with the atoms; but the dwarf was afraid that his voice of thunder, and still more that of Micromegas, might deafen the mites without conveying any meaning. They had to diminish its strength; and accordingly, placed in their mouths instruments like little tooth-picks, the tapering end of which was brought near the ship. Then the Sirian, holding the dwarf on his knees, and the vessel with her crew upon his nail, bent his head down and spoke in a low voice, thus at last, with the help of all these precautions and many others besides, beginning to address them:

"Invisible insects, whom the hand of the Creator has been pleased to produce in the abyss of the infinitely little, I thank him for having deigned to reveal to me secrets which seemed inscrutable. It may be the courtiers of my country would not condescend to look upon you, but I despise no one, and I offer you my protection."

If ever anyone was astonished, it was the people who heard these words, nor could they guess whence they came. The ship's chaplain repeated the prayers used in exorcism, the sailors swore, and the philosophers constructed theories; but whatever theories they constructed, they could not guess who was speaking to them The dwarf of Saturn, who had a softer voice than Micromegas, then told them in a few words with what kind of beings they had to do. He gave them an account of the journey from Saturn, and made them acquainted with the character of Mr. Micromegas; and, after having pitied them for being so small, he asked them if they had always been in that wretched condition little better than annihilation, what they found to do on a globe that appeared to belong to whales, if they were happy, if they increased and multiplied, whether they had souls, and a hundred other questions of that nature.

A philosopher of the party, bolder than the rest of them, and shocked that the existence of his soul should be called in question, took observations of the speaker with a quadrant from two different stations, and, at the third, spoke as follows:

"Do you then suppose, sir, because a thousand fathoms extend between your head and your feet, that you are—"

"A thousand fathoms!" cried the dwarf; "good heavens! How is it that he knows my height? A thousand fathoms! He is not an inch off. What! Has that atom actually measured me? He is a geometrician, he knows my size; while I, who cannot see him except through a microscope, am still ignorant of his!"

"Yes, I have taken your measure," said the man of science; "and I will now proceed, if you please, to measure your great companion."

The proposal was accepted; His Excellency lay down at full length, for, if he had kept himself upright, his head would have reached too far above the clouds. Our philosophers then planted a tall tree in a place which Dr. Swift would have named without hesitation, but which I refrain from naming out of my great respect for the ladies. Then by means of a series of triangles joined together, they came to the conclusion that the object before them was in reality a young man whose length was one hundred and twenty thousand statute feet.

Thereupon Micromegas uttered these words:

"I see more clearly than ever that we should judge of nothing by its apparent importance. O God, who has bestowed intelligence upon things which seemed so despicable, the infinitely little is as much your concern as the infinitely great; and, if it is possible that there should be living things smaller than these, they may be endowed with minds superior even to those of the magnificent creatures whom I have seen in the sky, who with one foot could cover this globe upon which I have alighted."

One of the philosophers replied that he might with all confidence believe that there actually were intelligent beings much smaller than man. He related, not indeed all the fables that Virgil has told about the bees, but the results of Swammerdam's discoveries, and Réaumur's dissections.[16] Finally, he informed him that there are animals which bear the same proportion to bees that bees bear to men, or that the Sirian himself bore to those huge creatures of which he spoke, or that those great creatures themselves bore to others before whom they seemed mere atoms. The conversation grew more and more interesting, and Micromegas spoke as follows.

VII

CONVERSATION WITH THE MEN

"O intelligent atoms, in whom the eternal Being has been pleased to make manifest his skill and power, you must doubtless taste joys of perfect purity on this your globe; for, having so little matter, and seeming to be all spirit, you must pass your lives in love and meditation, which is the true life of spiritual beings. I have nowhere beheld genuine happiness, but here it is to be found, without a doubt."

On hearing these words, all the philosophers shook their heads, and one of them, more frank than the others, candidly confessed that, with the exception of a small number held in low estimation among them, all the rest of mankind were a multitude of fools, knaves, and miserable wretches.

"We have more matter than we need," said he, "the cause of much evil, if evil proceeds from matter; and we have too much mind, if evil proceeds from the mind. Are you aware, for instance, that at this very moment while I am speaking to you, there are a hundred thousand fools of our species who wear hats, slaying a hundred thousand fellow-creatures who wear turbans, or being massacred by them, and that over almost all the earth such practices have been going on from time immemorial?"

The Sirian shuddered, and asked what could be the cause of such horrible quarrels between those miserable little creatures.

"The dispute is all about a heap of mud," said the philosopher, "no bigger than your heel. Not that a single one of those millions of men who get their throats cut has the slightest interest in this clod of earth. The only point in question is whether it shall belong to a certain man who is called *Sultan*, or to another who, I know not why, is called *Cæsar*. Neither the one nor the other has ever seen, or is ever likely to see, the little corner of ground which is involved; and hardly one of those animals, who are cutting each other's throats, has ever seen the animal for whom they fight so desperately."

"Ah! wretched creatures!" exclaimed the Sirian with indignation; "can anyone imagine such frantic ferocity! I should like to take two or three steps, and crush the whole swarm of these ridiculous assassins."

"Do not give yourself the trouble," answered the philosopher; "they are working hard enough to destroy themselves. I assure you that at the end of ten years, not a hundredth part of those wretches will be left; even if they had never drawn the sword, famine, fatigue, or intemperance will sweep them almost all away. Besides, it is not they who deserve punishment, but rather those arm-chair barbarians, who from the privacy of their cabinets, and during the process of digestion, command the massacre of a million men, and afterwards ordain a solemn thanksgiving to God."

The traveller, moved with compassion for the tiny human race, among whom he found such astonishing contrasts, said to the gentlemen who were present:

"Since you belong to the small number of wise men, and apparently do not kill anyone for money, tell me, pray, how you occupy yourselves."

"We dissect flies," said the same philosopher, "we measure distances, we calculate numbers, we are agreed upon two or three points which we understand, and we dispute about two or three thousand of which we know nothing."

The visitors from Sirius and Saturn were immediately seized with a desire to question these intelligent atoms to learn on which subjects they were agreed.

"How far do you reckon it," said the latter, "from the Dog-star to the great star in Gemini?"

They all answered together: "Thirty-two degrees and a half."

"How far do you make it from here to the moon?"

"Sixty half-diameters of the earth, in round numbers."

"What is the weight of your air?"

He thought to lay a trap for them, but they all told him that

the air weighs about nine hundred times less than an equal vol
ume of distilled water, and nineteen thousand times less than
pure gold.[17]

The little dwarf from Saturn, astonished at their replies, was
now inclined to take for sorcerers the same people to whom he
had refused, a quarter of an hour ago, to allow the possession of
a soul.

Then Micromegas said:

"Since you know so well what is outside of yourselves, doubtless you know still better what is within you. Tell me what is the
nature of your soul, and how you form ideas."

The philosophers spoke all at once as before, but this time
they were all of different opinions. The oldest of them quoted
Aristotle, another pronounced the name of Descartes, this spoke
of Malebranche, that of Leibnitz, and another again of Locke.
The old Peripatetic said in a loud and confident voice:

"The soul is an entelechy and a reason for its having the power
to be what it is; as Aristotle expressly declares on page 633 of
the Louvre edition of his works Ἐντελεχεῖα ἐστι. . . ."

"I don't understand Greek very well," said the giant.

"No more do I," said the mite of a philosopher.

"Why, then," inquired the Sirian, "do you quote the man you
call Aristotle in that language?"

"Because," replied the sage, "it is right and proper to quote
what we do not comprehend at all in a language we least understand."

The Cartesian then interposed and said:

"The soul is pure spirit, which has received in its mother's
womb all metaphysical ideas, and which, on issuing thence, is obliged to go to school, as it were, and learn afresh all that it knew
so well, and which it will never know any more."

"It was hardly worth while, then," answered the eight-leagued
giant, "for your soul to have been so learned in your mother's
womb, if you were to become so ignorant by the time you have
a beard on your chin.—But what do you understand by spirit?"

"Why do you ask me that question?" said the philosopher; "I
have no idea of its meaning, except that they say it is not matter."

"At least you know what matter is?"

"Perfectly well," replied the man. "For instance, this stone is gray, is of such and such a form, has three dimensions, has weight and divisibility."

"Very well!" said the Sirian. "Now tell me, please, what this thing actually is which appears to you to be divisible, heavy, and of a gray color. You observe certain qualities; but do you know the intrinsic nature of the thing itself?"

"No," said the other.

"Then you do not know what matter is."

Thereupon Mr. Micromegas, addressing his question to another sage, whom he held on his thumb, asked him what the soul was, and what it did.

"Nothing at all," said the disciple of Malebranche; "it is God who does everything for me; I see and do everything through him; it is he who does all without my interference."

"You might just as well have no existence," replied the sage of Sirius.

"And you, my friend," he said to a follower of Leibnitz, who was there, "what is your soul?"

"It is," answered he, "a hand which points to the hour while my body chimes, or, if you like, it is the soul which chimes, while my body points to the hour; or, to put it in another way, my soul is the mirror of the universe, and my body is its frame: that is all clear enough."

A little student of Locke was standing near; and when his opinion at last was asked:

"I know nothing," said he, "of how I think, but I know that I have never thought except at the suggestion of my senses. That there are immaterial and intelligent substances I do not doubt; but that it is impossible for God to communicate thought to matter, I doubt very strongly. I adore the eternal power; it is not my part to limit it. I assert nothing, I content myself with believing that more is possible than people think."

The creature of Sirius smiled; he did not deem the last speaker the least wise; and the dwarf of Saturn would have clasped Locke's disciple in his arms were it not for their extreme disproportion. But unluckily a little animalcule was there in a square cap, who interrupted all the other philosophical mites,[18] saying that he knew the whole secret, that it was all to be found in the *Summa* of St. Thomas; he scanned the pair of celestial visitors from top to toe, and maintained that they and all their kind, their suns and stars, were made solely for man's benefit. At this speech our two travellers tumbled over each other, choking with that inextinguishable laughter which, according to Homer, is the special privilege of the gods; their shoulders shook, and their bodies heaved up and down, till, in those convulsions, the ship which the Sirian held on his nail fell into the Saturnian's breeches pocket. These two good people, after a long search, recovered it at last, and re-arranged it properly. The Sirian once more took up the little mites, and addressed them again with great kindness, though he was a little irritated at the bottom of his heart at seeing such infinitely insignificant atoms puffed up with an almost infinite pride. He promised to supply them with a fine book of philosophy, written in very minute characters for their special use, and in which they would find the essence of things. He actually gave them the volume before his departure. It was carried to Paris before the Academy of Sciences; but when the old secretary came to open it, he saw nothing but blank pages.

"Ah!" said he, "this is just what I expected."

I once met, on my travels, an old Brahmin, who was exceedingly wise, full of native intelligence, and profoundly learned; moreover, he was rich, and, in consequence, all the wiser still, for, being in want of nothing, he had no need to deceive anybody. His household was very well managed by three handsome wives who devoted themselves to pleasing him; and, when he was not entertaining himself with them, he was engaged in philosophy.

Near his house, a fine one adorned by attractive gardens, dwelt an old Hindu woman, bigoted, half-witted, and extremely poor.

One day the Brahmin said to me:

"Would that I had never been born!"

I asked him why, and he replied as follows:

"I have studied for forty years, and they are so many years wasted; I teach others and am myself ignorant of everything. This state of things fills my soul with such humiliation and disgust, that life is intolerable to me. I have been born into the world, I live in time, and I know not what time is; I find myself on a point between two eternities, as our sages say, and I have no conception of eternity. I am composed of matter, and I can think; yet I have never been able to learn what produces thought; I know not whether my understanding is a simple faculty within me, like that of walking or of digesting food, and whether I think with my head in the same way as I grasp with my hands. Not only is the essential cause of my powers of thought unknown to me, but that of my movements is equally obscure; I cannot tell why I exist; yet I am questioned every day on all these points, and I have to answer. I have nothing to say worth hearing; but I say much, and, after talking, I remain confused and ashamed of myself.

"It is even worse when people ask me if Brahma was produced by Vishnu, or if they are both eternal. Heaven is my witness that I know nothing about the matter, as my answers only too plainly show. 'Ah, reverend father,' they say, 'teach us how it is that evil floods the whole earth?' I am as much at a loss as those who ask me that question; I tell them sometimes that all is well and could not be better, but those who have been ruined and maimed in the wars do not believe a word of it, any more than I do myself. I retire into my own house crushed by the weight of my ignorance and my curiosity. I read our ancient books, and they only make my darkness greater. I speak to my companions; some tell me in reply that we must enjoy life and laugh at mankind; others think that they know something, and lose themselves in a maze of extravagant ideas. All increases the painful feeling that possesses me; and I am ready sometimes to fall into despair, when I consider that, after all my investigations, I know neither whence I come, nor what I am, nor where I go, nor what I will become."

I was really pained at the state of this good man; no one could be more rational than he was, nor more sincere. I conceived that the brighter the light of his understanding, and the keener the sensibility of his heart, the greater was his unhappiness.

The same day I saw the old woman who lived in his neighborhood, and I asked her if she had ever been distressed at not knowing how her soul was formed. She did not even understand my question; she had never reflected for a single moment of her life on any one of those points which tormented the Brahmin; she believed in the metamorphoses of Vishnu with all her heart, and provided she might sometimes have a little water from the Ganges with which to wash herself, she thought herself the most fortunate of women.

Struck with this poor creature's happiness, I returned to my philosopher, and said:

"Are you not ashamed of being unhappy, while at your very gate there is an old automaton who thinks about nothing and lives contented?"

"You are right," he answered; "I have told myself a hundred

times that I should be happy if I were as stupid as my neighbor, and yet somehow I have no wish to attain such happiness."

This reply of my Brahmin impressed me more than anything else. I examined my own heart and discovered that I would not care to be happy on condition of being an imbecile.

I referred the problem to some philosophers, and their opinions were the same as mine.

"For all that," said I, "there is a wild contradiction in this manner of thinking; for, after all, what is at issue? Happiness. What does it matter whether one is intelligent or stupid? Moreover, those who are contented with their existence are quite sure that they are so, whereas those who reason are by no means so sure that they reason well. It is clear then," said I, "that we should choose not to have common sense, if it contributes to our unhappiness in however small a degree."

Everybody agreed with me, and yet I found no one willing to accept the bargain to become an imbecile in order to be content. Hence I concluded that if we value happiness, we value reason even more.

But, after having reflected on this matter, it appears to me that to prefer reason to happiness is sheer madness. How can this contradiction be explained? Like all the others. Much can be said about that.

CANDIDE[20]

OR OPTIMISM

I

HOW CANDIDE WAS BROUGHT UP IN A NOBLE CASTLE AND HOW HE WAS EXPELLED FROM THE SAME

In the castle of Baron Thunder-ten-tronckh in Westphalia there lived a youth, endowed by Nature with the most gentle character. His face was the expression of his soul. His judgment was quite honest and he was extremely simple-minded; and this was the reason, I think, that he was named Candide. Old servants in the house suspected that he was the son of the Baron's sister and a decent honest gentleman of the neighborhood, whom this young lady would never marry because he could only prove seventy-one quarterings,[21] and the rest of his genealogical tree was lost, owing to the injuries of time. The Baron was one of the most powerful lords in Westphalia, for his castle possessed a door and windows. His Great Hall was even decorated with a piece of tapestry. The dogs in his stable-yards formed a pack of hounds when necessary; his grooms were his huntsmen; the village curate was his Grand Almoner. They all called him "My Lord," and laughed heartily at his stories. The Baroness weighed about three hundred and fifty pounds, was therefore greatly respected, and did the honors of the house with a dignity which rendered her still more respectable. Her daughter Cunegonde, aged seventeen, was rosy-cheeked, fresh, plump and tempting. The Baron's son appeared in every respect worthy of his father. The tutor Pangloss was the oracle of the house, and little Candide followed his lessons with all the candor of his age and character. Pangloss taught metaphysico-theologo-cosmolonigology. He proved admirably that there is no effect without a cause and that in this best of all possible worlds, My Lord the Baron's castle was the best of castles and his wife the best of all possible Baronesses. " 'Tis demonstrated," said he, "that things cannot be otherwise; for, since everything is made for an end, everything is necessarily for the best end. Observe that noses were made to wear spectacles; and so we have spectacles. Legs were visibly instituted to be breeched, and we have breeches. Stones were formed to be quarried and to build castles; and My Lord has a very noble castle; the greatest Baron in the province should have the best house; and as pigs were made to be eaten, we eat pork all the year round; consequently, those who have asserted that all is well talk nonsense; they ought to have said that all is for the best." Candide listened attentively and believed innocently; for he thought Mademoiselle Cunegonde extremely beautiful, although he was never bold enough to tell her so. He decided that after the happiness of being born Baron of Thunder-ten-tronckh, the second degree of happiness was to be Mademoiselle Cunegonde; the third, to see her every day; and the fourth to listen to Doctor Pangloss, the greatest philosopher of the province and therefore of the whole world. One day when Cunegonde was walking near the castle, in a little wood which was called The Park, she observed Doctor Pangloss in the bushes, giving a lesson in experimental physics to her mother's waiting-maid, a very pretty and docile brunette. Mademoiselle Cunegonde had a great inclination for science and watched breathlessly the reiterated experiments she witnessed; she observed clearly the Doctor's sufficient reason, the effects and the causes, and returned home very much excited, pensive, filled with the desire of learning, reflecting that she might be the sufficient reason of young Candide and that he might be hers. On her way back to the castle she met Candide and blushed; Candide also blushed. She bade him good-morning in a hesitating voice; Candide replied without knowing what he was saying. Next day, when they left the table after dinner, Cunegonde and Candide found themselves behind a screen; Cunegonde dropped her handkerchief, Candide picked it up; she innocently held his hand; the young man innocently kissed the young lady's hand with remarkable vivacity, tenderness and grace; their lips met, their eyes sparkled, their knees trembled, their hands wandered. Baron Thunder-ten-tronckh passed near the screen, and, observing this cause and effect, expelled Candide from the castle by kicking him in the backside frequently and hard. Cunegonde swooned; when she recovered her senses, the Baroness slapped her in the face; and all was in consternation in the noblest and most agreeable of all possible castles.

II

WHAT HAPPENED TO CANDIDE AMONG THE BULGARIANS [22]

Candide, expelled from the earthly paradise, wandered for a long time without knowing where he was going, turning up his eyes to Heaven, gazing back frequently at the noblest of castles which held the most beautiful of young Baronesses; he lay down to sleep supperless between two furrows in the open fields; it snowed heavily in large flakes. The next morning the shivering Candide, penniless, dying of cold and exhaustion, dragged himself towards the neighboring town, which was called Waldberghoff-trarbk-dikdorff. He halted sadly at the door of an inn. Two men dressed in blue noticed him. "Comrade," said one, "there's a well-built young man of the right height." They went up to Candide and very civilly invited him to dinner. "Gentlemen," said Candide with charming modesty, "you do me a great honor, but I have no money to pay my share." "Ah, sir," said one of the men in blue, "persons of your figure and merit never pay anything; are you not five feet five tall?" "Yes, gentlemen," said he, bowing, "that is my height." "Ah, sir, come to table; we will not only pay your expenses, we will never allow a man like you to be short of money; men were only made to help each other." "You are in the right," said Candide, "that is what Doctor Pangloss was always telling me, and I see that everything is for the best." They begged him to accept a few crowns, he took them and wished to give them an I O U; they refused to take it and all sat down to table. "Do you not love tenderly . . ." "Oh, yes," said he. "I love Mademoiselle Cunegonde tenderly."

"No," said one of the gentlemen. "We were asking if you do not tenderly love the King of the Bulgarians." "Not a bit," said he, "for I have never seen him." "What! He is the most charming of Kings, and you must drink his health." "Oh, gladly, gentlemen." And he drank. "That is sufficient," he was told. "You are now the support, the aid, the defender, the hero of the Bulgarians; your fortune is made and your glory assured." They immediately put irons on his legs and took him to a regiment. He was made to turn to the right and left, to raise the ramrod and return the ramrod, to take aim, to fire, to march double time, and he was given thirty strokes with a stick; the next day he drilled not quite so badly, and received only twenty strokes; the day after, he only had ten and was looked on as a prodigy by his comrades. Candide was completely mystified and could not make out how he was a hero. One fine spring day he thought he would take a walk, going straight ahead, in the belief that to use his legs as he pleased was a privilege of the human species as well as of animals. He had not gone two leagues when four other heroes, each six feet tall, fell upon him, bound him and dragged him back to a cell. He was asked by his judges whether he would rather be thrashed thirty-six times by the whole regiment or receive a dozen lead bullets at once in his brain. Although he protested that men's wills are free and that he wanted neither one nor the other, he had to make a choice; by virtue of that gift of God which is called *liberty*, he determined to run the gauntlet thirty-six times and actually did so twice. There were two thousand men in the regiment. That made four thousand strokes which laid bare the muscles and nerves from his neck to his backside. As they were about to proceed to a third turn, Candide, utterly exhausted, begged as a favor that they would be so kind as to smash his head; he obtained this favor; they bound his eyes and he was made to kneel down. At that moment the King of the Bulgarians came by and inquired the victim's crime; and as this King was possessed of a vast genius, he perceived from what he learned about Candide that he was a young metaphysician very ignorant in worldly matters, and therefore pardoned him with a clemency which will be praised in all newspapers and all ages. An honest surgeon healed Candide in three weeks with the ointments recommended by Dioscorides. He had already regained a little skin and could walk when the King of the Bulgarians went to war with the King of the Abares.

III

HOW CANDIDE ESCAPED FROM THE BULGARIANS AND WHAT BECAME OF HIM

Nothing could be smarter, more splendid, more brilliant, better drawn up than the two armies. Trumpets, fifes, hautboys, drums, cannons, formed a harmony such as has never been heard even in hell. The cannons first of all laid flat about six thousand men on each side; then the musketry removed from the best of worlds some nine or ten thousand blackguards who infested its surface. The bayonet also was the sufficient reason for the death of some thousands of men. The whole might amount to thirty thousand souls. Candide, who trembled like a philosopher, hid himself as well as he could during this heroic butchery. At last, while the two Kings each commanded a Te Deum in his camp, Candide decided to go elsewhere to reason about effects and causes. He clambered over heaps of dead and dying men and reached a neighboring village, which was in ashes; it was an Abare village which the Bulgarians had burned in accordance with international law. Here, old men dazed with blows watched the dying agonies of their murdered wives who clutched their children to their bleeding breasts; there, disembowelled girls who had been made to satisfy the natural appetites of heroes gasped their last sighs; others, half-burned, begged to be put to death. Brains were scattered on the ground among dismembered arms and legs. Candide fled to another village as fast as he could; it belonged to the Bulgarians, and Abarian heroes had treated it in the same way. Candide, stumbling over quivering limbs or across ruins, at last escaped from the theatre of war, carrying a little food in his knapsack, and never forgetting Mademoiselle Cunegonde. His provisions were all gone when he reached Holland; but, having heard that everyone in that country was rich and a Christian, he had no doubt at all but that he would be as well treated as he had been in the Baron's castle before he had been expelled on account of Mademoiselle Cunegonde's pretty eyes. He asked alms of several grave persons, who all replied that if he continued in that way he would be shut up in a house of correction to teach him how to live. He then addressed himself to a man who had been discoursing on charity in a large assembly for an hour on end. This orator, glancing at him askance, said: "What are you doing here? Are you for the good cause?" "There is no effect without a cause," said Candide modestly. "Everything is necessarily linked up and arranged for the best. It was necessary that I should be expelled from the company of Mademoiselle Cunegonde, that I ran the gauntlet, and that I beg my bread until I can earn it; all this could not have happened differently." "My friend," said the orator, "do you believe that the Pope is Anti-Christ?" "I had never heard so before," said Candide, "but whether he is or isn't, I am starving." "You don't deserve to eat," said the other. "Hence, rascal; hence, you wretch; and never come near me again." The orator's wife thrust her head out of the window and seeing a man who did not believe that the Pope was Anti-Christ, she poured on his head a full . . . O Heavens! To what excess religious zeal is carried by ladies! A man who had not been baptized, an honest Anabaptist named Jacques, saw the cruel and ignominious treatment of one of his brothers, a featherless two-legged creature with a soul; he took him home, cleaned him up; gave him bread and beer, presented him with two florins, and even offered to teach him to work at the manufacture of Persian stuffs which are made in Holland. Candide threw himself at the man's feet, exclaiming: "Doctor Pangloss was right in telling me that all is for the best in this world, for I am vastly more touched by your extreme generosity than by the harshness of the gentleman in the black cloak and his good lady." The next day when he walked out he met a beggar covered with sores, dull-eyed, with the end of his nose fallen away, his mouth awry, his teeth black, who talked huskily, was tormented with a violent cough and spat out a tooth at every cough.

IV

Candide, moved even more by compassion than by horror, gave this horrible beggar the two florins he had received from the honest Anabaptist, Jacques. The phantom gazed fixedly at him, shed tears and threw its arms round his neck. Candide recoiled in terror. "Alas!" said the wretch to the other wretch, "don't you recognize your dear Pangloss?" "What do I hear? You, my dear master! You, in this horrible state! What misfortune has happened to you? Why are you no longer in the noblest of castles? What has become of Mademoiselle Cunegonde, the pearl of young ladies, the masterpiece of Nature?" "I am exhausted," said Pangloss. Candide immediately took him to the Anabaptist's stable where he gave him a little bread to eat; and when Pangloss had recovered: "Well!" said he, "Cunegonde?" "Dead," replied the other. At this word Candide swooned; his friend restored him to his senses with a little bad vinegar which happened to be in the stable. Candide opened his eyes. "Cunegonde dead! Ah! best of worlds, where are you? But what illness did she die of? Was it because she saw me kicked out of her father's noble castle?" "No," said Pangloss. "She was disembowelled by Bulgarian soldiers, after having been raped to the limit of possibility; they broke the Baron's head when he tried to defend her; the Baroness was cut to pieces; my poor pupil was treated exactly like his sister; and as to the castle, there is not one stone standing on another, not a barn, not a sheep, not a duck, not a tree; but we were well avenged, for the Abares did exactly the same to a neighboring barony which belonged to a Bulgarian Lord." At this, Candide swooned again; but, having recovered and having said all that he ought to say, he inquired the cause and effect, the sufficient reason which had reduced Pangloss to so piteous a state. "Alas!" said Pangloss, " 'tis love; love, the consoler of the human race, the preserver of the universe, the soul of all tender creatures, gentle love." "Alas!" said Candide, "I am acquainted with this love, this sovereign of hearts, this soul of our soul; it has never brought me anything but one kiss and twenty kicks in the backside. How could this beautiful cause produce in you so abominable an effect?" Pangloss replied as follows: "My dear Candide! You remember Paquette, the maid-servant of our august Baroness; in her arms I enjoyed the delights of Paradise which have produced the tortures of Hell by which you see I am devoured; she was infected and perhaps is dead. Paquette received this present from a most learned monk, who had it from the source; for he received it from an old countess, who had it from a cavalry captain, who owed it to a marchioness, who derived it from a page, who had received it from a Jesuit, who, when a novice, had it in a direct line from one of the companions of Christopher Columbus. For my part, I shall not give it to anyone, for I am dying." "O Pangloss!" exclaimed Candide, "this is a strange genealogy! Wasn't the devil at the root of it?" "Not at all," replied that great man. "It was something indispensable in this best of worlds, a necessary ingredient; for, if Columbus in an island of America had not caught this disease, which poisons the source of generation, and often indeed prevents generation, we should not have chocolate and cochineal; it must also be noticed that hitherto in our continent this disease is peculiar to us, like theological disputes. The Turks, the Indians, the Persians, the Chinese, the Siamese and the Japanese are not yet familiar with it; but there is a sufficient reason why they in their turn should become familiar with it in a few centuries. Meanwhile, it has made marvelous progress among us, and especially in those large armies composed of honest, well-bred stipendiaries who decide the destiny of States; it may be asserted that when thirty thousand men fight a pitched battle against an equal number of troops, there are about twenty thousand with the pox on either side." "Admirable!" said Candide. "But you must get cured." "How can I?" said Pangloss. "I haven't a sou, my friend, and in the whole extent of this globe, you cannot be bled or receive an enema without paying or without someone paying for you." This last speech determined Candide; he went and threw himself at the feet of his charitable Anabaptist, Jacques, and drew so touching a picture of the state to which his friend was reduced that the good easy man did not hesitate to succor Pangloss; he had him cured at his own expense. In this cure Pangloss only lost one eye and one ear. He could write well and knew arithmetic perfectly. The Anabaptist made him his book-keeper. At the end of two months he was compelled to go to Lisbon on business and took his two philosophers on the boat with him. Pangloss explained to him how everything was for the best. Jacques was not of this opinion. "Men," said he, "must have corrupted nature a little, for they were not born wolves, and they have become wolves. God did not give them twenty-four-pounder cannons or bayonets, and they have made bayonets and cannons to destroy each other. I might bring bankruptcies into the account and Justice which seizes the goods of bankrupts in order to deprive the creditors of them." "It was all indispensable," replied the one-eyed doctor, "and private misfortunes make the public good, so that the more private misfortunes there are, the more everything is well." While he was reasoning, the air grew dark, the winds blew from the four quarters of the globe and the ship was attacked by the most horrible tempest in sight of the port of Lisbon.

V

STORM, SHIPWRECK, EARTHQUAKE, AND WHAT HAPPENED TO DR. PANGLOSS, TO CANDIDE AND THE ANABAPTIST JACQUES

Half the enfeebled passengers, suffering from that inconceivable anguish which the rolling of a ship causes in the nerves and in all the humours of bodies shaken in contrary directions, did not retain strength enough even to trouble about the danger. The other half screamed and prayed; the sails were torn, the masts broken, the vessel leaking. Those worked who could, no one co-operated, no one commanded. The Anabaptist tried to help the crew a little; he was on the main-deck; a furious sailor struck him violently and stretched him on the deck; but the blow he delivered gave the sailor so violent a shock that he fell head-first out of the ship. He remained hanging and clinging to part of the broken mast. The good Jacques ran to his aid, helped him to climb back, and from the effort he made was flung into the sea in full view of the sailor, who allowed him to drown without condescending even to look at him. Candide came up, saw his benefactor reappear for a moment and then be engulfed for ever. He tried to throw himself after him into the sea; he was prevented by the philosopher Pangloss, who proved to him that the Lisbon roads had been expressly created for the Anabaptist to be drowned in them. While he was proving this *a priori*, the vessel sank, and every one perished except Pangloss, Candide and the brutal sailor who had drowned the virtuous Anabaptist; the blackguard swam successfully to the shore and Pangloss and Candide were carried there on a plank. When they had recovered a little, they walked toward Lisbon; they had a little money by the help of which they hoped to be saved from hunger after having escaped the storm. Weeping the death of their benefactor, they had scarcely set foot in the town when they felt the earth tremble under their feet; the sea rose in foaming masses in the port and smashed the ships which rode at anchor. Whirlwinds of flame and ashes covered the streets and squares; the houses collapsed, the roofs were thrown upon the foundations, and the foundations were scattered; thirty thousand inhabitants of every age and both sexes were crushed under the ruins. Whistling and swearing, the sailor said: "There'll be something to pick up here." "What can be the sufficient reason for this phenomenon?" said Pangloss. "It is the last day!" cried Candide. The sailor immediately ran among the debris, dared death to find money, found it, seized it, got drunk, and having slept off his wine, purchased the favors of the first woman of good-will he met on the ruins of the houses and among the dead and dying. Pangloss, however, pulled him by the sleeve. "My friend," said he, "this is not well, you are disregarding universal reason, you choose the wrong time." "Blood and 'ounds!" he retorted, "I am a sailor and I was born in Batavia; four times have I stamped on the crucifix during four voyages to Japan; you have found the right man for your universal reason!" Candide had been hurt by some falling stones; he lay in the street covered with debris. He said to Pangloss: "Alas! Get me a little wine and oil; I am dying." "This earthquake is not a new thing," replied Pangloss "The town of Lima felt the same shocks in America last year; similar causes produce similar effects; there must certainly be a train of sulphur underground from Lima to Lisbon." "Nothing is more probable," replied Candide; "but, for God's sake, a little oil and wine." "What do you mean, probable?" replied the philosopher; "I maintain that it is proved." Candide lost consciousness, and Pangloss brought him a little water from a neighboring fountain. Next day they found a little food as they wandered among the ruins and regained a little strength. Afterwards they worked like others to help the inhabitants who had escaped death. Some citizens they had assisted gave them as good a dinner as could be expected in such a disaster; true, it was a dreary meal; the hosts watered their bread with their tears, but Pangloss consoled them by assuring them that things could not be otherwise. "For," said he, "all this is for the best; for, if there is a volcano at Lisbon, it cannot be anywhere else; for it is impossible that things should not be where they are; for all is well." A little, dark man, a familiar of the Inquisition, who sat beside him, politely took up the conversation, and said: "Apparently, you do not believe in original sin; for, if everything is for the best, there was neither fall nor punishment." "I most humbly beg your excellency's pardon," replied Pangloss still more politely, "for the fall of man and the curse necessarily entered into the best of all possible worlds." "Then you do not believe in free-will?" said the familiar. "Your excellency will pardon me," said Pangloss; "free-will can exist with absolute necessity; for it was necessary that we should be free; for in short, limited will . . ." Pangloss was in the middle of his phrase when the familiar nodded to his armed attendant who was pouring out port or Oporto wine for him.

VI

HOW A SPLENDID AUTO-DA-FÉ WAS HELD TO PREVENT EARTHQUAKES AND HOW CANDIDE WAS FLOGGED

After the earthquake which destroyed three-quarters of Lisbon, the wise men of that country could discover no more efficacious way of preventing a total ruin than by giving the people a splendid *auto-da-fé*.[23] It was decided by the university of Coimbre that the sight of several persons being slowly burned in great ceremony is an infallible secret for preventing earthquakes. Consequently they had arrested a Biscayan convicted of having married his fellow-godmother, and two Portuguese who, when eating a chicken, had thrown away the fat; after dinner they came and bound Dr. Pangloss and his disciple Candide, one because he had spoken and the other because he had listened with an air of approbation; they were both carried separately to extremely cool apartments, where there was never any discomfort from the sun; a week afterwards each was dressed in a sanbenito and their heads were ornamented with paper mitres; Candide's mitre and sanbenito were painted with flames upside down and with devils who had neither tails nor claws; but Pangloss's devils had claws and tails, and his flames were upright. Dressed in this manner they marched in procession and listened to a most pathetic sermon, followed by lovely plain-song music. Candide was flogged in time to the music, while the singing went on; the Biscayan and the two men who had not wanted to eat fat were burned, and Pangloss was hanged, although this is not the custom. The very same day, the earth shook again with a terrible clamor. Candide, terrified, dumbfounded, bewildered, covered with blood, quivering from head to foot, said to himself: "If this is the best of all possible worlds, what are the others? Let it pass that I was flogged, for I was flogged by the Bulgarians, but, O my dear Pangloss! The greatest of philosophers! Must I see you hanged without knowing why! O my dear Anabaptist! The best of men! Was it necessary that you should be drowned in port! O Mademoiselle Cunegonde! The pearl of women! Was it necessary that your belly should be slit!" He was returning, scarcely able to support himself, preached at, flogged, absolved and blessed, when an old woman accosted him and said: "Courage, my son, follow me."

VII

HOW AN OLD WOMAN TOOK CARE OF CANDIDE AND HOW HE REGAINED THAT WHICH HE LOVED

Candide did not take courage, but he followed the old woman to a hovel; she gave him a pot of ointment to rub on, and left him food and drink; she pointed out a fairly clean bed; near the bed there was a suit of clothes. "Eat, drink, sleep," said she, "and may our Lady of Atocha, my Lord Saint Anthony of Padua and my Lord Saint James of Compostella take care of you; I shall come back tomorrow." Candide, still amazed by all he had seen, by all he had suffered, and still more by the old woman's charity, tried to kiss her hand. " 'Tis not my hand you should kiss," said the old woman, "I shall come back to-morrow. Rub on the ointment, eat and sleep." In spite of all his misfortune, Candide ate and went to sleep. Next day the old woman brought him breakfast, examined his back and smeared him with another ointment; later she brought him dinner, and returned in the evening with supper. The next day she went through the same ceremony. "Who are you?" Candide kept asking her. "Who has inspired you with so much kindness? How can I thank you?" The good woman never made any reply; she returned in the evening but without any supper. "Come with me," said she, "and do not speak a word." She took him by the arm and walked into the country with him for about a quarter of a mile; they came to an isolated house, surrounded with gardens and canals. The old woman knocked at a little door. It was opened; she led Candide up a back stairway into a gilded apartment, left him on a brocaded sofa, shut the door and went away. Candide thought he was dreaming, and felt that his whole life was a bad dream and the present moment an agreeable dream. The old woman soon reappeared; she was supporting with some difficulty a trembling woman of majestic stature, glittering with precious stones and covered with a veil. "Remove the veil," said the old woman to Candide. The young man advanced and lifted the veil with a timid hand. What a moment! What a surprise! He thought he saw Mademoiselle Cunegonde, in fact he was looking at her, it was she herself. His strength failed him, he could not utter a word and fell at her feet. Cunegonde fell on the sofa. The old woman dosed them with distilled waters; they recovered their senses and began to speak: at first they uttered only broken words, questions and answers at cross purposes, sighs, tears, exclamations. The old woman advised them to make less noise and left them alone. "What! Is it you?" said Candide. "You are alive, and I find you here in Portugal! Then you were not raped? Your belly was not slit, as the philosopher Pangloss assured me?" "Yes, indeed," said the fair Cunegonde; "but those two accidents are not always fatal." "But your father and mother were killed?" " 'Tis only too true," said Cunegonde, weeping. "And your brother?" "My brother was killed too." "And why are you in Portugal? And how did you know I was here? And by what strange adventure have you brought me to this house?" "I will tell you everything," replied the lady, "but first of all you must tell me everything that has happened to you since the innocent kiss you gave me and the kicks you received." Candide obeyed with profound respect; and, although he was bewildered, although his voice was weak and trembling, although his back was still a little painful, he related in the most natural manner all he had endured since the moment of their separation. Cunegonde raised her eyes to heaven; she shed tears at the death of the good Anabaptist and Pangloss, after which she spoke as follows to Candide, who did not miss a word and devoured her with his eyes.

VIII

CUNEGONDE'S STORY

"I was fast asleep in bed when it pleased Heaven to send the Bulgarians to our noble castle of Thunder-ten-tronckh; they murdered my father and brother and cut my mother to pieces. A large Bulgarian six feet tall, seeing that I had swooned at the spectacle, began to rape me; this brought me to, I recovered my senses, I screamed, I struggled, I bit, I scratched, I tried to tear out the big Bulgarian's eyes, not knowing that what was happening in my father's castle was a matter of custom; the brute stabbed me with a knife in the left side where I still have the scar." "Alas! I hope I shall see it," said the naïve Candide. "You shall see it," said Cunegonde, "but let me go on." "Go on," said Candide. She took up the thread of her story as follows: "A Bulgarian captain came in, saw me covered with blood, and the soldier did not disturb himself. The captain was angry at the brute's lack of respect to him, and killed him on my body. Afterwards, he had me bandaged and took me to his billet as a prisoner of war. I washed the few shirts he had and did the cooking; I must admit he thought me very pretty; and I will not deny that he was very well built and that his skin was white and soft; otherwise he had little wit and little philosophy; it was plain that he had not been brought up by Dr. Pangloss. At the end of three months he lost all his money and got tired of me; he sold me to a Jew named Don Issachar, who traded in Holland and Portugal and had a passion for women. This Jew devoted himself to my person but he could not triumph over it; I resisted him better than the Bulgarian soldier; a lady of honor may be raped once, but it strengthens her virtue. In order to subdue me, the Jew brought me to this country house. Up till then I believed that there was nothing on earth so splendid as the castle of Thunder-ten-tronckh; I was undeceived. One day the Grand Inquisitor noticed me at Mass; he ogled me continually and sent a message that he wished to speak to me on secret affairs. I was taken to his palace; I informed him of my birth; he pointed out how much it was beneath my rank to belong to an Israelite. A proposition was made on his behalf to Don Issachar to give me up to His Lordship. Don Issachar, who is the court banker and a man of influence, would not agree. The Inquisitor threatened him with an *auto-da-fé*. At last the Jew was frightened and made a bargain whereby the house and I belong to both in common. The Jew has Mondays, Wednesdays and the Sabbath day, and the Inquisitor has the other days of the week. This arrangement has lasted for six months. It has not been without quarrels; for it has often been debated whether the night between Saturday and Sunday belonged to the old law or the new. For my part, I have hitherto resisted them both; and I think that is the reason why they still love me. At last My Lord the Inquisitor was pleased to arrange an *auto-da-fé* to remove the scourge of earthquakes and to intimidate Don Issachar. He honored me with an invitation. I had an excellent seat; and refreshments were served to the ladies between the Mass and the execution. I was indeed horror-stricken when I saw the burning of the two Jews and the honest Biscayan who had married his fellow-godmother; but what was my surprise, my terror, my anguish, when I saw in a sanbenito and under a mitre a face which resembled Pangloss's! I rubbed my eyes, I looked carefully, I saw him hanged; and I fainted. I had scarcely recovered my senses when I saw you stripped naked; that was the height of horror, of consternation, of grief and despair. I will frankly tell you that your skin is even whiter and of a more perfect tint than that of my Bulgarian captain. This spectacle redoubled all the feelings which crushed and devoured me. I exclaimed, I tried to say: 'Stop, Barbarians!' but my voice failed and my cries would have been useless. When you had been well flogged, I said to myself: 'How does it happen that the charming Candide and the wise Pangloss are in Lisbon, the one to receive a hundred lashes, and the other to be hanged, by order of My Lord the Inquisitor, whose darling I am? Pangloss deceived me cruelly when he said that all is for the best in the world.' I was agitated, distracted, sometimes beside myself and sometimes ready to die of faintness, and my head was filled with the massacre of my father, of my mother, of my brother, the insolence of my horrid Bulgarian soldier, the gash he gave me, my slavery, my life as a kitchen-wench, my Bulgarian captain, my horrid Don Issachar, my abominable Inquisitor, the hanging of Dr. Pangloss, that long *miserere* in counterpoint during which you were flogged, and above all the kiss I gave you behind the screen that day when I saw you for the last time. I praised God for bringing you back to me through so many trials, I ordered my old woman to take care of you and to bring you here as soon as she could. She has carried out my commission very well; I have enjoyed the inexpressible pleasure of seeing you again, of listening to you, and of speaking to you. You must be very hungry; I have a good appetite; let us begin by having supper." Both sat down to supper; and after supper they returned to the handsome sofa we have already mentioned; they were still there when Signor Don Issachar, one of the masters of the house, arrived. It was the day of the Sabbath. He came to enjoy his rights and to express his tender love.

IX

WHAT HAPPENED TO CUNEGONDE, TO CANDIDE, TO THE GRAND INQUISITOR AND TO A JEW

This Issachar was the most choleric Hebrew who had been seen in Israel since the Babylonian captivity. "What!" said he. "Bitch of a Galilean, isn't it enough to have the Inquisitor? Must this scoundrel share with me too?" So saying, he drew a long dagger which he always carried and, thinking that his adversary was unarmed, threw himself upon Candide; but our good Westphalian had received an excellent sword from the old woman along with his suit of clothes. He drew his sword, and although he had a most gentle character, laid the Israelite stone-dead on the floor at the feet of the fair Cunegonde. "Holy Virgin!" she exclaimed, "what will become of us? A man killed in my house! If the police come we are lost." "If Pangloss had not been hanged," said Candide, "he would have given us good advice in this extremity, for he was a great philosopher. In default of him, let us consult the old woman." She was extremely prudent and was beginning to give her advice when another little door opened. It was an hour after midnight, and Sunday was beginning. This day belonged to My Lord the Inquisitor. He came in and saw the flogged Candide sword in hand, a corpse lying on the ground, Cunegonde in terror, and the old woman giving advice. At this moment, here is what happened in Candide's soul and the manner of his reasoning: "If this holy man calls for help, he will infallibly have me burned; he might do as much to Cunegonde; he had me pitilessly lashed; he is my rival; I am in the mood to kill, there is no room for hesitation." His reasoning was clear and swift; and, without giving the Inquisitor time to recover from his surprise, he pierced him through and through and cast him beside the Jew. "Here's another," said Cunegonde, "There is no chance of mercy; we are excommunicated, our last hour has come. How does it happen that you, who were born so mild, should kill a Jew and a prelate in two minutes?" "My dear young lady," replied Candide, "when a man is in love, jealous, and has been flogged by the Inquisition, he is beside himself." The old woman then spoke up and said: "In the stable are three Andalusian horses, with their saddles and bridles; let the brave Candide prepare them; mademoiselle has moidores and diamonds; let us mount quickly, although I can only sit on one buttock, and go to Cadiz; the weather is beautifully fine, and it is most pleasant to travel in the coolness of the night." Candide immediately saddled the three horses. Cunegonde, the old woman and he rode thirty miles without stopping. While they were riding away, the Holy Hermandad arrived at the house; My Lord was buried in a splendid church and Issachar was thrown into a sewer. Candide, Cunegonde and the old woman had already reached the little town of Avacena in the midst of the mountains of the Sierra Morena; and they talked in their inn as follows.

X

HOW CANDIDE, CUNEGONDE AND THE OLD WOMAN ARRIVED AT
CADIZ IN GREAT DISTRESS, AND HOW THEY EMBARKED

"Who can have stolen my pistoles and my diamonds?" said Cunegonde, weeping. "How shall we live? What shall we do? Where shall we find Inquisitors and Jews to give me others?" "Alas!" said the old woman, "I strongly suspect a reverend Franciscan father who slept in the same inn at Badajoz with us; Heaven forbid that I should judge rashly! But he twice came into our room and left long before we did." "Alas!" said Candide, "the good Pangloss often proved to me that this world's goods are common to all men and that every one has an equal right to them. According to these principles the monk should have left us enough to continue our journey. Have you nothing left then, my fair Cunegonde?" "Not a maravedi," said she. "What are we to do?" said Candide. "Sell one of the horses," said the old woman. "I will ride postillion behind Mademoiselle Cunegonde, although I can only sit on one buttock, and we will get to Cadiz." In the same hotel there was a Benedictine friar. He bought the horse very cheap. Candide, Cunegonde and the old woman passed through Lucena, Chillas, Lebrixa, and at last reached Cadiz. A fleet was there being equipped and troops were being raised to bring to reason the reverend Jesuit fathers of

Paraguay, who were accused of causing the revolt of one of their tribes against the kings of Spain and Portugal near the town of Sacramento. Candide, having served with the Bulgarians, went through the Bulgarian drill before the general of the little army with so much grace, celerity, skill, pride and agility, that he was given the command of an infantry company. He was now a captain; he embarked with Mademoiselle Cunegonde, the old woman, two servants, and the two Andalusian horses which had belonged to the Grand Inquisitor of Portugal. During the voyage they had many discussions about the philosophy of poor Pangloss. "We are going to a new world," said Candide, "and no doubt it is there that everything is for the best; for it must be admitted that one might lament a little over the physical and moral happenings in our own world." "I love you with all my heart," said Cunegonde, "but my soul is still shocked by what I have seen and undergone." "All will be well," replied Candide; "the sea in this new world already is better than the seas of our Europe; it is calmer and the winds are more constant. It is certainly the new world which is the best of all possible worlds." "God grant it!" said Cunegonde, "but I have been so horribly unhappy in mine that my heart is nearly closed to hope." "You complain," said the old woman to them. "Alas! you have not endured such misfortunes as mine." Cunegonde almost laughed and thought it most amusing of the old woman to assert that she was more unfortunate. "Alas! my dear," said she, "unless you have been raped by two Bulgarians, stabbed twice in the belly, have had two castles destroyed, two fathers and mothers murdered before your eyes, and have seen two of your lovers flogged in an *auto-da-fé*, I do not see how you can surpass me; moreover, I was born a Baroness with seventy-two quarterings and I have been a kitchen wench." "You do not know my birth," said the old woman, "and if I showed you my backside you would not talk as you do and you would suspend your judgment." This speech aroused intense curiosity in the minds of Cunegonde and Candide. And the old woman spoke as follows.

XI

THE OLD WOMAN'S STORY

"My eyes were not always bloodshot and red-rimmed; my nose did not always touch my chin and I was not always a servant. I am the daughter of Pope Urban X and the Princess of Palestrina. Until I was fourteen I was brought up in a palace to which all the castles of your German Barons would not have served as stables; and one of my dresses cost more than all the magnificence of Westphalia. I increased in beauty, in grace, in talents, among pleasures, respect and hopes; already I inspired love, my breasts were forming; and what breasts! White, firm, carved like those of the Venus de' Medici. And what eyes! What eyelids! What black eyebrows! What fire shone from my two eye-balls, and dimmed the glitter of the stars, as the local poets pointed out to me. The women who dressed and undressed me fell into ecstasy when they beheld me in front and behind; and all the men would have liked to be in their place. I was betrothed to a ruling prince of Massa-Carrara. What a prince! As beautiful as I was, formed of gentleness and charms, brilliantly witty and burning with love; I loved him with a first love, idolatrously and extravagantly. The marriage ceremonies were arranged with unheard-of pomp and magnificence; there were continual fêtes, revels and comic operas; all Italy wrote sonnets for me and not a good one among them. I reached the moment of my happiness when an old marchioness who had been my prince's mistress invited him to take chocolate with her; less than two hours afterwards he died in horrible convulsions; but that is only a trifle. My mother was in despair, though less distressed than I, and wished to absent herself for a time from a place so disastrous. She had a most beautiful estate near Gaeta; we embarked on a galley, gilded like the altar of St. Peter's at Rome. A Salle pirate swooped down and boarded us; our soldiers defended us like soldiers of the Pope; they threw down their arms, fell on their knees and asked the pirates for absolution *in articulo mortis.* They were immediately stripped as naked as monkeys and my mother, our ladies of honor and myself as well. The diligence with which these gentlemen strip people is truly ad-

mirable; but I was still more surprised by their inserting a finger
in a place belonging to all of us where we women usually only
allow the end of a syringe. This appeared to me a very strange
ceremony; but that is how we judge everything when we leave
our own country. I soon learned that it was to find out if we
had hidden any diamonds there; 'tis a custom established from
time immemorial among the civilized nations who roam the seas.

"I have learned that the religious Knights of Malta never fail in
it when they capture Turks and Turkish women; this is an international law which has never been broken. I will not tell you
how hard it is for a young princess to be taken with her mother
as a slave to Morocco; you will also guess all we had to endure
in the pirates' ship. My mother was still very beautiful; our
ladies of honor, even our waiting-maids possessed more charms
than could be found in all Africa; and I was ravishing, I was
beauty, grace itself, and I was a virgin; I did not remain so long;
the flower which had been reserved for the handsome prince of
Massa-Carrara was ravished from me by a pirate captain; he was
an abominable Negro who thought he was doing me a great
honor. The Princess of Palestrina and I must indeed have been
strong to bear up against all we endured before our arrival in
Morocco! But let that pass; these things are so common that they
are not worth mentioning. Morocco was swimming in blood
when we arrived. The fifty sons of the Emperor Muley Ismael
had each a faction; and this produced fifty civil wars, of blacks
against blacks, browns against browns, mulattoes against mulattoes. There was continual carnage throughout the whole extent
of the empire. Scarcely had we landed when the blacks of a
party hostile to that of my pirate arrived with the purpose of
depriving him of his booty. After the diamonds and the gold,
we were the most valuable possessions. I witnessed a fight such
as is never seen in your European climates. The blood of the
northern peoples is not sufficiently ardent; their madness for
women does not reach the point which is common in Africa.
The Europeans seem to have milk in their veins; but vitriol and
fire flow in the veins of the inhabitants of Mount Atlas and the
neighboring countries. They fought with the fury of the lions,
tigers and serpents of the country to determine who should have

us. A Moor grasped my mother by the right arm, my captain's
lieutenant held her by the left arm; a Moorish soldier held one
leg and one of our pirates seized the other. In a moment nearly
all our women were seized in the same way by four soldiers.
My captain kept me hidden behind him; he had a scimitar in
his hand and killed everybody who opposed his fury. I saw my
mother and all our Italian women torn in pieces, gashed, massacred by the monsters who disputed them. The prisoners, my
companions, those who had captured them, soldiers, sailors,
blacks, browns, whites, mulattoes and finally my captain were all
killed and I remained expiring on a heap of corpses. As every
one knows, such scenes go on in an area of more than three
hundred square leagues and yet no one ever fails to recite the
five daily prayers ordered by Mahomet. With great difficulty I
extricated myself from the bloody heaps of corpses and dragged
myself to the foot of a large orange-tree on the bank of a stream;
there I fell down with terror, weariness, horror, despair and hunger. Soon afterwards, my exhausted senses fell into a sleep which
was more like a swoon than repose. I was in this state of weakness and insensibility between life and death when I felt myself
oppressed by something which moved on my body. I opened my
eyes and saw a white man of good appearance who was sighing
and muttering between his teeth: O *che sciagura d'essere senza
coglioni!* [24]

XII

CONTINUATION OF THE OLD WOMAN'S MISFORTUNES

"Amazed and delighted to hear my native language, and not less
surprised at the words spoken by this man, I replied that there
were greater misfortunes than that of which he complained. In a
few words I informed him of the horrors I had undergone and
then swooned again. He carried me to a neighboring house, had
me put to bed, gave me food, waited on me, consoled me, flattered me, told me he had never seen anyone so beautiful as I,
and that he had never so much regretted that which no one
could give back to him. 'I was born at Naples,' he said, 'and
every year they make two or three thousand children there into

capons; some die of it, others acquire voices more beautiful than women's, and others become the governors of States. This operation was performed upon me with very great success and I was a musician in the chapel of the Princess of Palestrina.' 'Of my mother,' I exclaimed. 'Of your mother!' cried he, weeping. 'What! Are you that young princess I brought up to the age of six and who even then gave promise of being as beautiful as you are?' 'I am! my mother is four hundred yards from here, cut into quarters under a heap of corpses . . .' I related all that had happened to me; he also told me his adventures and informed me how he had been sent to the King of Morocco by a Christian power to make a treaty with that monarch whereby he was supplied with powder, cannons and ships to help to exterminate the commerce of other Christians. 'My mission is accomplished,' said this honest eunuch, 'I am about to embark at Ceuta and I will take you back to Italy. *Ma che sciagura d'essere senza coglioni!*' I thanked him with tears of gratitude; and instead of taking me back to Italy he conducted me to Algiers and sold me to the Dey. I had scarcely been sold when the plague which had gone through Africa, Asia and Europe, broke out furiously in Algiers. You have seen earthquakes; but have you ever seen the plague?" "Never," replied the Baroness. "If you had," replied the old woman, "you would admit that it is much worse than an earthquake. It is very common in Africa; I caught it. Imagine the situation of a Pope's daughter aged fifteen, who in three months had undergone poverty and slavery, had been raped nearly every day, had seen her mother cut into four pieces, had undergone hunger and war, and was now dying of the plague in Algiers. However, I did not die; but my eunuch and the Dey and almost all the seraglio of Algiers perished. When the first ravages of this frightful plague were over, the Dey's slaves were sold. A merchant bought me and carried me to Tunis; he sold me to another merchant who re-sold me at Tripoli; from Tripoli I was re-sold to Alexandria, from Alexandria re-sold to Smyrna, from Smyrna to Constantinople. I was finally bought by an Aga of the Janizaries, who was soon ordered to defend Azov against the Russians who were besieging it. The Aga, who was a man of great gallantry, took his whole seraglio with him, and lodged

us in a little fort on the Islands of Palus-Maeotis, guarded by
two black eunuchs and twenty soldiers. He killed a prodigious
number of Russians but they returned the compliment as well.
Azov was given up to fire and blood, neither sex nor age was
pardoned; only our little fort remained; and the enemy tried to
reduce it by starving us. The twenty Janizaries had sworn never
to surrender us. The extermities of hunger to which they were
reduced forced them to eat our two eunuchs for fear of breaking their oath. Some days later they resolved to eat the women.
We had with us a most pious and compassionate Imam who
delivered a fine sermon to them by which he persuaded them
not to kill us altogether. 'Cut,' said he, 'only one buttock from
each of these ladies and you will have an excellent meal; if you
have to return, there will still be as much left in a few days;
Heaven will be pleased at so charitable an action and you will
be saved.' He was very eloquent and persuaded them. This horrible operation was performed upon us; the Imam anointed us
with the same balm that is used for children who have just been
circumcised; we were all at the point of death. Scarcely had
the Janizaries finished the meal we had supplied when the Russians arrived in flat-bottomed boats; not a Janizary escaped. The
Russians paid no attention to the state we were in. There are
French doctors everywhere; one of them who was very skilful,
took care of us; he healed us and I shall remember all my life
that, when my wounds were cured, he made propositions to me.
For the rest, he told us all to cheer up; he told us that the
same thing had happened in several sieges and that it was a law
of war. As soon as my companions could walk they were sent to
Moscow. I fell to the lot of a Boyar who made me his gardener
and gave me twenty lashes a day. But at the end of two years
this lord was broken on the wheel with thirty other Boyars owing to some court disturbance, and I profited by this adventure;
I fled; I crossed all Russia; for a long time I was servant in an
inn at Riga, then at Rostock, at Wismar, at Leipzig, at Cassel,
at Utrecht, at Leyden, at the Hague, at Rotterdam; I have
grown old in misery and in shame, with only half a backside,
always remembering that I was the daughter of a Pope; a hundred times I wanted to kill myself but I still loved life. This

ridiculous weakness is perhaps the most disastrous of our inclinations; for is there anything sillier than to desire to bear continually a burden one always wishes to throw on the ground; to look upon oneself with horror and yet to cling to oneself; in short, to caress the serpent which devours us until he has eaten our heart? In the countries it has been my fate to traverse and in the inns where I have served I have seen a prodigious number of people who hated their lives; but I have only seen twelve who voluntarily put an end to their misery: three Negroes, four Englishmen, four Genevans and a German professor named Robeck. I ended up as servant to the Jew, Don Issachar; he placed me in your service, my fair young lady; I attached myself to your fate and have been more occupied with your adventures than with my own. I should never even have spoken of my misfortunes, if you had not piqued me a little and if it had not been the custom on board ship to tell stories to pass the time. In short, Mademoiselle, I have had experience, I know the world; provide yourself with an entertainment, make each passenger tell you his story; and if there is one who has not often cursed his life, who has not often said to himself that he was the most unfortunate of men, throw me head-first into the sea."

XIII

HOW CANDIDE WAS OBLIGED TO SEPARATE FROM THE FAIR CUNEGONDE AND THE OLD WOMAN

The fair Cunegonde, having heard the old woman's story, treated her with all the politeness due to a person of her rank and merit. She accepted the proposition and persuaded all the passengers one after the other to tell her their adventures. She and Candide admitted that the old woman was right. "It was most unfortunate," said Candide, "that the wise Pangloss was hanged contrary to custom at an *auto-da-fé*; he would have said admirable things about the physical and moral evils which cover the earth and the sea, and I should feel myself strong enough to urge a few objections with all due respect." While each of the passengers was telling his story the ship proceeded on its way.

They arrived at Buenos Ayres. Cunegonde, Captain Candide and the old woman went to call on the governor, Don Fernando d'Ibaraa y Figueora y Mascarenes y Lampourdos y Souza. This gentleman had the pride befitting a man who owned so many names. He talked to men with a most noble disdain, turning his nose up so far, raising his voice so pitilessly, assuming so imposing a tone, affecting so lofty a carriage, that all who addressed him were tempted to give him a thrashing. He had a furious passion for women. Cunegonde seemed to him the most beautiful woman he had ever seen. The first thing he did was to ask if she were the Captain's wife. The air with which he asked this question alarmed Candide; he did not dare say that she was his wife, because as a matter of fact she was not; he dared not say she was his sister, because she was not that either; and though this official lie was formerly extremely fashionable among the ancients, and might be useful to the moderns, his soul was too pure to depart from truth. "Mademoiselle Cunegonde," said he, "is about to do me the honor of marrying me, and we beg your excellency to be present at the wedding." Don Fernando d'Ibaraa y Figueora y Mascarenes y Lampourdos y Souza twisted his moustache, smiled bitterly and ordered Captain Candide to go and inspect his company. Candide obeyed; the governor remained with Mademoiselle Cunegonde. He declared his passion, vowed that the next day he would marry her publicly, or otherwise, as it might please her charms. Cunegonde asked for a quarter of an hour to collect herself, to consult the old woman and to make up her mind. The old woman said to Cunegonde: "You have seventy-two quarterings and you haven't a shilling; it is in your power to be the wife of the greatest Lord in South America, who has an exceedingly fine moustache; is it for you to pride yourself on a rigid fidelity? You have been raped by Bulgarians, a Jew and an Inquisitor have enjoyed your good graces; misfortunes confer certain rights. If I were in your place, I confess I should not have the least scruple in marrying the governor and making Captain Candide's fortune." While the old woman was speaking with all that prudence which comes from age and experience, they saw a small ship come into the harbor; an Alcayde and some Alguazils were on board, and this is what had happened. The old woman had guessed correctly that it was a long-sleeved monk who stole Cunegonde's money and jewels at Badajoz, when she was flying in all haste with Candide. The monk tried to sell some of the gems to a jeweller. The merchant recognized them as the property of the Grand Inquisitor. Before the monk was hanged he confessed that he had stolen them; he described the persons and the direction they were taking. The flight of Cunegonde and Candide was already known. They were followed to Cadiz; without any waste of time a vessel was sent in pursuit of them. The vessel was already in the harbor at Buenos Ayres. The rumor spread that an Alcayde was about to land and that he was in pursuit of the murderers of His Lordship the Grand Inquisitor. The prudent old woman saw in a moment what was to be done. "You cannot escape," she said to Cunegonde, "and you have nothing to fear; you did not kill His Lordship; moreover, the governor is in love with you and will not allow you to be maltreated; stay here." She ran to Candide at once. "Fly," said she, "or in an hour's time you will be burned." There was not a moment to lose; but how could he leave Cunegonde and where could he take refuge?

XIV

HOW CANDIDE AND CACAMBO WERE RECEIVED BY THE JESUITS IN PARAGUAY

Candide had brought from Cadiz a valet of a sort which is very common on the coasts of Spain and in colonies. He was one-quarter Spanish, the child of a half-breed in Tucuman; he had been a choir-boy, a sacristan, a sailor, a monk, a postman, a soldier and a lackey. His name was Cacambo and he loved his master because his master was a very good man. He saddled the two Andalusian horses with all speed. "Come, master, we must follow the old woman's advice; let us be off and ride without looking behind us." Candide shed tears. "O my dear Cunegonde! Must I abandon you just when the governor was about to marry us! Cunegonde, brought here from such a distant land, what will become of you?" "She will become what she can," said Cacambo. "Women never trouble about themselves; God will see to her; Let us be off." "Where are you taking me? Where are we going? What shall we do without Cunegonde?" said Candide. "By St. James of Compostella," said Cacambo, "you were going to fight the Jesuits; let us go and fight for them; I know the roads, I will take you to their kingdom, they will be charmed to have a captain who can drill in the Bulgarian fashion; you will make a prodigious fortune; when a man fails in one world, he succeeds in another. 'Tis a very great pleasure to see and do new things." "Then you have been in Paraguay?" said Candide. "Yes, indeed," said Cacambo. "I was servitor in the College of the Assumption, and I know the government of *Los Padres* as well as I know the streets of Cadiz. Their government is a most admirable thing. The kingdom is already more than three hundred leagues in diameter and is divided into thirty provinces. *Los Padres* have everything and the people have nothing; 'tis the masterpiece of reason and justice. For my part, I know nothing so divine as *Los Padres* who here make war on the Kings of Spain and Portugal and in Europe act as their confessors; who here kill Spaniards and at Madrid send them to Heaven; all this delights me; come on; you will be the happiest of men. What a pleasure it will be to *Los Padres* when they know there is coming to them a captain who can drill in the Bulgarian manner!" As soon as they reached the first barrier, Cacambo told the sentry that a captain wished to speak to the Commandant. This information was carried to the main guard. A Paraguayan officer ran to the feet of the Commandant to tell him the news. Candide and Cacambo were disarmed and their two Andalusian horses were taken from them. The two strangers were brought in between two ranks of soldiers; the Commandant was at the end, with a three-cornered hat on his head, his gown tucked up, a sword at his side and a spontoon in his hand. He made a sign and immediately the two new-comers were surrounded by twenty-four soldiers. A sergeant told them that they must wait, that the Commandant could not speak to them, that the reverend provincial father did not allow any Spaniard to open his mouth in his presence or to remain more than three hours in the country. "And where is the reverend provincial father?" said Cacambo. "He is on parade after having said Mass, and you will have to wait three hours before you will be allowed to kiss his spurs." "But," said Cacambo, "the captain who is dying of hunger just as I am, is not a Spaniard but a German; can we not break our fast while we are waiting for his reverence?" The sergeant went at once to inform the Commandant of this. "Blessed be God!" said that lord. "Since he is a German I can speak to him; bring him to my arbor." Candide was immediately taken to a leafy summer-house decorated with a very pretty colonnade of green marble and gold, and lattices enclosing parrots, humming-birds, colibris, guinea-hens and many other rare birds. An excellent breakfast stood ready in gold dishes; and while the Paraguayans were eating maize from wooden bowls, out of doors and in the heat of the sun, the reverend father Commandant entered the arbor. He was a very handsome young man, with a full face, a fairly white skin, red cheeks, arched eyebrows, keen eyes, red ears, vermilion lips, a haughty air, but a haughtiness which was neither that of a Spaniard nor of a Jesuit. Candide and Cacambo were given back the arms which had been taken from them and their two Andalusian horses; Cacambo fed them with oats near the arbor, and kept his eye on them for fear of a surprise. Candide first kissed the hem of the Commandant's gown and then they sat down to table. "So you are a German?" said the Jesuit in that language. "Yes, reverend father," said Candide. As they spoke these words they gazed at each other with extreme surprise and an emotion they could not control. "And what part of Germany do you come from?" said the Jesuit. "From the filthy province of Westphalia," said Candide; "I was born in the castle of Thunder-ten-tronckh." "Heavens! Is it possible!" cried the Commandant. "What a miracle!" cried Candide. "Can it be you?" said the Commandant. " 'Tis impossible!" said Candide. They both fell over backwards, embraced and shed rivers of tears. "What! Can it be you, reverend father? You, the fair Cunegonde's brother! You, who were killed by the Bulgarians! You, the son of My Lord the Baron! You, a Jesuit in Paraguay! The world is indeed a strange place! O Pangloss! Pangloss! How happy you would have been if you had not been hanged!" The Commandant sent away the Negro slaves and the Paraguayans who were serving wine in goblets of rock-crystal. A thousand times did he thank God and

St. Ignatius; he clasped Candide in his arms; their faces were wet with tears. "You would be still more surprised, more touched, more beside yourself," said Candide, "if I were to tell you that Mademoiselle Cunegonde, your sister, whom you thought disembowelled, is in the best of health." "Where?" "In your neighborhood, with the governor of Buenos Ayres; and I came to make war on you." Every word they spoke in this long conversation piled marvel on marvel. Their whole souls flew from their tongues, listened in their ears and sparkled in their eyes. As they were Germans, they sat at table for a long time, waiting for the reverend provincial father; and the Commandant spoke as follows to his dear Candide.

XV

HOW CANDIDE KILLED HIS DEAR CUNEGONDE'S BROTHER

"I shall remember all my life the horrible day when I saw my father and mother killed and my sister raped. When the Bulgarians had gone, my adorable sister could not be found, and my mother, my father and I, two maid-servants and three little murdered boys were placed in a cart to be buried in a Jesuit chapel two leagues from the castle of my fathers. A Jesuit sprinkled us with holy water; it was horribly salt; a few drops fell in my eyes; the father noticed that my eyelids trembled, he put his hand on my heart and felt that it was still beating; I was attended to and at the end of three weeks was as well as if nothing had happened. You know, my dear Candide, that I was a very pretty youth, and I became still prettier; and so the Reverend Father Croust, the Superior of the house, was inspired with a most tender friendship for me; he gave me the dress of a novice and some time afterwards I was sent to Rome. The Father General wished to recruit some young German Jesuits. The sovereigns of Paraguay take as few Spanish Jesuits as they can; they prefer foreigners, whom they think they can control better. The Reverend Father General thought me apt to labor in his vineyard. I set off with a Pole and a Tyrolese. When I arrived I was honored with a sub-deaconship and a lieutenancy; I am now colonel and priest. We shall give the King of Spain's troops a warm reception, I guarantee they will be excommunicated and beaten. Providence has sent you to help us. But is it really true that my dear sister Cunegonde is in the neighborhood with the governor of Buenos Ayres?" Candide assured him on oath that nothing could be truer. Their tears began to flow once more. The Baron seemed never to grow tired of embracing Candide; he called him his brother, his saviour. "Ah! My dear Candide," said he, "perhaps we shall enter the town together as conquerors and regain my sister Cunegonde." "I desire it above all things," said Candide, "for I meant to marry her and I still hope to do so." "You, insolent wretch!" replied the Baron. "Would you have the impudence to marry my sister who has seventy-two quarterings! I consider you extremely impudent to dare to speak to me of such a foolhardy intention!" Candide, petrified at this speech, replied: "Reverend Father, all the quarterings in the world are of no importance; I rescued your sister from the arms of a Jew and an Inquisitor; she is under considerable obligation to me and wishes to marry me. Dr. Pangloss always said that men are equal and I shall certainly marry her." "We shall see about that, scoundrel!" said the Jesuit Baron of Thunder-ten-tronckh, at the same time hitting him violently in the face with the flat of his sword. Candide promptly drew his own and stuck it up to the hilt in the Jesuit Baron's belly; but, as he drew it forth smoking, he began to weep. "Alas! My God," said he, "I have killed my old master, my friend, my brother-in-law; I am the mildest man in the world and I have already killed three men, two of them priests." Cacambo, who was acting as sentry at the door of the arbor, ran in. "There is nothing left for us but to sell our lives dearly," said his master. "Somebody will certainly come into the arbor and we must die weapon in hand." Cacambo, who had seen this sort of thing before, did not lose his head; he took off the Baron's Jesuit gown, put it on Candide, gave him the dead man's square bonnet, and made him mount a horse. All this was done in the twinkling of an eye. "Let us gallop, master; every one will take you for a Jesuit carrying orders and we shall have passed the frontiers before they can pursue us." As he spoke these words he started off at full speed and shouted in Spanish: "Way, way for the Reverend Father Colonel . ."

XVI

WHAT HAPPENED TO THE TWO TRAVELERS WITH TWO GIRLS, TWO MONKEYS, AND THE SAVAGES CALLED OREILLONS

Candide and his valet were past the barriers before anybody in the camp knew of the death of the German Jesuit. The vigilant Cacambo had taken care to fill his saddle-bag with bread, chocolate, ham, fruit, and several bottles of wine. On their Andalusian horses they plunged into an unknown country where they found no road. At last a beautiful plain traversed by streams met their eyes. Our two travelers put their horses to grass. Cacambo suggested to his master that they should eat and set the example. "How can you expect me to eat ham," said Candide, "when I have killed the son of My Lord the Baron and find myself condemned never to see the fair Cunegonde again in my life? What is the use of prolonging my miserable days since I must drag them out far from her in remorse and despair? And what will the Journal de Trévoux say?" [25] Speaking thus, he began to eat. The sun was setting. The two wanderers heard faint cries which seemed to be uttered by women. They could not tell whether these were cries of pain or of joy; but they rose hastily with that alarm and uneasiness caused by everything in an unknown country. These cries came from two completely naked girls who were running gently along the edge of the plain, while two monkeys pursued them and bit their buttocks. Candide was moved to pity; he had learned to shoot among the Bulgarians and could have brought down a nut from a tree without touching the leaves. He raised his double-barrelled Spanish gun, fired, and killed the two monkeys. "God be praised, my dear Cacambo, I have delivered these two poor creatures from a great danger; if I committed a sin by killing an Inquisitor and a Jesuit, I have atoned for it by saving the lives of these two girls. Perhaps they are young ladies of quality and this adventure may be of great advantage to us in this country." He was going on, but his tongue clove to the roof of his mouth when he saw the two girls tenderly kissing the two monkeys, shedding tears on their bodies and filling the air with the most piteous cries. "I did not expect so much human kindliness," he said at last to

Cacambo, who replied: "You have performed a wonderful master-piece; you have killed the two lovers of these young ladies." "Their lovers! Can it be possible? You are jesting at me, Cacambo; how can I believe you?" "My dear master," replied Cacambo, "you are always surprised by everything; why should you think it so strange that in some countries there should be monkeys who obtain ladies' favors? They are quarter men, as I am a quarter Spaniard." "Alas!" replied Candide, "I remember to have heard Dr. Pangloss say that similar accidents occurred in the past and that these mixtures produce Aigypans, fauns and satyrs; that several eminent persons of antiquity have seen them; but I thought they were fables." "You ought now to be con-vinced that it is true," said Cacambo, "and you see how people behave when they have not received a proper education; the only thing I fear is that these ladies may get us into difficulty." These wise reflections persuaded Candide to leave the plain and to plunge into the woods. He ate supper there with Cacambo and, after having cursed the Inquisitor of Portugal, the gover-nor of Buenos Ayres and the Baron, they went to sleep on the moss. When they woke up they found they could not move; the reason was that during the night the Oreillons, the inhabitants of the country, to whom they had been denounced by the two ladies, had bound them with ropes made of bark. They were surrounded by fifty naked Oreillons, armed with arrows, clubs and stone hatchets. Some were boiling a large cauldron, others were preparing spits and they were all shouting: "Here's a Jesuit, here's a Jesuit! We shall be revenged and have a good dinner; let us eat Jesuit, let us eat Jesuit!" "I told you so, my dear master," said Cacambo sadly. "I knew those two girls would play us a dirty trick." Candide perceived the cauldron and the spits and exclaimed: "We are certainly going to be roasted or boiled. Ah! What would Dr. Pangloss say if he saw what the pure state of nature is? All is well, granted; but I confess it is very cruel to have lost Mademoiselle Cunegonde and to be spitted by the Oreillons." Cacambo never lost his head. "Do not despair," he said to the wretched Candide. "I understand a little of their dialect and I will speak to them." "Do not fail," said Candide, "to point out to them the dreadful inhumanity of cooking men and how very unchristian it is." "Gentlemen," said Cacambo, "you mean to eat a Jesuit today? 'Tis a good deed; nothing could be more just than to treat one's enemies in this fashion. Indeed the law of nature teaches us to kill our neighbor and this is how people behave all over the world. If we do not exert the right of eating our neighbor, it is because we have other means of making good cheer; but you have not the same resources as we, and it is certainly better to eat our enemies than to abandon the fruits of victory to ravens and crows. But, gentlemen, you would not wish to eat your friends. You believe you are about to place a Jesuit on the spit, and 'tis your defender, the enemy of your enemies you are about to roast. I was born in your country; the gentleman you see here is my master and, far from being a Jesuit, he has just killed a Jesuit and is wearing his clothes; which is the cause of your mistake. To verify what I say, take his gown, carry it to the first barrier of the kingdom of *Los Padres* and inquire whether my master has not killed a Jesuit officer. It will not take you long and you will have plenty of time to eat us if you find I have lied. But if I have told the truth, you are too well acquainted with the principles of public law, good morals and discipline, not to pardon us." The Oreillons thought this a very reasonable speech; they deputed two of their notables to go with all diligence and find out the truth. The two deputies acquitted themselves of their task like intelligent men and soon returned with the good news. The Oreillons unbound their two prisoners, overwhelmed them with civilities, offered them girls, gave them refreshment, and accompanied them to the frontiers of their dominions, shouting joyfully: "He is not a Jesuit, he is not a Jesuit!" Candide could not cease from wondering at the cause of his deliverance. "What a nation," said he. "What men! What manners! If I had not been so lucky as to stick my sword through the body of Mademoiselle Cunegonde's brother I should infallibly have been eaten. But, after all, there is something good in the pure state of nature, since these people, instead of eating me, offered me a thousand civilities as soon as they knew I was not a Jesuit."

XVII

ARRIVAL OF CANDIDE AND HIS VALET IN THE COUNTRY
OF ELDORADO AND WHAT THEY SAW THERE

When they reached the frontiers of the Oreillons, Cacambo said
to Candide: "You see this hemisphere is no better than the
other; take my advice, let us go back to Europe by the shortest
road." "How can we go back," said Candide, "and where can
we go? If I go to my own country, the Bulgarians and the
Abares are murdering everybody; if I return to Portugal I shall
be burned; if we stay here, we run the risk of being spitted at
any moment. But how can I make up my mind to leave that
part of the world where Mademoiselle Cunegonde is living?"
"Let us go to Cayenne," said Cacambo, "we shall find Frenchmen there, for they go all over the world; they might help us.
Perhaps God will have pity on us." It was not easy to go to
Cayenne. They knew roughly the direction to take, but mountains, rivers, precipices, brigands and savages were everywhere
terrible obstacles. Their horses died of fatigue; their provisions
were exhausted; for a whole month they lived on wild fruits
and at last found themselves near a little river fringed with
cocoanut-trees which supported their lives and their hopes.
Cacambo, who always gave advice as prudent as the old woman's,
said to Candide: "We can go no farther, we have walked far
enough; I can see an empty canoe in the bank, let us fill it
with cocoanuts, get into the little boat and drift with the current; a river always leads to some inhabited place. If we do not
find anything pleasant, we shall at least find something new."
"Come on then," said Candide, "and let us trust to Providence."
They drifted for some leagues between banks which were sometimes flowery, sometimes bare, sometimes flat, sometimes steep.
The river continually became wider; finally it disappeared under
an arch of frightful rocks which towered up to the very sky.
The two travelers were bold enough to trust themselves to the
current under this arch. The stream, narrowed between walls,
carried them with horrible rapidity and noise. After twenty-four
hours they saw daylight again; but their canoe was wrecked on
reefs; they had to crawl from rock to rock for a whole league

and at last they discovered an immense horizon, bordered by inaccessible mountains. The country was cultivated for pleasure as well as for necessity; everywhere the useful was agreeable. The roads were covered or rather ornamented with carriages of brilliant material and shape, carrying men and women of singular beauty, who were rapidly drawn along by large red sheep whose swiftness surpassed that of the finest horses of Andalusia, Tetuan, and Mequinez. "This country," said Candide, "is better than Westphalia." He landed with Cacambo near the first village he came to. Several children of the village, dressed in torn gold brocade, were playing horseshoes outside the village. Our two men from the other world amused themselves by looking on; their horseshoes were large round pieces, yellow, red and green which shone with peculiar lustre. The travellers were curious enough to pick up some of them; they were of gold, emeralds and rubies, the least of which would have been the greatest ornament in the Mogul's throne. "No doubt," said Cacambo, "these children are the sons of the King of this country playing horseshoes." At that moment the village schoolmaster appeared to call them into school. "This," said Candide, "is the tutor of the Royal Family." The little beggars immediately left their game, abandoning their horseshoes and everything with which they had been playing. Candide picked them up, ran to the tutor, and presented them to him humbly, giving him to understand by signs that their Royal Highnesses had forgotten their gold and their precious stones. The village schoolmaster smiled, threw them on the ground, gazed for a moment at Candide's face with much surprise and continued on his way. The travelers did not fail to pick up the gold, the rubies and the emeralds. "Where are we?" cried Candide. "The children of the King must be well brought up, since they are taught to despise gold and precious stones." Cacambo was as much surprised as Candide. At last they reached the first house in the village, which was built like a European palace. There were crowds of people round the door and still more inside; very pleasant music could be heard and there was a delicious smell of cooking. Cacambo went up to the door and heard them speaking Peruvian; it was his maternal tongue, for everyone knows that Cacambo was born in a village of Tucuman where nothing else is spoken. "I will act as your interpreter," he said to Candide, "this is an inn, let us enter." Immediately two boys and two girls of the inn, dressed in cloth of gold, whose hair was bound up with ribbons, invited them to sit down to the table d'hôte. They served four soups each garnished with two parrots, a boiled condor which weighed two hundred pounds, two roast monkeys of excellent flavor, three hundred colibris in one dish and six hundred humming-birds in another, exquisite ragouts and delicious pastries, all in dishes of a sort of rock-crystal. The boys and girls brought several sorts of drinks made of sugar-cane. Most of the guests were merchants and coachmen, all extremely polite, who asked Cacambo a few questions with the most delicate discretion and answered his in a satisfactory manner. When the meal was over, Cacambo, like Candide, thought he could pay the reckoning by throwing on the table two of the large pieces of gold he had picked up; the host and hostess laughed until they had to hold their sides. At last they recovered themselves. "Gentlemen," said the host, "we perceive you are strangers; we are not accustomed to seeing them. Forgive us if we began to laugh when you offered us in payment the stones from our highways. No doubt you have none of the money of this country, but you do not need any to dine here. All the hotels established for the utility of commerce are paid for by the government. You have been ill-entertained here because this is a poor village; but everywhere else you will be received as you deserve to be." Cacambo explained to Candide all that the host had said, and Candide listened in the same admiration and disorder with which his friend Cacambo interpreted. "What can this country be," they said to each other, "which is unknown to the rest of the world and where all nature is so different from ours? Probably it is the country where everything is for the best; for there must be one country of that sort. And, in spite of what Dr. Pangloss said, I often noticed that everything went very ill in Westphalia."

XVIII

WHAT THEY SAW IN THE LAND OF ELDORADO

Cacambo informed the host of his curiosity, and the host said: "I am a very ignorant man and am all the better for it; but we have here an old man who has retired from the court and who is the most learned and most communicative man in the kingdom." And he at once took Cacambo to the old man. Candide now played only the second part and accompanied his valet. They entered a very simple house, for the door was only of silver and the paneling of the apartments in gold, but so tastefully carved that the richest decorations did not surpass it. The antechamber indeed was only encrusted with rubies and emeralds; but the order with which everything was arranged atoned for this extreme simplicity. The old man received the two strangers on a sofa padded with colibri feathers, and presented them with drinks in diamond cups; after which he satisfied their curiosity in these words: "I am a hundred and seventy-two years old and I heard from my late father, the King's equerry, the astonishing revolutions of Peru of which he had been an eye-witness. The kingdom where we now are is the ancient country of the Incas, who most imprudently left it to conquer part of the world and were at last destroyed by the Spaniards. The princes of their family who remained in their native country had more wisdom; with the consent of the nation, they ordered that no inhabitants should ever leave our little kingdom, and this it is that has preserved our innocence and our felicity. The Spaniards had some vague knowledge of this country, which they called Eldorado, and about a hundred years ago an Englishman named Raleigh came very near to it; but, since we are surrounded by inaccessible rocks and precipices, we have hitherto been exempt from the rapacity of the nations of Europe who have an inconceivable lust for the pebbles and mud of our land and would kill us to the last man to get possession of them." The conversation was long; it touched upon the form of the government, manners, women, public spectacles and the arts. Finally Candide, who was always interested in metaphysics, asked through Cacambo whether the country had a religion. The

old man blushed a little. "How can you doubt it?" said he.
"Do you think we are ingrates?" Cacambo humbly asked what
was the religion of Eldorado. The old man blushed again. "Can
there be two religions?" said he. "We have, I think, the religion
of every one else; we adore God from evening until morning."
"Do you adore only one God?" said Cacambo, who continued to
act as the interpreter of Candide's doubts. "Manifestly," said the
old man, "there are not two or three or four. I must confess
that the people of your world ask very extraordinary quetions."
Candide continued to press the old man with questions; he
wished to know how they prayed to God in Eldorado. "We do
not pray," said the good and respectable sage, "we have nothing
to ask from him; he has given us everything necessary and we
continually give him thanks." Candide was curious to see the
priests; and asked where they were. The good old man smiled.
"My friends," said he, "we are all priests; the King and all the
heads of families solemnly sing praises every morning, accompanied by five or six thousand musicians." "What! Have you no
monks to teach, to dispute, to govern, to intrigue and to burn
people who do not agree with them?" "For that, we should have
to become fools," said the old man; "here we are all of the same
opinion and do not understand what you mean with your
monks." At all this Candide was in an ecstasy and said to himself: "This is very different from Westphalia and the castle of
His Lordship the Baron; if our friend Pangloss had seen Eldorado, he would not have said that the castle of Thunder-ten-
tronckh was the best of all that exists on the earth; certainly,
a man should travel." After this long conversation the good old
man ordered a carriage to be harnessed with six sheep and gave
the two travelers twelve of his servants to take them to court.
"You will excuse me," he said, "if my age deprives me of the
honor of accompanying you. The King will receive you in a
manner which will not displease you and doubtless you will
pardon the customs of the country if any of them disconcert
you." Candide and Cacambo entered the carriage; the six sheep
galloped off and in less than four hours they reached the King's
palace, which was situated at one end of the capital. The portal
was two hundred and twenty feet high and a hundred feet

wide; it is impossible to describe its material. Anyone can see the prodigious superiority it must have over the pebbles and sand we call *gold* and *gems*. Twenty beautiful maidens of the guard received Candide and Cacambo as they alighted from the carriage, conducted them to the baths and dressed them in robes woven from the down of colibris; after which the principal male and female officers of the Crown led them to his Majesty's apartment through two files of a thousand musicians each, according to the usual custom. As they approached the throne-room, Cacambo asked one of the chief officers how they should behave in his Majesty's presence; whether they should fall on their knees or flat on their faces, whether they should put their hands on their heads or on their backsides; whether they should lick the dust of the throne-room; in a word, what was the ceremony? "The custom," said the chief officer, "is to embrace the King and to kiss him on either cheek." Candide and Cacambo threw their arms round his Majesty's neck; he received them with all imaginable favor and politely asked them to supper. Meanwhile they were carried to see the town, the public buildings rising to the very skies, the market-places ornamented with thousands of columns, the fountains of rose-water and of liquors distilled from sugar-cane, which played continually in the public squares paved with precious stones which emitted a perfume like that of cloves and cinnamon. Candide asked to see the law courts; he was told there were none, and that nobody ever went to law. He asked if there were prisons and was told there were none. He was still more surprised and pleased by the palace of sciences, where he saw a gallery two thousand feet long, filled with instruments of mathematics and physics. After they had explored all the afternoon about a thousandth part of the town, they were taken back to the King. Candide sat down to table with his Majesty, his valet Cacambo and several ladies. Never was there a better supper, and never was anyone wittier at supper than his Majesty. Cacambo explained the King's witty remarks to Candide and even when translated they still appeared witty. Among all the things which amazed Candide, this did not amaze him the least. They enjoyed this hospitality for a month. Candide repeatedly said to Cacambo: "Once again, my friend, it is quite true that the castle where I was born cannot be compared with this country; but then Mademoiselle Cunegonde is not here and you probably have a mistress in Europe. If we remain here, we shall only be like everyone else; but if we return to our own world with only twelve sheep laden with Eldorado pebbles, we shall be richer than all the kings put together; we shall have no more Inquisitors to fear and we can easily regain Mademoiselle Cunegonde." Cacambo agreed with this; it is so pleasant to be on the move, to show off before friends, to make a parade of the things seen on one's travels, that these two happy men resolved to be so no longer and to ask his Majesty's permission to depart. "You are doing a very silly thing," said the King. "I know my country is small; but when we are comfortable anywhere we should stay there; I certainly have not the right to detain foreigners, that is a tyranny which does not exist either in our manners or our laws; all men are free, leave when you please, but the way out is very difficult. It is impossible to ascend the rapid river by which you miraculously came here and which flows under arches of rock. The mountains which surround the whole of my kingdom are ten thousand feet high and are perpendicular like walls; they are more than ten leagues broad, and you can only get down from them by way of precipices. However, since you must go, I will give orders to the directors of machinery to make a machine which will carry you comfortably. When you have been taken to the other side of the mountains, nobody can proceed any farther with you; for my subjects have sworn never to pass this boundary and they are too wise to break their oath. Ask anything else of me you wish." "We ask nothing of your Majesty," said Cacambo, "except a few sheep laden with provisions, pebbles and the mud of this country." The King laughed. "I cannot understand," said he, "the taste you people of Europe have for our yellow mud; but take as much as you wish, and much good may it do you." He immediately ordered his engineers to make a machine to hoist these two extraordinary men out of his kingdom. Three thousand learned scientists worked at it; it was ready in a fortnight and only cost about twenty million pounds sterling in the money of that country. Candide and Cacambo were placed on the machine; there were two large red sheep saddled and bridled for them to ride on when they had passed the mountains, twenty pack sheep laden with provisions, thirty carrying presents of the most curious productions of the country and fifty laden with gold, precious stones and diamonds. The King embraced the two vagabonds tenderly. Their departure was a splendid sight and so was the ingenious manner in which they and their sheep were hoisted on to the top of the mountains. The scientists took leave of them after having landed them safely, and Candide's only desire and object was to go and present Mademoiselle Cunegonde with his sheep. "We have sufficient to pay the governor of Buenos Ayres," said he, "if Mademoiselle Cunegonde can be bought. Let us go to Cayenne, and take ship, and then we will see what kingdom we will buy."

XIX

WHAT HAPPENED TO THEM AT SURINAM AND HOW CANDIDE MADE THE ACQUAINTANCE OF MARTIN

Our two travelers' first day was quite pleasant. They were encouraged by the idea of possessing more treasures than all Asia, Europe and Africa could collect. Candide in rapture carved the name of Cunegonde on the trees. On the second day two of the sheep stuck in a marsh and were swallowed up with their loads; two other sheep died of fatigue a few days later; then seven or eight died of hunger in a desert; several days afterwards others fell off precipices. Finally, after they had traveled for a hundred days, they had only two sheep left. Candide said to Cacambo: "My friend, you see how perishable are the riches of this world; nothing is steadfast but virtue and the happiness of seeing Mademoiselle Cunegonde again." "I admit it," said Cacambo, "but we still have two sheep with more treasures than the King of Spain will ever have, and in the distance I see a town I suspect is Surinam, which belongs to the Dutch. We are at the end of our troubles and the beginning of our happiness." As they drew near the town they came upon a Negro lying on the ground wearing only half his clothes, that is to say, a pair of blue cotton drawers; this poor man had no left leg and no right hand. "Good heavens!" said Candide to him in Dutch, "what are you doing there, my friend, in that horrible state?" "I am waiting for my master, the famous merchant Monsieur Vanderdendur." "Was it Monsieur Vanderdendur," said Candide, "who treated you in that way?" "Yes, sir," said the Negro, "it is the custom. We are given a pair of cotton drawers twice a year as clothing. When we work in the sugar-mills and the grindstone catches our fingers, they cut off the hand; when we try to run away, they cut off a leg. Both these things happened to me. This is the price paid for the sugar you eat in Europe. But when my mother sold me for ten patagons on the coast of Guinea, she said to me: 'My dear child, give thanks to our fetishes, always worship them, and they will make you happy; you have the honor to be a slave of our lords the white men and thereby you have made the fortune of your father and mother.' Alas! I do not know whether I made their fortune, but they certainly did not make mine. Dogs, monkeys and parrots are a thousand times less miserable than we are; the Dutch fetishes who converted me tell me that we are all of us, whites and blacks, the children of Adam. I am not a genealogist, but if these preachers tell the truth, we are all second cousins. Now, you will admit that no one could treat his relatives in a more horrible way." "O Pangloss!" cried Candide. "This is an abomination you had not guessed; this is too much, in the end I shall have to renounce optimism." "What is optimism?" said Cacambo. "Alas!" said Candide, "it is the mania of maintaining that everything is well when we are wretched." And he shed tears as he looked at his Negro; and he entered Surinam weeping. The first thing they inquired was whether there was any ship in the port which could be sent to Buenos Ayres. The person they addressed happened to be a Spanish captain, who offered to strike an honest bargain with them. He arranged to meet them at an inn. Candide and the faithful Cacambo went and waited for him with their two sheep. Candide, who blurted everything out, told the Spaniard all his adventures and confessed that he wanted to elope with Mademoiselle Cunegonde. "I shall certainly not take you to Buenos Ayres," said the captain. "I should be hanged and you would, too. The fair Cunegonde is his Lord-

ship's favorite mistress." Candide was thunderstruck; he sobbed
for a long time; then he took Cacambo aside. "My dear friend,"
said he, "this is what you must do. We have each of us in our
pockets five or six millions worth of diamonds; you are more
skilful than I am; go to Buenos Ayres and get Mademoiselle
Cunegonde. If the governor makes any difficulties give him a
million; if he is still obstinate give him two; you have not killed
an Inquisitor so they will not suspect you. I will fit out another
ship, I will go and wait for you at Venice; it is a free country
where there is nothing to fear from Bulgarians, Abares, Jews or
Inquisitors." Cacambo applauded this wise resolution; he was in
despair at leaving a good master who had become his intimate
friend; but the pleasure of being useful to him overcame the
grief of leaving him. They embraced with tears. Candide urged
him not to forget the good old woman. Cacambo set off that
very same day; he was a very good man, this Cacambo. Candide
remained some time longer at Surinam waiting for another captain to take him to Italy with the two sheep he had left. He
engaged servants and bought everything necessary for a long
voyage. At last Monsieur Vanderdendur, the owner of a large
ship, came to see him. "How much do you want," he asked
this man, "to take me straight to Venice with my servants, my
baggage and these two sheep?" The captain asked for ten thousand piastres. Candide did not hesitate. "Oh! Ho!" said the prudent Vanderdendur to himself, "this foreigner gives ten thousand
piastres immediately! He must be very rich." He returned a moment afterwards and said he could not sail for less than twenty
thousand. "Very well, you shall have them," said Candide.
"Whew!" said the merchant to himself, "this man gives twenty
thousand piastres as easily as ten thousand." He came back again,
and said he could not take him to Venice for less than thirty
thousand piastres. "Then you shall have thirty thousand," replied
Candide. "Oho!" said the Dutch merchant to himself again,
"thirty thousand piastres is nothing to this man, obviously the
two sheep are laden with immense treasures; I will not insist
any further; first let me make him pay the thirty thousand
piastres, and then we will see." Candide sold two little diamonds,
the smaller of which was worth more than all the money the

captain asked. He paid him in advance. The two sheep were taken on board. Candide followed in a little boat to join the ship which rode at anchor; the captain watched his time, set his sails and weighed anchor; the wind was favorable. Candide, bewildered and stupefied, soon lost sight of him. "Alas!" he cried, "this is a trick worthy of the old world." He returned to shore, in grief; for he had lost enough to make the fortunes of twenty kings. He went to the Dutch judge; and, as he was rather disturbed, he knocked loudly at the door; he went in, related what had happened and talked a little louder than he ought to have done. The judge began by fining him ten thousand piastres for the noise he had made; he then listened patiently to him, promised to look into his affair as soon as the merchant returned, and charged him another ten thousand piastres for the expenses of the audience. This behavior reduced Candide to despair; he had indeed endured misfortunes a thousand times more painful; but the calmness of the judge and of the captain who had robbed him, stirred up his bile and plunged him into a black melancholy. The malevolence of men revealed itself to his mind in all its ugliness; he entertained only gloomy ideas. At last a French ship was about to leave for Bordeaux and, since he no longer had any sheep laden with diamonds to put on board, he hired a cabin at a reasonable price and announced throughout the town that he would give the passage, food and two thousand piastres to an honest man who would make the journey with him, on condition that this man was the most unfortunate and the most disgusted with his condition in the whole province. Such a crowd of applicants arrived that a fleet would not have contained them. Candide, wishing to choose among the most likely, picked out twenty persons who seemed reasonably sociable and who all claimed to deserve his preference. He collected them in a tavern and gave them supper, on condition that each took an oath to relate truthfully the story of his life, promising that he would choose the man who seemed to him the most deserving of pity and to have the most cause for being discontented with his condition, and that he would give the others a little money. The sitting lasted until four o'clock in the morning. As Candide listened to their adventures he remem-

bered what the old woman had said on the voyage to Buenos
Ayres and how she had wagered that there was nobody on the
boat who had not experienced very great misfortunes. At each
story which was told him, he thought of Pangloss. "This Pangloss," said he, "would have some difficulty in supporting his system. I wish he were here. Certainly, if everything is well, it is
only in Eldorado and not in the rest of the world." He finally
determined in favor of a poor man of letters who had worked
ten years for the booksellers at Amsterdam. He judged that there
was no occupation in the world which could more disgust a
man. This man of letters, who was also a good man, had
been robbed by his wife, beaten by his son, and abandoned by
his daughter, who had eloped with a Portuguese. He had just
been deprived of a small post on which he depended and the
preachers of Surinam were persecuting him because they thought
he was a Socinian. It must be admitted that the others were at
least as unfortunate as he was; but Candide hoped that this
learned man would help pass the time during the voyage. All
his other rivals considered that Candide was doing them a great
injustice; but he appeased them by giving each of them a hundred piastres.

XX

WHAT HAPPENED TO CANDIDE AND MARTIN AT SEA

So the old man, who was called Martin, embarked with Candide
for Bordeaux. Both had seen and suffered much; and if the ship
had been sailing from Surinam to Japan by way of the Cape
of Good Hope they would have been able to discuss moral and
physical evil during the whole voyage. However, Candide had
one great advantage over Martin, because he still hoped to see
Mademoiselle Cunegonde again, and Martin had nothing to
hope for; moreover, he possessed gold and diamonds; and, although he had lost a hundred large red sheep laden with the
greatest treasures on earth, although he was still enraged at
being robbed by the Dutch captain, yet when he thought of
what he still had left in his pockets and when he talked of
Cunegonde, especially at the end of a meal, he still inclined

towards the system of Pangloss. "But what do you think of all this, Martin?" said he to the man of letters. "What is your view of moral and physical evil?" "Sir," replied Martin, "my priests accused me of being a Socinian; but the truth is I am a Manichæan." "You are poking fun at me," said Candide, "there are no Manichæans left in the world." "I am one," said Martin. "I don't know what to do about it, but I am unable to think in any other fashion." "You must be possessed by the devil," said Candide. "He takes so great a share in the affairs of this world," said Martin, "that he might well be in me, as he is everywhere else; but I confess that when I consider this globe, or rather this globule, I think that God has abandoned it to some evil creature—always excepting Eldorado. I have never seen a town which did not desire the ruin of the next town, never a family which did not wish to exterminate some other family. Everywhere the weak loathe the powerful before whom they cower and the powerful treat them like flocks of sheep whose wool and flesh are to be sold. A million drilled assassins go from one end of Europe to the other murdering and robbing with discipline in order to earn their bread, because there is no more honest occupation; and in the towns which seem to enjoy peace and where the arts flourish, men are devoured by more envy, troubles and worries than the afflictions of a besieged town. Secret griefs are even more cruel than public miseries. In a word, I have seen so much and endured so much that I have become a Manichæan." "Yet there is some good," replied Candide. "There may be," said Martin, "but I do not know it." In the midst of this dispute they heard the sound of cannon. The noise increased every moment. Every one took his telescope. About three miles away they saw two ships engaged in battle; and the wind brought them so near the French ship that they had the pleasure of seeing the fight at their ease. At last one of the two ships fired a broadside so accurately and so low down that the other ship began to sink. Candide and Martin distinctly saw a hundred men on the main deck of the sinking ship; they raised their hands to Heaven and uttered frightful shrieks; in a moment all were engulfed. "Well!" said Martin, "that is how men treat each other." "It is certainly true," said Candide, "that there is something diabolical in this affair." As he was speaking, he saw something of a brilliant red swimming near the ship. They launched a boat to see what it could be; it was one of his sheep. Candide felt more joy at recovering this sheep than grief at losing a hundred all laden with large diamonds from Eldorado. The French captain soon perceived that the captain of the remaining ship was a Spaniard and that the sunken ship was a Dutch pirate; the captain was the very same who had robbed Candide. The immense wealth this scoundrel had stolen was swallowed up with him in the sea and only a sheep was saved. "You see," said Candide to Martin, "that crime is sometimes punished; this scoundrel of a Dutch captain has met the fate he deserved." "Yes," said Martin, "but was it necessary that the other passengers on his ship should perish too? God punished the thief, and the devil punished the others." Meanwhile the French and Spanish ships continued on their way and Candide continued his conversation with Martin. They argued for a fortnight and at the end of the fortnight they had got no further than at the beginning. But after all, they talked, they exchanged ideas, they consoled each other. Candide stroked his sheep. "Since I have found you again," said he, "I may very likely find Cunegonde."

XXI

CANDIDE AND MARTIN APPROACH THE COAST OF FRANCE AND ARGUE

At last they sighted the coast of France. "Have you ever been to France, Monsieur Martin?" said Candide. "Yes," said Martin, "I have traversed several provinces. In some half the inhabitants are crazy, in others they are too artful, in some they are usually quite gentle and stupid, and in others they think they are clever; in all of them the chief occupation is making love, the second scandal-mongering and the third talking nonsense." "But, Monsieur Martin, have you seen Paris?" "Yes, I have seen Paris; it is a mixture of all the species; it is a chaos, a throng where everybody hunts for pleasure and hardly anybody finds it, at least so far as I could see. I did not stay there long; when I arrived there I was robbed of everything I had by pickpockets at Saint-Germain's fair; they thought I was a thief and I spent a week in prison; after which I became a printer's reader to earn enough to return to Holland on foot. I met the scribbling rabble, the intriguing rabble and the fanatical rabble. We hear that there are very polite people in the town; I am glad to think so." "For my part, I have not the least curiosity to see France," said Candide. "You can easily guess that when a man has spent a month in Eldorado he cares to see nothing else in the world but Mademoiselle Cunegonde. I shall go and wait for her at Venice; we will go to Italy by way of France; will you come with me?" "Willingly," said Martin. "They say that Venice is only for the Venetian nobles but that foreigners are nevertheless well received when they have plenty of money; I have none, you have plenty, I will follow you anywhere." "By the way," said Candide, "do you think the earth was originally a sea, as we are assured by that large book belonging to the captain?" "I don't believe it in the least," said Martin, "any more than all the other whimsies we have been pestered with recently!" "But to what end was this world formed?" said Candide. "To infuriate us," replied Martin. "Are you not very much surprised," continued Candide, "by the love those girls of the country of the Oreillons had for those two monkeys, whose adventure I told you?" "Not in the least," said Martin. "I see nothing strange in their passion; I have seen so many extraordinary things that nothing seems extraordinary to me." "Do you think," said Candide, "that men have always massacred each other, as they do today? Have they always been liars, cheats, traitors, brigands, weak, flighty, cowardly, envious, gluttonous, drunken, grasping, and vicious, bloody, backbiting, debauched, fanatical, hypocritical and stupid?" "Do you think," said Martin, "that sparrow-hawks have always eaten the pigeons they came across?" "Yes, of course," said Candide. "Well," said Martin, "if sparrow-hawks have always possessed the same nature, why should you expect men to change theirs?" "Oh!" said Candide, "there is a great difference; free-will . . ." Arguing thus, they arrived at Bordeaux.

XXII

WHAT HAPPENED TO CANDIDE AND MARTIN IN FRANCE

Candide remained in Bordeaux only long enough to sell a few Eldorado pebbles and to provide himself with a two-seated post-chaise, for he could no longer get on without his philosopher Martin; but he was very much grieved at having to part with his sheep, which he left with the Academy of Sciences at Bordeaux. The Academy offered as the subject for a prize that year the cause of the redness of the sheep's fleece; and the prize was awarded to a learned man in the North, who proved by A plus B minus C divided by z that the sheep must be red and die of the sheep-pox. However all the travelers Candide met in taverns on the way said to him: "We are going to Paris." This general eagerness at length made him wish to see that capital; it was not far out of the road to Venice. He entered by the Faubourg Saint-Marceau and thought he was in the ugliest village of Westphalia. Candide had scarcely reached his inn when he was attacked by a slight illness caused by fatigue. As he wore an enormous diamond on his finger, and a prodigiously heavy strong-box had been observed in his baggage, he immediately had with him two doctors he had not asked for, several intimate friends who would not leave him and two devotees who kept making him broth. Said Martin: "I remember that I was ill too when I first came to Paris; I was very poor; so I had no friends, no devotees, no doctors, and I got well." However, with the aid of medicine and blood-letting, Candide's illness became serious. An inhabitant of the district came and gently asked him for a note payable to bearer in the next world; Candide would have nothing to do with it. The devotees assured him that it was a new fashion; Candide replied that he was not a fashionable man. Martin wanted to throw the inhabitant out the window; the clerk swore that Candide should not be buried; Martin swore that he would bury the clerk if he continued to annoy them. The quarrel became heated; Martin took him by the shoulders and turned him out roughly; this caused a great scandal, and they made an official report on it. Candide got better; and during his convalescence he had very

good company to supper with him. They gambled for high
stakes. Candide was vastly surprised that he never drew an ace;
and Martin was not surprised at all. Among those who did the
honors of the town was a little abbé from Périgord, one of those
assiduous people who are always alert, always obliging, impudent, fawning, accommodating, always on the look-out for the arrival of foreigners, ready to tell them all the scandals of the
town and to procure them pleasures at any price. This abbé
took Candide and Martin to the theatre. A new tragedy was
being played. Candide was seated near several wits. This did
not prevent his weeping at perfectly played scenes. One of the
argumentative bores near him said during an interval: "You have
no business to weep, this is a very bad actress, the actor playing
with her is still worse, the play is still worse than the actors;
the author does not know a word of Arabic and yet the scene
is in Arabia; moreover, he is a man who does not believe in
innate ideas; tomorrow I will bring you twenty articles written
against him." "Sir," said Candide to the abbé, "how many plays
have you in France?" "Five or six thousand," he replied. "That's
a lot," said Candide, "and how many good ones are there?"
"Fifteen or sixteen," replied the other. "That's a lot," said Martin. Candide was greatly pleased with an actress who took the
part of Queen Elizabeth in a rather dull tragedy which is sometimes played. "This actress," said he to Martin, "pleases me very
much; she looks rather like Mademoiselle Cunegonde; I should
be very glad to pay her my respects." The abbé offered to introduce her to him. Candide, brought up in Germany, asked
what was the etiquette, and how queens of England were
treated in France. "There is a distinction," said the abbé, "in the
provinces we take them to a tavern; in Paris we respect them
when they are beautiful and throw them in the public sewer
when they are dead." "Queens in the public sewer!" said Candide. "Yes, indeed," said Martin, "the abbé is right; I was in Paris
when Mademoiselle Monime departed, as they say, this life; she
was refused what people here call the *honors of burial*—that is
to say, the honor of rotting with all the beggars of the district
in a horrible cemetery; she was buried by herself at the corner
of the Rue de Burgoyne; which must have given her extreme

pain, for her mind was very lofty." [26] "That was very impolite,"
said Candide. "What do you expect?" said Martin. "These people are like that. Imagine all possible contradictions and incom-
patibilities; you will see them in the government, in the law-
courts, in the churches and the entertainments of this absurd nation." "Is it true that people are always laughing in Paris?" said
Candide. "Yes," said the abbé, "but it is with rage in their hearts,
for they complain of everything with roars of laughter and they
even commit with laughter the most detestable actions." "Who
is that fat pig," said Candide, "who said so much ill of the play
I cried at so much and of the actors who gave me so much
pleasure?" "He is a living evil," replied the abbé, "who earns
his living by abusing all plays and all books; he hates anyone
who succeeds, as eunuchs hate those who enjoy; he is one of
the serpents of literature who feed on filth and venom; he is a
scribbler." "What do you mean by a scribbler?" said Candide.
"A scribbler of periodical sheets," said the abbé. "A Fréron." [27]
Candide, Martin and the abbé from Périgord talked in this manner on the stairway as they watched everybody going out after
the play. "Although I am most anxious to see Mademoiselle
Cunegonde again," said Candide, "I should like to sup with
Mademoiselle Clairon, for I thought her admirable." The abbé
was not the sort of man to know Mademoiselle Clairon, for she
saw only good company. "She is engaged this evening," he said,
"but I shall have the honor to take you to the house of a lady
of quality, and there you will learn as much of Paris as if you
had been here for four years." Candide, who was naturally curious, allowed himself to be taken to the lady's house at the far
end of the Faubourg Saint-Honoré; they were playing faro;
twelve gloomy punters each held a small hand of cards, the
dog-eared register of their misfortunes. The silence was profound,
the punters were pale, the banker was uneasy, and the lady of
the house, seated beside this pitiless banker, watched with lynx's
eyes every double stake, every seven-and-the-go, with which each
player marked his cards; she had them un-marked with severe
but polite attention, for fear of losing her customers; the lady
called herself Marquise de Parolignac. Her fifteen-year-old
daughter was among the punters and winked to her to let her

know the tricks of the poor people who attempted to repair the cruelties of fate. The abbé from Périgord, Candide and Martin entered; nobody rose, nobody greeted them, nobody looked at them; everyone was profoundly occupied with the cards. "Her Ladyship, the Baroness of Thunder-ten-tronckh, was more civil," said Candide. However the abbé whispered in the ear of the Marquise, who half rose, honored Candide with a gracious smile and Martin with a most noble nod. Candide was given a seat and a hand of cards, and lost fifty thousand francs in two hands; after which they supped very merrily and everyone was surprised that Candide was not more disturbed by his loss. The lackeys said to each other, in the language of lackeys: "He must be an English Milord." The supper was like most suppers in Paris; first there was a silence and then a noise of indistinguishable words, then jokes, most of which were insipid, false news, false arguments, some politics and a great deal of scandal; there was even some talk of new books. "Have you seen," said the abbé from Périgord, "the novel by Gauchat, the doctor of theology?" "Yes," replied one of the guests, "but I could not finish it. We have a crowd of silly writings, but all of them together do not approach the silliness of Gauchat, doctor of theology. I am so weary of this immensity of detestable books which inundates us that I have taken to faro." "And what do you say about the *Mélanges* by Archdeacon T.?" [28] said the abbé. "Ah!" said Madame de Parolignac, "the tiresome creature! How carefully he tells you what everybody knows! How heavily he discusses what is not worth the trouble of being lightly mentioned! How witlessly he appropriates other people's wit! How he spoils what he steals! How he disgusts me! But he will not disgust me any more; it is enough to have read a few pages by the Archdeacon." There was a man of learning and taste at table who confirmed what the marchioness had said. They then talked of tragedies; the lady asked why there were tragedies which were sometimes played and yet were unreadable. The man of taste explained very clearly how a play might have some interest and hardly any merit; in a few words he proved that it was not sufficient to bring in one or two of the situations which are found in all novels and which always attract the spectators;

but that a writer of tragedies must be original without being bizarre, often sublime and always natural, must know the human heart and be able to give it speech, must be a great poet but not let any character in his play appear to be a poet, must know his language perfectly, speak it with purity, with continual harmony and never allow the sense to be spoilt for the sake of the rhyme. "Anyone," he added, "who does not observe all these rules may produce one or two tragedies applauded in the theatre, but he will never be ranked among good writers; there are a very few good tragedies; some are idylls in well-written and well-rhymed dialogue; some are political arguments which send one to sleep, or repulsive amplifications; others are the dreams of an enthusiast, in a barbarous style, with broken dialogue, long apostrophes to the gods (because he does not know how to speak to men), false maxims and turgid commonplaces." Candide listened attentively to these remarks and thought highly of the speaker; and, as the marchioness had been careful to place him beside her, he leaned over to her ear and took the liberty of asking her who was the man who talked so well. "He is a man of letters," said the lady, "who does not play cards and is sometimes brought here to supper by the abbé; he has a perfect knowledge of tragedies and books and he has written a tragedy which was hissed and a book of which only one copy has ever been seen outside his bookseller's shop and that was one he gave me." "The great man!" said Candide. "He is another Pangloss." Then, turning to him, Candide said: "Sir, no doubt you think that all is for the best in the physical world and in the moral, and that nothing could be otherwise than as it is?" "Sir," replied the man of letters, "I do not think anything of the sort. I think everything goes awry with us, that nobody knows his rank or his office, nor what he is doing, nor what he ought to do, and that except at supper, which is quite gay and where there appears to be a certain amount of sociability, all the rest of their time is passed in senseless quarrels: Jansenists with Molinists, lawyers with churchmen, men of letters with men of letters, courtiers with courtiers, financiers with the people, wives with husbands, relatives with relatives—'tis an eternal war." Candide replied: "I have seen worse things; but a wise

man, who has since had the misfortune to be hanged, taught
me that it is all for the best; these are only the shadows in
a fair picture." "Your wise man who was hanged was poking
fun at the world," said Martin; "and your shadows are horrible
stains." "The stains are made by men," said Candide, "and they
cannot avoid them." "Then it is not their fault," said Martin.
Most of the gamblers, who had not the slightest understanding
of this kind of talk, were drinking; Martin argued with the man
of letters and Candide told the hostess some of his adventures.
After supper the marchioness took Candide into a side room and
made him sit down on a sofa. "Well!" said she, "so you are
still madly in love with Mademoiselle Cunegonde of Thunder-
ten-trꞏnckh?" "Yes, madame," replied Candide. The marchioness
replied with a tender smile: "You answer like a young man
from Westphalia. A Frenchman would have said: 'It is true that
I was in love with Mademoiselle Cunegonde, but when I see
you, madame, I fear that I should cease to love her.'" "Alas!
madame," said Candide, "I will answer as you wish." "Your
passion for her," said the marchioness, "began by picking up her
handkerchief; I want you to pick up my garter." "With all my
heart," said Candide; and he picked it up. "But I want you to
put it on again," said the lady; and Candide put it on again.
"You see," said the lady, "you are a foreigner; I sometimes make
my lovers in Paris languish for a fortnight, but I give myself
to you the very first night, because one must do the honors of
one's country to a young man from Westphalia." The fair lady,
having perceived two enormous diamonds on the young foreigner's hands, praised them so sincerely that they passed from Candide's fingers to the fingers of the marchioness. As Candide went
home with his abbé from Périgord, he felt some remorse
at having been unfaithful to Mademoiselle Cunegonde. The
abbé sympathized with his distress; he had only had a small
share in the fifty thousand francs Candide had lost at cards
and in the value of the two half-given, half-extorted, diamonds. His plan was to profit as much as he could from the
advantages which his acquaintance with Candide might procure
for him. He talked a lot about Cunegonde and Candide told
him that he should ask that fair one's forgiveness for his in-

fidelity when he saw her at Venice. The abbé from Périgord redoubled his politeness and civilities and took a tender interest in all Candide said, in all he did, and in all he wished to do. "Then, sir," said he, "you are to meet her at Venice?" "Yes, sir," said Candide, "without fail I must go and meet Mademoiselle Cunegonde there." Then, carried away by the pleasure of talking about the person he loved, he related, as he was accustomed to do, some of his adventures with that illustrious Westphalian lady. "I suppose," said the abbé, "that Mademoiselle Cunegonde has a great deal of wit and that she writes charming letters." "I have never received any from her," said Candide, "for you must know that when I was expelled from the castle because of my love for her, I could not write to her; soon afterwards I heard she was dead, then I found her again and then I lost her, and now I have sent an express messenger to her two thousand five hundred leagues from here and am expecting her reply." The abbé listened attentively and seemed rather meditative. He soon took leave of the two foreigners, after having embraced them tenderly. The next morning when Candide woke up he received a letter composed as follows: "Sir, my dearest lover, I have been ill for a week in this town; I have just heard that you are here. I should fly to your arms if I could stir. I heard that you had passed through Bordeaux; I left the faithful Cacambo and the old woman there and they will soon follow me. The governor of Buenos Ayres took everything, but I still have your heart. Come, your presence will restore me to life or will make me die of pleasure." This charming, this unhoped-for letter, filled Candide with inexpressible joy; and the illness of his dear Cunegonde overwhelmed him with grief. Torn between these two sentiments, he took his gold and his diamonds and drove with Martin to the hotel where Mademoiselle Cunegonde was staying. He entered trembling with emotion, his heart beat, his voice was broken; he wanted to open the bed-curtains and to have a light brought. "Do nothing of the sort," said the waiting-maid. "Light would be the death of her." And she quickly drew the curtains. "My dear Cunegonde," said Candide, weeping, "how do you feel? If you cannot see me, at least speak to me." "She cannot speak," said the maid-servant. The lady then extended a plump hand, which Candide watered with his tears and then filled with diamonds, leaving a bag full of gold in the arm-chair. In the midst of these transports a police-officer arrived, followed by the abbé from Périgord and a squad of policemen. "So these are the two suspicious foreigners?" he said. He had them arrested immediately and ordered his bravoes to hale them off to prison. "This is not the way they treat travelers in Eldorado," said Candide. "I am more of a Manichæan than ever," said Martin. "But, sir, where are you taking us?" said Candide. "To the deepest dungeon," said the police-officer. Martin, having recovered his coolness, decided that the lady who pretended to be Cunegonde was a cheat, that the abbé from Périgord was a cheat who had abused Candide's innocence with all possible speed, and that the police-officer was another cheat of whom they could easily be rid. Rather than expose himself to judicial proceedings, Candide, enlightened by this advice and impatient to see the real Cunegonde again, offered the police-officer three little diamonds worth about three thousand pounds each. "Ah! sir," said the man with the ivory stick, "if you had committed all imaginable crimes you would be the most honest man in the world. Three diamonds! Each worth three thousand pounds each! Sir! I would be killed for your sake, instead of taking you to prison. All strangers are arrested here, but trust to me. I have a brother at Dieppe in Normandy, I will take you there; and if you have any diamonds to give him he will take as much care of you as myself." "And why are all strangers arrested?" said Candide. The abbé from Périgord then spoke and said: "It is because a scoundrel from Atrebatum listened to imbecilities;[29] this alone made him commit a parricide, not like that of May 1610, but like that of December 1594, and like several others committed in other years and in other months by other scoundrels who had listened to imbecilities." The police-officer then explained what it was all about. "Ah! the monsters!" cried Candide. "What! Can such horrors be in a nation which dances and sings! Can I not leave at once this country where monkeys torment tigers? I have seen bears in my own country; Eldorado is the only place where I have seen men. In God's name, sir, take me to Venice, where I am to wait for Mademoiselle

Cunegonde." "I can only take you to Lower Normandy," said the officer. Immediately he took off their irons, said there had been a mistake, sent his men away, took Candide and Martin to Dieppe, and left them with his brother. There was a small Dutch vessel in the port. With the help of three other diamonds the Norman became the most obliging of men and embarked Candide and his servants in the ship which was about to sail for Portsmouth in England. It was not the road to Venice; but Candide felt as if he had escaped from Hell, and he had every intention of taking the road to Venice at the first opportunity.

XXIII

CANDIDE AND MARTIN REACH THE COAST OF ENGLAND; AND WHAT THEY SAW THERE

"Ah! Pangloss, Pangloss! Ah! Martin, Martin! Ah! my dear Cunegonde! What sort of a world is this?" said Candide on the Dutch ship. "Something very mad and very abominable," replied Martin. "You know England; are the people there as mad as they are in France?" "'Tis another sort of madness," said Martin. "You know these two nations are at war for a few acres of snow in Canada, and that they are spending more on this fine war than all Canada is worth, it is beyond my poor capacity to tell you whether there are more madmen in one country than in the other; all I know is that in general the people we are going to visit are extremely melancholic." Talking thus, they arrived at Portsmouth. There were multitudes of people on the shore, looking attentively at a rather fat man who was kneeling down with his eyes bandaged on the deck of one of the ships in the fleet; four soldiers placed opposite this man each shot three bullets into his brain in the calmest manner imaginable; and the whole assembly returned home with great satisfaction. "What is all this?" said Candide. "And what Demon exercises his power everywhere?" He asked who was the fat man who had just been killed so ceremoniously. "An admiral," was the reply. "And why kill the admiral?" "Because," he was told, "he did not kill enough people. He fought a battle with a

French admiral and it was held that the English admiral was
not close enough to him." "But," said Candide, "the French
admiral was just as far from the English admiral!" "That is in-
disputable," was the answer, "but in this country it is a good
thing to kill an admiral from time to time to encourage the
others." [30] Candide was so bewildered and so shocked by what he
saw and heard that he would not even set foot on shore, but
bargained with the Dutch captain (even if he had to pay him
as much as the Surinam robber) to take him at once to Venice.
The captain was ready in two days. They sailed down the
coast of France; and passed in sight of Lisbon, at which Candide shuddered. They entered the Straits and the Mediterranean
and at last reached Venice. "Praised be God!" said Candide,
embracing Martin, "here I shall see the fair Cunegonde again. I
trust Cacambo as I would myself. All is well, all goes well, all
goes as well as it possibly could."

XXIV

PAQUETTE AND FRIAR GIROFLÉE

As soon as he reached Venice, he inquired for Cacambo in all
the taverns, in all the cafés, and of all the ladies of pleasure;
and did not find him. Every day he sent out messengers to all
ships and boats; but there was no news of Cacambo. "What!"
said he to Martin, "I have had time to sail from Surinam to
Bordeaux, to go from Bordeaux to Paris, from Paris to Dieppe,
from Dieppe to Portsmouth, to sail along the coasts of Portugal
and Spain, to cross the Mediterranean, to spend several months
at Venice, and the fair Cunegonde has not yet arrived! Instead
of her I have met only a jade and an abbé from Périgord!
Cunegonde is certainly dead and the only thing left for me is
to die too. Ah! It would have been better to stay in the Paradise
of Eldorado instead of returning to this accursed Europe. How
right you are, my dear Martin! Everything is illusion and calam-
ity!" He fell into a black melancholy and took no part in the
opera *à la mode* or in the other carnival amusements: not a lady
caused him the least temptation. Martin said: "You are indeed
simple-minded to suppose that a half-breed valet with five or six

millions in his pocket will go and look for your mistress at the other end of the world and bring her to you at Venice. If he finds her, he will take her for himself; if he does not find her, he will take another. I advise you to forget your valet Cacambo and your mistress Cunegonde." Martin was not consoling. Candide's melancholy increased, and Martin persisted in proving to him that there was llttle virtue and small happiness in the world except perhaps in Eldorado where nobody could go. While arguing about this important subject and waiting for Cunegonde, Candide noticed a young Theatine monk in the Piazza San Marco, with a girl on his arm. The Theatine looked fresh, plump and vigorous; his eyes were bright, his air assured, his countenance firm, and his step lofty. The girl was very pretty and was singing; she gazed amorously at her Theatine and every now and then pinched his fat cheeks. "At least you will admit," said Candide to Martin, "that those people are happy. Hitherto I have only found unfortunates in the whole habitable earth, except in Eldorado; but I wager that this girl and the Theatine are very happy creatures." "I wager they are not," said Martin. "We have only to ask them to dinner," said Candide, "and you will see whether I am wrong." He immediately accosted them, paid his respects to them, and invited them to come to his hotel to eat macaroni, Lombardy partridges, and caviar, and to drink Montepulciano, Lacryma Christi, Cyprus and Samos wine. The young lady blushed, the Theatine accepted the invitation, and the girl followed, looking at Candide with surprise and confusion in her eyes which were filled with a few tears. Scarcely had they entered Candide's room when she said: "What! Monsieur Candide does not recognize Paquette!" At these words Candide, who had not looked at her very closely because he was occupied entirely by Cunegonde, said to her: "Alas! my poor child, so it was you who put Dr. Pangloss into the fine state I saw him in?" "Alas! sir, it was indeed," said Paquette. "I see you have heard all about it. I have heard of the terrible misfortunes which happened to Her Ladyship the Baroness's whole family and to the fair Cunegonde. I swear to you that my fate has been just as sad. I was very innocent when you knew me. A Franciscan friar who was my confessor easily seduced me. The results were dreadful; I was obliged to leave the castle shortly after His Lordship the Baron expelled you by kicking you hard and frequently in the backside. If a famous doctor had not taken pity on me I should have died. For some time I was the doctor's mistress from gratitude to him. His wife, who was madly jealous, beat me every day relentlessly; she was a fury. The doctor was the ugliest of men, and I was the most unhappy of all living creatures at being continually beaten on account of a man I did not love. You know, sir, how dangerous it is for a shrewish woman to be the wife of a doctor. One day, exasperated by his wife's behavior, he gave her some medicine for a little cold and it was so efficacious that she died two hours afterwards in horrible convulsions. The lady's relatives brought a criminal prosecution against the husband; he fled and I was put in prison. My innocence would not have saved me if I had not been rather pretty. The judge set me free on condition that he take the doctor's place. I was soon supplanted by a rival, expelled without a penny, and obliged to continue the abominable occupation which to you men seems so amusing and which to us is nothing but an abyss of misery. I came to Venice to practice this profession. Ah! sir, if you could imagine what it is to be forced to caress impartially an old tradesman, a lawyer, a monk, a gondolier, an abbé; to be exposed to every insult and outrage; to be reduced often to borrow a petticoat in order to go and find some disgusting man who will lift it; to be robbed by one of what one has earned with another, to be despoiled by the police, and contemplate for the future nothing but a dreadful old age, a hospital and a dunghill, you would conclude that I am one of the most unfortunate creatures in the world." Paquette opened her heart in this way to Candide in a side room, in the presence of Martin, who said to Candide: "You see, I have already won half my wager." Friar Giroflée had remained in the dining room, drinking a glass while he waited for dinner. "But," said Candide to Paquette, "when I met you, you looked so gay, so happy; you were singing, you were caressing the Theatine so naturally; you seemed to me to be as happy as you are unfortunate." "Ah! sir," replied Paquette, "that is one more misery of our profession. Yesterday I was robbed and beaten by an officer, and today I must seem to be in a good humor to please a monk." Candide wanted to hear no more; he admitted that Martin was right. They sat down to table with Paquette and the Theatine. The meal was quite amusing and towards the end they were talking with some confidence. "Father," said Candide to the monk, "you seem to me to enjoy a fate which everybody should envy; the flower of health shines on your cheek, your face is radiant with happiness; you have a very pretty girl for your recreation and you appear to be very well pleased with your state of life as a Theatine." "Faith, sir," said Friar Giroflée, "I wish all the Theatines were at the bottom of the sea. A hundred times I have been tempted to set fire to the monastery and to go and be a Turk. My parents forced me at the age of fifteen to put on this detestable robe, in order that more money might be left to my cursed elder brother, whom God confound! Jealousy, discord, fury, inhabit the monastery. It is true, I have preached a few bad sermons which bring me in a little money, half of which is stolen from me by the prior; the remainder I spend on girls; but when I go back to the monastery in the evening I feel ready to smash my head against the dormitory walls, and all my colleagues are in the same state." Martin turned to Candide and said with his usual calm: "Well, have I not won the whole wager?" Candide gave two thousand piastres to Paquette and a thousand to Friar Giroflée. "I warrant," said he, "that they will be happy with that." "I don't believe it in the very least," said Martin. "Perhaps you will make them still more unhappy with those piastres." "That may be," said Candide, "but I am consoled by one thing; I see that we often meet people we thought we should never meet again; it may very well be that as I met my red sheep and Paquette, I may also meet Cunegonde again." "I hope," said Martin, "that she will one day make you happy; but I doubt it very much." "You are very hard," said Candide. "That's because I have lived," said Martin. "But look at these gondoliers," said Candide, "they sing all day long." "You do not see them at home, with their wives and their brats of children," said Martin. "The Doge has his troubles, the gondoliers have theirs. True, looking at it all round, a gondolier's lot is preferable to a Doge's; but I think the difference so slight that it is not worth examining." "They talk," said Candide, "about Senator Pococurante who lives in that handsome palace on the Brenta and who is hospitable to foreigners. He is supposed to be a man who has never known a grief." "I should like to meet so rare a specimen," said Martin. Candide immediately sent a request to Lord Pococurante for permission to wait upon him the next day.

XXV

VISIT TO THE NOBLE VENETIAN, LORD POCOCURANTE [31]

Candide and Martin took a gondola and rowed to the noble Pococurante's palace. The gardens were extensive and ornamented with fine marble statues; the architecture of the palace was handsome. The master of this establishment, a very wealthy man of about sixty, received the two visitors very politely but with very little cordiality, which disconcerted Candide but did not displease Martin. Two pretty and neatly dressed girls served them with very frothy chocolate. Candide could not refrain from praising their beauty, their grace and their skill. "They are quite good creatures," said Senator Pococurante, "and I sometimes make them sleep in my bed, for I am very tired of the ladies of the town, with their coquetries, their jealousies, their quarrels, their humors, their meanness, their pride, their folly, and the sonnets one must write or have written for them; but, after all, I am getting very tired of these two girls." After lunch, Candide was walking in a long gallery and was surprised by the beauty of the pictures. He asked what master had painted the two first. "They are by Raphael," said the Senator. "Some years ago I bought them at a very high price out of mere vanity; I am told they are the finest in Italy, but they give me no pleasure; the color has gone very dark, the faces are not sufficiently rounded and do not stand out enough; the draperies have not the least resemblance to material; in short, whatever they may say, I do not consider them a true imitation of nature. I shall only like a picture when it makes me think it is nature itself; and there are none of that kind. I have a great many pictures, but I never look at them now." While they waited for dinner, Pococurante gave them a concert. Candide thought the music delicious. "This noise," said Pococurante, "is amusing for half an hour; but if it lasts any longer, it wearies everybody although nobody dares to say so. Music nowadays is merely the art of executing difficulties and in the end that which is only difficult ceases to please. Perhaps I should like the opera more, if they had not made it a monster which revolts me. Those who please may go to see bad tragedies set to music, where the scenes are only composed to bring in clumsily two or three ridiculous songs which show off an actress's voice; those who will or can, may swoon with pleasure when they see a eunuch humming the part of Cæsar and Cato as he awkwardly treads the boards; for my part, I long ago abandoned such trivialities, which nowadays are the glory of Italy and for which monarchs pay so dearly." Candide demurred a little, but discreetly. Martin entirely agreed with the Senator. They sat down to table and after an excellent dinner went into the library. Candide saw a magnificently bound Homer and complimented the Illustrissimo on his good taste. "That is the book," said he, "which so much delighted the great Pangloss, the greatest philosopher of Germany." "It does not delight me," said Pococurante coldly; "formerly I was made to believe that I took pleasure in reading it; but this continual repetition of battles which are all alike, these gods who are perpetually active and achieve nothing decisive, this Helen who is the cause of the war and yet scarcely an actor in the piece, this Troy which is always besieged and never taken—all bore me extremely. I have sometimes asked learned men if they were as bored as I am by reading it; all who were sincere confessed that the book fell from their hands, but it must be in every library, as a monument of antiquity, and like those rusty coins which cannot be put into circulation." "Your Excellency has a different opinion of Virgil?" said Candide. "I admit," said Pococurante, "that the second, fourth and sixth books of his Æneid are excellent, but as for his pious Æneas and the strong Cloanthes and the faithful Achates and the little Ascanius and the imbecile king Latinus and the middle-class Amata and the insipid Lavinia, I think there could be nothing more frigid and disagreeable. I prefer Tasso and the childish tales of Ariosto." "May I venture to ask you, sir," said Candide, "if you do not take great pleasure in reading Horace?" "He has two maxims," said Pococurante, "which might be useful to a man of the world, and which, being compressed in energetic verses, are more easily impressed upon the memory; but I care very little for his Journey to Brundisium, and his description of a Bad Dinner, and the street brawlers' quarrel between—what is his name?—Rupilius, whose words, he says, were full of pus, and another person whose words were all vinegar. I was extremely disgusted with his gross verses against old women and witches; and I cannot see there is any merit in his telling his friend Mæcenas that, if he is placed by him among the lyric poets, he will strike the stars with his lofty brow. Fools admire everything in a celebrated author. I only read to please myself, and I only like what suits me." Candide, who had been taught never to judge anything for himself, was greatly surprised by what he heard; and Martin thought Pococurante's way of thinking quite reasonable. "Oh! There is a Cicero," said Candide. "I suppose you are never tired of reading that great man?" "I never read him," replied the Venetian. "What do I care that he pleaded for Rabirius or Cluentius. I have enough cases to judge myself; I could better have endured his philosophical works; but when I saw that he doubted everything, I concluded I knew as much as he and did not need anybody else in order to be ignorant." "Ah! There are eighty volumes of the Proceedings of an Academy of Sciences," exclaimed Martin, "there might be something good in them." "There would be," said Pococurante, "if a single one of the authors of all that rubbish had invented even the art of making pins; but in all those books there is nothing but vain systems and not a single useful thing." "What a lot of plays I see there," said Candide. "Italian, Spanish, and French!" "Yes," said the Senator, "there are three thousand and not three dozen good ones. As for those collections of sermons, which all together are not worth a page of Seneca, and all those large volumes of theology, you may well suppose that they are never opened by me or anybody else." Martin noticed some shelves filled with English books. "I should think," he said, "that a republican would enjoy most of those works written with so much freedom." "Yes," replied Pococurante, "it is good to write as we

think; it is the privilege of man. In all Italy, we write only
what we do not think; those who inhabit the country of the
Cæsars and the Antonines dare not have an idea without the
permission of a Dominican monk. I should applaud the liberty
which inspires Englishmen of genius if passion and party spirit
did not corrupt everything estimable in that precious liberty."
Candide, in noticing a Milton, asked him if he did not consider
that author to be a very great man. "Who?" said Pococurante.
"That barbarian who wrote a long commentary on the first chapter of Genesis in ten books of harsh verses? That gross imitator
of the Greeks, who disfigures the Creation, and who, while
Moses represents the Eternal Being as producing the world by
speech, makes the Messiah take a large compass from the heavenly cupboard in order to trace out his work? Should I esteem
the man who spoiled Tasso's hell and devil; who disguises Luci-
fer sometimes as a toad, sometimes as a pigmy; who makes him
repeat the same things a hundred times; makes him argue about
theology; and imitates seriously Ariosto's comical invention of
firearms by making the devils fire a cannon in Heaven? Neither
I nor anyone else in Italy could enjoy such wretched extravagances. The marriage of Sin and Death and the snakes which
sin brings forth nauseate any man of delicate taste, and his long
description of a hospital would only please a grave-digger. This
obscure, bizarre and disgusting poem was despised at its birth; I
treat it today as it was treated by its contemporaries in its own
country. But then I say what I think, and care very little
whether others think as I do." Candide was distressed by these
remarks; he respected Homer and rather liked Milton. "Alas?"
he whispered to Martin, "I am afraid this man would have a
sovereign contempt for our German poets." "There wouldn't be
much harm in that," said Martin. "Oh! What a superior man!"
said Candide under his breath. "What a great genius this Pococurante is! Nothing can please him." After they had thus reviewed all his books they went down into the garden. Candide
praised all its beauties. "I have never met anything more taste-
less," said the owner. "We have nothing but trifles; but tomorrow I shall begin to plant a garden on a more noble plan."
When the two visitors had taken farewell of his Excellency.

Candide said to Martin: "Now you will admit that he is the happiest of men, for he is superior to everything he possesses." "Do you not see," said Martin, "that he is disgusted with everything he possesses? Plato said long ago that the best stomachs are not those which refuse all food." "But," said Candide, "is there not pleasure in criticising, in finding faults where other men think they see beauty?" "That is to say," answered Martin, "that there is pleasure in not being pleased." "Oh! Well," said Candide, "then there is no one happy except me—when I see Mademoiselle Cunegonde again." "It is always good to hope," said Martin. However, the days and weeks went by; Cacambo did not return and Candide was so much plunged in grief that he did not even notice that Paquette and Friar Giroflée had not once come to thank him.

XXVI

HOW CANDIDE AND MARTIN SUPPED WITH SIX STRANGERS AND WHO THEY WERE

One evening when Candide and Martin were going to sit down to table with the strangers who lodged in the same hotel, a man with a face the color of soot came up to him from behind and, taking him by the arm, said: "Get ready to come with us, and do not fail." He turned round and saw Cacambo. Only the sight of Cunegonde could have surprised and pleased him more. He was almost wild with joy. He embraced his dear friend. "Cunegonde is here, of course? Where is she? Take me to her, let me die of joy with her." "Cunegonde is not here," said Cacambo. "She is in Constantinople." "Heavens! In Constantinople! But were she in China, I would fly to her; let us start at once." "We will start after supper," replied Cacambo. "I cannot tell you any more; I am a slave, and my master is waiting for me; I must go and serve him at table! Do not say anything; eat your supper, and be in readiness." Candide, torn between joy and grief, charmed to see his faithful agent again, amazed to see him a slave, filled with the idea of seeing his mistress again, with turmoil in his heart, agitation in his mind, sat down to table with Martin (who met every strange occurrence with the same

calmness), and with six strangers, who had come to spend the
Carnival at Venice. Cacambo, who acted as butler to one of the
strangers, bent down to his master's head towards the end of
the meal and said: "Sire, your Majesty can leave when you wish,
the ship is ready." After saying this, Cacambo withdrew. The
guests looked at each other with surprise without saying a word,
when another servant came up to his master and said: "Sire,
your Majesty's post-chaise is at Padua, and the boat is ready."
The master made a sign and the servant departed. Once more
all the guests looked at each other, and the general surprise
doubled. A third servant went up to the third stranger and said:
"Sire, believe me, your Majesty cannot remain here any longer;
I will prepare everything." And he immediately disappeared.
Candide and Martin had no doubt that this was a Carnival
masquerade. A fourth servant said to the fourth master: "Your
Majesty can leave when you wish." And he went out like the
others. The fifth servant spoke similarly to the fifth master. But
the sixth servant spoke differently to the sixth stranger who was
next to Candide, and said: "Faith, sire, they will not give your
Majesty any more credit nor me either, and we may very likely
be jailed to-night, both of us; I am going to look to my own affairs, good-bye." When the servants had all gone, the six strangers, Candide and Martin remained in profound silence. At last
it was broken by Candide. "Gentlemen," said he, "this is a curious jest. How is it you are all kings? I confess that neither Martin nor I are kings." Cacambo's master then gravely spoke and
said in Italian: "I am not jesting, my name is Achmet III. For
several years I was Sultan; I dethroned my brother; my nephew
dethroned me; they cut off the heads of my viziers; I am ending
my days in the old seraglio; my nephew, Sultan Mahmoud,
sometimes allows me to travel for my health, and I have come
to spend the Carnival at Venice." A young man who sat next to
Achmet spoke after him and said: "My name is Ivan; I was
Emperor of all the Russias; I was dethroned in my cradle; my
father and mother were imprisoned and I was brought up in
prison; I sometimes have permission to travel, accompanied by
those who guard me, and I have come to spend the Carnival at
Venice." The third said: "I am Charles Edward, King of Eng-

land; my father gave up his rights to the throne to me and I fought a war to assert them; the hearts of eight hundred of my adherents were torn out and dashed in their faces. I have been in prison; I am going to Rome to visit the King, my father, who is dethroned like my grandfather and me; and I have come to spend the Carnival at Venice." The fourth then spoke and said: "I am the King of Poland; the chance of war deprived me of my hereditary states; my father endured the same reverse of fortune; I am resigned to Providence like the Sultan Achmet, the Emperor Ivan and King Charles Edward, to whom God grant long life; and I have come to spend the Carnival at Venice." The fifth said: "I also am the King of Poland; I have lost my kingdom twice; but Providence has given me another state in which I have been able to do more good than all the kings of the Sarmatians together have been ever able to do on the banks of the Vistula; I also am resigned to Providence and I have come to spend the Carnival at Venice." It was now for the sixth monarch to speak. "Gentlemen," said he, "I am not so eminent as you; but I have been a king like anyone else. I am Theodore; I was elected King of Corsica; I have been called Your Majesty and now I am barely called Sir. I have coined money and do not own a farthing; I have had two Secretaries of State and now have scarcely a valet; I have occupied a throne and for a long time lay on straw in a London prison. I am much afraid I shall be treated in the same way here, although I have come, like your Majesties, to spend the Carnival at Venice." The five other kings listened to this speech with a noble compassion. Each of them gave King Theodore twenty sequins to buy clothes and shirts; Candide presented him with a diamond worth two thousand sequins. "Who is this man," said the five kings, "who is able to give a hundred times as much as any of us, and who gives it?" As they were leaving the table, there came to the same hotel four serene highnesses who had also lost their states in the chance of war, and who had come to spend the rest of the Carnival at Venice; but Candide did not even notice these newcomers. He could think of nothing but of going to Constantinople to find his dear Cunegonde.

XXVII

CANDIDE'S VOYAGE TO CONSTANTINOPLE

The faithful Cacambo had already spoken to the Turkish captain who was to take Sultan Achmet back to Constantinople and had obtained permission for Candide and Martin to come on board. They both entered this ship after having prostrated themselves before his miserable Highness. On the way, Candide said to Martin: "So we have just supped with six dethroned kings! And among those six kings there was one to whom I gave charity. Perhaps there are many other princes still more unfortunate. Now, I have only lost a hundred sheep and I am hastening to Cunegonde's arms. My dear Martin, once more, Pangloss was right, all is well." "I hope so," said Martin. "But," said Candide, "this is a very singular experience we have just had at Venice. Nobody has ever seen or heard of six dethroned kings supping together in a tavern." " 'Tis no more extraordinary," said Martin, "than most of the things which have happened to us. It is very common for kings to be dethroned; and as to the honor we have had of supping with them, 'tis a trifle not deserving our attention." Scarcely had Candide entered the ship when he threw his arms round the neck of his old valet, of his friend Cacambo. "Well!" said he, "what is Cunegonde doing? Is she still a marvel of beauty? Does she still love me? How is she? Of course you have bought her a palace in Constantinople?" "My dear master," replied Cacambo, "Cunegonde is washing dishes on the banks of Propontis for a prince who possesses very few dishes; she is a slave in the house of a former sovereign named Ragotsky, who receives in his refuge three crowns a day from the Grand Turk; but what is even sadder is that she has lost her beauty and has become horribly ugly." "Ah! beautiful or ugly," said Candide, "I am a man of honor and my duty is to love her always. But how can she be reduced to so abject a condition with the five or six millions you carried off?" "Ah!" said Cacambo, "did I not have to give two millions to Señor Don Fernando d'Ibaraa y Figueora y Mascarenes y Lampourdos y Souza, Governor of Buenos Ayres, for permission to bring away Mademoiselle Cunegonde? And did not a pirate bravely strip us of all the rest? And did not this pirate take us to Cape Matapan, to Milo, to Nicaria, to Samos, to Petra, to the Dardanelles, to Marmora, to Scutari? Cunegonde and the old woman are servants to the prince I mentioned, and I am slave to the dethroned Sultan." "What a chain of terrible calamities!" said Candide. "But after all, I still have a few diamonds; I shall easily deliver Cunegonde. What a pity she has become so ugly." Then, turning to Martin, he said: "Who do you think is the most to be pitied, the Sultan Achmet, the Emperor Ivan, King Charles Edward, or me?" "I do not know at all," said Martin. "I should have to be in your hearts to know." "Ah!" said Candide, "if Pangloss were here he would know and would tell us." "I do not know," said Martin, "what scales your Pangloss would use to weigh the misfortunes of men and to estimate their sufferings. All I presume is that there are millions of men on the earth a hundred times more to be pitied than King Charles Edward, the Emperor Ivan and the Sultan Achmet." "That may very well be," said Candide. In a few days they reached the Black Sea channel. Candide began by paying a high ransom for Cacambo and, without wasting time, he went on board a galley with his companions bound for the shores of Propontis, in order to find Cunegonde however ugly she might be. Among the galley slaves were two convicts who rowed very badly and from time to time the Levantine captain applied several strokes of a bull's pizzle to their naked shoulders. From a natural feeling of pity Candide watched them more attentively than the other galley slaves and went up to them. Some features of their disfigured faces appeared to him to have some resemblance to Pangloss and the wretched Jesuit, the Baron, Mademoiselle Cunegonde's brother. This idea disturbed and saddened him. He looked at them still more carefully. "Truly," said he to Cacambo, "if I had not seen Dr. Pangloss hanged, and if I had not been so unfortunate as to kill the Baron, I should think they were rowing in this galley." At the words Baron and Pangloss, the two convicts gave a loud cry, stopped on their seats and dropped their oars. The Levantine captain ran up to them and the lashes with the bull's pizzle were redoubled. "Stop! Stop, sir!" cried Candide. "I will give you as much money as you want." "What!

Is it Candide?" said one of the convicts. "What! Is it Candide?" said the other. "Is it a dream?" said Candide. "Am I awake? Am I in this galley? Is that my Lord the Baron whom I killed? Is that Dr. Pangloss whom I saw hanged?" "It is, it is," they replied. "What! Is that the great philosopher?" said Martin. "Ah! sir," said Candide to the Levantine captain, "how much money do you want for My Lord Thunder-ten-tronckh, one of the first Barons of the empire, and for Dr. Pangloss, the most profound metaphysician of Germany?" "Dog of a Christian," replied the Levantine captain, "since these two dogs of Christian convicts are Barons and metaphysicians, which no doubt is a high rank in their country, you shall pay me fifty thousand sequins." "You shall have them, sir. Row back to Constantinople like lightning and you shall be paid at once. But, no, take me to Mademoiselle Cunegonde." The captain, at Candide's first offer had already turned the bow towards the town, and rowed there more swiftly than a bird cleaves the air. Candide embraced the Baron and Pangloss a hundred times. "How was it I did not kill you, my dear Baron? And, my dear Pangloss, how do you happen to be alive after having been hanged? And why are you both in a Turkish galley?" "Is it really true that my dear sister is in this country?" said the Baron. "Yes," replied Cacambo. "So once more I see my dear Candide!" cried Pangloss. Candide introduced Martin and Cacambo. They all embraced and all talked at the same time. The galley flew; already they were in the harbor. They sent for a Jew, and Candide sold him for fifty thousand sequins a diamond worth a hundred thousand, for which he swore by Abraham he could not give any more. The ransom of the Baron and Pangloss was immediately paid. Pangloss threw himself at the feet of his liberator and bathed them with tears; the other thanked him with a nod and promised to repay the money at the first opportunity. "But is it possible that my sister is in Turkey?" said he. "Nothing is so possible," replied Cacambo, "since she washes the dishes of a prince of Transylvania." They immediately sent for two Jews; Candide sold some more diamonds; and they all set out in another galley to rescue Cunegonde.

XXVIII

WHAT HAPPENED TO CANDIDE, TO CUNEGONDE, TO PANGLOSS, TO MARTIN, ETC.

"Pardon once more," said Candide to the Baron, "pardon me, reverend father, for having thrust my sword through your body." "Let us say no more about it," said the Baron. "I admit I was a little too sharp; but since you wish to know how it was you saw me in a galley, I must tell you that after my wound was healed by the brother apothecary of the college, I was attacked and carried off by a Spanish raiding party; I was imprisoned in Buenos Ayres at the time when my sister had just left. I asked to return to the Vicar-General in Rome. I was ordered to Constantinople to act as almoner to the Ambassador of France. A week after I had taken up my office I met towards evening a very handsome young page of the Sultan. It was very hot; the young man wished to bathe; I took the opportunity to bathe also. I did not know that it was a most serious crime for a Christian to be found naked with a young Mahometan. A cadi sentenced me to a hundred strokes on the soles of my feet and condemned me to the galley. I do not think a more horrible injustice has ever been committed. But I should very much like to know why my sister is in the kitchen of a Transylvanian sovereign living in exile among the Turks." "But, my dear Pangloss," said Candide, "how does it happen that I see you once more?" "It is true," said Pangloss, "that you saw me hanged; and in the natural course of events I should have been burned. But you remember, it poured with rain when they were going to roast me; the storm was so violent that they despaired of lighting the fire; I was hanged because they could do nothing better; a surgeon bought my body, carried me home and dissected me. He first made a crucial incision in me from the navel to the collar-bone. Nobody could have been worse hanged than I was. The executioner of the holy Inquisition, who was a sub-deacon, was marvellously skilful in burning people, but he was not used to hanging them; the rope was wet and did not slide easily and it was knotted; in short, I still breathed. The crucial incision caused me to utter so loud a scream that the surgeon fell over backwards and, thinking he was dissecting the devil, fled away in terror and fell down the staircase in his flight. His wife ran in from another room at the noise; she saw me stretched out on the table with my crucial incision; she was still more frightened than her husband, fled, and fell on top of him. When they had recovered a little, I heard the surgeon's wife say to the surgeon: 'My dear, what were you thinking of, to dissect a heretic? Don't you know the devil always possesses them? I will go and get a priest at once to exorcise him.' At this I shuddered and collected the little strength I had left to shout: 'Have pity on me!' At last the Portuguese barber grew bolder; he sewed up my skin; his wife even took care of me, and at the end of a fortnight I was able to walk again. The barber found me a situation and made me lackey to a Knight of Malta who was going to Venice; but, as my master had no money to pay me wages, I entered the service of a Venetian merchant and followed him to Constantinople. One day I took it into my head to enter a mosque; there was nobody there except an old Imam and a very pretty young devotee who was reciting her prayers; her breasts were entirely uncovered; between them she wore a bunch of tulips, roses, anemones, ranunculus, hyacinths and auriculas; she dropped her bunch of flowers; I picked it up and returned it to her with a most respectful alacrity. I was so long putting them back that the Imam grew angry and, seeing I was a Christian, called for help. I was taken to the cadi, who sentenced me to receive a hundred strokes on the soles of my feet and sent me to the galleys. I was chained on the same seat and in the same galley as My Lord the Baron. In this galley there were four young men from Marseilles, five Neapolitan priests and two monks from Corfu, who assured us that similar accidents occurred every day. His Lordship the Baron claimed that he had suffered a greater injustice than I; and I claimed that it was much more permissible to replace a bunch of flowers between a woman's breasts than to be naked with one of the Sultan's pages. We argued continually, and every day received twenty strokes of the bull's pizzle, when the chain of events of this universe led you to our galley and you ransomed us." "Well! my dear Pangloss," said Candide, "when you were hanged, dissected, stunned with blows and made to row in the galleys, did you always think that everything was for the best in this world?" "I am still of my first opinion," replied Pangloss, "for after all I am a philosopher; and it would be unbecoming for me to recant, since Leibnitz could not be in the wrong and pre-established harmony is the finest thing imaginable like the plenum and subtle matter."

XXIX

HOW CANDIDE FOUND CUNEGONDE AND THE OLD WOMAN AGAIN

While Candide, the Baron, Pangloss, Martin and Cacambo were relating their adventures, reasoning upon contingent or non-contingent events of the universe, arguing about effects and causes, moral and physical evil, free-will and necessity, and the consolations to be found in the Turkish galleys, they came to the house of the Transylvanian prince on the shores of Propontis. The first objects which met their sight were Cunegonde and the old woman hanging out towels to dry on the line. At this sight the Baron grew pale. Candide, that tender lover, seeing his fair Cunegonde sunburned, blear-eyed, flat-breasted, with wrinkles round her eyes and red, chapped arms, recoiled three paces in horror, and then advanced from mere politeness. She embraced Candide and her brother. They embraced the old woman; Candide bought them both. In the neighborhood was a little farm; the old woman suggested that Candide should buy it, until some better fate befell the group. Cunegonde did not know that she had become ugly, for nobody had told her so; she reminded Candide of his promises in so peremptory a tone that the good Candide dared not refuse her. He therefore informed the Baron that he was about to marry his sister. "Never," said the Baron, "will I endure such baseness on her part and such insolence on yours; nobody shall ever reproach me with this infamy; my sister's children could never enter the noble assemblies of Germany. No, my sister shall never marry anyone but a Baron of the Empire." Cunegonde threw herself at his feet and bathed them in tears; but he was inflexible. "Madman," said Candide, "I rescued you from the galleys, I paid your ransom and your sister's; she was washing dishes here, she is ugly, I am so kind as to make her my wife, and you pretend to oppose me! I should kill you again if I listened to my anger." "You may kill me again," said the Baron, "but you shall never marry my sister while I am alive."

XXX

CONCLUSION

At the bottom of his heart Candide had not the least wish to marry Cunegonde. But the Baron's extreme impertinence determined him to complete the marriage, and Cunegonde urged it so warmly that he could not retract. He consulted Pangloss, Martin and the faithful Cacambo. Pangloss wrote an excellent memorandum by which he proved that the Baron had no rights over his sister and that by all the laws of the empire she could make a left-handed marriage with Candide. Martin advised that the Baron should be thrown into the sea; Cacambo decided that he should be returned to the Levantine captain and sent back to the galleys, after which he would be returned by the first ship to the Vicar-General at Rome. This was thought to be very good advice; the old woman approved it; they said nothing to the sister; the plan was carried out with the aid of a little money and they had the pleasure of duping a Jesuit and punishing the pride of a German Baron.

It would be natural to suppose that when, after so many disasters, Candide was married to his mistress, and living with the philosopher Pangloss, the philosopher Martin, the prudent Cacambo and the old woman, having brought back so many diamonds from the country of the ancient Incas, he would lead the most pleasant life imaginable. But he was so cheated by the Jews that he had nothing left but his little farm; his wife, growing uglier every day, became shrewish and unendurable; the old woman was ailing and even more bad-tempered than Cunegonde. Cacambo, who worked in the garden and then went to Constantinople to sell vegetables, was overworked and cursed his fate. Pangloss was in despair because he did not shine in some German university. As for Martin, he was firmly convinced that people are equally uncomfortable everywhere; he accepted things patiently

Candide, Martin and Pangloss sometimes argued about metaphysics and morals. From the windows of the farm they often watched the ships going by, filled with effendis, pashas, and cadis, who were being exiled to Lemnos, to Mitylene and Erzerum. They saw other cadis, other pashas and other effendis coming back to take the place of the exiles and to be exiled in their turn. They saw the neatly impaled heads which were taken to the Sublime Porte. These sights redoubled their discussions; and when they were not arguing, the boredom was so excessive that one day the old woman dared to say to them: "I should like to know which is worse, to be raped a hundred times by Negro pirates, to have a buttock cut off, to run the gauntlet among the Bulgarians, to be whipped and flogged in an *auto-da-fé*, to be dissected, to row in a galley, in short, to endure all the miseries through which we have passed, or to remain here doing nothing?" " 'Tis a great question," said Candide.

These remarks led to new reflections, and Martin especially concluded that man was born to live in the convulsions of distress or in the lethargy of boredom. Candide did not agree, but he asserted nothing. Pangloss confessed that he had always suffered horribly; but, having once maintained that everything was for the best, he had continued to maintain it without believing it.

One thing confirmed Martin in his detestable principles, made Candide hesitate more than ever, and embarrassed Pangloss. And it was this. One day there came to their farm Paquette and Friar Giroflée, who were in the most extreme misery; they had soon wasted their three thousand piastres, had left each other, made up, quarrelled again, been put in prison, escaped, and finally Friar Giroflée had turned Turk. Paquette continued her occupation everywhere and now earned nothing by it. "I foresaw," said Martin to Candide, "that your gifts would soon be wasted and would only make them the more miserable. You and Cacambo were once bloated with millions of piastres and you are no happier than Friar Giroflée and Paquette." "Ah! Ha!" said Pangloss to Paquette, "so Heaven brings you back to us, my dear child? Do you know that you cost me the end of my nose, an eye and an ear! What a plight you are

. in! Ah! What a world this is!" This new occurrence caused them to philosophize more than ever.

In the neighborhood there lived a very famous Dervish, who was supposed to be the best philosopher in Turkey; they went to consult him; Pangloss was the spokesman and said: "Master, we have come to beg you to tell us why so strange an animal as man was ever created." "What has it to do with you?" said the Dervish. "Is it your business?" "But, reverend father," said Candide, "there is a horrible amount of evil in the world." "What does it matter," said the Dervish, "whether there is evil or good? When his highness sends a ship to Egypt, does he worry about the comfort or discomfort of the rats in the ship?" "Then what should we do?" said Pangloss. "Hold your tongue," said the Dervish. "I flattered myself," said Pangloss, "that I should discuss with you effects and causes, this best of all possible worlds, the origin of evil, the nature of the soul and pre-established harmony." At these words the Dervish slammed the door in their faces.

During this conversation the news went round that at Constantinople two viziers and the mufti had been strangled and several of their friends impaled. This catastrophe made a prodigious noise everywhere for several hours. As Pangloss, Candide and Martin were returning to their little farm, they came upon an old man who was taking the air under a bower of orange-trees at his door. Pangloss, who was as curious as he was argumentative, asked him what was the name of the mufti who had just been strangled. "I do not know," replied the old man. "I have never known the name of any mufti or of any vizier. I am entirely ignorant of the occurrence you mention; I presume that in general those who meddle with public affairs sometimes perish miserably and that they deserve it; but I never inquire what is going on in Constantinople; I content myself with sending there for sale the produce of the garden I cultivate." Having spoken thus, he took the strangers into his house. His two daughters and his two sons presented them with several kinds of sherbet which they made themselves, caymac flavored with candied citron peel, oranges, lemons, limes, pineapples, dates, pistachios and Mocha coffee which had not been mixed with the bad coffee of Batavia and the Isles. After which this good Mussulman's two daughters perfumed the beards of Candide, Pangloss and Martin. "You must have a vast and magnificent estate?" said Candide to the Turk. "I have only twenty acres," replied the Turk. "I cultivate them with my children; and work keeps at bay three great evils: boredom, vice and need."

As Candide returned to his farm he reflected deeply on the Turk's remarks. He said to Pangloss and Martin: "That good old man seems to me to have chosen an existence preferable by far to that of the six kings with whom we had the honor to sup." "Exalted rank," said Pangloss, "is very dangerous, according to the testimony of all philosophers; for Eglon, King of the Moabites, was murdered by Ehud; Absalom was hanged by the hair and pierced by three darts; King Nadab, son of Jeroboam, was killed by Baasha; King Elah by Zimri; Ahaziah by Jehu; Athaliah by Jehoiada; the Kings Jehoiakim, Jeconiah and Zedekiah were made slaves. You know in what manner died Crœsus, Astyages, Darius, Denys of Syracuse, Pyrrhus, Perseus, Hannibal, Jugurtha, Ariovistus, Cæsar, Pompey, Nero, Otho, Vitellius, Domitian, Richard II of England, Edward II, Henry VI, Richard III, Mary Stuart, Charles I, the three Henrys of France, the Emperor Henry IV. You know . . ." "I also know," said Candide, "that we should cultivate our garden." "You are right," said Pangloss, "for, when man was placed in the Garden of Eden, he was placed there *ut operaretur eum* to dress it and to keep it; which proves that man was not born for idleness." "Let us work without theorizing," said Martin; " 'tis the only way to make life endurable."

The whole small fraternity entered into this praiseworthy plan, and each started to make use of his talents. The little farm yielded well. Cunegonde was indeed very ugly, but she became an excellent pastry-cook; Paquette embroidered; the old woman took care of the linen. Even Friar Giroflée performed some service; he was a very good carpenter and even became a man of honor; and Pangloss sometimes said to Candide: "All events are linked up in this best of all possible worlds; for, if you had not been expelled from the noble castle, by hard kicks in your backside for love of Mademoiselle Cunegonde, if you had not been clapped into the Inquisition, if you had not wandered about America on foot, if you had not stuck your sword in the Baron, if you had not lost all your sheep from the land of Eldorado, you would not be eating candied citrons and pistachios here." "That's well said," replied Candide, "but we must cultivate our garden."

POETRY

POEM ON THE LISBON EARTHQUAKE[32]

PREFACE

If the question concerning physical evil ever deserves the attention of men, it is in those melancholy events which put us in mind of the weakness of our nature; such as plagues, which carry off a fourth of the inhabitants of the known world; the earthquake which swallowed up four hundred thousand of the Chinese in 1699, that of Lima and Callao, and, more recently, that of Portugal and the kingdom of Fez. The maxim, "whatever is, is right," appears somewhat extraordinary to those who have been eye-witnesses of such calamities. All things are doubtless arranged and set in order by Providence, but it has long been too evident, that all has not been arranged so as to promote our present happiness.

When the celebrated Pope published his "Essay on Man," and expounded in immortal verse the systems of Leibnitz, Lord Shaftesbury and Lord Bolingbroke, his system was attacked by a crowd of theologians of a variety of different communions. They revolted against these new propositions, "whatever is, is right"; and that "man always enjoys that measure of happiness which is suited to his being," etc. There are few writings that may not be condemned, if considered in one light, or approved of, if considered in another. It would be much more reasonable to pay attention only to the beauties and improving parts of a work, than to try to put an odious construction on it; but it is one of the imperfections of our nature to put a bad interpretation on whatever can be so interpreted, and to run down whatever has been successful.

In a word, it was the opinion of many, that the axiom, "whatever is, is right," was subversive of the foundation of our established ideas. "If it be true," said they, "that whatever is, is right, it follows that human nature has not degenerated. If the general order requires that everything should be as it is, human nature has not been corrupted, and consequently could have had no occasion for a redeemer. If this world, such as it is, be the best of possible worlds, we have no room to hope for a happier future state. If all the evils by which man is overwhelmed, are a general good, all civilized nations have been wrong in seeking the origin of moral and physical evil. If a man devoured by wild beasts, causes the well-being of those beasts, and contributes to the order of the universe; if the misfortunes of individuals are only the consequence of this general and necessary order, we are nothing more than wheels which serve to keep the great machine in motion; we are not more precious in the eyes of God, than the animals by whom we are devoured."

These are the conclusions which were drawn from Pope's poem; and these very conclusions increased the fame and success of the work. But it should have been seen from another point of view. Readers should have considered the reverence for Divinity, the resignation to his supreme will, the useful morality, and the spirit of toleration, which are the heart of this excellent poem. This the public has done, and the work being translated by men equal to the task, has completely triumphed over critics, though it turned on matters of so delicate a nature.

It is the nature of overviolent censurers to give importance to the opinions which they attack. A book is decried on account of its success, and a thousand errors are imputed to it. What is the consequence of this? Men, disgusted with these invectives, take for truths the very errors which these critics think they have discovered. Censure raises phantoms so as to combat them, and indignant readers embrace these very phantoms.

Critics have declared, "Pope and Leibnitz teach fatalism"; the partisans of Leibnitz and Pope have said, on the other hand, "If Leibnitz and Pope teach fatalism, they are in the right, and we should believe in all this invincible fatality."

Pope had said that "whatever is, is right," in a sense that might very well be admitted, and his followers maintain the same proposition in a sense that may very well be contested.

The author of the poem, "The Lisbon Earthquake," does not write against the illustrious Pope, whom he always loved and admired; he agrees with him in almost every particular, but fully aware of the misery of men, he declares against the abuse of this old maxim, "whatever is, is right." He maintains that more ancient and sad truth acknowledged by all men, that *there is evil upon earth*; he acknowledges that the words "whatever is, is right," if understood in an absolute sense, and without any hope of a future state, only insult us in our present misery.

If, when Lisbon, Moquinxa, Tetuan, and other cities were swallowed up with so great a number of their inhabitants in the month of November, 1755, philosophers had cried out to the wretches, who with difficulty escaped from the ruins, "All is well; the heirs of those who have perished will increase their fortunes; masons will earn money by rebuilding the houses, beasts will feed on the corpses buried under the ruins; it is the necessary effect of necessary causes; your particular misfortune is nothing, you contribute to the general good," such a harangue would doubtless have been as cruel as the earthquake was fatal, and this is what the author of the poem upon the destruction of Lisbon has said.

He acknowledges with all mankind that there is evil as well as good on the earth; he owns that no philosopher has ever been able to explain the origin of moral and physical evil. He asserts that Bayle, the greatest master of the art of reasoning that ever wrote, has only taught to doubt, and that he combats himself; he owns that man's understanding is as weak as his life is miserable. He sets forth all of the philosophical systems in a few words. He says that revelation alone can untie the great knot which all the philosophers have only rendered more puzzling; he says that nothing but the hope of a development of our being in a new order of things can console us for our present misfortunes, and that the goodness of Providence is the only refuge man can take in the darkness of his reason, and in the calamities of his weak and mortal nature.

P.S. It is always unfortunately necessary to warn readers to dis-

tinguish between the objections which an author proposes
to himself and his answers to those objections, and not to mistake
what he refutes for what he adopts.

AN INQUIRY INTO THE MAXIM, "WHATEVER IS, IS RIGHT"

Oh wretched man, earth-fated to be cursed;
Abyss of plagues, and miseries the worst!
Horrors on horrors, griefs on griefs must show,
That man's the victim of unceasing woe,
And lamentations which inspire my strain,
Prove that philosophy is false and vain.
Approach in crowds, and meditate awhile
Yon shattered walls, and view each ruined pile,
Women and children heaped up mountain high,
Limbs crushed which under ponderous marble lie;
Wretches unnumbered in the pangs of death,
Who mangled, torn, and panting for their breath,
Buried beneath their sinking roofs expire,
And end their wretched lives in torments dire.
Say, when you hear their piteous, half-formed cries,
Or from their ashes see the smoke arise,
Say, will you then eternal laws maintain,
Which God to cruelties like these constrain?
Whilst you these facts replete with horror view,
Will you maintain death to their crimes was due?
And can you then impute a sinful deed
To babes who on their mothers' bosoms bleed?
Was then more vice in fallen Lisbon found,
Than Paris, where voluptuous joys abound?
Was less debauchery to London known,
Where opulence luxurious holds her throne?
Earth Lisbon swallows; the light sons of France
Protract the feast, or lead the sprightly dance.
Spectators who undaunted courage show,
While you behold your dying brethren's woe;
With stoical tranquillity of mind
You seek the causes of these ills to find;

But when like us Fate's rigors you have felt,
Become humane, like us you'll learn to melt.
When the earth gapes my body to entomb,
I justly may complain of such a doom.
Hemmed round on every side by cruel fate,
The snares of death, the wicked's furious hate,
Preyed on by pain and by corroding grief
Suffer me from complaint to find relief.
'Tis pride, you cry, seditious pride that still
Asserts mankind should be exempt from ill.
The awful truth on Tagus' banks explore,
Rummage the ruins on that bloody shore,
Wretches interred alive in direful grave
Ask if pride cries, "Good Heaven thy creatures save."
If 'tis presumption that makes mortals cry,
"Heaven on our sufferings cast a pitying eye."
All's right, you answer, the eternal cause
Rules not by partial, but by general laws.
Say what advantage can result to all,
From wretched Lisbon's lamentable fall?
Are you then sure, the power which could create
The universe and fix the laws of fate,
Could not have found for man a proper place,
But earthquakes must destroy the human race?
Will you thus limit the eternal mind?
Should not our God to mercy be inclined?
Cannot then God direct all nature's course?
Can power almighty be without resource?
Humbly the great Creator I entreat,
This gulf with sulphur and with fire replete,
Might on the deserts spend its raging flame,
God my respect, my love weak mortals claim;
When man groans under such a load of woe,
He is not proud, he only feels the blow.
Would words like these to peace of mind restore
The natives sad of that disastrous shore?
Grieve not, that others' bliss may overflow,
Your sumptuous palaces are laid thus low;

Your toppled towers shall other hands rebuild;
With multitudes your walls one day be filled;
Your ruin on the North shall wealth bestow,
For general good from partial ills must flow;
You seem as abject to the sovereign power,
As worms which shall your carcasses devour.
No comfort could such shocking words impart,
But deeper wound the sad, afflicted heart.
When I lament my present wretched state,
Allege not the unchanging laws of fate;
Urge not the links of the eternal chain,
'Tis false philosophy and wisdom vain.
The God who holds the chain can't be enchained;²⁶
By His blest will are all events ordained:
He's just, nor easily to wrath gives way,
Why suffer we beneath so mild a sway:³⁴
This is the fatal knot you should untie,
Our evils do you cure when you deny?
Men ever strove into the source to pry,
Of evil, whose existence you deny.
If he whose hand the elements can wield,
To the winds' force makes rocky mountains yield;
If thunder lays oaks level with the plain,
From the bolts' strokes they never suffer pain.
But I can feel, my heart oppressed demands
Aid of that God who formed me with His hands.
Sons of the God supreme to suffer all
Fated alike; we on our Father call.
No vessel of the potter asks, we know,
Why it was made so brittle, vile, and low?
Vessels of speech as well as thought are void;
The urn this moment formed and that destroyed,
The potter never could with sense inspire,
Devoid of thought it nothing can desire.
The moralist still obstinate replies,
Others' enjoyments from your woes arise,
To numerous insects shall my corpse give birth,
When once it mixes with its mother earth:

Small comfort 'tis that when Death's ruthless power
Closes my life, worms shall my flesh devour.
Remembrances of misery refrain
From consolation, you increase my pain:
Complaint, I see, you have with care repressed,
And proudly hid your sorrows in your breast.
But a small part I no importance claim
In this vast universe, this general frame;
All other beings in this world below
Condemned like me to lead a life of woe,
Subject to laws as rigorous as I,
Like me in anguish live and like me die.
The vulture urged by an insatiate maw,
Its trembling prey tears with relentless claw:
This it finds right, endowed with greater powers
The bird of Jove the vulture's self devours.
Man lifts his tube, he aims the fatal ball
And makes to earth the towering eagle fall;
Man in the field with wounds all covered o'er,
Midst heaps of dead lies weltering in his gore,
While birds of prey the mangled limbs devour,
Of Nature's Lord who boasts his mighty power.
Thus the world's members equal ills sustain,
And perish by each other born to pain:
Yet in this direful chaos you'd compose
A general bliss from individuals' woes?
Oh worthless bliss! in injured reason's sight,
With faltering voice you cry, "What is, is right"?
The universe confutes your boasting vain,
Your heart retracts the error you maintain.
Men, beasts, and elements know no repose
From dire contention; earth's the seat of woes:
We strive in vain its secret source to find.
Is ill the gift of our Creator kind?
Do then fell Typhon's cursed laws ordain
Our ill, or Arimanius' doom to pain?
Shocked at such dire chimeras, I reject
Monsters which fear could into gods erect.

But how conceive a God, the source of love,
Who on man lavished blessings from above,
Then would the race with various plagues confound,
Can mortals penetrate His views profound?
Ill could not from a perfect being spring,
Nor from another, since God's sovereign king;
And yet, sad truth! in this our world 'tis found,
What contradictions here my soul confound!
A God once dwelt on earth amongst mankind,
Yet vices still lay waste the human mind;
He could not do it, this proud sophist cries,
He could, but he declined it, that replies;
He surely will, ere these disputes have end,
Lisbon's foundations hidden thunders rend,
And thirty cities' shattered remnants fly,
With ruin and combustion through the sky,
From dismal Tagus' ensanguined shore,
To where of Cadiz' sea the billows roar.
Or man's a sinful creature from his birth,
And God to woe condemns the sons of earth;
Or else the God who being rules and space,
Untouched with pity for the human race,
Indifferent, both from love and anger free,
Still acts consistent to His first decree:
Or matter has defects which still oppose
God's will, and thence all human evil flows;
Or else this transient world by mortals trod,
Is but a passage that conducts to God.
Our transient sufferings here shall soon be o'er,
And death will land us on a happier shore.
But when we rise from this accursed abyss,
Who by his merit can lay claim to bliss?
Dangers and difficulties man surround,
Doubts and perplexities his mind confound.
To nature we apply for truth in vain,
God should His will to human kind explain.
He only can illume the human soul,
Instruct the wise man, and the weak console.

Without Him man of error still the sport,
Thinks from each broken reed to find support.
Leibnitz can't tell me from what secret cause
In a world governed by the wisest laws,
Lasting disorders, woes that never end
With our vain pleasures real sufferings blend;
Why ill the virtuous with the vicious shares?
Why neither good nor bad misfortune spares?
I can't conceive that "what is, ought to be,"
In this each doctor knows as much as me.
We're told by Plato, that man, in times of yore,
Wings gorgeous to his glorious body wore,
That all attacks he could unhurt sustain,
By death ne'er conquered, ne'er approached by pain.
Alas, how changed from such a brilliant state!
He crawls 'twixt heaven and earth, then yields to fate.
Look round this sublunary world, you'll find
That nature to destruction is consigned.
Our system weak which nerves and bone compose,
Cannot the shock of elements oppose;
This mass of fluids mixed with tempered clay,
To dissolution quickly must give way.
Their quick sensations can't unhurt sustain
The attacks of death and of tormenting pain,
This is the nature of the human frame,
Plato and Epicurus I disclaim.
Nature was more to Bayle than either known:
What do I learn from Bayle, to doubt alone?
Bayle, great and wise, all systems overthrows,
Then his own tenets labors to oppose.
Like the blind slave to Delilah's commands,
Crushed by the pile demolished by his hands.
Mysteries like these can no man penetrate,
Hid from his view remains the book of fate.
Man his own nature never yet could sound,
He knows not whence he is, nor whither bound.
Atoms tormented on this earthly ball,
The sport of fate, by death soon swallowed all.

But thinking atoms, who with piercing eyes
Have measured the whole circuit of the skies;
We rise in thought up to the heavenly throne,
But our own nature still remains unknown.
This world which error and o'erweening pride,
Rulers accursed between them still divide,
Where wretches overwhelmed with lasting woe,
Talk of a happiness they never know,
Is with complaining filled, all are forlorn
In seeking bliss; none would again be born.
If in a life midst sorrows past and fears,
With pleasure's hand we wipe away our tears,
Pleasure his light wings spreads, and quickly flies,
Losses on losses, griefs on griefs arise.
The mind from sad remembrance of the past,
Is with black melancholy overcast;
Sad is the present if no future state,
No blissful retribution mortals wait,
If fate's decrees the thinking being doom
To lose existence in the silent tomb.
All may be well; that hope can man sustain,
All now is well; 'tis an illusion vain.
The sages held me forth delusive light,
Divine instructions only can be right.
Humbly I sigh, submissive suffer pain,
Nor more the ways of Providence arraign.
In youthful prime I sung in strains more gay,
Soft pleasure's laws which lead mankind astray.
But times change manners; taught by age and care
Whilst I mistaken mortals' weakness share,
The light of truth I seek in this dark state,
And without murmuring submit to fate.
A caliph once when his last hour drew nigh,
Prayed in such terms as these to the most high:
"Being supreme, whose greatness knows no bound,
I bring thee all that can't in Thee be found;
Defects and sorrows, ignorance and woe."
Hope he omitted, man's sole bliss below.

LITERARY CRITICISM

Author's Preface

It may be considered somewhat presumptuous that, having spent only 18 months in England, I have ventured to write in a language which I speak very badly and which I can hardly understand in conversation. It seems to me that I am now doing what I used to do at school when I would write in Latin and in Greek; for I am sure that we pronounced these languages wretchedly and that we would be completely unable to understand them if they who use them followed the correct pronunciation of the Romans and Greeks. Furthermore, I consider the English language a learned language, worthy of the same application on the part of the French that the English give to the study of the French language.

For myself, I have studied the English language as a duty. I have agreed to give an account of my stay in England, and I have no desire to imitate Sorbière, who after spending but three months in this country, without knowing anything about its customs or its language, decided to write an account which is nothing else but a flat and miserable satire of a nation he knew nothing about.[36]

Most of our European travelers speak ill of their neighbors while they lavish praise on the Persians and the Chinese. It is because we naturally like to reduce those who can easily be compared with us, and to raise in esteem those whom distance protects from our jealousy.

A travel narrative, however, is written to instruct men and not to encourage their malice. It seems to me that in this sort of composition one should chiefly try to point out all of the useful things and all of the great men of the country described, so that his fellow citizens may benefit from knowing them. A traveler who writes from this point of view is a noble merchant who imports to his own country the talents and virtues of other nations.

Let others give an exact description of Saint Paul's Cathedral, Westminster, and the like; I will look at England from other points of view. I consider it as the country which has produced a Newton, a Locke, a Tillotson, a Milton, a Boyle, and many other unusual men, dead or still living, whose glory in the profession of arms, in politics, or in letters, deserves to be extended beyond the limits of that island.

As for this *Essay on Epic Poetry*, it is a discourse which I am publishing as a sort of introduction to my epic poem, *Henriade*, soon to appear.

I

OF THE DIFFERENT TASTES AMONG NATIONS

Almost all of the arts have been overwhelmed by a prodigious number of rules, most of which are useless or false. We find lessons everywhere, but few examples. Nothing is easier than to speak as a master of things one cannot execute: there are a hundred treatises on poetry for every poem. We see masters of eloquence; and hardly any orators. The world is full of critics who, by means of commentaries, definitions, distinctions, have managed to obscure the clearest and simplest kinds of knowledge. It seems that men like only difficult ways. Each science, each study, has its unintelligible jargon, which seems to have been invented only to keep others away. What barbarous names! What pedantic stupidities would be crammed into the head of a young man not very long ago in order to give him, in a year or two, a completely false notion of eloquence, which he could have really come to know in a few months through the reading of a few good books. The way in which the art of thinking has long been taught is assuredly directly opposed to the gift of thought.

But it is especially on poetry that commentators and critics have lavished their teachings. They have laboriously written volumes on a few lines created in fun by the poets' imagination. They are tyrants who wish to subject to their laws a free nation which they know nothing about. Thus these false legislators have often managed only to confuse everything in the states which they wished to rule.

Most of them have written weighty discourses on what one ought to feel with rapture; and even if their rules were just, how useless they would be! Homer, Virgil, Tasso, Milton, these have scarcely obeyed any teachings but those of their own genius. So many so-called rules, so many restrictions, would serve only to get in the way of the activity of great men, and rules would be of slight help indeed to those who lack talent. A man on his way must run, and not drag along on crutches. Almost every critic has sought in Homer for rules that are assuredly not there. But as this Greek poet composed two poems of an absolutely different character, the critics have had a hard time making Homer consistent with himself. Virgil coming next, combining in his work the plan of the *Iliad* and that of the *Odyssey*, they must again seek out new expedients to adjust their rules to the *Aeneid*. They have done about the same thing as the astronomers who daily invented imaginary circles and created or destroyed a crystal heaven or two at the slightest difficulty.

If one of those men who are called wise and who believe themselves to be such, came and told you: "An epic poem is a long fable invented to teach a moral truth, and in which a hero achieves a great action, with the help of the gods, in the space of a year"; you would have to tell him: Your definition is quite false, for without looking to see if Homer's *Iliad* is in accord with your rule, the English have an epic poem whose hero, far from coming to the end of a great enterprise through divine aid, in the space of a year, is deceived by the devil and by his wife in a single day, and is driven out of the earthly paradise for having disobeyed God. Yet this poem is considered by the English on a par with the *Iliad*, and many prefer it to Homer, with some justice.

"But," you will tell me, "isn't an epic poem, then, the account of an unhappy adventure?" Not at all. This definition would be as false as the other. Sophocles' *Oedipus*, Corneille's *Cinna*,

Racine's *Athalie,* Shakespeare's *Julius Caesar,* Addison's *Cato,* Maffei's *Merope,* Quinault's *Roland,* are all fine tragedies, and I venture to say, are all quite different in character; we would need some kind of separate definition for each of them.

In all of the arts we must be watchful of those deceptive definitions, by which we risk excluding all the beauties that are unknown to us or which custom has not yet made familiar. It is not the same with the arts, and especially with those dependent on the imagination, as it is with products of nature. We can define metals, minerals, elements, animals, because their nature is always the same; but almost all of the works of men change with the imagination that produces them. Customs, languages, the taste of the most neighboring peoples, indeed, the same country cannot be recognized after a passage of three or four centuries. Among the arts that depend purely on the imagination, there are as many revolutions as there are in governments: while men try to stabilize them, they change in a thousand different ways.

The music of the ancient Greeks, as nearly as we can judge, was very different from our own. That of the Italians of today is nothing like that of Luigi or Carissimi: Persian airs clearly would not please European ears. But without going so far afield, a Frenchman accustomed to our operas cannot help laughing the first time he hears an Italian recitative. The same is true of an Italian at the Paris opera; and both are wrong in the same way, failing to realize that the recitative is nothing more than a musical declamation; that the character of the two languages is very different; that neither the accent nor the tone is the same; that this difference is apparent in conversation, and even more in the tragic theatre, and should consequently be very much present in music. We follow pretty well the architectural rules of Vitruvius; yet the houses built in Italy by Palladio and in France by our own architects, resemble those of Pliny and Cicero no more than our clothes resemble theirs.

But to return to examples closer to our subject, what was tragedy among the Greeks? A chorus which was almost always present in the theatre; no divisions of acts; very little action, and even less of plot. Among the French, tragedy is ordinarily a succession of conversations in five acts with a love plot. In England, tragedy is really an action; and if the authors of this country combined a natural style, with decence and regularity, with the activity that animates their plays, they would certainly triumph over the Greeks and the French.

Were we to examine all of the other arts, we would not find one which does not receive its peculiar contours from the different genius of the various countries which cultivate it.

What then should be our concept of epic poetry? The word *epic* comes from the Greek ἔπος, which means *discourse*. Custom has applied this term especially to accounts in verse of heroic adventures; just as the word *oratio* of the Romans, which also meant *discourse*, was subsequently used only for ceremonial speeches; and as the title, *imperator*, which once belonged to army generals, was subsequently conferred only on the rulers of Rome.

An epic poem, considered in itself, is thus an account in verse of heroic adventures. It makes no difference whether the action be simple or complex; whether it last for a month or a year or longer; whether the scene is fixed in a single place, as in the *Iliad*; whether the hero travels from sea to sea, as in the *Odyssey*; whether he is happy or unfortunate, angry like Achilles or pious like Aeneas; whether there is one principal character or several; whether the action takes place on land or on sea; on the coast of Africa, as in the *Lusiads*; in America, as in the *Araucana*; in heaven, in hell, beyond the limits of our world, as in Milton's *Paradise Lost*: in any case, the poem will always be an epic poem, a heroic poem, unless one finds a new title proportionate to its merit. If you have scruples, said the famous Addison, over giving the title of an epic poem to Milton's *Paradise Lost*, call it if you like a divine poem, give it whatever name you like, so long as you grant that it is a work just as admirable in its kind as the *Iliad*.

Let us never quarrel over names. Will I refuse the name of comedies to the plays of Congreve or Calderón because they are not in the French style? The arts are much broader than one may think. A man who has read only the ancient writers disdains everything written in modern languages; and he who knows only his own language is like those who, never having been outside of the French court, think that the rest of the world counts for very little and that he who has seen Versailles has seen everything.

But the crux of the matter and of the difficulty is to know on what the civilized nations of the world are in agreement and on what they differ. An epic poem must everywhere be based on judgment and embellished by the imagination: what belongs to good sense likewise belongs to all the nations of the world. Any one will tell you that an action that is single and simple, that develops easily and gradually, and does not require fatiguing concentration, will please more than a confused heap of monstrous adventures. It is generally desired that this careful unity be adorned with a variety of episodes that are like the limbs of a robust and well-proportioned body. The greater the action, the more it will please men, whose weakness is to be enchanted by all that is outside of ordinary experience. It is especially important that this action be interesting, for every one likes to be stirred; and a poem perfect in every other way, if it does not move us, will be insipid in any age or country. It must be a whole, for no one is satisfied with a part of what he has been promised.

These are the principal rules that nature dictates to all the nations that cultivate the written word; but as for the contrivance of the marvellous, the intervention of celestial power, the nature of episodes, all that depends on tyranny and custom and on that instinct called taste, on these matters there are a thousand different opinions and certainly no general rules.

"But," you will exclaim, "are there not beauties of taste that please all peoples equally?" Certainly, and in large number. From the age of the Renaissance, which took the ancients for its models, Homer, Demosthenes, Virgil, and Cicero have in some way or other reunited under their laws all the peoples of Europe, and have made of so many different nations a single republic of letters; but in the midst of this general agreement the customs of each nation introduce a characteristic taste into each country.

In the best modern writers you can sense the character of their country through the imitation of classical antiquity: their flowers and their fruits are warmed and ripened by the same sun; but from the land which nourishes them they receive different tastes, colors, and forms. You can recognize an Italian, a Frenchman, an Englishman, a Spaniard, by his style, just as by his facial features, his pronunciation, his manners. The sweetness and softness of the Italian language has made its way into the genius of Italian authors. The pomp of words, metaphors, a majestic style, these, it seems to me, generally speaking, are the stamp of Spanish writers. Force, energy and boldness are more proper to the English; they are especially fond of allegories and comparisons. The French for their part have more clarity, exactness and elegance: they risk little; they have neither the English strength, which seems to them gigantic and monstrous, nor the Italian sweetness, which they hold degenerates into an effeminate softness.

From all of these differences rises that disgust and disdain that the various nations have for one another. To examine more closely this difference between the tastes of neighboring peoples, let us now consider their style.

In Italy these verses, imitated from Lucretius in the third stanza of the first canto of *Jerusalem Delivered*, are rightly approved:[37]

> Così all'egro fanciul porgiamo aspersi
> Di soave licor gli orli del vaso:
> Succhi amari ingannato intanto ei beve,
> E dall' inganno suo vita riceve.

This comparison of the charm of fables enclosing useful teachings with a bitter medicine given to a child out of a bottle lined with honey, would not be tolerated in a French epic poem. We read with pleasure in Montaigne that one should flavor good meat with honey to give it to children. But this image, which pleases us in its familiar style, would not seem to us worthy of the majesty of the epic.

Here is another selection, deservedly approved by every one: it is from the thirty-sixth stanza of the sixteenth canto of *Jerusalem Delivered*, when Armida begins to suspect her lover's flight:

> Volea gridar: Dove, o crudel, me sola
> Lasci? Ma il varco al suon chiuse il dolore:
> Sì che tornò le flebile parola
> Più amara indietro a rimbombar sul core.

These four Italian lines are very touching and very natural; but were they translated literally, they would make nonsense in French. "She wished to cry: Cruel one, why have you left me alone? But grief closed the way to her voice; and these painful words drew back with more bitterness, and resounded in her heart."

Let us take another example drawn from one of the most sublime sections of Milton's singular poem which I have already mentioned; it is from the first book (lines 56-67), in the description of Satan and hell.

> . . . Round he throws his baleful eyes
> That witness'd huge affliction and dismay
> Mix'd with obdurate pride and stedfast hate:
> At once, as far as angels ken, he views
> The dismal situation waste and wild;
> A dungeon horrible on all sides round,
> As one great furnace flam'd; yet from those flames
> No light, but rather darkness visible
> Serv'd only to discover sights of woe,
> Regions of sorrow, doleful shades, where peace
> And rest can never dwell, hope never comes
> That comes to all, etc.

Antonio de Solis in his excellent *History of the Conquest of Mexico*, after having stated that the place where Montezuma consulted his gods was a large subterranean vault where tiny holes scarcely allowed light to enter, adds: "O permitian solamente la (luz), que bastava, para que se viesse la obscuridad." "Or they let only enough light come in that was needed to see the darkness." These visible shadows of Milton are not condemned in England, and the Spanish do not censure the same idea in the passage of de Solis. It is quite certain that the French would not allow such liberties. It is not enough to say that one may excuse the license of these expressions; French exactitude will admit nothing that is in need of an excuse.

So as to leave no doubt on this subject, permit me to join one more example to those I have cited: I will take it from pulpit oratory. When a man like Father Bourdaloue preaches before a congregation of the Anglican Church, and in enlivening a mournful discourse by a noble gesture, exclaims: "Yes, Christians, you have been quite correct; but the blood of that poor wretch whom you let suffer; but the blood of those unfortunates whose cause you did not take into your hands; that blood will fall on you, and your good behavior will serve only to make its voice more powerful in asking God for vengeance of your faithlessness. Ah, my dear listeners, etc." These pathetic words, vigorously pronounced and accompanied by large gestures, would make an English listener laugh. For just as in the theatre they like full expressions and movements strong in eloquence, so in the pulpit they enjoy an unadorned simplicity. A sermon in France is a long declamation scrupulously divided into three parts, and recited with enthusiasm. In England a sermon is a solid dissertation and sometimes a dry one, read to the people without gesture and without any raising of the voice. In Italy it is a spiritual comedy. This is quite enough to show how great the differences are among national tastes.

I know that there are many who would not agree with this view. They say that reason and the passions are everywhere the same. This is true, but they are expressed everywhere differently. In every country men have a nose, two eyes and a mouth; yet the collection of features that makes for beauty in France would not do in Turkey, nor would a Turkish beauty in China; and what is most admired in Asia and Europe would be considered a monster in the Guineas. Since nature herself is so different, how can one impose general laws on arts over which custom, that is, inconsistency, has so much sway? Therefore, if we want to have a broader knowledge of these arts, we have to know how they are practiced in every nation. To know the epic it is not enough to have read Virgil and Homer, just as it is not enough, in tragedy, to have read Sophocles and Euripides.

We ought to admire what is universally beautiful among the ancients; we ought to direct ourselves to what was beautiful in their language and their manners; but one would go strangely astray if he wanted to follow them all the way. We do not speak the same language at all. Religion, which is almost always the foundation of epic poetry, is for us the opposite of their mythology. Our customs are more different from those of the heroes of the Trojan war than from those of the American Indians. Our battles, our sieges, our fleets, have not the slightest resemblance; our philosophy is completely the opposite of theirs. The invention of gun powder, of the compass, of printing, and so many other arts recently brought into the world, have to some degree changed the face of the universe. We must paint with true colors as did the ancients, but we must not paint the same things.

When Homer depicts his gods drunk with nectar and endlessly laughing at the bad grace with which Vulcan serves them drink, this was good in its time, when the gods were what fairies are for us; but surely no one would decide today to depict in a poem a troupe of angels and saints drinking and laughing at the table. What would be said of an author who would follow Virgil in introducing harpies that make off with his hero's dinner, and who would change old ships into beautiful nymphs? In a word, let us admire the ancients, but let our admiration not be a blind superstition: and let us not commit that injustice to ourselves and to human nature of closing our eyes to the beauties she places around us in order to examine and admire only her ancient productions, which we cannot judge with as much accuracy.

There are surely no monuments in Italy which deserve more attention from a traveler than Tasso's *Jerusalem Delivered*. Milton honors England as much as does the great Newton. It would undoubtedly be a great pleasure, and even of great advantage, for an intelligent man to examine all these different kinds of epic poems, born in centuries and countries remote from one another. It seems to me that there is a noble satisfaction in looking at the lifelike portraits of these famous characters, Greek, Roman, Italian, English, all dressed, if I may say so, in the fashion of their country.

It is an enterprise beyond my power to pretend to paint them; I will try simply to pencil out a sketch of their principal features: the reader will have to make up for the defects of this design. I shall only propose: he must judge; and his judgment will be just if he reads with impartiality and does not listen to the prejudices he received at school nor to that misunderstood self-esteem that makes us disdain all that is not part of our ways. He will see the birth, progress and decline of the art; he will see it then rise as if from its ruins; he will follow all its changes; he will distinguish what is beauty in every age and country from local beauties admired in one country and scorned in another. He will not have to ask Aristotle what he ought to think of an English or Portuguese writer, nor Perrault how he ought to judge the *Iliad*. He will not let himself be dominated by Scaliger or Le Bossu; but will draw his rules from nature, and from examples he will have before his eyes, and he will judge between the gods of Homer and the god of Milton, between Calypso and Dido, between Armida and Eve.

If the nations of Europe, instead of unjustly despising one another, wished to pay a less superficial attention to their neighbors' works and manners, not to laugh at them but to profit from them, perhaps from this mutual commerce of observations would arise that general good taste which is so fruitlessly sought.

TRANSLATOR'S PREFACE TO
JULIUS CAESAR,
TRAGEDY OF SHAKESPEARE

Having often heard Corneille and Shakespeare compared, I
thought it a good idea to show the different way they each make
use of subjects which might have some similarity. I have selected
the first acts of the death of Caesar, in which we may see a
conspiracy like that of *Cinna,* and indeed, which are concerned
only with a conspiracy until the end of the third act. The
reader will easily be able to compare the thoughts, style and
judgment of Shakespeare with the thoughts, style and judgment
of Corneille. The readers of all nations must choose between the
one and the other. A Frenchman and an Englishman would
perhaps be given to some partiality. To aid this contest we have
had to make an exact translation. We have rendered in prose
what is in prose in Shakespeare's tragedy; we have rendered in
blank verse what is in blank verse, and almost always line for
line. What is familiar and low is translated as familiar and low.
We have tried to rise and expand with the author when he expands, and when he is inflated and bombastic, we have taken
care not to be more nor less so.

A poet may be translated by expressing merely the substance
of his thoughts, but to make him known well, to give a just
idea of his language, we must translate not only his thoughts,
but all the accessories. If the poet has used a certain metaphor,
we must not substitute another metaphor; if he makes use of a

word that is low in his language, we must render it by a word that is low in our own. His work is a painting from which we must copy exactly the design, the attitudes, coloring, defects and beauties; otherwise you substitute your work for his.

We have in French imitations, sketches, extracts of Shakespeare, but no translation: apparently care has been taken not to offend our taste. For example, in the translation of *Othello*, Iago, at the beginning of the play, comes to warn the senator Brabantio that the Moor has carried off his daughter. The French writer makes Iago speak this way, in the French manner:

"I say, sir, that you are betrayed, and that the Moor is already in possession of your daughter's charms."

But here is how Iago speaks in the original English:

" 'Zounds, sir, you are one of those that will not serve God, if the devil bid you. Because we come to do you service and you think we are ruffians, you'll have your daughter cover'd with a Barbary horse; you'll have your nephews neigh to you; you'll have coursers for cousins, and gennets for germans.

Brabantio

"What profane wretch art thou?

Iago

"I am one, sir, that comes to tell you your daughter and the Moor are now making the beast with two backs.

Brabantio

"Thou art a villain, etc."

I do not say that the translator did wrong in sparing our eyes the reading of this passage; I say only that he has not made Shakespeare known, and that one cannot guess what is the genius of this author, of his times, of his language, from the imitations which we have been given under the name of *translation*. There are not six lines in a row in the French *Julius Caesar* which are found in the English *Caesar*. The translation given here is the most faithful ever made in our language of an ancient or a foreign poet. It is true that in the original one may find a few words that cannot be rendered literally in French, just as we have some words that the English cannot translate; but they are very few in number.

I have only one word to add, that blank verses cost only the trouble of dictation; this is no more difficult than writing a letter. If men decide to write tragedies in blank verse and to perform them in our theatre, tragedy is lost. As soon as you remove the difficulty, you remove the merit.

HISTORY

THE AGE OF LOUIS XIV [30]

I

INTRODUCTION

It is not merely the life of Louis XIV that we propose to write;
we have a wider aim in view. We shall endeavor to depict for
posterity, not the actions of a single man, but the spirit of men
in the most enlightened age the world has ever seen.

Every age has produced its heroes and statesmen; every nation
has experienced revolutions; every history is the same to one
who wishes merely to remember facts. But the thinking man,
and what is still rarer, the man of taste, numbers only four
ages in the history of the world; four happy ages when the arts
were brought to perfection and which, marking an era of the
greatness of the human mind, are an example to posterity.

The first of these ages, to which true glory belongs, is that of
Philip and Alexander, or rather of Pericles, Demosthenes, Aristotle, Plato, Apelles, Phidias, Praxiteles; and this honor was confined within the limits of Greece, the rest of the known world
being in a barbarous state.

The second age is that of Cæsar and Augustus, distinguished
moreover by the names of Lucretius, Cicero, Livy, Virgil, Horace,
Ovid, Varro and Vitruvius.

The third is that which followed the taking of Constantinople by Mahomet II. The reader may remember that the spectacle
was then witnessed of a family of mere citizens in Italy accom-
plishing what should have been undertaken by the kings of Europe. The scholars whom the Turks had driven from Greece

were summoned by the Medici to Florence; it was the hour of Italy's glory. The fine arts had already taken on new life there; and the Italians honored them with the name of virtue as the early Greeks had characterized them with the name of wisdom. Everything conduced to perfection. The arts, for ever transplanted from Greece to Italy, fell on favorable ground, where they flourished immediately. France, England, Germany and Spain, in their turn, desired the possession of these fruits; but either they never reached these countries or they degenerated too quickly.

Francis I encouraged scholars who were scholars and nothing else: he had architects, but neither a Michelangelo nor a Palladio; it was in vain that he endeavored to found Schools of Painting, for the Italian painters whom he employed made no French disciples. A few epigrams and fables made up the whole of our poetry. Rabelais was the only prose writer in fashion in the age of Henry II.

In a word, the Italians alone possessed everything, if one except music, which had not yet been brought to perfection, and experimental philosophy, equally unknown everywhere, and which Galileo at length brought to men's knowledge.

The fourth age is that which we call the age of Louis XIV; and it is perhaps of the four the one which most nearly approaches perfection. Enriched with the discoveries of the other three it accomplished in certain departments more than the three together. All the arts, it is true, did not progress further than they did under the Medici, under Augustus or under Alexander; but human reason in general was brought to perfection.

Rational philosophy only came to light in this period; and it is true to say that from the last years of Cardinal Richelieu to those which followed the death of Louis XIV, a general revolution took place in our arts, minds and customs, as in our government, which will serve as an eternal token of the true glory of our country. This beneficent influence was not merely confined to France; it passed over into England, and inspired a profitable rivalry in that intellectual and fearless nation; it imported good taste into Germany, and the sciences into Russia; it even revived Italy, who had begun to languish, and Europe has owed both her manners and the social spirit to the court of Louis XIV.

It must not be assumed that these four ages were exempt from misfortunes and crimes. The attainment of perfection in those arts practised by peaceful citizens does not prevent princes from being ambitious, the people from being mutinous, nor priests and monks from becoming sometimes turbulent and crafty. All ages resemble one another in respect of the criminal folly of mankind, but I only know of these four ages so distinguished by great attainments.

Prior to the age which I call that of Louis XIV, and which began almost with the founding of the *Académie française*, the Italians looked upon all those north of the Alps as barbarians; it must be confessed that to a certain extent the French deserved the insult. Their fathers joined the romantic courtesy of the Moors to Gothic coarseness. They practised scarcely any of the fine arts, which proves that the useful arts were neglected; for when one has perfected the necessary things, one soon discovers the beautiful and agreeable; and it is not to be wondered at that painting, sculpture, poetry, oratory and philosophy were almost unknown to a nation which, while possessing ports on the Atlantic Ocean and the Mediterranean, yet had no fleet, and which, though inordinately fond of luxury, had but a few coarse manufactures.

The Jews, the Genoese, the Venetians, the Portuguese, the Flemish, the Dutch, the English, in turn carried on the trade of France, who was ignorant of its first principles. When Louis XIII ascended the throne he did not possess a ship; Paris did not contain four hundred thousand inhabitants, and could not boast of four fine buildings; the other towns of the kingdom resembled those market towns one sees south of the Loire. The whole of the nobility, scattered over the country in their moat-surrounded castles, oppressed the people, who were engaged in tilling the land. The great highways were well-nigh impassable; the towns were without police, the state without money, and the government nearly always without credit among foreign nations. The fact must not be concealed that after the decadence of Charlemagne's descendants France had continued more or less in this state of weakness simply because she had hardly ever enjoyed good government.

If a state is to be powerful, either the people must enjoy a liberty based on its laws, or the sovereign power must be affirmed without contradiction. In France, the people were enslaved until the time of Philip Augustus; the nobles were tyrants until the time of Louis XI, and the kings, continually engaged in upholding their authority over that of their vassals, had neither the time to think of the welfare of their subjects nor the power to make them happy.

Louis XI did a great deal for the royal power, but nothing for the happiness and glory of the nation. Francis I inaugurated commerce, navigation, letters and the arts; but he did not succeed in making them take root in France, and they all perished with him. Henri-Quatre was about to redeem France from the calamities and barbarity into which she had been plunged by twenty years of dissension, when he was assassinated in his capital, in the midst of the people to whom he was on the point of bringing prosperity. Cardinal Richelieu, occupied with the humbling of the House of Austria, Calvinism and the nobles, did not possess a sufficiently secure position to reform the nation; but at least he inaugurated the auspicious work.

Thus for nine hundred years the genius of France had almost continually been cramped under a gothic government, in the midst of partitions and civil wars, having neither laws nor fixed customs, and changing every two centuries a language ever uncouth; her nobles undisciplined and acquainted solely with war and idleness; her clergy living in disorder and ignorance; and her people without trade, sunk in their misery.

The French also had no share in the great discoveries and wonderful inventions of other nations; printing, gunpowder, glassmaking, telescopes, the proportional compass, pneumatic machines, the true system of the universe—in such things they had no concern; they were engaged in tournaments while the Portuguese and Spaniards discovered and conquered new worlds to the east and west. Charles V was already lavishing on Europe the treasures of Mexico before a few subjects of Francis I discovered the uncultivated regions of Canada; but even from the slight accomplishments of the French at the beginning of the sixteenth century, one could see what they are capable of when they are led.

We propose to show what they became under Louis XIV.

Do not let the reader expect here, more than in the description of earlier centuries, minute details of wars, of attacks on towns taken and retaken by force of arms, surrendered and given back by treaties. A thousand events interesting to contemporaries are lost to the eyes of posterity and disappear, leaving only to view great happenings that have fixed the destiny of empires. Every event that occurs is not worth recording. In this history we shall confine ourselves to that which deserves the attention of all time, which paints the spirit and the customs of men, which may serve for instruction and to counsel the love of virtue, of the arts and of the fatherland.

The state of France and the other European States before the birth of Louis XIV has already been described: we shall here relate the great political and military events of his reign. The internal government of the kingdom, the most important matter for the people at large, will be treated separately. To the private life of Louis XIV, to the peculiarities of his court and of his reign, a large part will be devoted. Other chapters will deal with the arts, the sciences, and the progress of the human mind in this age. Finally, we shall speak of the Church, which has been joined to the government for so long a period, sometimes disturbing it, at other times invigorating it, and which, established for the teaching of morality, often surrenders herself to politics and the passions of mankind.

II

EUROPEAN STATES BEFORE LOUIS XIV

Already for a long time one could regard Christian Europe (except Russia) as a sort of great republic divided into several states, some monarchical, others of a mixed character; the former aristocratic, the latter popular, but all in harmony with each other, all having the same substratum of religion, although divided into various sects; all possessing the same principles of public and political law, unknown in other parts of the world. In obedience to these principles the European nations do not make their prisoners slaves, they respect their enemies' ambassadors, they agree as to the pre-eminence and rights of certain princes, such as the Emperor, kings and other lesser potentates, and, above all, they are at one on the wise policy of maintaining among themselves so far as possible an equal balance of power, ceaselessly carrying on negotiations, even in wartime, and sending each to the other ambassadors or less honorable spies, who can acquaint every court with the designs of any one of them, give in a moment the alarm to Europe, and defend the weakest from invasions which the strongest is always ready to attempt.

Since the time of Charles V the balance inclined to the side of the House of Austria. Towards the year 1630 this powerful House was mistress of Spain, Portugal, and the treasures of America; the Netherlands, the Milanese States, the Kingdom of Naples, Bohemia, Hungary, even Germany (one may say) had become her patrimony; and since so many states had become united under a single head of this House, it is credible that all Europe would at last have been subdued.

GERMANY

The German Empire is France's most powerful neighbor: it has a greater expanse, is not so rich in bullion perhaps, but more prolific in vigorous men inured to hard labor. The German nation is ruled in almost the same manner as France under the first kings of the House of Capet, who were the chiefs often ill-obeyed of a few great vassals and a large number of petty ones. Today, sixty free towns, known as imperial towns, nearly as many secular sovereigns, nearly forty ecclesiastical princes, either abbots or bishops, nine electors, among whom today one can count four kings, and finally the Emperor, the chief of these potentates, form this great Germanic body, which, thanks to German stolidity, has survived until the present day, with almost as much order as there was formerly confusion in the French government.

Each member of the Empire has his rights, his privileges, his duties; and the hardly acquired knowledge of so many laws, often disputed, has given rise to what is known in Germany as *the Study of Public Law*, for which the German nation is famed.

By himself the Emperor would be no more powerful and rich than a Venetian doge, for Germany, being divided into towns and principalities, allows the head of so many states only a highly-honored pre-eminence, without possessions, without money, and consequently without power.

He does not possess a single village in virtue of being Emperor. Nevertheless, this dignity, often as empty as it was supreme, had become so powerful in the hands of the Austrians, that it was often feared that they would transform what was a republic of princes into an absolute monarchy.

Two parties at that time divided Christian Europe, as they still do today, and especially Germany.

The first is that of the Catholics, more or less subjected to the Pope; the second is that of the enemies of the spiritual and temporal rule of the Pope and the Catholic prelates. The adher-ents of this party are called by the general name of Protestants, although they are made up of Lutherans, Calvinists, and others, who hate one another almost as much as they hate Rome. In Germany, Saxony, part of Brandenburg, the Palatinate, part of Bohemia, Hungary, the States of the House of Brunswick, Würtemberg and Hesse, observe the Lutheran religion, which is known as *evangelistic*. All the imperial free towns have embraced this sect, which seemed more suitable than the Catholic religion to people who were jealous of their liberty.

The Calvinists, scattered among the strongest party, the Lutherans, form only a moderate party; the Catholics compose the rest of the Empire and with the House of Austria as their head were undoubtedly the most powerful.

Not only Germany, but all the Christian States were still bleeding from the wounds they had received in numerous religious wars, a madness peculiar to Christians and unknown to pagans, the unfortunate result of a dogmatic spirit so long introduced into all classes of society. Few indeed are the points of difference which have resulted in civil war; and foreign nations (perhaps our own descendants) will find it hard to understand how our fathers were at one another's throats for so many years whilst at the same time preaching forbearance.

I have in a former work pointed out how Ferdinand was about to transform the German aristocracy into an absolute monarchy, and how he was on the point of being dethroned by Gustavus Adolphus. His son Ferdinand III who inherited his policy, and like him directed wars from the shelter of his study, reigned during the minority of Louis XIV.

Germany was far from being at that time so flourishing as she afterwards became; luxury was a thing unknown, and the comforts of life were very rare even among the greatest nobles. It was not until 1686 that they were introduced by French refugees who set up their manufactures there. This fertile and populous country lacked trade and money: the seriousness of their customs and the peculiar sluggishness of the Germans debarred them from those pleasures and agreeable arts which Italian acuteness had cultivated for so many years, and which French industry from that time began to bring to perfection. The Germans, rich at home, were poor abroad; and this poverty, added to the difficulty of mobilizing so many different peoples under the same standard at such short notice, rendered it almost impossible, as today, for them to carry on war for any length of time against their neighbors. Hence the French have nearly always made war on imperial soil against the Emperors. The difference of government and of national genius seems to render the French more adapted for attack and the Germans for defense.

SPAIN

Spain, ruled by the elder branch of the House of Austria, had, after the death of Charles V, inspired more terror than the German nation. The Kings of Spain were immeasurably more powerful and rich. The mines of Mexico and Potosi apparently supplied whatever was necessary to buy the freedom of Europe. This generation saw the scheme of a monarchy, or rather of a universal superiority over Christian Europe, begun by Charles V, and continued by Philip II.

The greatness of Spain under Philip III was nothing more than that of a vast body without substance, having more fame than power.

Philip IV, heir to his father's weakness, lost Portugal by carelessness, Roussillon through the weakness of his forces, and Catalonia by the abuse of despotism. Such kings could not for long be successful in their wars against France. If they gained certain advantages from the divisions and mistakes of their enemies, they lost them by their own incapacity. Moreover, they governed a people whose privileges allowed them to be disloyal; the Castilians had the right of not fighting outside their own country; the Aragonese ceaselessly contested their liberty against the Royal Council, and the Catalonians, who regarded their kings as their enemies, would not suffer them even to raise troops in their provinces.

Nevertheless, united with the empire, Spain was a formidable factor in the balance of Europe.

PORTUGAL

Portugal at this time again became a separate kingdom; John, Duke of Braganza, a prince commonly thought weak, had snatched this province from a king weaker than himself. The Portuguese cultivated commerce out of necessity as Spain neglected it out of pride; in 1641 they leagued themselves with France and Holland against Spain. This revolution in Portugal was worth more to France than the winning of the most decisive victories. The French ministry, which had contributed nothing to the event, reaped without effort the greatest advantage that one can have over an enemy, that of seeing her attacked by an irreconcilable power.

Portugal, shaking off the yoke of Spain, expanding her trade and increasing her power, recalls to mind the case of Holland, who enjoyed the same advantages in quite a different way.

THE UNITED PROVINCES

This small state, consisting of seven united provinces, a country abounding in pasture land but barren of grain, unhealthy, and almost swamped by the sea, had presented for nearly fifty years an almost unique example in the world of what love of liberty and indefatigable labor can accomplish. These far from wealthy people, numerically small, far less disciplined in war than the poorest Spanish troops, and who as yet counted for nothing in Europe, withstood the whole forces of their master and tyrant Philip II, evaded the schemes of various princes who wished to aid them in order to subdue them, and laid the foundations of a power that we have witnessed counterbalance the might of Spain herself. Despair, engendered by tyranny, first armed them; liberty exalted their courage and the princes of the House of Orange made them into excellent soldiers. Scarcely had they conquered their masters than they established a form of government which so far as it is possible maintains equality, the most natural right of men.

This state of so peculiar a nature was from its commencement closely allied with France: interest united them, they had the same enemies, and the great Henri-Quatre and Louis XIII had been the allies and protectors of Holland.

ENGLAND

England, much more powerful, assumed the supremacy of the seas and claimed to set a balance among the states of Europe; but Charles I, who had reigned since 1625, far from being able to support the weight of this balance already felt the scepter slipping from his grasp; he had wished to make his power independent of the laws of England and to change the religion of Scotland. Too obstinate to abandon his designs and too weak to execute them, a good husband, a good master, a good father, an honest man, but an ill-advised monarch, he became involved in a civil war, which, as we have shown elsewhere, at length caused him to lose his throne and his life on the scaffold in the course of an almost unprecedented revolution.

This civil war, begun during the minority of Louis XIV, prevented England for a time from interesting herself in the concerns of her neighbors; she lost alike her prosperity and her reputation; her trade was suspended; and other nations believed her to be buried beneath her own ruins, until suddenly she became more formidable than ever under the sway of Cromwell, who ruled her, the Bible in one hand and a sword in the other, wearing the mask of religion on his face, and disguising in his government the crimes of a usurper under the qualities of a great king.

ROME

This balance, which England had long flattered herself she had preserved among kings by her power, the court of Rome endeavored to maintain by her policy. Italy was divided as today into several sovereignties; that which the Pope possesses is large enough to make him respected as a prince and too small to make him formidable. The nature of his government does not tend to populate the country, which has indeed little money and trade; his spiritual authority, always somewhat involved with the temporal, is destroyed and abhorred by one-half of Christendom; and if by the other half he is regarded as a father, he has children who sometimes oppose him with both reason and success. The rule of France has been to regard him as a sacred but overreaching person, whose feet one must kiss, but whose hands one must sometimes bind. In all Catholic countries one may still see traces of the steps taken by the court of Rome towards a universal monarchy. All princes of the Catholic religion on their accession send to the Pope embassies of obedience, as they are called. Every crowned head has a cardinal in Rome who takes the name of protector. All bishoprics receive their bulls from the Pope, and in these bulls he addresses them as if he conferred such dignities by his power alone. All Italian, Spanish and Flemish bishops are pronounced bishops by divine permission and *that of the Holy See*. About the year 1682, many French prelates rejected this formula, unknown to earlier centuries; and in our time, in 1754, we have seen a bishop (Stuart Fitz-James, Bishop of Soissons) brave enough to omit it in a decree which deserves to be handed down to posterity; a decree, or rather a unique instruction, wherein it is expressly stated what no pontiff had yet dared to say, that all men, even unbelievers, are our brothers.

In fine, the Pope has preserved certain prerogatives in all Catholic countries which he certainly would not now obtain had time not previously given them to him. There is no kingdom in which there are not many benefices under his nomination, and as tribute he receives the first-year revenues of the consistorial benefices.

The monks, whose superiors are resident at Rome, are still the immediate subjects of the Pope, and are scattered throughout every state. Custom, which is all-powerful, and which is the cause of the world being ruled by abuses as well as by laws, has sometimes prevented princes from entirely removing danger, especially when it was related to matters considered as sacred. To take an oath to anyone but one's sovereign is a crime of high treason in the layman; it is an act of religion in the monk. The difficulty of knowing to what extent such a foreign sovereignty should be obeyed, the ease of allowing oneself to be won over, the pleasure of throwing off a natural yoke in order to accept one chosen by oneself, the spirit of disorder, the evil of the times, have only too often prompted whole religious orders to serve Rome against their own country.

The enlightened spirit that has prevailed in France for the last century and which has been diffused among nearly all classes has been the best remedy for this evil. Good books on this matter are of real service to kings and peoples, and one of the great changes thus brought about in our customs under Louis XIV is the conviction which the monks are beginning to have, that they are subjects of the king before being servants of the Pope.

Jurisdiction, that essential mark of sovereignty, still rests with the Roman pontiff. In spite of all the liberties of the Gallic Church, even France permits a final right of appeal to the Pope in certain ecclesiastical cases.

If one wishes to annul a marriage, to marry one's cousin or one's niece, to be released from one's vows, it is still to Rome and not to one's bishop that application must be made; to Rome where favors are bought and individuals from every country obtain dispensations at varying prices.

The right to confer these advantages, regarded by many people as the result of the most intolerable abuses, and by others as the relics of the most sacred rights, is always cunningly maintained. Rome looks after her credit with as much policy as the Roman republic employed in conquering half the known world.

Never did a court know better how to conduct itself in conformity with men and with the times. The popes are nearly always Italians grown old in the conduct of affairs, free from any blinding passions; their council is formed of cardinals of similar characters, all emboldened with the same spirit. From this council mandates are issued that extend to China and America; in this respect it embraces the whole world, and it could sometimes be said of it what a foreigner once said of the Roman senate: "I have seen a Council of Kings." The majority of our writers have justifiably cried out against the ambition of this court, but I do not know of one of them who has done sufficient justice to its prudence. I know of no nation that could have maintained so long in Europe so many prerogatives that were continually being challenged; any other court would have lost them, either by pride or weakness, by over-eagerness or indolence, but Rome, rarely failing to employ at the appropriate moment now firmness and now tact, has kept everything that was humanly possible for her to keep. We see her raging under the hand of Charles V, violent towards Henri III of France, by turns the enemy and friend of Henri IV, cunning with Louis XIII, openly opposed to Louis XIV at the time when he was to be feared, and often the secret enemy of the Emperors whom she distrusted more than the Turkish Sultans.

Rome retains today a few rights, many pretensions, a statecraft and patience, which is all that is left of her ancient power which six centuries ago attempted to bring the empire, nay all Europe, under the tiara.

Naples is an extant example of that right which the popes once seized with such ingenuity and magnificence, that of creating and bestowing kingdoms; but the King of Spain, the possessor of that state, left to the Roman court only the honor and the danger of having too powerful a vassal.

For the rest, the papal state was enjoying a prosperous peace, which had only been broken by the little war of which I have spoken elsewhere between the Cardinals Barberini, the nephews of Pope Urban VIII, and the Duke of Parma.

THE REST OF ITALY

The other provinces of Italy were occupied with various interests. Venice feared the Turks and the emperor; she was hard put to defend her mainland states from the claims of Germany and from the invasion of the Sultan. She was no longer that Venice once the mistress of the world's trade, who a hundred and fifty years before had aroused the envy of so many kings. The wisdom of her government remained, but the loss of her enormous trade deprived her of nearly all her power, and the city of Venice thus remained by reason of her situation invincible, but by reason of her decadence unable to make fresh conquests.

The State of Florence was enjoying peace and prosperity under the rule of the Medici; literature, the arts, and polite manners, which the Medici had created, still flourished. Tuscany, at that time, was to Italy what Athens had been to Greece.

Savoy, torn by civil war and overrun by French and Spanish troops, was at length completely united on the side of France, and contributed towards the weakening of the Austrian power in Italy.

The Swiss preserved as they do today their liberty without attempting to oppress others. They hired their forces to neighbors richer than themselves; they were poor, they were unacquainted with the sciences and arts which luxury had created, but they were prudent and happy.

THE NORTHERN STATES

The northern European states, Poland, Sweden, Denmark and Russia, were like the other powers continually suspicious of one another or openly at war. One might witness in Poland then as today the customs and government of the Goths and Franks— an elective king, nobles sharing his power, an enslaved people, weak infantry and a cavalry recruited from the nobles, no fortified towns and practically no trade. These people were attacked now by the Swedes or Russians, now by the Turks. The Swedes, constitutionally a still freer nation, admitting even peasants to the states-general, but at that time more under the subjection of their kings than Poland, were victorious nearly everywhere; Denmark, at one time formidable to Sweden, was now no longer so to any state; and her real greatness only commenced under her two kings, Frederick III and Frederick IV.

Russia was still in a state of barbarism.

THE TURKS

The Turks were no longer what they had been under the Selims, the Mahomets and the Solymans; effeminacy corrupted the seraglio, but did not banish cruelty. The Sultans were at one and the same time the most despotic of rulers in their seraglio and the least assured of their thrones and their lives. Osman and Ibrahim met their death by strangulation. Mustapha was twice deposed. Shaken by these shocks, the Turkish Empire was, moreover, attacked by the Persians; but, when the Persians allowed her breathing space and palace revolutions were at an end, that empire became formidable to Christendom; for, from the mouth of the Dnieper as far as the Venetian States, Russia, Hungary, Greece and the islands of the Mediterranean became in turn the prey of the Turkish forces; and from the year 1644 onwards they steadily prosecuted a war in Candia which was disastrous to the Christians. Such were the state of affairs, the forces and the aims of the chief European nations at the time of the death of Louis XIII, King of France.

THE SITUATION IN FRANCE

France, allied to Sweden, Holland, Savoy and Portugal, and possessing the goodwill of other neutral countries, was waging a war against the Empire and Spain, ruinous to both sides and disastrous to the House of Austria. It resembled many other wars that have been waged for centuries by Christian princes, in which millions of men are sacrificed and provinces laid waste in order finally to obtain a few small frontier towns whose possession is rarely worth the cost of conquest.

Louis XIII's generals had taken Roussillon. The Catalonians were about to go over to the side of France, the protectress of the liberty for which they fought against their own kings; but these triumphs did not prevent our enemies from taking Corbie in 1636 and advancing as far as Pontoise. Half the inhabitants of Paris had fled from fear, and Cardinal Richelieu, deep in his vast schemes for the humbling of the Austrian power, had been reduced to taxing the gates of Paris for each one to provide a lackey to go to the war and drive the enemy back from the gates of the capital. The French had thus done much damage to the Spaniards and Germans, and had suffered no less themselves.

The Forces of France after the Death of Louis XIII and the Manners of the Time

The wars had produced famous generals such as Gustavus Adolphus, Wallenstein, the Duke of Weimar, Piccolomini, Jean de Vert, the Marshal of Guébriant, the Princes of Orange and the Count d'Harcourt. Certain ministers of state had been no less conspicuous. The chancellor Oxenstiern, the Count-Duke of Olivares, and above all, Cardinal Richelieu, had attracted the attention of Europe. No century has lacked famous statesmen and warriors, for politics and warfare seem unhappily to be the two most natural professions to man, and he must always be either bargaining or fighting. The most fortunate is considered the greatest, and public opinion often ascribes to merit the happy chances of fortune.

War was not then waged as we have seen it waged in the time of Louis XIV: armies were not so numerous; after the siege of Metz, for instance, by Charles V, no general found himself at the head of fifty thousand men; towns were besieged and defended with fewer cannon than are used today, and the art of fortification was still in its infancy. Pikes and arquebuses were used, and the sword which has become useless in our time was employed a great deal. The old international rule of declaring war by a herald was still in use. Louis XIII was the last to observe this custom, when in 1635 he sent a herald-at-arms to Brussels to declare war upon Spain.

It is common knowledge that nothing was more usual at that time than to see priests in command of armies; the Cardinal Infant of Spain, the Cardinal of Savoy, Richelieu, La Valette, Sourdis, Archbishop of Bordeaux, Cardinal Theodore Trivulzio, commandant of the Spanish cavalry, had all donned the cuirass and fought in person. A Bishop of Mende had been many times an army commissary. The popes sometimes threatened these warrior priests with excommunication. Pope Urban VIII, when vexed with France, told Cardinal de la Valette that he would deprive him of his cardinal's hat if he did not lay down his arms; but once reconciled to France he overwhelmed him with benedictions.

Ambassadors, no less ministers of peace than ecclesiastics, made no difficulty about serving in the armies of allied powers, in whose service they were employed. Charnace, sent from France into Holland, commanded a regiment there in 1637, and later even the ambassador, d'Estrades, became a colonel in their service.

France had only about 80,000 foot-soldiers available in all. The navy, neglected for centuries, was restored a little by Cardinal Richelieu, but ruined again by Mazarin. Louis XIII had only about 45,000,000 livres of ordinary revenue; but money was at 26 livres to the mark; these 45,000,000 would amount to about 85,000,000 to-day, when the arbitrary value of the silver mark has risen to as much as 49½ livres, and that of pure silver to 54 livres 17 sous; a value that public interest and justice alike demand should never be changed.

Commerce, to-day spread widely abroad, was then in very few hands. The policing of the kingdom was wholly neglected, a sure proof of a far from prosperous administration. Cardinal Richelieu, mindful of his own greatness, which was itself bound up with that of the state, had begun to make France formidable abroad, but had not yet been able to bring prosperity to her at home. The great highways were neither kept in repair nor policed, and they were infested with brigands; the streets of

Paris, narrow, badly paved and covered with filth, were overrun with thieves. The parliamentary registers show that the city watch was at that time reduced to forty-five badly paid men, who, to crown all, totally neglected their work.

Since the death of Francis II France had been continually torn by civil wars or factions. The yoke had never been borne easily and voluntarily. The nobles had been bred up in the midst of conspiracies; such was indeed the art of the court, as since it has been that of pleasing the sovereign.

This spirit of discord and faction spread from the court to the smaller towns, and pervaded every community in the kingdom; everything was disputed, because there was nothing fixed, and even in the parishes of Paris the people were continually coming to blows; processions fought one another for the honor of their respective banners. More than once the canons of Notre-Dame were seen at grips with their brethren of the Sainte-Chapelle; members of parliament and of the chambers of accounts fought each other for pride of place in Notre-Dame on the day that Louis XIII placed his kingdom under the protection of the Virgin Mary.

Practically every commune in the kingdom was armed, practically every person was inspired by the passion for duelling. This gothic barbarism, sanctioned once by kings themselves, and become a part of the national character, contributed to the depopulation of the country as much as civil or foreign wars. It is not too much to say that in the course of twenty years, ten of which had been troubled by war, more French gentlemen were killed at the hands of their own countrymen than at the hands of their enemies.

We shall say nothing here with regard to the cultivation of the arts and sciences; that part of the history of our customs will be found in its proper place. We shall merely remark that the French nation was steeped in ignorance, not excepting those who held that they were not of the people.

People consulted astrologers, and, what is more, believed them. Every memoir of that period, from President de Thou's History onward, is prodigal of prophecies. The serious and austere Duke de Sully solemnly describes those which were made to Henri IV.

This credulity, the most infallible sign of ignorance, was so universal that care was taken to have an astrologer hidden near the bedchamber of Anne of Austria at the birth of Louis XIV.

What is hardly credible, but which is nevertheless vouched for by the abbé, Vittorio Siri, a very well-informed contemporary writer, is that Louis XIII was surnamed the *Just* from his infancy, because he was born under the sign of Libra.

The same ignorance which popularized the absurd phantom of judicial astrology gave credit to the belief in possession by the devil and sorcery; it was made a point of religion, and there was scarcely a priest who did not exorcise devils. The courts of justice, presided over by magistrates who ought to have been more enlightened than the vulgar herd, were occupied in judging sorcerers. The memory of Cardinal Richelieu will always be stained by the death of the celebrated curé of Loudun, Urbain Grandier, who was condemned to the stake as a magician, by a decree of the council. One is shocked that the minister and judges should have had the ignorance to believe in the devils of Loudun, or the barbarity to have condemned an innocent man to the flames. Posterity will always remember with amazement that the Maréchale d'Ancre was burnt as a sorcerer in the Place de la Grève.

One may still see in a copy of some registers of *Le Châtelet* the record of a trial begun in 1610, concerning a horse who had been laboriously trained by his master to perform very much like a modern circus animal; it was proposed to burn both master and horse.

We have said enough here to show in a general way the customs and the spirit of the age preceding that of Louis XIV

This lack of enlightenment in all classes of society favored superstitious practices even in the most upright which brought disgrace upon religion. The Calvinists, confusing the rational Catholic religion with the abuses emanating from it, became only the more determined in their hatred of our church.

As was typical of all the reformers, they opposed to our popular superstitions, often intimately allied to debauchery, a fierce austerity and harsh manners; thus the partisan spirit tore and debased France; and the social spirit that today makes this nation so renowned and so attractive was entirely unknown. There were no houses where men of ability might gather together for the purpose of communicating knowledge, no academies, no regular theatres. In short, customs, laws, the arts, society, religion, peace and war, were as nothing to what they afterwards became in the century known as the *Age of Louis XIV.*

XXV

INCIDENTS AND ANECDOTES OF THE REIGN OF LOUIS XIV

Anecdotes are the gleanings left over from the vast harvestfield of history; they are details that have been long hidden, and hence their name of *anecdotes*: the public is interested in them when they concern illustrious personages.

Plutarch's *Lives of Great Men* is a collection of anecdotes more entertaining than accurate; how could he have had definite knowledge of the private lives of Theseus and Lycurgus? The majority of the maxims which he puts into the mouths of his characters are noteworthy for their moral content rather than their historical truth.

Procopius's *Secret History of Justinian* is a satire prompted by motives of revenge; and although revenge may sometimes speak the truth, this satire, which contradicts his own official history of the reign, seems to be false in several instances. One is not allowed nowadays to imitate Plutarch, still less Procopius. Historical truths must first be proved before they can be admitted. When contemporaries who were mutual enemies such as Cardinal de Retz and Duke de La Rochefoucauld confirm the same fact in their Memoirs, the matter is placed beyond a doubt; when they contradict, one must doubt: the principle is that what is probable should not be accepted, unless several trustworthy contemporaries unanimously testify to its truth.

The most useful and valuable anecdotes are those left in the secret writings of great princes, their natural candor thus revealing itself in permanent records; such are those which I am about to relate of Louis XIV.

Domestic details gratify merely the inquisitive: weaknesses brought to light give pleasure but to the spiteful, except when these very weaknesses are instructive, either on account of the misfortunes which they have caused or the virtues which have redeemed them.

The secret memoirs of contemporaries must always be suspected of partiality: those who write one or two generations later must use the greatest care to omit the merely frivolous, to reduce exaggeration, and combat what has been dictated by motives of satire.

Louis XIV invested his court, as he did all his reign, with such brilliancy and magnificence, that the slightest details of his private life appear to interest posterity, just as they were the objects of curiosity to every court in Europe and indeed to all his contemporaries. The splendor of his rule was reflected in his most trivial actions. People are more eager, especially in France, to know the smallest incidents of his court, than the revolutions of some other countries. Such is the effect of a great reputation. Men would rather know what happened in the private council and court of Augustus than details of the conquests of Attila or of Tamerlane.

Consequently there are few historians who have failed to give an account of Louis XIV's early affection for the Baroness de Beauvais, for Mlle. d'Argencourt, for Cardinal Mazarin's niece, later married to the Count of Soissons, father of Prince Eugene; and especially for her sister, Marie Mancini, who afterwards married the High Constable Colonne.

He had not yet taken over the reins of government when such diversions occupied the idleness in which he was encouraged by Cardinal Mazarin, then ruling as absolute master. His attachment to Marie Mancini was in itself a serious matter, for he was sufficiently in love to be tempted to marry her, and yet sufficiently master of himself to abandon her. This victory gained over his passion was the earliest sign that he was born with a great soul. He gained a yet greater and more difficult victory in allowing Cardinal Mazarin to remain absolute master.

Gratitude prevented him from shaking off a yoke which was beginning to irk him. The anecdote was often quoted at court to the effect that after the cardinal's death he said: "I do not know what I should have done, if he had lived much longer."

He occupied his leisure in reading entertaining books, especially in the company of Marie Mancini, wife of the High Constable Colonne, a witty woman, like all her sisters. He delighted in poetry and novels, which in describing gallant and noble deeds secretly flattered his own character. He read Corneille's tragedies and thus formed his taste, which is nothing other than the result of good sense and the prompting of a rightly trained mind. The conversations of his mother and the ladies of the court contributed not a little to make him appreciate this supreme faculty of the intellect, and to bring to perfection in him that remarkable refinement of manners which from that time began to characterize the court. Anne of Austria had brought with her a certain dignified and haughty gallantry typical of the Spanish nation at that time, and had added a charm, a mildness and decorous freedom only to be found in France. The king made greater progress in this school of accomplishments from his eighteenth to twentieth year than he had ever made in the sciences under his tutor, the Abbé de Beaumont, afterwards Archbishop of Paris. He had been taught practically nothing. It was at least desirable that he should have been taught some history, and especially modern history; but the available histories were too badly written.

It was to be deplored that authors had as yet only succeeded in writing useless novels, and that important books were still remarkably unattractive. A *Translation of the Commentaries of Cæsar* was printed under Louis' name and one of *Florus* under that of his brother; but these princes had no other part in these books than that of having idly taken some passages from these authors for their exercises.

The tutor who had charge of the king's education under the first Marshal Villeroi was just such as he needed—learned and yet good-humored: the civil wars, however, disturbed his education, and Cardinal Mazarin was very willing that the king should receive but little instruction. When he became attached to Marie Mancini he quickly learned Italian for her sake, and later, at the time of his marriage, he studied Spanish with less success. The fact that his tutors had allowed him too much to neglect his studies in early youth, a shyness which arose from a fear of placing himself in a false position, and the ignorance in which he was kept by Cardinal Mazarin, gave the whole court to believe that he would always be ruled like his father, Louis XIII.

There was only one occasion on which those who can judge future events predicted what he would become; this was in 1665, following upon the suppression of the civil wars, and after his first campaign and coronation, when parliament again wished to assemble and discuss certain decrees; the king set out from Vincennes in hunting dress followed by all his court, entered parliament in top-boots, whip in hand, and uttered these words: "The misfortunes that your assemblies have brought about are well known; I order you to break up this assembly which has met to discuss my decrees. *M. le premier Président,* I forbid you to allow these meetings and a single one of you to demand them."

His figure, even now imposing, the nobility of his features, the masterful tone and air with which he spoke, impressed them more than did his rank, which up till then they had but little respected. These first signs of his greatness, however, seemed to wither almost immediately, and the fruits only became apparent after the cardinal's death.

Since the triumphant return of Mazarin the court was taken up with gaming, ballets and comedy, which, but lately born in France, had not yet the attained dignity of an art, and with tragedy, already become a sublime art in the hands of Pierre Corneille. A curé of Saint-Germain l'Auxerrois who inclined to the rigorous notions of the Jansenists had often written to the queen during the first few years of the regency, complaining of these performances. He maintained that anyone who attended them was doomed to perdition, and had even had this anathema signed by seven doctors of the Sorbonne; but the Abbé de Beaumont, the king's tutor, fortified himself by obtaining so many approvals from doctors that they outnumbered the condemnations of the stern curé. He thus calmed the scruples of the queen and, on becoming Archbishop of Paris, sanctioned the views he had upheld as an abbé. This fact is mentioned in the *Memoirs* of Mme. de Motteville, and as such may be taken as genuine.

It should be noted that since Cardinal Richelieu introduced

regular performances of plays at court, which have now made Paris the rival of Athens, not only was there a special bench for the Academy, which included several ecclesiastics among its members, but also one for the bishops.

In 1646 and 1654 Cardinal Mazarin had Italian operas performed by singers specially come from Italy on the boards of the Palais-Royal theatre and the Petit-Bourbon, not far from the Louvre. This new entertainment had been recently invented in Florence, a state then favored by fortune as well as by nature, and to which we owe the revival of several arts that had lain unknown for centuries, and even the creation of a few. There still remained in France a remnant of ancient barbarism which was opposed to the introduction of these arts.

The Jansenists, whom Richelieu and Mazarin endeavored to suppress, revenged themselves on the pleasures which those two ministers introduced into the country. Lutherans and Calvinists had behaved in the same way in the time of Pope Leo X. Indeed one had only to be an innovator to be austere. Men who overturn a whole nation to establish, often, an absurd doctrine, are the very ones to denounce innocent pleasures essential to a great city and arts which contribute to the glory of a nation. The suppression of the theatre is an idea more worthy of the age of Attila than of that of Louis XIV.

The dance, which may still be reckoned one of the arts since it is subject to rules and gives grace to the body, was one of the favorite amusements of the court. Louis XIII had only once danced in a ballet, in 1625; and that ballet was of an undignified character which gave no promise of what the arts would become in France thirty years later. Louis XIV excelled in stately measures, which suited the majesty of his figure without injuring that of his position. The ring jousts in which he sometimes engaged, and which were attended with great magnificence, strikingly displayed his dexterity in all kinds of military exercises. Everything breathed an air of luxury and magnificence so far as they were then known. It was little in comparison with what was seen when the king took the reins of government into his own hands; but it was something at which to marvel after the horrors of a civil war and the gloom of the melancholy and secluded life of Louis XIII. That sickly and disappointed prince had not been housed, furnished, or waited upon as befits a king. He did not possess more than a hundred thousand crowns' worth of crown jewels. Mazarin left but twelve hundred thousand; and today the crown jewels are worth about twenty million livres.

In 1660, the marriage of Louis XIV was attended by a display of magnificence and exquisite taste which was ever afterwards on the increase. He made his entry accompanied by his bride, and Paris beheld with respectful yet loving admiration the beautiful young queen as she advanced, drawn in a superb carriage of novel design; the king, on horseback at her side, was adorned with everything that art could add to enhance his manly and heroic beauty which attracted every eye.

At the meeting of the roads at Vincennes a triumphal arch was erected on a base of stone; time did not permit the whole to be built of lasting material, and it was consequently made only of plaster which has since been entirely demolished. Claude Perrault designed it. The gate of Saint-Antoine was rebuilt for the same occasion, a monument in poorer taste, but decorated with statues of considerable merit. All those who, after the Battle of Saint-Antoine, witnessed the dead or dying bodies of innumerable citizens brought back to Paris through that gate, at that time defended by a portcullis, and who now saw an entry so different, blessed God and gave thanks for so fortunate a change.

To celebrate the marriage the Italian opera *Ercole Amante* was performed at the Louvre by the orders of Cardinal Mazarin, but it failed to please the French. They were delighted only to see the king and queen dancing in it. The cardinal resolved to bring himself into prominence by providing a show more to the nation's taste. The Secretary of State Lyonne undertook to have a kind of allegorical tragedy written in the style of *Europe*, on which Cardinal Richelieu had worked. It was fortunate for the great Corneille that he was not chosen to complete this wretched sketch. The subject was that of *Lysis and Hesperia*—*Lysis* representing France and *Hesperia* Spain; and Quinault was entrusted with carrying it out. He had lately made a great reputation with a piece entitled *The False Tiberius*, which, poor though it was, had had a tremendous success. Matters faɪ d differently with *Lysis*. It was performed at the Louvre, and its only merit was the stage-machinery employed. The Marquis de Sourdeac, to whom was due at a later date the establishment of opera in France, had at this very time at his own expense arranged a performance of Pierre Corneille's *Golden Fleece* in his castle at Neubourg with suitable stage-machinery. Quinault, young and of pleasing appearance, had the court on his side, Corneille had his name and France. The result is that we owe opera and comedy in France to two cardinals.

The king's marriage was followed by one long series of fêtes, entertainments and gallantries. They were redoubled on the marriage of *Monsieur*, the king's eldest brother, to Henrietta of England, sister of Charles II, and they were not interrupted until the death of Cardinal Mazarin in 1661.

Several months after the death of that minister an event occurred which is without parallel, and, what is stranger, all historians omit to mention it. An unknown prisoner, of height above the ordinary, young, and of an extremely handsome and noble figure, was conveyed under the greatest secrecy to the castle of the Island of Sainte-Marguerite, lying in the Mediterranean off Provence. On the journey the prisoner wore a mask, the chin-piece of which had steel springs to enable him to eat while still wearing it, and his guards had orders to kill him if he uncovered his face. He remained on the island until an officer of the secret service by name Saint-Mars, governor of Pignerol, who was made governor of the Bastille in 1690, went in that year to Saint-Marguerite, and brought him to the Bastille still wearing his mask. The Marquis de Louvois visited him on the island before his removal, and remained standing while speaking to him, evidently regarding him with respect. The unknown prisoner was conducted to the Bastille, where he was accommodated as well as was possible in that citadel, being refused nothing that he asked for. His greatest desire was for linen and lace of extraordinary fineness. He used to play on the guitar. He was given the greatest delicacies and the governor rarely seated himself in his presence. An old physician in the Bastille who often attended this remarkable man in illness declared that he never saw his face, although he had often examined his tongue and the rest of his body. He was a wonderfully well-made man, said his physician; his skin was rather dark; he charmed by the mere tone of his voice, never complaining of his lot nor giving a hint of his identity.

The unknown man died in 1703 and was buried by night in the parish church of Saint Paul. What is doubly astonishing is that when he was sent to the Island of Sainte-Marguerite no man of any consequence in Europe disappeared. Yet such the prisoner was without a doubt, for during the first few days that he was on the island, the governor himself put the dishes on the table and then withdrew, locking the door after him. One day the prisoner wrote something with his knife on a silver plate and threw it out of the window in the direction of a boat lying by the bank almost at the foot of the tower. A fisherman, to whom the boat belonged, picked up the plate and carried it to the governor. In amazement the latter asked him, "Have you read what is written on this plate, and has anyone seen it in your hands?" "I cannot read," replied the fisherman, "I have just found it, and no one else has seen it." The peasant was detained until the governor was convinced that he had not read it and that the plate had not been seen. "Go now," he said to him; "you are a very lucky man not to be able to read." Among those who have had first-hand knowledge of this affair a very trustworthy one is still alive. M. de Chamillart was, however, the last minister to be acquainted with the strange secret. His son-in-law, the second Marshal La Feuillade, told me that when his father-in-law lay dying, he implored him on his knees to tell him the name of this man who had been known simply as *the man in the iron mask*. Chamillart replied that it was a state secret and that he had sworn never to reveal it. Lastly, there are still many of my contemporaries who can confirm the truth of the affair that I have described, than which I know none more extraordinary, and at the same time better authenticated.

Meanwhile Louis XIV was dividing his time between the pleasures befitting his age and the duties involved by his position. He used to hold a council every day, and would then work in secret with Colbert. This secret work brought about the downfall of the celebrated Fouquet, in which the Secretary of State, Guénégaud, Pellisson, Gourville, and so many others were involved. The fall of this minister, who was certainly less reproached than Cardinal Mazarin, shows that it is not everyone who can commit the same mistakes. His doom was already sealed when the king accepted an invitation to the magnificent fête which the minister held in his honor at his mansion at Vaux. This palace and the gardens had cost him eighteen millions, which would be worth about thirty-five today. He had twice built the palace and had bought three hamlets which were now contained in the enormous gardens, which had been planted in part by Le Nôtre, and were then regarded as the finest in Europe. The fountains of Vaux, afterwards less than mediocre in comparison with those of Versailles, Marli, and Saint-Cloud, were then considered marvelous. Nevertheless, however fine the mansion, an expenditure of eighteen millions—the accounts are still in existence—proves that his underlings had served him with as little regard for economy as he himself was serving the king. It could not be denied that Saint-Germain and Fontainebleau, the only country seats inhabited by the king, fell far short of the beauties of Vaux. Louis XIV felt this and it annoyed him. The arms and motto of Fouquet were to be seen on every side, consisting of a squirrel with the words: *Quo non ascendam?* The ambition of the motto did not tend to pacify him.

The courtiers noticed that the squirrel was depicted everywhere, and was followed by an adder, which was the emblem of Colbert. The entertainment surpassed those given by Cardinal Mazarin, not only in magnificence, but in refinement. Molière's *Fâcheux* was there performed for the first time. Pellisson had composed the prologue, which was much admired. So true is it that at court public entertainments often conceal or prepare the way for the downfall of individuals, that had it not been for the queen-mother Pellisson and Fouquet would have been arrested at Vaux on the very day of the fête. What still further increased the anger of the king was that Mlle. de La Vallière, for whom he was beginning to feel a genuine passion, had been the object of Fouquet's passing fancy, and the latter had spared no efforts to satisfy it. He had offered Mlle. de La Vallière two hundred thousand livres, but she had indignantly rejected the offer before even she had any design on the king's affections. Perceiving later what a powerful rival he had, Fouquet endeavored to become the confidant of her whom he could not possess, and thus but further exasperated the king.

Louis, in the first feeling of indignation, had been tempted to have Fouquet arrested in the middle of the very fête which was being held in his honor; but afterwards made use of an unnecessary dissimulation, almost as though the monarch, already all-powerful, was afraid of the party which Fouquet had gathered together.

He was the Attorney-General for parliament, an office which entitled him to the privilege of being tried by the combined chambers; but after so many princes, marshals and dukes had been tried by commissioners, it should have been surely possible to treat a magistrate in the same way, since it was thought wise to make use of unusual methods, such as without being unjust always leave behind them the flavor of injustice.

Colbert persuaded him to sell his office by a dishonorable trick. He was offered as much as 1,800,000 livres, which would be worth 3,500,000 today; and by a misunderstanding, he sold it for only 1,400,000 francs. The exorbitant amounts paid for seats in parliament, amounts which were later much reduced, prove that that body still commanded a considerable respect even in its decadence. The Duke de Guise, Grand Chamberlain to the king, had sold that office of the crown to the Duke de Bouillon for a mere 800,000 livres.

It was the Fronde and the civil war in Paris which so raised the price of judicial offices, while it was one of the greatest defects and misfortunes of a government long involved in debt, that France should be the only country where judicial offices were sold; it was, nevertheless, the result of the leaven of sedition and in itself an insult to the throne, that the office of the King's Attorney should cost more than the chief preferments of the crown.

Despite the fact that he had squandered state funds and appropriated them to his own use, Fouquet had, none the less, a certain greatness of soul. His depredations had all been used for public display and private liberality. In 1661 he handed over the price of his office to the royal treasury, but the magnanimous action did not save him. He who could have been arrested in Paris by a common police officer and two guards was cunningly lured to Nantes. The king paid him great attentions immediately before his downfall. I do not know why the majority of princes should have the custom of deceiving with false kindness those of their subjects of whom they wish to rid themselves. Duplicity at such a time is the opposite of greatness. It is never a virtue and only becomes a worthy expedient when it is entirely necessary. Louis XIV appeared to belie his usual character; but he had been told that Fouquet was making great fortifications at Belle-Isle, and that he probably possessed too many allies, both within and without the kingdom. But it was plain enough, when he was arrested and taken to the Bastille and Vincennes, that his party was nothing more than a few courtiers and greedy women, who were in receipt of pensions from him, and who forgot him immediately that he was no longer in a position to bestow them. Other friends remained, however, proving that he was worthy of them. The celebrated Mme. de Sévigné, Pellisson, Gourville, Mlle. Scudéri and several men of letters stoutly defended him, and by their zeal succeeded in saving his life.

The following verses of Hénault, the translator of Lucretius, against Colbert, Fouquet's persecutor, are well known:

> Base sordid minister, poor slave misplac'd,
> Who groan'st beneath the weight of state affairs,
> Devoted sacrifice to public cares,
> Vain phantom, with a weary title grac'd;
>
> The dangerous point of envied greatness see;
> Of fallen Fouquet behold the sad remains,
> And while his fall rewards thy secret pains,
> Dread a more dismal fate prepared for thee.
>
> Those pangs he suffers thou one day may'st feel.
> Thy giddy station dread, the court and fortune's wheel;
> Against him cease thy prince's ire to feed.

From power's steep summit few unhurt descend;
Thyself, perhaps, shall soon his mercy need,
Then seek not all his rigor to extend.

M. Colbert, on hearing of this libelous sonnet, asked if the king was offended by it. He was told that he was not. "Then neither am I," replied the minister.

One must never be deceived by such well-considered replies, or by public declarations which are belied by the speaker's actions.

Colbert appeared to be moderate, but in reality he sought Fouquet's death with extraordinary ferocity. A man may be a good minister and yet vindictive. It is a pity that Colbert could not be as magnanimous as he was wary.

One of the most implacable of Fouquet's enemies was Michel Le Tellier, then Secretary of State and his rival in favor. He it was who afterwards became chancellor. To read his funeral oration and then compare it with his conduct, one can but conclude that a funeral oration is nothing more than a piece of declamatory oratory. The chancellor, Séguier, president of the commission, was, however, of all Fouquet's judges the one who sought his death with the greatest fury, and who treated him with the greatest harshness.

It must be admitted that to bring an action against Fouquet was in itself to disparage the memory of Cardinal Mazarin. None had embezzled state funds with a freer hand, and, as a sovereign power, he had appropriated to himself several sources of state revenue. He had traded in army munitions in his own name and reaped good profits. "By means of *lettres-de-cachet*," said Fouquet in his defense, "he imposed enormous taxes on the various districts, a thing which had never been done before except by him and for his own profit, and which, according to the ordinances, is punishable by death." It was thus that the cardinal had amassed immense wealth, which he himself no longer enjoyed.

I have heard the late M. de Caumartin, comptroller of finance, relate that in his youth, some years after the cardinal's death, he had been to Mazarin's palace, where his heir, the Duke, and the Duchess Hortense were living, and that he saw there a huge inlaid cupboard occupying the whole of one wall of his study. The keys had long since been lost, and the drawers had remained, unopened. Amazed at such indifference, M. de Caumartin suggested to the Duchess de Mazarin that they might perhaps find some curios in the cupboard. It was thereupon opened, and found to be completely filled with doubloons, tokens and gold medallions. For more than a week Mme. de Mazarin threw handfuls of them out of the windows to people in the streets.

The fact that Cardinal Mazarin had abused his despotic power was no justification for Fouquet, but the irregularity of the proceedings taken against him, the length of the trial, the obvious and disgusting animosity of Chancellor Séguier towards him, the very passage of time which calms down the anger of the public, replacing it by pity for the wretch concerned, and finally the representations, always more powerful in favor of an unfortunate man than are the steps taken against him—all this, I repeat, was the means of saving his life. The trial dragged on for three years, from 1661 to 1664. Of the twenty-two judges who presided, not more than nine voted for the death penalty; the remaining thirteen, some of whom had accepted presents from Gourville, voted for perpetual banishment.

The king commuted the sentence to a less severe one. Such harsh treatment was consistent neither with the ancient laws of the realm nor with those of humanity. What most revolted the minds of citizens was that the chancellor exiled one of the judges, named Roquesante, who was chiefly responsible for inclining the court of justice to mercy. Fouquet was imprisoned in the Castle of Pignerol, and all historians agree in saying that he died there in 1680, but Gourville asserts in his *Memoirs* that he was released from prison some time before his death. The Countess de Vaux, his daughter-in-law, had already acquainted me with this fact; yet his family believe the contrary. Thus no one can be certain where this unfortunate man died, he whose least actions had been imposing at the time of his greatness.

Guénégaud, the Secretary of State, who had sold his office to Colbert, was also prosecuted by the Chamber of Justice, and was deprived of the greater part of his fortune. One of the most singular sentences of that court was that passed on a bishop of Avranches, who was fined twelve thousand francs. His name was Boislève; he was the brother of a taxfarmer, with whom he had shared bribes.

Saint-Evremond, who had been attached to Fouquet, was involved in his downfall. Colbert, searching everywhere for proofs against the man he wished to ruin, seized upon some papers entrusted to Mme. du Plessis-Bellière, and found among them an autograph letter of Saint-Evremond relating to the Peace of the Pyrenees. The facetious document was read to the king and was judged treasonable. Colbert, scorning to avenge himself on an unknown man like Hénault, persecuted in Saint-Evremond a friend of Fouquet, whom he hated, and a wit whom he feared. The king went to the extreme length of punishing an innocent piece of raillery directed long ago at Cardinal Mazarin, for whom he felt no regret, and whom the whole court had insulted, slandered and denounced with impunity for several years. Of the thousand libels written against that minister, the least virulent alone was punished, and that only after his death.

Saint-Evremond, who found a retreat in England, lived and died as a free man and a philosopher. His friend, the Marquis de Miremond, told me some time ago in London that there was another reason for his disgrace, one which Saint-Evremond would never reveal. When Louis XIV gave him permission to return to his native land at the close of his life, the philosopher disdained to regard such permission as a concession; he showed that one's country is where one can live, and as such he breathed the native air of London.

The new Minister of Finance, under the simple title of Comptroller-General, justified the severity of his prosecutions by restoring an order which his predecessors had sadly troubled, and working ceaselessly for the good of the state.

The court became the center of pleasures, and a model for all other courts. The king prided himself on giving entertainments which should put those of Vaux in the shade.

Nature herself seemed to take a delight in producing at this

moment in France men of the first rank in every art, and in
bringing together at Versailles the most handsome and well-
favored men and women that ever graced a court. Above all his
courtiers Louis rose supreme by the grace of his figure and the
majestic nobility of his countenance. The sound of his voice,
at once dignified and charming, won the hearts of those whom
his presence had intimidated. His bearing was such as befitted
himself and his rank alone, and would have been ridiculous
in any other. The awe which he inspired in those who spoke
with him secretly flattered the consciousness of his own superiority. The old officer who became confused and faltered in his
speech when asking a favor, finally breaking off with "Sire, I
have never trembled thus before your enemies," had no difficulty
in obtaining what he asked.

Court society had not yet, however, perfected its taste. Anne
of Austria, the queen-mother, was beginning to prefer retirement;
the reigning queen hardly knew any French; generosity was as
yet her only merit.

The king's sister-in-law, an English princess, brought to the
court the charms of pleasant and vivacious conversation soon
rendered more solid by the reading of good books, and a taste
as sure as it was fastidious. She perfected her knowledge of the
language, which at the time of her marriage she still wrote but
ill. She inspired a new spirit of emulation and introduced a
charm and gentility of manners into the court such as the rest
of Europe had scarcely conceived. *Madame* had all the wit of
her brother Charles II, set off by the charms of her sex, and
by the gift and desire to please. A certain gallantry pervaded the
court of Louis XIV which propriety rendered but more piquant.
That of the court of Charles II was more conspicuous but also
degraded by its coarseness.

At first *Madame* and the king frequently indulged in such
intimate coquetries and secret familiarities as were denoted by
certain little attentions oft repeated. The king sent verses to her;
and she replied to them. It happened that the same man was
at once the confidant of the king and *Madame* in this ingenious
correspondence. This was the Marquis de Dangeau. The king
engaged him to write for him, and the princess employed him

to reply to the king. He thus served both without letting either suspect that he was employed by the other, and this was one of the causes of his success.

The knowledge of the affair threw the royal family into alarm, and the king replaced this over-free correspondence with a respect and friendship which were never altered.

When *Madame* afterwards engaged Racine and Corneille upon the tragedy of *Bérénice*, she was thinking not only of the king's breach with the High Constable Colonne, but of the restraint she had herself imposed upon his fondness for her, for fear it should become dangerous. Louis XIV is adequately described in these two lines of Racine's *Bérénice*:

> His birth howe'er obscure, his race unknown,
> The world in him its sovereign chief would own.

These diversions made way for the ardent and obstinate passion which he entertained for Mlle. de La Vallière, a maid of honor of *Madame*. With her he enjoyed the rare felicity of being loved for himself alone. For two years she was the secret object of all the gay entertainments and fêtes given by the king. One of the king's young gentlemen-in-waiting, named Belloc, composed some verses which were mingled with the dance and performed both before the queen and before *Madame*—verses which gave mysterious utterance to the secret of their hearts, which soon ceased to be a secret.

All the public entertainments given by the king were paid by way of homage to his mistress. In 1662, a tournament was held, opposite the Tuileries, in an immense enclosure, which still retains the name of *Place du Carrousel (Tournament Square)*. There were five troops of horse. The king headed the Romans; his brother, the Persians; the Prince de Condé, the Turks; his brother the Duke d'Enghien, the Indians; the Duke de Guise, the Americans. This last was Balafré's grandson. He was famous everywhere for the fatal daring with which he had attempted to capture Naples. In everything he was remarkable —for his imprisonment, his duels, his romantic love affairs, his prodigality and his adventures. He seemed to belong to another age. Seeing him pass with the great Condé, people cried: "There go the heroes of history and fable."

Forgetful of their sorrows for the time being, the queen-mother, the reigning queen, and the Queen of England, Charles I's widow, were seated under a canopy watching the show. The Count de Sault, son of the Duke de Lesdiguières, gained the prize and received it at the hands of the queen-mother. These entertainments brought into vogue more than ever the taste for devices and emblems which the tournaments had formerly brought into fashion and which now survived them.

An antiquary of the name of Douvrier devised at this time for Louis XIV the emblem of a sun darting its rays on to a globe, with the words: *Nec Pluribus Impar*. The idea was partly copied from a Spanish device made for Philip II, and more suited to that king, who possessed the finest parts of the New World and so much territory in the Old, than to a young King of France whose expectations were as yet unrealized. The device had a wonderful success, and the king's coat of arms, the crown furniture, tapestries and statuary were all ornamented with it, but the king never wore it at his tournaments. Louis XIV was unjustly censured for the pompousness of this device, as though he had chosen it himself, and its signification was perhaps more justly criticized. The device does not illustrate the meaning of the motto, nor does the motto convey a sense sufficiently distinctive and precise. For what may be explained in several ways is not worth explaining in any. Devices, the remnants of ancient chivalry, are well suited to fêtes, and are agreeable when the allusions are appropriate, novel and witty. But it is better to be without them than to tolerate poor or vulgar ones, such as that of Louis XII, which was the emblem of a hog, with the words: "Meddle and smart for it." Devices bear the same relation to inscriptions as masquerades to stately ceremonies.

The fête of Versailles, held in 1664, surpassed the tournament fête by its remarkable character, its splendor, and by pleasures that charmed the mind, which, mingling with the magnificence of the entertainments, added a style and refinement with which no fête had hitherto been embellished. Versailles had become a delightful abode, but had not yet acquired that magnificence which it was afterwards to know.

(1664) On the fifth of May the king proceeded to Versailles with the court, which comprised six hundred people, all of whose expenses were defrayed, as well as those of their suites, as also were the expenses of those who were engaged in preparing the entertainment. Nothing was wanting at these fêtes save monuments specially erected in their honor, such as those raised by the Greeks and Romans; but the speed with which theatres, amphitheatres and porticos, ornamented with as much magnificence as taste, were erected, was a marvel, which added to the illusion and which, transformed afterwards in a thousand ways, still further enhanced the charm of the spectacle.

The proceedings began with a kind of tournament. Those who were to take part appeared on the first day as if for a review; they were preceded by heralds-at-arms, pages and equerries, who carried their devices and shields; and on these shields were written, in letters of gold, verses composed by Perigni and Benserade. The latter, especially, had a remarkable talent for such polite verses, in which he made delicate and pointed allusions to people's characters, to personages of antiquity or of the legends which were being represented, and to the love-affairs that animated the court. The king impersonated Roger; all the crown diamonds sparkled on his dress and on the horse that he was riding. Stationed beneath triumphal arches the queens and three hundred ladies watched his entrance.

All eyes were fixed on the king, but he observed none but those of Mlle. de La Vallière. The fête was for her alone; and she enjoyed it lost amid the crowd.

The procession was followed by a golden chariot, eighteen feet high, fifteen feet broad and twenty-four feet long, representing the chariot of the sun. The four ages, of gold, silver, brass and iron; the heavenly signs, the seasons, the hours, followed this chariot on foot. All of them bore their characteristic emblems. Shepherds followed, carrying the barricades, which were placed in position to the fanfare of trumpets, followed at intervals by the playing of musettes and violins. Several personages who followed the chariot of Apollo approached the queens and recited verses suited to the occasion, the season, the king and the ladies. When the courses were finished and night fell, four thousand great torches illuminated the space where the entertainments were given. The tables were served by two hundred persons, representing the seasons, Fauns, Sylvans and Dryads, together with shepherds, vintagers and reapers. Pan and Diana advanced on a moving mountain and, descending, placed on the tables the most delicious fruits that field and forest could produce. Behind the tables, a theatre shaped in a semi-circle, filled with performers, rose suddenly to view. The arcades surrounding the tables and the theatre were adorned with five hundred green and silver candelabra filled with candles, and a gold balustrade encircled this vast enclosure.

These fêtes, surpassing those invented in any novel, lasted seven days. Four times did the king carry off the prize for the games, and then allowed the other knights to compete for the prizes he had won and afterwards abandoned.

La Princesse d'Élide, though not one of the best comedies of Molière, proved one of the pleasantest diversions of these fêtes: it pleased by an infinite number of delicate allegories of contemporary fashions, and by allusions which add much to the amusement of such fêtes, but which are lost for posterity. The court was still infatuated with the delusions of judicial astrology; more than one prince imagined with arrogant superstition that nature honored him to the point of inscribing his destiny in the stars. Victor Amadeus, Duke of Savoy, father of the Duchess of Burgundy, had an astrologer attendant upon him even after his abdication. Molière had the temerity to attack this delusion in *Les Amants Magnifiques*, given at another fête in 1670.

There was also a court jester, as in *La Princesse d'Élide*. These wretches were still greatly in fashion. They were a relic of barbarism, which lasted longer in Germany than anywhere else. The need of amusement, the difficulty of obtaining agreeable and honorable entertainments in an age of ignorance and bad taste, were responsible for the invention of this melancholy pleasure, degrading to the human mind. The fool who attended Louis XIV at that time had belonged to the Prince de Condé;

his name was Angeli. The Count de Grammont said that of all the fools who engaged themselves in the prince's service, Angeli was the only one who had made his fortune. The buffoon was not lacking in wit. It was he who said "that he did not go to hear sermons preached because he did not like the *bawling* and did not understand the arguments."

(1664) Molière's farce entitled *Le Mariage Forcé* was also played at this fête. But what was truly admirable was the first performance of the first three acts of *Tartuffe*. The king wished to see this masterpiece before it was even finished. He afterwards defended it against those false bigots who wished to move heaven and earth to suppress it, and it will continue to live, as I have already said elsewhere, so long as there is good taste and a hypocrite in France.

The greater part of such brilliant ceremonies usually appeals only to sight and hearing. Mere pomp and show last but for a day; but when masterpieces of art, such as *Tartuffe*, enrich such fêtes, they leave behind them an enduring memory.

One still calls to mind certain features of the allegories of Benserade, which enlivened the ballets of that period. I shall quote only the following lines addressed to the king representing the sun:

> With you, I doubt we must not prate
> Of Daphne's scorn and Phaeton's fate;
>   He too aspiring, she inhuman,
> In snares like these you cannot fall,
> For who will dream that e'er you shall
>   Be fool'd by man or shunn'd by woman?

The chief glory of these amusements, which brought taste, polite manners and talents to such perfection in France, was that they did not for a moment detach the monarch from his incessant labors. Without such toil he could but have held a court, he could not have reigned: and had the magnificent pleasures of the court outraged the miseries of the people, they would only have been detestable; but the same man who gave these entertainments had given the people bread during the famine of 1662. He had bought up corn, which he sold to the rich at a low price, and which he gave free to poor families at the gate of the Louvre; he had remitted three millions of taxes to the people; no part of the internal administration was neglected, and his government was respected abroad. The King of Spain was obliged to allow him precedence; the Pope was forced to give him satisfaction; Dunkirk was acquired by France by a treaty honorable to the purchaser and ignominious to the seller; in short, all measures adopted after he had taken up the reins of government were either honorable or useful; thereafter, it was fitting that he should give such fêtes.

In 1664, the arrival of Chigi, the legate *a latere*, Pope Alexander VII's nephew, in the midst of all these rejoicings at Versailles, to give satisfaction to the king for the outrages committed by the Pope's guards, provided a new spectacle at court. Such great ceremonies are as so many fêtes to the public. The honors accorded to Chigi made the satisfaction that he rendered still more striking. Seated on a dais, he received the homage of the higher courts, of the corporations of towns, and of the clergy. He entered Paris to the firing of cannon, with the great Condé on his right-hand side, and that prince's son on his left; and attended by all this pomp, he came to humble himself, Rome and the Pope, before a king who had not so much as drawn a sword. After being received in audience, he dined with Louis XIV, everyone being occupied in treating him with magnificence and in procuring amusements for him. The Doge of Genoa was afterwards treated, albeit with fewer honors, with the same desire to please, which the king combined with his regal dignity.

All this conferred an air of grandeur on the court of Louis XIV, which eclipsed that of any other court in Europe. He desired that the glory which emanated from his own person should be reflected by all who surrounded him, so that all the nobles should be honored but no one powerful, not even his brother or *Monsieur le Prince*. It was with this object in view that he passed judgment in favor of the peers in their long-standing feud with the presidents of parliament. The latter claimed the prerogative of speaking before the peers and had assumed possession of this right. Louis decided at an extraordinary council that when the king was present at a meeting of the High Chamber in its judicial capacity peers should speak before the presidents, as though owing this prerogative directly to his presence; and in the case of assemblies which are not judicial bodies he allowed the old custom to hold good.

For the purpose of distinguishing his chief courtiers, blue cassocks had been devised, embroidered in gold and silver. Permission to wear them was a great favor for men who were swayed by vanity. They were in nearly as great demand as the collar of the order of Saint-Louis. It may be mentioned, since it is here a question of small details, that cassocks were at that time worn over a doublet ornamented with ribbons, and over this cassock a shoulder-belt was fastened, from which hung the sword. A kind of lace neck-band was also worn, and a hat adorned with two rows of feathers. This fashion, which lasted until 1684, prevailed throughout the whole of Europe, with the exception of Spain and Poland. Already nearly every country took a pride in imitating the court of Louis XIV.

He introduced into his household a system which still obtains, regulated the ranks and offices, and created new posts in attendance on his person, such as the Grand Master of the Wardrobe. He restored the tables instituted by Francis I and increased their number. Twelve of these were set apart for officers who dined in the royal presence, and were laid with as much nicety and profusion as those of many sovereigns: he desired all foreigners to be invited, and his consideration was extended to them during the whole of his reign. He was responsible for another attention still more subtle and refined. When the pavilions of Marli were built in 1679 all the ladies found a complete toilet set in their apartments; nothing that was essential to ease and luxury was forgotten: anyone who was fresh from travel could give meals in his own private room, and they were served with the same care as those of his master. Such small matters only acquire value when they are accompanied by great ones. Splendor and generosity characterized everything that he did. He made a present of two hundred thousand francs to the daughters of his ministers on their marriage.

What gave him the greatest glory in Europe was his liberality, which was unprecedented. The idea was suggested to him by a conversation with the Duke de Saint-Aignan, who related to him how Cardinal Richelieu had sent presents to certain foreign scholars who had written in his praise. The king did not wait to be praised, but sure of his desert he bade his ministers, Lyonne and Colbert, make a choice of a number of Frenchmen and foreigners upon whom he wished to confer marks of his generosity. Having written to foreign countries and acquired as much information as he could on so delicate a matter, where it was a question of making a selection among contemporaries, Lyonne first made a list of sixty persons; some of them received presents, and others annuities, according to their station, needs and merits.

(1663) Allacci, the librarian of the Vatican; Count Graiani, Secretary of State to the Duke of Modena; the illustrious Viviani, mathematician to the Grand Duke of Florence; Vossius, historiographer of the United Provinces; the celebrated mathematician, Huygens; a Dutch resident in Sweden, who was none other than Heinsius: finally, even certain professors of Altdorf and Helmstadt, towns almost unknown to the French—all these were astonished to receive letters from M. Colbert, in which he informed them that while the king was not their sovereign, yet he begged them to accept him as their patron. The tone of these letters was varied according to the importance of the person addressed, and they were all accompanied either by liberal gifts or by annuities.

Among the French singled out for these honors were Racine, Quinault and Fléchier, afterwards Bishop of Nîmes, and still quite young; they all received gifts. It is true that Chapelain and Cotin received annuities, but it was Chapelain whom the minister Colbert had particularly consulted. These two men, whose poetry has been so decried, were not without merit. Chapelain was extremely well-read, and what is more surprising, he had taste and was one of the most enlightened of critics. True, such talent is far removed from genius. Science and intelligence may guide an artist, but they cannot in any way create him. No one in France enjoyed so great a reputation during their lives as Ronsard and Chapelain. The fact is that Ronsard lived in a time of barbarism and the nation had scarcely emerged from this state during the life of Chapelain. Costar, the schoolfellow of Balzac and Voiture, called Chapelain the first of the heroic poets.

Boileau was not included in this generous scheme; as yet he had only written satires, and, as is well known, his satires attacked the very scholars whom the minister consulted. Some years afterwards the king honored him without consulting anyone.

So liberal were the gifts distributed in foreign countries that Viviani had a house built in Florence with the money he had received from Louis XIV. Over the portals he inscribed in gold letters the words: *Aedes a Deo datae*—an allusion to the cognomen of Heaven-born which the public voice had bestowed on the prince from his birth.

It may easily be imagined what effect this extraordinary lavishness had upon the rest of Europe; and when one considers all the notable things achieved by the king soon afterwards, the most severe and particular of critics must acquiesce in the extravagant praises showered upon him. Nor were the French the only people to eulogize him. Twelve panegyrics on Louis XIV were delivered in various towns in Italy—marks of respect which were prompted neither by hope nor fear, and which were brought to the king's notice by the Marquis Zampieri.

He did not cease to bestow his patronage upon literature and the arts. Proofs of this will be found in the special gift of about four thousand louis made to Racine, in the fortunes of Boileau, Quinault and especially Lulli, and of all those artists who dedicated their works to him. He also gave a thousand louis to Benserade for the engraving of the copper-plates for his *Metamorphoses* of Ovid, translated into rondeaus—a misplaced liberality which betokened only the sovereign's generosity. He was rewarding Benserade for the trivial merit of his ballets.

Several writers have ascribed this patronage of the arts and the magnificence of Louis XIV solely to Colbert; but the only credit that can be attributed to him in the matter was that of encouraging his master's magnanimity and judgment. That minister, who had a wonderful talent for financial affairs, commerce, navigation, and the maintenance of order, did not possess the

king's insight and nobility of soul; he lent himself eagerly to
the plan, but was far from inspiring in Louis what was nature's
gift.

In view of this it is difficult to see upon what grounds certain
writers have reproached that monarch with avarice. A prince,
who has estates entirely detached from the revenues of the state,
may be miserly just as any other man; but a King of France,
who is, in reality, but the distributor of his subjects' wealth,
can scarcely be afflicted with this vice. He may be lacking in
consideration and in the desire to reward merit, but these are
things for which Louis XIV cannot be reproached.

At the very time when he began to encourage talent by his
patronage, Count Bussy-Rabutin was severely punished for the
use he made of his. He was thrown into the Bastille in 1665,
the pretext of his imprisonment being his book, *Les Amours des
Gaules*. The real cause, however, was the ballad in which the
king was too much compromised, and which was now brought
to light again to ruin Bussy-Rabutin to whom it was attributed:

> Beyond expression sure this is,
> When Deodatus fondly kisses
> That beak so delicate and dear,
> Replete with charms from ear to ear.

His works were not of sufficient value to make up for the
mischief that they did. His use of language was pure, and he
had talent, but he was also too conceited and used his talents
but to make fresh enemies. Louis XIV would have acted generously had he pardoned him: as it was he avenged a personal
injury while appearing to yield to the opinion of society. Count
Bussy-Rabutin was released at the end of eighteen months; but
he was deprived of his post, and disgraced for the remainder of
his life, vainly professing a devotion to Louis XIV which neither
the king nor anyone else believed sincere.

XXVIII

FURTHER ANECDOTES

Louis XIV concealed his sorrows in public; people saw no difference in him, but in private the shock of so many misfortunes

overcame him, and he was convulsed with grief. He suffered all these family losses at the conclusion of a disastrous war, before he was even assured of peace, and at a time when his whole kingdom was plunged in misery. Yet he was not seen for one moment to be overcome by his misfortunes.

The remainder of his life was sad. The disorganization of state finances, which he was unable to repair, estranged many hearts. The complete confidence he placed in the Jesuit, Le Tellier, a turbulent spirit, stirred them to rebellion. It is remarkable that the people who forgave him all his mistresses could not forgive this one confessor. In the minds of the majority of his subjects he lost during the last three years of his life all the prestige of the great and memorable things he had accomplished.

With the loss of nearly all his children, his affection redoubled for his legitimized sons, the Duke of Maine and the Count of Toulouse, and he proclaimed them and their descendants, in default of princes of the blood royal, heirs to the throne by an edict which was passed in 1714 without protest. He thus tempered by a natural law the rigor of the conventional laws, which deprive children born out of wedlock of all rights to the paternal succession. Kings, however, dispense with this law. He thought himself justified in doing for his own flesh and blood what he had done on behalf of several of his subjects: especially was he justified in doing for two of his children what he had persuaded parliament to pass unopposed for the princes of the House of Lorraine. A year later, in 1715, he decreed that the rank of his illegitimate sons should be equal to that of princes of the blood royal. The lawsuit which the princes of the blood afterwards instituted against the legitimized princes is well known. The latter preserved, however, for themselves and their children the honors accorded by Louis XIV. As to the position of their descendants, that will depend upon their age, their merit, and their fortune.

On his return from Marli towards the middle of the month of August 1715, Louis XIV was attacked by the illness which ended his life. His legs swelled, and signs of gangrene began to show themselves. The Earl of Stair, the English ambassador, wagered, after the fashion of his country, that the king would not outlive the month of September. The Duke of Orleans, on the journey from Marli, had been left completely to himself, but now the whole court gathered round his person. During the last days of the king's illness, a quack physician gave him a cordial which revived him. He managed to eat, and the quack assured him that he would recover. On hearing this news the crowd of people that had gathered round the Duke of Orleans diminished immediately. "If the king eats another mouthful," said the Duke of Orleans, "we shall have no one left." But the illness was mortal. Arrangements were made for granting the absolute regency to the Duke of Orleans. In his will, ratified by parliament, the king had only given him very limited powers; or rather he had only made him president of the council of regency, in which he would have nothing more than the casting vote. Nevertheless, he said to him: "I have conserved to you all the rights to which your birth entitles you." He had overlooked the fundamental law which during a minority confers unlimited powers on the heir presumptive to the throne. This supreme power, which is liable to be abused, is dangerous; but a divided authority is no less so. He imagined that having been obeyed so unhesitatingly during his life, he would be so after his death, and forgot that the will of his own father had been broken.

(1 September, 1715) There is no one who does not know with what greatness of soul he perceived death approaching, saying to Mme. de Maintenon, "I had thought that it was more difficult to die," and to his servants, "Why do you weep? did you think me immortal?"—quietly giving his orders concerning many things, even the preparations for his own funeral. Whoever has many to witness his death dies always with a high heart.

During his last illness Louis XIII had set to music the *De Profundis*, which was to be sung at his funeral. The fortitude with which Louis XIV met his end was unattended by the pomp which had characterized his whole life. His courage even led him to the length of confessing his own faults, and his successor always kept written at the head of his bed the remarkable words which that monarch spoke to him, clasping him in his arms on the bed; these words are far other than those commonly reported in all the histories, and I give here an exact copy of them:

"You will soon be the monarch of a great kingdom. What I most strongly enjoin upon you is never to forget your obligations to God. Remember that you owe all that you are to Him. Endeavor to preserve peace with your neighbors. I have been too fond of war; do not imitate me in that, neither in my too great extravagance. Take counsel in all things and always seek to know the best and follow it. Let your first thoughts be devoted to helping your people, and do what I have had the misfortune not to be able to do myself. . . ."

This speech is very different from the narrow-mindedness attributed to him in certain memoirs.

He has been accused of wearing certain relics during the last years of his life. His own sentiments were exalted, but his confessor, who was of a different cast of mind, had persuaded him to adopt such unseemly habits, now quite gone out of fashion, in order to bring him more completely under his influence; moreover, these relics, which he was foolish enough to wear, had been given to him by Mme. de Maintenon.

Though the life and death of Louis XIV were alike glorious, he was not mourned as he deserved. The love of novelty, the advent of a minority, during which everyone thought to make his fortune, the disputes over the *Constitution*, which embittered men's minds, all led to the news of his death being received with a feeling of even less than indifference. The same people who, in 1686, had implored Heaven with tears to bring about the recovery of their king, were now seen to follow his funeral procession with very different feelings. It is related that when quite young his mother said to him one day: "My son, imitate your grandfather and not your father." The king having asked her why: "Because," she said, "people wept at the death of Henri IV, but laughed at that of Louis XIII."

Though he has been accused of being narrow-minded, of being too harsh in his zeal against Jansenism, too arrogant with foreigners in his triumphs, too weak in his dealings with certain women, and too severe in personal matters; of having lightly undertaken wars, of burning the Palatinate, and of persecuting the reformers—nevertheless, his great qualities and noble deeds when placed in the balance eclipse all his faults. Time, which modifies men's opinions, has put the seal upon his reputation, and, in spite of all that has been written against him, his name is never uttered without respect, nor without recalling to the mind an age which will be forever memorable. If we consider this prince in his private life, we observe him indeed too full of his own greatness, but affable, allowing his mother no part in the government but performing all the duties of a son, and observing all outward appearances of propriety towards his wife; a good father, a good master, always dignified in public, laborious in his study, punctilious in business matters, just in thought, a good speaker, and agreeable though aloof.

I have remarked elsewhere that he never uttered those words which have been imputed to him, when the first gentleman-in-waiting and the grand master of the wardrobe were disputing the honor of attending on him, "What matters it which of my valets waits on me?" Such a rude speech could never come from a man so refined and considerate as he was, and is scarcely consistent with what he said one day to the Duke de La Rochefoucauld on the subject of his debts: "Why not speak to your friends?"—a very different expression, which in itself was worth much, and which was accompanied by a gift of fifty thousand crowns.

It is not even true that he wrote to the Duke de La Rochefoucauld: "I compliment you as your friend on the office of Grand Master of the Wardrobe, which I confer on you as your king." Historians have exhibited this letter as to his credit. They do not perceive how indelicate, how ill-bred it is to tell a person whose master one is, that one is his master. It would be suitable were a king writing to a subject who had rebelled; it is what Henri IV might have said to the Duke de Mayenne before they were completely reconciled. Rose, the secretary of the council, wrote this letter, but the king had too much good taste to send it. It was this good taste which made him alter the pretentious inscriptions which the academician, Charpentier, placed on Lebrun's pictures in the gallery of Versailles: *The unbelievable passage of the Rhine: The marvelous capture of Valenciennes,* and so on. The king thought that *The capture of Valenciennes: The passage of the Rhine* would say yet more. Charpentier was quite right in embellishing these records of his country with inscriptions in our own tongue; it was excessive adulation and not the use of the vulgar tongue that spoiled his work.

Certain replies and witticisms of Louis XIV have been preserved which are of very little account. It is said that when he decided to suppress Calvinism in France, he exclaimed: "My grandfather loved the Huguenots and did not fear them; my father loved them not at all, but feared them; as for myself, I neither love nor fear them."

In 1658, on giving the office of First President of the Parliament of Paris to M. de Lamoignon, at that time Master of Requests, he said to him: "Did I know a better man or a more worthy subject, I would have chosen him." He made use of nearly the same expressions to Cardinal de Noailles, on making him Archbishop of Paris. What constitutes the merit of these words is that they were true and that they stimulated the practice of virtue.

It is said that an imprudent preacher one day addressed him personally at Versailles, an audacious act which would not have been permissible if done to a private individual, far more so to a king. It is alleged that Louis XIV contented himself with saying to him: "My father, I certainly like to take my share of a sermon, but I do not like to have it forced upon me." Whether he uttered these words or not, they may serve as a lesson.

He always expressed himself in a noble manner and with precision, striving to speak and act in public as behoved a sovereign. When the Duke of Anjou was departing to reign in Spain, he said to him, to show the unity which was henceforth to join the two nations: "The Pyrenees no longer exist."

Assuredly nothing reveals his character so well as the following memoir, the whole of which was written entirely by his own hand:

"Kings are often compelled to do things against their inclination, which offend their natural sense of right. They must take delight in pleasing people, and must often punish and thus lose the goodwill of persons whom they would naturally wish well. The interests of the state must come first. In any affair of importance, where it is possible to do better they should force themselves to do so, so that they may not have to reproach themselves afterwards; but I have been prevented by certain private interests, which have turned aside the regard I should have had for the greatness, the good and the power of the state. Vexed questions often present themselves; delicate problems which it is difficult to unravel, and on which one has but vague ideas. So long as one is in that condition it is permissible to remain undecided; but so soon as one makes up his mind about anything and believes he sees the better course, it must be taken. By so doing I have often been successful in what I have undertaken. The errors I have made and which have caused me infinite sorrow, have occurred as a result of easy-going and because I have allowed myself to be too much led by the advice of others. Nothing is so dangerous as weakness of whatever kind. In order to rule others, one must lift oneself above them, and, after hearing all sides, one must rely on his own judgment, which must be arrived at without prejudice, always taking care not to order or perform anything that is unworthy of oneself, of the character one bears, or of the dignity of the state. Well-intentioned princes who have some knowledge of their duties either through experience or study, and who take great pains to make themselves competent, find so many different things by which they can make themselves known, that they must pay special attention to each and general application to all. One must be on one's guard against oneself, beware of one's predilections, and always watch over one's temper. A king's profession is a great, noble and gratifying one, if he feels himself to be worthy of properly performing all the duties which he undertakes; but it is not free from troubles, fatigue and anxiety. Suspense is sometimes disheartening, and after taking a reasonable time to consider a question, one has to make up one's mind, and take the course that seems the best.

"A king works for himself, when he has the state in mind; the welfare of the one enhances the glory of the other: when the state is prosperous, exalted and powerful, he who is the cause of it is rendered glorious by it, and as compared with his subjects must still derive greater enjoyment from all that is most agreeable in life. If he commit an error, he must retrieve his mistake as soon as ever possible, nor should any consideration prevent him from so doing, not even for the sake of doing a kindness.

"In 1671, a man died who had the post of secretary of state, in charge of the foreign department. He was a capable man, but not without defects; he left no suitable man to occupy this post, which is a very important one.

"For some time I was in doubt as to whom I should appoint to this office, and after careful consideration I decided that a man who had had long experience in embassies would best fill the post.

"I ordered him to be sent for; my choice was approved by everyone, which does not always happen; and when he arrived, I appointed him to the post. I only knew of him by reputation, and by the fact that he had executed satisfactorily the commissions with which I had entrusted him; but the post I had given him proved too big and involved for him. I had not made the most of my opportunities, as I might have done, merely through being easy-going and good-natured. At length, I was compelled to order his resignation, since everything that passed through his hands lost the dignity and authority essential in carrying out the orders of a King of France. Had I made up my mind to remove him sooner, I should have escaped the inconveniences which have since occurred and I should not have to blame myself for my kindness to him which was prejudicial to the state. I have stated this in detail in order to give an example of what I have mentioned above."

This valuable memoir, hitherto unpublished, is a witness to posterity of the integrity and magnanimity of his mind. It might even be said that he judges himself too severely, that no blame was attached to him for appointing M. de Pomponne, since his choice of that minister was determined by his services and reputation, and was confirmed by universal approval; and if he blamed himself for his choice of M. de Pomponne, who at least had the good fortune to serve his country in her time of great glory, what would he not have to reproach himself with as regards M. de Chamillart, whose ministry was so ill-fated and so universally condemned?

He wrote several memoirs in this vein, either for his own benefit or for the instruction of the Dauphin, the Duke of Burgundy. These reflections were set down after the events. He would have approached more nearly the perfection to which he was worthy of aspiring, had he been able to frame a philosophy superior to ordinary politics and prejudices; a philosophy such as in the course of centuries has been practiced by so few sovereigns, and which one can pardon kings for not being acquainted with, since so many private individuals are ignorant of it.

The following are some of the precepts he gave to his grandson, Philip V, on his departure for Spain. They were written in haste, with a carelessness that lays bare the mind of the writer more surely than a studied speech.

"Love the Spanish and all your subjects attached to your crown and person. Do not favor those who flatter you most: esteem those who for the common good risk your displeasure. It is in them you find your true friends.

"Make your subjects happy, and with this end in view, do not make war until you are forced to do so, and have carefully considered and weighed the reasons in your council.

"Endeavor to restore your finances; keep a watch on the Indies and on your fleets; give thought to trade and continue in a close union with France, nothing being so advantageous to our two powers as such a union which nothing can resist.

"If you are compelled to make war, put yourself at the head of your armies.

"Contrive to restore order in your armies everywhere, and begin with those in Flanders.

"Never put pleasure before duty; but prepare for yourself a kind of program which will allow you some hours of liberty and amusement.

"There are few more innocent amusements than hunting and the pleasures of a country house, provided you do not spend too much on it.

"Give your undivided attention to affairs when you are consulted; listen carefully to the opening of any business, but reserve your decision.

"When you have acquired more knowledge, remember that it is you who have to decide; but no matter how experienced you are, always listen to every opinion and argument of your council, before making that decision.

"Do all that is possible to become well acquainted with the most important people, so that you may make use of them at the opportune moment.

"Always endeavor to have Spaniards for your viceroys and governors.

"Treat everyone with good humor; never say unpleasant things to anyone; but honor people of distinction and merit.

"Show your gratitude towards the late king and towards all those who were responsible for choosing you to succeed him.

"Place great trust in Cardinal Porto Carrero and show your gratitude to him for the way in which he has behaved.

"I think that you should do a great deal for the ambassador who has been so successful in his solicitations on your behalf, and who was the first to kneel to you as one of your subjects.

"Do not forget Bedmar; he is an accomplished man and able to serve you well.

"Put complete faith in the Duke d'Harcourt; he is a clever and honest man, and will only advise you with regard to your own duties.

"Keep all the French in order.

"Treat your own servants well, but do not be too familiar with them, and trust them still less. Employ them so long as they serve you well, dismiss them for the slightest fault, and never uphold them against the Spaniards.

"Have as little to do with the dowager queen as you may. See to it that she leaves Madrid, but does not leave Spain. Wherever she may be, keep a watch on her doings and prevent her from meddling with any of your affairs. Suspect those who have too much intercourse with her.

"Keep always an affection towards your family. Remember their sorrow at parting with you. Carry on constant correspondence with them on all matters both great and small Ask us for anything you are in want of or desire to have, and which you lack; we will ask the same of you.

"Never forget that you are a Frenchman and what may befall you. When you have got children who will ensure the Spanish succession, visit your kingdoms, go to Naples and Sicily; go on to Milan, and come back through Flanders; that will give you an opportunity of seeing us again; in the meanwhile, visit Catalonia, Aragon and other parts. See what must be done for Ceuta.

"Throw money to the people when you are in Spain, and especially when you enter Madrid.

"Do not appear surprised at the extraordinary people you will find there. Do not scoff at them. Every country has its peculiar manners, and you will soon become accustomed to what at first sight seems so astonishing.

"Avoid as much as you can granting favors to those who lay out money to obtain them. Give opportunely and freely, and hardly ever accept presents, unless they be quite trifling. If it happen that you cannot avoid accepting them, requite the donors with more generous gifts after the lapse of a few days.

"Have a casket in which you can put any special thing, and let no one have the key but yourself.

"I conclude with the most important advice I can give you. See to it that you are the ruler. You must be master; never have a favorite nor a prime minister. Consult your council and listen to what they have to say, but decide for yourself. God, who has made you a king, will give you the necessary wisdom, so long as your intentions are good."

The mind of Louis XIV was rather precise and dignified than witty; and indeed one does not expect a king to say notable things, but to do them. What is necessary to every man in office is never to let anyone leave his presence discontented, and to make himself agreeable to all who approach him. One may not be able to confer benefits at every moment, but one can always say pleasant things. Louis made a successful practice of doing so.

Between him and his court there existed a continual intercourse in which was seen on the one side all the graciousness of a majesty which never debased itself, and on the other all the delicacy of an eager desire to serve and please which never approached servility. He was considerate and polite, especially to women, and his example enhanced those qualities in his courtiers; he never missed an opportunity of saying things to men which at once flattered their self-esteem, stimulated rivalry, and remained long in their memory.

One day, the Duchess of Burgundy, who was still quite young, seeing at supper a very ugly officer, joked long and loudly about his ugliness. "I think, Madame," said the king in a still louder voice, "that he is one of the handsomest men in my kingdom, for he is one of the bravest."

A staff officer, rather brusque in his manners, which had not become softened even at the court of Louis XIV, had lost an arm in battle; the king had compensated him for the loss of an arm so far as one can compensate anyone for such a loss, but the officer complained, "I would that I had lost the other one as well, when I should no longer be able to serve your majesty." "I should be very sorry for you and for myself," the king replied, and followed up his words by bestowing some favors on him. He was so averse to saying disagreeable things, which are like fatal arrows in the mouth of a prince, that he would not even allow himself the most innocent and mildest of jests, while ordinary individuals perpetrate every day the cruelest and most bitter ones.

He delighted and was skilled in ingenious pursuits, such as improvisations and the composing of pleasing songs; and sometimes he also improvised little parodies on airs such as the following:

> Here's Phil, my younger brother,
> With Chancellor Serrant;
> He seldom makes a pother,
> He likes the wise Boifranc
> Much better than the other;

and the following, which he composed one day when dismissing his council:

> The Council in vain at his elbow appears
> When his bitch comes across; from all business he'll fly,

> Nought else he minds or sees or hears,
> When once the hounds are in full cry.

These trifles at least serve to show that such exercises of the wits formed one of the pleasures of the court, that he entered into such pleasures and that he knew how to live in private as a man, as well as sustain the part of monarch in the theatre of the world.

Although his letter to the Archbishop of Rheims, concerning the Marquis de Barbesieux, is written in an extremely careless manner, it does more honor to his character than the cleverest thoughts could have done to his wit. He had conferred on that young man the post of Secretary of State for War, which his father, the Marquis de Louvois, had held before him. Soon dissatisfied with the conduct of his new secretary of state, he wished to remonstrate with him without humiliating him too much. To this end he appealed to his uncle, the Archbishop of Rheims, and begged him to admonish his nephew. In his letter he is like a master who knows all, or like a father speaking of his son.

"I know," he said, "what I owe to the memory of M. de Louvois; but if your nephew does not mend his ways I shall be compelled to take measures. I shall be sorry to do so, but it will be necessary. He has talents, but does not make good use of them. He gives too many supper parties to the princes, instead of working: he neglects his duty for pleasure; he keeps officers waiting too long in his antechamber; is arrogant in his speech with them and sometimes harsh."

That is what I remember of the letter, which I once saw in the original. It plainly shows that Louis XIV was not ruled by his ministers, as has been thought, and that he knew how to control his ministers.

He was fond of praise, and it is desirable that a king should be so, since then he strives to deserve it. But Louis XIV did not always welcome it when it was inordinate.

When the French Academy, which always gave him a list of the subjects proposed for prizes, named the following: *Of all the king's virtues, which is the one that is the most estimable?* the king blushed, and preferred not to have such a subject discussed. He tolerated the prologues of Quinault, but it was when he was at the height of his glory, at a time when the nation in its intoxication overlooked his own. Virgil and Horace, out of gratitude, and Ovid, with contemptible weakness, lavished much higher praises on Augustus, and, when one recalls to mind the proscriptions, much less deserved.

Had Corneille said to one of the courtiers in Cardinal Richelieu's apartment: "Tell his reverence the cardinal that I know more about poetry than he does," the minister would never have forgiven him; yet that is what Boileau said aloud to the king in a dispute which arose over some verses which the king thought good, and of which Boileau disapproved. "He is right," said the king, "he does know more about it than I do." The Duke of Vendôme had a boon companion, Villiers, one of those men of pleasure who made a merit of cynical license. He lodged him in his apartment at Versailles, and he was commonly known as Villiers-Vendôme. Villiers loudly disapproved of Louis XIV's tastes in music, painting, architecture and gardens. Did the king plant a grove, furnish an apartment, or erect a fountain, Villiers found everything badly arranged, and expressed his opinion in no measured terms. "It is strange," said the king, "that Villiers should have singled out my house, in order to come and mock at everything that I do there."

Meeting him one day in the gardens: "Well," he said to him, showing him one of his latest contrivances, "this, I suppose, does not happen to please you?" "No," replied Villiers. "Nevertheless," replied the king, "there are many people who are far from displeased with it." "That may well be," retorted Villiers, "each to his own taste." Laughingly the king replied: "One cannot please everyone."

One day, when Louis XIV was playing backgammon, a dispute arose over a move. A discussion ensued, and the courtiers remained silent. Count Grammont arrived on the scene. "Give us your decision," said the king to him. "Sire, it is you who are in the wrong," said the count. "And how can you say so, when you do not know what move I made?" "Well, sire, do you not see that had there been any doubt at all about it, all these gentlemen would have decided in your favor?"

The Duke d'Antin made himself conspicuous in that age by his remarkable gift, not for saying flattering things, but for performing them. The king went to pass the night at Petit Bourg, and remarked what a pity it was that a large avenue of trees hid the view of the river. The duke had them cut down during the night. The king on awakening was astonished at no longer seeing the trees of which he had disapproved. "It is because your majesty disapproved of them that you no longer see them," replied the duke.

We have also related elsewhere how the same man, having observed that the king took a dislike to a somewhat extensive wood bordering the canal at Fontainebleau, took the opportunity when he was out walking, and all being ready, gave orders for the wood to be felled, and the whole of it was immediately cut down. These are the acts of a clever courtier, not of a flatterer.

Louis XIV has been accused of intolerable pride, because the base of his statue in the *Place des Victoires* is encircled with slaves in chains. But it was not he who erected that statue, nor the one in the *Place de Vendôme*. That in the *Place des Victoires* commemorates the greatness of soul of the first Marshal La Feuillade and his gratitude towards his sovereign. It cost him five hundred thousand livres, which would be worth a million to-day, and the town added as much again to have it erected. It is evident therefore that it was as much a mistake to ascribe the pompousness of that statue to Louis XIV, as to assume that the marshal's magnanimity was nothing else than vanity and flattery.

People could talk of nothing but the four slaves; but they represent vices repressed as much as nations conquered—the abolition of the duel and the suppression of the heresy; inscriptions also witness to this effect. They also record the union of the seas, the Peace of Nimeguen, and betoken acts of service rather than warlike exploits. Moreover, it is a time-honored practice for sculptors to carve figures of slaves at the base of the statues of kings. It would be better still to represent there free and happy citizens; but, after all, slaves are to be seen at the base of the statues of the beloved Henri IV and Louis XIII in Paris; also at Leghorn beneath the statue of Ferdinand de' Medici, who certainly enslaved no nation, and in Berlin, under the statue of an Elector who repulsed the Swedes, but gained no conquests.

France's neighbors and even the French themselves have very unjustly made Louis XIV responsible for this practice. The inscription: *Viro immortali, To the immortal man,* has been deemed idolatrous, as if that word signified aught else but the immortality of his glory. Viviani's inscription over his house in Florence: *Aedes a deo datae, A house bestowed by a god,* would seem much more idolatrous; yet it is only an allusion to the title of *Heaven-sent* and to Virgil's lines, *Deus nobis haec otia fecit* (*Ecl.* 1. v. 6).

With regard to the statue in the *Place de Vendôme,* it was the city which erected it. The Latin inscriptions which occupy the four sides of the base are more grossly flattering than those on the statue in the *Place des Victoires.* There one reads that it was only against his will that Louis XIV ever took up arms. On his death-bed he most solemnly refuted this extravagant compliment with words which will be remembered long after such inscriptions are forgotten, inscriptions which were merely the despicable work of certain men of letters.

The king had intended that the buildings surrounding this square should be constructed for his public library. The square was very large; it had at first three sides, forming the three fronts of an immense palace, whose walls were already built, when in 1701 the city was forced by the hardness of the times to build houses for private individuals on the ruins of the half-completed palace. The Louvre has consequently not been finished; and the fountain and obelisk which Colbert wished to have built opposite to the gate of Perrault exist only on paper; the beautiful gate of Saint-Gervais is thus left in gloom; and the greater part of the monuments of Paris leave much to be desired.

The nation would rather that Louis XIV had preferred his Louvre and capital to the palace of Versailles, which the Duke de Créqui called a worthless favorite. Posterity gratefully admires the great things he did for the public; but criticism tempers our admiration when we see what defects there are in the splendor of Louis XIV's country house.

It follows from what we have related, that in everything this ınonarch loved grandeur and glory. A prince who, having accomplished as great things as he, could yet be of plain and simple habits, would be the first among kings, and Louis XIV the second.

If he repented on his death-bed of having lightly gone to war, it must be owned that he did not judge by events; for of all his wars the most legitimate and necessary, namely, the war of 1701, was the only one unsuccessful.

By his marriage he had, besides *Monseigneur*, two sons and three daughters who died in infancy. He was more fortunate in his amours; only two of his natural children died in infancy; eight others survived and were legitimized, and five of them had issue. There was also a young girl, in attendance on Mme. de Montespan, an unacknowledged daughter, whom he married to a gentleman of the name of La Queue, who lived near Versailles.

There was every reason to suspect that one of the nuns at the convent of Moret was his daughter. She was very dark-skinned and resembled him in many ways besides. The king endowed her with twenty thousand crowns when placing her in this convent, and the belief she entertained that she was of high birth made her so haughty that her superiors complained of it. When on a journey to Fontainebleau Mme. de Maintenon visited the convent of Moret, and with the idea of instilling more modesty in this nun, she did what she could to dissuade her from the notion which was responsible for her haughtiness.

"Madame," that person said to her, "that a lady of your quality should take the trouble to come here especially to tell me that I am not the king's daughter, convinces me that I am." This anecdote is still related at the convent of Moret.

The description of so many details may be repellent to a philosopher; but curiosity, a failing that is common to all men, almost ceases to be so when it has for its object times and men who attract the notice of posterity.

XXXI

SCIENCE

This happy age, which saw the birth of a revolution in the human mind, gave at its commencement no signs of such a destiny; to begin with philosophy, there seemed no likelihood in the time of Louis XIII that it would extricate itself from the chaos in which it was plunged. The Inquisition in Italy, Spain and Portugal had linked philosophical errors with religious dogmas; the civil wars in France and the Calvinist disputes were not more calculated to elevate human reason than was the fanaticism in England at the time of Cromwell. No sooner did a canon of Thorn[40] resuscitate the ancient planetary system of the Chaldeans, so long buried in oblivion, than its truth was condemned at Rome; and the Brotherhood of the Holy Office, composed of seven cardinals, having pronounced the movement of the earth, without which there can be no true science of astronomy, not merely heretical, but absurd, and the great Galileo having asked forgiveness, at the age of seventy, for having spoken the truth, there seemed no likelihood that truth could be established upon earth.

Chancellor Bacon had pointed out the way from afar; Galileo had discovered the laws of falling bodies; Torricelli was on the point of discovering the weight of the air surrounding us, and various experiments had been made at Magdeburg. Ignoring these few attempts, the schools persisted in their folly, and the world in its ignorance. Then came Descartes; he did the opposite of what he should have done; instead of studying Nature, he sought to interpret her. He was the greatest geometrician of his age; but geometry leaves the mind where it finds it. Descartes' geometry was too much given to flights of fancy. He who was the foremost among mathematicians wrote scarcely anything else but philosophic romances. A man who scorned to make experiments, who never quoted Galileo, who thought to build without materials, could erect but an imaginary structure.

All that was romantic in his book succeeded, while the scraps of truth intermingled in these new extravagances were at first contested. But at length this modicum of truth prevailed, thanks to the system he had introduced. Before him no one had had a thread in the labyrinth; he at least provided one which others made use of, when he himself had gone astray. It was much to destroy the delusions of Peripateticism, though it was by the introduction of others. Each strove for mastery; each fell in due season, leaving reason to raise itself on their ruins. About 1655, Cardinal Leopold de' Medici had founded a society for making experiments in Florence, under the name of *del Cimento*. In that country of the arts it was already felt that one could only understand anything of the vast edifice of Nature by examining it piece by piece. After Galileo's death, and from the time of Torricelli, this Academy rendered great services.

In England under Cromwell's somber rule, a few philosophers met together for the purpose of seeking truth in peace, while elsewhere fanaticism suppressed all truth. Recalled to the throne of his forefathers by a repentant and fickle nation, Charles II presented letters patent to this budding academy; but this was the government's only gift. The Royal Society, or rather the Free Society of London, worked for the honor of working. We owe to this body the discoveries on the nature of light, the principle of gravitation, the aberrations of fixed stars, astronomical geometry, and a hundred other discoveries, which would justify one in calling this age the *Age of the English*, as well as the *Age of Louis XIV*.

In 1666 M. Colbert, jealous of this new glory, and anxious that France should share it, at the request of several scholars obtained permission from Louis XIV to found an Academy of Science. Like the English society and the French Academy, it was a free institution until 1699. By offering liberal annuities, Colbert attracted Domenico Cassini from Italy, Huygens from Holland and Roemer from Denmark. Roemer determined the velocity of the solar rays; Huygens discovered the ring and one of the satellites of Saturn, and Cassini the other four. We owe to Huygens, if not the original invention of pendulum clocks, at any rate the correct principles underlying the regularity of their movements, principles which he deduced from a wonderful geometrical system.

By the rejection of every system a certain amount of knowledge in every branch of true physics was gradually acquired. People were astonished to see a system of chemistry which did not profess either to search for the philosopher's stone or to prolong life beyond the natural limits; a system of astronomy which did not predict future events, and a system of medicine which was independent of the phases of the moon. Putrefaction was no longer thought to breed spontaneously insects and plants.

There was an end of miracles when Nature was better understood and she was studied in all her productions.

Geography was astonishingly developed. The observatory built by Louis XIV's orders was hardly finished, when, in 1669, Domenico Cassini and Picard set to work to determine the meridian line. In 1683 it was continued as far as Roussillon. This was the most glorious achievement of astronomy and was sufficient in itself to immortalize the age.

In 1672 scientists were sent to Cayenne to make some useful observations. On this voyage there was first originated the notion of the oblateness of the earth's sphere, which was afterwards proved by the great Newton; this led the way for those more famous voyages which have since rendered Louis XV's reign illustrious.

In 1700 Tournefort was sent out to the Levant, the object of his voyage being to collect plants for the royal garden, hitherto neglected, but now restored to its proper state in which it has become worthy of the curiosity of Europe. The royal library, already numerous, was enriched by more than thirty thousand volumes under Louis XIV, and this example has been so well followed in our days that it now contains more than one hundred and eighty thousand volumes. The law school, which had been closed for a century, was reopened. Chairs were founded in every university in France for the teaching of French law. It seemed right that others should not be taught, and that the admirable Roman laws, embodied with those of the country, should form the whole jurisprudence of the nation.

The publishing of journals originated during this reign. It is well known that the *Journal des Savants*, first issued in 1665, was the forerunner of all similar works, which at the present day circulate all over Europe, and into which, as into the most useful things, too many abuses have crept.

The *Academy of Belles-Lettres*, first formed in 1663 by some members of the French Academy for the purpose of having medallions struck to commemorate and hand down to posterity the achievements of Louis XIV, became useful to the public when it was no longer solely occupied with its monarch, and began to undertake researches into antiquity, and exercise a judicious criticism on ideas and events. It did very much for history what the Academy of Sciences did for physics; it dissipated error.

The spirit of learning and criticism which spread from place to place imperceptibly destroyed much of the prevalent superstition. To this dawn of reason was due the king's declaration in 1672, which forbade tribunals hearing simple accusations of sorcery. No one would have dared to do this in the reign of Henri IV or Louis XIII, and while people have still been tried for sorcery since 1672, judges have as a usual rule only condemned the accused as blasphemers, or in certain cases as poisoners in addition.

It had hitherto been very common to try sorcerers by throwing them bound into the water; if they floated, they were judged guilty. Many of the judges in the provinces had ordered such trials, and they long continued among the common people. Every shepherd was a sorcerer, and amulets and charmed rings were worn in the towns. Hazel twigs were definitely thought to have the power of revealing the sources of springs, treasures and thieves, and in more than one province of Germany the belief in their efficacy is still strong. There was hardly a person who did not have his horoscope cast. People spoke of nothing but magic secrets; almost everything was illusion. Solemn treatises were written on these subjects by scholars and magistrates, among whom was to be found a group of demonologists. There were tests by which real magicians could be distinguished, and those really possessed, from impostors; in short, up to that period hardly anything had been adopted from antiquity save its errors.

Superstitious notions were so deeply rooted in men's minds that even as late as 1680 people were alarmed at comets. Scientists hardly dared to controvert this universal dread. Jacques Bernouilli, one of the greatest mathematicians in Europe, when questioned about these comets by prejudiced persons, replied that a comet's head could not be a sign of divine wrath, because the head remains unchanged, but that the tail might certainly mean such a thing.

Yet in point of fact neither the head nor the tail remains unchanged. It was left to Bayle to write his famous book against popular superstition, a book which, read in the light of human reason of today, seems less caustic than when it first appeared.

One would not think that sovereigns would be under any obligation to philosophers. Yet it is true that the philosophic spirit which has penetrated practically every class of society save the lowest, has done much to promote the rights of sovereigns. Disputes which would once have produced excommunications, interdicts and schisms, have had no such effect. It has been said that the peoples would be happy could they have philosophers for kings, but it is also true to say that kings are so much the happier when many of their subjects are philosophers.

It must be admitted that this spirit of reason, which is beginning to control education in the large towns, was powerless to prevent the frenzied acts of the fanatics of the Cevennes or to prevent the populace of Paris from rioting before a tomb at Saint-Medard, or to settle disputes as bitter as they were frivolous between men who should have known better; but before this century such disputes would have brought about disturbances in the state; the greatest citizens would have believed in the miracles of Saint-Medard, and fanaticism, so far from being confined to the regions of the Cevennes, would have spread to the towns.

All branches of science and literature were utilized in this century, and so many writers contributed to extend the enlightenment of the human spirit that those who would have been accounted marvellous in former ages, were now lost in the crowd. Their individual glory is slight on account of their number, but the glory of their age is all the greater.

XXXII

LITERATURE AND THE ARTS

The philosophy of reason did not make such great progress in France as in England and in Florence, and while the Academy of Sciences contributed greatly to the enlightenment of the human mind, it did not place France in front of other nations. All the great discoveries and the great truths originated elsewhere.

But in rhetoric, poetry, cultural, didactic or merely amusing books, the French were the legislators of Europe. There was no longer taste in Italy. True rhetoric was everywhere unknown, religion ridiculously expounded in the pulpit and cases absurdly argued in the courts.

Preachers quoted Virgil and Ovid; barristers, St. Augustine and St. Jerome. The genius had not yet been found to give to the French language the turn of phrase, the numbers, the propriety of style and the dignity it afterwards possessed. A few verses of Malherbe showed only that it was capable of grandeur and force; but this was all. Men of talent who could write excellently in Latin, such as President de Thou and a certain chancellor de L'Hospital, wrote but indifferently in their own language, which proved to be a refractory medium in their hands. French was as yet but noteworthy for a certain simple directness which had constituted the sole merit of Joinville, Amyot, Marot, Montaigne, Regnier and the *Satire Ménippée*. This *naïveté* was very near to carelessness and coarseness.

Jean de Lingendes, Bishop of Mâcon, unknown today, since he omitted to publish his works, was the first orator to speak in the grand style. His sermons and funeral orations, though stained with the rust of his time, were a model of later orators, who imitated and surpassed him. The funeral oration on Charles Emmanuel, Duke of Savoy, surnamed "the Great" by his countrymen, delivered by Lingendes in 1630, contained such grand flights of eloquence, that long afterwards Fléchier took the whole of the exordium, as well as the text and several considerable passages, to embellish his famous funeral oration on the Vicomte de Turenne.

At this period Balzac gave number and harmony to prose. It

is true that his letters were bombastic effusions; he wrote thus to the first Cardinal de Retz: "You have just grasped the sceptre of kings and the rose-colored livery." Speaking of the perfumed waters, he wrote thus to Boisrobert, from Rome: "I am curing myself by swimming in my chamber in the midst of perfumes." With all these faults, he charmed the ear. Rhetoric has such power on men that Balzac was praised in his day for having discovered that small, neglected, but necessary branch of art which consists in the harmonious choice of words, even though he often employed it out of place.

Voiture gave some idea of the airy charm of the epistolary style, which is not the best since it consists of nothing more than wit. His two volumes of letters are a jumble of conceits containing not a single instructive letter, not one which comes from the heart, not one that paints the manners of the time and the characters of men; they show not so much the use of wit as its abuse.

The language gradually became more refined and took on a permanent form. The change was due to the French Academy, and above all to Vaugelas. His *Translation of Quintius Curtius*, which appeared in 1646, was the first good book to be written in a pure form, and there are few of its expressions and idioms which have become obsolete.

Olivier Patru, who followed him closely, did much to rule and purify the language, and though not considered to be deeply versed in the law, he displayed a conciseness, clarity, propriety and elegance of diction in his speeches, such as had never before been known at the Bar.

One of the works which most contributed to form the taste of the nation and give it a spirit of nicety and precision was the little collection of *Maxims* by François, Duke de La Rochefoucauld. Although there is but one real truth expressed in this book, namely, that "self-love is the mainspring of every action," yet the thought is presented under so many various aspects, that it is nearly always striking. It is not so much a book as materials to embellish a book. The little collection was read with eagerness; and it accustomed people to think and to express their thoughts in a vivid, concise and elegant manner. It was a merit which no other writer had had before in Europe, since the revival of letters.

The first book of genius, however, to appear in prose, was the collection of *Provincial Letters*, in 1656. Every variety of style is to be found there. After the lapse of a century, there is not a single word which has undergone that alteration of meaning which so often changes a living language. To this work must be ascribed the moment when the language became fixed. The Bishop of Lucon, son of the celebrated Bussi, told me that when he asked the Bishop of Meaux what book he would rather have written had he not written his own, Bossuet replied: *"The Provincial Letters."* They have lost much of their pertinence now that the Jesuits have been suppressed and the objects of their disputes come into contempt.

The good taste which distinguishes this book from beginning to end, and the vigor of the final letters, did not at first reform the loose, slovenly, incorrect and disconnected style which for long afterwards characterized the writings and speeches of nearly all authors, preachers and barristers.

One of the first to display a reasoned eloquence in the pulpit was Bourdaloue, about 1668. It was a new departure. After him came other pulpit orators, such as Massillon, Bishop of Clermont, who brought to their addresses greater elegance and finer and more penetrating descriptions of the manners of the age; but not one of them eclipsed him. His style was vigorous rather than florid, without any touch of fancy, so that it seemed that he was more inclined to convince people than to touch their hearts, and he never sought to please.

One may sometimes wish that in banishing bad taste from the pulpit which it degraded, he had also done away with the practice of preaching from a text. For, to speak at some length on a quotation of a line or two, to strain oneself to keep the whole of the sermon centered on those two lines, seems a work unworthy of the solemn office of a minister. The text becomes a sort of device, or rather enigma, which is unraveled by the sermon. The Greeks and the Romans were ignorant of such a practice. It was introduced during the decadence of letters, and course of time has hallowed it

The custom of dividing all subjects under two or three headings, some of which, such as a question of morals, require no division, and others, such as matters of controversy, require many more, remains a tiresome custom, which Bourdaloue found in common use and with which he himself complied.

He had been preceded by Bossuet, afterwards Bishop of Meaux. Bossuet, who became so great a man, was affianced in his youth to Mlle. Desvieux, a girl of remarkably fine character. His talent for theology, and that remarkable gift of eloquence which characterized it, showed themselves at such an early age that his parents and friends persuaded him to give himself to the Church alone. Mlle. Desvieux herself urged him to this course, preferring the glory that he was sure to obtain to the happiness of living with him. He had preached when quite young in 1662 before the king and queen-mother, long before Bourdaloue was known. His sermons, aided by a noble and impressive delivery, the first to be heard at court that approached the sublime manner, met with such great success that the king wrote to his father, the comptroller of Soissons, to congratulate him on possessing such a son.

However, on Bourdaloue's appearance, Bossuet was no longer considered the foremost preacher. He was already himself given to the composition of funeral orations, a kind of oratory which requires an imagination and majestic dignity which approaches poetry, from which art, indeed, something must always be borrowed, though with discretion, when one aspires to the sublime. The funeral oration on the queen-mother, which he delivered in 1667, brought him the bishopric of Condon; but the oration was not worthy of him, and, like his sermons, was not printed. The funeral panegyric on the Queen of England, widow of Charles I, which he delivered in 1669, appears in every detail a masterpiece. The subjects of such pieces of rhetoric are happy in proportion to the misfortunes which the dead experienced. They may be compared to tragedies where it is the misfortunes of the principal characters that interest us most. The funeral panegyric of *Madame*, carried off in the flower of life, who actually breathed her last in his arms, gained the greatest and rarest of triumphs, that of drawing tears from the eyes of courtiers. He was obliged to stop after the words: "O ill-fated, horrible night! when suddenly, like a clap of thunder, echoed the dire ·news: *Madame* is dying. *Madame* is dead. . . ." The listeners burst into sobs, and the orator's voice was lost amidst the sighs and weeping of the congregation.

The French were the only people who succeeded in this kind of oratory. Some time afterwards, the same man introduced a new style, which could hardly have succeeded save in his own hands. He applied the art of oratory to history itself, a literary genre which would seem incapable of admitting it. His *Discourse on Universal History*, written for the Dauphin's education, has neither precedent nor imitators. While the system which he adopts to reconcile the Jewish chronology with that of other nations has met with certain opposition among scholars, his style has met with nothing but admiration. The lofty vigor with which he describes the manners and customs, the government, the rise and fall of great empires, is astonishing, as are the vigorous, true and lively strokes with which he paints and passes judgment on the nations.

Nearly all the works which added luster to this age were of a kind unknown to the ancients. *Télémaque* is of the number. Fénelon, the pupil and friend of Bossuet, and afterwards against his will his rival and enemy, wrote this singular book, which resembles now a novel and now a poem, and in which a modulated prose takes the place of verse. Apparently his aim was to treat the novel as Bossuet had treated history, lending it a fresh dignity and charm and, above all, drawing from fiction a moral beneficial to mankind, and hitherto entirely overlooked in nearly all fictitious compositions. It has been thought that he wrote the book to serve as an exercise for the instruction of the Duke of Burgundy and other French princes, whose tutor he was, in the same way as Bossuet had written his *Universal History* for the education of *Monseigneur*. But his nephew, the Marquis de Fénelon, who inherited the graces of that celebrated man and who was killed at the Battle of Raucoux, assured me to the contrary. It would certainly have been unseemly for a priest to have taught the loves of Calypso and Eucharis as his first lessons to the royal princes.

This work was not written until he had retired to his arch-bishopric of Cambrai. Full of classical learning and endowed with a lively and sensitive imagination, he invented a style which could belong to none other than himself, and which flowed easily and fluently. I have seen the original manuscript, and there are not ten erasures in it. He wrote it in three months, in the midst of his unfortunate disputes on Quietism, little sus-pecting how superior such recreation was to his more learned occupation. It is said that a servant stole a copy of the manu-script and had it printed. If that is so, the Archbishop of Cam-brai owes the great reputation he has in Europe to that dishonest act, but to that act was also due the loss of any hope of favor at court for ever.

People pretend to discern in *Télémaque* a veiled criticism of Louis XIV's government. Sesostris, displaying too much pomp in the hour of triumph, Idomeneus reveling in luxury at Salentini and forgetting the necessities of life, were thought to represent the king, although after all it is impossible for anyone to in-dulge in superfluous luxury except by a superabundance of the products of the needful arts.

In the eyes of malcontents the Marquis de Louvois seemed represented under the name of Protesilas, vain, harsh and proud, an enemy of the great captains who served the state but not the minister.

The Allies who had united against Louis XIV in the war of 1688, and later caused his throne to totter in the war of 1701, joyfully recognized him in the character Idomeneus, whose ar-rogance disgusted all his neighbors. These allusions made a pro-found impression, aided, as they were, by a harmonious style, which insinuates in so delicate a manner the advantages of peace and moderation. Foreigners and even the French themselves, weary of so many wars, saw with malicious relief a satire in a book written for the purpose of inculcating virtue. Innumerable editions were brought out. I have myself seen forty in the Eng-lish language. It is true that after the death of that monarch, who had been so feared, so envied, so respected by all, and so hated by a few, when human malice had at length surfeited its appetite for those alleged allusions which cast a slur upon his conduct, the critics of a sterner taste treated *Télémaque* with some severity. They blamed its wearisomeness, its details, its too little connected adventures, and its oft-repeated and little-varied descriptions of country life, but this book has always been considered one of the finest monuments of a brilliant age.

The *Characters* of La Bruyère may be regarded as a production of a unique kind. No examples of such a work are to be found in the classics any more than of *Télémaque*. The public were struck by a style at once rapid, terse and vigorous, by picturesque expressions, in a word, by a totally new use of the language which did not, however, break its rules; and the numerous allusions contained in the work crowned its success. When La Bruyère showed the manuscript of his work to M. de Malezieu, the latter said to him: "Here is something which will bring you many readers and many enemies." When the generation that was attacked in this book had passed away, its reputation declined. Nevertheless, as there are some books which belong to all time and to all countries, it is probable that it will never be forgotten. *Télémaque* had some imitators; the *Characters* of La Bruyère had many more. It is easier to write short descriptions of things that strike us, than to compose a lengthy work of imagination which is both pleasing and instructive.

The delicate art of introducing charm into a philosophical work was as yet an innovation; of which the first example was *La Pluralité des Mondes* of Fontenelle, and a dangerous one, since the true dress of philosophy is method, clarity and, above all, truth. The fact that this work is partly based on the chimerical hypothesis of Descartes' vortices is sufficient to preclude it from being ranked among the classics by posterity.

Among these literary novelties mention should be made of the works of Bayle, who compiled a kind of dictionary of logic. It was the first work of its kind in which one may learn how to think. One must abandon to the fate of all second-rate books the articles in this collection which contain such unimportant facts as are alike unworthy of Bayle, of a serious reader and of posterity. For the rest, in thus counting Bayle among the authors who gave lustre to the age of Louis XIV, though he was a refu-

gee in Holland, I am but conforming to a decree of the parliament of Toulouse, which proclaimed the validity of his will in
France despite the rigor of the laws, and expressly stated "that
such a man could not be regarded as a foreigner."

This is no time to expatiate upon the large number of good
books which were produced in this age; we shall only dwell on
those works which are characterized by new or remarkable genius, and which distinguish this age from others. The eloquence
of Bossuet and Bourdaloue, for example, was not and could
not be that of a new Cicero, it was of a new order and excel-
lence. If there is anything to approach the Roman orator it is
the three memorials composed by Pellisson for Fouquet. They
are in the same manner as some of Cicero's orations, a medley
of legal matters and state affairs, judiciously treated with an art
that never obtrudes and diffused with passages of touching eloquence.

Historians there were, but no Livy. The style of the *Conspiracy of Venice* is comparable to that of Sallust. It is obvious
that the Abbé of Saint-Réal had taken that writer for his model,
and it is possible that he has surpassed him. All the other writings which we have just mentioned seem of a new creation. It is
that above all which distinguishes this illustrious age; for, as for
scholars and commentators, the sixteenth and seventeenth centuries had produced them in shoals; but true genius in any
genre had not yet been developed.

Who would think that such masterpieces of prose would probably never have been written, had they not been preceded by
poetry? Yet such is the progress of the human spirit in every
nation, verses were everywhere the earliest children of genius
and the first masters of eloquence.

Nations do not differ from the individual. Plato and Cicero
began by writing poetry. People knew by heart the few fine
stanzas of Malherbe, when it was not possible to quote a noble
and sublime passage of prose, and in all probability if Pierre
Corneille had not lived the genius of prose-writers would not
have been developed.

Corneille is the more highly to be admired in that when he

began to compose his tragedies he had but wretched models to guide him; that these models were admired made it still more difficult for him to choose the right path, and to dishearten him still further they were approved by Cardinal Richelieu, the patron of men of letters, though not of good taste. He remunerated such wretched scribblers as are customarily importunate, and, with an arrogance of mind which well became him in other affairs, he was inclined to disdain those in whom he perceived with a certain envy signs of real genius, such as will never bow the knee to idle patronage. It is rare indeed that a powerful man, himself an artist, is seen to give his protection to the artists who best deserve it.

Corneille had to contend with his age, his rivals, and Cardinal Richelieu. I do not propose to repeat here what has been written about *The Cid*; I shall merely remark that the Academy, in passing judgment between Corneille and Scudéri, was overmindful of Cardinal Richelieu's good favor when it censured the love of Chimène. To love her father's murderer and yet seek to revenge that murder was admirable. To have made her master her love would have been to break one of the fundamental laws of the tragic art, which is chiefly concerned with conflicts of the heart, but at that time the art was itself unknown to all except the author.

The Cid was not the only work of Corneille which Cardinal Richelieu sought to depreciate. The Abbé d'Aubignac tells us that that minister disapproved also of *Polyeucte*.

The Cid was after all a highly embellished imitation of *Guillem de Castro*, and in several passages a translation. *Cinna*, which followed it, was unique. I knew an old servant of the house of Condé, who told me that the great Condé, at the age of twenty, being present at the first performance of *Cinna*, shed tears at these words of Augustus:

> I am the world's great master and my own;
> I am, I will be. Memory and time
> Shall this last, greatest victory record.
> I triumph over wrath too justly rous'd,
> And latest age the conquest shall applaud
> Cinna, let us be friends: 'tis I who ask it.

They were the tears of a hero. The great Corneille causing the great Condé to weep with admiration constitutes a truly commemorative epoch in the history of the human spirit.

The number of plays unworthy of his genius which he composed years later did not prevent the nation from regarding him as a great man, just as the faults of Homer have never prevented his being sublime. It is the privilege of true genius, and especially of the genius who opens up a new avenue of thought, to make mistakes with impunity.

Corneille had formed himself alone; but Louis XIV, Colbert, Sophocles and Euripides all contributed to form Racine. An ode which he composed at the age of eighteen on the occasion of the king's marriage brought him a present which he had not expected, and this decided him to become a poet. His reputation was steadily increased, while that of Corneille has suffered a slight eclipse. The reason is that Racine in all his works after *Alexandre* is always elegant, always correct, always true; he speaks to the heart; and Corneille not infrequently fails in all these respects. Racine was far in advance of both the Greeks and Corneille in his knowledge of the passions, and carried the music of his verse and the elegance of his·style to the highest perfection attainable. These men taught the nation to think, to feel, and to express their thoughts. Their audiences, whom they alone had enlightened, at length became relentless critics of the very men who had instructed them.

In the time of Cardinal Richelieu there were few persons in France competent to detect the faults of *The Cid*; yet in 1702, when *Athalie*, a masterpiece of the theatre, was performed at the house of the Duchess of Burgundy, the courtiers thought themselves sufficiently qualified to condemn it. Time has avenged the author; but the great man died without enjoying the success of his finest work. A numerous party long took pride in being prejudiced against Racine. Mme. de Sévigné, the first letter-writer of her age, who had no rival in the sprightly recounting of trifles, always thought that Racine *would not go far*.

She judged him like coffee, of which she said: "People will soon grow tired of it." Reputations can ripen by the passage of time alone.

By the singular good-fortune of the age Molière was the contemporary of Corneille and Racine. It is not true to say that when Molière appeared he found the stage entirely lacking in good comedies. Corneille himself had presented *Le Menteur* (*The Liar*), a play of character and intrigue, borrowed like *The Cid* from the Spanish theatre; and Molière had written but two of his great masterpieces, when Quinault presented to the public *La Mère Coquette* (*The Mother as Coquette*), a comedy of both character and intrigue, and indeed a model of intrigue. It appeared in 1664; and was the first comedy in which those who were afterwards known as *Marquises* were caricatured. The majority of the great lords at the Court of Louis XIV were eager to imitate the grand air, the majesty and dignity of their masters. Those who were in a lower position copied the haughty manners of their betters, until at last there were many who carried this air of superiority and overweening conceit to the highest point of absurdity.

The failing lasted long. Molière attacked it often and contributed to rid the public of such self-important mediocrities, as well as of the affectation of the *précieuses* (*affected young women*), the pedantry of the *femmes savantes* (*learned ladies*), and the robe and Latin jargon of the doctors. Molière was, one may say, the legislator over the good manners of society. I am speaking here only of the service he rendered to his age; his other merits are sufficiently well known.

Such an age was worthy of the consideration of future ages; an age in which the heroes of Corneille and Racine, the characters of Molière, the symphonies of Lulli, all of them novelties to the nation, and (since we are here concerned only with the arts) the eloquence of Bossuet and Bourdaloue, were appreciated by Louis XIV, by *Madame* noted for her good taste, by such men as Condé, Turenne, Colbert and a host of eminent men in every department of life. There will never again be such an era in which a Duke de La Rochefoucauld, the author of the *Maxims*, after discoursing with a Pascal and an Arnauld, goes to the theatre to witness a play of Corneille.

Boileau attained to the level of these great men, not with his early satires, for posterity will not give a second glance to the

Embarras de Paris, and to the names of the Cassaignes and Cotins, but by the exquisite epistles with which he has instructed posterity, and especially by the *Art Poétique*, in which Corneille could have found much to learn.

La Fontaine, far less chaste in style, and far less faultless in his language, but unique in the simplicity and grace which are typical of his work, placed himself by the simplest of writings almost on a level with these sublime writers.

As the originator of a wholly new style, rendered but more difficult by its apparent ease, Quinault was worthy to be placed among his illustrious contemporaries. It is well known how unjustly Boileau sought to disparage him.

Boileau had never sacrificed on the altar of the Graces; and all his life he attempted, though in vain, to belittle a man whose true worth was recognized by them alone. The sincerest praise that we can give a poet is to remember his verses: whole scenes from Quinault are known by heart, a tribute which no Italian opera could obtain. French music has retained a simplicity which is no longer appreciated by other nations; but the natural and beautiful simplicity, which is so frequently and charmingly shown in Quinault, still delights everyone in Europe who is conversant with our language and possesses a cultured taste.

Were a poem like *Armide* or *Atys* to be discovered in antiquity, with what idolatry would it be received! But Quinault was a modern.

All these great men were known and protected by Louis XIV, with the exception of La Fontaine. His excessive simplicity of life, which was carried to the length of personal negligence, caused him to be slighted by a court whose favors he did not seek; but he was welcomed by the Duke of Burgundy and received kindnesses from that prince in his old age. Despite his genius, he was almost as artless as the heroes of his fables. A priest of the Oratory, named Pouget, took great credit to himself for having treated that man of such guileless character, as though he were speaking to the Marquise de Brinvilliers or La Voisin. His tales are all borrowed from Poggio, Ariosto and the Queen of Navarre. If desire be dangerous, pleasantries do not make it so. His admirable fable of the *Animals afflicted with*

the Plague, who accuse themselves of their misdeeds, might be
applied to La Fontaine himself. All is pardoned to the lions,
wolves and bears, and an innocent animal is sacrificed for having
eaten a blade or two of grass.

In the company of these men of genius, who will be the delight and instruction of future ages, there sprang up a host of
schools of pretty wits who produced innumerable elegant works
of minor importance, that contribute to the amusement of cultured people, just as there have been many pleasing painters
whom one would not put beside such painters as Poussin, Lesueur, Lebrun, Lemoine and Vanloo.

But towards the end of Louis XIV's reign two men rose above
the crowd of mediocre talents and acquired great reputations.
The one was La Motte Houdar, a man of a wise and generous
rather than of a lofty spirit, a careful and methodical prose-
writer, but often lacking favor and grace in his poetry, and even
that correctness which it is only permissible to sacrifice for the
sublime. At first he wrote fine stanzas rather than fine odes.
His talent deteriorated soon afterwards; but many beautiful fragments which remain to us in more than one genre, will place
him for ever above the rank of authors that may be ignored. He
proved that in the art of letters a writer of the second rank may
yet do good service.

The other was Rousseau, a man of less intellect, less delicacy
and less ease than La Motte, but with a greater talent for the
art of versifying. His odes were imitations of La Motte, but they
excelled in elegance, in variety, and in fancy. His psalms
equalled in grace and harmony the sacred songs of Racine. His
epigrams are more highly finished than those of Marot. He was
far less successful in opera, which requires delicacy of feeling, in
comedies, in which humor is indispensable, and in moral epistles,
which must delineate the truth; for he lacked all those qualities.
Thus he failed in those branches which were foreign to him.

He would have corrupted the French language if others had
imitated the *Marotic* style which he employed in serious works.
But fortunately his adulteration of the purity of our language
with the outworn forms of two centuries earlier proved only a
passing phase. Some of his epistles are rather strained imitations

of Boileau, but are not based on sufficiently clear ideas or acknowledged truths: *"Truth alone can please."*

This genius degenerated considerably in foreign countries, whether age and misfortunes had impaired his talents, or whether, his principal merit consisting in the choice of words and happy turns of phrase, a merit more rare and necessary in a great writer than might be thought, he was no longer within reach of the same assistance. Far from his native country, he might count among his misfortunes the lack of any severe critics.

His continued ill-fortune was the outcome of an ungovernable self-pride, too near inclined to jealousy and spite. His fate cannot but be a striking lesson to every man of talent; but he is to be considered here only as a writer who contributed not a little to the honor of letters.

Scarcely any great genius arose after the halcyon days of these great writers, and towards the time of the death of Louis XIV. Nature herself seemed to be reposing.

The path was difficult at the beginning of the age because no one had yet trodden it; it is difficult today because it has been beaten flat. The great men of the past age taught us how to think and speak; they told us things which we knew not. Those who succeed them can hardly say anything that is not known already. In short, a kind of distaste has arisen from a very surfeit of masterpieces.

Thus the age of Louis XIV suffered the same fate as those of Leo X, Augustus and Alexander. The ground which in those illustrious periods produced so many fruits of genius had been long prepared. Both moral and physical causes have been searched in vain to provide reason for this slow fecundity, followed by a long period of sterility. The true reason is that among the nations who cultivate the fine arts many years must elapse before the language and taste become purified. Once these first steps have been made men of genius begin to appear; rivalry and public favor incite fresh efforts and stimulate all talents. Each artist seizes upon the natural beauties which are proper to his particular genre. Any man who thoroughly examines the theory of the arts of pure genius must know, if he has anything of talent himself, that the prime beauties, the great natural opportunities which are suited to the nation for which the author is working are few in number. The subjects available and their appropriate elaboration have much narrower limits than might be thought. The Abbé Dubos, a man of great judgment, who wrote a treatise on poetry and painting about the year 1714, was of the opinion that in the whole of French history there was but a single subject for an epic poem, the destruction of the League by Henri-Quatre. He should have added that since embellishments of the epic theme, such as were well suited to the Greeks, the Romans and the Italians of the fifteenth and sixteenth centuries, are prohibited among the French, and the gods of fable, oracles, invulnerable heroes, monsters, sorceries, metamorphoses and romantic adventures no longer held to be fit subjects, the beauties appropriate to the epic poem are confined within a very narrow circle. If, therefore, it happens that any artist seizes upon the only embellishments suited to the times, the subject and the nation, and who carries out what others have attempted, those who come after him will find the ground already occupied.

It is the same with the art of tragedy. It is a mistake to believe that the great tragic passions and emotions can be infinitely varied in new and striking ways. Everything has its limits.

High comedy has no less its own. In human nature there are at the most a dozen characters that are really comic and that are marked by striking qualities. The Abbé Dubos, lacking talent, believes that men of talent can discover a whole host of new characters; but nature would first have to make them. He imagines that the little differences that distinguish one man from another can be as successfully treated as the fundamental qualities. It is true that there are numberless shades of differences, but the number of brilliant colors is small; and it is these primary colors of which a great artist does not fail to make use.

The eloquence of the pulpit, and especially funeral orations, provide a case in point. Moral truths once eloquently expressed, descriptions of human misery and human weaknesses, of the vanity of greatness and the ravages of death, once painted by able fingers, and all becomes commonplace. One is reduced to imitating them or going astray. An adequate number of fables having once been written by a La Fontaine, any additions to them can but point the same moral and relate almost the same adventures. Genius can thus flourish but in a single age and must then degenerate.

The other branches of literature whose subject-matter is, as it were, being continually renewed, such as history and natural science, which require only hard work, judgment and common sense, can more easily maintain their position; and the plastic arts such as painting and sculpture can avoid degeneration when those in power, like Louis XIV, take care to employ only the best artists. For in painting and in sculpture, the same subjects can be treated a hundred times; artists still paint the Holy Family, though Raphael expended all the genius of his art on this subject; but one would not be permitted to treat again the themes of *Cinna*, *Andromaque*, *L'Art Poétique* and *Tartuffe*.

It must be noted that, the past age having enlightened the present, it has become so easy to write mediocre stuff that we have been flooded out with books and, what is worse, with serious though useless books; but among this multitude of mediocre writing an evil becomes a necessity in a city at once large, wealthy and idle, in which one party of citizens being continually occupied in entertaining the other, there have appeared, from time to time, excellent works of history, of reflection or of that light literature which is the recreation of all sorts of minds.

Of all the nations, France has produced the greatest number of such works. Its language has become the language of Europe; everything has contributed to this end; the great writers of the age of Louis XIV, and their successors the exiled Calvinist ministers, who brought their eloquence and logic into foreign countries; above all, a Bayle, who, writing his works in Holland, has had them read by every nation; a Rapin de Thoyras, who has written in French the only good history of England; a Saint-Evremond, whose acquaintance was sought by every person of the Court of London: the Duchess de Mazarin, to please whom was everyone's ambition; Mme. d'Olbreuse, later Duchess von Zell, who carried with her into Germany all the graces of her country. The social spirit is the natural heritage of the French; it is a merit and a pleasure of which other nations have felt the need. The French language is of all languages that which expresses with the greatest ease, exactness and delicacy all subjects of conversation which can arise among gentlefolk; and it thus contributes throughout all Europe to one of the most agreeable diversions of life.

XXXIII

THE ARTS (*continued*)

The arts which do not solely depend upon the intellect had made but little progress in France before the period which is known as the age of Louis XIV. Music was in its infancy; a few languishing songs, some airs for the violin, the guitar and the lute, composed for the most part in Spain, were all that we possessed. Lulli's style and technique were astonishing. He was the first in France to write bass counterpoint, middle parts and figures. At first some difficulty was experienced in playing his compositions, which now seem so easy and simple. At the present day there are a thousand people who know music, for one who knew it in the time of Louis XIII; and the art has been perfected by this spread of knowledge. To-day, there is no great town which has not its public concerts: yet at that time Paris itself had none; the king's twenty-four violins comprised the sum total of French music.

The familiarity with music and its dependent arts has so increased that towards the end of Louis XIV's reign the practice of dancing figures to music was instituted, so that at the present day it may be truly said that people dance at sight.

There were several very great architects during the regency of Marie de' Medici. She had the Palace of Luxembourg built in the Tuscan style, in honor of her country and for the adornment of our own. The same de Brosse, whose gate of Saint-Gervais is still standing, built a palace for this queen, which she never occupied. Cardinal Richelieu, with all his greatness of mind, was far from having as good taste in such matters as she. The cardinal's palace, which is now the Palais-Royal, is indeed a proof of this. We had great hopes when we saw the fine façade of the Louvre being built, which is such as to make one long to see the palace completed. Many citizens built themselves magnificent houses, more distinguished for the exquisite taste of the interior rather than of the exterior, and gratifying the luxury of private individuals even more than adorning the city.

Colbert, the Mæcenas of all the arts, founded an Academy of Architecture in 1671. A Vitruvius is not enough, one must have an Augustus to employ him.

Municipal officials should also have an ardor for the arts, an ardor which must be enlightened. Had there been two or three mayors like President Turgot, the city of Paris would not be disgraced by such a badly built and badly situated town hall, by such a small and badly laid-out square, famous only for its gibbets and its bonfires; by the narrowness of the streets in the busiest quarters—in short, by this relic of barbarism in the midst of splendor and in the very home of all the arts.

Painting began with Poussin in the reign of Louis XIII. No account need be taken of the indifferent painters who preceded him. Since his time every age has had its great painters, though not in that profusion which is one of Italy's glories; but without stopping to dwell upon Lesueur, who owned no master, or Lebrun, who rivaled the Italians in design and execution, we have had more than thirty painters who have bequeathed works of art very worthy of regard. Foreigners are beginning to take them from us. The galleries and apartments of one great king I have seen filled with nothing else but French pictures, whose value we should perhaps be loath to recognize. In France I have seen a picture of Santerre refused for twelve thousand livres. There is scarcely to be found in Europe a larger painting than the ceiling of Lemoine at Versailles, and I know not whether there are any more beautiful. Since then we have had Vanloo, considered even in foreign countries as the finest painter of his time.

Not only did Colbert organize the Academy of Painting as it is today, but in 1667 he persuaded Louis XIV to establish one in Rome. A palace was purchased in that capital for the residence of the director, and pupils who have won prizes at the Paris Academy are sent there to study, the expenses of their journey and board being defrayed by the king; they there copy ancient works of art, and study the works of Raphael and Michelangelo. The desire to imitate both ancient and modern Rome is in itself a noble homage to the eternal city, and the homage has still been rendered even since the enormous collections of Italian paintings amassed by the king and the Duke of Orleans, and the masterpieces of sculpture which France has produced, have enabled us to dispense with the necessity of seeking masters abroad.

It is chiefly in sculpture that we have excelled, and in the art of casting colossal equestrian figures in a single mould.

Should posterity discover one day fragments of such works of art as the baths of Apollo, buried under ruins, or exposed to the ravages of the weather in the thickets of Versailles; or the tomb of Cardinal Richelieu in the Sorbonne chapel, too little noticed by the public; or the equestrian statue of Louis XIV made in Paris to grace the city of Bordeaux; or the Mercury which Louis XV presented to the King of Prussia; and many other works of art equal to those that I have mentioned, one cannot but think that these productions of our time would find a place among the finest of Greek antiquity.

We have equalled the ancients in our medallions. Warin was the first to raise this art from mediocrity towards the end of the reign of Louis XIII. Those dies and stamps now arranged in historical order in the corridors of the Louvre gallery are a marvelous sight. They are worth about two millions, and the greater part of them are masterpieces.

The art of engraving precious stones was no less successfully cultivated. That of reproducing pictures, and of perpetuating them by means of copper plates, and thus handing down to posterity all kinds of representations of nature and of art, was still in a very imperfect state in France previous to this age. It is one of the most pleasing and useful of arts. We owe its discovery to the Florentines, who invented it towards the middle of the fifteenth century, and it has made even greater progress in France than in the country of its origin, because a greater number of works of that class were produced there. Collections of royal engravings often formed the most magnificent gift of the king to ambassadors. The chasing of gold and silver, which requires a knowledge of designing, and good taste, was brought to the highest degree of perfection to which it is possible for the skill of man to attain.

Now that we have surveyed all the arts which contribute to the pleasures of the people and the glory of the state, we cannot pass over in silence the most useful of all the arts, and one in which the French excelled all other nations in the world; I mean the art of surgery, whose progress was so rapid and far-famed in this age, that people came to Paris from the ends of Europe for any cure or operation that required exceptional skill. Not only was France almost the only country in which first-rate surgeons were to be found, but it was in that country alone that the requisite instruments were properly made; France provided all her neighbors with them, and I have heard from the mouth of the celebrated Cheseldon, the greatest surgeon in London, that it was he who first began to make in London, in 1715, the instruments of his art. Medicine, which helped to improve surgery, did not reach a higher degree of perfection in France than in England, or under the famous Boerhaave in Holland; medicine indeed, like natural science, was perfected by making use of the discoveries of our neighbors.

The foregoing is, on the whole, a faithful account of the progress of the human spirit in France during that age which began in the time of Cardinal Richelieu, and ended in our days. It will be with difficulty surpassed, and, if in some ways it be eclipsed, it will remain the model of more fortunate ages, to which it will have given birth.

XXXIV

THE USEFUL ARTS AND SCIENCES IN EUROPE DURING THE REIGN OF LOUIS XIV

We have sufficiently intimated throughout the whole of this history that the national disasters which fill it, and which followed one another almost without a break, are in the long run erased from the register of time. The details and devices of politics sink into oblivion; but sound laws, institutions, and achievements in the sciences and the arts remain for ever.

The crowd of foreigners who travel to Rome today, not as pilgrims, but as men of taste, find few traces of Gregory VII or Boniface VIII; they admire the temples built by men like Bramante and Michelangelo, the pictures of Raphael and the sculpture of Bernini; if they are men of intelligence, they read Ariosto and Tasso and honor the ashes of Galileo. In England Cromwell's name is but spoken of now and then; people no longer discuss the Wars of the *White Rose*, but they will study Newton for years at a time, and no one is surprised to read in his epitaph that *he was the glory of the human race*, though one would be much surprised to find in England the memory of any statesman accorded such an honor.

I would gladly have it in my power to do justice to all the great men who, like Newton, gave luster to their country during the last hundred years. I have called that period the age of Louis XIV, not only because that monarch gave greater encouragement to the arts than all his fellow-kings together, but also because in his lifetime he outlived three generations of the kings of Europe. I have set the limits of this epoch at some years before Louis XIV and some years after him; for it was during this space of time that the human spirit has made most progress.

From 1660 to the present day the English have made greater progress in all the arts than in all preceding ages. I will not here repeat what I have said elsewhere of Milton. It is true that some critics disapprove of his fantastic descriptions, his paradise of fools, his alabaster walls which encircle the earthly paradise; his devils, who transform themselves from giants into pygmies that they may take less room in council, seated in a vast hall of gold erected in hell; his cannons fired from heaven, his mountains hurled at the heads of foes; his angels on horseback, angels who are cut in two and their dissevered bodies as quickly joined together again. His long descriptions and repetitions are considered tedious; it is said that he has equalled neither Ovid nor Hesiod in his long description of the way in which the earth, the animals and mankind were created. His dissertations on astronomy are condemned as too dry and the creations of his fancy as being extravagant, rather than marvelous, and more disgusting than impressive; such is a long passage upon chaos; the love of Sin and Death and the children of their incest; and Death, "who turns up his nose to scent across the immensity of chaos the change that has come over the earth, like a crow scenting a corpse"—Death, who smells out the odor of the Fall, who strikes with his petrifying hammer on cold and dry; and cold and dry with hot and moist, transformed into four fine army generals, lead into battle their embryonic atoms like light-armed infantry. Criticism indeed exhausts itself, but never praise. Milton remains at once the glory and wonder of England; he is compared to Homer, whose defects are as great, and he is preferred to Dante, whose conceptions are yet more fantastic.

Among the large number of pleasing poets who graced the reign of Charles II, such as Waller, the Earl of Dorset and the Earl of Rochester, the Duke of Buckingham and many others, we must single out Dryden, who distinguished himself in every branch of poetry; his works are full of details both brilliant and true to nature, lively, vigorous, bold and passionate, merits in which none of his own nation equals him nor any of the ancients surpass him. If Pope, who succeeded him, had not written late in life his *Essay on Man*, he could not be compared to Dryden.

No other nation has treated moral subjects in poetry with greater depth and vigor than the English; there lies, it seems to me, the greatest merit of her poets.

There is another kind of elegant writing which requires at once a mind more cultured and more universal; such was Addison's; he achieved immortal fame with his *Cato*, the only English tragedy written from beginning to end in an elegant and lofty style, and his other moral and critical works breathe a perfect taste; in all he wrote, sound sense appears adorned by a lively fancy, and his manner of writing is an excellent model for any country. Dean Swift left several passages whose like is not to be found among the writers of antiquity—a Rabelais made perfect.

The English have hardly any examples of funeral orations; it is not their custom to praise their kings and queens in churches; but pulpit oratory, which was in London coarse before the reign of Charles II, suddenly improved. Bishop Burnet admits in his *Memoirs* that it was brought about by imitating the French. Perhaps they have surpassed their masters; their sermons are less formal, less pretentious and less declamatory than those of the French.

It is, moreover, remarkable that this insular people, separated from the rest of the world and so lately cultured, should have acquired at least as much knowledge of antiquity as the Italians have been able to gather in Rome, which was for so long the meeting-place of the nations. Marsham penetrated the mysteries of ancient Egypt. No Persian had such a knowledge of the Zoroastrian religion as the scholar Hyde. The Turks were unacquainted with the history of Mahomet and the preceding centuries, and its interpretation was left to the Englishman Sale, who turned his travels in Arabia to such good profit.

There is no other country in the world where the Christian religion has been so vigorously attacked and so ably defended as in England. From Henry VIII to Cromwell men argued and fought, like that ancient breed of gladiators who descended into the arena sword in hand and a bandage on their eyes. A few slight differences in creed and dogma were sufficient to cause frightful wars, but from the Restoration to the present day when every Christian tenet has been almost annually attacked, such disputes have not aroused the least disturbance; science has taken the place of fire and sword to silence every argument.

It is above all in philosophy that the English have become the teachers of other nations. It is no mere question of ingenius systems. The false myths of the Greeks should have disappeared long ago and modern myths should never have appeared at all. Roger Bacon broke fresh ground by declaring that Nature must be studied in a new way, that experiments must be made; Boyle devoted his life to making them. This is no place for a dissertation on physics; it is enough to say that after three thousand years of fruitless research, Newton was the first to find and demonstrate the great natural law by which all elements of matter are mutually attracted, the law by which all the stars are held in their courses. He was indeed the first to see the light; before him it was unknown.

His principles of mathematics, which include a system of physics at once new and true, are based on the discovery of the calculus, incorrectly called *infinitesimal*, a supreme effort of geometry, and one which he made at the age of twenty-four. It was a great philosopher, the learned Halley, who said of him "that it is not permitted to any mortal to approach nearer to divinity."

A host of expert geometricians and physicists were enlightened by his discoveries and inspired by his genius. Bradley discovered the aberration of the light of fixed stars, distant at least twelve billion leagues from our small globe.

Halley, whom I have quoted above, though but an astronomer, received the command of one of the king's ships in 1698. It was on this ship that he determined the position of the stars of the Antarctic Pole, and noted the variations of the compass in all parts of the known globe. The voyage of the Argonauts was in comparison but the crossing of a bark from one side of a river to the other. Yet Halley's voyage has been hardly spoken of in Europe.

The indifference we display towards great events become too familiar, and our admiration of the ancient Greeks for trivial ones, is yet another proof of the wonderful superiority of our age over that of the ancients. Boileau in France and Sir William Temple in England obstinately refused to acknowledge such a superiority; they were eager to disparage their own age, in order to place themselves above it: but the dispute between the ancients and the moderns has been at last decided, at any rate in the field of philosophy. There is not a single ancient philosopher whose works are taught today to the youth of any enlightened nation.

Locke alone should serve as a good example of the advantage of our age over the most illustrious ages of Greece. From Plato to Locke there is indeed nothing; no one in that interval de veloped the operations of the human mind, and a man who knew the whole of Plato and only Plato, would know little and that not well.

Plato was indeed an eloquent Greek; his *Apologia of Socrates* stands a service rendered to philosophers of every nation; he should be respected, as having represented ill-fortuned virtue in so honorable a light and its persecutors in one so odious. It was long thought that ethics so admirable could not be associated with metaphysics so false; he was almost made a Father of the Church for his *Ternaire*, which no one has ever understood. But what would be thought today of a philosopher who should tell us that one substance is the same as *any other*; that the world is a figure of twelve pentagons; that fire is a pyramid which is connected with the earth by numbers? Would it be thought convincing to prove the immortality and transmigration of the soul by saying that sleep is born of wakefulness and wakefulness of sleep, the living from the dead and the dead from the living? Such reasonings as these have been admired for many centuries, and still more fantastic ideas have since been employed in the education of mankind.

Locke alone has developed the *human understanding* in a book where there is naught but truths, a book made perfect by the fact that these truths are stated clearly.

To complete our review of the superiority of the past century over all others, we may cast our eyes towards Germany and the North. Hevelius of Danzig was the first astronomer to study deeply the planet of the moon; no man before him surveyed the heavens with greater care: and of all the great men that the age produced, none showed more plainly why it should be justly called the age of Louis XIV. A magnificent library that he possessed was destroyed by fire; upon which the King of France bestowed on the astronomer of Danzig a present which more than compensated him for the loss.

Mercator of Holstein was the forerunner of Newton in geometry; and the Bernouillis in Switzerland were worthy pupils of that great man. Leibnitz was for some time regarded as his rival.

The celebrated Leibnitz was born at Leipzig; and died, full of learning, in the town of Hanover; like Newton, worshiping a god, and seeking counsel of no man. He was perhaps the most universal genius in Europe: a historian assiduous in research; a sagacious lawyer, enlightening the study of law with science, foreign to that subject though it seem; a metaphysician sufficiently open-minded to endeavor to reconcile theology with metaphysics; even a Latin poet, and finally a mathematician of sufficient caliber to dispute with the great Newton the invention of the infinitesimal calculus, so that for some time the issue remained uncertain.

It was the golden age of geometry; mathematicians frequently challenged one another, that is to say, they sent each other problems to be solved, almost as the ancient kings of Asia and Egypt are reported to have sent each other riddles to divine. The problems propounded by the geometricians were more difficult than the ancient riddles; and in Germany, England, Italy and France, not one of them was left unsolved. Never was intercourse between philosophers more universal; Leibnitz did much to encourage it. A republic of letters was being gradually established in Europe, in spite of different religions. Every science, every art, was mutually assisted in this way, and it was the academies which formed this republic. Italy and Russia were allied by literature. The Englishman, the German and the Frenchman went to Leyden to study. The celebrated physician Boerhaave was consulted both by the Pope and by the Czar. His greatest pupils attracted the notice of foreigners and thus became to some extent the physicians of the nation; true scholars in every branch drew closer the bonds of this great fellowship of intellect, spread everywhere and everywhere independent. This intercourse still obtains, and is indeed one of the consolations for those ills which political ambition scatters throughout the earth.

Italy throughout this century preserved her ancient glory, though she produced no new Tassos nor Raphaels; it is enough to have produced them once. Men like Chiabrera, and later Zappi and Filicaia, showed that refinement is still a characteristic of that nation. Maffei's *Merope* and the dramatic works of Metastasio are worthy monuments of the age.

The study of true physics, founded by Galileo, was still pursued despite the opposition of an ancient and too hallowed philosophy. Men like Cassini, Viviani, Manfredi, Bianchini, Zanotti and many others spread the same light in Italy which was already lighting other countries; and, while admitting that the chief rays of this beacon came from England, let it be said that Italian teachers at least did not hide their eyes from the gleam.

All branches of literature were cultivated in this ancient home of the arts, and with as great success save in those subjects where a liberty of thought unknown to Italy gives wider scope. This age, above all, was better acquainted with antiquity than all preceding ages. Italy provided more such monuments than all the rest of Europe, and every fresh excavation has but extended the boundaries of knowledge.

We owe this progress to a few learned men, a few geniuses scattered in small numbers in various parts of Europe, nearly all of them unhonored for many years and often persecuted; they enlightened and consoled the world when it was devastated by war. The names of all those who thus gave luster to Germany, England and Italy may be found elsewhere. A foreigner is perhaps little able to appreciate the merits of all these illustrious men. It is enough, here, if we have shown that during the past century mankind, from one end of Europe to the other, has been more enlightened than in all preceding ages.

AN ESSAY
ON THE MANNERS AND SPIRIT
OF NATIONS [41]

AND ON THE PRINCIPAL EVENTS OF HISTORY
FROM CHARLEMAGNE TO LOUIS XIII

INTRODUCTION

Containing the Plan of the Work
with a summary account of what the Western
nations originally were, and the reasons for
beginning this *Essay* with the Orient

You are at length resolved, then, to surmount your disgust from
reading modern history since the decline of the Roman Empire,
and to gain a general idea of the nations which inhabit and
ravage the face of the earth. All that you seek to learn in this
immensity of matter, is only that which deserves to be known;
the spirit, the manners and customs of the principal nations,
supported by facts which one cannot ignore. The aim of this
work is not to know the precise year in which the brutal sovereign of a barbarous people was succeeded by a prince unworthy
of being known. If a man could have the misfortune to encumber
his head with the chronological series of all the dynasties which
have existed, all his knowledge would be a jumble of words. As
it is laudable to know the great actions of those sovereigns who
have made their peoples better and happier, so is it reasonable
to ignore vulgar reigns, which serve only to burden the memory.
What advantage can you derive from the minute details of a
number of petty interests and connections which no longer sur-

vive; of families long extinct that contested the possession of provinces now swallowed up in mighty kingdoms? Almost every city now has its own particular history, whether true or false, more voluminous and more detailed than that of Alexander the Great. There is more writing in the archives of a single convent, than in the annals of the Roman Empire.

A reader must limit himself and select from these immense collections which serve only to confuse. They constitute a vast store-house, from which you take what is necessary for your own occasions.

The illustrious Bossuet, who, in his discourse on a phase of universal history has seized its true spirit, at least in what he says of the Roman Empire, left off at the reign of Charlemagne. Your design is by beginning with this era, to make a picture of mankind; but you must often go back to earlier times. That eloquent writer, in briefly mentioning the Arabians, who founded such a mighty empire, and established such a flourishing religion, speaks of them only as a deluge of barbarians. He seems to have written solely to insinuate that everything in the world was made for the Jewish nation; that if God gave the Asian Empire to the Babylonians, it was to punish the Jews; if God made Cyrus reign, it was to avenge them; if God sent forth the Romans, it was again to chastise these Jews. This may be; but the greatness of Cyrus and the Romans have still other causes, and Bossuet himself did not omit them in speaking of the spirit of nations.

It might well be wished that he did not completely forget the ancient peoples of the Orient, like the Indians and Chinese, who were so important before the other nations were formed.

Fed as we are by the produce of their country, clothed with their materials, amused by the games which they invented, even instructed by their old moral fables, why should we neglect to know the spirit of those nations which our European traders have constantly visited, ever since they first found the way to their coasts?

In your philosophical inquiries concerning this globe, you naturally direct your first attention to the East, the cradle of the arts, to which the western world owes everything.

The oriental and southern climes owe everything to nature;

whereas we, in these northern regions, owe all to time, to commerce, and to belated industry. The old countries of the Celts, Allobroges, Picts, Germans, Sarmatians, and Scythians, produced nothing but wild fruits, rocks, and forests. Sicily, indeed, is said to have produced a small quantity of oats; but as for wheat, rice, and delicious fruits, they grew on the borders of the Euphrates, in China, and in India. The most fertile countries were the first inhabited, and the first regulated by police. The whole Levant, from Greece to the extremities of our hemisphere, was famous long before we knew so much of it as to realize that we were savages. If we want to know anything of our ancestors, the Celts, we must have recourse to the Greeks and Romans, nations of a much later date than the Asiatics.

For example, although the Gauls bordering on the Alps, along with the inhabitants of these mountains, settled on the banks of the Po, from where they penetrated to Rome three hundred and sixty-one years after the founding of that city, and even besieged the capital, we should never have known of this expedition but for the Romans. Though other Gauls, about one hundred years later, invaded Thessaly and Macedonia, and advanced to the coast of the Euxine Sea, all the information we have of this adventure, is from the Greeks; and they have neither told us who those Gauls were, nor what route they followed. In our own country there is not the slightest trace of these migrations, which resemble those of the Tartars: they only prove that we were a numerous but not a civilized people. The Grecian colony that founded Marseilles six hundred years before the Christian era, could not polish Gaul: the Greek language did not extend beyond their own territory.

Gauls, Germans, Spaniards, Britons, Sarmatians, we know nothing about ourselves that happened over eighteen centuries ago, except for the little we learn from the records of conquerors. We do not even have fables, we have not dared to invent an origin. The vain idea that all the West was peopled by Gomer, the son of Japhet, is a fiction of the East.

If the ancient Tuscans, who instructed the first inhabitants of Rome, knew something more than the other peoples of the West, they either owed that knowledge to the Greek colonies that settled among them, or rather, because it has always been the peculiar property of that soil to produce men of genius, just as the territory of Athens was more suitable for the arts than those of Thebes and Lacedæmon. But what monuments do we have of ancient Tuscany? None at all. We exhaust ourselves in vague conjectures on some unintelligible inscriptions which have escaped the injuries of time, and which probably belong to the first centuries of the Roman republic. As for the other nations of Europe, we have nothing in their old language anterior to the Christian era.

Maritime Spain was discovered by the Phœnicians, as the Spaniards have since discovered America. The Tyrians, the Carthaginians, and the Romans were in turn enriched by the treasures of the earth which that country produced. The Carthaginians benefited from mines, but they were less rich than those of Mexico and Peru; time had exhausted them as it will exhaust those of the new world. Pliny declares that the Romans, in the space of nine years, drew from these mines eight thousand marks of gold, and about twenty-four thousand of silver. It must be admitted that those pretended descendants of Gomer made a very bad use of the various advantages which their country produced, for they were subjugated by the Carthaginians, the Romans, the Vandals, the Goths, and the Arabs.

What we learn of the Gauls from Julius Cæsar and other Roman authors, gives us the idea of a people in need of being subdued by an enlightened nation. The dialects of the Celtic language were frightful. The emperor Julian, in whose reign it was still spoken, says in his *Misopogon* that they resembled the croaking of ravens. In Cæsar's time, their manners were as barbarous as their language. The druids, gross impostors made for the people whom they governed, sacrificed human victims, whom they burned in large and hideous statues of straw. The female druids plunged their knives into the hearts of prisoners, and predicted future events from the flowing of their blood. The vast stones, a little hollowed, found on the confines of Gaul and Germany, are said to be the altars on which those sacrifices were made. These are the only monuments of ancient Gaul. Those who inhabited the coasts of Biscay and Gascony sometimes fed on human flesh. We must turn our eyes with horror from these savage times, which are the shame of human nature.

Let us count among the follies of the human imagination, the notion entertained in our days, that the Celts were descended from the Hebrews. They sacrificed their own species, it is said, because Jephthah sacrificed his daughter. The druids were clad in white, in imitation of the Jewish priests: like these, they had a high priest. The female druids were representatives of Moses' sister and Deborah. The poor wretch pampered at Marseilles, and offered as a sacrifice, crowned with flowers, and loaded with curses, originated from the scape-goat. They go so far as to find some resemblance between a few Celtic and Hebrew words, equally ill pronounced; and thence conclude that the Jews and the Celts are of the same family. Thus reason is insulted in our universal histories, and the little knowledge we might have of antiquity stifled under a heap of forced conjectures.

The Germans nearly resembled the Gauls in their morals: like them they sacrificed human victims; like them they decided their private disputes by single combat; the only difference was, that the Germans were coarser and less industrious than their neighbors. Caesar, in his memoirs, tells us that their magicians always fixed the day of combat. He states that when one of their kings, Ariovistus, brought a hundred thousand of his wandering Germans to pillage the Gauls, he who wished to enslave them and not pillage them sent two Roman officers to enter into conference with this barbarian: Ariovistus put them in irons. He adds that the two officers were destined to be sacrificed to the Germans' gods and were about to be, when he delivered them by his victory.

The families of all these savages had, in Germany, as their only domicile, wretched cottages, at one end of which the father, mother, sisters, brothers, and children lay huddled together, naked, upon straw; while at the other end was their cattle. These, however, are the same people whom we shall soon see in possession of Rome! Tacitus praises the manners of the Germans, but in the same way as Horace extolls the savages known as Getae; neither one knew anything about those they were praising, and wanted only to satirize Rome. The same Tacitus, in the midst of his eloges, admits that everyone knows that the Germans would rather live on plunder than cultivate the earth; and after pillaging their neighbors, they return to their homes to eat and sleep. It is the life of our present-day highway men and cut-purses, whom we punish with the wheel and the rope; and this is what Tacitus had the nerve to praise in order to make the court of the Roman emperors detested, through contrast with Germanic virtue! A mind so just as yours should regard Tacitus as an ingenious satirist, as profound in his ideas as he is concise in his expressions, who wrote the criticism rather than the history of his country, and who would deserve our admiration had he been impartial.

When Cæsar invaded Britain, he found that island still more savage than Germany: the natives scarcely took the trouble to cover their nakedness with skins. The women belonged in common to all the men of the same district. The habitations were willow cabins; and the ornaments of both sexes were figures painted on their bodies, by pricking the skin and pouring the juice of herbs over it, an art still practiced by the savages in America.

That human nature was for a long series of ages plunged in this state so nearly resembling that of brutes, and even inferior to it in many respects, is only too true. The reason, as has been said, is that it is not in human nature for man *to desire what he does not know.* He has always needed not only a prodigious space of time but also lucky circumstances in order to raise himself above the level of animal life.

You have, therefore, great reason for resolving to go at once to those nations which were first civilized. Long before the empires of China and India commenced, perhaps the world produced nations that were learned, polished, and powerful; and these were, perhaps, plunged again, by deluges of barbarians, into that first state of ignorance and brutality which is called the state of nature.

The taking of Constantinople was alone sufficient to annihilate the spirit of ancient Greece. The Goths destroyed the genius of the Romans. The coast of Africa, formerly so rich and flourishing, is nothing now but the haunt of bandits. Changes still more ex-

traordinary must have happened in less favorable climates. Physical and moral causes must have joined; for although the ocean
cannot have entirely changed its bed, it is certain that vast tracts
of lands have been by turns overflowed and forsaken by the sea.
Nature must have been exposed to many scourges and vicissi-
tudes. The most beautiful and most fertile soils of western Europe, all of the low lands watered by the rivers of the Rhine, the
Meuse, the Seine, the Loire, have been covered by the ocean
for a prodigious number of centuries; you have already seen this
in the *Philosophy of History*.

We will say again that it is not so certain that the mountains
which cross the old and new world were formerly plains covered
by the seas, because:

1. Many of these mountains are fifteen thousand feet and more
above sea level.

2. If there had been a time when these mountains did not
exist, where would the streams have come from which are so
necessary to animal life? These mountains are the waters' reser-
voirs. In the two hemispheres they move in different directions:
they are, as Plato says, the bones of this great animal called *the
earth*. We observe that the slightest plants have an invariable
structure; why should the earth be exempt from the general law?

3. If the mountains were thought to have carried the seas, it
would be a contradiction in the order of nature, a violation of the
laws of gravitation and hydrostatics.

4. The ocean's bed is hollow and in its crest one finds no
chains of mountains from one end to the other or from east to
west, as we see on earth. Hence we must not conclude that this
globe was long a sea just because several parts of the globe were
water. We must not conclude that water covered the Alps and
the Andes just because it covered lower Gaul, Greece, Germany,
Africa and India. We can hardly assert that Mount Taurus was
navigable because the Philippine archipelago and the Moluccas
were a continent. It is very likely that high mountains have always been very much as they are. How many books do not state
that a ship's anchor has been found on the summit of the Swiss
mountains? Yet this is as false as all the stories found in these
books.

Let us admit in physics only that which is proven, and in history, that which is of the greatest and most recognized probability. It may well be that mountainous countries have undergone, through volcanoes and earthquakes, as many changes as the low countries; but wherever rivers have had their sources, there have been mountains. A thousand local revolutions have certainly changed a part of the globe, both physically and morally, but we do not know them; and men have decided to write history so late that the human race, old though it is, seems new to us.

Besides, you begin your investigations at an age when the chaos of our Europe begins to take a form, after the fall of the Roman empire. Let us survey the world together; let us see in what condition it was then, by studying it in the same way in which it seems to have been civilized: that is, from the oriental countries to our own, and let us direct our first attention to a people who had a continuous history in a language already fixed, when we did not even possess writing.

PHILOSOPHICAL WRITINGS

PHILOSOPHICAL LETTERS[42]

OR ENGLISH LETTERS

FIFTH LETTER
ON THE ANGLICAN RELIGION

England is truly the country of sects. An Englishman, in virtue of his liberty, goes to Heaven his own way. And yet, notwithstanding that every one is permitted to serve God after his own way, the true Religion of the nation, that in which a man makes his fortune, is the sect of Episcopalians, called the Anglican Church, or simply "the Church." No one can possess an employment, either in England or Ireland, unless he be ranked among the faithful of the Church of England. This reason—which carries its conviction with it—has converted so many nonconformists that not a twentieth part of the nation is out of the pale of the established Church.

The English clergy has retained a great number of Catholic ceremonies, and, in particular, that of receiving their tithes with a most scrupulous exactness. They have also the pious ambition of aiming at superiority.

Moreover, they make a religious merit of inspiring their flock with a holy zeal against every one who dissents from their church. This zeal burned fiercely under the Tories during the last years of Queen Anne's reign; but produced no greater mischief than the breaking of the windows of some few heretic meeting-houses; for the rage of religious sects ceased in England with the civil wars, and was under Queen Anne no more than the murmurings of a sea, whose billows still heaved, after a violent storm. When the Whigs and the Tories laid waste their native country, in the same manner as the Guelphs and Ghibellines formerly did Italy, it was absolutely necessary for both parties to call religion to their aid. The Tories were for Episcopacy, the Whigs for abolishing it; but they contented themselves with only limiting its power when they became masters.

When the Earl of Oxford and Lord Bolingbroke used to drink the health of the Tory cause, the Church of England considered these noblemen as defenders of its holy privileges. The lower house of convocation, a kind of house of commons, composed wholly of the clergy, had some credit at that time; at least, the members of it had the liberty of meeting to discuss ecclesiastical matters; to sentence, from time to time, to the flames, all impious books, that is, books written against themselves. The ministry, which is composed of Whigs at present, does not now so much as allow these gentlemen to assemble; so that they are at this time reduced—in the obscurity of their respective parishes —to the dull occupation of praying for the prosperity of that government, whose tranquillity they would not unwillingly disturb. With respect to the bishops, who are twenty-six in all, they still maintain their seats in the house of lords in spite of the Whigs; because the ancient abuse of considering them as barons still subsists; but they have no more power than the dukes and peers in the parliament of Paris. There is a clause in the oath they are obliged to take to the government, that puts these gentlemen's Christian patience to a severe trial.

They promise that they shall be of the Church of England, as by law established. There is hardly a bishop, dean, or other dignitary, but imagines himself so by divine right; and consequently it cannot but be a great mortification to them to be obliged to confess that they owe their dignities to a pitiful law made by profane laymen. A monk (Father Courayer) wrote a book, not long ago, to prove the validity and succession of English ordinations. This book was forbidden in France; but think you the English ministry were pleased with it? No such thing. Those cursed Whigs do not care a straw whether the Episcopal succession among them has been interrupted or not; or whether Bishop Parker was consecrated in a tavern (as some pretend) or in a church; they prefer that the bishops derive their authority from the parliament rather than from the apostles. Lord B—— observed that the notion of divine right would only serve to make tyrants in lawn sleeves and linens, but that the law made citizens.[43]

With respect to the morals of the English clergy, they are more regular than those of France, and for this reason: all the clergy are educated in the universities of Oxford and Cambridge, far from the corruption of the capital. They are not called to the dignities of the Church till very late, at a time of life when men have no other passion but avarice, and their ambition lacks sustenance. Employments are here bestowed, both in church and in the army, as the rewards for long services; and one does not see boys made bishops or colonels immediately upon their leaving school. Besides, most of the clergy are married. The bad manners contracted at the university and the little commerce men of this profession have with the women, commonly oblige a bishop to confine himself to his own. Clergymen sometimes go to the tavern, because custom allows it, and if they get drunk, it is with great propriety, and without giving the least scandal.

That undefinable mixed kind of mortal who is neither of the clergy nor the laity; in a word, the thing called *abbé* in France, is a species utterly unknown in England. All the clergy here are very much reserved and most of them are pedants. When these are told, that in France young fellows, distinguished for their dissolute ways and raised to the prelacy by female intrigues, make love publicly, amuse themselves with writing tender songs, give carefully prepared and long dinners every day, and after the feast is over, withdraw to invoke the assistance of the Holy Spirit, and boldly assume the title of successors to the apostles; when the English, I say, are told these things, they thank God that they are Protestants. But these are shameless heretics, who deserve to fry in hell with all the devils, as Master Rabelais says; and, for this reason, I shall trouble myself no more about them.

SIXTH LETTER

ON THE PRESBYTERIANS

The Church of England is confined wholly to England and Ireland. Presbyterianism is the established religion in Scotland.

This Presbyterianism is exactly the same as Calvinism, as it was established in France, and is now professed at Geneva. As the priests of this sect receive but very wretched stipends from their churches, and consequently cannot live in the same luxurious manner as bishops, they very naturally exclaim against honors to which they cannot attain. Imagine the haughty Diogenes trampling under foot the pride of Plato. The Scotch Presbyterians greatly resemble that proud and beggarly reasoner. Diogenes did not treat Alexander with half the insolence with which they treated King Charles II. For when they took up arms in his cause against Cromwell, who had deceived them, they compelled that poor king to undergo hearing four sermons every day; they forbade him to play; they reduced him to a state of penance; so that Charles very soon grew weary of being king of these pedants, and made his escape from them with as much joy as a youth does from school.

In presence of the young and sprightly French graduate, who bawls for a whole morning together in the divinity school, and sings in the evening with the ladies, a Church of England clergyman is a Cato. But this Cato is a very gallant when compared with a Scotch Presbyterian. The latter affects a solemn gait, an angry countenance, wears a broad-brimmed hat and a long cloak over a short coat, preaches through the nose, and calls by the name of "Whore of Babylon" all churches where the ministers are so fortunate as to have an income of fifty thousand pounds a year, and where the people are good enough to suffer this, and give them the titles of "my lord," "your grace," or "your eminence."

These gentlemen, who have also some churches in England, have brought an appearance of gravity and austerity into fashion in this country. To them is owing the sanctification of Sunday in the three kingdoms. People are forbidden to work or take any recreation on that day, which is being twice as severe as the Catholic Church. No operas, plays, or concerts are allowed in London on Sundays; and even cards are so expressly forbidden, that none but persons of quality, and those we call genteel, play on that day; the rest of the nation go either to church, to the tavern, or to women of pleasure.

Though the Episcopal and Presbyterian sects are the two prevailing ones in Great Britain, yet all others are very welcome to come and settle in it, and they live very sociably together, though most of their preachers hate one another almost as cordially as a Jansenist damns a Jesuit.

Go into the Royal Exchange in London, a place more respectable than many courts; there you will see the representatives of all nations assembled for the benefit of mankind. There the Jew, the Mahometan, and the Christian transact business together, as though they were all of the same religion, and give the name of infidels only to bankrupts; there the Presbyterian confides in the Anabaptist, and the Anglican depends upon the Quaker's word. At the breaking up of this peaceful and free assembly, some withdraw to the synagogue, and others to take a drink. This man goes and is baptized in a great tub in the name of the Father, Son, and Holy Ghost; that man has his son's foreskin cut off, and has some Hebrew words—to the meaning of which he himself is an utter stranger—to be mumbled over the infant; others retire to their churches, and there wait the inspiration of heaven with their hats on; and all are satisfied.

If there were only one religion in England, there would be fear of despotism; if there were but two, the people would cut one another's throats; but there are thirty, and they all live happy, and in peace.

EIGHTH LETTER

ON PARLIAMENT

The members of the English Parliament are fond of comparing themselves, on all occasions, to the old Romans.

Not long ago, Mr. Shipping opened a speech in the house of commons with these words: "The majesty of the people of England would be wounded." The singularity of this expression occasioned a loud laugh; but this gentleman, far from being disconcerted, repeated the statement in a resolute tone of voice, and the laughter ceased. I must own that I see no resemblance between the majesty of the people of England and that of the Romans, and still less between the two governments. There

is in London a senate, some of whose members are accused—
doubtless very unjustly—of selling their votes on certain occasions, as was done at Rome; and this is the whole resemblance.
In other respects, the two nations appear to be entirely different,
with regard both to good and to evil. The Romans never knew
the terrible madness of religious wars. This abomination was reserved for devout preachers of humility and patience. Marius and
Sulla, Cæsar and Pompey, Antony and Augustus, did not draw
their swords against one another to determine whether their
priest should wear his shirt over his robe, or his robe over his
shirt; or whether the sacred chickens should both eat and drink,
or eat only, in order to take the augury. The English have formerly destroyed one another, by sword or rope, for disputes of as
trifling a nature. The Episcopalians and the Presbyterians quite
turned the heads of these gloomy people for a time; but I believe they will hardly be so foolish again, as they seem to have
grown wiser at their own expense; and I do not perceive the
least inclination in them to murder one another any more for
syllogisms.

Here follows a more essential difference between Rome and
England, which throws the advantage entirely on the side of the
latter; namely, that the civil wars of Rome ended in slavery, and
those of the English in liberty. The English are the only people
on earth who have been able to regulate the power of kings by
resisting them, and who, by a series of struggles, have at length
established that wise form of government where the prince is
all-powerful to do good, and at the same time is restrained from
committing evil; where the nobles are great without insolence
and without vassals; and where the people share in the government without confusion.

The house of lords and the house of commons divide the leg-
islative power under the king; but the Romans had no such balance. Their patricians and plebeians were continually at odds,
without any intermediate power to reconcile them. The Roman
senate, which had the unjust and reprehensible pride to wish to
exclude the plebeians from having any share in the affairs of
government, could find no other artifice to effect their design
than to occupy them in foreign wars. They considered the people

as wild beasts, whom they were to let loose upon their neighbors, for fear they should turn upon their masters. Thus the greatest defect of the government of the Romans was the means of making them conquerors; and, by being unhappy at home, they became masters of the world, till in the end their divisions made them slaves.

The government of England, from its nature, can never attain to so exalted a pitch, nor can it ever have so fatal an end. It has not in view the splendid folly of making conquests, but only the prevention of their neighbors from conquering. The English are jealous not only of their own liberty, but even of that of other nations. The only reason of their quarrels with Louis XIV was because they thought him ambitious. They made war on him out of the goodness of their heart, certainly with nothing to gain by it.

It has not been without some cost that liberty has been established in England, and the idol of arbitrary power has been drowned in seas of blood; nevertheless, the English do not think they have purchased their laws at too high a price. Other nations have not had fewer troubles, have not shed less blood, but then the blood they spilled in defense of their liberty served only to enslave them the more.

That which becomes a revolution in England is only sedition in other countries. A city in Spain, in Barbary, or in Turkey takes up arms in defense of its privileges, and immediately it is stormed by mercenary troops, punished by executioners, and the rest of the nation kiss their chains. The French think that the government of this island is more tempestuous than the seas which surround it; in which, indeed, they are not mistaken: but then this happens only when the king raises the storm by attempting to seize the ship, of which he is only the pilot. The civil wars of France lasted longer, were more cruel, and productive of greater crimes, than those of England: but none of these civil wars had a wise liberty for their object.

In the detestable times of Charles IX and Henry III the whole affair was only whether the people should be slaves to the Guises. As to the last war of Paris, it deserves only to be hooted at. It makes us think we see a crowd of schoolboys rising up in arms against their master, and afterward being whipped for it. Cardinal de Retz, who was witty and brave, but employed those talents badly; who was rebellious without cause, factious without design, and the head of a party without an army, intrigued for the sake of intriguing, and seemed to foment the civil war for his amusement. The parliament did not know what he wanted, nor what he did not want. He levied troops, and the next instant cashiered them; he threatened; he begged pardon; he set a price on Cardinal Mazarin's head, and afterward congratulated him publicly. Our civil wars under Charles VI were bloody and cruel, those of the League execrable, and that of the Fronde ridiculous.

That for which the French chiefly reproach the English is the murder of King Charles I, who was treated by his conquerors as he would have treated them, had he been lucky.

After all, consider, on one side, Charles I, defeated in a pitched battle, imprisoned, tried, sentenced to die in Westminster Hall; and, on the other, the emperor Henry VII poisoned by his chaplain in receiving the sacrament; Henry III of France stabbed by a monk, the minister of the fury of a whole party; thirty different plots contrived to assassinate Henry IV, several of them put into execution, and the last depriving France of this great king. Weigh all these wicked attempts, and then judge.

TENTH LETTER

ON COMMERCE

Commerce, which has enriched the citizens of England, has helped make them free, and this freedom has in turn extended commerce; hence the greatness of the state. It is commerce which gradually established the naval forces that have made the English the masters of the sea. They have now close to two hundred war ships. Posterity will perhaps be surprised to learn that a little island which has but a small quantity of lead, tin, clay and wool became so powerful through its commerce that it could send in 1723 three fleets to three extremities of the world at the same time, one to Gibraltar, conquered and maintained by its arms; another to Porto-Bello, to deprive the king of Spain of the enjoyment of the treasures of the Indies; and the third to the Baltic Sea to prevent the powers of the north from fighting.

When Louis XIV made Italy tremble, and his armies, already in possession of Savoy and Piedmont, were on the point of taking Turin, Prince Eugene had to march from the remotest parts of Germany to the assistance of the duke of Savoy. He had no money, without which cities can neither be taken nor defended. He had recourse to the English merchants. In half an hour's time they lent him fifty millions, with which he liberated Turin, beat the French, and wrote this short note to those who had lent him the money: "Gentlemen, I have received your money, and flatter myself I have employed it to your satisfaction."

All this gives an English merchant a just pride, and causes him, not without reason, to compare himself to a citizen of Rome. Thus the younger son of a peer of the realm does not disdain trade. Lord Townshend, secretary of state, has a brother who is satisfied with being a merchant in the city. At the time when Lord Oxford ruled all England, his younger brother was a merchant at Aleppo, whence he would not depart, and where he died.

This custom, which is now unhappily dying out, appears monstrous to a German, whose head is full of the hereditary privilege of his family. They can never conceive how it is possible that the son of an English peer should be no more than a rich and powerful bourgeois, while in Germany everyone is a prince. I have known more than thirty highnesses of the same name, whose whole fortunes and estate put together amounted to a few coats of arms and their pride.

In France anybody is a marquis who wants to be; and whoever comes from the obscurity of some remote province with money in his pocket and a name that ends with "*ac*" or "*ille*," can say "A man of my quality and rank"; and hold merchants in the most sovereign contempt. The merchant hears his profession spoken of scornfully so often, that he is foolish enough to blush because of it. I do not know, however, which is the most useful to his country, a powdered lord, who knows to a minute when the king rises or goes to bed, perhaps to stool, and who gives himself airs of importance in playing the part of a slave in the antechamber of some minister; or a merchant, who enriches his country, and from his office sends his orders to Surat or Cairo, thereby contributing to the happiness of the world.

ELEVENTH LETTER

INOCULATION

The rest of Europe, that is, the Christian part of it, very gravely assert that the English are fools and madmen; fools, because they give smallpox to their children, in order to keep them from getting it; madmen, because with perfect ease they give their children a dreadful disease, with the aim of preventing a possible evil. The English, on their side, call the rest of Europe unnatural and cowardly; unnatural, in leaving their children exposed to death from smallpox; and cowardly, in fearing to give their children a trifling pain. In order to determine which of the two is in the right, I shall now relate the history of this famous practice, which is discussed outside of England with so much dread.

The women of Circassia have from time immemorial been accustomed to giving their children smallpox, even as early as at six months of age, by making an incision in the arm, and afterward inserting in this incision a pustule carefully taken from the body of some other child. This pustule so insinuated produces in the body of the patient the same effect that leaven does in a piece of dough; that is, it ferments in it, and communicates to the mass of blood the qualities with which it is impregnated. The pustules of the child infected in this manner with smallpox serve to convey the same disease to others. It is perpetually circulating through the different parts of Circassia; and when, unluckily, there is no infection of smallpox in the country, it creates the same uneasiness as an unhealthy season would have occasioned.

What has given rise to this custom in Circassia, and which seems so strange to other nations, is, however, a cause common to all the nations on the face of the earth; that is, the tenderness of mothers, and motives of interest.

The Circassians are poor, and their daughters are beautiful; hence, they are the principal article of their foreign commerce.

It is they who supply beauties for the harems of the grand seigneur, the sufi of Persia, and others who are rich enough to purchase and to maintain these precious commodities. These people train their children in the complete art of dancing lasciviously and of arousing by the most voluptuous artifices, the desire of those haughty lords to whom they are destined. These poor creatures repeat their lesson every day with their mothers, in the same manner as our girls do their catechism; that is, without understanding a thing about it.

Now it often happened that a father and mother, after having taken great pains in giving their children a good education, suddenly see their hopes frustrated. Smallpox getting into the family, one daughter perhaps died; another lost an eye; a third recovered, but with a disfigured nose; so that the poor folk were hopelessly ruined. Often, too, when there was an epidemic, commerce was interrupted for several years which caused notable decline in the seraglios of Turkey and Persia.

A commercial people are always very much alert to their interests, and never neglect knowledge that may be of use in the carrying on of their trade. The Circassians found that of a thousand persons there was hardly one that was ever twice infected by smallpox completely formed; that there had been instances of a person's having had a slight touch of it, or something resembling it, but there never were any two cases known to be dangerous; in short, never has the same person been known to have been twice infected with this disorder. They also noticed that when the disease is mild, and the eruption has only to pierce through a thin and delicate skin, it leaves no mark on the face. From these natural observations they concluded, that if a child of six months or a year old was to have a mild kind of smallpox, not only would the child certainly survive, but it would get better without bearing any marks of it, and would be immune during the rest of its life.

Hence it followed, that to save the life and beauty of their children, their only method would be to give them the disease early, which they did, by inserting into the child's body a pustule taken from the body of one infected with smallpox, the most completely formed, and at the same time the most favorable kind that could be found. The experiment could hardly fail. The Turks, a very sensible people, soon adopted this practice; and, at this day, there is scarcely a pasha in Constantinople who does not inoculate his children while they are at the breast.

There are some who pretend that the Circassians formerly learned this custom from the Arabians. We will leave this point in history to be elucidated by some learned Benedictine, who will not fail to compose several large volumes upon the subject, together with the necessary proof. All I have to say of the matter is that, in the beginning of the reign of George I, Lady Mary Wortley Montague, one of the most celebrated ladies in England for her strong and solid good sense, happening to be with her husband at Constantinople, resolved to give smallpox to a child she had had in that country. In vain did her chaplain remonstrate that this practice was not Christian, and could only be expected to succeed with infidels; my lady Wortley's son recovered, and was presently as well as could be wished. This lady, on her return to London, communicated the experiment she had made to the princess of Wales, now queen of Great Britain. It must be admitted that, setting crowns and titles aside, this princess is certainly born for the encouragement of arts, and for the good of the human race. She is an amiable philosopher seated on a throne, who has improved every opportunity of instruction, and has never lost any occasion of showing her generosity. It is she who, on hearing that a daughter of Milton was still living, and in extreme misery, immediately sent her a valuable present; she it is who encourages the celebrated Father Courayer; in a word, it is she who deigned to become the mediator between Dr. Clarke and Mr. Leibnitz. As soon as she heard of inoculation for smallpox, she had it tried on four criminals under sentence of death, who were thus doubly indebted to her for their lives: for she not only rescued them from the gallows, but, by means of this artificial attack of smallpox, prevented them from having it in the natural way, which in all probability they would have had, and of which they might have died at a more advanced age.

The princess, thus assured of the utility of this proof, had her own children inoculated. All England followed her example; and from that time at least ten thousand children are indebted for their lives to Lady Mary Wortley Montagu, as are all the girls for their beauty.

Out of every hundred persons, at least sixty contract smallpox; of these sixty, twenty die, in the most favorable times, and twenty more wear disagreeable marks of this cruel disease as long as they live. Here is then a fifth part of the human race killed, or, at least, horribly disfigured. Among the vast numbers inoculated in Great Britain, or in Turkey, none are ever known to die, except such as were in a very ill state of health, and doomed to die in any case. No one is marked by it; no one is ever infected a second time, supposing the inoculation to be perfect. It is, therefore, certain that, had some French lady imported this secret from Constantinople into Paris, she would have rendered an everlasting service to the nation. The duke de Villequier, father of the present duke d'Aumont, a nobleman of the most robust constitution, would not have been cut off in the flower of his age.

The prince de Soubise, who enjoyed the most remarkable state of good health ever known, would not have been carried off at twenty-five; nor would the grandfather of Louis XV have been laid in his grave by it in his fiftieth year. The twenty thousand persons who died at Paris in 1723 would have been now alive. What shall we say then? Is it that the French do not love life? Are they indifferent to beauty? It is true that we are a very odd kind of people! It is possible that in ten years we may think of adopting this British custom, provided the doctors and curates allow it; or, perhaps, the French will inoculate their children, out of sheer whim, should those islanders leave it off, out of natural inconstancy.

I learn that the Chinese have practised this custom for a hundred years; the example of a nation that is considered the wisest and the best governed in the universe, is a strong prejudice in its favor. It is true, the Chinese follow a method peculiar to themselves; they make no incision, but take smallpox up the nose in powder, just as we do a pinch of snuff: this method is more pleasant, but amounts to much the same thing, and serves equally to prove that had inoculation been practised in France, it would have saved the lives of thousands.

TWELFTH LETTER

ON LORD BACON

It is not long since the ridiculous and threadbare question was discussed in a celebrated assembly; who was the greatest man, Cæsar or Alexander, Tamerlane or Cromwell?

Somebody said that it must undoubtedly be Sir Isaac Newton. This man was right; for if true greatness consists in having received from heaven a powerful genius, and in using it to enlighten one's self and others, a man like Newton—and such a one is hardly to be met with in ten centuries—is surely the greatest man; and those statesmen and conquerors which no age has ever been without, are commonly but so many illustrious villains. It is the man who sways our minds by the prevalence of reason and the native force of truth, not they who make slaves through violence; the man who knows the universe, not those who disfigure it, that claims our respect.

Therefore, as you desire to be informed of the great men that England has produced, I shall begin with the Bacons, the Lockes, and the Newtons. The generals and ministers will come after them in their turn.

I must begin with the celebrated baron Verulam, known to the rest of Europe by the name of Bacon, which was his family name. He was the son of a keeper of the seals, and was for a considerable time chancellor under James I. Notwithstanding the intrigues of court and the occupations of his office, which would have required his whole attention, he found the time to be a great philosopher, a good historian, and an elegant writer; and what is yet more wonderful is that he lived in an age where the art of writing well was hardly known, and where sound philosophy was still less so. As is the way among mankind, he was more valued after his death than while he lived. His enemies were at the court of London; his admirers were in all of Europe.

When Marquis d'Effiat brought Princess Mary, daughter of Henry the Great, over to be married to King Charles, this minister paid Bacon a visit, who being then ill in bed, received him with close curtains. "You are like the angels," said d'Effiat to him; "we hear much talk of them, and while everybody thinks them quite superior to men, we are never favored with a sight of them."

You have been told in what manner Bacon was accused of a crime which is very far from being the sin of a philosopher; of being corrupted by money; and how he was sentenced by the house of peers to pay a fine of about four hundred thousand livres of our money, besides losing his office of chancellor and the rank of a peer.

At present the English revere his memory to such a degree that they will not admit that he was guilty. Should you ask me what I think of it, I will make use of a saying I heard from Lord Bolingbroke. They happened to be talking of the avarice of which the duke of Marlborough had been accused, and cited several instances of it, for the truth of which they appealed to Lord Bolingbroke, who being his sworn enemy, might, perhaps, quite properly say what he thought. "He was," said he, "so great a man that I have forgotten his vices."

I shall, therefore, limit myself to those qualities which have acquired for Chancellor Bacon the esteem of all Europe.

The most singular, as well as the best of all his works, is that which is now the least read, and the most useless: I mean his *Novum Scientiarum Organum*. This is the scaffold by means of which the edifice of the new philosophy was built; and when the building was at least partially completed, the scaffold was no longer of any use.

Chancellor Bacon was unacquainted with nature, but he knew and pointed out all the paths which lead to her. He had very early despised what the Universities call philosophy; and he did everything in his power that those bodies, instituted for the perfection of human reason, might cease to mar it, by their *"quiddities,"* their *"horror of a vacuum,"* their *"substantial forms,"* with the rest of that jargon which ignorance and a ridiculous combination of religion had consecrated.

He is the father of experimental philosophy. It is true that wonderful discoveries had been made before his time: the mariner's compass, the art of printing, that of engraving, the art of painting in oil, that of making glass, the art of restoring in some measure sight to old men, by means of spectacles, the secret of making gunpowder, etc. They had gone in search of, discovered, and conquered a new world. Who would not have thought that these sublime discoveries had been made by the greatest philosophers, and in times much more enlightened than ours? By no means; for these great changes took place in the age of the most stupid barbarity. Chance alone brought forth almost all these inventions, and it is even possible that chance had a great share in the discovery of America; at least, it has been believed that Christopher Columbus undertook this voyage on the faith of a captain of a ship who had been cast by a storm on one of the Caribbean islands.

Be this as it may, men had learned to go from one end of the world to the other; they learned how to destroy cities with an artificial thunder much more terrible than the real; but they were still ignorant of the circulation of the blood, the weight of the air, the laws of motion, light, the number of our planets, etc. And a man capable enough to maintain a thesis on the "Categories of Aristotle," the *universale a parte rei*, or some other foolishness, was considered as a prodigy.

The most wonderful and useful inventions are by no means those which do most honor to the human mind.

It is to a mechanical instinct which exists in most men that we owe the arts, and in no way whatever to sound philosophy.

The discovery of fire, the arts of making bread, of melting and working metals, of building houses, the invention of the shuttle, are infinitely more useful than printing and the compass; yet these arts were invented by men who were still savages.

What astonishing things have the Greeks and Romans since done in mechanics? Yet men believed, in their time, that the heavens were of crystal, and the stars were little lamps that sometimes fell into the sea; and one of their greatest philosophers, after much research, had at length discovered that the stars were pebbles that had become detached from the earth.

In a word, there was not a man who had any idea of experimental philosophy before Chancellor Bacon; and of all the physical experiments which have been made since his time, there is hardly a single one which has not been pointed out in his book. He had even made a good number of them himself. He constructed several sort of pneumatic machines, by which he discovered the elasticity of the air; he had long attempted the discovery of its weight, and was even at times very near to it, when it was laid hold of by Torricelli. A short time after, experimental physics began to be cultivated in almost all parts of Europe. This was a hidden treasure, which Bacon had suspected, and which all the philosophers, encouraged by his promises tried to unearth.

But what surprises me most is to see in his book a discussion, in specific terms, of that new attraction of which Newton passes for the inventor.

"We must inquire," said Bacon, "whether there be not a certain magnetic force, which operates reciprocally between the earth and other heavy bodies, between the moon and the ocean, between the planets, etc."

In another place he says: "Either heavy bodies are impelled toward the centre of the earth, or they are mutually attracted by it, and in this latter case it is evident that the nearer falling bodies approach the earth, the more forcibly are they attracted by it. We must try to see," he continues, "if the same pendulum clock goes faster on the top of a mountain, or at the bottom of a mine. If the force of the weight diminishes on the mountain, and increases in the mine, it is probable the earth has a real attracting quality."

This precursor in philosophy was also an elegant writer, a historian, and a wit.

His moral essays are in high regard; but they are made rather to instruct than to please; and as they are neither a satire on human nature, like the *Maxims* of La Rochefoucauld, nor a school of skepticism, like Montaigne; they are less read than these two ingenious books.

His *History of Henry* VII passed for a masterpiece; but I am much mistaken if it can be compared with the history of our illustrious M. de Thou.

In speaking of that famous impostor Perkin, a Jew by birth, who assumed so boldly the name of Richard IV, king of England, encouraged by the duchess of Burgundy, and who disputed the crown with Henry VII, the Chancellor Bacon expresses himself in these terms: "About this time King Henry was beset with evil spirits, by the magic of the duchess of Burgundy, who conjured up from hell the ghost of Edward IV, in order to torment King Henry. When the duchess of Burgundy had instructed Perkin, she began to consider in what region of Heaven she should make this comet appear, and resolved immediately that it should burst forth on the horizon of Ireland."

I think our sage de Thou seldom gives in to this hocus-pocus, which used formerly to pass for the sublime, but which at present is properly called "nonsense."

THIRTEENTH LETTER

ON LOCKE

Perhaps never was there a wiser mind, a more methodical understanding, nor a more exact logician, than Locke, even though he was not a great mathematician. He never could bring himself to undergo the drudgery of calculation, nor the dryness of mathematical truths, which present nothing tangible to the mind; and no one has proved better than he, that a man, without the aid of geometry, might still possess the geometrical spirit. The great philosophers before his time had decided positively what the human soul was; but as they were wholly ignorant of the matter, it was but reasonable they should all be of different opinions.

In Greece, the cradle of arts and of errors, where the greatness and folly of the human mind were pushed so far, they reasoned on the soul exactly as we do.

The divine Anaxagoras, who had altars erected to him for teaching men that the sun was bigger than the Peloponnessus, that snow was black, that the sky was of stone, affirmed that the soul was an *aerial* spirit, though immortal.

Diogenes, a different person from him who became a cynic after having been a counterfeiter, asserted that the soul was a portion of the very substance of God, a notion which was at least striking.

Epicurus maintained the soul is composed of parts, in the same manner as bodies. Aristotle, whose works have been interpreted a thousand different ways, because they were unintelligible, was of the opinion, if we may trust some of his disciples, that the understanding of all men was but one and the same substance.

The divine Plato, master of the divine Aristotle, and the divine Socrates, master of the divine Plato, said that the soul was at the same time corporeal and eternal. The dæmon of Socrates had, no doubt, let him into the secret of this matter. There are actually some who claim that a fellow who boasted of having a private spirit of his own was most assuredly either knave or fool; but these people are too demanding.

As for our Fathers of the Church, several of them in the first centuries were of the opinion that the human soul, as well as the Angels, and God himself, were all corporeal.

The world is every day improving. St. Bernard, as Father Mabillon admits, taught, with respect to the soul, that after death it did not behold God in heaven, but was obliged to rest satisfied with conversing with the humanity of Jesus Christ. He was not believed this time on his bare word. The adventure of the crusade had somewhat discredited his oracles. A thousand Scholastics came after him: there was the irrefragable doctor, the subtle doctor, the angelic doctor, the seraphic doctor, the cherubimical doctor, all of whom were absolutely sure of knowing the soul perfectly, but who have, for all that, spoken of it exactly as if they did not want anyone to understand of what they spoke.

Our Descartes, born to discover the errors of antiquity, but also to substitute his own in their place, and dragged along by that systematic spirit which blinds the greatest men, imagined he had demonstrated that the soul was the same thing as thought, in the same way, according to him, as matter is the same as extension. He firmly maintained that the soul always thinks, and that at its arrival in the body, it is provided with all of the metaphysical notions, knowing God, space, infinity, having all the abstract ideas, filled with wonderful knowledge which it unhappily loses the moment it comes out of its mother's womb.

Father Malebranche, of the Oratory, in his sublime illusions, not only admits of innate ideas, but he has no doubt of our seeing everything in God; and that God Himself, so to speak, is our soul.

After so many reasoners had made this romance of the soul,

one truly wise man appeared, who has modestly given us its history. Locke has exposed human reason, just as a learned anatomist would have explained the functions of the body. He is aided throughout by the light of physics; he sometimes dares to speak in a positive manner, but he also dares to doubt. Instead of defining at once what we do not know, he examines, by degrees, what we want to know. He takes a child from the moment of its birth; he follows all the stages of its understanding; he views what it possesses in common with animals, and in what it is superior to them. Above all, he consults his own experience, the consciousness of his thought.

"I leave," says he, "those who are possessed of more knowledge than I am to determine whether our souls exist before or after the organization of the body; but cannot help acknowledging that the soul that has fallen to my share is one of those coarse material kinds which does not always think, and I am even so unhappy as not to be able to conceive how it should be more indispensably necessary that the soul should always think, than that the body should always be in motion."

For my part, I am proud of the honor of being as stupid on this point as Locke. Nobody shall every persuade me that I always think; and I don't find myself in the least more disposed than he to think that, a few weeks after I was conceived, my soul was very learned, and acquainted with a thousand things that I forgot the moment I came into the world, and that I possessed to very little good purpose in the uterus, so much valuable knowledge, which escaped me the instant it could have been of any advantage, and which I have never since been able to recover.

Locke, after demolishing the notion of innate ideas; having renounced the vain belief that the mind always thinks, establishes the fact, that all our ideas come through the senses; examines our simple and compound ideas; accompanies the mind in all its operations; shows the imperfection of all the languages spoken by men, and what abuse of terms we commit every moment.

He finally proceeds to consider the extent, or rather the nothingness, of human knowledge. This is the chapter in which he has the boldness to advance, though in a modest manner, that

We shall never be able to determine, whether a purely material being is capable of thought or not.

This sagacious proposition seemed to more than one theologian as a scandalous assertion that the soul is material and mortal.

Some Englishmen, devout in their manner, gave the alarm. The superstitious are in society what cowards are in an army; they infect the rest with their own panic. They cried out that Locke wanted to turn all religion topsy-turvy: there was, however, not the smallest question of religion in the affair, the matter was purely philosophical, and altogether independent of faith and revelation. They had only to examine, without rancor, whether it were a contradiction to say: *matter can think*, and God is able to endow matter with thought. But it is common with theologians to begin by pronouncing that God is offended, whenever we happen not to think as they do. The case is pretty much like that of the bad poets, who exclaimed that Boileau insulted the king, because he made fun of them.

Doctor Stillingfleet has acquired the reputation of a moderate theologian, only because he has refrained from abuse in his controversy with Locke. He ventured to enter the lists with him, but was vanquished, because he reasoned like a doctor; while Locke, like a philosopher acquainted with the strength and weakness of human understanding, fought with arms of whose temper he was perfectly well assured.

If I may dare to speak after Locke on so delicate a subject, I would say: For a long time men have argued about nature and the immortality of the soul. With respect to its immortality, it is impossible to demonstrate it, for there is still much dispute over its nature, and it is certain that we must know a created being completely in order to decide if it is immortal or not. Human reason is so little capable of demonstrating by itself the immortality of the soul, that religion has been obliged to reveal it to us. The common welfare of all men demands that we believe the soul to be immortal; faith orders that we do so; no more is needed, and the matter is decided. It is not the same with respect to man's nature. It matters little to religion of what substance the soul is composed, provided that it is virtuous; it is like a watch we are given to take care of: the workman does not tell us what the watchspring is made of.

I am a body and I think: I know nothing more Shall I attribute to an unknown cause what I can so easily attribute to the only immediate cause that I know? Here all the schoolmen interrupt my argument and say: "A body is made up only of extension and solidity and can have only movement and shape. Now, out of movement and shape, extension and solidity, a thought cannot come. Hence the soul cannot be matter." This great process of reasoning so often repeated is reduced uniquely to this: "I know absolutely nothing about matter; I can imperfectly guess at a few of its properties. Now I do not know at all if these properties may be joined to thought; hence, because I know nothing at all, I assert positively that matter is not able to think." Here you have clearly the reasoning process of the School. Locke would say quite simply to these gentlemen:"At least confess that you are as ignorant as I; neither your imagination nor my own can conceive how a body may have ideas; and do you understand any better how a substance, whatever it may be, has ideas? You do not conceive either of matter or of mind; how do you dare to assert anything?"

The superstitious man comes in his turn and says that for the good of their souls we must burn those who suspect that we can think with the sole aid of the body. But what would such persons say if they were the ones guilty of irreligion? In fact, who is the man who would dare to assert, without an absurd impiety, that it is impossible for the Creator to give thought and feeling to matter? See, if you please, to what a pass you are reduced, you who thus limit the power of the Creator! Animals have the same organs as we, the same feelings, the same perceptions; they have memory, they combine several ideas. If God could not animate matter and give it feeling, it must be true either that animals are pure machines or that they have a spiritual soul.

It seems to me almost demonstrated that animals can not be mere machines. Here is my proof: God has given them precisely the same organs of feeling as we have; hence, if they do not feel, God has made something useless. Now God, by your own admission, does nothing in vain; hence he has not invented so many organs of feeling so that there be no feeling; hence animals are certainly not pure machines.

Animals, according to you, cannot have a spiritual soul; hence, in spite of you, there is nothing else to say, except that God has given the organs of animals, which are matter, the faculty of feeling and perceiving, which you call their instinct.

Well then! What could prevent God from communicating to our finer organs this faculty of feeling, perceiving and thinking, that we call human reason? Whichever way you turn, you are obliged to admit your ignorance and the immense power of the Creator. Do not, then, rebel against the sage and modest philosophy of Locke; far from being contrary to religion, it serves it as a proof, should religion have need of it; for what philosophy is more religious than that which, while affirming only what it conceives clearly and admitting its weakness, tells you that we must have recourse to God as soon as we examine first principles?

Besides, we must never fear that any philosophical belief can harm a nation's religion. Our mysteries in vain run counter to our demonstrations; they are no less revered by Christian philosophers, who know that the objects of reason and faith are of a different nature. Never will philosophers create a religious sect. Why? Because they do not write for the whole people, and they are without enthusiasm.

Divide the human race into twenty parts: nineteen will be composed of those who work with their hands and who will never know if there was a Locke in the world; in the twentieth part which remains, how few men will be found who read! And among those who read, there are twenty who read the Roman authors for every one who studies philosophy. The number of those who think is excessively small, and these do not care to disturb the world.

It is not Montaigne or Locke or Bayle or Spinoza or Hobbes or Shaftesbury or Collins or Toland or the like who have kindled the flame of discord in their land; it is rather the theologians, who, having first had the ambition of becoming heads of a sect, soon came to have that of becoming heads of a faction. Indeed, all of the books of modern philosophers put together will never make as much noise in the world as did the dispute of the Franciscans over the form of their sleeve and cowl.

EIGHTEENTH LETTER

ON TRAGEDY

The English had a regular theatre, as well as the Spaniards, while the French had only platforms. Shakespeare, who passed for the English Corneille, flourished about the time of Lope de Vega. He created the theatre. His genius was at once strong and abundant, natural and sublime, but without the smallest spark of taste, and without the slightest knowledge of the rules. I will venture to tell you a bold but yet undoubted truth; which is, that the merit of this author has been the ruin of the English stage: there are in him scenes so perfectly beautiful, and passages so full of the great and terrible, spread up and down those monstrous farces of his which they have christened tragedies, that his pieces have always been played with prodigious success. Time, which alone makes men's reputation, serves at length to consecrate their very defects. The greater part of those extravagant passages and bombast have, in the course of two hundred years, acquired the right to pass for the sublime. Almost all modern authors have copied him, though what succeeded in Shakespeare is hissed in them; and you can well imagine that the veneration they entertain for this ancient increases in proportion to their contempt of the moderns. They never once reflect that it is absurd to imitate him; and the ill success of those copiers makes him thought inimitable.

You know that in the tragedy of the "Moor of Venice," a very touching piece, a husband smothers his wife on the stage, and the poor woman dies asserting her innocence. You are not ignorant that in "Hamlet" a couple of grave-diggers dig a grave upon the stage, singing and drinking at their work, and making the low jokes common to this sort of people, about the skulls they throw up; but what will most astonish you is that these fooleries have been imitated in the reign of Charles II, which was the reign of politeness, and the golden age of the fine arts.

Otway, in his "Venice Preserved," introduced the senator Antonio, and his courtesan, Aquilina, in the midst of the horrors of Bedamar's conspiracy; the old senator plays all the tricks of an old impotent crazy lecher. He mimics by turns a bull, and a dog, and he bites his mistress' legs, who alternately whips and kicks him. These buffooneries, made to please the rabble, have since been omitted in the representation of this piece; but in "Julius Caesar," the idle jests of Roman shoemakers and cobblers are still introduced on the stage with Cassius and Brutus. This is because Otway's foolishness is modern, while Shakespeare's is ancient.

You will, no doubt, lament that those who have hitherto spoken to you of the English stage, and particularly of this celebrated Shakespeare, have pointed out only his errors, and that no one has translated those striking passages in this great man which atone for all his faults. To this I shall answer that it is very easy to recount in prose the absurdities of a poet, but very difficult to translate his fine verses; those who set themselves up as critics of celebrated writers generally compile volumes; but I had rather read two pages which present only their beauties; for I shall always concur with all men of good taste, that there is more to be learned in a dozen verses of Homer or Virgil, than in all the criticism that has been written on these two great men.

I have ventured to translate some passages of the best English poets: here is one of Shakespeare's. Be indulgent to the copy, in honor to the original; and always remember, that when you see a translation, you perceive only a faint copy of a beautiful picture.

I have selected the soliloquy in the tragedy of "Hamlet," which is universally known, and begins with this line: "To be, or not to be: that is the question." It is Hamlet, prince of Denmark, who speaks.

> *Demeure; il faut choisir, & passer à l'instant*
> *De la vie à la mort, ou de l'être au néant.*
> *Dieux cruels! s'il en est, éclairez mon courage.*
> *Faut-il vieillir courbé sous la main qui m'outrage,*
> *Supporter ou finir mon malheur & mon sort?*
> *Qui suis-je? Qui m'arrête? Et qu'est-ce que la mort?*
> *C'est la fin de nos maux, c'est mon unique asile;*
> *Après de longs transports, c'est un sommeil tranquille.*
> *On s'endort, et tout meurt; mais un affreux réveil*

Doit succéder peut-être aux douceurs du sommeil.
On nous menace, on dit, que cette courte vie
De tourments éternels est aussitôt suivie.
O mort! moment fatal! affreuse éternité!
Tout cœur à ton seul nom se glace épouvanté!
Eh! qui pourrait sans toi supporter cette vie?
De nos Prêtres menteurs bénir l'hypocrisie?
D'une indigne maîtresse encenser les erreurs?
Ramper sous un Ministre, adorer ses hauteurs?
Et montrer les langueurs de son âme abattue,
A des amis ingrats, qui détournent la vue?
La mort serait trop douce en ses extrémités.
Mais le scrupule parle, et nous crie, "Arrêtez."
Il défend à nos mains cet heureux homicide,
Et d'un Héros guerrier, fait un chrétien timide, etc.

Do not imagine that I have rendered the English word for word—woe be to those literal translators, who, by translating every single word, enervate the sense! It is in this case that we may truly say, "The letter kills, and the spirit giveth life."

I shall now give you a passage from the famous tragedian, Dryden, an English poet who flourished in the reign of Charles II; an author more fertile than judicious, who would have preserved an unblemished reputation, if he had written only the tenth part of his works, and whose great fault was wanting to be universal.

The passage begins thus:

> When I consider life, 'tis all a cheat;
> Yet, fooled by hope, men favor the deceit . . .

De desseins en regrets et d'erreurs en désirs
Les mortels insensés promènent leur folie,
Dans des malheurs présents, dans l'espoir des plaisirs.
Nous ne vivons jamais, nous attendons la vie.
Demain, demain, dit-on, va combler tous nos vœux;
Demain vient, et nous laisse encor plus malheureux.
Quelle est l'erreur, hélas! du soin qui nous dévore?
Nul de nous ne voudrait recommencer son cours:
De nos premiers moments nous maudissons l'aurore,
Et de la nuit qui vient, nous attendons encore
Ce qu'ont en vain promis les plus beaux de nos jours, etc.

It is in these detached sentences that the English tragedies have hitherto excelled. Their pieces, almost always barbarous, void of decency, order, and probability, have yet, amid this night of darkness, astonishing illuminations. Their style is too stiff, too unnatural, too much copied from the Hebrew writers, and too full of Asiatic bombast; but also it must be admitted that the mind is transported to an amazing height, soaring on the movement of the metaphorical style which adorns the English language, even though the route be irregular.

The famous Addison was the first Englishman who wrote a rational tragedy written with elegance from one end to the other. His tragedy of "Cato" is a masterpiece in its diction and in the beauty of its verses. The role of Cato is to my mind well above that of Cornélie in Corneille's *Pompée*; for Cato is great without bombast, and Cornélie, who is not a necessary character in the play, sometimes approaches nonsense. Addison's Cato seems to me the finest character in any theatre but the other roles in the play are not of the same order, and this well-written work is disfigured by a cold love intrigue which expands a deadly languor over the piece.

The custom of introducing love, right or wrong, into dramatic works, passed over from Paris to London about the year 1660, with our ribbons and wigs. The ladies, who there as well as here embellish the theatre, would no longer suffer any other conversation but of love. The sage Addison had the effeminate complaisance to bend the severity of his character to the manners of his time, and spoiled a masterpiece in order to please.

Since his time plays have become more regular, the people more difficult, the authors more timid. I have seen very decent, but very flat, new plays. The brilliant monsters of Shakespeare please a thousand times more than the modern wisdom. The poetic genius of the English resembles, at this day, a spreading tree planted by nature, shooting forth at random a thousand branches, and growing with unequal strength; it dies if you force its nature, or shape it into a regular tree, fit for the gardens of Marly.

NINETEENTH LETTER

ON COMEDY

I do not know why the wise and ingenious Muralt, author of
Letters on the English and on the French, takes the trouble, while
discussing comedy, to criticize a writer named Shadwell. This
author was very much despised in his day; he surely was not the
poet of decent men. His plays, admired for a while by the common sort, were disdained by men of good taste, and are like so
many plays that I have seen in France, to attract the rabble and
to revolt the reader, on which one might say:

> All Paris condemns them, and all Paris pursues them.

It would seem too that Muralt should have told us about an excellent writer who was living at that time: Wycherly, who for a
long while was the declared lover of the most famous mistress of
Charles II. This man, who spent his life in high society, knew its
vices and foibles perfectly, and painted them with the boldest
strokes and in the truest colors.

He made a misanthrope, imitated from Molière. Here Wycherly's strokes are stronger and bolder than is true of our misanthrope; but also they have less smoothness and order. The English author corrected the only weakness in Molière's play: the
lack of intrigue and of plot interest. The English play is interesting and its plot is ingenious; undoubtedly it is too bold for our
customs. The hero is a captain of a ship, of great courage and
frankness, and scorn for mankind. He has a sincere and prudent
friend whom he mistrusts, and a mistress, by whom he is tenderly
beloved, whom he disdains, while he places all his confidence in
a false friend, the most worthless of men, and gives his heart to a
flirt, the most perfidious of her sex. He believes, however, that
this woman is a Penelope, and this false friend a Cato. He sets
out on an expedition against the Dutch, and leaves all his money,
jewels, and other effects, in the hands of this woman to the care
of this friend he so firmly relies on; while the true friend, whom
he mistrusts, embarks with him, and the lady, to whom he has not
deigned to pay the least regard, disguises herself in the habit of a

page and performs the voyage with him, without revealing her sex the whole time.

Having lost his ship in an engagement, the captain returns to London in the utmost distress, accompanied by his friend and the page, without knowing the friendship of the one, or the love of the other. He goes immediately to that paragon of women from whom he expects to receive his strong box, and a proof of her fidelity. He finds her married to the honest rogue he had confided in, and his treasure has been handled in a similar way. The good man will hardly believe that so virtuous a woman could be guilty of such deeds, when the better to convince him of it, this honest lady falls in love with the little page, and attempts to take him away by force: but as it is necessary in a dramatic piece that justice should take place, vice be punished and virtue rewarded, at the close of the play, the captain, disguised in place of the page, goes to the bed of his inconstant mistress, cuckolds his treacherous friend, runs him through the body, recovers the remains of his effects, and marries his page. You will observe that this piece is interlarded with an old litigious woman, related to the captain, who is one of the merriest creatures, and one of the best characters, on the stage.

Wycherly has taken another piece from Molière not less bold and singular; it is a sort of "School for Wives."

The principal character in the piece is a droll libertine, the terror of the husbands of London; who, to make sure of his business, spreads a rumor, that, in a late illness, his surgeons had found it necessary to make him a eunuch. With this fine reputation, the husbands grant him free access to their wives, and his only difficulty is where to fix his choice. He gives the preference to a little country-girl, who has a great share of innocence, with a natural warmth of temperament, by which she makes her husband a cuckold with a good will and readiness that far exceeds the malice of more expert ladies. This piece is not indeed the school of morality; but it is in truth the school of wit and true comic humor.

The comedies of Sir John Vanbrugh are more agreeable but less ingenious. The knight was a man of pleasure, and besides, a poet and an architect. It is remarked, that he wrote as he built:

a little clumsily: it was he who built the famous castle of Blenheim, the heavy but durable monument of our unfortunate battle of Hochstedt. If the apartments were only as large as the walls are thick, this mansion would be convenient enough.

In Sir John Vanbrugh's epitaph, *the earth is invoked to lie heavy on him, who, when living, had laid such heavy loads upon it.*

This gentleman took a tour into France just before the war of 1701, and was put into the Bastille, where he remained some time, without knowing what it was that had procured him this mark of distinction from our ministry. He wrote a comedy in the Bastille, and, what is in my opinion very remarkable, there is not in all the piece the least stroke against the country where he suffered this violence.

Of all the English writers, the late Mr. Congreve has carried the glory of the comic theatre to the highest pitch. He wrote but few pieces, but they are all excellent of their kind. The laws of the drama are rigorously observed in them; they are full of nuanced characters elegantly varied; not a single bad joke, not the least indecency, is introduced; you find in every part the language of politeness with the actions of knaves; which proves that he knew the world, and kept what is called good company. He was old and almost dying when I knew him; he had one defect, that of insufficiently valuing his first profession of a writer, which made his reputation and his fortune. He spoke to me of his works as bagatelles beneath him, and asked me, in our first conversation, to view him only as a very ordinary gentleman. I replied that if he had the misfortune to be only a gentleman, like all the others, I should never have come to see him, and I was very shocked by this misplaced vanity.

His comedies are the most sprightly and correct, Sir John Vanbrugh's the gayest, and Wycherly's the boldest.

It is to be observed, that none of these five wits have spoken ill of Molière: it is only the English writers of no repute that have vilified this great man. It was the bad musicians of Italy who despised Lulli, but a Buononcini praised him and did him justice, just as a Mead did for a Helvetius and a Silva.

England still has good writers of comedy such as Steele or

Cibber, an excellent playwright and also poet of the king, a title that may seem ridiculous, but which yields an income of a thousand gold pieces and handsome privileges. Our great Corneille did not have as much.

Do not expect from me any details of these English plays of which I am so great a partisan, nor that I should give you a single *bon mot* or jest from Congreve or Wycherly. One cannot laugh in a translation. If you would be acquainted with the English comedy, you must go to London and reside there three years. You must learn the language perfectly, and constantly frequent the theatre. I take no great pleasure in reading Plautus or Aristophanes, because I am neither Greek nor Roman. The delicate turn of phrase, the allusion, and the manner, are all lost for a foreigner.

It is not the same in tragedy; that consists alone of great passions, and heroic stupidities consecrated by the stale error of legend and history. Œdipus and Electra belong as much to us, to the English, and to the Spaniards, as to the Greeks. But true comedy is the living picture of the absurdities of a country; and, if you do not know the nation well, you can hardly judge of the painting.

TWENTY-THIRD LETTER

ON THE CONSIDERATION OWED TO MEN OF LETTERS

Neither in England nor in any other country does one find institutions in favor of the fine arts such as in France. Almost everywhere there are universities, but it is in France alone that we find useful encouragement for astronomy, for all branches of mathematics, for medicine, for research into antiquity, for painting, sculpture and architecture. Louis XIV immortalized his name by his foundations, and this immortality did not cost him two hundred thousand francs a year.

I admit that I have been greatly surprised that the English parliament, which decided to promise twenty thousand guineas to the man that would make the impossible discovery of the longitudes, never thought of imitating Louis XIV in his magnificence with respect to the arts.

In truth merit in England has found other rewards more hon-

orable for the nation. So great is the respect this people have for
talent that a man of merit always makes his fortune there. Addison in France would have belonged to some Academy and might
have obtained, through the influence of some woman, a pension
of twelve hundred francs, or else he might have been imprisoned
on the pretext that certain strokes in his tragedy of *Cato* were
directed against some man in power. In England he was secretary of state. Newton was warden of the royal mint; Congreve
held an important post; Prior was an ambassador; Swift is a Dean
in Ireland and is much more greatly respected than the primate.
If Pope's religion does not permit him to have an official position, it did not prevent his translation of Homer from bringing
him two hundred thousand francs. I have seen in France the
author of *Rhadamiste* nearly die of hunger, and the son of one of
the greatest men France ever had, and who began to follow in his
father's footsteps, would have been reduced to misery without
the patronage of Fagon.[44] What most encourages the arts in England is the consideration in which they are held: the portrait of
the prime minister hangs over the fire-place of his office, but I
have seen Pope's in twenty homes.

Newton was honored during his life, and also after his death
as he should have been. The greatest men of his country disputed
the honor of being among his pall-bearers. Go into Westminster
Abbey. It is not the tombs of kings that are admired there; but
monuments which the gratitude of the nation has erected to the
greatest men who have contributed to its glory. You see their
statues as those of Sophocles and Plato were seen in Athens, and
I am convinced that the mere sight of the glorious monuments
has quickened more than one mind and formed more than
one great man.

The English have even been blamed for going too far in the
honors they bestow on mere merit; they have been criticized for
burying in Westminster the celebrated actress, Mrs. Oldfield,
with almost the same honors paid to Newton. Some have claimed
that they honored the memory of this actress in this way so as to
make us feel even more the barbarous and cowardly injustice for
which they condemn us: throwing the body of Mademoiselle Lecouvreur into a common sewer.

But I can assure you that the English, in the funeral pomp of Mrs. Oldfield, buried in their Saint-Denis, consulted only their taste; they are very far from imputing any infamy to the art of Sophocles and Euripides, and from cutting off from the body of their citizens those who dedicate themselves to reciting before them the works by which their nation is glorified.

In the time of Charles I and at the beginning of those civil wars begun by rigorous fanatics who were themselves finally the victims, there was a good deal of writing denouncing plays, especially because Charles I and his wife, daughter of our Henry the Great, liked them very much.

A doctor named Prynne, incredibly scrupulous, who would have thought himself damned had he worn a cassock instead of a short cloak, and who would have liked to see one half of the human race massacre the other half for the glory of God and true belief, took it upon himself to write a wretched book against the rather good comedies that were played every day in all innocence before the king and queen. He cited the authority of rabbis and some passages from Saint Bonaventura to prove that the *Oedipus* of Sophocles was the work of the evil spirit, that Terence was excommunicated *ipso facto*; and he added that without doubt Brutus, who was a most severe Jansenist, assassinated Caesar only because Caesar, who was a high priest, had composed a tragedy of *Oedipus*; finally, he said that all who attend a stage play were excommunicants who denied their chrism and baptism. This was an outrage to the king and the royal family. In those days the English respected Charles I; they would not permit anyone to speak of excommunicating the same prince whom they later decapitated. Prynne was summoned to appear before the star chamber and was condemned to see his fine book burned by the hangman and to have his ears cut off. His trial is a matter of public record

They are very careful, in Italy, not to condemn the opera or to excommunicate Signor Senesino or Signora Cuzzoni. For myself, I could wish that we might suppress in France I know not what bad books written against the stage; for when the Italians and the English learn that we brand with the greatest infamy an art in which we excel, that a spectacle performed by nuns and in convents is condemned as impious, that the plays in which Louis

XIV and Louis XV have acted are dishonored, that pieces reviewed by the severest judges and performed before a virtuous queen are declared the work of the devil; when, I say, foreigners will learn of this insolence, this lack of respect for royal authority, this gothic barbarity that some dare to call Christian severity, what do you expect them to think of our country? And how can they imagine, either that our laws sanction an art declared so infamous, or that some will dare to stamp with such infamy an art authorized by the laws, rewarded by the sovereigns, cultivated by great men and admired by nations; and that in the same book store you can find the declamation of Father Le Brun against our plays along side of the immortal works of Racine, Corneille, and Molière?

TREATISE ON TOLERANCE[45]

I

A BRIEF ACCOUNT OF THE DEATH OF JEAN CALAS

The murder of Jean Calas, committed in Toulouse with the sword of justice, the 9th of March, 1762, is one of the most singular events that calls for the attention of the present age and of posterity. We soon forget the crowd of victims who have fallen in the course of innumerable battles, not only because this is a destiny inevitable in war, but because those who thus fell might also have given death to their enemies, and did not lose their lives without defending themselves. Where the danger and the advantage are equal, our wonder ceases, and even pity itself is in some measure lessened; but where the father of an innocent family is delivered up to the hands of error, passion, or fanaticism; where the accused person has no other defense but his virtue; where the arbiters of his destiny have nothing to risk in putting him to death but their having been mistaken, and where they may murder with impunity by decree, then every one is ready to cry out, every one fears for himself, and sees that no person's life is secure in a court erected to watch over the lives of citizens, and every voice unites in demanding vengeance.

In this strange affair, we find religion, suicide, and parricide. The object of inquiry was, whether a father and a mother had murdered their own son in order to please God, and whether a brother had murdered his brother, or a friend his friend; or whether the judges had to reproach themselves with having broken on the wheel an innocent father, or with having acquitted a guilty mother, brother, and friend.

Jean Calas, a person of sixty-eight years of age, had followed the profession of a merchant in Toulouse for upwards of forty years, and was known by all as a good parent in his family. He was a Protestant, as was also his wife, and all his children, one son only excepted, who had abjured heresy, and to whom the father allowed a small annuity. Indeed, he appeared so far removed from that absurd fanaticism which destroys the bonds of society, that he even approved of the conversion of his son, Louis Calas, and he had for thirty years a maid-servant, who was a zealous Catholic, and who had brought up all his children.

Another of his sons, whose name was Marc-Antoine, was a man of letters, but, at the same time, of a restless, gloomy, and violent disposition. This young man finding that he could neither succeed nor enter into business as a merchant, for which indeed he was very unfit, nor be admitted to the bar as a lawyer, because he lacked the certificates of his being a Catholic, resolved to end his life, and gave some intimation of his design to one of his friends. He confirmed himself in his resolution by reading everything that had been written upon the subject of suicide.

At length, one day, having lost all his money in gambling, he chose that as a most proper opportunity for executing his design. A friend named Lavaisse, a young man of nineteen years of age, the son of a famous lawyer of Toulouse, and a youth esteemed by every one who knew him, happened to come from Bordeaux the evening before.[46] He went by chance to dine with the Calas family at their house. Old Calas, his wife, Marc-Antoine, their eldest son, and Pierre their second son, all ate together that evening; after supper was over, they retired into another room, when Marc-Antoine suddenly disappeared. After some time, young Lavaisse took his leave, and Pierre Calas accompanied him downstairs; when they came near the store they saw Marc-Antoine hanging in his shirt behind the door, and his coat folded up and laid upon the counter. His shirt was not in the least rumpled, and his hair was well combed. There was no wound on his body, nor any other mark of violence.

We shall not here enter into all the minute circumstances with which the lawyers have filled their briefs; nor shall we describe the grief and despair of the unhappy parents; their cries were heard by the whole neighborhood. Lavaisse and Peter Calas, almost beside themselves, ran, the one to fetch a surgeon, and the other an officer of justice.

While they were thus employed, and old Calas and his wife were sobbing in tears, the people of Toulouse gathered in crowds about the house. The Toulousians are a superstitious and headstrong people; they look upon their brothers who are not of the same religion as themselves, as monsters. It was at Toulouse that a solemn thanksgiving was ordered for the death of Henry III and that the inhabitants took an oath to murder the first person who should propose to acknowledge that great and good prince Henry IV for their sovereign. This same city still continues to solemnize, by an annual procession and bonfires, the day on which, about two hundred years ago, it ordered the massacre of four thousand of its citizens as heretics. In vain has the council issued six decrees prohibiting this detestable holiday. The Toulousians still continue to celebrate it as a high festival.

Some fanatic among the mob cried out that Jean Calas had hanged his own son; this cry, taken up, became in an instant unanimous; some persons added that the deceased was to have made his abjuration the next day; that his own family and young Lavaisse had murdered him out of hatred for the Catholic religion. No sooner was this opinion stated than it was fully believed by every one; and the whole town was persuaded that it is one of the articles of the Protestant religion for a father or mother to murder their own son, if he attempts to change his faith.

When minds are once aroused, they are not easily appeased. It was now imagined that all the Protestants of Languedoc had assembled together the preceding night, and had chosen by a plurality of voices one of their sect for an executioner; that the choice had fallen upon young Lavaisse; that this young man had, in less than four and twenty hours, received the news of his election, and had come from Bordeaux to assist Jean Calas, his wife, and their son Pierre, to murder a son, a brother, and a friend.

The Sieur David, magistrate of Toulouse, excited by these rumors, and desirous of bringing himself into notice by the ready execution of his office, took a step contrary to all the established rules and ordinances, by ordering the Calas family, together with their Catholic maid-servant and Lavaisse, to be put in irons.

After this a legal declaration was published which was no less vicious. Matters were carried still farther; Marc-Antoine Calas had died a Calvinist, and as such, if he had laid violent hands on himself, his body ought to have been dragged on a hurdle; he was buried with the greatest funeral pomp in the church of St. Stephen, in spite of the curate who entered his protest against this profanation of holy ground.

There are in Languedoc four orders of penitents, the white, the blue, the gray, and the black, who wear a long capuchin or hood, having a mask of cloth falling down over the face, in which are two holes to see through. These orders wanted the Duke of Fitz-James to become one of their body, but he refused. On the present occasion the white penitents performed a solemn service for Marc-Antoine Calas as for a martyr; nor was the festival of a martyr ever celebrated with greater pomp by any church: but then this pomp was truly terrible. Beneath a magnificent canopy was placed a skeleton which was made to move and which represented Marc-Antoine Calas, holding in one hand a branch of palm, and, in the other, the pen with which he was to sign his adjuration of heresy, and which in fact wrote the death-warrant of his father.

And now nothing more remained to be done for this wretch who had been his own murderer but the office of canonization; all the people looked on him as a saint; some invoked him, some went to pray at his tomb, some besought him to work miracles, while others gravely recounted those he had already performed: A monk pulled out one or two of his teeth, in order to have some lasting relics. An old woman, somewhat deaf, declared that she had heard the sound of bells; and a priest was cured of an apoplectic fit, after taking a stout emetic. Protocols were drawn up of these stupendous miracles, and the author of this account has in his possession an affidavit to prove that a young man of Toulouse went mad for having prayed several nights successively at the tomb of the new saint, without having been able to obtain the miracle he requested of him.

Among the order of the white penitents were some magistrates. The death of Jean Calas seemed then inevitable.

But what more particularly hastened his fate was the approach of that singular festival, which, as I have already observed, the Toulousians celebrate every year, in commemoration of the massacre of four thousand Huguenots; the year 1762 happened to be the *annum seculare* of this deed. The inhabitants were busied in making preparations for the solemnity; this circumstance added fresh fuel to the heated imagination of the people; every one cried out that a scaffold for the execution of the Calas family would be the greatest ornament of the ceremony; and that Providence itself seemed to have brought these victims to be sacrificed to our holy religion. Twenty persons heard these speeches, and others still more violent. And this, in the present age! this at a time when philosophy has made so great a progress! and while the pens of a hundred academies are employed in inspiring gentleness of manners. It should seem that enthusiasm enraged at the recent success of reason, fought under her standard with redoubled fury.

Thirteen judges met every day to try this cause; they had not, they could not, have any proof against this family; but mistaken religion took the place of proofs. Six of the judges persisted obstinate, resolved to sentence Jean Calas, his son, and Lavaisse, to be broken on the wheel, and his wife to be burned at the stake; the other seven judges, rather more moderate, were at least for having the accused examined. The debates were frequent and long. One of the judges, convinced in his mind of the innocence of the accused and of the impossibility of the crime, spoke warmly in their favor; he opposed the zeal of humanity to that of cruelty, and openly pleaded the cause of the Calas family in all the houses of Toulouse where misguided religion demanded with incessant cries the blood of these unfortunates. Another judge, well known for his violence, went about the town, raving with as much fury against the accused as his brother had been earnest in defending them. In short, the contest became so warm that both were obliged to enter protests against each other's proceedings, and retire into the country.

But by a strange fatality, the judge who had been on the favorable side had the delicacy to persist in his exceptions, and the other returned to give his vote against those on whom he could no longer sit as judge; and it was his single vote which carried the sentence to the wheel, there being eight voices against five, one of the six merciful judges being at last, after much contestation, brought over to the more rigorous side.

In my opinion, in cases of parricide, and where the head of a family is to be given over to the most dreadful punishment, the sentence ought to be unanimous, inasmuch as the proofs of so unheard of a crime ought to be of such a manner as to satisfy all the world: the least shadow of a doubt in a case of this nature should be sufficient to make the judge tremble who is about to pass sentence of death. The weakness of our reason, and the insufficiency of our laws, become every day more obvious; but surely there cannot be a greater example of this wretchedness than that a single vote should be sufficient to condemn a fellow-citizen to be broken alive on the wheel. The Athenians required at least fifty voices, over and above the majority of the judges, before they would dare to pronounce sentence of death. What does all this show? That we know, quite uselessly, that the Greeks were wiser and more humane than ourselves.

It appeared impossible that Jean Calas, who was an old man of sixty-eight, and had been long troubled with a swelling and weakness in his legs, should have been able by himself to have strangled his son and hanged him, a stout young fellow of eight and twenty, and more than commonly robust; therefore he must absolutely have been assisted in this act by his wife, his other son, Pierre Calas, Lavaisse, and by the servant-maid, and they had been together the whole night of this fatal adventure. But this supposition is altogether as absurd as the other; for can any one believe that a servant, who was a zealous Catholic, would have permitted Huguenots to murder a young man whom she herself had brought up, for his attachment to a religion to which she herself was devoted? That Lavaisse would have come purposely from Bordeaux to murder his friend, of whose pretended conversion he knew nothing? That an affectionate mother would have joined in laying violent hands on her own son? And lastly, how could they all together have been able to strangle a young man stronger than them all, without a long and violent struggle, or without his making such a noise as must have been heard by the whole neighborhood, without repeated blows passing between them, without any marks of violence, or without any of their clothes being torn.

It was evident that if this murder could have been committed, the accused persons were all equally guilty, because they did not leave each other's company an instant the whole night; but then it was equally evident that they were not guilty, and that the father alone could not be so, and yet, by the sentence of the judges, the father alone was condemned to expire on the rack.

The motive on which this sentence was passed was as unaccountable as all the rest of the proceeding. Those judges who had given their opinion for the execution of Jean Calas persuaded the others that this poor old man, unable to support the torments, would, under the blows of torturers, make a full confession of his crime and that of his accomplices. They were confounded, when the old man, dying on the wheel, called God as a witness of his innocence, and besought him to forgive his judges!

They were afterwards obliged to pass a second decree, which contradicted the first, namely to set at liberty the mother, her son Pierre, young Lavaisse, and the maid-servant; but one of the counsellors having made them aware that this latter decree contradicted the other, and that they condemned themselves, inasmuch as it was proved that all the accused parties had been constantly together during the whole time the murder was supposed to be committed, the setting at liberty of the survivors was an incontestable proof of the innocence of the master of the family whom they had ordered to be executed. They then determined to banish Pierre Calas, the son, which was an act as ill-grounded and absurd as any of the rest, for Pierre Calas was either guilty or not guilty of the murder; if he was guilty, he should have been broken on the wheel in the same manner as his father; if he was innocent, there was no reason for banishing him. But the judges, frightened by the punishment of the father, and by that tender piety with which he had died, thought to save their honor by making people believe that they showed mercy to the son; as if this was not a new degree of prevarication; and they thought that no bad consequences could arise from banishing this young man, who was poor and destitute of friends. His exile was not a great injustice after that which they had been already so unfortunate as to commit.

They began by threatening Pierre Calas in his prison cell that they would treat him as they had his father, if he would not abjure his religion. This the young man has declared on oath.

As Pierre was going out of the town, he was met by one of the abbés with a converting spirit, who made him return back to Toulouse, where he was shut up in a convent of Dominicans, and there compelled to perform all the functions of a convert to the Catholic religion; this was in part what his persecutors wanted; it was the price of his father's blood, and the religion they thought they were avenging seemed satisfied.

The daughters were taken from their mother, and shut up in a convent. This unhappy woman, who had been, as it were, sprinkled with the blood of her husband, who had held her eldest son lifeless within her arms, had seen the other banished, her daughters taken from her, herself stripped of her property, and left alone in the world destitute of bread, and bereft of hopes, was almost weighed down to the grave by the excess of her misfortunes. Some persons, who had maturely weighed all the circumstances of this horrible adventure, were so struck with them that they pressed Madame Calas, who now led a life of retirement and solitude, to exert herself, and go and demand justice at the foot of the throne. At this time she was scarcely able to sustain herself; besides, having been born in England and brought over to a distant province in France when very young, the very name of the city of Paris frightened her. She imagined that in the capital of the kingdom they must be still more savage than in Toulouse; at length, however, the duty of avenging the memory of her husband got the better of her weakness. She arrived in Paris half dead, and was surprised to find herself received with tenderness, sympathy, and offers of assistance.

In Paris reason always triumphs over fanaticism, however great, whereas in the provinces fanaticism almost always triumphs over reason.

M. de Beaumont, a famous lawyer of the Parliament of Paris, immediately took up her cause and drew up an opinion, which was signed by fifteen other lawyers. M. Loiseau, equally famous for his eloquence, likewise drew up a brief in favor of the family; and M. Mariette, solicitor to the council, drew up a formal statement of the case, which struck every one who read it with conviction.

These three generous defenders of the laws and of innocence made the widow a present of all the profits arising from the publication of these pleas,[47] which filled not only Paris but all Europe with pity for this unfortunate woman, and every one cried aloud for justice to be done her. The public passed sentence on this affair long before it was determined by the council.

This pity made its way even to the Cabinet, notwithstanding the continual round of business, which often excludes pity and the familiarity of seeing unhappiness, which too frequently steels the heart even more. The daughters were restored to their mother, and all three in deep mourning, and in sobs, drew sympathetic tears from the eyes of their judges.

Nevertheless, this family had still some enemies for this was an affair of religion. Several persons, whom in France we call devout, declared publicly that it was much better to suffer an old Calvinist, though innocent, to be broken upon the wheel, than to force eight counsellors of Languedoc to admit that they had been mistaken; these people made use of this very expression: "That there were more magistrates than Calases"; by which they inferred that the Calas family ought to be sacrificed to the honor of the magistracy. They never reflected that the honor of a judge, like that of another man, consists in making reparation for his faults. In France no one believes that the pope, assisted by his cardinals, is infallible. One may also believe that eight judges of Toulouse are not. Every sensible and disinterested person declared that the decree of the court of Toulouse would be quashed anywhere in Europe, even though particular considerations might prevent it from being declared void by the council.

Such was the state of this surprising affair when it caused certain impartial, but sensible, persons to form the design of laying before the public a few reflections upon tolerance, indulgence, and commiseration, which the Abbé Houtteville in his bombastic and declamatory work, which is false in all the facts, calls a *monstrous dogma*, but which reason calls the *portion of human nature.*

Either the judges of Toulouse, carried away by the fanaticism of the mob, caused the innocent head of a family to be tortured to death, a thing which is without example; or this father and his wife murdered their eldest son, with the assistance of another son and a friend, which is altogether contrary to nature. In either case, the abuse of the most holy religion has produced a great crime. It is therefore to the interest of mankind to examine if religion should be charitable or savage.

XXI

VIRTUE IS BETTER THAN LEARNING

The fewer dogmas, the fewer disputes; and the fewer disputes, the fewer misfortunes: if this is not true, I am mistaken.

Religion is instituted to make us happy in this life and the next. But what is required to make us happy in the life to come? To be just.

To be happy in this life, as much as the wretchedness of our nature will permit, what do we need? To be indulgent.

It would be the height of madness to pretend to bring all mankind to think exactly in the same manner about metaphysics. We might, with much greater ease, conquer the whole universe by force of arms than subject the minds of all the inhabitants of one single village.

Euclid found no difficulty in persuading every one of the truths of geometry. And why? Because there is not one of them which is not a self-evident corollary of this simple axiom: "Two and two make four." But is it not altogether the same for the mixture of metaphysics and theology.

When Bishop Alexander and Arius the priest began first to dispute in what manner the *Logos* proceeded from the Father, the Emperor Constantine wrote to them in the following words reported by Eusabius and Socrates: "You are great fools to dispute about things you can not understand."

If the two contending parties had been wise enough to agree that the emperor was right, Christendom would not have been drenched in blood for three hundred years.

And, indeed, what can be more foolish, or more horrible than to address mankind in this manner: "My friends, it is not sufficient that you are faithful subjects, dutiful children, tender parents, and good neighbors; that you practice every virtue; that you are friendly, grateful, and worship Jesus-Christ in peace; it is furthermore required of you that you should know how a thing is begotten from all eternity and if you cannot distinguish the *omousian* in the hypostasis, we declare to you that you will be burned for all eternity; and in the meantime we will begin by cutting your throats"?

If such a decision as this had been presented to Archimedes, Posidonius, Varro, Cato, or Cicero, what answer do you think they would have made?

Constantine, however, did not persevere in silencing the two parties; he might easily have summoned the chiefs of the disputes before him, and have demanded of them by what authority they disturbed the peace of mankind. "Are you," he might have said, "members of the divine family? What is it to you whether the *Logos Son* was made or begotten, provided that you are faithful to it; that you preach a virtuous morality and practise it if you can? I have committed many faults in my lifetime, and so have you; you are ambitious, and so am I; it has cost me many falsehoods and cruelties to gain the empire; I have murdered almost all my relatives; but I now repent: I want to expiate my crimes by restoring peace to the Roman Empire; do not prevent me from doing the only good action which can possibly make my former cruel ones forgotten; help me to end my days in peace." Perhaps Constantine might not have prevailed over the disputants, and perhaps he might have been pleased with presiding over a council in a long crimson robe, with his forehead glittering with jewels.

This, however, opened the way to all those dreadful calamities which overran the West from Asia. Out of every contested verse there issued a fury armed with an interpretation and a dagger, who made men stupid and cruel. The Huns, the Heruli, the Goths, and Vandals, who came afterwards, did infinitely less harm, and the greatest they did was that of afterwards engaging in the same fatal disputes.

XXII

OF UNIVERSAL TOLERANCE

It does not require any great art or studied elocution to prove that Christians ought to tolerate one another. I will go even further and say that we ought to look upon all men as our brothers. What! call a Turk, a Jew, and a Siamese, my brother? Yes, of course; for are we not all children of the same father, and the creatures of the same God?

But these people despise us and call us idolaters! Well, then, I should tell them that they are very wrong. And I think that I could stagger the headstrong pride of an imaum, or a talapoin, were I to speak to them something like this:

"This little globe, which is no more than a point, rolls, together with many other globes, in that immensity of space in which we are lost. Man, who is about five feet high, is certainly a very inconsiderable part of the creation; but one of those hardly visible beings says to some of his neighbors in Arabia or South Africa: Listen to me, for the God of all these worlds has enlightened me. There are about nine hundred millions of us little insects who inhabit the earth, but my ant-hill alone is cherished by God who holds all the rest in horror for all eternity; those who live with me upon my spot will alone be happy, and all the rest eternally wretched."

They would stop me and ask, "What madman could have made so foolish a speech?" I should then be obliged to answer them, "It is yourselves." After which I should try to pacify them, but that would not be very easy.

I might next address myself to the Christians and venture to say, for example, to a Dominican, one of the judges of the inquisition: "Brother, you know that every province in Italy has a jargon of its own and that they do not speak in Venice and Bergamo as they do in Florence. The Academy della Crusca has fixed the standard of the Italian language; its dictionary is an absolute rule, and Buonmattei's Grammar is an infallible guide, from neither of which we ought to depart; but do you think that the president of the Academy, or in his absence Buonmattei, could in conscience order the tongues of all the Venetians and Bergamese, who persisted in their own dialect, to be cut out?"

The inquisitor would reply: "There is a very wide difference; here the salvation of your soul is concerned; and it is entirely for your good that the directory of the inquisition orders that you be seized, upon the deposition of a single person, though of the most infamous character; that you have no lawyer to plead for you, nor even be acquainted with the name of your accuser; that the inquisitor promise you favor, and afterwards condemn you; that he make you undergo five different kinds of torture, and that afterwards you be either whipped, sent to the galleys, or burned at the stake. Father Ivonet, and the doctors, Cuchalon, Zanchinus Campegius, Roias, Felynus, Gomarus, Diabarus, and Gemelinus are exactly of this opinion, and this pious practice will not admit of contradiction."

To all of which I should take the liberty of making the following reply: "My brother, you may perhaps be in the right; I am perfectly well convinced of the great good you would do me; but may I not be saved without all this?"

It is true that these absurd horrors do not daily stain the face of the earth; but they have been frequent, and one might easily collect instances enough to make a volume much larger than that of the Holy Gospels, which condemn such practices. It is not only very cruel to persecute in this short life those who do not think in the same way as we do, but I very much doubt if there is not an impious boldness in pronouncing them eternally damned. In my opinion, it little befits such insects of a summer's day as we are thus to anticipate the decrees of the Creator. I am very far from opposing the maxim, "outside the church there is no salvation;" I respect it and all that it teaches, but, after all, do we know all the ways of God, and all the extent of his mercy? Are we not permitted to hope in him, as well as to fear him? Is it not sufficient if we are faithful to the Church? Must every individual usurp the rights of Divinity and determine, before it, the eternal fate of all men?

When we wear mourning for a king of Sweden, Denmark, England or Prussia, do we say that we are in mourning for a damned soul that is burning eternally in hell? There are about forty millions of inhabitants in Europe who are not members of the Church of Rome; should we say to every one of them, "Sir, since you are infallibly damned, I shall neither eat, converse, nor have any connections with you?"

Is there an ambassador of France who, when he is presented to the Grand Seigneur for an audience, will seriously say to himself, his highness will infallibly burn for all eternity for having submitted to circumcision? If he really thought that the Grand Seigneur was a mortal enemy of God, and the object of his vengeance, could he converse with such a person; ought he to be sent to him? With what man could we carry on any commerce, or perform any of the civil duties of society, if we were indeed convinced that we were conversing with persons destined to eternal damnation?

O different worshippers of a peaceful God! if you have a cruel heart, if, while you adore he whose whole law consists of these few words, "Love God and your neighbor," you have burdened that pure and holy law with false and unintelligible disputes, if you have lighted the flames of discord sometimes for a new word, and sometimes for a single letter of the alphabet; if you have attached eternal punishment to the omission of a few words, or of certain ceremonies which other people cannot comprehend, I must say to you with tears of compassion for mankind: "Transport yourselves with me to the day on which all men will be judged and on which God will do unto each according to his works.

"I see all the dead of past ages and of our own appearing in his presence. Are you very sure that our Creator and Father will say to the wise and virtuous Confucius, to the legislator Solon, to Pythagoras, Zaleucus, Socrates, Plato, the divine Antonins, the good Trajan, to Titus, the delights of mankind, to Epictetus, and to many others, models of men: Go, monsters, go and suffer torments that are infinite in intensity and duration. Let your punishment be eternal as I am. But you, my beloved ones, John Châtel, Ravaillac, Damiens, Cartouche, etc. who have died according to the prescribed rules, sit forever at my right hand and share my empire and my felicity."

You draw back with horror at these words; and after they have escaped me, I have nothing more to say to you.

XXIII

PRAYER TO GOD

No longer then do I address myself to men, but to you, God of all beings, of all worlds, and of all ages; if it may be permitted weak creatures lost in immensity and imperceptible to the rest of the universe, to dare to ask something of you, you who have given everything, and whose decrees are immutable as they are eternal. Deign to look with pity on the errors attached to our nature; let not these errors prove ruinous to us. You have not given us hearts to hate ourselves with, and hands to kill one another. Grant then that we may mutually aid each other to support the burden of a painful and transitory life; that the trifling differences in the garments that cover our frail bodies, in our insufficient languages, in our ridiculous customs, in our imperfect laws, in our idle opinions, in all our conditions so disproportionate in our eyes, and so equal in yours, that all the little variations that differentiate the atoms called *men* not be signs of hatred and persecution; that those who light candles in broad daylight to worship you bear with those who content themselves with the light of your sun; that those who dress themselves in a white robe to say that we must love you do not detest those who say the same thing in cloaks of black wool; that it may be all the same to adore you in a dialect formed from an ancient or a modern language; that those whose coat is colored red or violet, who rule over a little parcel of a little heap of mud of this world, and who possess a few round fragments of a certain metal, enjoy without pride what they call *grandeur* and *riches*, and may others look on them without envy: for you know that there is nothing in all these vanities to inspire envy or pride.

May all men remember that they are brothers! May they hold

in horror tyranny exerted over souls, just as they do the violence which forcibly seizes the products of peaceful industry! And if the scourge of war is inevitable, let us not hate one another, let us not destroy one another in the midst of peace, and let us use the moment of our existence to bless, in a thousand different languages, from Siam to California, your goodness which has given us this moment.

A COMMENTARY ON THE BOOK,

Of Crimes and Punishments[48]

II

OF PUNISHMENTS

The misfortunes of the wretched in the face of the severity of the law have induced me to look at the criminal code of nations. The humane author of the essay, *Of Crimes and Punishments*, is only too right in complaining that punishment is much too often out of proportion to the crime, and sometimes detrimental to the nation it was intended to serve.

Ingenious punishments, in which the human mind seems to have exhausted itself in order to make death terrible, seem rather the inventions of tyranny than of justice.

The punishment of the wheel was first introduced in Germany in times of anarchy, when those who seized royal power wished to terrify, by the device of an unheard-of torture, whoever would dare to rise up against them. In England they used to rip open the belly of a man convicted of high treason, tear out his heart, slap his cheeks with it, and then throw it into the fire. And what, very frequently, was this crime of high treason? During the civil wars, it was to have been faithful to an unfortunate king, and sometimes had to be explained according to the doubtful rights of a conqueror. In time, manners became milder; it is true that they continue to tear out the heart, but it is always after the death of the criminal. The torture is terrible but the death is easy, if death can ever be easy.

IX

OF WITCHES

In 1749 a woman was burned in the Bishopric of Wurtzburg, convicted of being a witch. This is an extraordinary phenomenon in the age in which we live. Is it possible that people who boast of their reformation and of trampling superstition under foot, who indeed supposed that they had reached the perfection of reason, could nevertheless believe in witchcraft, and this more than a hundred years after the so-called reformation of their reason?

In 1652 a peasant woman named Michelle Chaudron, living in the little territory of Geneva, met the devil going out of the city. The devil gave her a kiss, received her homage, and imprinted on her upper lip and right breast the mark that he customarily bestows on all whom he recognizes as his favorites. This seal of the devil is a little mark which makes the skin insensitive, as all the demonographical jurists of those times affirm.

The devil ordered Michelle Chaudron to bewitch two girls. She obeyed her master punctually. The girls' parents accused her of witchcraft before the law. The girls were questioned and confronted with the accused. They declared that they felt a continual pricking in certain parts of their bodies and that they were possessed. Doctors were called, or at least, those who passed for doctors at that time. They examined the girls. They looked for the devil's seal on Michelle's body—what the statement of the case called *satanic marks*. Into them they drove a long needle, already a painful torture. Blood flowed out, and Michelle made it known, by her cries, that satanic marks certainly do not make one insensitive. The judges, seeing no definite proof that Michelle Chaudron was a witch, proceeded to torture her, a method that infallibly produces the necessary proofs: this wretched woman, yielding to the violence of torture, at last confessed every thing they desired.

The doctors again looked for the satanic mark. They found a little black spot on one of her thighs. They drove in the needle. The torment of the torture had been so horrible that the poor creature hardly felt the needle; thus the crime was established. But as customs were becoming somewhat mild at that time, she was burned only after being hanged and strangled.

In those days every tribunal of Christian Europe resounded with similar arrests. The faggots were lit everywhere for witches, as for heretics. People reproached the Turks most for having neither witches nor demons among them. This absence of demons was considered an infallible proof of the falseness of a religion.

A zealous friend of public welfare, of humanity, of true religion, has stated in one of his writings on behalf of innocence, that Christian tribunals have condemned to death over a hundred thousand accused witches. If to these judicial murders are added the infinitely superior number of massacred heretics, that part of the world will seem to be nothing but a vast scaffold covered with torturers and victims, surrounded by judges, guards and spectators.

X

OF CAPITAL PUNISHMENT

It is an old saying that a man after he is hanged is good for nothing, and that the punishments invented for the welfare of society should be useful to that society. It is clear that twenty vigorous thieves, condemned to hard labor at public works for the rest of their life, serve the state by their punishment; and their death would serve only the executioner, who is paid for killing men in public. Only rarely are thieves punished by death in England; they are transported overseas to the colonies. The same is true in the vast Russian empire. Not a single criminal was executed during the reign of the autocratic Elizabeth. Catherine II who succeeded her, endowed with a very superior mind, followed the same policy. Crimes have not increased as a result of this humanity, and almost always, criminals banished to Siberia become good men. The same thing has been noticed in the English colonies. This happy change astonishes us, but nothing is more natural. These condemned men are forced to work constantly in order to live. Opportunities for vice are lacking; they marry and have children. Force men to work and you make them honest. It is well known that great crimes are not committed in the country, except, perhaps, when too many holidays bring on idleness and lead to debauchery.

A Roman citizen was condemned to death only for crimes affecting the welfare of the state. Our teachers, our first legislators, respected the blood of their fellow citizens; we lavish that of ours.

This dark and delicate question has been long discussed: whether judges may punish by death when the law does not expressly require this punishment. This question was solemnly debated before Emperor Henri IV. He judged, and decided that no magistrate could have this power.

There are some criminal cases that are so unusual or so complicated, or are accompanied by such strange circumstances, that the law itself has been forced in more than one country to leave these singular cases to the discretion of the judges. If there really should be one instance in which the law permits a criminal to be put to death who has not committed a capital offense, there will be a thousand instances in which humanity, which is stronger than the law, should spare the life of those whom the law has sentenced to death.

The sword of justice is in our hands; but we ought to blunt it more often than sharpen it. It is carried in its sheath before kings, to warn us that it should be rarely drawn.

There have been judges who loved to make blood flow; such was Jeffreys in England; such in France was a man who was called *coupe-tête*. Men like these were not born to be judges; nature made them to be executioners.

XIX

OF SUICIDE

The famous Duverger de Hauranne, abbé of St. Cyran, considered the founder of Port Royal, wrote around 1608 a treatise on suicide which has become one of the rarest books in Europe.

The Decalogue, he says, orders us not to kill. The murder of one's self seems to be just as much included in this precept as the murder of some one else. Now, if there are situations in which it is right to kill some one else, there are also situations in which it is right to kill one's self; however, a man should attempt to take his own life only after first consulting his reason.

Public authority, which serves in place of God, may dispose of our life. Human reason may also serve in place of Divine reason: a ray of the eternal light.

St. Cyran extends this argument to great length, which could be taken as sheer sophistry; but when he comes to an explanation and to particulars, it is more difficult to answer him. One might, he states, kill himself for the good of his prince, his country, or his family.

It is indeed true that we cannot condemn such men as Codrus and Curtius. Surely no ruler would dare to punish the family of a man wholly dedicated to his prince; indeed, there is no sovereign who would dare not to reward such a man. St. Thomas said the same thing well before St. Cyran. But we do not need Thomas or Bonaventura or Hauranne to know that a man who dies for his country is worthy of our praise.

The abbé of St. Cyran concludes that it is permitted to do for one's self what it is worthy to do for another. It is generally well known what Plutarch, Seneca, Montaigne, and a hundred other philosophers allege in favor of suicide. It is a common subject and an exhausted one. I do not claim here to present a defense of an action condemned by the laws; but neither the Old Testament nor the New ever forbade a man to depart from life when he could no longer bear it. No Roman law condemned self-murder. On the contrary, here is the law of Emperor Marcus Aurelius, which was never revoked.

"If your father or your brother, convicted of no crime, kills himself either to remove himself from grief or through weariness of life, or in despair or in madness, his will is valid, or if he dies intestate, his heirs inherit according to law."

Despite this humane law of our ancient masters, we still rip apart and pierce with a stake the body of a man who dies voluntarily; we render his memory infamous; we dishonor his family to the extent that we can; we punish the son for having lost his father, and the widow for being deprived of her husband. We even confiscate the possessions of the deceased, which is tantamount to plundering the patrimony of the living to whom it belongs. This custom, like many others, is derived from our canon law, which deprives those who die a voluntary death of the rights of burial. The conclusion drawn from this fact is that no one can inherit on earth the property of a man who is deemed to have no inheritance in heaven. The canon law in the section, *De Pœnitentia*, assures us that Judas committed a greater sin in hanging himself than in betraying our Lord Jesus Christ.

XXII

OF CRIMINAL AND OTHER FORMS OF PROCEDURE

If one day humane laws soften in France some of our too rigorous customs, but without giving greater facility to crime, it is likely that there will also be a reform of those articles of procedure in which our legislators were animated by too severe a zeal. Criminal law in many respects seems to have been contrived only for the ruin of the accused. It is the only uniform law in the kingdom; should it not be as favorable to the innocent as it is terrifying to the guilty? In England, a mere false arrest is compensated by the official who ordered it; but in France, the innocent man who has been flung into a dungeon and has suffered torture, has no consolation to hope for, no damages to seek against any one; he remains with a permanently ruined reputation in society. The innocent man condemned! And why? Because he was dragged out of his home and imprisoned! He ought to arouse only pity and respect. The discovery of crimes demands severity: it is a war that humane justice wages against iniquity; but there is generosity and compassion even in war. The soldier is compassionate; must the man of law be savage?

Let us here compare on a few points the criminal procedure of the Romans with our own.

With the Romans, witnesses were heard in public, in the presence of the accused, who could answer them, even question them or have them cross-examined by a lawyer. This procedure was noble and frank; it was full of Roman magnanimity.

With us, everything is done in secret. A single judge, with his clerk, hears each witness separately, one after another. This practice, established by François I, was authorized by the commissioners who drew up the laws of Louis XIV, in 1670. Nothing but a misunderstanding was responsible for it.

They imagined, in reading the code, *de Testibus*, that the words *testes intrare judicii secretum* meant that witnesses were interrogated in secret. But *secretum* here means the judge's chamber. It would not be correct Latin to say *intrare secretum* for "speaking in secret." A solecism was responsible for this part of our jurisprudence.

Witnesses are usually of the very dregs of the population, and the judge, in private conversation with them, can make them say anything he likes. These witnesses are heard a second time, still in secret, for what is known as the reading of the testimony. And if, after this reading, they retract what they had earlier said, or if they change their testimony in any essentials, they are punished for perjury. So that when a simple-minded fellow, who cannot express himself well but whose heart is in the right place, remembers that he has said too much or too little, that he has misunderstood the judge or that the judge has misunderstood him, and out of a principle of justice takes back what he had said, he is punished as a criminal, and is often forced to adhere to false testimony, only out of fear of perjury.

If he runs away, the accused exposes himself to conviction, whether the crime be proven or not. Some writers on jurisprudence, it is true, maintain that in such instances a man should not be condemned if his crime has not been clearly established; but others, less enlightened, and perhaps more generally followed, have a contrary opinion: they venture to say that the flight of the accused is proof of the crime; that the contempt he displays for justice, in refusing to appear before it, is worthy of the same punishment he would receive were he convicted. Thus, according to the school of jurists to which the judge may happen to belong, an innocent man will be acquitted or condemned.

It is a great abuse of French jurisprudence that it often regards as laws the sometimes cruel fantasies and errors of unprincipled men, who have substituted their feelings for laws.

Two ordinances were promulgated during the reign of Louis XIV which are in force throughout the entire kingdom. In the first, concerned with civil procedure, judges are forbidden to give judgment when the petition is not proved; but in the second, which governs criminal procedure, there is no provision that the accused will be discharged if no evidence is brought against him. This is a strange business! The law states that a man sued for money shall be condemned to pay only if the debt be allowed; but when life is in question, it is a moot point if a man who refuses to go before the court must be condemned when the crime has not been proven; and the law does not resolve this difficulty.

When the accused has taken to flight, you proceed to seize and take inventory of his property; you do not even wait for the proceedings to be finished. You still have no proof, you do not yet know if he is innocent or guilty, and you begin by forcing immense expenses on him!

It is a penalty, you say, as punishment of his disobedience of a legal summons. But does not the extreme severity of your criminal procedure force him to this disobedience?

A man is accused of a crime. At once you lock him up in a wretched dungeon; you allow him no communication with any one; you load him down with irons as if you had already found him guilty. The witnesses who testify against him are heard in secret; he is confronted with them only for a moment; before hearing their testimony he must state his objections to them in detail; at the same time, he must name everyone who might support these objections, none of which are admitted after the reading of the testimony. If he shows the witnesses that they may have exaggerated certain facts or omitted others, or have been mistaken in some of their details, the fear of punishment will make them persist in their perjury. If circumstances described by the accused during interrogation be reported differently by the witnesses, that will be quite enough for ignorant or prejudiced judges to condemn an innocent man.

What man is there who is not terrified by this procedure? What just man can be certain of not being crushed by it? O judges! If you want accused innocent men not to flee, give them the means of defending themselves.

The law seems to require the magistrate to behave towards the accused man as an enemy rather than a judge. The judge has the power of ordering the confrontation of the accused by the witness, or of omitting it. How can so necessary a thing as the confrontation of witnesses be an arbitrary matter.

If a crime is in question, the accused can not have a lawyer; hence he decides to flee, a step which every maxim of the law urges upon him; but in running away, he may be condemned whether the crime is proven or not. Thus a man sued for money is condemned to pay only if the debt be allowed; but when life is at stake, a man can be condemned by default even though the crime has not been established. Is it, then, that the law considers money more than it does life! O judges! Consult pious Antoninus and good Trajan; they forbade the absent to be condemned.

Indeed, your law allows an embezzler or a crooked bankrupt to have recourse to the counsel of a lawyer; and very often, an honorable man is deprived of this aid. If even a single instance can be found in which an innocent man might be acquitted through the help of an attorney, is it not clear that the law which deprives him of such help is unjust?

The president of the royal commission, de Lamoignon, said in speaking against this law, "The lawyer or counsel customarily allowed accused men is not a privilege granted by ordinances or laws: it is a liberty acquired by natural right, older than any human laws. Nature teaches every man that he must depend on the talents of others when he cannot find his own way, and to call on help when he does not feel strong enough to defend himself. Our laws have taken so many advantages away from the accused that it is altogether just to conserve for them what remains, especially the right to counsel, which is the most essential part. For if one compares our procedure with

that of the Romans and of other nations, he will find that none
are so rigorous as that observed in France, particularly since the
ordinance of 1539."

This procedure has been even more severe since the ordinance
of 1670. It would have been much more mild if most of the
commissioners had thought like de Lamoignon.

The parliament of Toulouse has a very unusual way of dealing with proof by witnesses. In other places half-proofs are admitted, which are at bottom only doubts: for everyone knows
there are no such things as half-truths; but at Toulouse they
allow quarter-proofs and eighth-proofs. Hearsay, for example,
might be considered a quarter-proof, and another piece of hearsay, more vague still, an eighth-proof. So that eight rumors,
which are only a single echo of an unfounded report, can serve
as a complete proof. And it was more or less on this principle
that Jean Calas was condemned to be broken on the wheel.
Roman laws required proofs to be *luce meridiana clariores*.[49]

XXIII

THE IDEA OF A REFORM

The magistracy is itself so respectable that the only country in
the world where it can be bought and sold prays to be delivered from this practice. Men hope that a jurist might come
by his merit to deliver that justice which he formerly defended
in person and through his writings. Perhaps there will then
arise, by dint of fortunate labors, a regular and uniform judicial
system.

Will men always judge the same case differently in the provinces and in the capital? Must the same man be right in Brittany
and wrong in Languedoc? Indeed, there are as many systems of
law as there are cities; and even in the same parliament, the
rules of one house are not those of the next.

What prodigious inconsistency there is in the laws of the
same kingdom! In Paris, a man who has resided in the city
for a year and a day is considered a citizen. In Franche-Comté,
a free man who has lived for a year and a day in a house
held in mortmain becomes a slave; his collateral relations can

not inherit the property he may have acquired elsewhere; and his own children are reduced to beggary if they spend a year away from the house in which the father has died. The province is called "frank," but what frankness!

When limits are to be fixed between civil authority and ecclesiastical custom, what interminable disputes arise! What are these limits? Who will reconcile the eternal contradictions of the treasury and the bench? And finally, why in certain countries are sentences passed without explanation? Is it shameful to give the reasons for a verdict? Why do not they who judge in the king's name present their death sentences to the king before execution?

No matter which way we look, we find contradiction, harshness, uncertainty, arbitrary power. In this age we are trying to make everything perfect; let us try, then, to perfect the laws on which our lives and fortunes depend.

ABBÉ

In common speech we may say, "Where are you going, *Monsieur l'Abbé?*" Do you know that the word *abbé* signifies father? If you become one you render a service to the state; you doubtless perform the best work that a man can perform; you give birth to a thinking being: in this action there is something divine.

But if you are only *Monsieur l'Abbé* because you have had your head shaved, wear a small collar, and a short cloak, and are waiting for a fat benefice, you do not deserve the name of *abbé*.

The ancient monks gave this name to the superior whom they elected; the *abbé* was their spiritual father. What different things do the same words signify at different times! The spiritual *abbé* was once a poor man at the head of others equally poor; but the poor spiritual fathers have since had incomes of two hundred or four hundred thousand pounds, and there are poor spiritual fathers in Germany who have regiments of guards.

A poor man, making a vow of poverty, and in consequence becoming a sovereign? We have already said and must repeat a thousand times, this is intolerable. The laws exclaim against such an abuse; religion is indignant at it, and the really poor, who want food and clothing, appeal to heaven at the door of *Monsieur l'Abbé.*

But I hear the *abbés* of Italy, Germany, Flanders, and Burgundy ask: "Why are not we to accumulate wealth and honors? Why are we not to become princes? The bishops are, who were originally poor, like us; they have enriched and elevated themselves; one of them has become superior even to kings; let us imitate them as far as we are able."

Gentlemen, you are right. Invade the land; it belongs to him whose strength or skill obtains possession of it. You have made ample use of the times of ignorance, superstition, and madness, to strip us of our inheritances, and trample us under your feet, that you might fatten on the substance of the unfortunate. Tremble lest the day of reason arrive.

ARIUS

Here is an incomprehensible question, which, for more than sixteen hundred years, has furnished exercise for curiosity, for sophistic subtlety, for animosity, for the spirit of cabal, for the fury of dominion, for the rage of persecution, for blind and bloody fanaticism, for barbarous credulity, and which has produced more horrors than the ambition of princes, which ambition has occasioned very many. Is Jesus the Word? If He be the Word, did He emanate from God in time or before time? If He emanated from God, is He co-eternal and consubstantial with Him, or is He of a similar substance? Is He distinct from Him, or is He not? Is He made or begotten? Can He beget in his turn? Has He paternity? or productive virtue without paternity? Is the Holy Ghost made? or begotten? or produced? or proceeding from the Father? or proceeding from the Son? or proceeding from both? Can He beget? can He produce? is His hypostasis consubstantial with the hypostasis of the Father and the Son? and how is it that, having the same nature—the same essence as the Father and the Son, He cannot do the same things done by these persons who are Himself?

Assuredly, I understand nothing of this; no one has ever understood any of it, and that is why we have slaughtered one another.

The Christians tricked, cavilled, hated, and excommunicated one another, for some of these dogmas inaccessible to human intellect, before the time of Arius and Athanasius. The Egyptian Greeks were remarkably clever; they would split a hair into four, but on this occasion they split it only into three. Alexandros, bishop of Alexandria, thought proper to preach that God, being necessarily individual—single—a monad in the strictest sense of the word, this monad is triune.

The priest Arios or Arious, whom we call Arius, was quite scandalized by Alexandros's monad, and explained the thing in quite a different way. He cavilled in part like the priest Sabellius, who had cavilled like the Phrygian Praxeas, who was a great caviller. Alexandros quickly assembled a small council of those of his own opinion, and excommunicated his priest. Eusebius, bishop of Nicomedia, took the part of Arius. Thus the whole Church was in flame.

The Emperor Constantine was a villain; I confess it—a parricide, who had smothered his wife in a bath, cut his son's throat, assassinated his father-in-law, his brother-in-law, and his nephew; I cannot deny it—a man puffed up with pride and immersed in pleasure; granted—a detestable tyrant, like his children; *transeat*—but he was a man of sense. He would not have obtained the Empire, and subdued all his rivals, had he not reasoned justly.

When he saw the flames of civil war lighted among the scholastic brains, he sent the celebrated Bishop Ozius with dissuasive letters to the two belligerent parties. "You are great fools," he expressly tells them in this letter, "to quarrel about things which you do not understand. It is unworthy the gravity of your ministry to make so much noise about so trifling a matter."

By "so trifling a matter," Constantine meant not what regards the Divinity, but the incomprehensible manner in which they were striving to explain the nature of the Divinity. The Arabian patriarch, who wrote the *History of the Church of Alexandria*, makes Ozius, on presenting the emperor's letter, speak in nearly the following words:

"My brethren, Christianity is just beginning to enjoy the blessings of peace, and you would plunge it into eternal discord. The emperor is only too right to tell you that you *quarrel about a very trifling matter*. Certainly, had the object of the dispute been essential, Jesus Christ, whom we all acknowledge as our legislator, would have mentioned it. God would not have sent his son on earth, to return without teaching us our catechism. Whatever he has not expressly told us is the work of men and error is their portion. Jesus has commanded you to love one another, and you begin by disobeying him and hating one another and stirring up discord in the empire. Pride alone has given birth to these disputes, and Jesus, your Master, has commanded you to be humble. Not one among you can know whether Jesus is made or begotten. And in what does his nature concern you, provided your own is to be just and reasonable? What has the vain science of words to do with the morality which should guide your actions? You cloud our doctrines with mysteries—you, who were designed to strengthen religion by your virtues. Would you leave the Christian religion a mass of sophistry? Did Christ come for this? Cease to dispute worship, humble yourselves, edify one another, clothe the naked, feed the hungry, and pacify the quarrels of families, instead of giving scandal to the whole empire by your dissensions."

Ozius addressed an obstinate audience. The Council of Nicea was assembled and the Roman Empire was torn by a civil war. This war brought on others and mutual persecution has continued from age to age, down to our own day.

BEAUTIFUL, BEAUTY

Ask a toad what is beauty—the great beauty, the *to kalon;* he will answer that it is the female with two great round eyes coming out of her little head, her large flat mouth, her yellow belly, and brown back. Ask a Negro of Guinea; beauty is to him a black, oily skin, sunken eyes; and a flat nose.

Ask the devil; he will tell you that the beautiful consists in a pair of horns, four claws, and a tail. Then consult the philosophers; they will answer you with jargon; they must have something conformable to the archetype of the essence of the beautiful—to the *to kalon.*

I was once watching a tragedy while seated near a philosopher. "How beautiful that is," said he. "What do you find beautiful?" asked I. "It is," said he, "that the author has attained his object." The next day he took his medicine, which did him some good. "It has attained its object," cried I to him; "it is a beautiful medicine." He comprehended that it could not be said that a medicine is beautiful, and that to give anything the name *beautiful* it must cause admiration and pleasure. He admitted that the tragedy had inspired him with these two sentiments, and that it was the *to kalon,* the beautiful.

We made a journey to England. The same piece was played, and, although ably translated, it made all the spectators yawn. "Oh, oh!" said he, "the *to kalon* is not the same with the English as with the French." He concluded after many reflections that "the beautiful" is often most relative, as that which is decent at Japan is indecent at Rome; and that which is the fashion at Paris is not so at Peiping; and he was thereby spared the trouble of composing a long treatise on the beautiful.

CANNIBALS

We have spoken of love. It is hard to pass from people kissing to people eating one another. It is, however, but too true that there have been cannibals. We have found them in America; they are, perhaps, still to be found; and the Cyclops were not the only individuals in antiquity who sometimes fed on human flesh. Juvenal relates that among the Egyptians—that wise people, so renowned for their laws—those pious worshippers of crocodiles and onions—the Tentyrites ate one of their enemies who had fallen into their hands. He does not tell this tale on hearsay; the crime was committed almost before his eyes; he was then in Egypt, and not far from Tentyra. On this occasion he quotes the Gascons and the Saguntines, who formerly fed on the flesh of their countrymen.

In 1725 four savages were brought from the Mississippi to Fontainebleau, with whom I had the honor of conversing. There was among them a lady of the country, whom I asked if she had eaten men; she answered, with great simplicity that she had. I appeared somewhat scandalized; on which she excused herself by saying that it was better to eat one's dead enemy than to leave him to be devoured by wild beasts, and that the conquerors deserved to have the preference. We kill our neighbors in battles, or skirmishes; and, for the meanest consideration, provide meals for the crows and the worms. There is the horror; there is the crime. What matters it, when a man is dead, whether he is eaten by a soldier, or by a dog or a crow?

We have more respect for the dead than for the living. It would be better to respect both the one and the other. The nations called well-governed have done right in not putting their vanquished enemies on the spit; for if we allowed to eat our neighbors, we should soon eat our countrymen, which would be rather unfortunate for the social virtues. But well-governed nations have not always been so; they were all for a long time savage; and, in the infinite number of revolutions which this globe has undergone, mankind have been sometimes numerous and sometimes scarce. It has been with human beings as it now is with elephants, lions, or tigers, the race of which has very much decreased. In times when a country was but thinly inhabited by men, they had few arts; they were hunters. The custom of eating what they had killed easily led them to treat their enemies like their stags and their boars. It was superstition that caused human victims to be sacrificed; it was necessity that caused them to be eaten.

Which is the greater crime—to assemble piously in order to plunge a knife into the heart of a girl adorned with ribbons, or to eat a worthless man whom we have killed in our own defense?

Yet we have many more instances of girls and boys sacrificed than of girls and boys eaten. Almost every nation of which we know anything has sacrificed boys and girls. The Jews immolated them. This was called the Anathema; it was a real sacrifice; and in *Leviticus* it is ordained that the living souls which shall be given over to sacrifice shall not be spared; but it is not in any manner prescribed that they shall be eaten; this is only threatened. Moses, as we have seen, tells the Jews that unless they observe his ceremonies they shall not only have the itch, but the mothers shall eat their children. It is true that in the time of Ezekiel the Jews must have been accustomed to eat human flesh; for, in his thirty-ninth chapter, he foretells to them that God will cause them to eat not only the horses of their enemies, but moreover the horsemen and the rest of the warriors. This is definite. And, indeed, why should not the Jews have been cannibals? It was the only thing wanting to make the people of God the most abominable people upon earth.

I have read in anecdotes of English history in Cromwell's time that a woman who kept a tallow chandler's shop in Dublin sold excellent candles, made of the fat of Englishmen. After some time one of her customers complained that the candles were not so good. "Sir," said the woman, "it is because we are short of Englishmen." I ask which were the most guilty—those who massacred the English, or the poor woman who made candles of their fat?

CHAIN OF CREATED BEINGS

The first time I read Plato and saw this gradation of beings rising from the lowest atom to the supreme Being, this scale filled me with admiration; but when closely regarded, this phantom disappears, as apparitions were wont to vanish at the crowing of the cock.

The imagination is pleased at first to see the imperceptible transition from brute matter to organized matter, from plants to zoophytes, from zoophytes to animals, from animals to men, from men to genii, from these genii, clad in a light aërial body, to immaterial substances of a thousand different orders, rising from beauty to perfection, up to God himself. This hierarchy is very pleasing to good men who think they see the pope and his cardinals, followed by the archbishops and bishops, after whom are the vicars, curates and priests, the deacons and subdeacons, then come the monks, and the capuchins bring up the rear.

But there is, perhaps, a somewhat greater distance between God and his most perfect creatures than between the holy father and the dean of the sacred college. The dean may become pope, but can the most perfect genii created by the supreme Being become God? Is there not infinity between them?

Nor does this chain, this pretended gradation, any more exist in vegetables and animals; the proof is that some species of plants and animals have been entirely destroyed. We have no more murex. The Jews were forbidden to eat griffin and ixion, these two species, whatever Bochart may say, have probably disappeared from the earth. Where, then, is the chain?

Supposing that we had not lost some species, it is evident that they may be destroyed. Lions and rhinoceroses are becoming very scarce.

It is very probable that there have been races of men who are no longer to be found. Why should they not have existed as well as the whites, the blacks, the Kaffirs, to whom nature has given an apron of their own skin, hanging from the belly to the middle of the thigh; the Samoyeds, whose women have nipples of a beautiful ebony, etc.

Is there not a manifest void between the ape and man? Is it not easy to imagine a two-legged animal without feathers having intelligence without our shape or the use of speech—one which we could tame, which would answer our signs, and serve us? And again, between this new species and man, cannot we imagine others?

Beyond man, divine Plato, you place in heaven a string of celestial substances, in some of which we believe because faith so teaches us. But what reason had you to believe in them? It does not appear that you had spoken with the genius of Socrates, and though the good Heres rose again on purpose to tell you the secrets of the other world, he told you nothing of these substances.

In the sensible universe the pretended chain is no less interrupted.

What gradation, I pray you, is there between planets? The moon is forty times smaller than our globe. Traveling from the moon through space, you find Venus, about as large as Earth. From thence you go to Mercury, which revolves in an ellipsis very different from the circular orbit of Venus; it is twenty-seven times smaller than the Earth, the Sun is a million times larger, and Mars is five times smaller. The latter goes his round in two years, his neighbor Jupiter in twelve, and Saturn in thirty; yet Saturn, the most distant of all, is not so large as Jupiter. Where is the pretended gradation?

And then, how, in so many empty spaces, do you extend a

chain connecting the whole? There can certainly be no other
than that which Newton discovered—that which makes all the
globes of the planetary world gravitate towards one another in
this immense void.

Oh, much admired Plato! You have told us nothing but
fables and we have seen a philosopher arise, on an island where
in your day men went naked, who has taught the world truths
that are as great as your imaginings are puerile.

CONFESSION

It is still a question whether confession, viewed only from a
political point of view, has done more good than harm.

Confession was practiced as part of the mysteries of Isis, Orpheus and Ceres before the high priest and the initiates; for
since these mysteries were in fact expiations, it had to be admitted that there were crimes to expiate.

Christians adopted the confession in the early centuries of the
Church, as they virtually took over the rituals of antiquity,
along with the temples, altars, incense, tapers, processionals, holy
water, priestly garments, many formulae out of the mysteries—
the *Sursum corda*, the *Ite missa est*, and many others.[51] The
scandal of the public confession of a woman in Constantinople
in the fourth century, brought on the abolition of the confession.

The secret confession that one man makes to another was
instituted in the West only around the seventh century. Abbés
began by requiring their monks to come to them twice a year
to confess all their faults. It was these abbés who invented the
formula: "I absolve you to the extent that I am able and that
you have need of it." It seems that it would have been more
respectful of the supreme Being, and more just to say: "May he
pardon your faults and mine."

The good that the confession has done is to have sometimes
obtained restitutions from petty thieves. The evil is to have
sometimes, in times of political strife, forced the penitent to become rebellious and blood-thirsty in spirit. The Guelph priests
refused absolution to the Ghibellines, and the Ghibelline priests

took care not to absolve the Guelphs. The murderers of the Sforza, the Medici, the princes of Orange, the kings of France, made ready for their acts by the sacrament of confession.

Louis XI and Brinvilliers confessed as soon as they had committed a great crime, and they confessed often, like gourmands who take medicine so as to have a better appetite.

If there is anything astounding, it is a bull of Pope Gregory XV, promulgated by His Holiness on August 30, 1622, in which he orders the revelation of confessions in certain cases.

The answer of the Jesuit Coton to Henri IV will last longer than the Jesuit order: "Would you reveal the confession of a man resolved to assassinate me?" "No; but I would place myself between him and you."

COUNTRY

A country is a composition of many families; and as a family is communally supported on the principle of self-love, when one has no opposing interest, he extends the same self-love to his town or his village, which is called his country. The greater a country becomes, the less we love it; for love is weakened by diffusion. It is impossible to love a family so numerous that we hardly know it.

He who is burning with ambition to be edile, tribune, prætor, consul, or dictator, exclaims that he loves his country, while he loves only himself. Every man wishes to be sure of sleeping quietly at home, and of preventing any other man from possessing the power of sending him to sleep elsewhere. Every one would be certain of his property and his life. Thus, all forming the same wishes, the particular becomes the general interest. The welfare of the republic is spoken of, while all that is signified is love of self.

It is impossible that a state was ever formed on earth which was not governed in the first instance as a republic: it is the natural course of human nature. At first a few families assembled for protection against bears and wolves; those who had grains exchanged them with those who had only wood.

On the discovery of America, all the people were found divided into republics; there were but two kingdoms in all that part of the world. Of a thousand nations, but two were found subjugated.

It was the same in the ancient world; all was republican in Europe before the little kingdoms of Etruria and of Rome. There are yet republics in Africa. Tripoli, Tunis, Algeria, in the north, are republics of pirates. The Hottentots, towards the south, still live as people are said to have lived in the first ages of the world—free, equal, without masters, without subjects, without money, and almost without wants. The flesh of their sheep feeds them; they are clothed with their skins; huts of wood and clay form their habitations. They are the most dirty of all men, but they feel it not, but live and die more easily than we do.

There remain eight republics in Europe without monarchs— Venice, Holland, Switzerland, Genoa, Lucca, Ragusa, Geneva, and San Marino. Poland, Sweden, and England may be regarded as republics under a king, but Poland is the only one of them which takes this name.

But which of the two is to be preferred for a country—a monarchy or a republic? The question has been debated for four thousand years. Ask the rich, and they will tell you an aristocracy; ask the people, and they will reply a democracy; kings alone prefer royalty. Why, then, is almost all the earth governed by monarchs? Put that question to the rats who proposed to hang a bell around the cat's neck. In truth, the genuine reason is, as we have said, that men are rarely worthy of governing themselves.

It is sad that often, to be a good patriot, we must become the enemy of the rest of mankind. That good citizen, the ancient Cato, always said, in speaking to the senate, "Such is my opinion, and Carthage must be destroyed." To be a good patriot is to wish our own country enriched by commerce, and powerful in arms. It is clear that one country cannot gain without another losing, and cannot conquer without making men unfortunate.

Such is the condition of mankind, that to wish the greatness of our own country is often to wish evil to our neighbors. He who could wish that his country should always remain neither greater nor smaller, neither richer nor poorer, would be a citizen of the universe.

DAVID

If a young peasant, while looking for asses finds a kingdom, this is a most unusual event; if another peasant cures his king in a fit of madness by playing the harp, the instance is also very rare; but when this little harpist becomes king because he has chanced to meet a village priest who empties a bottle of olive oil on his head, the event is even more wonderful.

When and by whom were these marvels written? I have no idea, but I am quite sure that it was neither by a Polybius nor a Tacitus. I hold in great reverence the worthy Jew, whoever he may have been, who wrote the true history of the powerful Hebrew kingdom for the instruction of the universe, dictated to by the God of all the worlds who inspired this good Jew; but I am vexed that my friend David begins by assembling a band of thieves numbering 400; that at the head of this troupe of honest men he makes an agreement with Abimelech, the high priest, who arms him with the sword of Goliath and gives him consecrated bread (I *Kings*, chapter xxi, v. 13).

I am a little upset that David, the annointed of the Lord, the man after the heart of God, a rebel against Saul, another annointed of the Lord, goes off with 400 bandits to impose a levy on the land, goes off to rob honest Nabal; and immediately after Nabal is found dead, David marries his widow without delay (I *Kings*, chapter xxv, v. 10-11).

I have some scruples over his conduct with the great king Achis, owner, if I am not mistaken, of five or six villages in the canton of Geth. David, then at the head of 600 bandits, made the rounds of the allies of his benefactor, Achis: he plundered everything, he killed everyone: old men, women, children at their mother's breast. And why did he massacre children at their mother's breast? "It was," says the divine Jewish author, "for fear lest the children bear news to king Achis." (I *Kings*, chapter xxvii, v. 8-9-11).

The bandits rose up against him and wanted to stone him. What did this Mandarin Jew do? He consulted the Lord, and the Lord told him that he must go and attack the Amelekites, that there the bandits will gain large booty and enrich themselves (I *Kings*, chapter xxx).

Meanwhile, the annointed of the Lord, Saul, lost a battle against the Philistines and killed himself. A Jew brought the news to David. David, who apparently did not have anything with which to give the *buona nuncia* to the messenger, had him killed as his reward (II *Kings*, chapter i, v. 10).

David took over the whole kingdom. He surprised the little town or the village of Rabbath and had every inhabitant killed by rather extraordinary devices: they were sawed in two; they were torn in pieces by iron plows; they were burned in brick furnaces; an altogether noble and generous way of making war (II *Kings*, chapter xii).

After these fine expeditions there was a famine of three years in the land. I readily believe it, for with the manner in which good David made war, the grounds must have been cultivated badly.

The people consulted the Lord and asked him why there was a famine. The answer was really simple: it was clearly because, in a country which barely can produce wheat, when the workers have been baked in furnaces and sawed in two there are very few people left to till the soil; but the Lord answered that it was because Saul had formerly killed some Gabaonites.

What did good David do? He assembled the Gabaonites; he told them that Saul was very wrong to make war on them; that Saul was in no way like himself, after God's own heart; that it was just to punish Saul's race; and he gave them seven of Saul's grandchildren to hang, who were hanged because there had been a famine (II *Kings*, chapter xxi).

It is a pleasure to see how that imbecile Dom Calmet justifies and sanctifies all these acts that would make one shake with horror were they not incredible.

I will say nothing here of the abominable murder of Uriah and the adultery of Bathsheba: it is rather well known, and the ways of God are so different from those of men that he has allowed Jesus Christ to be descended from this infamous Bath-sheba, all being purified by this holy mystery.

I do not ask now how Jurieu had the insolence to persecute the wise Bayle for not having approved all of the deeds of good king David; but I ask how it was permitted that a man like Jurieu molest a man like Bayle.

DOGMAS

On Feb. 18, 1763, of the vulgar era, the sun entering the sign of the fishes, I was transported to heaven, as all my friends can bear witness. The mare Borac, of Mahomet, was not my steed, neither was the fiery chariot of Elijah my carriage. I was not carried on the elephant of Somonocodom, the Siamese; on the horse of St. George, the patron of England; nor on St. Anthony's pig. I avow with frankness that my journey was made I know not how.

It will be easily believed that I was dazzled; but it will not so easily be credited that I witnessed the judgment of the dead. And who were the judges? They were—do not be displeased at it—all those who have done good to man. Confucius, Solon, Socrates, Titus, the Antonines, Epictetus, all the great men who, having taught and practiced the virtues that God requires, seemed to be the only persons possessing the right of pronouncing his decrees.

I shall not describe on what thrones they were seated, nor how many millions of celestial beings were prostrate before the creator of all worlds, nor what a crowd of the inhabitants of these innumerable worlds appeared before the judges. I shall not even give an account of several little interesting peculiarities which were exceedingly striking.

I remarked that every spirit who pleaded his cause and displayed his noble sentiments, had beside him all the witnesses of his actions. For example, when Cardinal Lorraine boasted of having caused some of his opinions to be adopted by the Council of Trent, and demanded eternal life as the price of his orthodoxy, there immediately appeared around him twenty ladies of the court, all bearing on their foreheads the number of their *rendezvous* with the cardinal. I also saw those who had concerted with him the foundations of the infamous League. All the accomplices of his perverse designs surrounded him.

Over against Cardinal Lorraine was Calvin, who boasted, in his coarse dialect, of having trampled upon the papal idol, after others had overthrown it. "I have written against painting and sculpture," said he; "I have made it apparent that good works are of no use at all, and I have proved that it is diabolical to dance a minuet. Send away Cardinal Lorraine quickly, and place me by the side of St. Paul."

As he spoke there appeared by his side a wood pile in flames; a dreadful spectre, wearing round his neck a Spanish frill, arose half burned from the midst of the fire, with dreadful cries. "Monster," he exclaimed; "execrable monster, tremble! recognize that Servetus, whom you caused to perish by the most cruel torments, because he had disputed with you on the manner in which three persons can form one substance." Then all the judges commanded that Cardinal Lorraine should be thrown into the abyss, but that Calvin should be punished still more rigorously.

I saw a prodigious crowd of the dead, each of which said, "I have believed, I have believed!" but on their forehead it was written, "I have acted," and they were condemned.

The Jesuit Le Tellier appeared boldly with the bull *Unigenitus* in his hand. But there suddenly arose at his side a heap of two thousand *lettres-de-cachet*. A Jansenist set fire to them, and Le Tellier was burned to the bones and the Jansenist, who had no less intrigued than the Jesuit, had his share of the flames.

I saw approach, from right and left, troops of fakirs, talapoins, bonzes, and black, white, and gray monks, who all imagined that, to make their court to the supreme Being, they must either sing, whip themselves, or walk all naked. "What good have you done to men?" was the query. A dead silence followed this question. No one dared to answer; and they were all conducted to the mad-houses of the universe, the largest buildings imaginable.

One cried out, "We must believe in the metamorphoses of

Xaca!" Another said, "In those of Sammonocodom." "Bacchus stopped the sun and moon!" said this one. "The gods resuscitated Pelops!" said the other. "Here is the bull *in cœna Domini!*" said a newcomer—and the officer of the court exclaimed, "To Bedlam, to Bedlam!"

When all these cases had been examined, I heard this proclamation: "BY THE ETERNAL CREATOR, PRESERVER, REWARDER, REVENGER, PARDONER, etc., be it known to all the inhabitants of the hundred thousand millions of millions of worlds that it hath pleased us to form, that we never judge any sinners in reference to their own shallow ideas, but only according to their actions; for such is our Justice."

I own that this was the first time I ever heard such an edict; all those which I had read, on the little grain of sand on which I was born, ended with these words: *For such is our pleasure.*"

END, FINAL CAUSES

It would appear that a man must be supposed to have lost his senses before he can deny that stomachs are made for digestion, eyes to see, and ears to hear.

On the other hand, a man must have a strange love of final causes, to assert that stone was made for building houses, and that silkworms are produced in China so that we may wear satins in Europe.

But, it is urged, if God has evidently done one thing by design, he has then done all things by design. It is ridiculous to admit Providence in the one case and to deny it in the others. Everything that is done was forseen, was arranged. There is no arrangement without an object, no effect without a cause; all, therefore, is equally the result, the product of a final cause; it is therefore as correct to say that noses were made to wear spectacles, and fingers to be adorned with rings, as to say that the ears were formed to hear sounds, the eyes to receive light.

I believe that we can easily clear up this difficulty. When the effects are invariably the same in all times and places, and when these uniform effects are independent of the beings to which they attach, then there is visibly a final cause.

All animals have eyes and see; all have ears and hear; all have mouths with which they eat, stomachs, or something similar, by which they digest their food; all have an orifice for expelling excrement; all have an instrument for generation; and these natural gifts operate without any intermixture of art. Here are final causes clearly established; and to deny a truth so universal would be a perversion of the faculty of reason.

But stones, in all times and places, do not constitute the materials of buildings. All noses do not bear spectacles; all fingers do not carry a ring; all legs are not covered with silk stockings. A silkworm, therefore, is not made to cover my legs, in the way that your mouth is made for eating, and your rear for the toilet-seat. There are, therefore, we see, immediate effects produced from final causes, and effects of a very numerous description, which cannot be called by this name.

But the one and the other are both in the plan of general Providence; undoubtedly nothing is made in spite of it, or even without it. Everything belonging to nature is uniform, immutable, and the immediate work of the Master. It is he who has established the laws by which the moon contributes three-fourths to the cause of the flux and reflux of the ocean, and the sun the remaining fourth. It is he who has given a rotational motion to the sun, in consequence of which that orb communicates its rays of light in the short space of five and a half minutes to the eyes of men, crocodiles, and cats.

But if, after many centuries, we decided to invent shears and spits, to clip the wool of sheep with the one, and to roast them with the other in order to eat them, what else can be inferred but that God formed us in such a manner that, at some time or other, we could not help becoming industrious and carnivorous?

Sheep, undoubtedly, were not made expressly to be roasted and eaten, since many nations abstain from this horror. Mankind are not created essentially to massacre one another, since the Brahmins and Quakers kill no one. But the clay out of which we are kneaded frequently produces massacres, as it produces calumnies, vanities, persecutions, and impertinences. It is not precisely that the formation of man is the final cause of our madnesses and follies, for a final cause is universal, and invariable in every age and place; but the horrors and absurdities of the human race are nevertheless part of the eternal order of things. When we thresh our corn, the flail is the final cause of the separation of the grain. But if that flail, while threshing my grain, crushes to death a thousand insects, that occurs not by the determination of my will, nor, on the other hand, is it by mere chance; the insects were, on this occasion, actually under my flail, and had to be there.

It is a consequence of the nature of things that a man should be ambitious; that he should sometimes discipline a number of other men; that he should be a conqueror, or that he should be defeated; but never can it be said: Man was created by God to be killed in war.

The organs with which nature has supplied us cannot always be final causes in action, with an invariable effect. The eyes which are bestowed for seeing are not constantly open. Every sense has its time of rest. There are some senses that are even unused. An unfortunate imbecilic female, for example, shut up in a cloister at the age of fourteen, closes forever the door from which a new generation should emerge; but the final cause subsists nevertheless: it will operate as soon as it is free.

ENTHUSIASM

This Greek word signifies *emotion of the bowels, internal agitation*. Was the word invented by the Greeks to express the shocks experienced by the nerves, the dilation and shrinking of the intestines, the violent contractions of the heart, the precipitous course of those fiery spirits which mount from the bowels to the brain whenever we are strongly and vividly affected?

Or was the term *enthusiasm*, after painful affection of the bowels, first applied to the contortions of the Pythia, who, on the Delphian tripod, received the inspiration of Apollo in a place apparently intended for the receipt of body rather than of spirit?

What do we understand by enthusiasm? How many shades

are there in our affections! Approbation, sensibility, emotion, distress, impulse, passion, transport, insanity, fury, rage. Such are the stages through which the miserable soul of man is liable to pass.

A geometrician attends the representation of an affecting tragedy. He merely remarks that it is a judicious performance. A young man who sits next to him is so moved that he notices nothing; a lady sheds tears over it; another young man is so transported that to his great misfortune he goes home determined to compose a tragedy himself. He has caught the disease of enthusiasm.

The centurion or military tribune who considers war simply as a profession by which he is to make his fortune, goes to battle coolly, like a roofer ascending the roof of a house. Cæsar wept at seeing the statue of Alexander.

Ovid speaks of love only in a lively way. Sappho expressed the enthusiasm of this passion, and if it be true that it cost her her life, her enthusiasm must have advanced to madness.

The spirit of party tends astonishingly to excite enthusiasm; there is no faction that has not its devoted and possessed partisans.

Enthusiasm is especially the accompaniment of misunderstood devotion. The young fakir who fixes his eye on the tip of his nose when saying his prayers, gradually grows in devotional ardor until he at length believes that if he burdens himself with chains of fifty pounds weight the supreme Being will be grateful to him. He goes to sleep with an imagination totally absorbed by Brahma, and is sure to have a sight of him in a dream. Occasionally even in the intermediate state between sleeping and waking, sparks radiate from his eyes; he beholds Brahma resplendent with light; he falls into ecstasies, and the disease frequently becomes incurable.

What is most rarely to be met with is the combination of reason with enthusiasm. Reason consists in constantly seeing things as they really are. He, who, under the influence of intoxication, sees objects double is at the time deprived of his reason.

Enthusiasm is precisely like wine, it has the power to excite such a ferment in the blood-vessels, and such strong vibrations in the nerves, that reason is completely destroyed by it. But it may also occasion only light shocks so as not to convulse the brain, but merely to render it more active, as is the case in great outbursts of eloquence and more especially in sublime poetry. Reasonable enthusiasm is the lot of great poets.

This reasonable enthusiasm is the perfection of their art. It is this which formerly occasioned the belief that poets were inspired by the gods, a notion which was never applied to other artists.

How is reasoning to control enthusiasm? A poet should, in the first instance, make a sketch of his design. Reason then holds the crayon. But when he wants to animate his characters and to communicate to them the nature of the passions, then his imagination is heated, enthusiasm acts and urges him on like a fiery courser in his career. But his course is traced regularly.

EQUALITY

What does a dog owe a dog, a horse owe a horse? Nothing. No animal depends upon his fellow beast; but as man has received the ray of Divinity we call *reason*, what has been the result? To be enslaved almost the whole world over.

If the earth were in fact what it might be supposed to be—if men found upon it everywhere an easy and certain subsistence, and a climate congenial to their nature, it would clearly have been impossible for one man to subjugate another. Let the globe be covered with wholesome fruits; let the air on which we depend for life convey to us no diseases and premature death; let man require no other lodging than the deer or roe, in that case the Genghis Khans and Tamerlanes will have no other attendants than their own children, who will be worthy enough to assist them in their old age.

In that state of nature enjoyed by all undomesticated quadrupeds, and by birds and reptiles, men would be just as happy as they are. Domination would be a mere chimera—an absurdity which no one would think of, for why should servants be sought for when no service is required?

If it should enter the mind of any individual of a tyrannical disposition and nervous arm to enslave his less powerful neighbor, his success would be impossible; the oppressed would be a hundred leagues away before the oppressor had completed his preparations.

All men, then, would necessarily have been equal had they been without wants; it is the misery attached to our species which subordinates one man to another; not inequality is the real misfortune, but dependence. It is of little consequence for one man to be called His Highness and another His Holiness, but it is hard for me to be the servant of another.

A numerous family has cultivated a good soil, two small neighboring families live on lands unproductive and barren. It will therefore be necessary for the two poor families to serve the rich one, or to destroy it. This is easily accomplished. One of the two indigent families goes and offers its services to the rich one in exchange for bread, the other makes an attack upon it and is conquered. The serving family is the origin of domestics and laborers, the beaten one is the origin of slaves.

It is impossible in our melancholy world to prevent men living in society from being divided into two classes: one, the rich who command; the other, the poor who obey; and these two are subdivided into various others, which have also their respective shades of difference.

All the poor are not absolutely unhappy. The greater number are born in that state, and constant labor prevents them from too strongly feeling their situation; but when they do feel it, then wars follow such as those of the popular party against the senate at Rome, and those of the peasantry in Germany, England, and France. All these wars ended sooner or later in the subjection of the people, because the powerful have money, and in a state money commands everything; I say in a state, for the case is different between nation and nation. That nation which makes the best use of iron will always subjugate another that has more gold but less courage.

Every man is born with an eager inclination for power, wealth, and pleasure, and also with a great taste for indolence. Every man, consequently, would wish to possess the fortunes

and the wives or daughters of others, to be their master, to
subject them to his caprices, and to do nothing, or at least
nothing but what is perfectly agreeable. You clearly perceive that
with such amiable dispositions, it is as impossible for men to be
equal as for two preachers or divinity professors not to be jealous
of each other.

The human race, constituted as it is, cannot exist unless there
be an infinite number of useful individuals who possess nothing
at all; for most certainly a man in easy circumstances will not
leave his own land to come and cultivate yours; and if you
want a pair of shoes you will not get a lawyer to make them
for you. Equality, then, is at the same time the most natural
and the most chimerical thing possible.

As men carry everything to excess if they have it in their
power to do so, this inequality has been pushed too far; it has
been maintained in many countries that no citizen has a right
to quit that region in which he chanced to be born. The meaning of such a law must evidently be: "*This country is so
wretched and ill-governed we prohibit every man from quitting
it, for fear that otherwise all would leave it.*" Do better; arouse
in all your subjects a desire to stay with you, and in foreigners
a desire to come and settle among you.

Every man, at the bottom of his heart, has a right to consider
himself entirely equal to other men, but it follows not that a
cardinal's cook should take it upon him to order his master to
prepare his dinner. The cook, however, may say: "I am a man
as well as my master; I was born like him in pain, and shall
die like him in anguish, attended by the same common ceremonies. We both perform the same animal functions. If the
Turks get possession of Rome, and I then become a cardinal
and my master a cook, I will take him into my service." This
language is perfectly reasonable and just, but, while waiting for
the Grand Turk to get possession of Rome, the cook is bound
to do his duty, or all human society is subverted.

With respect to a man who is neither a cardinal's cook nor
invested with any office whatever in the state—with respect to
an individual who has nothing and is disgusted at being everywhere received with an air of protection or contempt, who sees

quite clearly that many men of quality and title have not more knowledge, wit, or virtue than himself, and is wearied by being occasionally in their waiting room, what ought such a man to do? He ought to stay away.

FANATICISM

Fanaticism is to superstition what delirium is to fever, what rage is to anger. He who has ecstasies and visions, who takes dreams for realities, and his own imaginations for prophecies is an enthusiast; he who reinforces his madness by murder is a fanatic. John Diaz of Nuremberg was completely convinced that the pope was the Antichrist of the Apocalypse and had the sign of the beast. His brother Bartholomew, who left Rome in order to murder his brother, and who in fact killed him for the love of God, was one of the most abominable fanatics that superstition ever formed.

Polyeucte, who went to the temple on a day of solemn festival, to throw down and destroy the statues and ornaments, was a fanatic less horrible than Diaz, but not less foolish. The assassins of Francis, duke of Guise, of William, prince of Orange, of King Henry III, of King Henry IV, and various others, were equally possessed, equally ill from the same fury as Diaz.

The most detestable example of fanaticism is that exhibited on the night of St. Bartholomew, when the people of Paris rushed from house to house to stab, slaughter, throw out of the window, and tear in pieces their fellow citizens who did not go to mass.

There are some cold-blooded fanatics; such as those judges who sentence men to death for no other crime than that of thinking differently from themselves, and these are so much the more guilty and deserving of the execration of mankind, as, not laboring under madness like the Clements, Châtels, Ravaillacs, and Damiens, they might be capable of listening to reason.

Once fanaticism has infected a brain, the disease is almost incurable. I have seen convulsionaries who, while speaking of the miracles of Saint Paris, gradually grew heated in spite of themselves. Their eyes became inflamed, their limbs shook, fury disfigured their face, and they would have killed anyone who contradicted them.

There is no other remedy for this epidemic malady than that philosophical spirit which, extending itself from one to another, at length softens the manners of men and prevents the access of the disease. For when the disorder has made any progress, we should, without loss of time, flee from it, and wait till the air has become purified. Law and religion are not enough against the spiritual pestilence. Religion, indeed, far from affording proper nourishment, is turned by the diseased minds into poison. These wretches have ceaselessly in their minds the example of Ehud, who assassinated the king of Eglon; of Judith, who cut off the head of Holofernes while in bed with him; of Samuel, hewing in pieces King Agag. They do not see that these instances, which are respectable in antiquity, are abominable at the present day. They derive their fury from religion, which itself condemns them.

Laws are yet more powerless against these paroxysms of rage. To oppose laws to cases of such a description would be like reading a decree of council to a man in a frenzy. Such persons are fully convinced that the holy spirit which animates them is above all laws; that their enthusiasm is the only law which they must obey.

What can be said in answer to a man who says he will rather obey God than men, and who consequently feels certain of meriting heaven by cutting your throat?

Fanatics are nearly always under the direction of knaves, who place the dagger in their hands. These knaves resemble Montaigne's Old Man who, it is said, made imbeciles enjoy the joys of paradise, and promised them a whole eternity of such pleasures if they would go and assassinate all those that he should point out to them. There has been only one religion in the world which has not been polluted by fanaticism and that is the religion of the learned in China. The sects of philosophers were not merely exempt from this plague, but they were the remedy to it: for the effect of philosophy is to render the soul tranquil, and fanaticism and tranquillity are totally incompatible. That our holy region has been so frequently corrupted by this infernal fury must be imputed to the folly and madness of mankind.

> Thus of his plumage
> Icarus abused the use;
> He received it for his welfare,
> He used it for his ruin.
>
> (BERTAUD, Bishop of Séez).

FREEDOM OF THOUGHT

Towards the year 1707, the time at which the English gained the battle of Saragossa, protected Portugal, and for some time gave a king to Spain, Lord Boldmind, a general officer who had been wounded, was at the waters of Barèges. He there met with Count Medroso, who having fallen from his horse behind the baggage, a league and a half from the field of battle, also came to take the waters. He was a familiar of the Inquisition, while Lord Boldmind was only familiar in conversation. One day after their wine, he held this dialogue with Medroso:

BOLDMIND: You are then the sergeant of the Dominicans? You practice a villainous trade.

MEDROSO: It is true; but I would rather be their servant than their victim, and I have preferred the unhappiness of burning my neighbor to that of being roasted myself.

BOLDMIND: What a horrible alternative! You were a hundred times happier under the yoke of the Moors, who freely suffered you to abide in all your superstitions, and who, conquerors though they were, did not assume the strange right of putting souls in irons.

MEDROSO: What do you expect? It is not permitted us either to write, speak, or even to think. If we speak, it is easy to misinterpret our words, and still more our writings; and as we cannot be condemned in an *auto-da-fé* for our secret thoughts, we are threatened with being burned eternally by the order of God himself, if we think like the Jacobins. They have persuaded the government that if we had common sense the entire state would be in flames, and the nation would become the most miserable upon earth.

BOLDMIND: Do you believe that we English who cover the seas with vessels, and who go to gain battles for you in the south of Europe, can be so unhappy? Do you perceive that the Dutch, who have stripped you of almost all your discoveries in India, and who at present are ranked as your protectors, are cursed by God for having given entire liberty to the press, and for trading in thoughts? Was the Roman Empire less powerful because Cicero wrote freely?

MEDROSO: Who is this Cicero? I have never heard his name mentioned. We are not concerned with Cicero but with our holy father the pope and with Saint Anthony of Padua, and I have always heard that the Catholic religion is lost if men begin to think.

BOLDMIND: It is not for you to believe it; for you are sure that your religion is divine, and that the gates of hell cannot prevail against it. If that is the case, nothing will ever destroy it.

MEDROSO: No; but it may be reduced to very little; and it is through having thought, that Sweden, Denmark, all your island, and the half of Germany groan under the frightful misfortune of not being subjects of the pope. It is even said that, if men continue to follow their false lights, they will soon have merely the simple adoration of God and of virtue. If the gates of hell ever prevail so far, what will become of the Holy Office?

BOLDMIND: If the first Christians had not had freedom of thought, does it not follow that there would not have been Christianity?

MEDROSO: What do you mean? I do not follow you.

BOLDMIND: I readily believe it. I mean that if Tiberius and the first emperors had been Jacobins, they would have hindered the first Christians from having pens and ink; and had it not been long permitted in the Roman Empire to think freely, it would be impossible for the Christians to establish their dogmas. If, therefore, Christianity was formed only through freedom of thought, by what contradiction, by what injustice, would you now destroy the liberty on which alone it is founded?

When some affair of interest is proposed to us, do we not examine it for a long time before we conclude? What interest in the world is so great as our eternal happiness or misery? There are a hundred religions on earth which all condemn us if we believe your dogmas, which they call impious and absurd; therefore, why not examine these dogmas?

MEDROSO: How can I examine them? I am not a Jacobin.

BOLDMIND: You are a man, and that is enough.

MEDROSO: Alas! you are much more of a man than I am.

BOLDMIND: You have only to teach yourself to think; you were born with a mind, you are a bird in the cage of the Inquisition, the Holy Office has clipped your wings, but they can grow again. He who knows not geometry can learn it: all men can instruct themselves. It is shameful to put your soul into the hands of those to whom you would not trust your money. Dare to think for yourself.

MEDROSO: It is said that if everyone thought for himself, it would produce strange confusion.

BOLDMIND: Quite the contrary. When we see a play, every one freely gives his opinion of it, and the public peace is not thereby disturbed; but if some insolent protector of a bad poet would force all men of taste to proclaim that to be good which appears to them bad, blows would follow, and the two parties would throw apples at one another's heads, as once happened at London. Tyrants of the mind have caused a large part of the misfortunes of the world. We are happy in England only because every one freely enjoys the right to speak his opinion.

MEDROSO: We too are very peaceful at Lisbon, where no person dares speak his.

BOLDMIND: You are peaceful, but you are not happy: it is the peace of galley-slaves, who row in cadence and in silence.

MEDROSO: You believe, then, that my soul is in the galleys?

BOLDMIND: Yes, and I would deliver it.

MEDROSO: But if I am happy in the galleys?

BOLDMIND: Then you deserve to be there.

GOD

In the reign of Arcadius, Logomachos, a theologue of Constantinople, went into Scythia and stopped at the foot of Mount Caucasus in the fruitful plains of Zephirim, on the borders of

Colchis. The good old man Dondindac was in his great hall between his large sheepfold and his extensive barn; he was on his
knees with his wife, his five sons and five daughters, his kinsmen
and servants; and all were singing the praises of God, after a
light meal. "What are you doing, idolater?" said Logomachos to
him. "I am not an idolater," said Dondindac. "You must be an
idolater," said Logomachos, "for you are not a Greek. Come, tell
me what you were singing in your barbarous Scythian jargon?"
"All tongues are alike to the ears of God," answered the
Scythian; "we were singing his praises." "Very extraordinary!"
returned the theologue; "a Scythian family praying to God without having been instructed by us!" He soon entered into conversation with the Scythian Dondindac; for the theologue knew a
little Scythian, and the other a little Greek. This conversation
has been found in a manuscript preserved in the library of Constantinople.

LOGOMACHOS: Let us see if you know your catechism. Why
do you pray to God?

DONDINDAC: Because it is just to adore the supreme Being,
from whom we have everything.

LOGOMACHOS: Not bad for a barbarian. And what do you ask
of him?

DONDINDAC: I thank him for the blessings I enjoy, and even
for the trials which he sends me; but I am careful to ask nothing
of him; for he knows our wants better than we do; besides, I
should be afraid of asking for fair weather while my neighbor
was asking for rain.

LOGOMACHOS: Ah! I thought he would say some sort of nonsense. Let us begin farther back. Barbarian, who told you that
there is a God?

DONDINDAC: All nature tells me.

LOGOMACHOS: That is not enough. What idea have you of
God?

DONDINDAC: The idea of my creator, of my master, who will
reward me if I do good, and punish me if I do evil.

LOGOMACHOS: Trifles! trash! Let us come to essentials. Is God
infinite *secundum quid*,[52] or according to essence?

DONDINDAC: I don't understand you.

LOGOMACHOS: Savage beast! Is God in one place, or out of every place, or in every place?

DONDINDAC: I know not . . . just as you please.

LOGOMACHOS: Ignoramus! . . . Can he cause that which has not been to have been, or that a stick not have two ends? Does he see the future as future, or as present? How does he draw being from nothing, and how reduce being to nothing?

DONDINDAC: I have never examined these things.

LOGOMACHOS: What a stupid fellow! Well, I must lower myself, come nearer to your level. Tell me, friend, do you think that matter can be eternal?

DONDINDAC: What matters it to me whether it exists from all eternity or not? I do not exist from all eternity. God must still be my master. He has given me the notion of justice; it is my duty to follow it: I do not want to be a philosopher; I wish to be a man.

LOGOMACHOS: One has a great deal of trouble with these hardheads. Let us proceed step by step. What is God?

DONDINDAC: My sovereign, my judge, my father.

LOGOMACHOS: That is not what I ask. What is his nature?

DONDINDAC: To be mighty and good.

LOGOMACHOS: But is he corporeal or spiritual?

DONDINDAC: How should I know that?

LOGOMACHOS: What; do you not know what a spirit is?

DONDINDAC: Not in the least. What good would that knowledge do me? Should I be more just? Should I be a better husband, a better father, a better master, or a better citizen?

LOGOMACHOS: You must absolutely be taught what a spirit is. Listen. It is—it is—it is—I will say what another time.

DONDINDAC: I much fear that you will tell me what it is not rather than what it is. Permit me, in turn, to ask you one question. Some time ago, I saw one of your temples: why do you paint God with a long beard?

LOGOMACHOS: That is a very difficult question, and requires preliminary instruction.

DONDINDAC: Before I receive your instruction, I must tell you what happened to me one day. I had just built a closet at the end of my garden, when I heard a mole arguing with an ant:

"Here is a fine structure," said the mole; "it must have been a very powerful mole that performed this work." "You jest," returned the ant; "the architect of this edifice is an ant of mighty genius." From that time on, I resolved never to dispute.

IDEA

What is an idea?

It is an image painted in my brain.

Are all your thoughts, then, images?

Certainly; for the most abstract ideas are only the consequences of all the objects that I have perceived. I utter the word *being* in general, only because I have known particular beings; I utter the word *infinity*, only because I have seen certain limits, and because I push back those limits in my mind as far as I can. I have ideas in my head only because I have images.

And who is the painter of this picture?

It is not myself; I cannot draw with sufficient skill; the being that made me, makes my ideas.

You must, then, be of Malebranche's opinion, that we see all in God?

I am at least certain of this, that if we do not see things in God, we see them in consequence of his all-powerful action.

And how does this action occur?

I have already told you repeatedly in our conversations, that I do not know a single word about the subject, and that God has not communicated his secret to any one. I am completely ignorant of that which makes my heart beat and my blood flow through my veins; I am ignorant of the principle of all my movements, and yet you want me to tell you how I feel and how I think! This is unreasonable.

But you at least know whether your faculty of having ideas is joined to extension?

Not in the least. It is true that Tatian, in his discourse to the Greeks, says the soul is evidently composed of a body. Irenæus, in the twenty-fifth chapter of his second book, says that the Lord has taught that our souls preserve the figure of our body in order to retain its memory. Tertullian asserts, in his second book on the *Soul*, that it is a body. Arnobius, Lactantius, Hilary, Gregory of Nyssa, and Ambrose, are precisely of the same opinion. It is claimed that other Fathers of the Church assert that the soul is without extension, and that in this respect they adopt the opinion of Plato; this, however, may well be doubted. With respect to myself, I dare not venture to form an opinion; I see nothing but incomprehensibility in either system; and, after a whole life's meditation on the subject, I am not advanced a single step beyond where I was on the first day.

The subject, then, was not worth thinking about?

That is true; the man who enjoys knows more of it, or at least knows it better, than he who reflects; he is more happy. But what do you expect? It depended not upon myself to admit or reject all those ideas which have crowded into my brain in conflict with each other, and which actually converted my medullary cells into their battlefield. After a hard-fought contest between them, I have obtained nothing but uncertainty from their remains.

It is a melancholy thing to possess so many ideas, and yet to have no precise knowledge of the nature of ideas.

It is, I admit; but it is much more melancholy, and very much more foolish, for a man to believe he knows what in fact he does not.

INQUISITION

The Inquisition is well known to be an admirable and truly Christian invention for increasing the power of the pope and monks, and rendering the population of a whole kingdom hypocrites.

St. Dominic is usually considered as the person to whom the world is principally indebted for this institution. In fact, we still have a patent granted by that great saint, expressed precisely in his own words: "I, brother Dominic, reconcile to the Church Roger, the bearer of these presents, on condition of his being whipped by a priest on three successive Sundays from the entrance of the city to the church doors; of his abstaining from meat all his life; of his fasting for the space of three Lents in a year; of his never drinking wine; of his wearing the *san-benito* with crosses; of his reciting the breviary every day, and ten paternosters in the course of the day, and twenty at midnight; of his preserving perfect chastity, and of his presenting himself every month before the parish priest, etc.; the whole under pain of being treated as heretical, perjured, and impenitent."

Although Dominic was the real founder of the Inquisition, yet Louis de Paramo, one of the most respectable writers and most brilliant luminaries of the Holy Office, relates, in the second chapter of his second book, that God was the first institutor of the Holy Office, and that he exercised the power of the preaching brethren against Adam. In the first place Adam is cited before the tribunal: "*Adam, ubi es?*" And in fact, adds Paramo, the want of this citation would have rendered the whole procedure of God null and void.

The dresses formed of skins, which God made for Adam and Eve, were the model of the *san-benito*, which the Holy Office requires to be worn by heretics. It is true that, according to this argument, God was the first tailor; it is not, however, the less evident that he was the first inquisitor.

Adam was deprived of all the immovable property he possessed in the terrestrial paradise, and hence the Holy Office confiscates the property of all whom it condemns.

Louis de Paramo remarks, that the inhabitants of Sodom were burned as heretics because sodomy is a formal heresy. He thence passes to the history of the Jews: and in every part of it discovers the Holy Office.

Jesus Christ is the first inquisitor of the new law; the popes were inquisitors by divine right; and they afterwards communicated their power to St. Dominic.

He afterwards estimates the number of all those whom the Inquisition has put to death; he states it to be considerably above a hundred thousand.

His book was printed in 1598, at Madrid, with the approbation of doctors, the praise of bishops, and the privilege of the king. We can, at the present day, scarcely form any idea of horrors at once so extravagant and abominable; but at that period nothing appeared more natural and edifying. All men resemble Louis de Paramo when they are fanatics.

Paramo was a simple man, very exact in dates, omitting no interesting fact, and calculating with precision the number of human victims immolated by the Holy Office throughout the world.

He relates, with great naïveté, the establishment of the Inquisition in Portugal, and agrees perfectly with four other historians who have treated that subject. Here is what they unanimously report.

Pope Boniface IX had long before, at the beginning of the fifteenth century, delegated some Dominican friars to go to Portugal, from one city to another, to burn heretics, Moslems, and Jews; but they were itinerant and not stationary; and even the kings sometimes complained of the vexations caused by them. Pope Clement VII wanted to give them a fixed residence in Portugal, as they had in Aragon and Castile. Difficulties arose between the court of Rome and that of Lisbon; tempers became irritated, the Inquisition suffered by it, and was far from being perfectly established.

In 1539, there appeared at Lisbon a legate of the pope, who came, he said, to establish the holy Inquisition on immovable foundations. He delivered his letters to King John III from Pope Paul III. He had other letters from Rome for the chief officers of the court; his patents as legate were duly sealed and signed; and he exhibited the most ample powers for creating a grand inquisitor and all the judges of the Holy Office. He was, however, in fact an impostor of the name of Saavedra, who had the talent of counterfeiting signatures, seals, and coats-of-arms. He had acquired the art at Rome, and was perfected in it at Seville, at which place he arrived in company with two other sharpers. His train was magnificent, consisting of more than a hundred and twenty servants. To defray this enormous expense, he and his associates borrowed large sums at Seville in the name of the apostolic chamber of Rome; everything was handled with the most consummate skill.

The king of Portugal was at first astonished at the pope's

despatching a legate to him without any previous announcement to him of his intention. The legate boldly observed that in a concern so urgent as that of establishing the inquisition on a firm foundation, His Holiness could admit of no delays, and that the king might consider himself honored by the holy father's having appointed a legate to be the first person to announce his intention. The king did not venture to reply. The legate on the very same day appointed a grand inquisitor, and sent about collectors to receive the tithes; and before the court could obtain clarification from Rome, the legate had already burned two hundred victims at the stake, and collected more than two hundred thousand crowns.

However, the marquis of Villanova, a Spanish nobleman, of whom the legate had borrowed at Seville a very considerable sum upon forged bills, determined, if possible, to repay himself by force, instead of going to Lisbon and exposing himself to the intrigues and influence of the impostor. The legate was at this time on the borders of Spain. The marquis marched there with fifty armed men, carried him off prisoner, and conducted him to Madrid.

The whole imposture was speedily discovered at Lisbon; the Council of Madrid condemned the legate Saavedra to be flogged and sent to the galleys for ten years; but the most admirable circumstance was, that Pope Paul IV subsequently confirmed all that the impostor had established; out of the plenitude of his divine power he rectified all the little irregularities of the proceedings, and rendered sacred what before was merely human. "What matter the arm which God condescends to use?"

Such was the manner in which the Inquisition became established at Lisbon; and the whole kingdom admired Providence.

For what follows, the methods of procedure adopted by this tribunal are generally known; it is well known how strongly they are opposed to the false equity and blind reason of all other tribunals in the world. Men are imprisoned on the mere accusation of the most infamous persons; a son may denounce his father, a wife her husband; the accused is never confronted with the accusers; and the property of the person convicted is confiscated for the benefit of the judges: such at least was the way the Inquisition was conducted down to our own times. Surely in this we must perceive something divine; for it is incomprehensible that men would have submitted to this yoke patiently.

At length Count Aranda has obtained the blessings of all Europe by paring the nails and filing the teeth of the monster; but it still breathes.

LENT

QUESTIONS ABOUT LENT

Did the first who were advised to fast put themselves under this regimen by order of the physician, for indigestion?

The want of appetite which we feel in grief—was it the first origin of fast days prescribed in melancholy religions?

Did the Jews take the custom of fasting from the Egyptians, all of whose rites they imitated, including flagellation and the scape-goat?

Why fasted Jesus for forty days in the desert, where he was tempted by the devil—by the "Chathbull"? St. Matthew remarks that after this Lent he was hungry; therefore he was not hungry during the fast.

Why, in days of abstinence, does the Roman Church consider it a crime to eat animals, and a good work to be served with soles and salmon? The rich Papist who has five hundred francs worth of fish upon his table will be saved, and the poor wretch dying with hunger, who has eaten four sous worth of salt pork, will be damned.

Why must we ask permission of our bishop to eat eggs? If a king ordered his people never to eat eggs, would he not be thought the most ridiculous of tyrants? What strange aversion have bishops to omelets?

Can we believe that among Papists there have been tribunals imbecile, cowardly, and barbarous enough to condemn to death poor citizens, who committed no other crime than that of having eaten horseflesh in Lent? The fact is but too true; I have in my hands a sentence of this kind. What is strange is that the judges who passed such sentences believed themselves superior to the Iroquois.

Idiotic and cruel priests, to whom do you order Lent? Is it to the rich? they take good care to observe it. Is it to the poor? they keep Lent all the year. The unhappy peasant scarcely ever eats meat, and has not the means to buy fish. Fools that you are, when will you correct your absurd laws?

LETTERS, MEN OF LETTERS, OR LEARNED MEN

In barbarous times when the Franks, Germans, Bretons, Lombards, and Spanish Moors knew neither how to read nor write, we instituted schools and universities almost entirely composed of ecclesiastics, who, knowing only their own jargon, taught this jargon to those who would learn it. Academies were not founded until long after; they have despised the follies of the schools, but they have not always dared to oppose them, because there are follies which we respect when they are attached to respectable things.

Men of letters who have rendered the most service to the small number of thinking beings scattered over the earth are isolated scholars, true sages shut up in their closets, who have neither publicly disputed in the universities, nor said things by halves in the academies; and such have almost all been persecuted. Our miserable race is so created that those who walk in the beaten path always throw stones at those who would show them a new way.

Montesquieu says that the Scythians put out the eyes of their slaves that they might be more attentive to the making of their butter. It is thus that the Inquisition acts, and almost everyone is blinded in the countries where this monster reigns. In England people have had two eyes for more than a hundred years. The French are beginning to open one eye—but sometimes men in place will not even permit us to be one-eyed.

These miserable statesmen are like Doctor Balouard of the Italian comedy, who will only be served by the fool Harlequin, and who fears to have too penetrating a servant.

Compose odes in praise of Lord Superbus Fatus, madrigals for his mistress; dedicate a book of geography to his porter, and you will be well received. Enlighten men, and you will be crushed.

Descartes is obliged to quit his country; Gassendi is calumniated; Arnauld drags out his days in exile; all the philosophers are treated as the prophets were among the Jews.

Who would believe that in the eighteenth century, a philosopher has been dragged before the secular tribunals, and treated as impious by reasoning theologians, for having said that men could not practise the arts if they had no hands? I expect that they will soon condemn to the galleys the first who shall have the insolence to say that a man could not think if he had no head; "For," a learned bachelor will say to him, "the soul is a pure spirit, the head is only matter; God can place the soul in the heel as well as in the brain; therefore I denounce you as a blasphemer."

The greatest misfortune of a man of letters is not perhaps to be the object of the jealousy of his colleagues, the victim of cabals, and the despised of the powerful of the world—it is to be judged by fools. Fools sometimes go very far, particularly when fanaticism is joined to ineptitude, and ineptitude to the spirit of vengeance. Further, the great misfortune of a man of letters is generally to be isolated. A citizen buys a public office, and is maintained by his fellows. If any injustice is done to him, he soon finds defenders. The literary man is without help; he resembles the flying fish; if he rises a little, the birds devour him; if he dives, the fishes eat him up.

Every public man pays tribute to malignity; but he is repaid in coins and honors. The man of letters pays the same tribute without getting anything in return; he descends into the arena for pleasure, and thereby condemns himself to the beasts.

LOVE

Amor omnibus idem.[53] Here we must have recourse to physics. Love is the material of nature embroidered by the imagination. If you wish to form an idea of love, look at the sparrows in your

garden; look at your pigeons; contemplate the bull when introduced to the heifer; look at that powerful and spirited horse
which two of your grooms are conducting to the mare that quietly awaits him, and turns her tail aside to receive him; observe
the flashing of his eyes, notice the strength and loudness of his
neighing, the leaps, the bows, the ears erect, the mouth opening with convulsive gaspings, the distended nostrils, the inflamed
breath of the raised and waving mane, and the imperious movement with which he rushes towards the object which nature has
destined for him; do not, however, be jealous of his happiness;
but reflect on the advantages of the human species; they afford
ample compensation in love for all those which nature has conferred on animals—strength, beauty, lightness, and rapidity.

There are even some animals who are not acquainted with
sexual pleasure. Fishes are deprived of this enjoyment. The female deposits her millions of eggs on the waters, and the male
that meets them passes over them and impregnates them with
his sperm, without bothering to notice what female they belong
to.

The greater part of those animals which copulate enjoy
pleasure only by a single sense; and when appetite is satisfied,
all is over. No animal but you is acquainted with embraces.
Your whole body is susceptible; your lips particularly experience
a pleasure which never wearies, and which belongs only to your
species; finally, you can surrender yourself at all seasons to love,
while animals possess only limited periods. If you reflect on
these pre-eminences, you will agree with the Earl of Rochester's
remark, "Love would impel a whole nation of atheists to worship
Divinity."

As men have been endowed with the talent of perfecting
whatever nature has granted them, they have perfected love.
Propriety and care, while making the skin more delicate, increase
the pleasure of touch, and proper attention to their well-being
makes the organs of pleasure more sensitive.

All the other feelings enter afterwards into that of love, like
metals which amalgamate with gold; friendship and esteem come
to its support; and talents both of body and of mind are new
and strengthening bonds:

Nam facit ipsa suis interdum femina factis,
Morigerisque modis, et mundo corpore culta
Ut facile insuescat secum vir degere vitam.[54]
    —LUCRETIUS, iv.

Self-love, above all, tightens these bonds. Men pride themselves in the choice they have made; and crowds of illusions are the ornament of that work, whose foundation is laid by nature.

Here are the advantages you possess over the animals. But, if you enjoy delights of which they are ignorant, how many vexations are you exposed to, from which they are free! The most dreadful of these is that nature has poisoned the pleasures of love and sources of life over three-quarters of the world by a terrible disease, to which man alone is subject, and which infects only his organs of procreation.

It is not the same plague as with other diseases, which are the natural consequences of excess. It was not introduced into the world by debauchery. The Phrynes and Laises, the Floras and Messalinas, were never attacked by it. It originated in islands where men lived together in innocence, and thence spread throughout the Old World.

If nature could in any instance be accused of despising her own work, contradicting her own plan, and counteracting her own views, it would be in this instance. Is this the best of all possible worlds? And, if Cæsar and Antony and Octavius never had this disease, was it not possible to prevent Francis the First from dying of it? No, it is said; things were so ordered all for the best; I would like to think so, but it is hard.

OPTIMISM

It made a good deal of noise in the schools and even among thinking men, when Leibnitz, paraphrasing Plato, built his edifice of the best of all possible worlds, and imagined that everything was for the best. He asserted in the north of Germany that God could make but a single world.

Plato had left him the liberty of making five worlds; because, said he, there are five regular solids in geometry, the tetrahedron, the cube, the hexahedron, the dodecahedron, and the icosahedron. But as our world has not the form of any of Plato's five bodies, God must be allowed a sixth way.

Let us leave divine Plato. Leibnitz, who was surely a better geometrician and a deeper metaphysician, thereby rendered a great service to mankind in making it see that we should all be quite content, and that God could not possibly do more for us; that he had necessarily made the best choice, without any doubt of all possible choices.

Some cried out to him, "What will become of original sin?" "It will become what it can," Leibnitz and his friends said; but publicly, he wrote that original sin would necessarily enter into the best of worlds.

What! to be chased from a delicious place, where we might have lived for ever were it not for the eating of an apple? What! to produce in misery wretched children, who will suffer everything, and in return produce others to suffer after them? What! to experience all diseases, feel all vexations, die in pain, and for refreshment be burned to all eternity—is this lot the best possible? It certainly is not too good for us, and in what manner can it be good for God?

Leibnitz felt that nothing could be said to these objections; hence he wrote fat books, in which he did not even understand himself.

Lucullus, in good health, partaking of a good dinner with his friends and his mistress in the hall of Apollo, may deny the existence of evil; but let him put his head out of the window and he will behold wretches; let him have a fever, and he will be one himself.

I do not like to quote; it is ordinarily a thorny business. What precedes and what follows the passage quoted is too frequently neglected; and thus a thousand objections may arise. I must, notwithstanding, quote Lactantius, a Father of the Church who, in his thirteenth chapter on the anger of God, makes Epicurus speak as follows: "God either wants to take away evil from the world and cannot; or he can, and does not want to; or he neither can nor will; or, lastly, he both wants to and can. If he is willing to remove evil and cannot, then he is not omnipotent, which is contrary to the nature of God; if he can, but will not remove it, that is meanness which is no less contrary to his nature; if he is neither able nor willing, then he is both mean and powerless; lastly, if both able and willing (the only one of these alternatives appropriate to God), how does evil come to be on earth?"

The argument is weighty, and Lactantius replies to it very poorly by saying that God wills evil, but has given us wisdom to secure the good. It must be admitted that this answer is very weak in comparison with the objection; for it implies that God could bestow wisdom only by producing evil—a pleasant wisdom truly!

The origin of evil has always been an abyss, the depth of which no one has been able to sound. It was this which reduced so many ancient philosophers and legislators to have recourse to two principles—the one good, the other wicked. Typhon was the evil principle among the Egyptians, Ariman among the Persians. The Manichæans, as we know, adopted this theory; but as these people have never spoken either of a good or of a bad principle, we cannot take their word for it.

Among the absurdities abounding in this world, and which may be placed among the number of our evils, that is not the least which presumes the existence of two all-powerful beings, combating to see which shall prevail in this world, and making a treaty like the two physicians in Molière: "Give me the emetic, and I will give you the lancet."

Basilides, after the platonists, in the first century of the Church, claimed that God gave the making of our world to his inferior angels, and these, being inexpert, have constructed it as we can see. This theological fable is demolished by the overwhelming objection that it is not in the nature of an all-powerful and all-wise God to entrust the construction of a world to incompetent architects.

Simon, who felt the force of this objection, forestalls it by saying that the angel who presided over the workmen is damned for having done his business so badly; but the roasting of this angel does not help us.

The adventure of Pandora among the Greeks scarcely meets the objection better. The box in which every evil is enclosed, and at the bottom of which remains hope, is indeed a charming allegory; but this Pandora was made by Vulcan only to avenge himself on Prometheus, who had made a man out of clay.

The Indians have succeeded no better. God having created man, gave him a drug which would insure him permanent health. The man loaded his ass with the drug, and the ass being thirsty, the serpent directed him to a fountain, and while the ass was drinking, stole the drug for himself.

The Syrians imagined that man and woman, having been created in the fourth heaven, resolved to eat a cake in lieu of ambrosia, their natural food. Ambrosia exhaled by the pores; but after eating cake, they had to go to the wash-room. The man and the woman requested an angel to direct them to a toilet. Behold, said the angel, this little planet which is almost of no size at all; it is situated about sixty million leagues from this place, and is the privy of the universe—go there as quickly as you can. The man and woman obeyed the angel and came here, where they have ever since remained; and it is from this time on that the world has been as we now find it.

The Syrians will eternally be asked why God allowed man to eat the cake and experience such a host of dreadful ills.

I pass with speed from the fourth heaven to Lord Bolingbroke, so as not to be bored. This writer, who doubtless was a great genius, gave to the celebrated Pope his plan of *All for the best*, as it is found word for word in the posthumous works of Lord Bolingbroke, and previously included by Lord Shaftesbury in his *Characteristics*. Read in Shaftesbury the chapter of the "Moralists," and you will find these words:

"Much may be replied to these complaints of the defects of nature—How came it so powerless and defective from the hands of a perfect being?—But I deny that it is defective. . . . Beauty is the result of opposites, and universal concord springs out of a perpetual conflict. . . . It is necessary that everything be sacrificed to other things—vegetables to animals, and animals to the earth. . . . The laws of the central power and of gravitation, which give to the celestial bodies their weight and motion, are not to be deranged for the sake of a pitiful animal, who, protected as he is by the same laws, will soon be reduced by them to dust."

Bolingbroke, Shaftesbury, and Pope, their spokesman, resolve the question no better than the rest. Their *All for the best* says no more than that all is governed by immutable laws; who did not know that? We learn nothing when we notice, in the manner of little children, that flies are created to be eaten by spiders, spiders by swallows, swallows by hawks, hawks by eagles, eagles to be killed by men, men by one another, to afford food for worms, and at last, at the rate of about a thousand to one, to be the prey of devils everlastingly.

There you have a constant and regular order established among animals of all kinds—a universal order. When a stone is formed in my bladder, the mechanical process is admirable; sandy particles pass gradually into my blood; they are filtered by the veins; and passing the urethra, deposit themselves in my bladder; where, collecting by an excellent Newtonian attraction, a stone is formed, which gradually increases, and I suffer pains a thousand times worse than death by the finest arrangement in the world. A surgeon, perfect in the art of Tubal-Cain, thrusts into me a sharp instrument; and cutting into the perineum, seizes the stone with his pincers, which break during the endeavors, by the necessary laws of mechanism; and owing to the same mechanism, I die in frightful torments. *All this is for the best*, being the evident result of unalterable physical principles. I die in accordance with them, which I know as well as you.

If we were insensitive, there would be nothing to say against this system of physics; but this is not the point in question. We ask if there are not physical evils, and whence they originate. "There is no absolute evil," says Pope in the fourth part of his *Essay on Man*; "or if there are particular evils, they compose a general good."

It is a singular general good which is composed of the stone and the gout—of all sorts of crime and sufferings, and of death and damnation.

The fall of man is the plaster we apply to all these particular maladies of body and soul, which you call the *general health*; but Shaftesbury and Bolingbroke make fun of original sin. Pope says nothing about it; but it is clear that their system saps the foundations of the Christian religion, and explains nothing at all.

Yet, this system has been since approved by many theologians, who willingly admit contradictions. Be it so; we ought to leave to everyone the privilege of reasoning in his own way upon the deluge of ills which overwhelm us. It is just to allow incurable patients to eat what they please. "God," says Pope, "beholds, with an equal eye, a hero perish or a sparrow fall; the destruction of an atom, or the ruin of a thousand planets; the bursting of a bubble, or the dissolution of a world."

This, I must confess, is a pleasant consolation. Who does not find a comfort in the declaration of Lord Shaftesbury, who asserts, "that God will not derange his eternal laws for so miserable an animal as man?" It must be confessed at least that this pitiful creature has a right to cry out humbly, and to seek, while lamenting to understand why these eternal laws are not made for the well-being of every individual.

This system of *all for the best* represents the author of all nature as a powerful and malevolent monarch, who cares not for the destruction of four or five hundred thousand men, nor of the others who spend the rest of their days in penury and tears, provided he succeeds in his designs.

Far therefore from consoling, the doctrine that this is the best of all possible worlds is a hopeless one for the philosophers who embrace it. The question of good and evil remains in inextricable chaos for those who seek to fathom it in good faith. It is mere sport for disputants; they are captives who play with their chains. For unreasoning people, it resembles the fish which are transported from a river to a reservoir; they do not suspect that they are to be eaten during Lent. Thus we ourselves know nothing at all of the causes of our destiny.

Let us place at the end of every chapter of metaphysics the two letters used by the Roman judges when they did not understand a case. N. L. *non liquet*—it is not clear.

PERSECUTION

I will not call Diocletian a persecutor, for he protected the
Christians for eighteen years; and if, during his latter days, he
did not save them from the resentment of Galerius, he was
thereby only a prince seduced, like many others, by intrigue and
cabal, into a conduct unworthy of his character.

I will still less give the name of persecutor to Trajan or Antoninus. I should regard myself as uttering blasphemy.

What is a persecutor? He whose wounded pride and furious
fanaticism arouse princes and magistrates against innocent men,
whose only crime is that of being of a different opinion. "Impudent man! you have worshipped God; you have preached and
practised virtue; you have served man; you have protected the
orphan, have helped the poor; you have changed deserts, in
which slaves dragged on a miserable existence, into fertile lands
peopled by happy families; but I have discovered that you despise me, and have never read my controversial work. You know
that I am a rogue; that I have forged G's signature, that I have
stolen. You might tell these things; I must anticipate you. I will,
therefore, go to the confessor of the prime minister, or the magistrate: I will show them, with outstretched neck and twisted
mouth, that you hold an erroneous opinion in relation to the
cells in which the Septuagint was studied; that you have even
spoken disrespectfully ten years ago of Tobit's dog, which
you asserted to have been a spaniel, while I proved that it was
a greyhound. I will denounce you as the enemy of God and
man!" Such is the language of the persecutor; and if precisely
these words do not issue from his lips, they are engraven on his
heart with the pointed steel of fanaticism steeped in the bitterness of envy.

It was thus that the Jesuit Le Tellier dared to persecute Cardinal de Noailles, and that Jurieu persecuted Bayle.

When the persecution of the Protestants began in France, it
was not Francis I, nor Henry II, nor Francis II, who spied on
these unfortunate people, who hardened themselves against them
with reflective fury, and who delivered them to the flames in
the spirit of vengeance. Francis I was too much engaged with the

Duchess d'Étampes; Henry II, with his ancient Diana, and Francis II was too much a child. Who, then, began these persecutions? Jealous priests, who served the prejudices of magistrates and the policy of ministers.

If these kings had not been deceived, if they had foreseen that persecution would produce fifty years of civil war, and that one half of the nation would be exterminated by the other, they would have extinguished with their tears the first wood piles which they allowed to be lighted.

O God of mercy! If any man can resemble that evil being who is described as ceaselessly employed in the destruction of your works, is it not the persecutor?

PHILOSOPHER

Philosopher, *lover of wisdom*, that is, *of truth*. All philosophers have had this two-fold character; there is not one among those of antiquity who did not give examples of virtue to mankind, and lessons of moral truth. They might all be mistaken on physics; but that is of so little importance to the conduct of life, that philosophers had no need of it. Ages were required to discover a part of the laws of nature. A single day is sufficient to enable a sage to know the duties of man.

The philosopher is no enthusiast; he does not set himself up for a prophet; he does not say he is inspired by the gods. I shall not therefore place in the rank of philosophers the ancient Zoroaster, or Hermes, or Orpheus, or any of those legislators of whom the countries of Chaldæa, Persia, Syria, Egypt, and Greece boast. Those who called themselves the sons of gods were the fathers of imposture; and if they employed falsehood to inculcate truths, they were unworthy of inculcating them; they were not philosophers; they were at best only prudent liars.

By what fatality, disgraceful perhaps to the nations of the West, has it happened that we are obliged to travel to the end of the East in order to find a sage of simple manners and character, without arrogance and without imposture, who taught men how to live happily six hundred years before our era, at a period when the whole of the North was ignorant of the use of letters, and when the Greeks had scarcely begun to distinguish them-selves by wisdom? That sage is Confucius who, as a legislator, never wanted to deceive men. What finer rule of conduct has ever been given since his time, throughout the earth? "Rule a state as you rule a family; a man cannot govern his family well without giving a good example.

"Virtue should be common to the laborer and the monarch.

"Be active in preventing crimes, that you may lessen the trou-ble of punishing them.

"Under the good kings Yao and Xu, the Chinese were good; under the bad kings Kie and Chu, they were wicked.

"Do to another as to thyself.

"Love mankind in general, but cherish those who are good. Forget injuries, but never benefits.

"I have seen men incapable of the sciences, but never any in-capable of virtue."

Let us acknowledge that no legislator ever announced to the world more useful truths.

A multitude of Greek philosophers taught afterwards a moral-ity equally pure. Had they limited themselves to their vain sys-tems of physics, their names would be mentioned at the present day only in derision. If they are still respected, it is because they were just, and because they taught mankind to be so.

It is impossible to read certain passages of Plato, and particu-larly the admirable exordium of the laws of Zalcucus, without experiencing an ardent love of honorable and generous actions. The Romans have their Cicero who alone is perhaps worth more than all the philosophers of Greece. After him come men more respectable still, but whom we may almost despair of imitating; these are Epictetus in slavery, and the Antonines and Julian on the throne.

Where is the citizen to be found among us who would de-prive himself, like Julian, Antoninus, and Marcus Aurelius, of all the refinements of our soft and effeminate modes of living? Who would, like them, sleep on the bare ground? Who would restrict himself to their frugal habits? Who would, like them, march bareheaded and barefooted at the head of armies, exposed sometimes to the burning sun, and at other times to the freezing wind? Who would, like them, keep perfect mastery of all his passions? We have among us devout men, but where are the sages? where are the inflexible, just, and tolerant spirits?

There have been arm-chair philosophers in France; and all of them, with the exception of Montaigne, have been persecuted. It seems to me the last degree of the malignity of our nature to attempt to oppress these very philosophers who would correct it.

I can easily conceive of the fanatics of one sect slaughtering those of another; that the Franciscans should hate the Dominicans, and that a bad artist should intrigue for the destruction of an artist that surpasses him; but that the sage Charron should have been threatened with the loss of life; that the learned and generous Ramus should have been assassinated; that Descartes should have been obliged to withdraw to Holland in order to escape the rage of the ignorant; that Gassendi should have been often compelled to retire to Digne, far distant from the calumnies of Paris, these are events to the eternal shame of a nation.

One of the philosophers most persecuted, was the immortal Bayle, the honor of human nature. I shall be told that the name of Jurieu, his slanderer and persecutor, has become execrable; I acknowledge that it is so; that of the Jesuit Le Tellier has also become so; but is it less true that the great men whom he oppressed ended their days in exile and poverty?

One of the pretexts used to reduce Bayle to poverty, was his article on *David*, in his useful dictionary. He was reproached with not praising actions which were in themselves unjust, bloody, atrocious, contrary to good faith, or grossly offensive to decency.

Bayle certainly has not praised David for having, according to the Hebrew historians, collected six hundred vagabonds overwhelmed with debts and crimes; for having pillaged his countrymen at the head of these bandits; for having resolved to massacre Nabal and his whole family, because he refused to pay contributions to him; for having hired out his services to King Achis, the enemy of his country; for having afterwards betrayed Achis; for having sacked the villages allied to that king; for having massacred in these villages every human being, including even infants at the breast, for fear lest anyone be found on a future day to give testimony of his depredations, as if an infant could have possibly disclosed his villainy; for having destroyed all the inhabitants of some other villages under saws, and iron harrows, and axes, and in brick-kilns; for having wrested the throne from Ishbosheth, the son of Saul, by an infamous act; for having stripped of his property and afterwards put to death Mephibosheth, the grandson of Saul, and son of his own friend and protector, Jonathan; or for having delivered up to the Gibeonites two other sons of Saul, and five of his grandsons who perished by the gallows.

I do not speak of the extreme looseness of David, his concubines, his adultery with Bathsheba, and the murder of Uriah.

What then! Is it possible that the enemies of Bayle should have expected him to praise all these cruelties and crimes? Ought he to have said: Go, princes of the earth, and imitate the man after God's own heart; massacre without pity the allies of your benefactor; destroy or give over to destruction the whole family of your king; sleep with all the women, while you are pouring out the blood of the men; and you will be a model of human virtue, especially if they say that you have composed a book of psalms?

Was not Bayle perfectly correct in his observation, that if David was the man after God's own heart, it must have been by his penitence, and not by his crimes? Did not Bayle perform a service to the human race when he said, that God, who undoubtedly dictated the Jewish history, has not consecrated all the crimes recorded in that history?

However, Bayle was in fact persecuted, and by whom? By the very men who had been elsewhere persecuted themselves; by refugees who in their own country would have been given over to the flames; and these refugees were opposed by other refugees called Jansenists, who had been driven from their own country by the Jesuits; who have at length been themselves driven from it in their turn.

Thus all persecutors declare mortal war against each other, while the philosopher, oppressed by all of them, is content to pity them.

It is not generally known that Fontenelle, in 1713, was on

the point of losing his pensions, his office, and his liberty, for having published in France, twenty years before, the learned Van Dale's *Treatise on Oracles*, in which he had taken particular care to cut out anything that could arouse to fanaticism. A Jesuit had written against Fontenelle; he had not deigned to reply, and that was enough for the Jesuit Le Tellier, confessor to Louis XIV, to accuse Fontenelle to the king, of atheism.

But for M. d'Argenson, the son of a crooked solicitor of Vire —a son worthy of such a father, as he was detected in forgery himself—would have exiled, in his old age, the nephew of Corneille.

It is so easy for a confessor to seduce his penitent, that we ought to bless God that Le Tellier did not do even more harm. There are two situations in which seduction and calumny cannot be resisted . . . the bed and the confessional.

We have always seen philosophers persecuted by fanatics. But can it be really possible that men of letters too should be mixed up in such a business, and that they should often sharpen the weapons against their brothers, by which they are themselves almost universally wounded?

Unhappy men of letters! Is it your job to turn informers? See if the Romans ever found a Garasse, a Chaumieux, or a Hayer, to accuse a Lucretius, a Posidonius, a Varro, or a Pliny.

How low to be a hypocrite! how horrible it is to be a vicious hypocrite! There were no hypocrites in ancient Rome, which considered us a small number of its subjects. There were impostors, I admit, but not religious hypocrites, which are the most cowardly and most cruel of all. Why don't we see any in England, and how does it arise that they still exist in France? Philosophers, you will solve this problem easily.

PREJUDICES

Prejudice is an opinion without judgment. Thus, throughout the world, children are inspired freely with opinions, before they can judge.

There are universal and necessary prejudices, and these even constitute virtue. In all countries, children are taught to acknowledge a rewarding and punishing God; to respect and love their fathers and mothers; to regard theft as a crime, and lying as a vice, before they can tell what is a virtue or a vice.

Prejudices, therefore, may be very good, such as those judgment will confirm when we reason.

Feeling is not simply prejudice, it is something much stronger. A mother does not love her son because she is told that she must love him; fortunately, she cherishes him in spite of herself. It is not through prejudice that you run to the aid of an unknown child about to fall down a precipice, or to be devoured by a beast.

But it is through prejudice that you will respect a man dressed in certain clothes, walking gravely, and talking in the same way. Your parents have told you that you must bow to this man; you respect him before you know whether he merits your respect; you grow in age and knowledge; you perceive that this man is a charlatan, steeped in pride, interest, and artifice; you despise that which you revered, and prejudice yields to judgment. Through prejudice, you believed the fables of your infancy: you are told that the Titans made war against the gods, that Venus was in love with Adonis; at twelve years of age you take these fables for truths; at twenty, you regard them as ingenious allegories.

Let us examine, in a few words, the different kinds of prejudices, in order to put order into our ways. We shall perhaps be like those who, in the time of the enterprise of John Law, realized that they had banked upon imaginary riches.

Prejudices of the Senses

Is it not an amusing thing, that our eyes always deceive us, even when we see very well, and that on the contrary our ears do not? When your attentive ear hears: "You are beautiful; I love you," it is very certain that the words are not: "I hate you; you are ugly." But when you see a smooth mirror—it can be demonstrated that you are deceived: it is a very rough surface. You see a sun of about two feet in diameter; it is demonstrated that it is a million times larger than the earth.

It seems that God has put truth into your ears, and error into your eyes; but study optics, and you will see that God has not deceived you, and that it was impossible for objects to appear to you otherwise than you see them in the present state of things.

Physical Prejudices

The sun rises, the moon also, the earth is immovable: these are natural physical prejudices. But that crabs are good for the blood, because when boiled they are of the same color; that eels cure paralysis, because they frisk about; that the moon influences our diseases, because an invalid was one day observed to have an increase of fever during the waning of the moon: these ideas and a thousand others were the errors of ancient charlatans, who judged without reasoning and who, being themselves deceived, deceived others.

Historical Prejudices

Most histories have been believed without examination, and this belief is a prejudice. Fabius Pictor tells us that, several centuries before him, a vestal of the town of Elba, going to draw water in her pitcher, was raped; that she was delivered of Romulus and Remus; that they were nourished by a she-wolf, etc. The Roman people believed this fable; they did not examine whether at that time there were vestals in Latium; whether it was likely that the daughter of a king should go out of her convent with a pitcher, or whether it was probable that a she-wolf should suckle two children instead of eating them. Prejudice established it.

A monk writes that Clovis, being in great danger at the battle of Tolbiac, made a vow to become a Christian if he escaped; but is it natural that he should address a foreign god on such an occasion? Would not the religion in which he was born have acted the most powerfully? Where is the Christian who, in a battle against the Turks, would not rather address himself to the Holy Virgin, than to Mahomet? He adds, that a pigeon brought the holy vial in his beak to anoint Clovis, and that an angel brought the oriflamme to conduct him. The prejudiced believed all the little tales of this kind. Those who know human nature know well that the usurper Clovis, and the usurper Rollo, or Rol, became Christians to govern the Christians more securely; as the Turkish usurpers became Moslems to govern the Moslems more securely.

Religious Prejudices

If your nurse has told you, that Ceres presides over corn, or that Vishnu and Xaca became men several times, or that Sammonocodom cut down a forest, or that Odin expects you in his hall near Jutland, or that Mahomet, or some other, made a journey to heaven; finally, if your preceptor afterwards stuffs into your brain what your nurse has imprinted on it, you will possess it for life. If your judgment would rise above these prejudices, your neighbors, and above all, the ladies, exclaim "impiety!" and frighten you; your dervish, fearing to see his revenue diminished, accuses you before the cadi; and this cadi, if he can, causes you to be impaled, because he would command fools, and he believes that fools obey better than others. And this state of affairs will last until your neighbors and the dervish and the cadi begin to understand that stupidity is good for nothing, and that persecution is abominable.

SELF-LOVE

A beggar of the suburbs of Madrid boldly asked alms. A passer-by said to him: Are you not ashamed to carry on this infamous trade, when you can work? Sir, replied the mendicant, I ask you for money, and not for advice; and turned his back on him with Castilian dignity. This gentleman was a haughty beggar; his vanity was wounded by very little: he asked alms for love of himself, and would not suffer the reprimand from a still greater love of himself.

A missionary, travelling in India, met a fakir loaded with chains, naked as a monkey, lying on his stomach, and lashing himself for the sins of his countrymen, the Indians, who gave him a few coins. What a renunciation of self! said one of the spectators. Renunciation of myself! said the fakir; learn that I only lash myself in this world to serve you the same in the next, when you will be the horses and I the rider.

Those who said that love of ourselves is the basis of all our feelings and actions were right; and as no one has written to prove to men that they have a face, there is no need to prove to them that they possess self-love. This self-love is the instrument of our preservation; it is something like the means for the perpetuation of the race. It is necessary, it is dear to us, it gives us pleasure, and we must conceal it.

STATES, GOVERNMENTS

WHICH IS THE BEST?

I have not hitherto known anyone who has not governed some state. I speak not of messieurs the ministers, who really govern; some two or three years, others six months, and others six weeks; I speak of all other men, who, at supper or in their office, unfold their systems of government, reform armies, the Church, the law, and finances.

The Abbé de Bourzeis began to govern France towards the year 1645, in the name of Cardinal Richelieu, and wrote the *Political Testament*, in which he says that he would enlist the nobility into the cavalry for three years, make the parliaments pay the poll-tax, and deprive the king of the produce of the excise tax. He asserts, above all, that to enter a country with fifty thousand men, it is essential, for the sake of economy, that a hundred thousand should be raised. He affirms that, "Provence alone has more seaports than Spain and Italy together."

The Abbé de Bourzeis had not travelled. Besides, his work abounds with anachronisms and errors; and as he makes Cardinal Richelieu sign in a manner in which he never signed, so he makes him speak as he had never spoken. Moreover, he takes a whole chapter to say that "reason should be the rule of a state," and in endeavoring to prove this discovery. This work of obscurities, this bastard of the Abbé de Bourzeis, has long passed for the legitimate offspring of the Cardinal Richelieu; and all members of the academy, in their speeches of reception, do not fail to praise extravagantly this political masterpiece.

The Sieur Gatien de Courtilz, seeing the success of the *Testament Politique* of Richelieu, published at The Hague the *Testament de Colbert*, with a fine letter of M. Colbert to the king.

It is clear that if this minister made such a testament, it would have been suppressed; yet this book has been quoted by several authors.

Another ignoramus, of whose name we are ignorant, did not fail to produce the *Testament de Louis*, still worse, if possible, than that of Colbert. An abbé of Chevremont also made Charles, duke of Lorraine, write a testament. We have had the political testaments of Cardinal Alberoni, Marshal de Belle-Isle, and finally that of Mandrin.

M. de Bois-Guillebert, author of the *Détail de la France*, published in 1695, produced the impracticable project of the royal tithe under the name of the marshal de Vauban.

A madman named La Jonchère, lacking bread, wrote, in 1720, a project of finance, in four volumes; and some fools have quoted this production as a work of La Jonchère, the treasurer-general, imagining that a treasurer could not write a bad book on finance.

But it must be confessed that very wise men, perhaps very worthy to govern, have written on the administration of states in France, Spain, and England. Their books have done much good; not that they have corrected ministers who were in place when these books appeared, for a minister does not and cannot correct himself. He has completed his growth; no more instruction, no more counsel. He has not time to listen. The current of affairs carries him away; but good books form young people, destined for their places; they form princes, the succeeding generation is instructed.

The strength and weakness of all governments has been narrowly examined in recent times. Tell me, then, you who have travelled, who have read and seen, in what state, under what sort of government, would you be born? I conceive that a great landed lord in France would have no objection to be born in Germany: he would be a sovereign instead of a subject. A peer of France would be very glad to have the privileges of the English peerage: he would be a legislator.

The lawyer and financier would find himself better off in France than elsewhere.

But what country would a wise and free man choose, a man of small fortune and without prejudices?

A rather learned member of the council of Pondicherry came into Europe, by land, with a brahmin, more learned than most brahmins are. "How do you find the government of the Great Mogul?" said the counsellor. "Abominable," answered the brahmin; "how can you expect a state to be happily governed by Tartars? Our rajahs, our omras, and our nabobs are very contented, but the citizens are by no means so; and millions of citizens are something."

The counsellor and the brahmin traversed all Upper Asia, reasoning on their way. "I reflect," said the brahmin, "that there is not a republic in all this vast part of the world." "There was formerly that of Tyre," said the counsellor, "but it did not last long; there was another towards Arabia Petræa, in a little nook called Palestine, if we can honor with the name of republic a horde of thieves and usurers, sometimes governed by judges, sometimes by a sort of kings, sometimes by high priests; who became slaves seven or eight times, and were finally driven from the country which they had usurped."

"I fancy," said the brahmin, "that we should find very few republics on earth. Men are seldom worthy of governing themselves. This happiness should only belong to little people, who conceal themselves in islands, or between mountains, like rabbits who steal away from carnivorous animals; but at length they are discovered and devoured."

When the travellers arrived in Asia Minor, the counsellor said to the brahmin, "Would you believe that there was a republic formed in a corner of Italy, which lasted more than five hundred years, and which possessed this Asia Minor, Asia, Africa, Greece, the Gauls, Spain, and the whole of Italy?" "It was therefore soon turned into a monarchy?" said the brahmin. "You have guessed it," said the other; "but this monarchy fell, and every day we write fine dissertations to discover the causes of its decline and fall." "You take a great deal of trouble," said the Indian: "this empire fell because it existed. All must fall. I hope that the same will happen to the empire of the Great Mogul."

"By the way," said the European, "do you believe that more honor is required in a despotic state, and more virtue in a republic?" The term honor being first explained to the Indian, he replied, that honor was more necessary in a republic, and that there is more need of virtue in a monarchical state. "For," said he, "a man who pretends to be elected by the people, will not be so, if he is dishonored; while at court he can easily obtain a place, according to the maxim of a great prince, that to succeed, a courtier should have neither honor nor humor. With respect to virtue, it is prodigiously required in a court, in order to dare to tell the truth. The virtuous man is much more at his ease in a republic, having nobody to flatter."

"Do you believe," said the European, "that laws and religions are made for climates, the same as furs are needed at Moscow, and gauze materials at Delhi?" "Yes, doubtless," said the brahmin; "all laws which concern physics are calculated for the meridian which we inhabit; a German requires only one wife, and a Persian must have two or three. Rites of religion are of the same nature. If I were a Christian, how would you have me say mass in my province, where there is neither bread nor wine? With regard to dogmas, it is another thing; climate has nothing to do with them. Did not your religion begin in Asia, from which it was driven? Does it not exist towards the Baltic Sea, where it was unknown?"

"In what state, under what dominion, would you most like to live?" said the counsellor. "Under any but my own," said his companion, "and I have found many Siamese, Tonquinese, Persians, and Turks who have said the same." "But, once more," said the European, "what state would you choose?" The brahmin answered, "That in which the laws alone are obeyed." "That is an old answer," said the counsellor. "It is not the worse for that," said the brahmin. "Where is this country?" said the counsellor. The brahmin replied, "We must seek it."

THEIST

The theist is a man firmly persuaded of the existence of a supreme Being as good as he is powerful, who has formed all existing, living, feeling and reflecting beings; who perpetuates their species, who punishes crimes without cruelty and rewards virtuous actions with goodness.

The theist does not know how God punishes, how he favors, how he pardons; for he is not rash enough to flatter himself with knowing how God acts; but he knows that God acts and that he is just. The difficulties of the existence of Providence have no effect on his faith, for they are only great difficulties, not proofs. He submits to this Providence, although he perceives only some of its effects and externals: and judging what he does not see from what he sees, he thinks that this Providence exists in all places and in all ages.

United in this principle with the rest of the universe, he embraces no sect for they all contradict themselves. His religion is the oldest and the most wide-spread, for the simple adoration of a God preceded all the systems in the world. He speaks a language that all peoples understand, even though they do not agree among themselves. He has brothers from Peking to Cayenne, and he counts every wise man as his brother. He believes that religion consists neither in the opinions of unintelligible metaphysics nor in vain display, but in adoration and in justice. To do good, that is his ceremony; to submit to God, that is his doctrine. The mohammedan cries out to him, "Look out if you do not make the pilgrimage to Mecca!" "Misfortune will befall you," the Franciscan tells him, "if you do not make a visit to Notre-Dame de Lorette!" He laughs at Lorette and at Mecca; but he helps the poor and he defends the oppressed.

TOLERANCE

What is tolerance? It is the portion of humanity. We are all full of weakness and errors; let us mutually pardon our follies. This is the first law of nature.

When, at the stock exchange of Amsterdam, of London, of Surat, or of Bassora, the Gueber, the Banian, the Jew, the Mahometan, the Chinese Deist, the Brahmin, the Greek Catholic, the Roman Catholic, the Protestant, and the Quaker traffic together, they do not lift the dagger against each other in order to gain souls for their religion. Why then have we been cutting one another's throats almost without interruption since the first Council of Nicea?

Constantine began by issuing an edict which allowed all religions, and ended by persecuting. Before him, tumults were excited against the Christians, only because they began to constitute a faction in the state. The Romans permitted all kinds of worship, even those of the Jews, and of the Egyptians, for whom they had so much contempt. Why did Rome tolerate these religions? Because neither the Egyptians, nor even the Jews, aimed at exterminating the ancient religion of the empire, or ranged through land and sea for proselytes; they thought only of making money; but it is undeniable, that the Christians wished their own religion to be the dominant one. The Jews would not permit the statue of Jupiter at Jerusalem, but the Christians wished it not to be in the capital. St. Thomas had the candor to avow, that if the Christians did not dethrone the emperors, it was because they could not. Their opinion was that the whole earth ought to be Christian. They were therefore necessarily enemies to the whole earth, until it was converted.

Among themselves, they were the enemies of each other on all their points of controversy. Was it first of all necessary to regard Jesus Christ as God? Those who denied it were anathematized under the name of Ebionites, who themselves anathematized the adorers of Jesus.

Did some among them wish all things to be in common, as it is claimed they were in the time of the apostles? Their adversaries called them Nicolaites, and accused them of the most infamous crimes. Did others profess a mystical devotion? They were termed Gnostics, and attacked with fury. Did Marcion dispute on the Trinity? He was treated as an idolater.

Tertullian, Praxeas, Origen, Novatus, Novatian, Sabellius, Donatus, were all persecuted by their brothers, before Constantine; and scarcely had Constantine made the Christian religion the ruling one, when the Athanasians and the Eusebians tore each other to pieces; and from that time to our own days, the Christian Church has been deluged with blood.

The Jewish people were, I confess, a very barbarous nation.

They mercilessly cut the throats of all the inhabitants of an unfortunate little country upon which they had no more claim than they have upon Paris or London. However, when Naaman was cured of leprosy by being plunged seven times in the Jordan, when, in order to show his gratitude to Elisha, who had taught him the secret, he told him he would adore the God of the Jews out of gratitude, he reserved himself the liberty to adore also the God of his own king; he asked Elisha's permission to do so, and the prophet did not hesitate to grant it. The Jews adored their God, but they were never astonished that every nation had its own. They approved of Chemos having given a certain district to the Moabites, provided their God would give them one also. Jacob did not hesitate to marry the daughters of an idolater. Laban had his God, as Jacob had his. There are examples of tolerance among the most intolerant and cruel people of antiquity. We have imitated them in their absurd passions, and not in their indulgence.

It is clear that every private individual who persecutes a man, his brother, because he is not of the same opinion, is a monster. This admits of no difficulty. But the government, the magistrates, the princes!—how do they conduct themselves towards those who have a faith different from their own? If they are powerful foreigners, it is certain that a prince will form an alliance with them. The Most Christian Francis I will league himself with the Moslems against the Most Catholic Charles V. Francis I will give money to the Lutherans in Germany, to support them in their rebellion against the Emperor; but he will begin, according to custom, by having the Lutherans in his own country burned. He pays them in Saxony from policy; he burns them in Paris from policy. But what follows? Persecutions make proselytes. France will soon be filled with new Protestants. At first they will submit to be hanged; afterwards they will hang in their turn. There will be civil wars; then Saint Bartholomew will come; and this corner of the world will be worse than all that the ancients and moderns have ever said of hell.

Lunatics, who have never been able to worship purely the God who made you! Wretches, whom the example of the Noachides, the Chinese sages, the Parsees, and all the wise, has not availed to guide! Monsters, who need superstitions, just as the gizzard of a raven needs carrion! We have already told you, and we have nothing else to say, if you have two religions among you, they will massacre each other; if you have thirty, they will live in peace. Look at the Grand Turk: he governs Guebers, Banians, Greek Catholics, Nestorians, and Roman Catholics. The first who would excite a tumult is impaled; and all is peaceful.

II

Of all religions, the Christian ought doubtless to inspire the most tolerance, although hitherto the Christians have been the most intolerant of all men.

Jesus, having deigned to be born in poverty and lowliness like his brethren, never condescended to practise the art of writing. The Jews had a law written with the greatest minuteness, and we have not a single line from the hand of Jesus. The apostles were divided on many points. St. Peter and St. Barnabas ate forbidden meats with the new Christians, and abstained from them with the Jewish Christians. St. Paul reproached them with this conduct; and this same St. Paul, the Pharisee, the disciple of the Pharisee Gamaliel—this same St. Paul, who had persecuted the Christians with fury, and who after breaking with Gamaliel became a Christian himself—nevertheless, went afterwards to sacrifice in the temple of Jerusalem, during his apostolic vacation. For eight days he observed publicly all the ceremonies of the Judaic law which he had renounced; he even added devotions and purifications which were superabundant; he completely Judaized. The greatest apostle of the Christians did, for eight days, the very things for which men are condemned to the stake among a large portion of Christian nations.

Theudas and Judas were called Messiahs, before Jesus: Dositheus, Simon, Menander, called themselves Messiahs after Jesus. From the first century of the Church, and before even the name of Christian was known, there were a score of sects in Judæa.

The contemplative Gnostics, the Dositheans, the Cerintheins, existed before the disciples of Jesus had taken the name of

Christians. There were soon thirty Gospels, each of which belonged to a different society; and by the close of the first century thirty sects of Christians might be reckoned in Asia Minor, in Syria, in Alexandria, and even in Rome.

All these sects, despised by the Roman government, and concealed in their obscurity, nevertheless persecuted each other in the underground where they lurked; that is to say, they reproached one another. This is all they could do in their abject condition: they were almost wholly composed of the dregs of the people.

When at length some Christians had embraced the dogmas of Plato, and mingled a little philosophy with their religion, which they separated from the Jewish, they insensibly became more considerable, but were always divided into many sects, without there ever having been a time when the Christian church was reunited. It took its origin in the midst of the divisions of the Jews, the Samaritans, the Pharisees, the Sadducees, the Essenians, the Judaites, the disciples of John, and the Therapeutæ. It was divided in its infancy; it was divided even amid the persecutions it sometimes endured under the first emperors. The martyr was often considered by his brethren as an apostate; and the Carpocratian Christian expired under the sword of Roman executioners, excommunicated by the Ebionite Christian, which Ebionite was anathematized by the Sabellian.

This horrible discord, lasting for so many centuries, is a very striking lesson that we ought mutually to forgive each other's errors: discord is the great evil of the human species, and toleration is its only remedy.

There is nobody who does not assent to this truth, whether meditating coolly in his closet, or examining the truth peacefully with his friends. Why, then, do the same men who in private admit indulgence, benevolence, and justice, rise up in public so furiously against these virtues? Why? It is because their interest is their god; because they sacrifice all to that monster whom they adore.

I possess dignity and a power which ignorance and credulity have founded. I trample on the heads of men prostrate at my feet; if they should rise and look me in the face, I am lost; they must, therefore, be kept bound down to earth with chains of iron.

Thus have men reasoned whom ages of fanaticism have rendered powerful. They have other persons in power under them, and these latter again have underlings, who all enrich themselves with the spoils of the poor, fatten themselves with his blood, and laugh at his imbecility. They all detest tolerance, as contractors enriched at the expense of the public are afraid to open their accounts, and as tyrants dread the name of liberty. To crown all, finally, they encourage fanatics who cry aloud: "Respect the absurdities of my master; tremble, pay, and be silent."

Such was the practice for a long time in a great part of the world; but now, when so many sects are balanced by their power, what side must we take among them? Every sect, we know, is a mere title of error; while there is no sect of geometricians, of algebraists, of arithmeticians; because all the propositions of geometry, algebra, and arithmetic, are true. In all the other sciences, one may be mistaken. What Thomist or Scotist theologian would dare to say seriously that he is sure of his grounds?

If there is any sect which recalls the time of the first Christians, it is undeniably that of the Quakers. Nothing resembles the apostles more. The apostles received the spirit. The Quakers receive the spirit. The apostles and disciples spoke three or four at once in the assembly on the third floor; the Quakers do as much on the ground floor. Women were permitted to preach, according to St. Paul, and they were forbidden according to the same St. Paul: the Quakeresses preach by virtue of the first permission.

The apostles and disciples swore by yea and nay; the Quakers will not swear in any other form.

There was no rank, no difference of dress, among apostles and disciples; the Quakers have sleeves without buttons, and are all clothed alike.

Jesus Christ baptized none of his apostles; the Quakers are not baptized.

It would be easy to push the parallel farther; it would be still easier to demonstrate how much the Christian religion of our day differs from the religion which Jesus practiced. Jesus was a Jew, and we are not Jews. Jesus abstained from pork, because it is unclean, and from rabbit, because it ruminates and its foot is not cloven; we boldly eat pork, because it is not unclean for us, and we eat rabbit which has the cloven foot and does not ruminate.

Jesus was circumcised, and we retain our foreskin. Jesus ate the Paschal lamb with lettuce. He celebrated the feast of the tabernacles; and we do nothing of this. He observed the sabbath, and we have changed it; he sacrificed, and we never sacrifice.

Jesus always concealed the mystery of his incarnation and his dignity; he never said he was equal to God. St. Paul says expressly, in his *Epistle to the Hebrews*, that God created Jesus inferior to the angels; and in spite of St. Paul's words, Jesus was acknowledged as God at the Council of Nicea.

Jesus has not given the pope either the March of Ancona or the Duchy of Spoleto; and yet the pope possesses them by divine right.

Jesus did not make a sacrament of marriage or of deaconry; and, with us, marriage and deaconry are sacraments.

If we would attend closely to the fact, the Catholic, apostolic, and Roman religion is, in all its ceremonies and in all its dogma, the reverse of the religion of Jesus.

But what! Must we all Judaize, because Jesus Judaized all his life? If we were allowed to reason logically in matters of religion, it is clear that we ought all to become Jews, since Jesus Christ, our saviour, was born a Jew, lived a Jew and died a Jew, and since he expressly said, that he accomplished and fulfilled the Jewish religion. But it is still more clear that we ought mutually to tolerate one another, because we are all weak, inconsequential, subject to change, to error. Ought a reed, blown by the wind into the mire, say to a neighboring reed blown in a contrary direction: "Creep the way I do, wretch, or I will request that you be seized and burned?"

WAR

Famine, plague, and war are the three most famous ingredients of this vile world. In famine we can include all the bad food that poverty forces on us, to shorten our life in the effort of sustaining it.

Plague includes all of the contagious diseases, which number two or three thousand. These two presents come to us from Providence. But war, which combines all of these gifts, comes to us from the imagination of three or four hundred persons scattered over this globe under the name of princes or ministers, and it is perhaps for this reason that in several dedications they are called living images of Divinity.

The most determined of flatterers will readily agree that war always brings pestilence and famine in its wake, from the little that he may have seen in the hospitals of the armies of Germany, or the few villages he may have passed through in which some great exploit of war has been performed.

That is doubtless a very fine art which ruins countries, destroys habitations, and in a normal year causes the death of from forty to a hundred thousand men. This invention was first cultivated by nations assembled for their common good; for instance, the parliament of the Greeks declared to the parliament of Phrygia and neighboring nations, that they intended to depart on a thousand fishers' barks, to exterminate them if they could.

The assembled Roman people judged that it was to their interest to go and fight, before harvest, against the people of Veii or the Volscians. And some years later, all the Romans, angered at all the Carthaginians, fought them for a long time on sea and land. It is not exactly the same at present.

A genealogist proves to a prince that he descends in a direct line from a count, whose parents made a family compact, three or four hundred years ago, with a house, whose very memory does not even exist. This house had distant pretensions to a province, of which the last possessor died of apoplexy. The prince and his council easily conclude that this province is theirs by divine right. This province, which is some hundred leagues away from him, in vain protests that it knows him not; that it has no desire to be governed by him; that to give laws to its people, he must at least have their consent; these discourses do not even reach as far as the ears of the prince, whose right is incontestable. He immediately assembles a great number of men who have nothing to lose, dresses them in coarse blue cloth, borders their hats with broad white ribbon, makes them turn to the right and left, and marches to glory.

Other princes who hear of this expedition take part in it, each according to his power, and cover a small extent of country with more mercenary murderers than Genghis Khan, Tamerlane, and Bajazet employed in their train.

Distant people hear that they are going to fight, and that they may gain five or six sous a day, if they will come along; they divide themselves into two bands, like reapers, and offer their services to whoever will employ them.

These multitudes fall upon one another, not only without having any interest in the affair, but without knowing what it is all about.

We see at once five or six belligerent powers, sometimes three against three, sometimes two against four, and sometimes one against five; all equally detesting one another, uniting with and attacking by turns; all agree in a single point, that of doing all the harm possible.

The most wonderful part of this infernal enterprise is that each chief of the murderers has his colors blessed, and solemnly invokes God before going to exterminate his neighbor. If a chief has only the good fortune to kill two or three thousand men, he does not thank God for it; but when he has exterminated about ten thousand by fire and sword, and, to complete the work, some town has been levelled with the ground, they then sing a long song in four parts, composed in a language unknown to all who have fought, and moreover replete with barbarisms. The same song serves for marriages and births, as well as for murders; which is unpardonable, particularly in the nation most famous for new songs.

Natural religion has a thousand times prevented citizens from committing crimes. A well-born spirit has not the inclination for it; a tender one is alarmed at it, representing to itself a just and avenging God. But artificial religion encourages all the cruelties exercised by troops, conspiracies, seditions, pillages, ambuscades, surprises of towns, robberies, and murder. Each marches gaily to crime, under the banner of his saint.

A certain number of orators are everywhere paid to celebrate these murderous days; some are dressed in a long tight black coat, with a short cloak; others have a shirt above a gown; some wear two pieces of material hanging over their shirts. All of them speak for a long time, and quote that which was done of old in Palestine, as applicable to a combat in Veteravia.

The rest of the year these people declaim against vices. They prove, in three points and by antitheses, that ladies who lay a little carmine upon their cheeks will be the eternal objects of the eternal vengeances of the Eternal; that *Polyeucte* and *Athalie* are works of the demon; that a man who, for two hundred crowns a day, has his table furnished with fresh seafish during Lent, infallibly works his salvation; and that a poor man who eats two sous and a half worth of mutton, will go forever to all the devils.

Of five or six thousand declamations of this kind, there are three or four at most, composed by a Gaul named Massillon, which an honest man may read without disgust; but in all these discourses, you will scarcely find two in which the orator dares to say a word against the scourge and crime of war, which contains all other scourges and crimes. The unfortunate orators speak incessantly against love, which is the only consolation of mankind, and the only way of reconstructing it; they say nothing of the abominable efforts which we make to destroy it.

You have made a very bad sermon on impurity, O Bourdaloue! —but none on these murders, varied in so many ways; on these rapines and robberies; on this universal rage which devours the world. All the united vices of all ages and places will never equal the evils produced by a single campaign.

Miserable physicians of souls! you exclaim, for five quarters of an hour, over some pricks of a pin, and say nothing on the disease which tears us into a thousand pieces! Philosophers! moralists! burn all your books. While the caprice of a few men causes thousands of our brothers to be murdered, that part of the human race dedicated to heroism will be the most dreadful thing in all nature.

What becomes of humanity, beneficence, modesty, temperance, mildness, wisdom, and piety, and what difference do they all make to me, while half a pound of lead, sent from the distance of six hundred steps, pierces my body, and I die at twenty years of age, in inexpressible torments, in the midst of five or six thousand dying men, while my eyes which open for the last time, see the town in which I was born destroyed by fire and sword, and the last sounds which reach my ears are the cries of women and children expiring under the ruins, all for the pretended interests of a man whom we do not know?

What is worse, war is an inevitable scourge. If we take notice, all men have worshipped the god Mars. Sabaoth, among the Jews, signifies the god of arms; but Minerva, in Homer, calls Mars a furious god, out of his mind, infernal.

DIALOGUES AND
SHORTER PIECES

ACCOUNT OF THE SICKNESS, CONFESSION AND DEATH OF THE JESUIT BERTHIER [55]

It was on October 12, 1759, that Brother Berthier unfortunately went from Paris to Versailles, along with Brother Coutu who usually accompanied him. Berthier had placed several copies of the *Journal de Trévoux* in the carriage, in order to give them to his male and female protectors; such as the maid of Madame the nurse, an officer of the table, one of the king's apprentice pharmacists, and to several other gentlemen who have a high regard for talent. On the way Berthier had a few spells of nausea; his head became heavy: he yawned frequently. "I don't know what's the matter," he said to Coutu, "I've never yawned so much." "My reverend Father," answered Brother Coutu, "it's only something given back." "What! What do you mean with this 'something given back'?" said Brother Berthier. "The fact is," said Brother Coutu, "that I am yawning too, and I don't know why because I have read nothing all day long and you have not spoken to me during the time that I've been traveling with you." While speaking these words, Brother Coutu yawned more than ever. Berthier answered with unending yawns. The coachman turned around and seeing them yawning in this way, began to yawn also; the disease spread to all who passed by, and in all the nearby houses, everyone yawned. Thus the mere presence of a learned man has sometimes so great an influence on others!

Meanwhile, a slight cold sweat came over Berthier. "I don't know what's wrong with me," he said; "I feel like ice." "I can well believe it," said the Brother companion. "What! You can well believe it!" said Berthier; "What do you mean by that?" "I mean that I am frozen too," said Coutu. "I am sleepy," said Berthier. "That doesn't surprise me a bit," said the other. "Why is that?" said Berthier. "It's because I'm sleepy too," his companion said. There they were, both seized by a soporific and lethargic malady, and in this condition they stopped before the carriage gate at Versailles. The coachman, while opening the door for them, tried to wake them from their deep sleep; he couldn't do so. Help was sent for. The companion, more robust than Brother Berthier, at last gave some signs of life; but Berthier was colder than ever. Some court physicians, coming from dinner, passed near the carriage, and were implored to take a look at the sick man. One of them, having felt his pulse, went off saying that he no longer had practiced medicine from the time he came to court. Another, having examined him more carefully, declared that the illness came from the gall bladder, which was always too full; a third asserted that it all came from the brain, which was too empty.

While they were arguing, the patient became worse; convulsions were beginning to present dangerous indications, and already the three fingers which hold a pen were drawn back, when a chief physician, who had studied under Mead and Boerhaave, and who knew more than the others, opened Berthier's mouth with a nipple and after carefully reflecting on the odor he exhaled, declared that he was poisoned.

At this word everyone became excited. "Yes, gentlemen," he continued, "he is poisoned; you need only feel his skin to see that the exhalations of a cold poison have made their way through the pores; and I maintain that this poison is worse than a mixture of hemlock, black hellebore, opium, solanum, and henbane. Coachman, could it not be that you put some sort of package into your carriage for our pharmacists?" "No sir," answered the coachman, "this is the only package that I put there by order of the reverend Father." Then he searched around inside and drew out two dozen copies of the *Journal de Trévoux*. "Well, gentlemen, was I wrong?" said this great physician.

All who were present admired his prodigious wisdom; everyone recognized the origin of the disease. They burned the pernicious package on the spot under the patient's nose, and, as the heavy particles were lightened by the action of the fire, Berthier was relieved a little; but as the disease had already made great progress and had attacked the head, the danger still persisted. The doctor decided to make him swallow a page of the *Encyclopedia* in white wine, to restore the humours of the thickened bile to motion; an enormous evacuation resulted; but the head was still horribly heavy, dizziness continued, and the few words he could articulate meant nothing. For two hours he remained in this condition, after which it was necessary to have him confess.

Two priests were walking along the street of the Franciscans, and were approached. The first refused: "In no way," he said, "do I wish to concern myself with the soul of a Jesuit, it's too risky a business: I want nothing to do with those people, neither in matters of this world nor of the next. Let he who wants to confess a Jesuit; it won't be me." The second was not so difficult. "I will undertake this operation," he said; "some advantage can be gotten out of anything."

At once he was led into the room to which the patient had just been carried; and as Berthier still could not speak distinctly, the confessor questioned him. "My reverend Father, do you believe in God?" "Now that is a strange question," said Berthier. "Not so strange," said the other; "there is belief and belief: to be sure of believing as one should, he must love God and his neighbor; do you love them sincerely?" "I make a distinction," said Berthier. "No distinctions, if you please," replied the confessor; "no absolution if you do not begin with these two duties." "Very well, yes," said the man confessing, "since you force me to it, I love God, and my neighbor as I can."

"Haven't you often read bad books?" said the confessor. "What do you mean by bad books?" "I do not mean," the confessor said, "books that are merely boring, like the *Roman History* of Brothers Catrou and Rouille, and your schoolboy tragedies, and your books entitled *Of Belles Lettres,* and the *Louisiade* of your colleague Lemoine, and the verses of your Ducerceau about shallot-sauce, and his noble stanzas on the messenger from Mans, and his thanks to the Duke of Maine for liver paste, and your

Think About It Carefully, and all the niceties of monkish wit;
I mean the imaginings of Brother Bougeant, condemned by the
parliament and by the Archbishop of Paris; I mean the pretty
writings of Brother Berruyer, who changed the Old and the
New Testament into a fashionable novel in the style of *Clelia*,
so rightly condemned at Rome and in France; I mean the theology of Brother Busembaum and Brother Lacroix,[56] who have so
greatly improved upon all that Brother Guignard had written,
and Brother Gueret, and Brother Garnet, and Brother Oldcorn,
and so many others; I mean Brother Jouvency, who delicately
compared the President of Harlai to Pilate, the parliament to
the Jews, and Brother Guignard to Jesus Christ, because a citizen
who was too carried away, but imbued with a just horror against
an advocate of parricide, decided to spit in the face of Brother
Guignard, murderer of Henri IV, at the time that this impenitent monster refused to ask pardon of the King and of
justice; I mean, finally, the innumerable crowd of your casuists,
whom the eloquent Pascal let off too easily, and especially your
Sanchez, who in his book, *De Matrimonio*, has made a collection
of all that Aretino and the *Portier des Chartreux* would have
trembled to say. If you have happened to have read such things,
your salvation is in great danger."

"I make a distinction," replied the man under question. "I
must say once more, no distinctions," declared the questioner.
"Have you read all these books, yes or no?" "Sir," said Berthier,
"I am entitled to read them because of the eminent position
which I occupy in the Society." "What! And what is this great
position?" said the confessor. "Well," replied Berthier, "it is I, if
you must know, who am the author of the *Journal de Trévoux*."

"What! You are the author of that work which damns so
many people?" "Sir, sir, my work damns no one; into what sin
can it make one fall, if you please?" "Ah, Brother," said the
confessor, "don't you know that whoever calls his brother a fool
is liable to the fire of hell? Now you have the misfortune to
make any one who reads you prone to call you a fool. How
often have I seen good men who, after reading but two or three
pages of your work, throw it into the fire, furious with rage!
"What an impertinent author!" they say; "the ignorant fool!

the boob! the ass!" And it does not stop there: their feelings of charity are completely extinguished and they evidently risk their salvation. Judge of how many evils you have been the cause! There are perhaps almost fifty people who read you, and they are fifty souls whom you endanger every month. What especially arouses anger among the faithful ones is that confidence with which you decide on everything you do not understand. This vice clearly has its source in two mortal sins: the one is pride and the other, avarice. Is it not true that you write for money, and that you are filled with pride when you wretchedly criticize Abbé Velly, Abbé Coyer and Abbé d'Olivet, and all our good writers? I can not give you absolution, unless you make a firm promise never again during your lifetime to work on the *Journal de Trévoux*."

Brother Berthier did not know what to reply; his mind was not clear, and he held on savagely to his two favorite sins. "What! You hesitate!" said the confessor; "reflect that in a few hours it will all be over for you: can a man still cherish his passions when he must renounce satisfying them forever? On the day of judgment will you be asked if you succeeded or not in writing the *Journal de Trévoux?* Is that why you were born? Is it in order to bore us that you have taken the vow of chastity, humility and obedience? Dry tree, stunted tree, soon to be reduced to ashes, take advantage of the moment that remains to you; once more, bring the fruits of penitence; detest above all the spirit of calumny that has possessed you up to the present time; try to have as much religion as those whom you accuse of being without religion. Know, Brother Berthier, that piety and virtue do not consist in believing that when your François Xavier let his crucifix fall into the sea, a crab humbly brought it back to him. A man can be good, and yet doubt that this Xavier was in two places at the same time; your books may say so; but, my Brother, it is permissible to believe nothing of what is in your books."

"By the way, Brother, didn't you write to Brother Malagrida and his accomplices? [57] Really I had forgotten that little sin: do you believe, then, that because in the past it cost Henri IV only a tooth, and today cost the King of Portugal only an arm, that you can save yourself with the direction of intention? You think that those are venial sins, and as long as the *Journal de Trévoux* is sold, you care very little about the rest."

"I make a distinction, sir," said Berthier. "More distinctions!" said the confessor; "very well; I make no distinctions and I forthwith refuse you absolution."

As he uttered these words, Brother Coutu ran up, running, out of breath, sweating, panting, stinking. He learned who it was that had the honor of confessing his reverend Father. "Stop, stop," he exclaimed, "no sacraments, my reverend Father, no sacraments, I implore you, my dear reverend Father Berthier, die without sacraments; you are with the author of the *Nouvelles ecclésiastiques*,[58] he is the fox confessing the wolf: you are lost if you have told the truth."

Astonishment, shame, pain, anger, rage for a moment revived the patient's spirits. "You the author of the *Nouvelles ecclésiastiques!*" he exclaimed; "and you have trapped a Jesuit!" "Yes, my friend," replied the confessor with a bitter smile. "Give me back my confession, rogue," said Berthier; "give me back my confession at once. Ah, so it is you, the enemy of God, of kings and even of the Jesuits; it is you who came to take advantage of my condition: traitor, if only you had apoplexy and I could give you extreme unction! Do you really think that you are less boring and less fanatical than I? Yes, I have written stupidities, I admit; I have made myself detestable and hateful, I confess; but you, aren't you the lowest and most execrable of all scribblers in whose hands madness has placed a pen? Tell me if your account of convulsions is not equal to our *Curious and Edifying Letters?* I admit that we want to dominate everywhere; and you, you want to smash everything. We want to seduce all of the powers; and you, you would excite sedition against them. It is true that the courts of justice have had our books burned, but have they not had yours burned too? We are all in prison in Portugal, true enough; but have not the police pursued you a hundred times, you and your accomplices? If I have been foolish enough to write against enlightened men who disdained to crush me, did you not have the same impertinence? Aren't both of us made ridiculous, and should we not admit that in this century, the sink-hole of centuries, we both are the vilest insects of all that swarm amidst the scum of this mire?" All this the force of truth drew out of the mouth of Brother Berthier. He spoke like a man inspired; his eyes, filled with a dark fire, rolled wildly; his mouth became twisted; foam covered it, his body stiffened, his heart fluttered: soon a complete crumbling away followed these convulsions, and he tenderly squeezed the hand of Brother Coutu. "I admit," he said, "that there are many poor things in my *Journal de Trévoux;* but we must excuse human weakness." "Ah, my reverend Father, you are a saint," said Brother Coutu; "you are the first writer who has ever admitted that he was dull; go, die in peace; mock at the *Nouvelles ecclésiastiques;* die, my reverend Father, and be sure that you will accomplish miracles."

Thus passed Brother Berthier from this life to the next, October 12, at half past five in the evening.

OF THE HORRIBLE DANGER
OF READING [59]

We, Youssouf Cheribi, by the grace of God mufti of the Holy
Ottoman Empire, light of lights, elected of the elect, to all of
the faithful to whom these presents come, stupidity and benediction.

As it happens that Saïd-Effendi, former ambassador of the
Gate Sublime to a little state called *Frankrom*, located between
Spain and Italy, has informed us of the pernicious use of printing, having discussed this news with our venerable brothers
and cadis and imans of the imperial city of Stamboul, and especially with the fakirs well known for their zealous activity
against the mind, it has seemed good to Mahomet and to us to
condemn, proscribe, anathematize the aforesaid infernal invention of printing, for the reasons set forth below.

1. This ease of communicating thoughts clearly tends to dis-
sipate ignorance, which is the guardian and safety of well policed states.

2. It is to be feared that among the books brought from the
West, there may be some dealing with agriculture and the ways
of improving mechanical techniques, which works could ulti-
mately, to the displeasure of God, awaken the ingenuity of our
farmers and manufacturers, arouse their industry, increase their
riches, and some day inspire in them some elevation of soul and
love of public welfare, feelings absolutely opposed to correct
doctrine.

3. It would finally result that we would have histories free of

the marvelous which keeps the nation in a happy stupidity. These books would have the imprudence of according justice to good and to bad actions, and to recommend equity and love of country, all of which is plainly contrary to the rights of our position.

4. It might come about, in the course of time, that wretched philosophers, under the fallacious but punishable pretext of enlightening men and making them better, would come to teach us dangerous virtues which the people should never know.

5. By increasing the respect for God and by scandalously saying in print that he fills all with his presence, they could decrease the number of pilgrims to Mecca, to the great detriment of the salvation of souls.

6. It will no doubt come about that as a result of reading western writers who deal with contagious diseases and with the way of preventing them, we would be unfortunate enough to safeguard ourselves from the plague, which would be an enormous crime against the dictates of Providence.

For these reasons and others, for the edification of the faithful and for the good of their souls, we forbid them to ever read any book, under pain of eternal damnation. And for fear lest they be seized by the diabolical temptation to instruct themselves, we forbid mothers and fathers to teach their children how to read. And to prevent any violation of our law, we expressly forbid them to think, under pain of the same penalties; we enjoin all true believers to denounce officially any one who might pronounce four phrases in consecutive order from which a clear and distinct sense can be inferred. We command that in all conversation our subjects make use of terms that mean nothing, according to the ancient usage of the Gate Sublime.

And to prevent any thought from entering as contraband into the sacred imperial city, we specially commission the chief doctor of His Excellency, born in a swamp of the northern Occident; which doctor, having already killed four august members of the Ottoman royal family, is more interested than any one else in preventing any introduction of knowledge into the country; we herewith give him power to have seized any idea which might present itself, in writing or by mouth, at the gates of the city, and to bring us this idea with its hands and feet bound, so that we may inflict on it such punishment as we please.

Given in our palace of stupidity, the 7th day of the moon of Muharem, in the year 1143 of the hegira.

CONVERSATION OF LUCIAN,
ERASMUS AND RABELAIS [60]

IN THE ELYSIAN FIELDS

Some time ago Lucian, despite his distaste for everything coming from the frontiers of Germany, made the acquaintance of Erasmus. He did not believe that a Greek should lower himself to speak with a Batavian; but as this Batavian seemed to him a deceased of such good company, they had this conversation together:

LUCIAN: You say then that you practiced the same profession in a barbarous country that I practiced in the most civilized on earth; you made fun of everything?

ERASMUS: Alas! I certainly would have liked to; it would have been a great consolation for a poor theologian such as I was; but I could not take the same liberties as you.

LUCIAN: That astounds me: men rather like to be shown their stupidities in a general way, so long as no one is designated in particular; each one then ascribes his own follies to his neighbor, and every one laughs at one another's expense. Wasn't it that way with your contemporaries?

ERASMUS: There was a vast difference between the ridiculous men of your time and of mine: you had to do with gods represented in the theatre, and with philosophers who were believed even less than the gods; but I on the other hand was surrounded by fanatics, and I had to take great care not to be burned by some or murdered by others.

LUCIAN: How can you laugh about these alternatives?

ERASMUS: I hardly ever laughed at all; and I passed for a

much more pleasant fellow than I really was: they thought I was very gay and very clever, because at that time every one was sad. Men were profoundly occupied with empty ideas that made men quarrelsome. A man who believed that a body could be in two places at once was ready to massacre another who explained the same thing in a different way. There were worse things: a man of my sort who absolutely would not take part among these two factions would have been viewed as a monster.

LUCIAN: Those barbarians with whom you lived were really strange men. In my day, the Getes and Massagetes were gentler and more reasonable. And what then was your profession in the horrible country in which you lived?

ERASMUS: I was a Dutch monk.

LUCIAN: Monk! What profession is that?

ERASMUS: That of having none, of contracting by an inviolable oath to be useless to mankind, to be absurd and slavish, and to live at the expense of others.

LUCIAN: There you have a really wretched profession! How with so much intelligence could you embrace a condition which dishonors human nature? I do not speak about living at the expense of others, but to take an oath to deny common sense and to lose your liberty!

ERASMUS: It happened that as I was very young and had neither parents nor friends, I let myself be seduced by rogues who sought to increase the number of their kind.

LUCIAN: What! Were there many men of that sort?

ERASMUS: There were in Europe around six or seven hundred thousand.

LUCIAN: Good heavens! The world has surely become quite stupid and barbaric since I have left it. Horace was quite right when he said that things would get worse as they went along: *Progenium vitiosiorem.*

ERASMUS: What consoles me is that every one, in the age I lived in, had climbed to the very summit of madness; some of them will have to come down, and among them will be a few who will at last regain a little reason.

LUCIAN: I doubt that very much. Tell me, if you please, what were the principal follies of your time?

ERASMUS: Here you are, a long list of them which I always have along; read it.

LUCIAN: It is very long. (*Lucian reads and bursts out laughing. Rabelais comes up.*)

RABELAIS: Gentlemen, when some one laughs, I am welcome. What is it about?

LUCIAN AND ERASMUS: About extravagances.

RABELAIS: Ah, I am your man.

LUCIAN (*To Erasmus*): Who is this unusual fellow?

ERASMUS: He is a man who was bolder than I, and more agreeable; but he was only a priest and could take more liberty than could I, being a monk.

LUCIAN (*To Rabelais*): Did you, like Erasmus, take an oath to live at the expense of others?

RABELAIS: Doubly so, for I was a priest and a doctor. I was born very wise, I became as learned as Erasmus; and seeing that wisdom and learning lead together only to the hospital or the gallows; seeing too that this somewhat pleasant fellow, Erasmus, was sometimes persecuted, I decided to be madder than all my compatriots together; I composed a great book of scurvy tales, full of filth, in which I turned to ridicule all the superstitions, all the ceremonies, all that was worshipped in my country, every occupation, from that of king and pope to that of doctor of theology, which is the lowest of all: I dedicated my book to a cardinal, and I made even those who despised me laugh.

LUCIAN: What is a cardinal, Erasmus?

ERASMUS: He is a priest garbed in red, who is paid an income of a hundred thousand crowns for doing nothing at all.

LUCIAN: You will at least grant me that those cardinals were reasonable men. Not all of your fellow citizens must have been as crazy as you say they were.

ERASMUS: Let Monsieur Rabelais allow me to have the floor. The cardinals had another sort of madness: that of dominating; and as it is easier to subjugate fools than intelligent men, they wished to crush reason, which was beginning to stir a little. Monsieur Rabelais, whom you see, imitated the first Brutus, who pretended insanity in order to escape the defiance and tyranny of the Tarquins.

LUCIAN: Everything you tell me confirms my opinion that it was better to live in my century than in yours. These cardinals you mentioned were thus masters of the whole world, since they commanded madmen?

RABELAIS: No; there was an old fool over them.

LUCIAN: What was he called?

RABELAIS: A *papegaut*. This man's madness was that he held himself to be infallible and thought himself to be the master of kings; and he had this said and repeated so often, and exclaimed so frequently by monks, that finally almost all Europe believed him.

LUCIAN: Ah, but you certainly are ahead of us in madness. The fables of Jupiter, Neptune and Pluto, which I made so much fun of, were respectable along side of the stupidities with which your world was infatuated. I can not see how you could have managed to ridicule, in safety, men who must have feared ridicule even more than conspiracy. For a man does not make fun of his masters with impunity, and I was wise enough not to say a single word about the Roman emperors. Your nation adored a *papegaut!* You allowed this *papegaut* all the stupidities imaginable, and your nation tolerated it! Was your country, then, so patient?

RABELAIS: I have to tell you what my nation was. It was an amalgamation of ignorance, superstition, stupidity, cruelty and nonsense. They began by hanging and roasting all those who spoke seriously against cardinals and *papegauts*. The land of the Welsh, of which I am a native, was bathed in blood; but as soon as the executions had taken place, the whole country began to dance, to sing, to make love, to drink and to laugh. I took my fellow citizens at their weak point; I talked about drinking, I told filthy tales, and in this way I got away with everything. Intelligent men understood my cleverness and liked me for it; coarser men saw only filth and enjoyed it; far from persecuting me, every one liked me.

LUCIAN: You make me want very much to see your book. Haven't you a copy in your pocket? And you, Erasmus, could you also lend me your jests? (*Hereupon Erasmus and Rabelais*

give their works to Lucian, who reads a few passages from them.
and meanwhile, these two philosophers converse.)

RABELAIS (*To Erasmus*): I have read your writings although
you have not read mine, because I came a little after you. You
were perhaps too reserved in your raillery, and I too bold in
mine; but at present we both think the same. As for myself, I
laugh when I see a doctor arrive in these parts.

ERASMUS: And I pity him, and say: There is an unfortunate who wore himself out his whole life long in making mistakes, and who will gain nothing here in leaving off error.

RABELAIS: What do you say! Is it nothing to be undeceived?

ERASMUS: It is very little when you can no longer undeceive
others. The greatest of pleasures is to show the way to friends
who have gone astray, and dead men ask the way from no one.

Erasmus and Rabelais talked for a long time. Lucian returned
after reading the chapter of the burnt rumps and some pages
from *In Praise of Folly*. Afterwards, having met Doctor Swift,
all four went off to dine together.

André Destouches was a very agreeable musician in the brilliant reign of Louis XIV, before music was perfected by Rameau, and before it was corrupted by those who prefer difficulty overcome to the natural and graceful.

Before making use of these talents he had been a musketeer, and before that, in 1688, he went to Siam with the Jesuit Tachard, who gave him many signs of his affection, for the amusement he afforded on board the ship; and Destouches spoke with admiration of Father Tachard for the rest of his life.

In Siam he became acquainted with the prime minister, whose name was Croutef, and he committed to writing most of the questions which he asked of Croutef, and the answers of that Siamese. Here they are, as we have found them in his papers:

ANDRÉ DESTOUCHES: How many soldiers have you?

CROUTEF: Eighty thousand, very meanly paid.

ANDRÉ DESTOUCHES: And how many buddhist priests?

CROUTEF: A hundred and twenty thousand, very idle and very rich. It is true that in the last war we were badly beaten, but our priests have lived sumptuously, built fine houses, and kept pretty girls.

ANDRÉ DESTOUCHES: Nothing could be wiser and more considered. And your finances, in what state are they?

CROUTEF: In a very bad state. We have, however, about ninety thousand men employed to render them prosperous, and if they have not succeeded, it has not been their fault, for there is not one of them who does not honorably seize all that he can get, and strip and plunder those who cultivate the ground for the good of the state.

ANDRÉ DESTOUCHES: Bravo! And is not your jurisprudence as perfect as the rest of your administration?

CROUTEF: It is much superior. We have no laws, but we have five or six thousand volumes on the laws. We are governed in general by customs; for it is known that a custom, having been established by chance, is the wisest principle that can be imagined. Besides, all customs being necessarily different in different provinces, like clothes and hair styles, the judges may choose at their pleasure a custom which prevailed four hundred years ago or one which prevailed last year. It is a variety of legislation which our neighbors are forever admiring. It is a sure fortune to practitioners, a resource for all pleaders who are destitute of honor, and an infinite amusement for the judges, who can, with safe consciences, decide cases without understanding them.

ANDRÉ DESTOUCHES: But in criminal cases at least, you have laws which may be depended upon?

CROUTEF: God forbid! We condemn men to exile, to the galleys, to be hanged; or we can discharge them, according to our whim. We sometimes complain of the arbitrary power of the prime minister, but we want all our judgments to be arbitrary.

ANDRÉ DESTOUCHES: That is just. And the torture, do you put people to the torture?

CROUTEF: It is our greatest pleasure. We have found it an infallible secret to save a guilty person, who has vigorous muscles, strong and supple legs, nervous arms, and firm loins, and we gaily break on the wheel all those innocent persons to whom nature has given weak organs. It is thus we conduct ourselves with wonderful wisdom and prudence. As there are half proofs, I mean half truths, it is clear there are persons who are half innocent and half guilty. We begin, then, by making them half dead; we then go to lunch; afterwards comes whole death, which gives us great consideration in the world, which is one of the most valuable advantages of our offices.

ANDRÉ DESTOUCHES: It must be allowed that nothing can be more prudent and humane. Pray tell me what becomes of the property of the condemned?

CROUTEF: The children are deprived of it. For you know that nothing can be more equitable than to punish all the descendants for a single fault of a parent.

ANDRÉ DESTOUCHES: Yes. It is a great while since I have heard of this jurisprudence.

CROUTEF: The people of Laos, our neighbors, admit neither torture, nor arbitrary punishments, nor different customs, nor the horrible deaths which are in use among us; but we regard them as barbarians who have no idea of good government. All Asia is agreed that we dance much better than they do, and that, consequently, it is impossible they should come near us in jurisprudence, in commerce, in finance, and, above all, in the military art.

ANDRÉ DESTOUCHES: Tell me, I beseech you, by what steps men arrive at the magistracy in Siam.

CROUTEF: By ready money. You can see that it would be impossible to be a good judge if a man did not have with him thirty or forty thousand pieces of silver. It is in vain a man may be perfectly acquainted with all our customs; it is to no purpose that he has pleaded five hundred cases with success—that he has a mind filled with rightness, and a heart replete with justice; no man can become a magistrate without money. This, I say, is what distinguishes us from all the peoples of Asia, and particularly from the barbarous inhabitants of Laos, who have the madness to reward all kinds of talents, and not to sell any employment.

André Destouches, who was a little absent-minded, like all musicians, said to the Siamese that most of the airs which he had just sung sounded a little discordant to him, and he wished to be informed about real Siamese music. But Croutef, full of his subject, and enthusiastic about his country, continued in these words:

"What does it matter that our neighbors, who live beyond our mountains, have better music than we have, or better pictures, provided that we always have wise and humane laws? It is in that area that we excel. For example, there are a thousand instances in which, when a woman gives birth to a dead baby, we correct the loss of the child by hanging the mother, so that henceforth she is clearly unable to have a miscarriage.

"If a man has adroitly stolen three or four hundred thousand pieces of gold we respect him, and we go and dine with him. But if a poor servant clumsily takes three or four pieces of copper out of his mistress' box we never fail of putting that servant to death in the public square: first, lest he should not correct himself; secondly, that he may not have it in his power to produce a great number of children for the state, one or two of whom might possibly steal a few little pieces of copper, or become great men; thirdly, because it is just to fit the punishment to the crime, and it would be ridiculous to give any useful employment in prison to a person guilty of so enormous a crime.

"But we are still more just, more merciful, more reasonable in the chastisements which we inflict on those who have the audacity to make use of their legs to go wherever they choose. We treat those warriors so well who sell us their lives, we give them so prodigious a salary, they have so considerable a part in our conquests, that they must be the most criminal of all men to wish to return to their parents on the recovery of their reason because they had enlisted in a state of intoxication. To make them stay in one place, we fire about a dozen lead balls in their heads, after which they become infinitely useful to their country.

"I will not speak of a great number of excellent institutions which do not go so far as to shed the blood of men, but which make life so pleasant and agreeable that it is impossible the guilty should avoid becoming good men. If a farmer has not been able to pay promptly a tax which exceeds his ability to pay, we sell the pot in which he cooks his food; we sell his bed in order that, being relieved of all his superfluities, he may be in a better condition to cultivate the earth."

ANDRÉ DESTOUCHES: That is extremely harmonious! A beautiful concert.

CROUTEF: To comprehend our profound wisdom you must know that our fundamental principle is to acknowledge in many places as our sovereign a shaven-headed foreigner who lives at the distance of nine hundred miles from us. When we give some of our best lands to any of our priests, which it is very prudent for us to do, that Siamese priest must pay the revenue of his first year to that shaven-headed Tartar, without which it is clear that we would have no harvest.

But the time, the happy time, is no more when that tonsured priest induced one-half of the nation to cut the throats of the other half in order to decide whether Sammonocodom had played at leap-frog or at some other game; whether he had been disguised as an elephant or as a cow; if he had slept three hundred and ninety days on the right side or on the left. Those great questions, which so essentially affect morality, agitated all minds; they shook the world; blood flowed over them; women were massacred on the bodies of their husbands; they smashed their little infants on the stones with a devotion, a grace, a contrition truly angelic. Woe to us! degenerate offspring of pious ancestors, who no longer offer such holy sacrifices! But, heaven be praised, there are yet among us at least a few good souls who would imitate them if they were permitted.

ANDRÉ DESTOUCHES: Tell me, I beseech you, sir, if in Siam you divide the major tone into two commas, or into two semi-commas, and if the progress of the fundamental sounds are made by one, three, and nine?

CROUTEF: By Sammonocodom, you are laughing at me. You have no manners. You have questioned me on the form of our government, and you talk to me about music!

ANDRÉ DESTOUCHES: Music has to do with everything. It was the foundation of all the politics of the Greeks. But I beg your pardon; you have not a good ear, and we will return to our subject. You said that in order to produce a perfect harmony—

CROUTEF: I was telling you that formerly the tonsured Tartar pretended to dispose of all the kingdoms of Asia, which occasioned something very different from perfect harmony. But a great good resulted from it; for people were then more devout toward Sammonocodom and his elephant than they are now, for, at the present time, every one pretends to common sense with an indiscretion truly pitiable. However, things go on; people amuse themselves, they dance, they play, they dine, they eat, they make love; this makes every man shudder who has good intentions.

ANDRÉ DESTOUCHES: And what more do you war t? All you need is good music. When you have that, you can boldly call yourself the happiest nation on earth.

DIALOGUES BETWEEN A, B AND C[62]

Eighth Conversation: OF BODILY SERFS

B: It seems to me that Europe today is like a great fair. In it we can find everything that is considered necessary for life. There are the civil guards to watch over the safety of the shops; there are sharpers who win the money of fools at dice; good-for-nothings who ask for alms; and marionettes in the market square.

A: All that, as you can see, is a matter of convention; and these conventions of the fair are based on man's needs, on his nature, on the development of his intelligence, on the first cause that animates the operation of second causes. I am convinced that the same is true in a republic of ants: we always see them in action without being quite sure of what they are doing; they seem to be running around at random, and they probably think the same of us; they have their fair as we have ours. As for myself, I am not altogether discontented with my shop.

C: Among the conventions which displease me in this great world fair, there are particularly two which arouse my anger: the fact that slaves are sold there, and the existence of quack charlatans who are paid much too much. Montesquieu pleased me no end in his chapter on Negroes. He is quite comical; he triumphs while making fun of our injustice.

A: It is quite true that we do not have the natural right to seize and tie up a citizen of Angola in order to take him away to work under the lash of whip-cords at our sugar mills in the Barbadoes, quite unlike the natural right we have to lead to the chase a hunting dog we have fed; but we have the right of convention. Why is this Negro sold? Or why does he let himself be sold? I have purchased him, he belongs to me; what wrong do I do him? He works like a horse, I feed him badly, I clothe him in the same way, he is beaten when he disobeys; is there anything here to get excited about? Do we treat our soldiers any better? Haven't they completely lost their freedom, like the Negro? The only difference between the Negro and the soldier is that the soldier costs a good deal less. A handsome Negro comes at the present time to at least 500 gold pieces, and a good soldier will cost barely 50. Neither the one nor the other can leave the place in which he is confined; either one is beaten for the slightest fault. Their salaries are just about the same; and the Negro has the advantage over the soldier of in no way risking his life and of being accompanied by his Negress and little Negroes.

B: Do you believe that a man can sell his liberty, which has no price?

A: Everything has its price. Too bad for him if he sells me cheaply something so precious. You can say that he is an imbecile, but do not say that I am a rogue.

C: It seems to me that Grotius highly approves of slavery. He even finds the condition of a slave much more advantageous than of a workingman, not always sure of his daily bread.

B: But Montesquieu considers servitude as a kind of sin against nature. Here we have a free Dutch citizen who wants slaves, and a Frenchman who will have nothing to do with them; he does not even believe in the right to make slaves in war.

A: And what other right could there be in war than that of the stronger? Suppose that I am in America engaged in a battle with the Spaniards. A Spaniard wounds me, and I am about to kill him; he says to me, "Good Englishman, do not kill me, and I will serve you." I accept the proposition, I do him this favor, and I feed him onions and garlic; every evening he reads *Don Quixote* to me at my bedside: what harm is there in that, if you please? If I give myself up to a Spaniard on the same conditions, how can I reproach him? As the Emperor Justinian says, there is nothing in a bargain but what men put into it.

Does not Montesquieu himself admit that there are peoples

of Europe among whom it is very common for a man to sell himself, for example, the Russians?

B: It is true that he says so and that he quotes from Captain Jean Perry's *Present State of Russia*; but he quotes rather casually. Jean Perry says exactly the opposite. Here are his own words: "The Czar has ordered that no one in the future call himself his slave, his *golup*, but only *raab*, which means subject. It is true that the people gain no real advantage from this, for they are still slaves to this day."

As a matter of fact, all the farmers and all the inhabitants of lands belonging to the nobles or the priests are slaves. If the Russian Empress began to create free men, she would thereby make her name immortal.

Besides, to the shame of humanity, the farmers, artisans and bourgeois who are not citizens of large cities are still slaves, land serfs, in Poland, Bohemia, Hungary, in many provinces in Germany, in most of the Franche-Comté, in a fourth part of Burgundy; and what is altogether contradictory is that they are the slaves of priests. There are some bishops who have little beside land serfs of mortmain in their territory: this is humanity, this is Christian charity. As for slaves taken in war, we can see that the religious knights of Malta have only slaves from Turkey or the African coast enchained to the oars of their Christian galleys.

A: By the Lord, if bishops and churchmen have slaves, I want to have them too.

B: It would be better that no one should have them.

C: This will happen without fail when the perpetual peace of the Abbé de Saint-Pierre will be ratified by the Great Turk and all the powers, and when the city of arbitration will be built along side of the hole that is to pierce the center of the earth, so that men may know exactly how they should behave on its surface.

Ninth Conversation: OF SPIRITUAL SERFS

B: If you permit physical slavery, at least you will not permit spiritual slavery?

A: Let us please understand one another. In no way do I

admit physical slavery as a principle of society. I only say that it is better for a man who has been conquered to be a slave than to be killed, should he love life more than liberty.

I say that the Negro who sells himself is mad, and that the father who sells his Negro child is savage, but I am much too sensitive a man to buy this Negro and make him work at my sugar mill. My interest is in his well-being, so that he may work. I will be humane toward him and I will not expect more gratitude from him than from my horse, to whom I am obliged to give oats if I want him to serve me. I am with my horse very much the same as God is with man. If God has made man to live for a few moments in the stable of the earth, he has to obtain food for him: for it would be absurd for God to have endowed man with hunger and a stomach, and have forgotten to feed him.

c: And what if your slave is useless to you?

a: I would give him his freedom without reservations, even if he should become a monk.

b: But spiritual slavery, what about that?

a: What do you mean by spiritual slavery?

b: I mean the way used to bend the spirit of our children, just as women in the Carribean knead their infants' heads; to begin by teaching them to stammer nonsense that we ourselves make fun of; to make them believe stupidities as soon as they are able to believe anything at all; to take all possible care in this way to make a nation idiotic, weak, and barbarous; and finally, to institute laws that prevent men from writing, speaking and even thinking, just as Arnolphe in Molière's comedy insists that there be no writing table in his home except for him, and wants to make a ninny out of Agnès in order to enjoy her.

a: If there were ever laws like this in England, I would either lead a good conspiracy designed to abolish them, or else I would flee my island forever after having first set it on fire.

c: Yet it is good that every one does not say what he thinks. A man should not insult either in writing or in speech the powers and laws to whose protection he owes his fortune, his freedom, and all the pleasures of life.

a: No, to be sure, and we should punish bold seditious men,

but just because men might abuse writing, should they be forbidden its use? It would be just the same as making you deaf to prevent you from hearing bad arguments. Men rob in the street; should we for that reason prevent people from walking around? Men say stupid and harmful things; must we forbid speaking? In our country any one can write what he thinks, at his risk and peril; it is the only way for a man to speak to his country. If it is found that you have spoken foolishly, the nation will hiss you; if seditiously, it will punish you; if wisely and nobly, it will love and reward you. The liberty of addressing men with the pen is established in England as it is in Poland; it is so established in the low countries, and in Sweden in imitation of our practice. It should be so established in Switzerland, for otherwise Switzerland is not worthy of freedom. There is no liberty among men unless there is the freedom of expressing thought.

c: And if you were born in modern Rome?

a: I would have erected an altar to Cicero and to Tacitus, men of ancient Rome; I would have mounted this altar and with the hat of Brutus on my head and his dagger in my hand, I would have recalled the people to the natural rights they have lost; I would have re-established the tribunal as did Nicholas Rienzi.

c: And you would have ended like him.

a: Perhaps; but I can not express to you the horror aroused in me by the slavery of the Romans during my last visit; I trembled in seeing monks at the capital. Four of my friends have outfitted a ship in order to seek out the useless ruins of Palmyra and Balbec; I have been tempted a hundred times to arm a dozen ships at my expense to reduce to ruins the improvements of the inquisitors in countries where man is enslaved by these monsters. My hero is Admiral Blake. Sent by Cromwell to sign a treaty with Jean de Bragance, King of Portugal, this prince excused himself from concluding the treaty because the grand inquisitor would not allow any dealings with heretics. "Leave it to me," said Blake; "he will come aboard my ship to sign the treaty." This monk had his palace on the Tagus, opposite our fleet. The Admiral fired a broadside of cannon balls at it; the inquisitor came to beg his pardon, and signed the treaty on his knees. In this matter the Admiral did only half of what he should have done; he should have forbidden any inquisitor from tyrannizing over souls and burning bodies, just as the Persians, and after them the Greeks and Romans forbade the Africans from human sacrifice.

B: You speak like a true Englishman.

A: Like a man, and like every man would speak if he dared. Shall I tell you what is the greatest weakness of the human race?

C: It would be a pleasure; I love to know my kind.

A: This weakness is to be stupid and cowardly.

C: Yet every nation shows courage in war.

A: Yes, like horses that tremble at the first beat of the drum, and who advance proudly when they are disciplined by a hundred drumbeats and a hundred whip-lashes.

A servant of Louis XV told me that while his master, the king, was dining one day at Trianon with a small group, the conversation turned first on hunting and then on gun powder. Someone said that the best powder is made with equal parts of saltpeter, sulphur and coal. The Duke de La Vallière, who knew better, argued that to make a good gun powder all you needed was one part of sulphur and one of coal to five parts of saltpeter that had been well filtered, well evaporated, and well crystallized.

"It is funny," said the Duke de Nivernois, "that we amuse ourselves daily by killing partridges in the park at Versailles, and sometimes by killing men or by being killed ourselves at the frontier, without knowing exactly with what we kill."

"Alas! We are reduced to that state for most things of this world," answered Madame de Pompadour; "I do not know what the rouge I put on my cheeks is made of, and I should be very much embarrassed if someone asked me how the silk hose I am wearing is made."

"It is a pity," the Duke de La Vallière then said, "that His Majesty confiscated our encyclopedic dictionaries, each of which cost us a hundred gold pieces: there we would quickly find the answer to all our questions."

The king justified the confiscation: he had been warned that the twenty-one folio volumes that were found on all the ladies' dressing tables were the most dangerous thing in the world for the French kingdom; and he wanted to know for himself if this were true before allowing anyone to read this work. At the end of the dinner he sent three of his servants for a copy, each of whom returned carrying seven volumes with great difficulty.

They saw at the article "Powder" that the Duke de La Vallière was right; and soon Madame de Pompadour learned the difference between the old Spanish rouge that the ladies of Madrid used to color their cheeks, and the rouge of Parisian ladies. She learned that Greek and Roman ladies were painted with purple that came from seashells, and that consequently our scarlet was the purple of the ancients; she learned that there was more saffron in Spanish rouge, and more cochineal in the French.

She saw how her stockings were manufactured; and the operation of this process delighted her with wonder. "Oh, the fine book!" she exclaimed. "Sire, did you confiscate this storehouse of useful things so as to possess it alone and be the only wise man of your kingdom?"

They all jumped at the volumes like the daughters of Lycomedes at Ulysses' jewels; every one found at once what he was looking for. Those who had lawsuits were surprised to find there the judgment of their cases. The king read all the rights of the crown. "But really," he said, "I don't know why I was told so many bad things about this work."

"Well, don't you see, Sire," said the Duke de Nivernois, "it's because it is very good? Men do not attack the mediocre and the dull of whatever sort. If women try to ridicule a newcomer, it is certain that she is prettier than they."

All the while the others kept leafing through the pages, and the Count de C . . . said aloud: "Sire, you are too fortunate that there should be under your reign men capable of knowing all the arts and of transmitting them to posterity. Everything is here, from how to make a pin to how to make and direct your canons; from the infinitely small to the infinitely great. Thank God for having made men born in your kingdom who have thus served the entire universe. Other nations must either buy the *Encyclopedia* or copy it. Take all my property if you like; but give me back my *Encyclopedia*."

"Yet they say," replied the king, "that there are many faults in this so necessary and so admirable work."

"Sire," rejoined the Count de C . . . , "there were two spoiled sauces at your dinner; we did not eat them, and we ate very well. Would you like to have the whole dinner thrown out the window because of these two sauces?"

The king felt the strength of reason; every one recovered his property: it was a happy day.

Envy and ignorance did not hold themselves beaten; these two immortal sisters continued their outcries, their schemes, their persecutions: ignorance is very learned in these matters.

What happened? Foreigners brought out four editions of this French work, banned in France, and made about eighteen hundred thousand gold pieces.

Frenchmen, try henceforth to understand your interests better.

DIALOGUES OF EVHÉMÈRE [64]

First Dialogue: ON ALEXANDER

CALLICRATUS: Well, wise Evhémère, what have you seen or your travels?

EVHÉMÈRE: Stupidities.

CALLICRATUS: What! You have followed the route of Alexander the Great and you are not ecstatic with admiration.

EVHÉMÈRE: You mean with pity?

CALLICRATUS: Pity for Alexander!

EVHÉMÈRE: For who else, then? I saw him only in India and in Babylon, where I hurried, like the others, in the vain hope of instructing myself. I was told that in fact, he had begun his campaigns like a hero, but he finished them like a madman: I saw this demigod, who has become the cruelest of savages after having been the most humane of the Greeks. I saw the sober disciple of Aristotle changed into a miserable drunkard. I was quite close to him when, on leaving the dinner table, he decided to put the superb temple of Esthekar to the fire, to please the whim of a wretched prostitute named Thaïs. I followed him in his madness in India; finally I saw him die in the flower of his age at Babylon, having gotten as dead drunk as the lowest of the wretches in his army.

CALLICRATUS: There is a great man who is really very little!

EVHÉMÈRE: There is no other kind; they are just like the magnet whose properties I discovered: on one side they attract and on the other they repel.

CALLICRATUS: Alexander repels me furiously when in his drunkenness he burns a city I do not know this Esthekar you

mentioned; I know only that this extravagant man and crazy
Thaïs had burned Persepolis for their amusement.

EVHÉMÈRE: Esthekar is exactly what the Greeks call Persepolis.
Our Greeks like to dress the whole universe in the Greek fashion. They have given the Zom-Bodpo River the name of Indos;
they have called another river Hydaspe; none of the cities besieged and taken by Alexander is known by its real name; even
that of India is their invention: the oriental nations called it
Odhu. It is in this way that in Egypt they made the cities of
Heliopolis, Crocodilopolis, and Memphis. As long as they find a
sonorous phrase, they are happy. In this way they have deceived
the whole world, by naming gods and men.

CALLICRATUS: There is no great harm in that. I do not complain about those who have deceived the world in this way; I
complain about those who destroy it. I have no use for your
Alexander, who goes from Greece to Seleucia to Egypt to the
Caucasus and thence to the Ganges, always killing those he
meets, whether they are enemies, friends, or indifferent to him.

EVHÉMÈRE: It is only a matter of give and take. If he went to
kill the Persians, the Persians had apparently come to kill the
Greeks; if he hastened to the Caucasus, to the vast spaces inhabited by the Scythians, these Scythians had twice ravaged Greece
and all Asia. Every nation has at one time or another robbed,
imprisoned, and exterminated one another. Who says *soldier* says
thief. Every country robs its neighbors in the name of its god.
Do we not today see our neighbors, the Romans, desert their
seven hills to rob the Volscians, the Antiates, the Samnites?
Soon they will come to pillage us, if they can manage to make
ships. As soon as they know that their neighbor, Etruria, has a
little wheat and barley stored away, they will have the priests
of Jupiter declare that it is just to go and rob the Etrurians. This
robbery becomes a holy war. They have oracles that command
murder and rapine. The Etrurians also have their oracles that
promise them they will steal the Romans' straw. Today Alexander's successors steal for themselves the provinces they had stolen
for their master-thief. Such has been, such is, and such always
will be the human species. I have travelled over half the world
and I have seen nothing but follies, misfortunes and crimes.

CALLICRATUS: May I ask you if among so many peoples you have found one that is just?

EVHÉMÈRE: Not one.

CALLICRATUS: Tell me then, which is the most stupid and the meanest?

EVHÉMÈRE: The most superstitious.

CALLICRATUS: Why is the most superstitious the meanest?

EVHÉMÈRE: It is because superstition makes men do out of duty what others do either by habit or in a fit of madness. An ordinary savage, such as a Greek, a Roman, a Scythian, a Persian, when he has killed and robbed to his heart's content, drunk all the wine of those he has just killed and raped all the daughters of the fathers he has massacred, having need of nothing else, becomes peaceful and humane by way of relaxation. He hears the pity which nature has placed in the depths of the human heart. He is like the lion who leaves off the pursuit of his prey when he is no longer hungry; but the superstitious man is like the tiger who kills and rends, even when he is sated. The worshipper of Pluto said to him: "Slaughter all the adorers of Mercury, burn all their homes, kill all their cattle." My holy man would deem it a sacrilege if he left alive a single child or cat in the land of Mercury.

CALLICRATUS: What! Are there people so abominable on the face of the earth and Alexander did not exterminate them instead of journeying to the Ganges to attack peaceful and humane men who, from what I've been told, were the inventors of philosophy?

EVHÉMÈRE: Not really; he passed like a flash of lightning through the tiny lands of the barbarous fanatics I have just spoken about; and as fanaticism does not exclude meanness and cowardice, these wretches craved his pardon, flattered him, gave him a part of the gold they had stolen, and gained his permission to steal even more.

CALLICRATUS: The human race is then a very horrible species?

EVHÉMÈRE: There are a few sheep among the great number of these animals; but most of them are wolves and foxes.

CALLICRATUS: I should like to know why there is this enormous difference within the same species.

EVHÉMÈRE: They say that it is because the foxes and wolves eat the lambs.

CALLICRATUS: No, this world is too miserable and too dreadful; I want to know why there are so many calamities and so much stupidity.

EVHÉMÈRE: So do I. It has been a long time since I dreamed about cultivating my garden in Syracuse.

CALLICRATUS: Well, what have you dreamed about? Tell me, please, in just a few words, if this earth was always inhabited by men; if the earth itself always existed; if we have a soul; if this soul is eternal, as is said of matter; if there is one god or several; what they do and what they are good for. What is virtue? What is order and disorder? What is nature? Has she laws? Who made them? Who invented society and the arts? What is the best government? And especially, what is the best way to escape the perils that surround every man at every moment? We will take up the other problems another time.

EVHÉMÈRE: You have enough there for at least ten years, talking ten hours a day.

CALLICRATUS: Yet all of this was discussed yesterday at the home of beautiful Eudoxia by the most agreeable men of Syracuse.

EVHÉMÈRE: Very well, and what was concluded?

CALLICRATUS: Nothing. There were two worshippers by sacrifice, one of Ceres and the other of Juno, who finally came to insults. Come now, tell me without hesitation what you think. I promise not to beat you, and certainly not to denounce you to the worshipper of Ceres.

EVHÉMÈRE: Good. Come and question me tomorrow: I will try to answer you; but I do not promise to satisfy you.

LETTERS

LETTERS

To CATHERINE OLYMPE DUNOYER [65]

November 28, 1713

I am here as the King's prisoner. They may rob me of my life, but not of my love for you. Yes, my adorable mistress, I will see you to-night, though it bring my head to the block. For God's sake, do not write to me in so sombre a vein: live, and be cautious: beware of your mother as your most dangerous enemy: beware of everyone, trust nobody: be ready when the moon rises; I shall leave this house incognito, shall take a coach or a chaise, and we will fly like the wind to Scheveningen. I will bring ink and paper, and we will write the necessary letters. But if you love me, take heart: summon all your resolution and coolness: keep strict watch on yourself in your mother's presence: try to get hold of your portrait; and be sure that the threat of the greatest punishments will not keep me from serving you. No, nothing is capable of detaching me from you. Our love is founded on virtue and will last as long as our life. You had better tell the shoemaker to order a chaise—no, on second thought I had rather you did not trust him. Be ready at four o'clock. I will wait for you near your street. Goodbye: all I risk for you is nothing: you are worth infinitely more. Goodbye, my dear heart.

To CATHERINE OLYMPE DUNOYER

This Wednesday evening, December 13, 1713

I only heard yesterday, my dear, that you were ill—as a result of all the worry I have given you. Alas! that I should be at once the cause of your sufferings and powerless to relieve them! I have never felt so keen a grief—and I have never so thoroughly deserved one: I do not know what is the matter with you: everything adds to my fears: you love me, and do not write to me —I know from that you must be really ill. What a melancholy position for two lovers to be in!—one in bed, the other a prisoner. I can offer you nothing but wishes, while waiting for your recovery and my freedom. I should implore you to get better, if you had it in your power to do me that favor: but at least you can take care of yourself, and that is the greatest pleasure you can give me. I believe I have begged you in every letter I have ever written to you to take care of your health which is so dear to me. I could bear all my own misfortunes joyfully if you could get the better of yours. My departure is again postponed. M. de M., who has just come into my room, forbids me to go on writing. Goodbye, my dear mistress, goodbye, my dear heart! May you be as happy for ever as I am miserable now! Goodbye, my dear; try to write to me.

To CATHERINE OLYMPE DUNOYER

Paris, February 10, 1714

My dear . . . , every time you miss writing to me makes me imagine that you have not received my letters, for I cannot believe that absence can have an effect on you which it never can have on me, and as I love you for ever, I am persuaded that you still love me. Tell me two things: first, if you have received my last two letters, and if I am still in your heart. Be sure to say if you have received my last letter which I wrote on January 23rd, in which I was rash enough to mention by name the Bishop of Evreux and other persons: tell me something definite in your reply to this letter; above all, I implore you to let me know how you are and how things go with you: address your letter to M. le Chevalier de Saint-Fort, at M. Alain's near the Place Maubert. Write me a longer letter than this one. It will always give me more pleasure to read one of your four page letters than you take in reading two lines of mine.

To MY LORD THE DUKE OF ORLEANS, REGENT [66]

1718

My Lord, will it be necessary for the poor Voltaire to have any other obligations to you than that of having been corrected by a year in the Bastille? He flattered himself that, after having put him in purgatory, you would remember him at the time when you are opening paradise to everyone. He takes the liberty of asking three favors of you: the first, to grant him the honor of dedicating to you the tragedy that he has just written; the second, to deign one day to hear parts of an epic poem concerning that ancestor of yours whom you most resemble; and the third, to realize that I have the honor of writing you a letter where the word subscription does not appear at all.

I am with profound respect, my Lord, of your Royal Highness, the very humble and very poor secretary of trifles.

To THE MINISTER OF THE DEPARTMENT OF PARIS [67]

April, 1726

M. de Voltaire ventures very humbly to point out that he has been assaulted by the brave Chevalier de Rohan, assisted by six cut-throats, behind whom he courageously stationed himself, and that ever since he has constantly endeavored to repair not his own honor, but that of the Chevalier, which has proved too difficult. If he came from Versailles, it is completely false that he went to ask for the Chevalier de Rohan-Chabot at the house of the Cardinal de Rohan.

It is very easy to prove the contrary, and he consents to remain in the Bastille his whole life if he is lying. He requests permission to eat at the table of the governor of the Bastille and to see his friends. He requests, with still more insistence, permission to go at once to England. If there is any doubt of his departure, a guard can be sent with him as far as Calais.

To M. THIERIOT [68]

October 26, 1726

I intend to send you two or three poems of Mr. Pope, the best poet of England, and at present of all the world. I hope you are acquainted enough with the English tongue to be sensible of all the charms of his works. For my part I look on his poem call'd the *Essay upon criticism* as superior to the *Art of poetry* of Horace; and his *Rape of the lock*, la boucle de cheveux (that is a comical one), is in my opinion above the *Lutrin* of Despreaux; I never saw so amiable an imagination, so gentle graces, so great variety, so much wit, and so refined knowledge of the world as in this little performance.

Now, my dear Tiriot, after having fully answered to what you asked about English books, let me acquaint you with an account of my for ever cursed fortune. I came again into England in the latter end of July very much dissastified with my secret voyage into France both unsuccesful and expensive. I had about me only some bills of exchange upon a Jew called Medina for the sum of about eight or nine thousand French livres reckoning all. At my coming to London, I found my damned Jew was broken; I was without a penny, sick to death of a violent ague, a stranger, alone, helpless, in the midst of a city wherein I was known to no body; my Lord and my Lady Bolingbroke were in the country; I could not make bold to see our ambassadour in so wretched a condition. I had never undergone such distress; but I am born to run through all the misfortunes of life. In these circumstances my star, that among all its direful influence spours allways on me some kind refreshment, sent to me an English gentleman unknown to me, who forced me to receive some money that I wanted. Another London citizen[69] that I had seen but once at Paris, carried me to his own country house, wherein I lead an obscure and charming life since that time, without going to London, and quite given over to the pleasures of indolence and of friendship. The true and generous affection of this man who sooths the bitterness of my life brings me to love you more and more. All the instances of friendship endear my friend Tiriot to me. I have seen often mylord and mylady Bolingbroke; I have found their affection still the same, even increased in proportion to my unhappiness; they offered me all, their money, their house; but I refused all, because they are lords, and I have accepted all from Mr. Falkener, because he is a single gentleman.

I had a mind at first to print our poor *Henry* at my own expenses in London, but the loss of my money is a sad stop to my design: I question if I shall try the way of subscriptions by the favour of the court, I am weary of courts, my Tiriot; all that is king, or belongs to a king, frights my republican philosophy, I won't drink the least draught of slavery in the land of liberty.

I have written freely to the abbot Desfontaines, it is true, and I will always do so, having no reason to lay myself under any restraint. I fear, I hope nothing from your country. All that I wish for, is to see you one day in London. I am entertaining myself with this pleasant hope; if it is but a dream, let me enjoy it, don't undeceive me, let me believe I shall have the pleasure to see you in London, [drawing] up the strong spirit of this unaccountable nation; you will translate their thoughts better when you live among them. You will see a nation fond of their liberty, learned, witty, despising life and death, a nation of philosophers; not but that there are some fools in England, every country has its madmen; it may be French folly is pleasanter than English madness, but by God English wisdom and English honesty is above yours. One day I will acquaint you with the character of this strange people, but t'is time to put an end to my English talkativeness. I fear you will take this long epistle for one of those tedious English books that I have advised you not to translate. Before I make up my letter, I must acquaint you with the reason of receiving yours so late; t'is the fault of my correspondent at Calais, master Dunoquet. So you must write to me afterwards at my lord Bolingbroke's house, London. This way is shorter and surer. Tell all who write to me that they ought to make use of this superscription.

I have written so much about the death of my sister to those who had writ to me on this account that I had almost forgotten to speak to you of her. I have nothing to tell you on that accident but that you know my heart and my way of thinking. I have wept for her death, and I would be with her. Life is but a dream full of starts of folly and of fancied and true miseries. Death awakes us from this painful dream, and gives us either a better existence or no existence at all. Farewell. Write often to me. Depend upon my exactness in answering you when I shall be fixed in London.

Write me some lines in English to show your improvement in your learning.

To A FIRST COMMISSIONER [70]

June 20, 1733

As you have it in your power, sir, to do some service to letters, I implore you not to clip the wings of our writers so closely, nor to turn into barn-door fowls those who, allowed a start, might become eagles; reasonable liberty permits the mind to soar—slavery makes it creep. Had there been a literary censorship in Rome, we should have had to-day neither Horace, Juvenal, nor the philosophical works of Cicero. If Milton, Dryden, Pope, and Locke had not been free, England would have had neither poets nor philosophers; there is something positively Turkish in proscribing printing; and hampering it *is* proscription. Be content with severely repressing defamatory libels, for they are crimes: but so long as those infamous *Calottes* are boldly published, and so many other unworthy and despicable productions, at least allow Bayle to circulate in France, and do not put him, who has been so great an honor to his country, among its contraband.

You say that the magistrates who regulate the literary customhouse complain that there are too many books. That is just the same thing as if the provost of merchants complained there were too many provisions in Paris. People buy what they choose. A great library is like the City of Paris, in which there are about eight hundred thousand persons: you do not live with the whole crowd: you choose a certain society, and change it. So with books: you choose a few friends out of the many. There will be seven or eight thousand controversial books, and fifteen or sixteen thousand novels, which you will not read: a heap of pamphlets, which you will throw into the fire after you have read them. The man of taste will only read what is good; but the statesman will permit both bad and good.

Men's thoughts have become an important article of commerce. The Dutch publishers make a million a year, because Frenchmen have brains. A feeble novel is, I know, among books what a fool, always striving after wit, is in the world. We laugh at him and tolerate him. Such a novel brings the means of life to the author who wrote it, to the publisher who sells it, to the moulder, the printer, the paper-maker, the binder, the carrier—and finally to the bad wine-shop where they all take their money. Further, the book amuses for an hour or two a few women who like novelty in literature as in everything. Thus, despicable though it may be, it will have produced two important things—profit and pleasure.

The theatre also deserves attention. I do not consider it a counter attraction to dissipation: that is a notion only worthy of an ignorant curé. There is quite time enough, before and after the performance, for the few minutes given to those passing pleasures which are so soon followed by disgust. Besides, people do not go to the theatre every day, and among our vast population there are not more than four thousand who are in the habit of going constantly.

I look on tragedy and comedy as lessons in virtue, good sense, and good behavior. Corneille—the old Roman of the French—has founded a school of Spartan virtue: Molière, a school of ordinary everyday life. These great national geniuses attract foreigners from all parts of Europe, who come to study among us, and thus contribute to the wealth of Paris. Our poor are fed by the production of such works, which bring under our rule the very nations who hate us. In fact, he who condemns the theatre is an enemy to his country. A magistrate who, because he has succeeded in buying some judicial post, thinks that it is beneath his dignity to see *Cinna*, shows much pomposity and very little taste.

There are still Goths and Vandals even among our cultivated people: the only Frenchmen I consider worthy of the name are those who love and encourage the arts. It is true that the taste for them is languishing: we are sybarites, weary of our mistresses' favors. We enjoy the fruits of the labors of the great men who have worked for our pleasure and that of the ages to come, just as we receive the fruits of nature as if they were our due. We have been eating acorns only for a century; the kings who taught us how to grow the purest wheat are indifferent to us. Nothing will rouse us from this nonchalance to great things which always goes side by side with our vivid interest in small.

Every year we take more pains over snuffboxes and nicknacks than the English took to make themselves masters of the seas, to make water rise by means of fire, and to calculate the aberration of light. The old Romans raised those marvels of architecture —their amphitheatres—for beasts to fight in: and for a whole century we have not built a single passable place for the representation of the masterpieces of the human mind. A hundredth part of the money spent on cards would be enough to build theatres finer than Pompey's: but what man in Paris has the public welfare at heart? We play, sup, talk scandal, write bad verses, and sleep, like fools, to recommence on the morrow the same round of careless frivolity. You, sir, who have at least some small opportunity of giving good advice, try and rouse us from this stupid lethargy, and, if you can, do something for literature, which has done so much for France.

To M. JACOB VERNET, AT GENEVA[71]

Paris, September 14, 1733

Your conversation, sir, made me desire very much to have a steady acquaintance with you. I see with great satisfaction that you are not one of those travelers who visit men of letters in passing by, as one goes to see statues and paintings—to satisfy a passing curiosity. You make me feel all the worth of your correspondence, and I tell you already—without any compliment— that you have found a friend in me: for on what can friendship be founded if not on esteem and on the affinity of tastes and feelings? You seem to me to be a philosopher who thinks freely and speaks wisely; you despise moreover this effeminate style, full of affectation and devoid of matter with which the frivolous authors of our French Academy have weakened our language. You love truth, and the vigorous style which alone belongs to truth. With all that, how can I not love you? It is for the impertinent style with which France is flooded today that there should be no indulgence; for men can be made to have good sense on these little things. But, in religious matters, we have, you and I, tolerance, because one can never make men have good sense on this score. I can accept everything in men provided that they are not persecutors. I would like Calvin if he had not had Servet burned; I would be the servant of the Council of Constance if it had not been for the faggots of John Huss.

The *English Letters* you mention are written in this spirit of liberty which perhaps will bring persecutions upon me in France, but which will win your esteem for me; they still circulate in English only, and I have done all I can to have the French edition supressed. I don't know whether I'll succeed; but consider, sir, the difference which exists between the English and the French: these *Letters* seemed philosophical to the readers of London only, and in Paris people call them impious without having seen them. Anyone who passes for a liberal here, soon passes for an atheist. The bigots and the frivolous minds—the ones, deceivers and the others, deceived—scream impiety at whosoever dares to think humanely, and just because a man has made a jest at the expense of the Quakers, our Catholics conclude that he does not believe in God.

To THE COMTE D'ARGENTAL [72]

May, 1734

Another importunity, another letter. Admit that I am more of a harasser than one harassed. The *lettre de cachet* has provoked me to write a thousand letters.

Nardi parvus onyx eliciet cadum.[73]

I beg of you to have this letter delivered to the Duchesse d'Aiguillon. I am sending it to you opened; have the kindness to see there my justification, and to seal it. A thousand pardons. Truly, since people are screaming so much about those cursed

Letters, I am actually sorry not to have said more about it. Come, come Pascal, leave it to me! You have a chapter on the prophecies where there isn't an ounce of good sense; wait and see!

Where were we, I beg of you? Please, a word concerning this excommunicated one. Will my book be burned, or I? [74] Do they want me to retract, like Saint Augustine? Do they want me to go to the devil? Write either at Demoulin's or at the Abbé Moussinot's, or rather to M. Pallu and tell him to keep all this a deep secret.

To FREDERICK, ROYAL PRINCE OF PRUSSIA

Cirey, October, 1737

My Lord, I have received the last letter with which Your Highness honored me, dated September 20. I am very eager to know if my last package and the one destined for Monsieur de Keyserlingk reached their address; I sent them about the beginning of August.

You bid me, sir, give you an account of my metaphysical doubts. I therefore take the liberty of sending you an extract from a paper *On Liberty.* Your Royal Highness will find it honest, even if ignorant: would to God all the ignorant were as truthful!

Perhaps humanity, the principle of all my thoughts, overpowered me in this work. Perhaps the idea I am always pursuing, that there is neither vice nor virtue: that neither punishment nor reward is necessary: that society would be (especially among philosophers) an interchange of wickedness and hypocrisy if man had not full and absolute liberty—perhaps, I say, this opinion has led me too far in this work. But if you find errors in my judgment, forgive them for the sake of the principle which gave them birth.

I always reduce, so far as I can, my metaphysics to morality. I have honestly sought, with all the attention of which I am capable, to gain some definite idea of the human soul, and I own that the result of all my researches is ignorance. I find a principle—thinking, free, active—almost like God himself: my reason tells me that God exists: but it also tells me that I cannot know what he is. Is it indeed likely that we should know what our soul is when we can form no idea of light if we have had the misfortune to be born blind? I see then, with regret, that all that has been written about the soul teaches us nothing at all.

After my vain groping to discover its nature, my chief aim has been to try at least to regulate it: it is the mainspring of our clock. All Descartes' fine ideas on its elasticity tell me nothing of the nature of the spring: I am ignorant even of the cause of that flexibility: however, I wind up my timepiece, and it goes passably well.

I examine man. We must see if, of whatsoever materials he is composed, there is vice and virtue in them. That is the important point with regard to him—I do not say merely with regard to a certain society living under certain laws: but for the whole human race; for you, sir, who will one day sit on a throne, for the wood-cutter in your forest, for the Chinese doctor, and for the savage of America. Locke, the wisest metaphysician I know, while he very rightly attacks the theory of innate ideas, seems to think that there is no universal moral principle. I venture to doubt, or rather, to elucidate the great man's theory on this point. I agree with him that there is really no such thing as innate thought: whence it obviously follows that there is no principle of morality innate in our souls: but because we are not born with beards, is it just to say that we are not born (we, the inhabitants of this continent) to have beards at a certain age? We are not born able to walk: but everyone, born with two feet, will walk one day. Thus, no one is born with the idea he must be just: but God has so made us that, at a certain age, we all agree to this truth.

It seems clear to me that God designed us to live in society —just as he has given the bees the instincts and the powers to make honey: and as our social system could not subsist without the sense of justice and injustice, he has given us the power to acquire that sense. It is true that varying customs make us attach the idea of justice to different things. What is a crime in Europe will be a virtue in Asia, just as German dishes do not please

French palates: but God has so made Germans and French that they both like good living. All societies, then, will not have the same laws, but no society will be without laws. Therefore, the good of the greatest number is the immutable law of virtue, as established by all men from Peiping to Ireland: what is useful to society will be good for every country. This idea reconciles the contradictions which appear in morality. Robbery was permitted in Lacedæmonia: why? because all goods were held in common, and the man who stole from the greedy, who kept for himself what the law gave to the public, was a social benefactor.

It is said that there are savages who eat men, and believe they do well. I say those savages have the same idea of right and wrong as ourselves. As we do, they make war from anger and passion: the same crimes are committed everywhere: to eat your enemies is but an extra ceremonial. The wrong does not consist in roasting, but in killing them: and I dare swear there is no cannibal who believes that he is doing right when he cuts his enemy's throat. I saw four savages from Louisiana who were brought to France in 1723. There was a woman among them of a very gentle disposition. I asked her, through an interpreter, if she had ever eaten the flesh of her enemies and if she liked it; she answered, Yes. I asked her if she would be willing to kill, or to have killed, any one of her fellow-countrymen in order to eat him: she answered, shuddering, visibly horrified by such a crime. I defy the most determined liar among travelers to dare to tell me that there is a community or a family where to break one's word is laudable. I am deeply rooted in the belief that, God having made certain animals to graze in common, others to come together only very rarely, and spiders to spin webs, each species has the tools necessary for the work it has to do. Man has received all he needs to live in society, just as he has received a stomach in order to digest, eyes in order to see, a soul in order to judge.

Put two men on the globe, and they will only call good, right, just, what will be good for them both. Put four, and they will only consider virtuous what suits them all: and if one of the four eats his neighbor's supper, or fights or kills him, he will

certainly raise the others against him. And what is true of these
four men is true of the universe. Here, my lord, you have the
foundation on which I have written this moral *Metaphysics*; but
as far as virtue is concerned, have I the right to speak of it before you?

> Virtues are the endowment
> You receive from heaven;
> Along side of such gifts
> Your ancestors' throne
> Is weak indeed.
> It is the man in you, the sage
> Who commands me by his law
> Ah! Were you only a king,
> You would not have my praise.

To JEANNE FRANÇOISE QUINAULT [75]

Cirey, August 16, 1738

> Charming Thalia, you want
> To revive and bring today
> My buried Melpomene
> Dark in the somber depths
> Of obscure philosophy.
> I swear to you it is a great effort
> For I feel that I am dead
> And miss life just a little.

You are very much the right person to work miracles; I need
them. I am far from sure that I have not finally abandoned the
dangerous longing to be judged by the public. There comes a
time, my dear Thalia, when the love of repose and the charms
of a quiet life carry all before them. Happy he who knows how
to escape early the seductions of fame, the storms of envy, the
thoughtless judgments of men! I have only too much reason to
repent of having labored for anything except peace. What have
I gained by twenty years' work? Nothing but enemies. That is
almost the only reward to be expected from the cultivation of

letters—contempt if one does not succeed, and hatred if one does. There is something degrading in success itself when we are forced to encourage those Italian mountebanks to turn the serious into ridicule and spoil good writing by buffoonery.

No one is better able than you to form an opinion on the profession you adorn. But is not your noble art just as much decried by bigots and equally looked down upon at Court? Is less contempt poured on a business which requires intelligence, education, talent, than on a study and art which teach only morality, decency, and the virtues?

I have always been indignant for both you and myself that work so difficult and so useful as ours should be repaid by so much ingratitude, but now my indignation has turned to despair. I shall never reform the abuses of the world: I had better give up trying. The public is a ferocious beast: one must chain him up or flee from him. Chains I have none, but I know the secret of retirement. I have found out the blessedness of quiet—which is true happiness. Shall I leave it to be torn to pieces by the Abbé Desfontaines and to be sacrificed by the Italian buffoons to the malignity of the public and the laughter of the rabble? I ought rather to persuade you to leave an ungrateful profession, that you may no more incite me to expose myself on the boards. I must add to all I have just said that I find it impossible to work well in my present state of discouragement. I need to be intoxicated with self-approval and enthusiasm—a wine I have mixed, and now no longer care to drink. Only you still have the power to make me drunk, but though you have a pious zeal to make converts, you will find plenty of more suitable subjects in Paris—younger, bolder, more talented. Seductive Thalia, leave me in peace! I shall love you just as much as if I owed to your energies the success of two plays a year. Do not tempt me: do not fan a flame I would extinguish: do not abuse your power! Your letter very nearly made me think of a plot for a tragedy: a second letter, and I shall be writing verses. Leave me my senses, I entreat you. Alas! I have so few! Goodbye; the little black dogs present their compliments. We call one Zamore and the other Alzire. What names! everything here suggests tragedy.

No one is more tenderly attached to you than I am.

Mme. du Châtelet's kindest regards.[76] Once again, Mademoiselle, count on my tender devotion and my gratitude.

To THE ABBÉ DUBOS [77]

Cirey, October 30, 1738

For a long time already I have been attached to you by the greatest esteem; I am now going to be attached to you out of gratitude. I'll not repeat to you here that your books should be the breviary of men of letters, that you are the most useful and judicious writer that I know; I am so pleased to see that you are the kindest that I am all taken up with this last idea.

I have been assembling material for a long time with the purpose in mind of writing the history of the century of Louis XIV. It is not solely the life of this prince that I am writing, it is not the annals of his reign, it is rather the history of the human mind drawn from the century which is the most glorious to the human mind.

This work is divided into chapters; there are about twenty devoted to a general history: they are twenty tableaux of the great events of the time. The principal figures are in the foreground of the picture; the mob is in the background. Woe to details! posterity neglects them all: they are a vermin which kills great works. What characterizes this century, what caused revolutions, what will be important in a hundred years, that is what I want to write about today.

There is one chapter for the private life of Louis XIV; two for the great changes made in the administration of the kingdom, in commerce, in finances; two for the ecclesiastical government, in which the Revocation of the Edict of Nantes and the business of the Régale are included; five or six for the history of the arts beginning with Descartes and finishing with Rameau.

I have no other memoirs for the general history except for about two hundred volumes of printed memoirs with which everyone is acquainted; it is only a question of forming a well proportioned body out of all these scattered parts, and to paint in true colors, but with a single stroke, what Larrey, Limiers, Lamberti, Roussel, etc., etc., falsified and spun out for volumes.

For the private life of Louis XIV I have the *Memoirs of the Marquis de Dangeau*, in forty volumes, from which I have extracted forty pages; I have what I have heard said to old courtiers, valets, great lords, and others, and I am bringing together the facts with which they are in agreement. I am abandoning the rest to the fabricators of conversations and anecdotes. I have an extract from the famous letter of the King concerning M. de Barbésieux, all of whose faults he mentions and which he forgives on behalf of the services of the father: all which characterizes Louis XIV much better than the flatteries of Pellisson.

I am rather well informed about the *man in the iron mask*, who died in the Bastille. I have spoken to people who served him.

There exists a kind of memorial, written in the hand of Louis XIV, which should be in the study of Louis XV. M. Hardion is undoubtedly acquainted with it; but I do not dare to ask for communication of it.

On the affairs of the Church, I have all the litter of the biased slanders, and I shall attempt to extract an ounce of honey from the wormwood of men such as Jurieu, Quesnel, Doucin, etc.

For the interior of the kingdom I am examining the memoirs of the intendants, and the good books which we have on this subject. The Abbé de Saint-Pierre has written a political journal about Louis XIV which I should like him to entrust to me very much. I do not know if he will perform this act of *benificence* in order to gain paradise.

As for the arts and sciences, it is a question, I believe, only of tracing the advance of the human mind in philosophy, in oratory, in poetry, in criticism; of indicating the progress of painting, of sculpture, of music, of the working in precious metals, of the manufacture of tapestries, of mirrors, of gold cloths, of watches. I only wish to paint, as I go along, the geniuses who have excelled in these domains. May God preserve me from using three hundred pages for the history of Gassendi! Life is too short, time too precious, to say useless things.

In a word, sir, you see my plan much better tnan ɪ could draw it for you. I am in no hurry to erect my structure:

> . . . Pendent opera interrupta, minaeque
> Murorum ingentes. . . .

If you deign to conduct me, I will be able to say then:

> . . . Æquataque machina cœlo[78]

Consider what you can do for me, for truth, for a century which counts you among its embellishments.

To whom will you deign to communicate your knowledge if not to a man who loves his country and truth, and who is endeavoring to write history neither as a flatterer, nor a panegyrist, nor a journalist, but a philosopher? The one who has so well unravelled the chaos of the origin of the French will help me without doubt to diffuse light on the most beautiful days of France. Think, sir, that you will be giving service to your disciple and to your admirer.

I shall be all my life, with as much gratitude as esteem, etc.

To M. MARTIN KAHLE

June ?, 1744

I am very pleased to hear, my good dean, that you have written a little book against me. You do me too much honor. On page 17 you reject the proof, from final causes, of the existence of God. If you had argued thus at Rome, the reverend father and governor of the Holy Palace would have condemned you to the Inquisition: if you had written thus against a theologian of Paris, he would have had your proposition censured by the sacred faculty: if against a fanatic, he would have abused you: but I have the honor to be neither a Jesuit, nor a theologian, nor a fanatic. I shall leave you to your opinion, and shall remain of mine. I shall always be convinced that a watch proves a watchmaker, and that the universe proves a god. I hope that you yourself understand what you say concerning space and eternity, ʋ ɛ necessity of matter, monads, and preordained harmony: and

I recommend you to look once more at what *I* said, finally, in the new edition, where I earnestly tried to make myself thoroughly understood—and in metaphysics that is no easy task.

You quote, à propos of space and infinity, the *Medea* of Seneca, the *Philippics* of Cicero, and the *Metamorphoses* of Ovid; also the verses of the Duke of Buckingham, of Gombaud, Regnier, Rapin, etc. I must tell you, sir, I know at least as much poetry as you do: that I am quite as fond of it: that if it were a question of verses we would have some very pretty sport: but I do not think them suitable to shed light on a metaphysical question, be they Lucretius' or the Cardinal de Polignac's. Furthermore, if ever you understand anything about monads, preordained harmony, and, to cite poetry,

> If Monsieur the dean can ever understand
> How everything, while full, can move itself

if you also discover how, while everything is necessary, man is free, you will do me a service if you will pass the information on to me When you have shown, in verse or otherwise, why so many men massacre one another in the best of all possible worlds, I shall be very much obliged to you.

I await your arguments, your verses, and your invectives; and assure you from the bottom of my heart that neither you nor I know anything about this matter. I have the honor to be, etc.

To M. DIDEROT

June, 1749

I thank you, sir, for the profound and brilliant work you have been so good as to send me:[79] the book I send you is neither the one nor the other, but in it you will find the anecdote of the man born blind set forth in greater detail than in the earlier editions. I am entirely of your opinion as to what you say respecting the judgment formed in such a case by ordinary men of average good sense, and that formed by philosophers. I am sorry that in the examples you quote you have forgotten the case of the blind who, receiving the gift of sight, saw men as trees walking.

I have read your book with great pleasure. It says much, and gives still more to be understood. I have long honored you as much as I despise the stupid vandals who condemn what they do not understand, and the wicked who unite themselves with the fools to denounce those who are trying to enlighten them.

But I confess I am not at all of the opinion of Saunderson, who denies a God because he was born sightless.[80] I am, perhaps, mistaken, but, in his place, I should recognize a great intelligence who had given me so many substitutes for sight, and perceiving, on reflection, the wonderful relations between all things, I should have suspected a workman, infinitely able. If it is very presumptuous to pretend to divine what he is, and why he has made everything that exists, so it seems to me very presumptuous to deny that he is. I am exceedingly anxious to meet and talk with you, whether you think yourself one of his works, or a particle drawn, of necessity, from matter, eternal and necessary. Whatever you are, you are a worthy part of that great whole which I do not understand. I very much wish, before I leave Lunéville, you would do me the honor to join a philosophers' feast at my table with a few other wise men. I am not one myself, but I have a passion for them when they are wise after your fashion. Rest assured, sir, that I appreciate your merits, and that to render them fuller justice I long to see you and assure you that I have the honor to be, etc.

To MADAME THE MARQUISE DU DEFFAND [81]

September 10, 1749

I have just seen a friend of twenty years die, who really loved you and who spoke to me two days before this fatal death of the pleasure that she would have of seeing you in Paris at her first trip. I had asked the Président Hénault to inform you of an accouchement which had seemed so singular and so fortunate; there was a long passage in my letter which was meant for you. Mme. du Châtelet had requested me to write to you, and I had thought that I was fulfilling my duty in writing to the Président Hénault. This unfortunate little girl of whom she was delivered, and who caused her death, didn't interest me enough. Alas! mad-

ame, we had turned this event into a joke, and it is in this unfortunate tone that, on her order, I had written to her friends. If
anything could increase the horrible condition in which I am, it
would be to have taken lightly an event whose consequences
empoison the remainder of my poor life. I didn't write to you to
tell you about her confinement, and here I am announcing to
you her death. I have recourse to your sensitive heart in my
grief. I am being dragged away to Cirey with M. du Châtelet.
From there I shall come back to Paris, without knowing what
will become of me, and hoping to rejoin her soon. Grant that
on arrival I may have the painful consolation of talking with you
about her, and of mourning at your feet a woman who, in spite
of her weaknesses, was worthy of our esteem.

To MADAME DENIS [82]

Berlin, December 18, 1752

I enclose, my dear, the two contracts from the Duke of Würtemberg: they secure you a little fortune for life. I also enclose my
will. Not that your prophecy that the King of Prussia *would
worry me to death* is going to be fulfilled. I have no mind to
come to such a foolish end: nature afflicts me much more than he
can, and it is only prudent that I should always have my valise
packed and my foot in the stirrup, ready to start for that world
where, happen what may, kings will be of small account.

As I do not possess here below a hundred and fifty thousand
mustaches at my service, I cannot pretend to make war. My
only plan is to desert honorably, to take care of my health, to
see you again, and forget this three years' nightmare. I am very
well aware that *the orange has been squeezed:* now we must
consider how to save the peel. I am compiling, for my instruction, a little Dictionary for the Use of Kings.

My friend means *my slave.*

My dear friend means *you are absolutely nothing to me.*

By *I will make you happy* understand *I will bear you as long
as I have need of you.*

Sup with me to-night means *I will make fun of you this evening.*

The dictionary might be long: quite an article for the *Encyclopædia*.

Seriously, all this weighs on my heart. Can what I have seen be true? To take pleasure in making bad blood between those who live together with him! To say to a man's face the kindest things—and then to write brochures upon him—and what brochures! To drag a man away from his own country by the most sacred promises, and then to ill-treat him with the blackest malice! What contradictions! And this is he who wrote so philosophically: whom I believed to be a philosopher! And whom I called the *Solomon of the North!*

You remember that fine letter which never succeeded in reassuring you? *You are a philosopher*, said he, *and so am I*. On my soul, sir, neither the one nor the other of us!

My dear child, I shall certainly never believe myself to be a philosopher until I am with you and my household gods. The difficulty is to get away from here. You will remember what I told you in my letter of November 1st. I can only ask leave on the plea of my health. It is not possible to say "I am going to Plombières" in December.

There is a man named Pérrard here: a sort of minister of the Gospel and born, like myself, in France: he asked permission to go to Paris on business: the King answered that he knew his affairs better than Pérrard himself, and that there was no need at all for him to go to Paris.

My dear child, when I think over the details of all that is going on here, I come to the conclusion that it cannot be true, that it is impossible, that I must be mistaken—that such a thing must have happened at Syracuse some three thousand years ago. What is true is that I sincerely love you and that you are my only consolation.

To JEAN-JACQUES ROUSSEAU
In Paris

August 30, 1755

Sir, I have received your new book against the human race, and I thank you for it.[83] You will please people by your manner of telling them the truth about themselves, but you will not alter them. The horrors of that human society—from which in our feebleness and ignorance we expect so many consolations—have never been painted in more striking colors: no one has ever been so witty as you are in trying to turn us into brutes: to read your book makes one long to go on all fours. Since, however, it is now some sixty years since I gave up the practice, I feel that it is unfortunately impossible for me to resume it: I leave this natural habit to those more fit for it than are you and I. Nor can I set sail to discover the aborigines of Canada, in the first place because my ill-health ties me to the side of the greatest doctor in Europe, and I should not find the same professional assistance among the Missouris: and secondly because war is going on in that country, and the example of the civilized nations has made the barbarians almost as wicked as we are ourselves. I must confine myself to being a peaceful savage in the retreat I have chosen—close to your country, where you yourself should be.

I agree with you that science and literature have sometimes done a great deal of harm. Tasso's enemies made his life a long series of misfortunes: Galileo's enemies kept him languishing in prison, at seventy years of age, for the crime of understanding the revolution of the earth: and, what is still more shameful, obliged him to forswear his discovery. Since your friends began the *Encyclopædia*, those who dare to be their rivals attack them as *deists, atheists*—even *Jansenists*.

If I might venture to include myself among those whose works have brought them persecution as their sole recompense, I could tell you of men set on ruining me from the day I produced my tragedy *Œdipe:* of a perfect library of absurd calumnies which have been written against me: of an ex-Jesuit priest whom I saved from utter disgrace rewarding me by defamatory libels: of a man yet more contemptible printing my *Age of Louis XIV* with *Notes* in which crass ignorance gave birth to the most abominable falsehoods: of yet another, who sold to a publisher some chapters of a *Universal History* supposed to be by me: of the publisher avaricious enough to print this shapeless mass of blunders, wrong dates, mutilated facts and names: and, finally, of men sufficiently base and craven to assign the production of this farago to me. I could show you all society poisoned by this class of person—a class unknown to the ancients—who, not being able to find any honest occupation—be it manual labor or service—and unluckily knowing how to read and write, become the brokers of literature, live on our works, steal our manuscripts, falsify them, and sell them. I could tell of some loose sheets of a gay trifle which I wrote thirty years ago (on the same subject that Chapelain was stupid enough to treat seriously) which are in circulation now through the breach of faith and the cupidity of those who added their own grossness to my *badinage* and filled in the gaps with a dullness only equalled by their malice; and who, finally, after twenty years, are selling everywhere a manuscript which, in very truth, is theirs and worthy of them only. I may add, last of all, that someone has stolen part of the material I amassed in the public archives to use in my *History of the War of* 1741 when I was historiographer of France; that he sold that result of my labors to a bookseller in Paris; and is as set on getting hold of my property as if I were dead and he could turn it into money by putting it up to auction. I could show you ingratitude, imposture, and rapine pursuing me for forty years to the foot of the Alps and the brink of the grave. But what conclusion ought I to draw from all these misfortunes? This only: that I have no right to complain: Pope, Descartes, Bayle, Camoens—a hundred others—have been subjected to the same, or greater, injustice: and my destiny is that of nearly everyone who has loved letters too well.

Confess, sir, that all these things are, after all, but little personal pin-pricks, which society scarcely notices. What matter to humankind that a few drones steal the honey of a few bees? Literary men make a great fuss of their petty quarrels: the rest of the world ignores them, or laughs at them.

They are, perhaps, the least serious of all the ills attendant on human life. The thorns inseparable from literature and a modest degree of fame are flowers in comparison with the other evils which from all time have flooded the world. Neither Cicero, Varro, Lucretius, Virgil, or Horace had any part in the proscriptions of Marius, Scylla, that profligate Antony, or that fool Lepidus; while as for that weak tyrant, Octavius Cæsar, cowardly entitled Augustus, he only became an assassin when he was deprived of the society of men of letters.

Confess that Italy owed none of her troubles to Petrarch or to Boccaccio; that Marot's jests were not responsible for the massacre of St. Bartholomew; or the tragedy of the *Cid* for the wars of the Fronde. Great crimes are always committed by great ignoramuses. What makes, and will always make, this world a vale of tears is the insatiable greediness and the indomitable pride of men, from Thamas Kouli-kan, who did not know how to read,[84] to a customhouse officer who can just count. Letters support, refine, and comfort the soul: they are serving you, sir, at the very moment you decry them: you are like Achilles declaiming against fame, and Father Malebranche using his brilliant imagination to belittle imagination.

If anyone has a right to complain of letters, I am that person, for in all times and in all places they have led to my being persecuted; still, we must needs love them in spite of the way they are abused—as we cling to society, though the wicked spoil its pleasantness; as we must love our country, though it treats us unjustly; and as we must love and serve the supreme Being, despite the superstition and fanaticism which too often dishonor his service.

M. Chappuis tells me your health is very unsatisfactory; you must come and recover here in your native place, enjoy its freedom, drink with me the milk of its cows, and browse on its grass.

I am yours most philosophically and with the most tender esteem, etc.

To M. TRONCHIN, OF LYONS

Les Délices, November 24, 1755

This is indeed a cruel piece of natural philosophy![85] We shall find it difficult to discover how the laws of movement produce such fearful disasters *in the best of all possible worlds*—where a hundred thousand ants, our neighbors, are crushed in a second on our ant-heaps, half of them dying undoubtedly in inexpres-

sible agonies, beneath débris from which it was impossible to
extricate them, families all over Europe reduced to beggary, and
the fortunes of a hundred merchants—Swiss, like yourself—swallowed up in the ruins of Lisbon. What a game of chance human
life is! What will the preachers say—especially if the Palace of
the Inquisition is left standing? I flatter myself that those reverend fathers, the Inquisitors, must have been crushed just like
other people. That ought to teach men not to persecute men:
for, while a few sanctimonious scoundrels are burning a few
fanatics, the earth opens and swallows up the one and the other.
I believe it is our mountains which save us from earthquakes.

To M. DIDEROT

January, 1758

Is it true, sir, that while you are doing a service for mankind, and
while you are enlightening it, those who believe themselves born
to blind it have permission to conduct a periodic libel against
you and against those who think as you do? What! the Garasses
are permitted to insult the Varros and the Plinys!

Some ministers of Geneva have had the madness, lastly, to
want to justify the judicial murder of Servet: the magistrate imposed silence upon them; the wiser ministers blushed for their
colleagues so openly mocked; and I don't know what Jesuit pedants will be permitted to insult their masters!

Are you not tempted to declare that you will interrupt the
Encyclopædia until you have received justice? The Guignards
have been hanged, and the new Garasses ought to be put to the
pillory.[86] Send me, I beg of you, the names of these wretches. I'll
treat them according to their merit in the new edition of the
General History that is in preparation. How sorry I am that you
are not writing the *Encyclopædia* in a free country. Must this
dictionary, one hundred times more useful than Bayle's, be ham-
pered by the very superstition which it ought to annihilate; must
one still treat kindly rascals who treat nothing kindly; should
the enemies of reason, the persecutors of the philosophers, the
murderers of our kings, still be allowed to speak in a century
such as ours.

It is said that these monsters want to make jokes, and that they claim to revenge religion, which is not attacked, with defamatory libels, which should be used to kindle the stakes of their sodomite priests, if one did not have as much indulgence as they have rage.

Your admirer and your partisan until death.

To M. [87]

Les Délices, January 5, 175,

It is as necessary, my dear friend, to preach tolerance among you as it is among us. With all due deference to you, if you could justify the English, Danish and Swedish penal laws you would be justifying at the same time our laws against you. They are all, I concede, equally absurd, inhuman, and contrary to good government: but we have simply imitated you. By your laws I am not allowed to buy a tomb in Sichem.[88] If one of your people prefers the mass to the sermon, for the salvation of his soul, he at once ceases to be a citizen, and loses everything—even his national rights. You do not allow any priest to celebrate mass in a low voice, in private, in any of your towns. Have you not driven out all ministers who cannot bring themselves to sign I know not what doctrinal formula? have you not exiled, for a mere yea and nay, those poor, peaceful Memmonites, in spite of the wise representations of the States General, who received them kindly? are there not still a large number of these exiles in the mountains in the diocese of Basle whom you do not permit to return? and has not a pastor been deposed because he objected to his flock being damned eternally? Confess, my dear philosopher, that you are no wiser than we are: and avow, too, that opinions have caused more trouble on this little globe than plagues and earthquakes. And yet you do not wish us to attack such opinions with our united strength! Would it not be a good thing for the world to overthrow the superstition which in all ages infuriates men one against the other? To worship God: to leave to every man freedom to serve him according to his own ideas: to love one's neighbors; enlighten them, if one can; pity them, if they are in error: to regard as immaterial, questions which would never have given trouble if no importance had been attached to them: this is my religion, which is worth all your systems and all your symbols.

I have not read any of the books of which you tell me, my dear philosopher: I keep to old works, which teach me something: from the new I learn very little. I confess that Montesquieu often lacks arrangement, in spite of his division into books and chapters: that he sometimes takes an epigram for a definition, and an antithesis for a new idea: that he is not always correct in his quotations: but he will remain for ever a profound and heaven-sent genius, who thinks and makes his readers think. His book should be the breviary of those called to rule others. He will endure, and the scribblers will be forgotten.

As to your writers on agriculture, I believe that a sensible peasant knows more about it than authors who, from the retirement of their libraries, issue instructions as to how the earth is to be ploughed. I plough, but I do not write on ploughing. Every age has had its hobby. On the revival of learning, people began by quarrelling with each other over dogmas and rules of syntax: a taste for rusty old coins has been succeeded by researches on metaphysics, which nobody understands. These unintelligible questions have been abandoned in favor of pneumatic and electrical machines, which do teach something: then everybody began collecting shells and fossils. After that, some modestly essayed to manage the universe: while others, equally modest, sought to reform empires by new laws. Finally, descending from the sceptre to the plough, new Triptolemies tried to teach men what everybody knows and does much better than they know how to talk about it. Such is the march of changing fashions: but my friendship for you will never change.

To MME. DU DEFFAND

Les Délices, April 12, 1760

I have not sent you, madam, any of those trifles with which you condescend to while away an idle moment. For more than six weeks I have broken with all humankind: I have buried myself in my own thoughts: then came the usual country employments, and then a fever. Taking all these things into consideration, you have had nothing, and most likely will have nothing, for some time.

You need, however, only write and say to me, "I want to be amused, I am well, in good humor, and I should like some trifles sent along to me," and you shall have a whole postbag—comic, scientific, historical, or poetic, just as pleases you best—on condition you throw it in the fire when read.

You were so enthusiastic over *Clarissa* that I read it as a relaxation from my work when I was ill: the reading made me feverish. It is cruel for a man as lively as I am to read nine whole volumes containing nothing at all, and serving no purpose whatever but to give a glimpse of Clarissa's love for a profligate like Lovelace. I said to myself: "Were all these people my friends and relatives, I could not take the least interest in them." I see nothing in the author but a clever man who knows the invincible curiosity of the human species, and who holds out hopes of gratifying it in volume after volume, in order to sell them. At last I found Clarissa in a brothel, in volume ten, and that greatly touched me.

Pierre Corneille's *Théodore*, who wants to get into La Fillon's from a Christian motive, does not approach *Clarissa*, either in its situations or in its pathos; but, save that part where the pretty English girl finds herself in that disreputable place, I confess that nothing in the novel gave me the least satisfaction, and I should be sorry to have to read it through again. The only good books, it seems to me, are those which can be re-read without weariness.

The only good books of that particular kind are those which set a picture constantly before the imagination, and soothe the ear by their harmony. People want music and painting, with a few little philosophical precepts thrown in now and again with a reasonable discretion. For this reason Horace, Virgil, and Ovid always please, save in the translations which spoil them.

After *Clarissa* I re-read some chapters of Rabelais, such as the fight of brother Jean des Entommeures, and the meeting of the council of Picrochole (I know them almost by heart): but I re-read them with the greatest pleasure, for they give a most vivid picture of life.

Not that I compare Rabelais with Horace: but if Horace is tne first writer of good epistles, Rabelais, at his best, is the first of buffoons. Two men of this kind in a nation are not needed: but one there must be. I am sorry I once said harsh things about him.

But there are pleasures superior to all this sort of thing: those of seeing the grass grow in the fields, and the abundant harvest ripen. That is man's true life: all the rest is illusion.

Forgive me, madam, for speaking to you of a pleasure en-joyed through the eyes: you only know the pleasures of the soul. The way you bear your affliction is wholly admirable: you enjoy, anyhow, all the advantages of society. It is true that often this comes to mean merely giving one's opinion on the news of the day; which, in the long run, seems to me exceedingly insipid. Only our tastes and passions make this world supportable. You replace the passions by philosophy, a poor substitute: while I replace them with the tender and respectful attachment I have always felt for you.

Wish your friend good health from me, and I hope he will not quite forget me.

To M. DE BASTIDE [89]

1760

I do not suppose, *Spectator of the World*, that you propose to fill your pages with facts concerning the physical world. Socrates, Epictetus, Marcus Aurelius, allowed all the spheres to gravitate one on the top of the other, that they might devote themselves to the regulation of manners. Are your speculations also thus concentrated on morality? But what do you expect from a morality which the teachers of the nations have already preached about with so much success?

I agree with you that it is somewhat of a reflection on human nature that money accomplishes everything and merit almost nothing: that the real workers, behind the scenes, have hardly a modest subsistence, while certain selected personages flaunt on the stage: that fools are exalted to the skies, and genius is in the gutter: that a father disinherits six virtuous children to make his first-born—often a scapegrace—heir to all his possessions: that a luckless wretch who comes to grief, or to any unhappy end in a foreign country, leaves the fortune of his natural inheritors to the treasury of that state.

It is sad to see—I confess it again—those who toil, in poverty, and those who produce nothing, in luxury; great proprietors who claim the very birds that fly and the fish that swim; trembling vassals who do not dare to free their houses from the wild boar that devours them; fanatics who want to burn everyone who does not pray to God after their own fashion; violence in high places which engenders violence in the people; might making right not only among nations but among individuals.

And it is this state of things, common to all lives and to all places, which you expect to change! Behold the folly of you moralists! Mount the pulpit with Bourdaloue, or wield the pen like La Bruyère, and you waste your time—the world will go its way! A government which could provide for all would do more in a year than the order of preaching friars has done since its institution.

In a very short space of time Lycurgus raised the Spartans above ordinary humanity. The force of Confucius' wisdom, two thousand years ago, is still felt in China.

But, as neither you nor I are made to govern, if you have such an itching for reform, reform our virtues, which in excess may well become prejudicial to the prosperity of the state. It is easier to reform virtues than vices. The list of exaggerated virtues would be a long one: I will mention a few, and you will easily guess the rest.

I observe, walking about the country, that the children of the soil eat much less than they require: it is difficult to conceive this immoderate passion for abstinence. It even looks as if they had got into their heads that it will be accounted to them for virtue if their beasts also are half-starved.

What is the result? Men and beasts waste away, their stock becomes feeble, work is suspended, and the cultivation of the land suffers.

Patience is another virtue carried to excess, perhaps, in the country. If the tax collectors limited themselves to executing the will of their lord, to be patient would be a duty: but if you question these good folk who supply us with bread, they will tell you that the manner in which the taxes are levied is a hundred times more onerous than the tax itself. Their patience ruins them and their landowners with them.

The evangelical pulpit has reproached kings and the great a hundred times for their harshness to the poor. The fault has been corrected—in excess. The royal antechambers overflow with servants better fed and better clothed than the lords of the parishes whence they come. This excess of charity robs the country of soldiers, and the land of laborers.

Spectator of the World, do not let the scheme of reforming our virtues shock you: the founders of religious orders have reformed each other.

Another reason for encouragement is that it is perhaps easier to discern an excess of good than to pronounce on the nature of evil. Believe me, dear *Spectator*, I cannot urge you too strongly to reform our virtues: men cling too tightly to their vices.

To M. D'ALEMBERT

Ferney, March 19, 1761

My very worthy and resolute philosopher, true scholar, true wit, man necessary to the century, see, I beg of you, in my *Epistle to Mme Denis*, a few of my answers to your vigorous letter.

So my dear archdeacon and arch-tedious Trublet is a member of the Academy! He will compile a fine speech made up of sentences taken from Lamotte. I should like you to answer him —that would make a fine contrast. I believe that you accuse wrongly *Cicero*-d'Olivet; he is not the kind of man who would lend his voice to the Almoner of Houdard and of Fontenelle. Blame everything on the Queen's superintendent.

What's especially distressing for human nature is that this Trublet is an atheist like Cardinal de Tencin, and that this wretch worked on the *Christian Journal* in order to enter the Academy under the Queen's protection. The philosophers are disunited—when the wolf happens to devour the little flock, the animals begin to eat one another. It's with your Jean-Jacques that I am most angry. This stark-raving man, who could have been something if he had let himself be guided by you, has taken it into his head to keep apart from the others: he writes against plays after composing a bad comedy; he writes against the France that nourishes him; he finds four or five rotted staves from Diogenes' barrel and puts himself inside to bark; he abandons his friends; he writes me the most impertinent letter that ever a fanatic scribbled. He informs me, in these very words: "You have corrupted Geneva as a reward for the asylum which she has afforded you"; as if I cared about alleviating the morals of Geneva, as if I needed an asylum, as if I had taken it in the city of *Socinian preachers*, as if I had some obligation to this city. I have not answered his letter, but M. de Ximenès has answered for me, and has crushed his wretched novel.[90] If Rousseau had been a reasonable man whom one could reproach solely for having written a bad book, he would not have been treated in this way. Let's go on to *Pancrace*-Colardeau. He is a courtier of Pompignan and of Fréron; it isn't a bad idea to plunge the muzzle of these servants into the mud of their masters.

My worthy philosopher, what will become of truth? what will become of philosophy? If the learned men choose to be bold, if they are courageous, if they are together, I will dedicate myself to them; but if they are divided, if they abandon the common cause, I will think no longer about anything except the plow, my oxen, and my sheep. But, while cultivating the earth, I will pray God that you always enlighten it, and you will be the only public I need.

What do you think about the square cap of *Midas*-Omer?

I embrace you tenderly.

To MADEMOISELLE ***

Aux Délices, April 15, 1762

It is true, mademoiselle, that in a reply I wrote to M. de Chazelles, I asked him for information about the horrible experience of Calas whose son has aroused my grief as much as my curiosity. I have given an account to M. de Chazelles of the feelings and outcries of all the foreigners around me; but I can not have spoken to him about my opinion of this cruel affair, since I have none. I am only acquainted with the pamphlets written in favor of the Calas, and that is not enough to venture to take sides.

I have wanted to inform myself in the capacity of a historian. An event as dreadful as that of a whole family being accused of parricide on religious grounds, a father expiring on the wheel for having strangled his own son with his hands, on the simple suspicion that this son wanted to give up the beliefs of Jean Calvin, a brother strongly charged with having helped to strangle his brother, a young lawyer suspected of having served as executioner in this unprecedented execution, this event, I say, belongs essentially to the history of the human mind and to the vast tableau of our rages and weaknesses, of which I have already given a sketch.

Thus I asked for information from M. de Chazelles, but I did not expect him to show my letter. Be that as it may, I am continuing to wish that the parliament of Toulouse will consent to make the trial of Calas public, as the trial of Damiens was published. One doesn't bother with custom when such extraordinary cases are concerned. These two trials interest mankind; and if something can arrest in men the madness of fanaticism, it is the publication and the proof of the parricide and of the sacrilege which have brought Calas to the wheel, and which leave the whole family a prey of the most violent suspicions. Such is my sentiment.

To M. AUDIBERT

MERCHANT IN MARSEILLE, AND MEMBER OF THE ACADEMY OF THE SAME CITY

Aux Délices, July 9, 1762

You have been able to see, sir, the letters of the widow Calas and of her son. I have been examining this case for three months; I can be mistaken, but it seems to me as clear as day that the furor of the cabal and the strangeness of destiny have concurred to have the most innocent and the most unfortunate of men judicially murdered on the wheel, to disperse his family, and to reduce it to mendicity. I am afraid that in Paris very little thought is given to this affair. In vain a hundred innocent men would be broken on the wheel; in Paris people will only talk about a new play, and think only about a good supper.

However, by dint of raising one's voice, a man can make himself heard by the hardest of hearing; and sometimes even the cries of the unfortunate reach as far as the court. The widow Calas is in Paris at the house of MM. Dufour and Mallet, rue Montmartre; the young Lavaysse is there also. I believe that he has changed his name; but the poor widow can arrange it so that you can talk with him. Will you please have the curiosity to see both of them; this is a tragedy which has a horrible and absurd dénouement, but its plot is not yet clearly defined.

Will you please get these two actors to talk, and draw from them all possible elucidations, and be so kind as to inform me of the principal striking things which you find out.

Tell me also, sir, I beg of you, if the widow Calas is in need; I do not doubt that MM. Tourton and Baur will join you in assisting her in this event.

I have taken it upon myself to pay the cost of the trial which she must bring before the King's council. I have sent her to M. Mariette, lawyer to the council, who requests the docket of the Toulouse proceedings before acting. The parliament, which appears ashamed of its judgment, has forbidden any communication of the documents, and even of the sentence. Only the King's strongest protection can force this parliament to bring the truth to light. We are doing everything in our power to secure this protection, and we believe that public outcry is the best way to succeed in obtaining it.

It seems to be that it is in the best interest of all men to examine this affair thoroughly, which, on one hand or the other, is the height of the most horrible fanaticism. To treat such an affair with indifference is to renounce humanity. I am sure of your zeal: it will inflame the zeal of others, without compromising you.

I embrace you tenderly, my dear friend, and am, with all the sentiments which you deserve, etc.

To M. BERTRAND

January 8, 1764

I shall never cease, my dear sir, to preach tolerance from the housetops, despite the complaints of your priests and the outcries of ours, until persecution is no more. The progress of reason is slow, the roots of prejudice lie deep. Doubtless, I shall never see the fruits of my efforts, but they are seeds which may one day germinate.

You are of the opinion, my dear friend, that jesting is not suitable to serious subjects. We Frenchmen are naturally lively: the Swiss are more serious. Is it possible that in the delightful canton of Vaud, which in itself inspires cheerfulness, solemnity is an effect of the government? Depend upon it, nothing is so efficacious in crushing superstition as ridicule. I do not confound superstition with religion, my dear philosopher. The former results from pride and folly; the latter from wisdom and reason. Superstition has always produced trouble and war; religion maintains brotherhood and peace. My friend Jean-Jacques will not allow comedy, and you set your face against innocent jests. In spite of your solemnity, I am yours most affectionately.

To THE MARQUISE du DEFFAND

Ferney, August 31, 1764

I have just learned, madame, that you have lost M. d'Argenson. If this news is true, I share your grief. We are all like prisoners condemned to death, who amuse themselves a little while in the prison yard until someone comes to dispatch them. This idea is truer than it is consoling. The first lesson I believe one must give men is to inspire them with courage of mind; and since we are born to suffer and to die, one must familiarize himself with this harsh destiny.

I should like very much to know if M. d'Argenson died as a philosopher or as a coward. The final moments are accompanied, in some parts of Europe, by circumstances so disgusting and so ridiculous that it is extremely difficult to know what the dying think. They all go through the same ceremonies. There were some Jesuits impudent enough to say that M. de Montesquieu died an imbecile, and they thought this example gave them the right to entice others to die in the same way.

One must admit that the ancients, our masters in everything, had a great advantage over us; they did not trouble life and death with subjections rendering both baneful. One lived, at the time of the Scipios and the Caesars, one thought, and one died as one wished; as for us, we are treated like marionettes.

I believe that you are enough of a philosopher, madame, to agree with me. If you are not, burn my letter; but always keep for me a little friendship during the time which I still have to crawl about on the heap of mud where nature has placed us.

To M. DAMILAVILLE

Ferney, March 1, 1765

My dear friend, I have devoured the new *Memoir* of M. de Beaumont on the innocence of the Calas; I have admired and wept over it, but it told me nothing I did not know; I have long been convinced, and it was I who was lucky enough to furnish the first proofs.

You would like to know how this protest of all Europe against the judicial murder of the unhappy Calas, broken on the wheel at Toulouse, managed to reach a little unknown corner of the world, between the Alps and the Jura, a hundred leagues from the scene of the fearful event.

Nothing more clearly reveals the existence of that imperceptible chain which links all the events of this miserable world.

At the end of March, 1762, a traveler, who had come through Languedoc and arrived in my little retreat two miles from Geneva, told me of the punishment of Calas, and assured me that he was innocent. I answered him that the crime was not a probable one, but that it was still more improbable that Calas' judges should, without any motive, break an innocent man on the wheel.

I heard the next day that one of the children of this unfortunate man had taken refuge in Switzerland, fairly near my cottage. His flight made me presume the guilt of the family. However, I reflected that the father had been condemned to death for having, by himself, murdered his son on account of his religion, and that, at the time of his death, this father was sixtynine years old. I never remember to have read of any old man being possessed by so horrible a fanaticism. I have always observed that this mania is usually confined to young people, with weak, heated, and unstable imaginations, inflamed by superstition. The fanatics of the Cevennes were madmen from twenty to thirty years of age, trained to prophesy since childhood. Almost all the convulsionists I had seen in any large numbers in Paris were young girls and boys. Among the monks the old are less carried away and less liable to the fury of the zealot than those just out of their novitiate. The notorious assassins, goaded by religious frenzy, have all been young people, as have all those who have pretended to be possessed—no one ever saw an old man exorcised. This reasoning made me doubt a crime, which was, moreover, unnatural. I was ignorant of its circumstances.

I had young Calas brought to my house. I expected to find him a religious enthusiast, such as his country has sometimes produced. I found a simple and ingenuous youth, with a gentle and very interesting expression, who, as he talked to me, made vain efforts to restrain his tears. He told me that he was at Nîmes, apprenticed to a manufacturer, when he heard that his whole family was about to be condemned to death at Toulouse, and that almost all Languedoc believed them guilty. He added that, to escape so fearful a disgrace, he had come to Switzerland to hide himself.

I asked him if his father and mother were of a violent character. He told me that they had never beaten any one of their children, and that never were parents more tender and indulgent.

I confess that no more was needed to give me a strong presumption in favor of the innocence of the family. I gathered fresh information from two merchants of Geneva, of proven honesty, who had lodged at the Calas' house in Toulouse. They confirmed me in my opinion. Far from believing the Calas famıly to be fanatics and parricides, I thought I saw that it was the fanatics who had accused and ruined them. I had long known of what party spirit and calumny are capable.

But what was my astonishment when, having written to Languedoc on the subject of this extraordinary story, Catholics and Protestants answered that there was no doubt as to the crime of the Calas! I was not disheartened. I took the liberty of writing to those in authority in the province, to the governors of neighboring provinces, and to ministers of state: all unanimously advised me not to mix myself up in such a horrible affair: everyone condemned me: and I persisted: this is what I did.

Calas' widow, from whom, to fill to the brim her cup of misery and insult, her daughters had been forcibly removed, had retired into solitude where she lived on the bread of tears, and awaited death. I did not enquire if she was, or was not, attached to the Protestant religion, but only if she believed in a God who rewarded virtue and punished crime. I asked her if she would sign a solemn declaration, as before God, that her husband died innocent: she did not hesitate. Nor did I. I asked M. Mariette to undertake the defense before the royal council. Mme. Calas had to be persuaded to leave her retirement and to undertake the journey to Paris.

It is then apparent that, if there are great crimes on the earth, there are as many virtues; and that, if superstition produces horrible sufferings, philosophy redresses them.

A lady, whose generosity is as noble as her birth, and who was staying at Geneva to have her daughters inoculated, was the first to help this unhappy family. French people living in this country seconded her: the traveling English distinguished themselves: there was a beneficent rivalry between the two nations as to which should give the more to virtue so cruelly oppressed.

As to the sequel, who knows it better than you? Who has served innocence with a zeal as faithful and courageous? Who has more generously encouraged the voice of those orators whom all France and Europe paused to hear? The days when Cicero justified, before an assembly of legislators, Amerinus accused of parricide, are with us again. A few people, calling themselves *pious*, have raised their voices against the Calas: but, for the first time since fanaticism was established, the voices of the wise have silenced them.

What great victories reason is winning among us! But would you believe, my dear friend, that the family of the Calas, so efficiently succored and avenged, was not the only one that religion accused of parricide—was not the only one sacrificed to the furies of religious persecution? There is a case yet more pitiable, because, while experiencing the same horrors, it has not had the same consolations: it has not found Mariettes, Beaumonts, and Loiseau.

There appears to be a horrible mania, indigenous to Languedoc, originally sown there by the inquisitors in the train of Simon de Montfort, which, ever since then, from time to time waves its banner.

A native of Castres, named Sirven, had three daughters. As the religion of the family is the so-called reformed religion, the youngest of the daughters was torn from the arms of her mother. She was put into a convent, where they beat her to help her learn her catechism. She went mad; and threw herself into a well at a place not far from her parents' house. The bigots thereupon made up their minds that her father, mother, and sisters had drowned the child. The Catholics of the province are absolutely convinced that one of the chief points of the Protestant religion is that the fathers and mothers are bound to hang, strangle, or drown any of their children whom they suspect of any leaning towards the Catholic religion. All this was precisely at the moment when the Calas were in irons and their scaffold was being prepared.

The story of the drowned girl reached Toulouse at once. Everyone declared it to be a fresh instance of murderous parents. The public fury grew daily: Calas was broken on the wheel: Sirven, his wife, and his daughter were accused. Sirven, terrified, just had time to flee, with his family ill. They went on foot, with no one to help them, across precipitous mountains, deep in snow. One of the daughters gave birth to an infant among the glaciers: and, dying, bore her dying child in her arms. They finally took the road to Switzerland.

The same fate which brought the children of the Calas to me, willed that the Sirvens should also appeal to me. Picture to yourself, my friend, four sheep accused by the butchers of having devoured a lamb: for that is what I saw. I despair of describing to you so much innocence and so much sorrow. What ought I to have done? and what would you have done in my place? Could I rest satisfied with sighing over human nature? I took the liberty of writing to the first president of Languedoc, a wise and good man: but he was not at Toulouse. I had one of my friends present a petition to the vice-chancellor. During this time, near Castres, the father, mother, and two daughters were executed in effigy: their property confiscated and dissipated, to the last sou.

Here was an entire family—honest, innocent, virtuous—left to disgrace and beggary among strangers: some, doubtless, pitied them: but it is hard to be an object of pity to one's grave! I was finally informed that remission of their sentence was a possibility. At first, I believed that it was the judges from whom that pardon must be obtained. You will easily understand that the family would sooner have begged their bread from door to door, or have died of want, than ask a pardon which admitted a crime too horrible to be pardonable. But how could justice be obtained? How could they go back to prison in a country where half the inhabitants still say that Calas' murder was just? Would there be a second appeal to the council? Would anyone try to rouse again the public sympathy which the misfortunes of the Calas has perhaps exhausted, and which would weary of refuting such accusations, of reinstating the condemned, and of confounding their judges?

Are not these two tragic events, my friend, so rapidly following each other, proofs of the inevitable decrees of fate, to which our miserable species is subject? A terrible truth, so much insisted on in Homer and Sophocles; but a useful truth, since it teaches us to be resigned and to learn to suffer.

Shall I add that, while the incredible disaster of the Calas and the Sirvens wrung my heart, a man, whose profession you will guess from what he said, reproached me for taking so much interest in two families who were strangers to me? "Why do you mix yourself up in such things?" he asked; 'let the dead bury their dead." I answered him, "I found an Israelite in the desert —an Israelite covered with blood; suffer me to pour a little wine and oil into his wounds: you are the Levite, leave me to play the Samaritan."

It is true that, as a reward for my trouble, I have been treated quite as a Samaritan: a defamatory libel appeared under the titles of A *Pastoral Instruction* and A *Charge*: but it may well be forgotten—a Jesuit wrote it. The wretch did not know then that I was myself giving shelter to a Jesuit! Could I prove more conclusively that we should regard our enemies as our brothers?

Your passions are the love of truth, humanity, the hatred of calumny. Our friendship is founded on the similarity of our characters. I have spent my life in seeking and publishing the truth which I love. Who else among modern historians has de fended the memory of a great prince against the abominable in ventions of a writer, whoever he may be, who might well be called the *traducer of kings, ministers, and military commanders,* and who now has not a single reader?

I have only done in the fearful cases of the Calas and the Sirvens what all men do: I have followed my bent. A philosopher's is not to pity the unhappy—it is to be of use to them.

I know how furiously fanaticism attacks philosophy, whose two daughters, *Truth* and *Tolerance*, fanaticism would destroy as it did Calas; while philosophy only wishes to disarm the off-spring of fanaticism, *Falsehood* and *Persecution*.

Men who do not reason try to bring into discredit those who do: they have confused the philosopher with the sophist; they have greatly deceived themselves. The true philosopher can be aroused against the calumny which so often attacks himself: he can overwhelm with everlasting contempt the vile mercenary who twice a month outrages reason, good taste, and virtue: he can even expose to ridicule, in passing, those who insult litera-ture in the sanctuary where they should have honored it: but he knows nothing of cabals, underhand dealings, or revenge. Like the sage of Montbar, like the sage of Voré, he knows how to make the land fruitful and those who dwell on it happier.

The true philosopher clears uncultivated ground, adds to the number of ploughs and, so, to the number of inhabitants; employs and enriches the poor; encourages marriages and finds a home for the orphan; does not grumble at necessary taxes, and puts the farmer in a condition to pay them promptly. He expects nothing from men, and does them all the good he can. He has a horror of hypocrisy, but he pities the superstitious; and, finally, he knows how to be a friend.

I perceive that I am painting your portrait: the resemblance would be perfect, were you so fortunate as to live in the country.

To M. D'ALEMBERT

April 5, 1766

My dear and great philosopher, in a jumble of letters which I received by way of Geneva, in my thoughtlessness, I opened the one that I am sending you. I noticed that it was addressed to you only after having been so stupid as to unseal it; very humbly I beg your pardon for having done so, protesting, on my word as a philosopher, that I have not read any of it. I had instructed in general that all those which were addressed to you from Italy should be removed. I only found this one in my bundle; I trust that it is not from the ruling pope; I presume that it is from a thinking being since it is for you.

There are few of these thinking beings. My former crowned disciple informs me that there is scarcely one in a thousand; that is about the number of the well-bred set, and, if there is presently a thousandth part of men who are reasonable, that will increase tenfold in ten years. The world is sharpening its wits enormously. We can foresee a great revolution in minds everywhere. You would not be able to believe the progress reason has made in a certain part of Germany. I'm not talking about the godless who embrace openly the system of Spinoza, I am talking about the honest people who have no fixed principles at all concerning the nature of things, who do not know what is, but who know very well what is not: there you have my true philosophers. I can assure you that among all those who came to see me, I found only two who were fools. It seems to me that men of wit have never been so feared in Paris as today. The inquisition on books is severe: I am informed that the subscribers have not yet received the *Encyclopaedic Dictionary*. That is not only being severe, it's being very unjust. If the delivery of this book is stopped, the subscribers are robbed, and the bookstores are ruined. I should certainly like to know what harm a book can do which costs one hundred crowns. Twenty *in-folio* volumes will never cause a revolution; it's the little portable 30 cent books which are to be feared. If the Gospel had cost twelve hundred sesterces, the Christian religion would never have been established.

As for myself, I have a copy of the *Encyclopaedia*, in my capacity of foreigner and Swiss. They don't mind if the Swiss are damned, but, from what I see, they keep a close watch on the salvation of the Parisians. If you could send me something to put the finishing touches on my damnation, you would give me a diabolic pleasure, for which I would be very grateful to you. I can no longer work, but I love to enjoy myself, and I want something which is stimulating.

I must tell you that I have just read Grotius' *De Veritate*, etc. I am certainly astonished by this man's reputation; I hardly know a more foolish book than his, except for the bombastic Houteville. In his time a reputation was acquired cheaply. There is a good article on *Hobbes* in the *Encyclopaedia*. Would to God that this whole work were written as well as your preliminary discourse!

Goodbye, my very dear philosopher: will it be said that I shall die without seeing you again?

To M. D'ALEMBERT

June 26, 1766

My worthy and amiable philosopher, I have seen him, this brave *Bite-them*,[91] who has bit them so well; he has the character of those true brave men who have as much sweetness as courage; he is visibly called to the apostolate. What fatality makes it possible for so many fanatic imbeciles to establish sects for fools while so many superior minds can hardly manage to establish a little school for reason? It's perhaps because they are learned; they lack enthusiasm, activity. All the philosophers are too lukewarm; they are content with laughing at the errors of men rather than crushing them. Missionaries run about the earth and the seas; philosophers must at least run about the streets; they must go sow the good seed from house to house. Preaching is better than the writings of the Fathers if you want to succeed. Fulfill these two great duties, my dear brother; preach and write, combat, convert, make the fanatics so odious and so despicable that the government will be ashamed to support them.

In the end, those who have gained honors and riches through a fanatic and persecuting sect will have to content themselves with the advantages, limit themselves to reveling in peace, and get rid of the idea of making their errors respectable. They will say to the philosophers: let us revel, and we will let you reason. Some day one will think in France as in England where religion is looked upon only as a political matter; but to reach that point, my dear brother, it will take work and time.

The Church of Wisdom is beginning to develop in our neighborhood where, twelve years ago the most somber fanaticism ruled. The provinces are becoming enlightened, the young magistrates are thinking boldly; there are Solicitor Generals who are anti-Omers. The book attributed to Fréret, and which perhaps is by Fréret, is doing a tremendous amount of good. There are many confessors, and I hope that there will be no martyrs. There is a great deal of political bickering in Geneva; but I know of no city where there are fewer Calvinists than in this city of Calvin. One is astonished by the progress that human reason has made in so few years. This little professor of stupidities called Vernet is the object of public scorn. His book against you and against the philosophers is the most unknown of books in spite of a pretended third edition. You certainly realize that the *Curious Letter of Robert Covelle*, which I have sent you, is intended only for the Geneva meridian and to mortify the pedant. He has a brother who possesses a farm on my land at Tournay; he comes there sometimes. I am counting on the pleasure of having him put to the pillory as soon as I have a little health; this is a jest which philosophers can allow them-

selves when such priests are concerned, and without being persecutors like them.

It seems to me that all those who have written against the
philosophers are punished in this world: the Jesuits have been
banished; Abraham Chaumeix has fled to Moscow; Berthier has
died from a cold poison;[92] Fréron has been dishonored on every
stage, and Vernet will be pilloried without fail.

In truth, you should punish all those scoundrels with one of
those half serious, half jesting books which you know how to
write so well. You can get wherever you like with ridicule; it is
the strongest of weapons, and no one wields it better than you.
It's a great pleasure to laugh while revenging oneself. If you do
not crush the *inf* . . . , you have missed your vocation. I can
no longer do anything. I have but a short time to live; I shall
die, if I can, laughing, but, unquestionably, loving you.

To M. D'ALEMBERT

July 18, 1766

Brother Damilaville has doubtless sent you, my dear philosopher,
the "Narrative" of Abbeville. I cannot conceive how thinking
beings can live in a land of apes who so often turn into tigers.
For my part, I am ashamed to be even on the frontier. Truly,
this is the moment to break all one's ties, and hide the shame
and horror of one's soul in some far off land. I have not been
able to get the report of the lawyers' consultation: you doubtless
have seen it—and shuddered. The time for joking has gone by:
witticisms do not accord with massacres. What! these Busirises in
wig and gown condemn to death by the most horrible tortures
children of sixteen! and that against the judgment of ten humane
and upright judges! And the nation allows it! People discuss it
for five minutes, and then go on to the Opéra-Comique: and
inhumanity, growing more and more insolent on the strength of
our silence, tomorrow will legally cut the throats for which her
fingers are itching—yours, first of all, for you have raised your
voice against her two or three times. Here, on one hand, is
Calas broken on the wheel; on the other, Sirven hanged; a little
further from home, a lieutenant-general gagged; and, a fortnight

later, five young men condemned to be burnt for follies which deserved Saint-Lazare. What is the use of the *Preface* of the King of Prussia? Can he remedy such horrible crimes as these? Is this the land of gaiety and philosophy? It is rather that of the Massacre of St. Bartholomew. The Inquisition would not have dared to decide as these Jansenist judges have decided. Tell me, I beg you, what is being said, since nothing is being done. It is a feeble consolation to know that such monsters are held in abhorrence, but it is the only one that remains to our impotence, and I pray you to let me have it. The Prince of Brunswick is beside himself with indignation, rage, and pity. Redouble these passions in my heart by two words in your handwriting sent, by *petite poste*, to brother Damilaville. Your friendship, and that of a few other thinking beings, is the only pleasure I have left.

N. B. The theologian Vernet complained to the Council of Geneva that he was being held up to ridicule: the Council offered him a written testimony to his morality—as if to say that he had not been a highway robber, nor even a pickpocket. This last part of the guarantee seems somewhat rash.

To M. DIDEROT

July 23, 1766

One cannot help writing to Socrates when the Melituses and the Anytuses are bathing in blood and lighting the stakes. A man like you must see only with horror the country where you have the misfortune to live. You really should come to a country where you would have complete freedom, not only to print what you would like, but to preach openly against superstitions as infamous as they are bloodthirsty. You would not be alone there, you would have companions and disciples. You could establish a pulpit there which would be the pulpit of truth. Your library would be transported by water and there would not be four leagues to go by land. In a word, you would leave slavery for freedom. I can not imagine how a sensitive heart and a righteous man can live in the country of monkeys which have become tigers. If the suggestion proposed to you satisfies your indignation and pleases your wisdom, let me know, and we will try to arrange everything in a manner worthy of you, in the greatest secrecy, and without compromising you. The country proposed to you is beautiful and within reach of everything. The Uranienbourg of Tycho Brahé would be less agreeable. He who has the honor of writing to you is filled with a respectful admiration for you, as much as with indignation and sorrow. Believe me, the learned men who have humanity must congregate far from the senseless barbarians.

To MR. HORACE WALPOLE

Ferney, July 15, 1768

Sir, I have not ventured to speak English for forty years, and you are perfectly at home in our language. I have seen letters from you, written as naturally as you think. Moreover, my age and my state of health do not allow me to write with my own hand. So you must accept my thanks in my own tongue.

I have just read the preface of your *History of Richard III* and found it all too short. When an author is so visibly in the right, and has in addition a philosophy so bold and a style so virile, I want more of him. Your father was a great statesman and a good orator, but I doubt if he could have written as you write. You cannot say, "My father is greater than I."

I have always agreed with you, sir, that ancient histories are untrustworthy. Fontenelle, the only man of the time of Louis XIV who was at once poet, philosopher, and scholar, declared that they were undoubtedly *fabrications*; and it must be admitted that Rollin has amassed many absurdities and contradictions.

After I had read the preface to your history, I read that to your novel.[93] You laugh a little at me therein; the French quite understand raillery; but I am going to answer you in all seriousness.

You have nearly succeeded in making your countrymen believe that I despise Shakespeare. I was the first writer who made Shakespeare known to the French: forty years ago I translated passages from his works, as from Milton's, Waller's, Rochester's,

Dryden's, and Pope's. I can assure you that before my time no one in France knew anything about English poetry: and had hardly ever heard of Locke. I have been persecuted for thirty years by hosts of fanatics for having said that Locke is the Hercules of metaphysics and that he defined the limits of the human understanding.

Fate willed that I should be the first to explain to my fellow-countrymen the discoveries of the great Newton, which many people among us still speak of as *the systems.* I have been your apostle and your martyr: truly, it is not fair that the English should complain of me.

I said, long ago, that if Shakespeare had lived in the time of Addison he would have added to his genius the elegance and purity which make Addison admirable. I stated that *his genius was his own, and his faults the faults of his age.* He is precisely, to my mind, like Lope de Vega, the Spaniard, and like Calderón. His is a fine but barbarous nature: he has neither regularity, nor propriety, nor art: in the midst of his sublimity he sometimes descends to grossness, and in the most impressive scenes, to buffoonery: his tragedy is chaos, illuminated by a hundred rays of light.

The Italians, who revived tragedy a century before the English and the Spanish, have not fallen into this fault: they have imitated the Greeks much better. There are no buffoons in *Œdipus* and the *Electra* of Sophocles. I strongly suspect that this grossness had its origin in our four fools. We were all a little uncivilized on this side of the Alps. Each prince had his regularly appointed fool. Ignorant kings, brought up by the ignorant, cannot know the noble pleasures of the mind: they degrade human nature to the point of paying people to talk nonsense to them. Thence comes it we have our *Mère Sotte*: and, before Molière, there was a court fool in nearly all comedies: an abominable custom.

I have, sir, it is true, said, just as you state, that there are serious comedies such as the *Misanthrope* which are masterpieces; that there are others which are very amusing, such as *Georges Dandin*; that drollery, gravity, pathos, may very well find place in the same comedy. I said that all styles were good, save the style which bores. Yes, sir, but grossness is not a style at all. *In my father's house are many mansions*: but I never pretended that it was reasonable to lodge in the same room Charles V and Don Japhet of Armenia, Augustus and a drunken sailor, Marcus Aurelius and a street mountebank. It seems to me that Horace so thought, in the noblest of all ages: consult his *Ars Poetica*. All enlightened Europe thinks the same today; and the Spanish are beginning to get rid of bad taste as well as the Inquisition—good sense proscribing the one as much as the other.

You know so well, sir, to what point the trivial and the low disfigure tragedy, that you reproach Racine for telling Antiochus, in *Bérénice*:

> This door is next to her apartment,
> And the other leads to the queen's.

To be sure, these are not heroic lines, but be good enough to observe that they are in an expository scene, which should be simple. This is not poetic beauty but a beauty of exactitude which fixes the place of the action, which alerts the spectator at once and lets him know that all of the characters will appear in this little room, common to the other apartments. Otherwise it would hardly be credible for Titus, Bérénice, and Antiochus always to speak in the same room.

Let the place of action be fixed and clear. Thus speaks the wise Boileau, the oracle of good taste, in his *Art Poétique*, a work at the very least equal to that of Horace. Our excellent Racine has almost never failed to keep this rule; and it is worthy of admiration that Athalie appears in the Jews' temple and in the very place where we have seen the high priest, without in any way offending probability.

You will pardon even more the famous Racine when you recall that the play *Bérénice* was in some ways the story of Louis XIV and our English princess, the sister of Charles II. They shared the same floor at Saint-Germain, and a salon separated their apartments.

I will add in passing that Racine presented the love affair of Louis XIV and his sister-in-law in his plays, and the monarch was grateful to him for it. A stupid tyrant would have punished him. I will also remark that this Bérénice, so tender, so delicate, so disinterested, to whom Racine claims that Titus owes all his virtues and who was on the point of becoming Empress, was only an insolent and debauched Jewess who slept openly with her brother, Agrippa II. Juvenal calls her the incestuous savage. In the third place, she was forty-four years old when Titus sent her away. My fourth observation is that this Jewish mistress of Titus is mentioned in the *Acts of the Apostles*. She was still young, according to the author of *Acts*, when she came to see the governor of Judea and when Paul, accused of having defiled the temple, defended himself by arguing that he had always been a good pharisee. But we will drop the history of Paul and the gallantries of Bérénice. Let us return to the rules of the theatre, which are more interesting for men of letters.

You free Britons, you do not observe the *unities of time, place, and action*. Truly, you do not improve matters: probability ought to count for something. It makes art more difficult: and difficulties overcome give pleasure and glory in any art form.

You must allow me, Englishman as you are, to plead the cause of my own nation. I so often tell it unpalatable truths, that it is only just I should caress it when I think it is in the right. Yes, sir, I have always believed, I now believe, and I always shall believe, that Paris is very superior to Athens in the matter of tragedies and comedies. Molière, and even Regnard, seem to me to excel Aristophanes as much as Demonsthenes excels our lawyers. I say boldly that I think all the Greek tragedies seem to me the work of school boys as compared with the *sublime scenes* of Corneille and the *perfect tragedies* of Racine. Admirer of the ancients as he was, Boileau himself thought this. He had no compunction in inscribing beneath the portrait of Racine that that great man had surpassed Euripides and equaled Corneille.

Yes, I believe I can prove that there are more men of taste in Paris than in Athens. We have more than thirty thousand souls in Paris who delight in the fine arts, and Athens had not ten thousand; the lower orders of the Athenians frequented theatres only when a performance was given gratis on some great.

or trivial, occasion. Our constant dealings with women have given us much greater delicacy of feeling, much more propriety of manners, and much more nicety of taste. Leave us our theatre, leave the Italians their *favole boscareccie;*[94] you are rich enough in other respects.

It is true that very bad pieces, absurdly intricate and barbarously written, have had, for a time, prodigious success in Paris, helped by a clique, party spirit, fashion, and the careless patronage of well-known persons. That is a passing madness; in a very few years the illusion fades. *Don Japhet d'Arménie* and *Jodelet* are relegated to the populace, and the *Siège de Calais* has no longer any repute outside Calais.

I must add one word on the rhyme with which you reproach me. Nearly all Dryden's pieces are in rhyme: which added to the difficulty of his task. The best remembered lines he ever wrote and the most widely quoted are rhymed: and I maintain again that, *Cinna, Athalie, Phèdre, Iphigénie* being in verse, any one who tried to shake off this yoke would, in France, be considered a weakling who had not the strength to support it.

As an old man, I will tell you an anecdote. I asked Pope one day why Milton had not versified his poem when all other poets versified theirs, in imitation of the Italians; he answered: "Because he could not."

I have confessed, sir, all that was in my heart. I own that I was much in the wrong in not paying attention to the fact that the Count of Leicester was first called Dudley: but if the fancy takes you to enter the House of Lords and change your name, I shall always remember the name of Walpole with the profoundest esteem.

Before despatching this letter, I have found time, sir, to read your *Richard III*. You would be an excellent *attorney-general*. You weigh all the pros and cons: still, I think I detect that you have a secret liking for the hunchback. You cannot help wishing he had been a pretty fellow, if not a fine fellow. Calmet, the Benedictine, wrote a long dissertation to prove that Christ had a handsome face. I wish I could agree with you that Richard III was neither so ugly nor so wicked as he is said to have been: but I should not have cared to have had anything to do with him. Your *white rose* and your *red rose* were full of fearful thorns for the nation.

Those gracious kings are all a pack of rogues.

Truly, the history of the Yorkists and Lancastrians, and many others, is much like reading the history of highway robbers. Your Henry VII was only a cut-purse, etc.

Yours, with respects, etc.

To M. D'ALEMBERT

September 4, 1769

Martin was a farmer with a large family, settled at Bleurville, in Barrois, on a farm of the Marche. Two years eight months ago a man was murdered on the highroad near the village of Bleurville. Some sharp person, having noticed on that same road, between Martin's house and the place where the murder was committed, the impress of a shoe, Martin was arrested, and his shoes fitting more or less into the prints, he was interrogated and tortured. After this preliminary, a witness came forward who had seen the murderer fleeing: Martin was confronted with the witness, who said he did not recognize him as the murderer: whereon Martin cried: "Thank God! Here is one person who says he does not recognize me!"

The judge, being very weak in his logic, thus interpreted the words: "Thank God! I have committed the murder, and have not been identified by the witness."

This judge, assisted by several local intellects, condemned Martin to the wheel, on an equivocal meaning. The case is sent up to La Tournelle of Paris: and the sentence being confirmed, Martin is executed in his own village. When he was stretched out on St. Andrew's cross, he asked permission of the sheriff's officer and the executioner to raise his arms to call heaven to witness to his innocence, as he could not make himself heard by the crowd. He was allowed that favor: after which, his arms, thighs, and legs were broken, and he was left to die on the wheel.

On July 26th of this year, a scoundrel, who was executed in the neighborhood, solemnly declared before he died that it was he who had committed the murder for which Martin had been broken on the wheel. However, notwithstanding, the little property of this innocent father of a family is confiscated and dissipated: the family was dispersed three years ago, and very likely does not even know that the father's innocence has at last been acknowledged.

This comes from Neufchâteau in Lorraine: two consecutive letters have confirmed the news.

What should I do, my dear philosopher? *Villars cannot be everywhere.* I can only lift my hands to heaven, like Martin, and take God to witness all the horrors which happen in his work of creation. I have enough to do with the Sirven family. The daughters are still in my neighborhood. I have sent the father to Toulouse: his innocence is as clearly demonstrated as a proposition of Euclid. The crass ignorance of a village doctor, and the still grosser ignorance of a subordinate judge, added to the grossness of fanaticism, has ruined a whole family, made them wanderers for six years, destitute, and begging their bread.

Finally, I trust that the Parliament of Toulouse will make it its honor and duty to show Europe that it is not always led away by appearances, and is worthy of the work it has to do. This affair gives me more trouble and anxiety than an old invalid can well bear: but I shall never let go until I am dead, for I am obstinate.

Happily, for about ten years now, the Parliament has appointed young men with much sense, well read, and who think as you do.

I am not surprised that your project on the progress of reason has failed. Do you think that the rivals of Marshal de Saxe would have liked it if he had defended a thesis on the progress of his military art in their presence?

I have seen Dr. Maty's son:

> Dignus, dignus est intrare
> In nostro *philosophico* corpore.[95]

I have just found among my papers a letter in Locke's handwriting, written just before his death to Lady Peterborough: it is pleasingly philosophical.

The Turks' affairs go ill. How I should like to see those scoundrels chased out of the country of Pericles and Plato: it is true, they are not persecutors, but they are brutes. God defend us from both the one and the other!

While I am in the process of wishing, I will ask permission of the good father Hayer to hope that there be no more Franciscans at the capital. Scipios and Ciceros would be much better there from my point of view. Sometimes I weep, sometimes I laugh over the human race. And you, my dear friend, you laugh all the time; consequently, you are wiser than I.

By the way, have you heard that the sentence of the Chevalier de la Barre has been condemned as abominable by four hundred Russian deputies appointed to frame a legal code? I believe that it will be spoken of in that code as an instance of the most horrible barbarity, and that it will be long cited throughout Europe to the eternal shame of our nation.

To M. PANCKOUCKE [96]

September 29, 1769

I strongly approve of your plan of writing a supplement for the *Encyclopaedia*. I hope that there are no more men like Abraham Chaumeix, and that those who condemned the theses against Aristotle, the emetic, the circulation of the blood, gravitation, inoculation, the fifteenth chapter of Belisarius, are so tired of their former blunders that they'll make no new ones. I dare hope even that finally some right to hospitality will be given in France to that stranger called *Truth*, and who has always been so badly received. The ministry will see that there is no glory in commanding a nation of fools, and that, if in the world there were a king of geniuses and a king of simpletons, the king of the geniuses would have precedence.

You are making fun of me, and you are insulting me, in offering me eighteen thousand francs to scribble off ideas for you to insert in your *in-folio*. You are making fun of me when you imagine that at the age of seventy-six I might be of some use to literature; and you are insulting me a little in offering me eighteen thousand francs for about six hundred pages. You know that I gave all my nonsense *free* to the Genevans; I will not sell it to the Parisians. I pity myself, or rather I pity them for persisting in searching for everything which might have been overlooked by me, and which does not deserve to be brought to light. You will pay the penalty, for I guarantee you that you will not sell this enormous pile of trash.

As for your *Encyclopaedia*, I could, within two or three months, begin to write the following articles for you: *Human Understanding, Eclogue, Elegy, Epic,* adding a few historical notes to M. Marmontel's article. *Proof, Fable;* one can make a pleasant comparison between the fables invented by Ariosto and imitated by La Fontaine. *Fanaticism* (the history of); that can be very interesting. *Woman;* a ridiculous subject which can become instructive and stimulating. *Fatality;* on this subject one can say some very striking things drawn from history. *Folly;* there are wise things to be said about fools. *Genius;* one can talk about it and yet not have any. *Language;* this article can be immense. *Jews;* one can put forth some very surprising ideas about their history without frightening people too much. *Law;* examine whether there are any fundamental laws. *Locke;* he must be justified for an error attributed to him in his article *Mortmain;* an excellent article will be furnished me on this barbarian jurisprudence. *Malebranche;* his system can provide some very surprising reflections. *Metempsychosis, Metamorphosis,* good subjects to treat.[97]

I will indicate to you the other subjects on which I will be able to work; but this is on the condition that I am alive, for I assure you that if I am dead you will not have a line from me.

As for the Italian who wants, so they say, to remodel, with the help of some Swiss, the *Encyclopaedia* written by French men, I have never heard of him here in my retreat.

To FREDERICK-WILLIAM [98]

Ferney, November 28, 1770

Monseigneur, the royal family of Prussia has excellent reasons for not wishing the annihilation of the soul. It has more right than anyone to immortality.

It is very true that we do not know any too well what the soul is: no one has ever seen it. All that we do know is that the eternal Lord of nature has given us the power of thinking, and of distinguishing virtue. It is not proved that this faculty survives our death: but the contrary is not proved either. It is possible, doubtless, that God has given thought to a monad which he will make think after we are gone; there is no inconsistency in this idea.

In the midst of all the doubts which we have discussed for four thousand years in four thousand ways, the safest course is to do nothing against one's conscience. With this secret, we can enjoy life and have nothing to fear from death.

Only charlatans are certain. We know nothing of first principles. It is surely very presumptuous to define God, the angels, spirits, and to pretend to know precisely why God made the world, when we do not know why we can move our arms at our pleasure.

Doubt is not a pleasant condition, but certainty is a ridiculous one.

What is most repellent in the *System of Nature* (after the recipe to make eels from flour), is the audacity with which it decides that there is no God, without even having tried to prove the impossibility. There is some eloquence in the book: but much more rant, and no sort of proof. It is a pernicious work, alike for princes and people:

If God did not exist, we would have to invent him.[99]

But all nature cries aloud that he does exist: that there is a supreme intelligence, an immense power, an admirable order, and everything teaches us our own dependence on it.

From the depth of our profound ignorance, let us do our best: this is what I think, and what I have always thought, amid all the misery and follies inseparable from seventy-seven years of life.

Your Royal Highness has a noble career before you. I wish you, and dare prophesy for you, a happiness worthy of yourself and of your heart. I knew you when you were a child, monseigneur; I came to your room when you had smallpox: I feared for your life. Your father honored me with much goodness; you condescend to shower on me the same favors which are the honor of my old age, and the consolation of those sufferings which must shortly end it. I am, with deep respect, etc.

To LORD CHESTERFIELD [100]

Ferney, September 24, 1771

Lord Huntington tells me that, of the five senses common to us all, you have only lost one, and that you have a good digestion; that is well worth a pair of ears.

I, rather than you, should be the person to decide whether it is worse to be deaf or blind or to have a weak digestion. I can judge these three conditions from personal experience; only for a long time I have not dared to come to decisions on trifles, much less on subjects so important. I confine myself to the belief that, if you have sunshine in the fine house you have built yourself, you will have bearable moments. That is all that we can hope for at our age, and, in fact, at any age. Cicero wrote a beautiful treatise on old age, but facts did not confirm his theories; his last years were very miserable. You have lived longer and more happily than he did. You have not had to deal with perpetual dictators or triumvirs. Your lot has been, and is still, one of the most desirable in this great lottery, where the prizes are so rare, and the greatest one, continual happiness, has never yet been gained by anybody.

Your philosophy has never been misled by the wild dreams which have confused heads otherwise strong enough. You have never been, in any way, either a charlatan or the dupe of charlatans and I count that as one of the most uncommon advantages that contributes to the shadow of felicity one can enjoy in this short life, etc.

To FREDERICK II, KING OF PRUSSIA

Ferney, August 31, 1775

Sire, I am sending back today to the feet of Your Majesty, your brave and wise officier D'Etallonde Morival, whom you were so kind to entrust to me for eighteen months. I assure you that one will not find in him at Potsdam the flighty and presumptuous air of our so-called French marquis. His conduct and his continual application to the study of tactics and to the art of engineering, the circumspection in his proceedings and in his words, the gentleness of his manners, his fine character, are strong enough proofs against the lunacy, as execrable as it is absurd, of the sentence of three village judges who condemned him ten years ago, along with the Chevalier de La Barre,[101] to a punishment which the Busirises would never have dared imagine.

After the Busirises of Abbeville, he will find in you a Solon. Europe knows that the hero of Prussia has been its legislator; and it is as legislator that you have protected virtue, delivered by fanaticism to the executioners. It is to be believed that we will see no more of these horrible atrocities in France, which until now were so strange and so frequent a contrast with our lightness; one will soon cease to say: *The gayest nation is the most barbarian.*

We have a very wise ministry, chosen by a king who is not less wise, and who desires well-being. This is what Your Majesty states in his last letter of the 13th. Most of our faults and misfortunes up to now have come from our subjection to ancient customs honored with the name of laws, in spite of our love for novelty. Our criminal jurisprudence, for example, is nearly all founded on what is called *canon law*, and on the ancient procedures of the Inquisition. Our laws are a hodge-podge of ancient barbarism badly corrected by new directives. Until now our government has always been what the city of Paris is: a collection of palaces and of hovels, of magnificence and of misery, of admirable beauties and of disgusting blemishes. Only a new city can be uniform in structure.

Your Majesty condescends to inform me that he deigns to travel with my poor works. I should like very much to be in their place, in spite of my eighty-two years. I am obliged to tell you that several of these children which are baptized with my name, are not mine. I know that you have a Lausanne edition in forty-two volumes, undertaken by two magistrates and two priests who have never consulted me. If by chance the twenty-third volume fell into your hands, you would see there about thirty little selections in verse quite worthy of the coachman of Vertamont. You do not need to have as much taste at Lausanne as at Potsdam.

What is mine hardly merits your attention much more. The mania of editors has buried me in masses of paper. Those people ruin themselves out of an excess of zeal. I have written to them a hundred times that you do not go to posterity with such heavy baggage. They have not kept this in mind; they have disfigured your letters and mine which have circulated in society. There I am in an *in-folio*, gnawed by rats and worms like a Church Father.

Your Majesty will see therefore my eternal quarrels with the Larchers, and brother Nonotte, and brother Fréron, and brother Paulian, those illustrious ex-Jesuits. These beautiful disputes must be extraordinarily boring for the conqueror of so many nations, and the historian of his country. The Jesuits declared war on me at the very time that your brothers the kings of France and Spain were punishing them. They were soldiers dispersed after their defeat who robbed a poor passer-by in order to have something to eat.

The Jesuits had to persecute me in conscience: for, before they were expelled from France and Spain, I had expelled them from my neighborhood. They had seized, on the Bern frontier, the belongings of seven gentlemen named MM. de Crassy, all brothers, all in the service of the king of France, all minors, all very poor. I had the good fortune to deposit the money necessary to enable them to return to their land usurped by the Jesuits. Saint Ignatius has not pardoned me for this impiety. Since this time, Fréron has been remaking the *Henriade* with La Beaumelle; Paulian has been writing against the Emperor Julian and against me; Nonotte has been accusing me, in two thick volumes, for taking it amiss that the great Constantine murdered in former times his father-in-law, his brother-in-law, his nephew, his son and his wife. I had the weakness to answer these sots: the editors have been foolish enough to reprint these sorry things which no one cares about.

I beg Your Majesty to do with this trash the same thing that I have seen him do with so many books: he took his scissors, cut out all the pages which bored him, kept those which could amuse him, and thereby reduced thirty volumes to one or two; an excellent method for curing us of the madness of writing too much.

There we have then, sire, the baron of Pöllnitz dead; he wrote too. That is the way we must all finish, the Frérons, the No-nottes, and I. Nothing at all will remain. Only certain names will be saved from annihilation, as, for example, a Gustavus-Adolphus, and another who is very superior, in my opinion, whose victorious hands I kiss, which have written things so ingenious and useful, which protect innocence and which spread favors.

To DR. TRONCHIN
AT THE ROYAL PALACE

Paris, February 17, 1778

The old Swiss whom Monsieur Tronchin was good enough to see at the home of Monsieur de Villette, advises him that the constant alternation of stangury and diabetes along with the total cessation of the peristaltic movement of the bowels, is a rather disagreeable and somewhat dangerous matter; a body so disordered can subsist only a few days longer by means of the same kindnesses that Monsieur Tronchin has shown.

Madame Denis' pills have recently done him much good, but they have not diminished any of his pains. A slight swelling in the legs, a swelling that is difficult to reduce in so dry a body, seems to announce the imminent destruction of this frail machine.

The old patient would be very happy to be able to receive Monsieur Tronchin for a moment before taking leave of every one.

He has seen Monsieur Franklin who came with his grandson, and told the boy to ask for the old man's blessing. The old man gave him his blessing in the presence of twenty persons, and said these words to him in benediction: *God and liberty.*

To DR. TRONCHIN

May, 1778

Your old patient has a fever. The legs of his glorious body are quite swollen and covered with red blotches. This morning he wanted to take himself to the temple of Esculapius; he could not.

To DR. TRONCHIN

May, 1778

The patient on the rue de Beaune was convulsed by a violent ⌐ough all night long and more. He vomited blood three times. Ie asks pardon for giving you so much trouble for a corpse.

To THE COUNT DE LALLY [102]

May 26, 1778

The dying man revives on learning this great news;[108] he embraces Monsieur de Lally tenderly; he sees that the king is the defender of justice: he dies content.

NOTEBOOKS

NOTEBOOKS 104

(SELECTIONS)

[*Some of the following items were written by Voltaire in English. These have not been corrected; they present few difficulties to the modern reader.*]

England is meeting of all religions as the Royal exchange is the rendez vous of all foreigners.

When I see Christians, cursing Jews, methings I see children beating their fathers.

Jewish relligion is mother of Christyanity, and grand mother of the mahometism.

One greatest error among christians is about the holy ghost. Formerly when a man was made a Lawyer in Jerusalem, he was so by these words, receive the holy ghost. Now one make use of the same words in making a priest.

T'is a meer fancy to believe the character of a priest is indelible. A lay man is made a clergy man only by designation. T'is an office wich can be revoked, and which was revoked effectually in the old ages of christianity, when a priest wanted church and fonction,

Go and teach all nations; this was said to all christians, before the distinction of clergy and layty.

For to get some authority over others one must make oneself as unlike them, as one can: t'is a sure way of dazling the eys of the crowd. So the priests appears in longue gown etc.

To have Lowis of gold and crowns, and to rekon in imaginary livres is a contrivance of the Kings and banquiers to get monney.

It seems that one doth deal in England with the quakers as with the Peers of the realm, wich give their verdict upon their honour, not upon their oath.

Theatre in England is without decency etc.

In England everybody is publik-spirited—in France everybody is concerned in his own interest only. An English man is full of taughts, French all in miens, compliments, sweet words and curious of engaging outside, overflowing in words, obsequious with pride, and very much self concerned under the appearance of a pleasant modesty. The English is sparing of words, openly proud and unconcerned. He gives the most quick birth, as he can, to his taughts, for fear of loosing his time.

There was a parson in France, who for to saunter away the time, was playing one day in the morning, at piquet, with his own whore. In the mean time, some good contrymen, and great many devotious women were at a loss round about the altar, in order to communicate, and waiting upon their kneels, for their parson. The clerc of the church comes in a great hurry to his master. Make haste, sais he, good sir, come to administer god to your people. The parson rises on a sudden, leaves off the game, kiss his whore, takes up his wafers box, but by mistake, he puts in its som counters of ivory of the same figure, wherewith he plai'd, and he runs to the altar. As he was distributing god in wafers, to the people, he gives to one old woman, an ivory counter instead of a wafer. This old jade, after having receiv'd her portion of god, sneaks into a secret part of the church to pray, and to collect herself. She wonders at first that she can't swallow up the host. She endeavours to chaw it, but in vain. At last she goes to the priest in the vestry. Good ser, sais she, I believe you gave me god the father, so he is tough, and hard.

Rara est concordia fratrum

Seldom brothers agree together. T'is for this reason sovereigns of Europe are stiled brothers to each other. They pursue, they deceive, they betray, the hate one another like true brothers, and after having fight with the utmost fury and having lay wast respectively their kingdoms, they take a solemn mourning upon the death one of another.

I think oft. of Mr. B. and Mr. P. There are both virtuous and learned; of equal wit and understanding, but quite contrary in their wais. P. loves retirement and silence, virtuous and learned for himself. B. more communicatif diffuses everiwhere his virtue and his knowledge. B. is a dark lanthorn; tho' it is illuminated within, it affords no manner of light, or advantage to such, as stood by it. The other is an ordinary lamp, which consumes and wastes itself for the benefit of every passenger.

M. B. was as great whoremaster as great statesman.[105] He was in the bloom of his youth, and of his whoring too, when queen Anna made him secretary of war. A swarm of strumpets were walking in St. James' park, when a sudden rumor was spred, h. st. was raised to that place which is worth five thousand pounds a year. All the whores cried out with joy, god bless us, five thousand pounds all among us.

Mr. Lock's reasonableness of christian relligion is really a new relligion.

No one disputes over the essential of religion, which is to do good; men dispute over unintelligible dogmas. If religion were content to say: be just, there would not be an unbeliever on the face of the earth. But the priests say believe, etc., and men do not believe at all.

Guesses

Perhaps we may rekon 8 senses.

We do not know what a soul is, we have no idea of the thing, therefore we ought not to admitt it.

We are not of another gender than the beasts but of another species.

Water, exercise, sobriety, may cure all diseases.

God cannot be proved, nor denied, by the mere force of our reason.

In the countries in which commerce is not well developed,

there is always some one who is extremely rich because the rest
are poor.

The same is true in matters of the spirit, in science and
philosophy The more an age is enlightened, the fewer the num-
be, of dominant geniuses, every one is comfortable, but hardly
anyone has an immense fortune.

Superiority of mind sometimes injures talent.

Galileo was obliged to retract by those mitred marionettes
who are today the tyrants and the shame of Italy.

On English Literature

Poetry in the oriental taste from the time that writing in common speech was fashionable with them.

Comedians honored from the time there first were comedies;
casuists scorned.

Bacon the inventor of the system of attraction.

Addison secretary of state.

I can not understand what matter is, and even less so what
is spirit.

If there is a god, if there is not, if the world is finite or
infinite, created or eternal, arranged by intelligence or by physical
laws, or even by chance.

I can not understand

> how I think,
> how I retain my thoughts,
> how I move,

The first principles to which my existence is attached are all
impenetrable. Hence it is not that which we must seek but
what is useful, and dangerous, to the human body, the laws by
which it moves, the art of increasing moving forces, not the
principles of movement.

To my lord Bolingb

How the French theater bears the price. Superior to the ancients,
no visards; and we have women. Then there must be love.

Critics are fleas, known because the bite.

Scenes in Schakespar. No plays.
We want action.
We deal in words.
We are naturals, so was Virgil, Horace.
English seem to go beyond nature.
We are slaves to good breeding.
Wit better rewarded in England
Mr la Motte errs about the temple in Andromache
Poetry, necessary, to us

Singular Judgments

The time which Euripides lived in was not more refined then the age which produced Bacon, Spenser, Queen Elisabeth, Shakespear.

Puerilities in Hamlet,
The same in Hippolitus.

You have the terror of the action peculiar to the Athenian theater, we have its elegance.

Our plays longer, then there must be a more intangled plot etc.

Why tragedi is of a more difficult access. Because when I have framed my plot, and write it in the best stile nothing is done, without poetry.

La Motte, Fontenelle writ without any trouble. Yrself, what stile, but how easi it flows. When one has bent his genius to think and used his hand to writing, trust the coming word. Four verses are more difficult to wrte wel than it was to Tulli to write his orations.

Love, duty, treason, ambition, jealousy, romances, intrigues, a child, a mistress lost and recovered. All that is old topik. No more digging in these exhausted mines.

Theater, in esteem

Paulus, Callistrate, Philonide among the Greecs.

The autors themselves acted, witness Aristophanes.

Amongst us quite the reverse, rewards for all sort of artificers, none for plays.

Remember Driden's injustice and thefts.

Read the Spectator.

In Rome, in Athenes, plays acted at certain times, among us all the year round.

Academy impoverish'd the language, because they do not deal in ideas.

The same subject, new turns, quaere phrases, bad stile, whipt creame. Had they handled other topics, they had succeeded better.

Reward for Surgeons, not for good books.

Differences between the Englh and French stage

One kills him self here; why shant he kill another? One is carried dead out of the scene, why not brought dead? Hippolitus appears wonded, in Euripides. Cato's son is brought in murdered.

Racine is the only tragic author who talks of love with decency.

Remember Smiths, and Euripides Hippolitus, with Shadwel and Dryden.

The Greek tragedies seem to be ancient basso relievo's, without the art of perspective.

Sophocles and Euripides, noble Scenes, few good plays, like Shakespear, and Homer, yet esteem'd with justice.

We can't help rhiming. One who would write a tragedy in prose is like one who would walk at a ball, in stead of dansing.

Ordinary history, which is only a mass of the deeds of men and consequently their crimes, has scarcely any value, and he who reads the daily newspaper will gain more in this respect than he who knows the whole of ancient history. Curiosity alone is satisfied.

Our tragedies are admirable but our spectacles are ridiculous and savage, our theatres wretched for the voice; until the present there has been no knowledge of theatrical architecture.

What a shame to have to play Mithridate and Tartuffe on a tennis court with a front platform and with gallants confused with the actors! Even in Holland there is a suitable theatre.

The story of the matron of Epheses is found in an old Chinese book.

The learned Ouang met a young wife weeping on the seashore. She was at her husband's tomb, and waved a large fan. "Why this fan, madame?" "Alas, my dear husband made me promise that I would re-marry only when this tomb would be dry, and I wave my fan in order to dry it." Ouang told this story to his wife who shuddered in horror and swore to him that she would never use a fan. Ouang contrived an illness and pretended to be dead. They put him in a coffin. At once there appeared a very handsome youth who came to study with the learned man, etc. He pleased. They were married. He fell into convulsions and his old valet made the lady believe that she needed a dead man's brain to cure him. The good woman then went to smash the head of her husband Ouang, who came out of the tomb.

A man cuts on earth the same figure as a louse a twelfth of an inch high and a fifth of that distance wide would make on a mountain of some 15,000 feet.

Detached Thoughts

To learn several languages is an affair for a year or two; to be eloquent in one's own demands half a life-time.

We do not fear to commit follies that cannot be discovered. That is why we boldly write Latin poems and sing motets, for the court of Augustus is not around to make fun of us.

Julius Caesar subjugated three hundred nations in Gaul. Had there been only one, perhaps he would not have conquered any.

The Jewish religion is the mother of Christianity, the grandmother of Mohammedanism, beaten by its son and its grand-son.

Most men are like the magnet; they have a side which repels and another which attracts.

Detached Thoughts

We are unhappy because of what we lack, and never happy by dint of what we have. To sleep, etc. is not happiness; not to sleep is unbearable.

Only weak men commit crimes; great and happy men have no need of them.

A Sermon Preached Before Fleas

My dear fleas, you are the cherished work of god; and this entire universe has been made for you. God created man only to serve as your food, the sun only to light your way, the stars only to please your sight, etc.

When we decide to translate we must choose our author as one chooses a friend, of a taste conforming to our own.

We admire Marot, Amiot, Rabelais, in the same way as we praise children when by chance they say a good thing. We approve them because we scorn their century, and children because we expect nothing from them at their age.

Let be damned for all eternity only those who wanted to make themselves gods.

Dreams are the intermediaries of the comedy played by human reason. The imagination, then finding itself alone, makes a parody of the play reason performed during the day.

A Tale Taken from the Book of Todos Joschut

Jesus, Peter and Judas had only one egg for their supper. Jesus said, "It's too little. Let's go to sleep, and he who has the most beautiful dream will eat the egg."

"I dreamed that I was in heaven at God's right hand," said Peter. "And I," said Jesus, "I dreamed that you were at my right." "As for me," said Judas, "I dreamed that I had eaten the egg." And in fact the rogue had eaten it.

Superstition is of all ages.

Xenophon during the retreat of the ten thousand said that they were bothered by the north wind and that they sacrificed to the wind. Young Cyrus at the head of his army and in the presence of the enemy asked his astrologer when the battle would take place.

A decree preventing money from leaving the country. An order to our subjects not to pay their debts.

The most perfect language is that containing the least that is arbitrary. It is the same as with government.

Cicero

He was not exiled as was Demosthenes for allowing himself to be corrupted but for having saved the country. He won a battle and despised its glory. He desired the glory of his true talent. He was a tender friend, a zealous citizen, the best philosopher of his time; intrepid in the days of the conspiracy. He died with resolution, but he did not commit suicide like Demosthenes. His was a different courage. The one prefered to dispose of his life; the other allowed an ingrate, whom he had saved, for whom he had pleaded, to be master of it. It is the fate of all public men always to find ingrates.

N.B. He said to Atticus, non mei inimici sed invidi perdiderunt.[106] I must make use of that and especially make it clearly understood that the success of plays in the theatre is in the subject and in the actors.

A historian is a chatter-box who pesters the dead.

Religion is not a restraint; on the contrary, it is an encouragement to crime. Every religion is based on expiations.

It is one of the superstitions of mankind to have imagined that virginity could be a virtue.

When Corneille, Racine, Molière wrote, they taught France. they said what men did not know. Today whatever one may do, he tells us only what we know.

Electra

N.B. Crebillon's Preface is as ridiculous as his play, but let's say nothing about it.

Greek works are like Greece, full of defects, superstitions, weakness, but the first people of the earth.

Actors of comedies were slaves in Rome, magistrates in Athens, excommunicated in France.

Thoughts on Happiness

Men who seek happiness are like drunkards who can never find their house but are sure that they have one.

The stoics should inspire a more firm and magnanimous virtue than our religion. They directed self-love to the love of virtue for itself. Christianity tells you after thirty years of crimes that a good confession is enough.

Portrait of Mr. Walpole

1742

Never was there a man whose actions were more severely and more publicly sifted than the present prime minister, who has governed a free and intelligent nation for so long a period of time, and in whom so many contradictions have been found that you can make a whole library out of what has been written for or against him. He has been the subject of most of the scribbling that has been done in his country for the past twenty years. I hope, for the love of our country, that his character is here presented with so much impartiality and judgment that our descendents will attest to it, and that finally our liberty may begin to serve a better end. I fear to fail only in the first quality, that of judgment, but even so, this will be no more at best than one more sheet of paper added to the hundred thousand on the same subject which have been torn up and cast aside. Meanwhile I may pleasantly flatter myself with the idea that the following portrait will be adopted by future historians.

Mr. Robert Walpole, prime minister of Great Britain, is a man of capacity but without genius; of a natural goodness, but certainly not virtuous; unbending, but certainly not courageous; moderate without being equitable. His virtues are in some measure exempt from the contamination of vices, which are ordinarily confused with similar virtues. He is a generous friend, and in no way a dangerous enemy. His defects in other areas are not compensated for by the good qualities he possesses. If he has undertaken no enterprises, it has not been by design. His private character is better than his public, and the man in him triumphs over his vices. His fortune is greater than his reputation. With so many good qualities, he did not permit himself to attract public hatred; with so much merit he could not guarantee himself free from ridicule. He might have been considered worthy of holding an eminent office even if he had never occupied one. He is more fit to hold the second place in a government than the first. His ministry was more advantageous to his family than to the nation, better for his own times than for posterity, more pernicious for the bad example it set than for its real accomplishments. During his administration commerce flourished, liberty declined, and learning fell into decay. As a man, I love him; as a lover of the arts I hate him; as an Englishman I wish for his overthrow and his fall.

Animals have a prodigious advantage over us: they forsee neither evils nor death.

It is the same with different works as with ordinary life. Business demands seriousness; pleasure, gaiety. But today people want to mix everything up: it is as though you would dress for a ball to attend a council of state. There must be peaceful moments in great works, just as in life after moments of passion, but not moments of disgust.

Happiness is a condition of the soul; consequently it cannot be durable. It is an abstract name composed of a few ideas of pleasure.

Man is the only animal that knows he must die. Sad knowledge, but necessary, since he has ideas. Thus there are misfortunes necessarily attached to the condition of being a man.

We must have a religion and not believe in the priests, just as we must have a diet and not believe in the doctors.

Man must be glad, they say, but of what?
If every one was satisfied, no one would work.
We must never be satisfied or uneasy: that is difficult.

It is not the superiority of genius that makes the great minister; it is character and temperament; an indefatigable body and courage of mind. Most men see clearly what they must do, but the boldness of soul that determines to act is rarer. We must clearly distinguish spirit and character. Deception, vengeance, false oaths, scorn for all that binds men, there you have character. Penetration, learning, invention, clarity, eloquence, there you have spirit. The soul is a stamp on which five hammers pound; each strikes a different place. There is no such thing as a mathematical point; hence the soul is extended, hence it is material. Must I strip a being of all the properties which strike my senses because the essence of this being is unknown to me? It may be that we become something else after our death: does a caterpillar suspect that it will become a butterfly?

All of the principal facts of history should be applied to morality and to the study of the world, otherwise reading is useless.

Literature has become immense, the number of books countless, universal knowledge impossible. The cultivated mind is no more than an echo, and the present age is only the disciple of the past century. We have made for ourselves a storehouse of ideas and expressions to which every one helps himself. Nothing is new; consequently everything languishes, and the multitude of authors brought about the decline.

The universities were instituted for the advancement of the sciences, and we can never know anything except by following a route contrary to the universities; thus Galileo, Descartes, Bacon, Dumoulin, etc. etc. Only schools of errors were instituted.

In 1619 at Longsaunoir a father burned his two sons accused of being sorcerers. He was believed absolved by the judge.

Force and weakness arrange the world. If there were only force, all men would be fighting; but god has given us weakness: thus the world is made up of asses who carry and of men who load.

Human sacrifices, to know if they were ever ordered by legislators. It seems that the Jewish people is the only one among whom these horrors are a matter of precept, and it is for this reason that they do not show their books to strangers, for fear lest the whole world exterminate so abominable a people.

In the Indies it is not a law that women must burn on the bodies of their husbands, but a religious act, founded on the hope of finding the husband again in another form, such as being a mare if the husband should be a stallion or a queen should he be a king.

It seems that the horrible custom of human sacrifice extends throughout the world. The first of these sacrifices known is that of Ilus reported in Sanconiathon.

The two Greeks and the two Gauls sacrificed by the Romans according to Plutarch.

At Tyre, at Carthage, according to Dionysus of Halicarnassus.

For the Gauls, see Caesar and Diodorus Siculus.

According to Arien, the Tribaliens before fighting Alexander immolated three girls, three boys, and three black rams.

In Homer twelve Trojans are sacrificed by Achilles at the funeral of Patroclus; but out of revenge rather than religion.

A girl thrown into the Nile, afterwards turned to bull-rushes. See Pausanias, Porfiry, Plutarch and Abbe Banier, volume 1. page 243.

It is very probable that these sacrifices were made only on great occasions. I do not see that it lies within human nature for a civilized people to allow the fathers of families to be in danger every year of seeing their sons or daughters sacrificed.

Obedience to the pope remains slavery. The bishop of Rome believed and made others believe that he succeeded to the throne of the Caesars. The same thing happened to —— as to St. Ignatius. He was a madman; clever men founded his society based on fanaticism.

Religion is between man and God a matter of conscience, between the sovereign and his subject a matter for the police, between man and man a matter of fanaticism or hypocrisy.

Man was not born vicious. All children are innocent, all youths are confiding and lavish of their friendship, married couples love their children, pity exists in every heart: only tyrants corrupt the world. Priests were invented as opposition to the tyrants. The priests were worse. What do men have left? Philosophy.

Assan, son of Ali, was taking a bath, and a slave happened to spill a vessel of boiling water on his body. Assan gave him money and said, there is one degree of paradise for those who do not get angry, one for those who forgive, and one for those who reward involuntary offenses.

At Lausanne, October 25, 1757

In one of my dreams I dined with Monsieur Touron who composed the words and music of the songs he sang to us. I composed in my dream these four lines:

> My dear Touron how you delight me
> By the sweetness of your accents
> How sweet and flowing are your verses
> You write them as you sing.

In another dream I recited the first canto of the Henriade quite differently from the way it is written. Yesterday I dreamed that they recited verses to us at dinner. Some one claimed they were too lively. I answered that verses were a holiday for the soul and that celebrations require adornments.

Thus while dreaming I have said things that I hardly would have said during the previous evening. Hence I must have reflective thoughts in spite of myself and without having the least to do with them. I had neither will nor liberty, and yet I combined ideas wisely and even with some genius. What am I then if not a machine?

NOTES

1   *Zadig* was originally entitled *Memnon, an Oriental Tale*, and was printed in Amsterdam in 1747. The definitive title dates from 1748. The text of *Zadig* here presented is based on the critical edition of Georges Ascoli (Paris, 1929). It is common for English translations to include two chapters, "The Dance" and "The Blue Eyes," found by Voltaire's editors among his papers after his death. These chapters may be authentic, but Voltaire did not incorporate them into his tale during his lifetime. Accordingly, this material along with other posthumous interpolations in *Zadig* has been omitted.

2   Thalestris was an Amazon queen who sought out Alexander the Great to make love to him and bear his child.

3   Yebor is an anagram of Bishop Boyer of Mirepoix who intrigued against Voltaire at the French court.

4   At this point some editors include the story of Irax, omitted by Voltaire in his revision of 1756 and thereafter, but reprinted in the posthumous edition of 1784-87.

5   Voltaire adds in a note: "Chinese words which properly mean: *Li*, natural light, reason; and *Tien*, heaven; and which also signify God."

6   *The Way the World Goes* first appeared in the collected works of Voltaire published in Dresden in 1748. It was probably written late in the preceding year.

7   The Pictavians here satirized are the inhabitants of Poitou in central France.

8   The "immense mansion" is an allusion to the Hôtel des Invalides in Paris.

9   Theona is in all likelihood a portrait of Madame du Châtelet.

10   *Micromegas* was first published in London in 1752. The conception of the tale may date from 1739. "Micromegas" means "the little great one."

11   A reference to William Derham's *Astro-Theology*, first published in 1715.

12   Voltaire has in mind Fontenelle, secretary of the Academy of Sciences, whose theories are parodied in the following chapter.

13   Voltaire here alludes to Huyghens, the discoverer of Saturn's rings.

14 Father Castel, best remembered for his color organ, was considered a charlatan by Voltaire.

15 Voltaire here refers to an expedition to Norway in 1736.

16 Swammerdam was a Dutch naturalist of the seventeenth century; the French scientist, Réaumur, was an elder contemporary of Voltaire.

17 Some editions read "nineteen hundred times less than pure gold."

18 An allusion to a doctor of the Sorbonne.

19 *The Story of a Good Brahmin* was first published in 1761 but was written at least two years earlier.

20 *Candide* was first published in 1759. Voltaire amused himself by repeatedly denying its authorship, even in letters to close friends. The condemnation of the book by the Council of Geneva may have influenced Voltaire's disavowal.

21 A quartering of nobility represents a generation.

22 The Bulgarians represent the Prussians in the Seven Years War.

23 An *auto-da-fé*, "act of faith," is a ceremony of burning heretics at the stake. Voltaire's description is based on contemporary accounts.

24 "What a pity to have no testicles!"

25 The Jesuit *Journal de Trévoux*, founded in 1701, frequently denounced Voltaire and his works.

26 Mademoiselle Monime is the actress Adrienne Lecouvreur. On her death in 1730 she was denied burial in consecrated ground. According to some reports, Voltaire helped to bury her secretly by night.

27 Fréron was a literary journalist of the day who ceaselessly scribbled attacks on Voltaire.

28 The allusion is to another of Voltaire's enemies, the Abbé Trublet.

29 A reference to Damiens' attempted assassination of Louis XV in 1755. Atrebatum is the Latin name for the region of Arras where Damiens was born. In May 1610 Ravaillac assassinated Henri IV; Châtel's attempt of 1594 was unsuccessful.

30 Voltaire here alludes to the execution of the English Admiral Byng in March 1757. He had interested himself in the case and made several appeals on behalf of Byng to English authorities and friends.

31 The name Pococurante means "caring little."

32 The *Poem on the Lisbon Earthquake* along with Voltaire's Preface was written in 1756. Between thirty and forty thousand persons are said to have been killed in the disaster which occurred on November 1, 1755. See Voltaire's letter of November 24 of that year to M. Tronchin of Lyons. The translation of the poem is taken from the contemporary edition of Tobias Smollett.

33 I have omitted a long note by Voltaire in which he rejects the concept of the chain of being set forth by Pope in his *Essay on Man*. See the article, "Chain of Created Beings," in the *Philosophical Dictionary*.

34 Voltaire adds in a footnote the statement of Saint Augustine: "*Sub*

Deo justo nemo miser nisi mereatur." "No one is wretched under a just God unless he deserves to be so." I have omitted Voltaire's other notes; for the most part, they are long restatements of the philosophical position set forth in the poem.

35   The *Essay on Epic Poetry* was first written in English and published in London in 1727. Voltaire made important revisions for the French version, which appeared in 1733. The section of the *Essay* here presented is a translation of the French text.

36   Samuel Sorbière, a seventeenth century French philosopher, published his *Account of a Journey to England* in 1664.

37   "Thus for sick little children
      We sweeten the edges of the bottle:
      So that, unsuspecting, they drink the bitter medicine,
      And gain their life through deception."

38   Voltaire's Preface to *Julius Caesar* was published in 1764 along with his translation of part of Shakespeare's play, to the beginning of Act III.

39   The first complete text of *The Age of Louis XIV* was published in Berlin in 1751, but the first draft dates from the closing years of the 1730's. In 1739 the first two chapters appeared in Paris and were confiscated by the French authorities. Discouraged, Voltaire put the project aside for several years, and finally published it in Berlin while at the court of Frederick the Great. He subsequently made numerous additions and corrections. The translation here presented is that of Martyn P. Pollack. Voltaire's notes have been omitted; they consist primarily of references to his sources.

40   The allusion is to Copernicus.

41   The *Essay on the Manners and Spirit of Nations* did not receive that title until the edition of 1769, but Voltaire's conception of a universal history dates at least from 1740. In that year he wrote the Introduction containing the plan of the work and addressed it to Madame du Châtelet to encourage her interest in his approach to history. The history was first published from 1753 to 1756.

42   The *Philosophical Letters* or *English Letters* were begun by Voltaire in England in 1726 and completed in France in 1730. They were published in France in 1734 and were at once condemned by the parliament and publicly burned by the hangman. Clandestine editions followed until 1742 when the *Philosophical Letters* were included in an edition of Voltaire's complete works. The text of the present selection is based on the edition of Naves, after that of Lanson.

43   Here again, in all likelihood, Voltaire is referring to Bolingbroke.

44   The impoverished authors are Crébillon and Louis Racine; both were much admired at the time Voltaire wrote this essay

45   The *Treatise on Tolerance* was published in 1763.

46   Voltaire adds in a note, "October 2, 1761."

47 Voltaire adds: "The editions were pirated in many towns, and Madame Calas lost the fruit of this generosity." Other notes by Voltaire, chiefly references to his sources, have been omitted.

48 Cesare Beccaria's essay, *Of Crimes and Punishments*, was published in Italy in 1764. A French translation by the Abbé Morellet appeared at the end of 1765. Voltaire's *Commentary* was composed and published in the following year. His interest in legal reform was undoubtedly quickened by the execution of the Chevalier de La Barre in July, 1766. See note 101, below.

49 "Shining more brightly than noon."

50 The *Philosophical Dictionary* first appeared in 1764. It was revised and enlarged by Voltaire on four separate occasions during his lifetime. After his death, his editors reprinted the work and added to it a large number of articles and essays from other writings. The present selection, based on the edition of Naves, is taken from those pieces that appeared under the title of the *Philosophical Dictionary* during the life of Voltaire.

51 *Sursum corda:* "Lift up your hearts"; *Ite missa est:* "Go, the service is finished."

52 "According to his properties."

53 "Love is the same to all men."

54 "Sometimes a woman may so act
By her clever ways and proper grooming
To make it easy for a man to pass his life with her."

55 *The Account of the Sickness, Confession, and Death of the Jesuit Berthier* appeared in 1759; only the first part of this satire is included. Guillaume-François Berthier, editor for several years of the *Journal de Trévoux*, was born in 1704 and actually died in 1782.

56 Voltaire adds in a note: "These two honest Jesuits say, in a fine book reprinted just a little while ago, that a citizen exiled by a prince can be legitimately assassinated only in the prince's territory; but that a prince exiled by the Pope, can be assassinated anywhere, because the Pope is sovereign of the earth; that a man charged with killing one who has been excommunicated can give this duty to another; that it is an act of charity to accept this commission, etc., pages 101, 102, 103."

57 Gabriel Malagrida was a Portuguese Jesuit compromised in a plot on the life of Joseph I of Portugal, which led to the expulsion of the Jesuits from that country in 759.

58 The *Nouvelles ecclésiastiques* was a Jansenist weekly, hence anti-Jesuit. It too was attacked by Voltaire for its fanaticism.

59 *Of the Horrible Danger of Reading* first appeared in 1765.

60 *The Conversation of Lucian, Erasmus and Rabelais* was first published in 1765.

61 *André Destouches in Siam* was first published in 1766. André Destouches was a French composer of the late seventeenth century

62 *The Dialogues Between A, B, and C* appeared in 1768. There are 17 dialogues in all, dealing primarily with political and philosophical subjects.

63 *Of the Encyclopedia* was first published in 1774.

64 *The Dialogues of Evhémère* first appeared in 1777. Evhémère or Ephemerus, a Greek philosopher of the fourth century B. C., was noted for his profoundly sceptical attitude toward the ancient gods, whom he viewed as superior men deified by their contemporaries.

65 At the age of 19 Voltaire accompanied the French Ambassador to Holland to The Hague, where he fell in love with Mademoiselle Du Noyer. She is sometimes referred to in modern editions as Pimpette or by her middle name, Olympe.

66 Voltaire was imprisoned in the Bastille in 1717 for having written satiric poetry against the Regent, to whom this letter is addressed. Not all of the poems charged to Voltaire were in fact by him. He remained in the Bastille for eleven months and was then released under police surveillance, in consequence of this appeal.

67 In December 1725 Voltaire publicly exchanged retorts with the Chevalier de Rohan, who consequently had Voltaire beaten by his servants. Voltaire was imprisoned in the Bastille in April 1726 to prevent him from taking revenge. As a result of this letter he was allowed to leave prison in May of that year, to go to Calais and thence to England.

68 Thieriot was one of Voltaire's longest and closest friends, and frequently managed Voltaire's business affairs in Paris. This letter is reprinted in Voltaire's English.

69 The "London citizen" was Everard Falkener, a well-to-do merchant who befriended Voltaire generously during his English exile.

70 The "First Commissioner" was the prime minister's assistant in charge of the censorship of books.

71 Jacob Vernet was a Calvinist minister at Geneva. At first he was on excellent terms with Voltaire, but was subsequently attacked by him for intolerance and fanaticism.

72 Count d'Argental, Minister of State, was one of Voltaire's closest friends and most frequent correspondents.

73 "A whole barrel-full in exchange for a flagon of nard."

74 Voltaire refers here to the *Philosophical Letters*. They were condemned by the French Parliament on June 10, 1734, and publicly burned.

75 Mademoiselle Quinault was a popular actress of the day, admired for her performances in light comedy.

76 Voltaire fell in love with Madame du Châtelet in 1733 and lived at her chateau at Cirey, in Lorraine, from 1734 until her death in 1749. Her influence on his reading, writing, and personal affairs was very great.

77 The Abbé Dubos was permanent secretary of the French Academy at the time of this letter. He is best known for his *Critical Reflections on Poetry and Painting*.

78 "No more do the unfinished towers rise, nor immense threatening walls. . . . And engines towering into the sky."

79 Voltaire here alludes to Diderot's *Letter on the Blind for the Use of Those Who See*.

80 Saunderson was a famous English mathematician, blind from infancy.

81 Madame du Deffand was one of the leading figures of Parisian salon society and a lively correspondent.

82 Madame Denis was Voltaire's niece. In 1749 she succeeded Madame du Châtelet as caretaker of Voltaire's personal affairs.

83 Rousseau had sent Voltaire a copy of his *Discourse on the Origin of Inequality*.

84 Thamas Kouli-kan was a military conqueror of central Asia of the early eighteenth century.

85 Voltaire's letter was written shortly after news had reached him of the Lisbon earthquake.

86 Guignard was a Jesuit implicated in the unsuccessful assassination attempt on Henri IV of 1594 and sentenced to death; Garasse was a violent Jesuit pamphleteer of the early seventeenth century.

87 This letter is probably addressed to a Calvinist minister friendly to Voltaire.

88 Voltaire means in Switzerland.

89 M. de Bastide was the editor of a new periodical, *The Spectator of the World*.

90 Voltaire had just written a violent attack on Rousseau's novel, *La Nouvelle Héloise*, and signed it by the name of Ximenès.

91 A pun on the name of Abbé Morellet, an enlightened cleric of the day, previously imprisoned for writing a pamphlet in defense of Diderot.

92 Voltaire here alludes to his satire of 1759; Berthier died in 1782.

93 The novel is *The Castle of Otranto*, published in 1765.

94 Pastoral novels.

95 A parody of the Finale of Molière's *The Would-Be Invalid*: "He is worthy of entering into our *philosophical* body."

96 Henri Panckoucke was a contemporary playwright admired by Voltaire.

97 Voltaire wrote most of these articles but published them in his *Questions on the Encyclopedia* and not in Panckoucke's new edition of the *Encyclopedia*.

98 Frederick-William II, the nephew and successor of Frederick the Great.

99 Quoted by Voltaire from his own poetry.

100 Voltaire had met Chesterfield along with Swift and Pope forty-five
     years earlier, during his stay in England.

101 In 1766 at Abbeville the Chevalier de La Barre was accused of
     having mutilated a crucifix and sung disrespectful songs during a
     religious procession. He was condemned to be burned at the stake.
     Instead, he was first decapitated; then a copy of Voltaire's *Philo-
     sophical Dictionary* was burned with his body.

102 This was Voltaire's last letter. It is addressed to the son of General
     Lally, who was executed in 1766 for allegedly having badly de-
     fended Pondichéry.

103 The parliamentary decree condemning General Lally had just
     been revoked.

104 Voltaire's *Notebooks* were published in two volumes in 1952,
     edited by Theodore Besterman. Many of Voltaire's jottings were
     written by him in English. Discontinuous selections have been
     separated.

105 Another allusion to Lord Bolingbroke, whose name was Henry St.
     John.

106 "Not my enemies but they who envy me will destroy me."

MODERN LIBRARY COLLEGE EDITIONS